Extension of Life

Extension of Life
Based on Actual Events

"Make the lie big.
Make it simple.
Keep saying it and
eventually they will believe it."

Adolf Hitler

By: Robert J. Bauman

Kravitz and Sons LLC
1301 Farmville Blvd, Suite 104
Greenville, NC 27834

Published by Kravitz and Sons LLC.

ISBN: 979-8-89639-022-0 (sc)
ISBN: 979-8-89639-021-3 (e)
Library of Congress Control Number: 2024924759

Table of Contents

FORWARD

I have written this in the first person as if it was my story but it is not. It is my father's story. When he came to America he vowed never again to hide the fact that he was Jewish as he had done before and during the war. To reinforce this, he changed his name back to Bauman.

To me, it is a story of courage. My father could easily have used the "extension" only for himself. Instead, he decided to help others, often putting him and our mother at risk. He made me swear that I would never tell anyone about his story as long as he was alive. I honored his request. It may have been because he did want to be associated with such a gory act as the emasculation of the dead. Or, it could have been his guilt for having worked with the Nazis in certain projects. I can only guess. However, being the oldest, he often took me aside and told me some of the stories of his activities which I found fascinating.

He died some years ago. About two months before he died he told me that he regretted that he had not told the complete story to someone to have as a record of what the group had accomplished. He took out a notebook that he had hidden for many years and gave it to me. He said that if I wanted to tell his story based on what he told me and what he had written in the notebook since the war ended, it would be the right thing to do.

My sister, brother and I had our own lives (thanks to him) and it seemed that I was always too busy to describe in detail the story of our father. Now that I have retired I have devoted the time necessary to reconstruct his life and activities in Vienna. I also traveled to Vienna and retraced his footsteps with the help of special knowledgeable guides, visited the neighboring countries he mentioned and visited his birthplace near Bruck, about 300 km east of Vienna.

With very few exceptions my father never knew what happened to the people he and his group saved. They specifically asked the people not to communicate with them after leaving Switzerland lest it tip off the Nazis if intercepted. Most complied with the request. He knew that many left Switzerland during the war as there were some Jewish organizations operating in Switzerland that helped Jews emigrate.

I also have to apologize that I am not totally positive that I have all of the right names, places and dates. My father never wrote anything down at the time for obvious reasons. When he started his notebook after coming to America he was working from memory plus some of the names and places were scrawled in German which made it even more difficult for me to read.

He also had a scrap book that he had brought with him from Austria. There were about fifteen envelopes pasted onto the scrap book pages. In each envelope he had saved some examples of the anti-Semitic paper money, postcards, documents, photographs and other memorabilia from the places or events that he had described. I have inserted a few of them in the book as examples to allow you to see them as well. Spacc did not permit showing all of the items that I originally wanted to include in the book.. The entire collection has been donated to the Houston Holocaust Museum (www.hmh.org).

My father believed that the group helped more than 450 Jews escape from Nazi-occupied Austria from 1939 to 1944. There were about 110 Jewish men and boys that used his "extension" along with their families during their escape. An additional 70 Jewish males and their families stayed in Vienna using the extension. They formed the network that worked with the group. In addition, there were about 160 Jewish men, women and children that were smuggled out of the country without the extensions. This does not include the 38 French Jews that were smuggled out of Austria when their transport train derailed in Vienna – nor does it include the one SS officer that was involved in the 1944 plot to kill Hitler who was smuggled out of Austria – as a Jew.

CHAPTER ONE

THE MOHEL MISSES THE MARK

"The Ten Commandments have lost their validity. Conscience is a Jewish invention; it is a blemish like circumcision."

Adolf Hitler

Bodies started to arrive at the morgue at around 9:30 Saturday morning. I was finishing some paperwork when the first ones arrived. I had been busy working since 7 AM in the basement as we were going to expand and add additional cold storage facilities and another laboratory. At ten o'clock Otto came down to the basement. "Have you heard the news? The German army has crossed the border at Braunau, Hitler's birthplace. The chancellor ordered the Austrian army to stand down. Not a shot was fired. They are on their way to Vienna as we speak! Most of the staff has taken to the streets to welcome them. There are rumors that Hitler is also coming today. I forgot you were down here until just now." I had not heard about any of this due to my self-imposed confinement but before I could comment he added, "By the way, there are two dead Jews in the holding room. Could you process them?" I went into the holding room where the bodies of two men were on two tables each covered with a sheet. Their wallets were on top of the sheet with their IDs beside them: Mikhail Goldblatt and Samuel Shimonson. I drew down the sheet.

The first body was an older, well-dressed man who had hung himself. The rope marks were quite distinct but his neck was not broken. Looking at his contorted face, it must have taken him a few minutes to die. The second man, also well-dressed, had shot himself in the mouth. The gun was also on top of the sheet. A cursory examination of the gun barrel, his right hand and his mouth confirmed that it was suicide. I thought nothing of it. The suicide of a

Jewish businessman in Vienna was not uncommon. These were hard times. One or two Jews, and an equal number of gentiles, typically committed suicide each month due to the extremely poor business conditions as they faced bankruptcy and ruin. I re-covered each body.

Since just about everyone had left the morgue to await the arrival of the Nazis, I decided that I would process them now before going out with the rest of the staff to wait for them to arrive in Vienna – an event to which I was certainly not looking forward. I should have left then. My mistake! Fifteen minutes later two ambulances arrived with four more suicides – all Jews. There was a family of three that died of a lethal injection apparently administered by the father as he was found with a syringe in his hand according to the ambulance attendant's report, and one man also with an apparent self-inflicted gunshot wound but this time to the right side of his head. Before the attendants could unload the ambulance, another one came in with three more bodies. During the next three hours, fifteen more bodies were brought to the morgue. All were Jews and all were suicides. They were from different districts although most were from the second district which had the largest Jewish population in Vienna. The attendants from the last ambulance with four bodies just left them at the entrance just inside the holding room as there were no more tables for them. They hastily told me that they had to get more bodies as they left the holding room. I asked Hans, one of the few remaining assistants to get whoever was left in the morgue to assist me by calling their relatives. This was very important. In the Jewish religion, a dead person has to be buried the next day. All of suicides had their identification papers on them. As the distraught family members of the deceased showed up they were led into a large waiting area. There were not enough seats so most had to stand and wait. I decided that I would go to the waiting room and explain the procedure to them. Before I could even go to the waiting room, one of the coroners came back to get something from his office and looked at the many bodies. He turned to me, not realizing that they were all Jewish, and asked, "So many deaths at one time? Was there a major accident? What was the cause of death for all of these people?" I turned to him and said one word – "Anschluss!"

That morning, Saturday, March 12, 1938, the Nazi army marched triumphantly into Austria – unopposed – as a prelude to the unification of Austria with Germany. Hitler's word for this annexation was Anschluss. As the army marched, they were welcomed by most of the population, even by Austrians of non-German descent. Tens of thousands of men, women and children lined the streets and highways waving Nazi flags, raising their right arm and yelling, "Heil Hitler!" Simultaneously, tens of thousands of men, women and children of Jewish descent cringed in fear and horror. For some the fear and horror were too much and they committed suicide, sometimes with family members. By nightfall, more than eighty Jews had committed suicide with some having also committed homicide in killing their spouses and, in two cases, their children.

As I walked back to the holding room I thought to myself, "There but for the Grace of God, many lies, a winter storm and an old mohel, go I."

For those of you that might not know what a Mohel (pronounced moy-il) is, I should let you know that it is the man that performs the rite of circumcision which is the cutting off of the loose piece of flesh called a foreskin that surrounds and covers the head of the penis. All Jewish baby boys in accordance with Jewish law (Genesis 17:10-11) are circumcised in a ceremony called a "bris". The bris typically takes place on the eighth day after a Jewish male is born and is a joyous occasion – a time for celebration. During the ceremony, the boy is officially given his Hebrew name, which for me was (Moshe).

For those that are the firstborn son in the family (which I was) there is yet another traditional ceremony called a "pidyon ha-ben". This translates as "the redemption of the first born son." It dates back to when the Israelites were slaves in Egypt. God, with Moses as his earthly representative, unleashed seven plagues upon Egypt in order to free the Jewish slaves. The last plague, and the most devastating, was the slaying of the first-born male in every Egyptian household while sparing the first-born male in every Jewish household. As a result, every first-born son in a Jewish family "belonged to God and was obligated to serve in the Temple" (Exodus 13:2). Without going into a lot of detail the tradition that arose was that you could redeem your first-born son from this obligation by paying five silver coins to a descendent from one of the twelve tribes of Israel, specifically the tribe of the priesthood which was from the tribe of Cohen. The pidyon ha-ben occurs on the thirty-first day after birth and is another occasion for celebration. For both ceremonies, my father decided that only Jewish people should attend – with one exception – he invited his close friend, Father Peters, the head priest at the St. Stephan's Church in Bruck where my father did volunteer medical service.

I was born on January 20, 1908 in Judendorf im Pinzgau, a small town in Austria about 120 kilometers from Salzburg close to Bruck on the Grossglocknerstrasse in Fusch. Pinzgau was one of five districts in the state of Salzburg. Salzburg was the capital city of the state of Salzburg. Fusch was a region in Pinzgau. Judendorf was originally founded by three Jewish families in the early 1600s. Over time the town was settled by non-Jewish (Gentile) families. By 1908 Jews were a very small minority in the town – and the surrounding area as well. Most of the population was of German descent since Salzburg bordered Germany and throughout its long history was often part of Germany. German was the official language in Austria. In the 1900 census, the population of the Fusch region was listed at 16,470. About 95 percent of the people in the Bruck area were of German origin. Of the remaining 5 percent, about 3 percent were of Swiss descent and the remaining 2 percent came from other countries. Catholics dominated the region followed by Lutherans and Protestants. The Jewish population accounted for less than 2 percent. Judendorf, like Bruck, was a popular ski and mountain hiking resort. Bruck also had a very good railway system which resulted in the Nazis using Bruck as a marshalling station during the war. The Bruck marshalling station was a primary target of the Allies towards the end of the war when most targets in Germany had been destroyed.

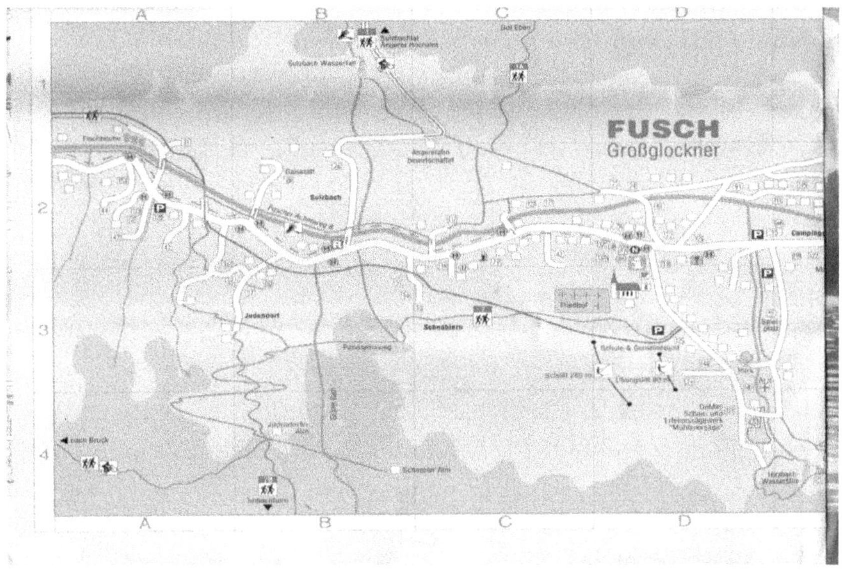

Current map showing Fusch/Bruck area on the Grossglockner Highway with Judendorf and Judendorfer Alm (A3 and B4); Bruck is to the west (not on map). Judendorf was completely destroyed during the war.

There was no synagogue in Judendorf let alone a Mohel so as soon as I was born a Mohel from Salzburg was called and asked to come to perform the circumcision ceremony which was scheduled for January 28th. Due to a very heavy snowstorm the day before the circumcision ceremony that made travel difficult, the Mohel did not arrive until about twenty minutes before the appointed time. He was very old, very cold, very tired and very shaky but a couple of rounds of schnapps eased his suffering. So, at the appointed hour he made the cut, which, due to his tired and now semi-inebriated condition, was less than perfect. Now obviously you are wondering in which direction he made his error. Did he take off too much or too little? Well, fortunately for me he erred on the right side and took off too little. My guess was that this was not the first time that he performed the ceremony in a semi-inebriated state so he compensated for his lower acumen by clipping the foreskin with some room to spare. This, of course was not noticed until a few years later. Being the first born son, my mother had no idea what the proper cut should look like. She only knew that it had taken place and, as she was prone to say, "It is what it is."

My father, Markus Bauman was a very private man who had some trouble while growing up and attending the local high school for being Jewish so when he went to Salzburg University and to medical school in Munich he kept a low non-Jewish profile until after he was graduated. This was particularly important in Munich which had a long history of anti-Semitism and was the birthplace of the Nazi Party. In other words, he pretended to be a Gentile and not a Jew, which he reinforced by adding a second "n" to his surname to become Baumann. The single "n" versus double "n" is an odd quirk in German nomenclature in that family names ending in a single "n" were invariably Jewish and those with two of them were invariably not Jewish. Upon graduation and interning in Munich, he returned to Judendorf and set up his own medical practice. He had known my mother, Helena, before he left for the university as they attended the same high school but they never dated. When he returned to Judendorf, he met her again at one of the Jewish holiday celebrations, Purim I believe, that was hosted by one of our neighbors. They started dating and were married about one year later. My sister, Elena, was born first; I was born a few years later.

My father was one of five doctors in the area of which he was the second Jewish doctor. Since he was known to be Jewish it affected his ability to attract Gentile patients which he needed since the Jewish community was quite small and they all went to the existing Jewish doctor who had been practicing in Judendorf for more than twenty years. This was not really a very strong issue. My grandfather was quite wealthy. He owned a drugstore in Judendorf and three other drugstores in the towns around Bruck. They did not have our family name on them as my grandfather did not want to overtly advertise that they were owned by a Jew so each of them had a different generic name. He thought that people would not realize that he owned all four stores. He also owned quite a bit of land east of Bruck which came to be called Judendorfer Alm (Jewish village pasture). He leased the land for grazing. Both of these are still on the current map of the area today even though Judendorf is long-gone and the pasture is no longer Jewish-owned. He paid for my father to attend medical school and helped him financially.

There was a very strong undercurrent of anti-Semitism that existed throughout the country for decades. This was brought to a head after the First World War particularly in 1919 and 1920 with the issuing of emergency paper money that was overtly anti-Semitic and another unfortunate event. But I am jumping ahead of myself.

Since my father did not have that many patients, he volunteered to do charity work at the church for the poor. There were not that many poor Jewish families in the area (actually none) so all of his charitable work in the St. Stephan's Catholic Church in Bruck where Father Peters was the head priest was for Gentiles. Father Peters was very appreciative of my father's help and showed no signs of caring that my father was Jewish. Three days a week my father operated a clinic in the church rectory administering to the poor often using supplies purchased at his own expense. Father Peters would often come to our house for dinner. I really liked him. He was older than my father and much taller and heavier with graying black hair, brown eyes and a hearty laugh. He was adored by his parishioners. His sense of humor and deep religious knowledge made his sermons entertaining – and his church crowded.

My mother was a great cook and she always prepared special Jewish dishes that Father Peters could not get anywhere else. Before and after dinner my father and Father Peters would discuss everything from religion to politics to social change to the price of bandages. They became close personal friends. This was the reason that Father Peters was invited to my bris and pidyon ha-ben. These were first-time observations for him into Jewish tradition and he was genuinely honored to be invited. My father also got along very well with the other church workers. They also appreciated his charitable efforts and often secretly sought him out for medical attention, for which he never charged. Every once in a while there was a knock on our door late at night by someone from the church saying that there was a medical emergency – a premature or troubled birth, an accident or just someone with a very high fever. He never refused, no matter what the hour or the weather.

While I was growing up I was often invited to listen to and eventually participate in the discussions between my father and Father Peters. Sometimes, if my father was busy, I would talk to Father Peters until my father finished what he was doing. I learned a lot about Catholicism from him. It was like having my own personal catechism class.

When I was eight years old, I started to take Hebrew lessons from a private tutor which also included a history of the Jewish people as written in the Old Testament. My father was very open with Father Peters and when he saw that I was very interested he allowed Father Peters to give me a copy of the New Testament. I bet we were the only Jewish family in Judendorf, and perhaps in all of Austria to have a copy. What's more, I actually read it and discussed some of the more interesting parts such as all of the miracles that Jesus performed and why there were no longer any miracles being performed. The Immaculate Conception and the Virgin Birth of Jesus were also topics of discussion along with the principles of confession, the rosary and absolution. I even memorized the Hail Mary and atoned for my sins by saying a number of Hail Marys when I was alone. The greater that I perceived my sin, the more Hail Marys I would say. Even though I was Jewish I felt that since the majority of the people in Judendorf and all of the neighboring towns were Catholic there had to be something quite powerful in their religion so it became my "two Gods are better than one" theory. I discussed religion with Father Peters who would often comment that he wished his parishioners and their children were as interested as I was.

The post World War I period was very bad for Germany, which had a direct impact on Austria. The Treaty of Versailles placed the entire blame for the war upon Germany and required Germany to compensate all of the winning countries for the war. Termed "war reparations" the amount was so staggering that there was no way that Germany could pay it and maintain any semblance of economic stability. The post-war Weimar government went through numerous economic crises. Austria, which was created as a result of the war by splitting Austria-Hungary, was similarly affected. Inflation was rampant and metal coins became more valuable for their metal content than for their intrinsic value as a medium of commerce. As a result, people hoarded coins containing certain metals during the war and for a few years after the war had ended. In addition, due to the rampant inflation, the government no longer minted coins. Coins disappeared so every city in Austria and Germany as well as many companies and businesses decided to print small value paper money to substitute for coins which were only for local use. These issues were called "notgeld" (not = emergency; geld = money). In Germany, the unit of currency was the Mark which was divided into 100 Pfennig (pennies). In Austria, the unit of currency was the Krone which was divided into 100 Heller.

The first notgeld issues during the war (1914-1918) were very simple consisting only of text with a simple design but as the coin shortage continued after the war, cities began to be more creative in subsequent issues with pictures of the towns, famous people, historical events, poetry, etc. Soon a new collecting hobby emerged. People wanted to get examples of the notgeld issued from other cities and towns. As a result, cities could actually make money by printing and selling money. Now cities were issuing sets of notgeld notes more for collectors than for actual circulation, often competing for sales. To differentiate themselves, they thought about different themes for the notes to increase sales and issued them in sets. As the issuing of notgeld proliferated, some cities and private merchants issued notes with anti-Semitic scenes and text. This further intensified anti-Semitism as it gave a sense of legitimacy to it.

I give you this background because there were many people in Austria and Germany who believed that the Jews were the cause of all of their economic problems. The Jews started and financed the war. The Jews profited from the war and have all the money. The Jews were profiting from the misfortune of the Austrian and German people after the war. The Jews were usurers and profiteers. This was a key theme of the National Socialist (Nazi) party as well.

Well, it was only a matter of time when some cities in Austria decided that they would also issue anti-Semitic notgeld that clearly identified the Jews as the source of their misery. Unfortunately, we lived near one of these cities. Some of the city officials were overtly anti-Semitic. They autocratically ruled the town council which did not have any Jewish members. If any Jews decided to run for office they would be told that it would be "a grave mistake" for them. They got the hint.

In 1920 just before Christmas a set of six notgeld notes was issued in Bruck with three designs. Each design had two different denominations. Two designs had a Christmas theme and one design had an anti-Semitic theme. One of the Christmas designs showed Santa Claus walking with a young girl and the other showed an angel dropping Christmas presents to some dancing children. The anti-Semitic note showed the devil taking a very rich Jew in a tuxedo and top hat to Hell. The Jew, who is much smaller than the devil, is chained to him by the wrist. Behind them are the sacks of money that the Jew had accumulated (cheated or stolen) from the Austrian people. The theme was quite clear: the Jews were responsible for their economic problems as they had all of the money and they should be banished to Hell (removed from Austria). All six had the same back design. They were signed by the Mayor (Bürgermeister), Anton Posch, and two members of the City Council. The set was very popular and was much sought after by collectors.

Notgeld from Bruck with Christmas and Anti-Semitic themes issued by the City Council of Bruck in the district of Pinzgau in 1920. (Source: Author's Personal Collection)

Things became decidedly worse in Judendorf after these notes were issued. Anti-Jewish graffiti was painted on Jewish headstones in the cemetery, on some Jewish stores, including my Grandfather's drug stores (so much for anonymity). My father lost most of his non-Jewish patients. Coincidentally, that was about the same time that my father was re-evaluating his future in Judendorf. He just did not have enough patients to make a good living and he did not want to continue to depend upon his father to support us. He had discussed this option with his father but his father really wanted us to stay since his wife, my grandmother, was not in good health – so my father deferred leaving. After the notgeld was issued, under pressure from parishioners, even the church stopped calling on him for his charitable medical aid except for emergencies. The three non-Jewish doctors got together and worked out a schedule to replace him at the clinic so the service to the poor would not stop – but they made it clear that they were not to be bothered at night or on weekends. Father Peters apologized profusely. My father understood and stoically accepted it. He continued to be available for emergency night and weekend calls. The only thing still really keeping him in Judendorf now was my sick grandmother and my grandfather who still asked that he stay and kept paying the bills. Since our grandmother was already in poor heath, the rash of anti-Semitic incidents worsened her condition. This was not the only incident.

One of the main tourist attractions in the area was Schloss Fischhorn, a thirteenth century castle located in Bruck. The Fischhorn family allowed tourists and townspeople into the castle during many weekends of the year and also allowed them to use the well-manicured gardens for picnics and family outings on selected weekends.

There was a fire at Schloss Fischhorn in 1920 that was blamed on a Jew. According to a city official, a Jewish man, a vagrant, was arrested for the crime. He confessed but before he was brought to trial he hung himself in the jail. The fire was extensive destroying quite a number of historic and personal items of the Fischhorn family. As a result they closed the castle to townspeople and tourists even after repairing the damage. This further intensified anti-Semitic feelings. Many townspeople that were formerly ambivalent were now openly anti-Semitic. Whether this was arson or accidental or whether the

Jewish man arrested for the crime was indeed guilty, was never really proven.

Anti-Semitic incidents escalated after the Bruck notes were issued and the fire. My mother was six-months pregnant when she was accosted in the street the day before Christmas by four young men. They pushed her around and called her names and accused her and our family of being Christ-killers and that she shouldn't be bringing another "dirty Jew bastard" into this world especially at this time of year when Jesus Christ was born. It was more mentally upsetting than it was physically harmful but the psychological impact was tremendous. This was the proverbial "straw that broke the camel's back" for him. That night, my parents talked it over and decided that they would leave Judendorf and move to a large city either in Austria or perhaps in another country such as Switzerland and change their name if necessary, but, in any case, not reveal that they were Jewish in the new city. They decided to wait until after my mother gave birth before moving which gave them time to carefully plan their relocation. This was not the only incident for our family. One had occurred to me some years earlier.

One day, when I was seven years old, as I was going to school, three older boys from the school chased me, grabbed me and pushed me to the ground. They stood over me calling me a "dirty Jew" and took my pocket watch that I had received as a birthday present from my grandfather just a few weeks before and some money. Before they left they pulled down my pants, pointed at my penis and laughed saying that I could run but I could not hide (that I was Jewish). They told me to keep my mouth shut or next time it would be worse. I wasn't hurt at all but I had no idea what they were talking about when they pulled down my pants so I asked my mother about it after telling her about my attack. I would not allow myself to be intimidated.

That night, my mother and father came into my room. He brought one of his medical books with him. My mother began the explanation. She told me the history of the Jewish people of Israel that had been persecuted for centuries due to their religious beliefs and sometimes overtly different customs and attire. I, of course, knew that I was Jewish but I did not know much about it. We were not very religious and, as there was no synagogue in Judendorf I had no knowledge of Jewish traditions and religious practices. Once in a while there were special occasions such as the Bar-Mitzvah of a relative or friend where a rabbi would come from Salzburg to perform the ceremony or we would go there – but that was the extent of it. A boy did not start Hebrew school until he was eight where he learned all about Judaism and prepared for his Bar-Mitzvah during the five years that he attended Hebrew school. My father picked up the story from my mother telling me about certain customs and the rite of circumcision. He showed me some circumcised and uncircumcised penises in the medical book. I looked down my pants and saw that I had a circumcised penis as the head of my penis was clearly visible and I could see the scar where the Mohel had made his cut as I pulled back my foreskin. My father was watching me do this and it was then that he first noticed that I had a much larger foreskin than normal. He turned to my mother and commented about it. They looked at each other and laughed as they remembered the day of my bris, the snow storm, the old mohel and his inebriated state when he performed his service. He turned to my mother and shook his head telling her that I wasn't really circumcised. She quickly turned away from me and looked up at him almost in shock. My father told her, "No. Our son was just circumed – only half the job was done." My mother realized he was joking and regained her composure and laughed. I did not laugh thinking that I had a serious problem and that I would have to go get the rest cut off but my father re-assured me that I did not. I was relieved. Every once in a while when I came down for breakfast, my father would greet me by saying. "How is my circumed son this morning?" This is how I learned about my not-so-perfect circumcision.

The next day my father went to the school with me. I knew the boys. They were brought to the principal's office. When they saw me and my father they really got scared. They were confronted and admitted the attack. They returned my watch and repaid the money that they took from me. The principal was going to punish them further including telling their parents, but my father interceded and asked that the incident just be forgotten. The boys were very thankful that it went no further. They, and their friends, never bothered me again but every once in a while when I went to the bathroom at night, I would stare at my penis looking at the circumcision scar and push my foreskin to completely cover the head of my penis to see what it would look like if I had not been circumcised but it would not stay in that position. As soon as I let go, the head reappeared.

One day while making a collage in my arts and crafts class, I had a really great idea. That night, I glued the loose foreskin over the head of my penis with some glue from the class but it looked so ridiculous in the morning that I started laughing so loud that my mother ran up to the bathroom to find out what was going on inside. Unfortunately, the glue was very strong so I hurt my penis pretty badly by pulling the foreskin off of the head of my penis. It took four days for the redness and swelling to go down and for it to stop itching. Until it healed, every day in school was torture as I wiggled and writhed trying to find a comfortable position for the irritated head of my penis to avoid rubbing it against my pants. One teacher asked if I had "ants in my pants" because I couldn't sit still. The class laughed but I can tell you that it was no laughing matter.

The next key ceremony for a Jewish boy is the Bar-Mitzvah. This occurs when a boy reaches the age of thirteen and moves overnight from puberty to adulthood which basically means in the Jewish religion that he becomes a "man." Bar-Mitzvah translates to "son of the commandment" (bar = son; mitzvah = commandment). It marks the transition from being a boy to being recognized by the Jewish community as an adult which also means that he can be counted in making a minion (quorum) in order for religious services to be held. In Jewish law, there must be eight male adults present to conduct religious services and a boy, until he has his bar-mitzvah at thirteen, cannot be one of the eight. Once bar-mitzvahed, he can even get married, which, of course, was a necessary pre-requisite to fathering a child, not that any thirteen year old actually got married – at least in modern times. This transition from a boy to a man was celebrated with friends and family that began with a religious ceremony in the synagogue on the Sabbath (Saturday) followed by a party with much food and drink. As there was no synagogue in the area, my father rented a hall in Bruck that was typically used for weddings. The party was usually held immediately after the ceremony or on Saturday night. The night parties were the most fun because the Sabbath was over and you could sing and dance and have entertainment. It was also much more expensive. Since my father was a doctor he was expected to have a night party, which we did (but my grandfather paid for it). So, on Saturday, January 22, 1921, I became a man. A rabbi came from Salzburg with a torah from his synagogue. This culminated my five years of studying with my tutor which included a special course in training for my bar-mitzvah. Depending upon the date, each bar-mitzvah boy has to read from a specific section of the torah. Actually, it was not just reading; it was recited in a singsong manner. Whether you could sing well or not, you had to sing the specific portion of the torah for that particular Sabbath. I started to learn how to sing this portion of the torah (called a haftorah) about three months before the ceremony. When the day finally came I was really ready. I was confident that I would do very well and I did. After the ceremony, everybody came up to me and congratulated me. Even the rabbi congratulated me before returning to Salzburg. However, I was a bit concerned. I knew that Father Peters had been invited but he was not there. He had promised me that he would come to the ceremony and the party. We had become good friends and he continued to explain many of the different aspects of Catholicism compared to Judaism to me while I was being tutored. At the time, I did not realize how valuable these discussions would be to me later in life. I thought that he must be very sick to have missed my bar-mitzvah and said a prayer for him to get better. Then I thought that perhaps he was just very busy with church stuff in the morning but would come for the party that night. He did not show up for the party either so I went back to the "he must be sick" rationale.

The party that night was great. I was able to see many relatives from other cities that I had not seen in many years some of whom had not attended the bar-mitzvah ceremony. It is not unusual for people to skip the ceremony and just come to the party. Since we were not a religious family, many of our relatives opted for the "party only" option electing to spend Saturday traveling to Judendorf rather than coming in the night before and having to pay for an extra night in a hotel. Some had to work on Friday so they had to travel on Saturday. In any case, it was really great to see them again. The typical bar-mitzvah party begins with a sumptuous open buffet served on a large table with traditional Jewish dishes such as chopped liver, stuffed cabbage and stuffed derma (don't ask!). This is followed by a multi-course sit-down dinner. Usually there was also an open bar throughout the night. There are traditional songs and dances of which hava-nagilah is a mandatory song. The mandatory dance is the horah where all of the people participating in the dance form a circle and dance first in one direction and then the other. It was an evening of great fun. Unfortunately, the events of 1920 caught up to us.

We were in the middle of dinner when without warning a group of men with ski masks over their faces and armed with clubs burst in the door and started hitting people and smashing the tables and anything else that was there. There were six of them. They were indiscriminate, attacking men, women and children screaming anti-Jewish epithets and telling everyone to get out of Bruck and Judendorf. They didn't club any of the women and children but did slap them and push them to the floor and threw food, wine and other drinks on the women's beautiful evening dresses. They ripped necklaces, rings, bracelets off of the women. They also robbed the men of their rings and watches when they fell to the floor. They only clubbed the men. All of the non-Jewish men that my father had invited were attacked for being "Jew-lovers." They were harder on them than on the Jewish people. Our family and friends from Salzburg were warned "not to show up in Bruck ever again" implying that further harm would befall them. They clearly knew who was Jewish and who was not as they sometimes called one of the people they were beating by name. I was with a few of my friends across the room from where they burst in. We were able to hide under a table. From under the table, I saw my father run to my pregnant mother who was in her eighth month when one of the attackers approached her. He picked up a chair and swung it hitting him in the back. He fell to the floor, obviously injured. Two of the other attackers picked him up and carried him out of the room. The attack only lasted about fifteen minutes. They were in and out very quickly and destroyed everything.

People were lying all around the room screaming and crying. The people that were not badly injured were helping those that were badly injured. None of the children were injured. Two of the women that had been slapped and pushed down to the floor were hurt. About fifteen men were hurt, four of them seriously with broken arms or legs and head wounds. My mother was unhurt but visibly shaken up. My father worried that she would have a miscarriage but she regained her composure quickly and they both went to the aid of the injured. My grandfather was hit in the arm as he raised it to protect his face and once on the thigh. He could hardly walk. My grandmother was not hurt but she was crying uncontrollably.

The police arrived about forty-five minutes later but did not appear to be that interested in doing anything. They nonchalantly took everyone's statement, called for more ambulances, told everyone to go home and promised a full investigation into the matter. I noticed that one of the policemen was stooped over holding his back in pain. He could hardly bend down. So much for the investigation!

My grandmother was never the same after the attack. She died about two months later which my father said was a result of the emotional shock and trauma. She hardly ate and jumped every time someone knocked on the door of their house. After her death, my grandfather fully supported and encouraged my father to leave Judendorf.

We found out the next day that Father Peters had been summoned to Salzburg the day before the bar-mitzvah on official church business that was supposed to only be for one day but he was kept there for three days as they asked him to deliver a sermon at one of the large churches on Sunday. He had sent a telegram to me through the local telegraph office but it was never delivered. He was genuinely devastated by the horrible event when he returned and offered every resource at his disposal to help. In retrospect, he suspected that he was purposely called away and kept there for more days than was necessary since the official church business was not very important.

As a young Jewish doctor with very few paying patients, my father was not really sacrificing that much in his decision to leave Judendorf. Realizing that simply moving to a large city would take time to build a practice and that as a doctor his background would be more thoroughly investigated in order to get a city license which would surely reveal that he was Jewish, he took the Civil Service

Exam as a Catholic and applied for a job as an assistant mortician at the city morgue in Vienna. One critical aspect of his choice was that it had to be a German speaking city and, given the stronger wave of anti-Semitism fomenting in Germany, Vienna became the city of choice. It was very large, was far enough away that meeting someone by chance from Judendorf was not very likely and there were numerous job opportunities. It also had the largest Jewish population in the country with more than 180,000 Jews so the likelihood of having the same level of anti-Semitic behavior was not likely (so he thought). This was just in case we were discovered as being Jewish and had to live openly as Jews. Another consideration for his choice was that the number of applicants for this type of work at a morgue was very small with none of the other applicants having a medical degree. Anyone with a medical degree went on to become a doctor. Surprisingly, no one asked why he was giving up his medical practice to work in the morgue. He scored high in the Civil Service exam and was immediately offered the job as an assistant mortician in the Vienna City Morgue, which he accepted.

My father now began to set up his new non-Jewish identity. Since his University diplomas were already issued to Markus Baumann, with the double n, he solicited the help of Father Peters who arranged for a variety of documents proving that he was Catholic. Baumann was not an uncommon name. There was one Baumann family living in Bruck and two Baumann families in neighboring towns that were related to each other. They had been living there for decades. One owned a guest house in St. Georgen and the second owned a shop in Bruck. The third was a dentist in Bruck. As they were longtime residents, all of the documents Father Peters obtained were actually legitimate. Father Peters provided original church membership cards, family baptism documents dating back three generations, other documents and receipts for donations (which he did actually make in appreciation for the documents) from the three Baumann families. He hoped that the families would not come looking for them. In February, my mother gave birth to Rebecca, named after her grandmother. At the suggestion of Father Peters, we went to Salzburg when she was due so she gave birth in a hospital there. Father Peters came to the hospital and attested that we were Catholic for the birth certificate. He also provided a Catholic baptism certificate when we returned to Judendorf.

In July of 1921 when I was thirteen and a half, my older sister was sixteen and my new sister was four months old, we moved to Vienna about 420 kilometers from Judendorf where we could start a new life – as a non-Jewish family. My father told me later that he had considered moving to England where we had some family, but his heritage, language and culture was Austrian/German and he wanted to remain in Austria should his father or any other member of the family need him. He would eventually inherit the three drugstores and the land that his father owned which he had decided he would sell and would therefore need to be in Austria.

When he had gone to the university and added an "n" to his name he did not tell his father. It was only when his father saw the diplomas that he learned of my father's action. He was very angry and would not speak to my father for a month but he mellowed and reluctantly accepted it. After the bar-mitzvah attack, my grandfather realized that my father had made the right decision. In supporting my father's decision to leave Judendorf he told the townspeople that he was sending my father to Berlin to study for an advanced medical degree in surgery. This would explain why we left Judendorf and would not raise any suspicions. He also gave my father a large amount of money to use as he saw fit. We found out later that when the Nazis took control of Austria my grandfather, who was eighty seven, and all of the Jewish people in Judendorf and surrounding towns were sent directly to Dachau located just outside of Munich where none of them survived. Judendorf was one of the few cities in Austria where Jews were sent directly to Dachau. This, I found out later, was due to the efforts of a certain city official who was an underground Nazi.

CHAPTER TWO

LIKE FATHER, LIKE SON

"It was easier for Jews to hide among Gentiles if they dressed, spoke, and acted like them. In Western and Southern Europe there was a high degree of acculturation and assimilation among Jews."

Hatikvah Holocaust Education Center website

My father started out as an assistant mortician when he arrived in Vienna but circumstances soon earned him a promotion. In fact, the first time that he distinguished himself was actually the first time that I was permitted to go to the morgue with him.

He was a workaholic at the morgue. He knew that he had to do very well to establish tenure and get promoted so that there would not be any danger of losing his job. His rationale was very simple. He had gotten this job using real documents that did not belong to him. The civil service background check was minimal. In fact, it was almost non-existent. Whoever ran the background check on him when he was hired at the morgue never went to Judendorf. He sent a few letters to the references that my father provided such as Father Peters, who had provided the documents, as well as some of my father's closest Gentile friends all of whom corroborated everything in his application almost to the exact words he used. This was not so surprising since my father gave them copies of the application. As a result of the test scores and the minimal background check, he was hired. His concern was that if he happened to lose this job and had to apply for another job in a related field (e.g., medical assistant at a hospital) that another, more-detailed background check with a visit to Judendorf could lead to the discovery that he was Jewish. The real documents were used without any changes. They were the actual records of the parents, grandparents and great grandparents of the other Baumann families. If someone went to Judendorf and Bruck and spoke to one of the other Baumann families thinking that they could be related he would learn the truth. There were too many loose ends. So, my father knew that his job performance at the morgue had to be exemplary to keep the job and avoid the need for another background check.

The main hospital was located in the first district near the University of Vienna. The Coroner's office and the main city morgue were located in a separate building behind the hospital. Birth certificates were stored at the hospital. As one might expect the death records office was in the morgue. In addition to being the central point for bodies in the first and three surrounding districts, the central morgue received the bodies when people died accidentally (e.g., traffic accidents), criminally (e.g., murder victim), suspiciously (e.g., suicide), legally (e.g., executed criminal), medically (communicable disease) or when no one could be found to immediately claim the body (e.g., a vagrant). Otherwise, the attending physician could certify the cause of death and have the body sent to a private funeral home. There were also three smaller morgues located in outlying districts. The central morgue had two separate sections. Every weekend one section would be closed for cleaning and to give the people working there at least one weekend off every two weeks. Autopsies were only performed where the deaths were of a suspicious nature (suicide) or if there were extenuating circumstances (murder). Often where foul play was suspected the Coroner or an Assistant Coroner was called to the scene of the death to verify conditions and attest to the cause of death or indicate that further investigation was needed. This was always done before the body was brought to the morgue although in many instances the body had been moved at the scene before the Coroner or Assistant Coroner arrived. If someone died from a sudden disease the protocol was to call the Coroner's office before moving the body to determine if the disease was contagious. The morgue also provided one additional service. If the family of the dead person could not afford the services of a private funeral home, there were some morticians that would perform the embalming procedure for a small fee. Since the salary for a mortician was not that high, this was a welcome supplement to their regular wages.

My mother worked as a secretary at one of the government agencies. We lived in a Catholic neighborhood and to perpetuate the "not being Jewish" ruse, my father joined the neighborhood Catholic Church, though he never went to mass. He did occasionally go to confession so the priests would at least know him but I have no idea what he confessed. They were very impressed with his knowledge of the Catholic religion (thanks to his conversations with Father Peters) and kept after him to come to church regularly and perhaps become a deacon but he politely declined saying that his duties at the morgue were quite intense and required weekend work. I never went to mass or confession as I was worried that I might say something to give our Jewish secret away.

Luckily, the subject of religion did not come up often at work but when it did, he was able to participate in the discussion with such a deep knowledge of Catholicism that no one ever suspected that he was Jewish. In fact, he was often asked by his co-workers for advice or clarification on a controversial point of Catholicism. In keeping with his Catholic pretension, he joined the Christian Social political party, which was anti-Semitic, but he was not active politically.

I attended the local public school in our neighborhood where I entered the eighth grade. I no longer participated in any sports on the advice of my father. As a team member I would have to take a shower with my teammates and my circumcised penis would reveal that there was a Jew amongst them. So we made up a story of my having rheumatic fever when I was younger and had some physical issues related to the disease that precluded sports activities. It worked.

My father would come home around 8 PM during the week and at 7 PM on the alternate weekends that he worked. After dinner he would sometimes talk to me about the more interesting events of the day such as the accident and murder victims brought in that day. I must admit that I had a morbid fascination of what my father did at the morgue. I asked many questions and repeatedly asked to go to work with him but was refused.

When I was fourteen a series of turning points occurred. First, I finally succeeded in getting my father to take me to the morgue with him. Secondly, events started to unfold that would change my life and everyone else's in Austria. In Germany, a politician by the name of Adolf Hitler started his rise to power as the leader of the National Socialist Worker's Party. He had just been arrested for an attempted coup and was sent to prison where he wrote Mein Kampf (My Struggle). Finally, when I was fourteen I entered Theresianische Akademie secondary (high) school.

So, for the first turning point! When I was fourteen I finally convinced my father to let me come to the morgue to see what he actually did. I had been pestering him to take me to the morgue ever since he got the job. It had sort of a morbid air of mystery and excitement about it that really interested me. Now, you may think that this was some kind of weird obsession but I don't really care. Anyway, during my first visit he took me into the autopsy room and started to perform an autopsy on an elderly man that had died from an overdose of sleeping pills. He was counting on me getting sick to my stomach and never again asking that I return to the morgue with him. On the contrary, not only did it not sicken me, I actually moved closer to watch and even asked some questions. He was amazed first that I did not get sick, second that I asked some questions and third that they were very good questions.

The man had ingested almost a whole bottle of very powerful sleeping pills. He was in bed when he was found by the maid that morning. Alongside the body there was a note written in a very shaky hand saying that he was taking his own life due to some business and personal problems. The suicide note was brought in with the body. A preliminary investigation by the police at his home ruled it a suicide. I looked at him lying on the autopsy table. He appeared to be in his mid-sixties with graying brown hair that was receding on his forehead. He was wearing monogrammed brown silk pajamas - an obvious sign that he was wealthy. My father removed his pajamas and began the autopsy. From the contents of his stomach, my father confirmed that he had indeed ingested many pills, more than enough to cause his death. However, when he examined the man's mouth he saw that there was a residue of white powder in his mouth between his teeth and around the upper part of his mouth between the lip and the gum. He tested the powder and confirmed that this was the sleeping powder from the pills. My father immediately called in the police and reported that the man had been murdered. The police were astonished. How could he be so sure? He explained that he based his conclusion on the following observances. There was a residue of the sleeping pill contents in his mouth. The man evidently chewed some of the pills prior to swallowing them. This was very unusual since the contents tasted horrible. In both accidental overdoses and intentional suicides the victim always swallows the pills whole with water and never chews them. This man was evidently being forced to take the pills, many at a time, and in his duress had chewed some of them. Secondly, the note was written with a very shaky handwriting. Typically, when a person chooses to commit suicide in a planned manner such as with sleeping pills, he takes the time to sit down and write the note in a steady hand with a well-thought-out explanation. The content of the dead man's letter was also a bit incoherent in that the reasons for his suicide were not that clear and concise, as if he were being forced to write what someone was telling him. The detectives listened attentively to the explanation offered by my father. They agreed with my father's diagnosis, thanked him and left to begin an investigation. A few days later I read in the paper that the man's oldest son had been arrested and had confessed that he murdered his father for his inheritance. He owed a lot of money as a result of a gambling addiction and when he asked his father for the money he was refused. He begged and pleaded with him but to no avail; the answer was still no. This was not the first time he had asked his father for money to pay off a gambling debt but it was the first time he was refused. Without the money he was going to be severely beaten by the men to whom he owed the money so it was either his father or him. As the eldest son he would get control of the business and quite a bit of money. He also knew that his mother would not refuse giving him money from her share of the inheritance should he ever need it – or else he could have her commit suicide as well. At the trial, my father testified about the residue in the victim's mouth. The only thing he changed about his testimony that day was that he said that the policemen that brought in the victim suspected foul play and all he did was to confirm their suspicions. The police investigating the case were commended for their diligence. Two of the detectives came to the morgue after the trial and thanked my father for his help and for not saying that initially that they thought it was suicide and were ready to close the case. By testifying the way that he did, the police received the full credit for breaking the case. When asked by the detectives why he did it, he just said that he felt that his job was to support the police and work with them not to try to take any credit for just doing his job. This incident made the rounds of all the police stations in Vienna. From that point on, whenever there was any important or high-profile crime my father, even though he was just an assistant mortician, was also asked to come to the scene of the crime along with the Coroner, before anything was touched or moved. My father had a keen sense of observation since he was a full medical doctor and could often discern some things that were missed by the Coroner and the police at the scene. In actuality, my father really had an ulterior motive for doing what he did. If he testified that he determined that it was murder and solved the case, his picture could have been in the Vienna newspapers and most likely newspapers in other cities which meant that he could have been recognized by someone from Judendorf that happened to see the picture. Moreover, it would have made the police look incompetent.

I learned three valuable lessons from this. The first was that people like being in the limelight whether they deserved it or not, so giving credit where credit wasn't due was an invaluable way to make friends and garner favors. The second was that with being a Jew in hiding, fame is not a benefit, it is a detriment as it could lead to discovery. The third was not to make anyone look stupid – or at least less intelligent than they were. If he had taken credit for solving the crime, the police would have looked foolish and could have become antagonists. This could have hurt him in the future.

Now, in addition to performing autopsies, my father often worked with the police providing forensic evidence of suicides, murders and accidental deaths. This gave him some very good contacts within the Vienna police department. Sometimes he was called to testify in some murder cases. He would always extol the expertise of the police which often was reported by the press. My father was promoted to mortician about two months after the first case was publicized and six months later he was promoted to Assistant Coroner, even though he did not have the tenure. When one of the Coroners retired one of the

Assistant Coroners was promoted my father got his position. There was no doubt in his mind that his relationship with the authorities was the key factor in his two rapid promotions. Another reason that he believed he was promoted was for protocol. He was only an Assistant Mortician but was often asked to go to the scene of a crime which was the function of an Assistant Coroner or a Coroner. They dare not refuse the request of the police so the most expedient way to resolve the issue was to promote my father.

Between the trials and the subsequent work with the police force on almost all of the important crimes or deaths where foul play was suspected, my father became somewhat of a local celebrity. Now, my mind was really made up. I was going to become a mortician like my father, work with the police to help them solve crimes and, perhaps, become a celebrity as well, even if it was within a limited group of people. Whenever he discovered anything out of the ordinary during an autopsy or post-mortem examination of the body, he would first report his findings to his superiors who would tell the police. His sharing of the limelight ingratiated him with his boss who obviously liked the limelight. Here again, his ulterior motive was to limit his exposure to the press to reduce the possibility of his picture being in the paper. This worked. Twice the Chief Coroner's picture was in the paper due to my father's work contributing to solving a high-profile crime. The police involved in the investigation always knew that it was my father who was the real brains behind the discovery. They were very happy when he was promoted to Assistant Coroner and made it a point to tell it to the three Coroners and the Chief Coroner, who knew it anyway. The Chief Medical Examiner in Vienna was also aware of my father's acumen and would sometimes privately consult with him as well on an important death.

So whenever there was a major crime and my father was involved he tried very hard not to get his name in the paper. When reporters were present at the scene of a high-profile crime, he always referred them to the police on the scene for the interviews and the photographs. One tactic that he often used was to give one of the policemen at the scene some important information about the crime that would be made public anyway so he would be of more interest to the press. Typically, the policeman on the beat never had his picture in the paper let alone be interviewed. So, when my father gave them some information that would not jeopardize the investigation, and deferred the press to that police officer, the officer loved it. It really made their families proud when their pictures were in the paper and they also liked seeing their family name in the press associated with an important crime even if there was no picture. As a result, my father's popularity with the rank and file of the police continued to grow.

Being the son of someone highly popular with the police had some fringe benefits as I was soon to learn. As a freshman, I was a very good, very smart and a very well-behaved student who did not participate in any sports. I maintained a low profile and did not have many friends. So, during my freshman year I basically was a nobody as my father was still building his reputation. He managed to help the police solve numerous cases using his forensic skills which was often well-publicized in spite of his desire not to be in the press. During the summer break he worked on two high-profile murders and was singled out by the Chief of Police in Vienna in a press interview.

As my father's son during my sophomore year I was able to overcome the nobody image – not by my actions alone – but by the actions of several aggressive girls who wanted to be associated with the son of someone famous. Many of the popular boys also wanted to hang around with a famous person's son. They all sought me out. A couple of them wanted me to take them to the morgue. I always refused.

In my junior year I reached the epitome of popularity. I was usually invited to a few parties but there was one that resulted in my being invited to every single party and social event that was held by anyone at school during the rest of my junior and all through my senior year. Sometimes I had to promise to go to two parties on the same night. This came about again due to me being my father's son.

In December I was invited to a party at one of the soccer player's house. We had become good friends as I often helped him with his schoolwork. His parents were away at a ski resort for the Christmas holidays. This was where they went on their honeymoon so it became . an annual event as they recaptured their honeymoon so he was never invited. Most of the time he was sent to relatives during their sojourn but his time none of the relatives were able to take him so they allowed him to stay home alone. Mark had strict instructions not to have any type of party while they were gone which he fully intended to ignore. He had a new girl friend whose birthday was December 28 and he really wanted to have sex with her so he decided to have a birthday party for her. At first, it was going to be small, but being on the soccer team, being one of the most popular guys in school and having a very large house the list of invitees grew and grew. Overall, there were about sixty of his closest friends and their dates at the party. It wasn't long before they started drinking. His father had a very well-stocked wet bar and wine cellar and there was an ice box in the basement that had a lot of beer in it. Other than having a little beer and wine at family gatherings, many of the students had not really had much alcohol so for many this was the first time that they had an unrestrained opportunity. Luckily, no one got violent or wild enough to damage anything but they did get loud – very loud. The record player was blasting, students were outside in the back and front yards singing, dancing and talking loudly. Pleas by the neighbors to quiet down were totally ignored. Mark was upstairs in his parent's bedroom with his new girlfriend. He had always wanted to have sex in his parent's bed which he was finally doing. With the door closed and locked and with the radio on, he was oblivious to the noise and the neighbor's complaints.

At about 11:30 the police were called. Four patrol cars came to the house with their sirens on. They stopped in front of the house and in the driveway. Apparently at least three neighbors finally called the police and reported riotous teenagers so they came in force. Most of the students just ran away at the sound of the approaching sirens but at least fifteen had stayed in the house oblivious to the sirens or just too drunk to move. They were caught including Mark and his girlfriend who emerged from his parent's bedroom covered only in some sheets. Mark was really upset. His parents would kill him especially since most of the boys and girls were underage. I was also caught. As we all sat in the living room I recognized a couple of the policemen. I went over to them and introduced myself. They told the others. They talked it over for about five minutes and decided to let us off with a warning and not report it. Mark was ecstatic. He sent everyone home except for me and some other members of his soccer team. We cleaned up the house and the front and back yards. Mark took his girlfriend home while we continued the cleanup. He came back about twenty minutes later and helped us finish cleaning. We finished by about 3 AM. We segregated the beer, wine and liquor bottles and counted them also listing the brand names since Mark knew he would have to replace them before his parents returned. We took up a collection to help him with the cost. I had saved the day. The word spread. After that night I was invited to every party held by any student in the school. I was their insurance policy.

The rest of high school was uneventful as was college – with just one exception. I did very well scholastically and had no trouble getting into the pre-med program at the University of Vienna. However, I knew that I needed to have some extra-curricular activities to ensure my entry into medical school. I still had to avoid sports because of my uncircumcised penis so I decided to join the college debating team in my junior year after doing miserable in chess. There was one particular debate that was significant. It was against the University of Berlin. They had the top college debating team in Europe for the past three out of four years and were undefeated for the year when they came to Vienna. The University of Vienna team had never won against any University of Berlin team. The subject of the debate, which was only revealed at the beginning of the debate, was: "Tenets of Faith: Defending the Immaculate Conception". The German team, as the visiting team, went first. They were very eloquent. They spoke about Mary being impregnated by an act of God. How Jesus was the Son of God born to Mary without having sexual relations with her husband, Joseph, or any man, and that Mary was a virgin at the time resulting in the Immaculate Conception. They went on about the life and death of Jesus and the Holy Trinity as a foundation of Christianity. They quoted passages from the Bible. When they finished the audience stood up and applauded. They were very, very polished. They were very, very eloquent. They were very, very convincing. But, they were very, very wrong.

The judges, one of whom was Cardinal Friedrich Gustav Piffl, the head of the Catholic Church in Austria, showed no emotion while the German team spoke, which was the rule. I found out later that he had selected the topic as the condition for him judging. He had been invited to stimulate attendance which was typically low. It worked as the hall was packed. As the German team proceeded I watched my other three teammates. They were clearly disheartened. They knew that we were not as eloquent or as knowledgeable on the bible where we could quote anything that the German team hadn't already quoted. I just sat there smiling. I knew that we had won after the first minute. I was going to be the third speaker but I passed a note to the team captain asking that I be allowed to go first and that if he agreed, we would win. He looked at me quizzically but agreed so when it was our team's turn, we switched seats and I started the debate.

My opening statement was a bit out of the ordinary. I basically started out by saying that the German team was absolutely fantastic. The audience agreed and gave them another round of applause. When the audience calmed down, I dropped the bomb. I said that while they were indeed eloquent they did not address the issue and that they were totally wrong. You could have heard a pin drop such was the silence that ensued. I started out by saying that the Immaculate Conception was not about Jesus, it was about Mary. It was that Mary was born without sin. Actually, the specific terminology was that Mary was born "without the stain of original sin" which enabled her to be the mother of Jesus. The birth of Jesus is called the "Virgin Birth" but the Immaculate Conception was solely about Mary. The Original Sin refers to the sin of Adam eating the apple from the Tree of Knowledge and being forced to leave Eden. Mary was spared this "stain of the original sin" by the "Grace of God" so she was immaculate. This is reinforced in the bible when the Angel Gabriel first greets Mary with, "Hail Mary, full of Grace, the Lord is with You." which I quoted from Luke 1:28. This is also recited in the opening statement of the rosary, which I also recited. I went on with some more quotes including some from Catholic texts not generally known by lay people also using some of the esoteric bits of knowledge that I had gleaned from Father Peters covering the first few centuries of Catholicism and the Immaculate Conception.

The entire audience was stunned. The German team was stunned. My teammates were stunned as were most of the judges, save one – Cardinal Piffl. Departing from the normal rules and procedures, he stood up when I had finished and glanced down at the team list, "You are Mr. Baumann?" he asked. "Yes," I replied. 'You are absolutely correct!" He proceeded to expound further on this issue even to the point of admonishing the German team. My teammates were able to pick up where I left off even though they were a bit repetitive. Actually, our team's performance was one of the best ever. The rest of the team was so ebullient, so self-confident after Cardinal Piffl spoke that they were exemplary. When we finished we also received a standing ovation. Now, debating was not a big thing at the University of Vienna but defeating the undefeatable University of Berlin team was the talk of the campus. It made the front page of the campus newspaper and was even reported in some of the local Vienna papers. For about two days we were celebrities. The debate was held on Thursday night and the campus newspaper was published on Friday. On Sunday there was a soccer game. The University of Vienna team won. We were immediately forgotten on Monday as all eyes, ears and thoughts were on the soccer team. However, Cardinal Piffl sent me a very nice letter on his personal stationary commending me for being a "devout Catholic" and on my "deep knowledge of the Catholic teachings" and that I was a "role model for young Catholic men and women in the university" as well. I sent a copy of the letter and newspaper articles to Father Peters thanking him for the many hours that we spent together. I am sure that he really enjoyed it. He sent back a note congratulating me and writing "if only the true believers paid as much attention as you it would make my life easier and more fulfilling," which he signed, "Your Proud Teacher!" in large script. He asked if I would consider "switching my curriculum from studying to be a mortician to becoming a priest?"

When I applied for admission to medical school in Vienna, I attached a copy of the campus newspaper and the other press clippings that reported on my role in winning the debate. I also attached a copy of the letter from Cardinal Piffl. I received an early admission acceptance letter with a congratulatory note from the Rector specifically citing the letter from Cardinal Piffl as a key factor in their early selection process and requesting if I could ask the Cardinal if he would give the invocation at the opening day induction ceremony for the new school term – which I did and which he gladly accepted.

While my term at the university was uneventful for me, it was not for many of the Jewish students. Jews accounted for about 30 percent of the student body and less than 10 percent of the population of Vienna and less than 3 percent of the total Austrian population. This disproportional ratio was an extremely sore point with the Catholic majority. They would beat up Jewish students, disrupt classes when Jewish students were answering questions or giving oral reports and even destroy personal property of some Jewish teachers. At times the violence was so bad that the Rector had to close the school. Cardinal Piffl often had to intercede on behalf of the Jews admonishing the students that were violent but this had little effect. The anti-Semitism of certain groups of students, especially members of the National Socialist (Nazi) Youth Group, was so strong that they risked suspension and even expulsion to mistreat Jewish students and teachers.

At medical school I was the only student not studying to be a doctor or some sort of specialist like a gynecologist. I was studying to be a mortician with the goal of becoming a Coroner. This made me the "odd fellow" but they knew about my father so they understood perfectly why I wanted to follow in his footsteps. Moreover, they did not view me as a threat to them in their highly competitive quest to become a doctor. Given this lack of competition, they were always willing to answer any question I had and share information with me. I think a few of them recognized that cooperating with me now and having me as a friend could be beneficial to them later when they were doctors. Another advantage in just becoming a mortician was that when I finished the three-year term of initial medical study I would be able to stop studying and apply for the position. The other medical students had at least two additional years of school plus a couple of years of internship. Here again, my term at the medical school was uneventful but my father was promoted to Coroner during my second year of medical school. As a result of his promotion, he was invited to speak at a conference on the investigation of causes of death where there was any suspicion of foul play. The conference was held in Munich. My father invited me to go with him. It was there that I really understood how strongly the Nazi Party promoted their prime doctrine of anti-Semitism. In addition to the anti-Semitic speeches and the slide shows showing that most criminals were full or part Jewish, the Nazis developed an ingenious way to link Jews to the economic crisis afflicting Germany. They handed out old banknotes that had lost their value during the period of post-war hyperinflation that were overprinted with anti-Semitic slogans and pictures.

Obsolete worthless inflation currency overprinted with anti-Semitic slogans. Author's Personal Collection

(right)

Surprise!

Swastika/Hitler/National Socialism (as a comet) (Surprised Jewish man)

God the righteous! A new comet is coming!

People come to Hitler and National Socialism

(left)

- **Gold, silver and bacon is what the Jews have and they leave us with this shit (worthless money)**
- **People, how long will you let this international Jewish conspiracy last**
- **Come to us, the National Socialist Party**

I was graduated with honors, took the civil service exam, passed it with a very high score and was accepted to the position of assistant mortician in the City Morgue of Vienna. This was done independently of my father's position and obvious influence but I was now able to work with him. My father was very proud that I was following in his footsteps. We became even closer. I was now 24 years old.

CHAPTER THREE

ASSASSINATION

"The best man cannot live in peace if his wicked neighbors will not leave him in peace."

> Engelbert Dollfuss, Chancellor of Austria, using a quote from Schiller to describe the Nazi uprising of June 1933 in a speech at a League of Nations Conference.

As 1932 unfolded, I was working closely with my father at the morgue. Every Sunday I would go to my parents' house where my mother cooked a traditional Jewish meal. To mask my being Jewish I never went to a Jewish restaurant, except on the odd occasion when one of my Jewish co-workers at the morgue invited me. Most of the time, I politely turned down their invitations. When I did go, I always had them explain the various items on the menu. Even though I got my job on my own merits and did very good work (if I don't say so myself) the fact that my father was such a renowned Coroner did have some benefits in the way I was treated by my peers and superiors. Recognizing this I felt that going out with my Jewish co-workers once in a while was a requirement just as it was going out with members of the Christian Social and Social Democrat political party members working at the morgue. I stopped short of going out with any one from the National Socialist (Nazi) or Pan-German party.

There was not one Sunday meal when the subject of politics, Nazis and the treatment of Jews in Vienna and Germany did not come up. The National Socialist Party in Austria was growing rapidly. Hitler was gaining much ground in Germany which was spreading to Austria. The last two years of the Weimar government had been a disaster. The world was still in a global recession that was led by the stock market crash in the United States in October 1929. It was even more pronounced in Germany because of the war reparations. There was absolutely no way Germany could recover with such a heavy debt burden. Unemployment exceeded 35 percent. Riots were commonplace and government officials were being assaulted or murdered in an ongoing power struggle. Hitler's Nazis promoted the violence both openly and secretly. In fact, Hitler reveled in it. This was the perfect breeding ground for attracting new members. His oratory skills were second to none – and he knew it. His message, which was repeated over and over again, was that the Jews and the Communists were the cause of their economic problems – not the Aryan German people; they were stabbed in the back, betrayed, by these groups. He had plans to rebuild the economy and eliminate the Jews and the Communists. Conditions were even worse in Austria. In 1931 the largest bank in Austria became insolvent. It was owned by the Rothschild family who were Jews. This added fuel to the fire. More than 400,000 people were unemployed. Austrian Nazis became very aggressive and very violent in Vienna. They sabotaged many infrastructure installations in an attempt to discredit the government. They also attacked many Jewish businesses, particularly in the second district, Leopoldstadt, which had the highest concentration of Jews. Anti-Semitism was clearly on the rise in Vienna.

But now there was a new hope for Austria. A new coalition government under President Miklas had just been formed with a consensus chancellor. He was Engelbert Dollfuss, a member of the anti-Semitic conservative Christian Social party. He instituted a number of reforms and work programs focusing on the economic strengths of the country such as agriculture and steel manufacture. However, there were some things beyond his, or for that matter, any leader's control. The Treaty of Versailles had broken apart Austria-Hungary into four separate countries: Austria, Czechoslovakia, Hungary and Yugoslavia. The major industrial area of the Austro-Hungarian Empire was Bohemia-Moravia which was now part of Czechoslovakia. Many Austrian businessmen had factories there. Some were sold and some were kept but the net result was that the jobs were in Bohemia-Moravia and not Austria.

The coalition was very fragile to say the least. The Christian Social Party only had a one vote majority in the Parliament. They needed the support of the minority parties to combat the belligerence of the Social Democrats who opposed most of the plans put forth by the Christian Social party.

This came to head in 1933. In March, there was a critical issue with an extremely close vote. The President of the lower house of Parliament, which was a non-voting position, resigned in order to cast his vote in this extremely close race. So did the two Vice-Presidents. At this point the lower House ceased to function since here was no leadership at all. Dollfuss saw his chance. He went to the President and requested that the Parliament be dissolved and that the two of them should rule the country together with military support. The crucial argument that he used to convince Miklas was that Adolf Hitler had just become the chancellor of Germany and was in the process of setting himself up as the supreme leader turning Germany into a dictatorship. With the Nazi Party gaining ground in Austria only a unified totalitarian government could cause positive economic change, stem their violence and block them from getting control of the country. Miklas agreed and ordered the police and the army to block the entrance of the Parliament and not let anyone enter from either the lower or the upper house of Parliament. Miklas dissolved Parliament following the guidelines set in the constitution but without setting the date for new elections. Dollfuss, as chancellor actually had more power in day-to-day operations than the President so he became the de facto dictator of Austria. He banned all political parties and replaced it with the Vaterländische Front (National Front), a coalition of "people that believed in Austria". To gain countrywide support he invited members of all political parties to put aside their partisan beliefs and join the National Front under his direct leadership. Many did join in the hope that the new government could finally solve some of the economic problems that could not be solved in the bipartisan parliament. The invitation to join the National Front was not extended to members of the National Socialist Party.

My father and I thought that this was a good move. First, only a strong government could get anything done to resolve the economic crisis. Every time something constructive was brought forth in

Parliament there was always some special interest group opposed to it. Debates lasted for weeks and eventually nothing was being done – or, if passed, there was so much corruption involved that less than 50 percent of the money found its way into the project. Second, Dollfuss was vehemently against Hitler and the National Socialist Party. As the saying goes, the enemy of my enemy is my friend. As such, in spite of being a member of the anti-Semitic Christian Social party, he garnered the open support of most Jews who made substantial financial contributions to the National Front when he toned down all anti-Semitic rhetoric. Many Jews even joined the National Front, especially the wealthier ones. We discussed joining but we mutually decided against it. Being Jews in hiding, maintaining a low profile was the best defense to prevent discovery.

Recognizing the importance of the financial support of the Jews in these troubled times Dollfuss censored anti-Semitic newspaper and magazine articles, ensured the safety of Jewish students at the universities and prohibited hotels, resorts and restaurants from discriminating against Jews. The government could easily revoke permits and licenses to such establishments putting them out of business. Compliance was wide-spread – as was the resentment against Jews for the forced policy changes. Some of these hotels and resorts gained Jewish members – but lost non-Jewish members, particularly those that had been openly anti-Semitic.

Dollfuss modeled the new government after the Italian dictatorship of Mussolini and visited him in Rome a number of times. Being quite egotistical, Mussolini was extremely flattered and pledged his support to Dollfuss and for the independence of Austria. A key reason for his support was that he preferred to have neutral Austria on his northern border rather than Germany. Dollfuss also had the support of the church and the military – but not everyone supported him.

An armed uprising by the Nazis occurred in June 1933 while Dollfuss was attending a League of Nations conference in London. It was quickly suppressed by the police and the army. Time magazine ran this account of the uprising:

"Under orders from Munich and Berlin, Austrian Nazis went to work last week. Attempts were made to assassinate at least ten high Austrian officials. Crowds of Nazi students that gathered in front of Vienna University were chased down the Ringstrasse by mounted police swinging their sabers. A huge bomb tore out the inside of a (Jewish-owned) department store. Lives of dozens of people were saved when a 30-lb. bomb failed to explode in a cafe in Vienna's Jewish quarter, the Leopoldstadt. Not so lucky was Frau Futterweit. Standing in the doorway of her little jewelry shop, an old silk stocking stuffed with newspapers and a hand grenade was flung at her from a passing car. Frau Futterweit tried to throw it back. It burst in her hands, killing her instantly. Eight passersby were wounded; one died in the hospital."

Against Austria's Nazi terror the Austrian Government struck back. Nazis to the number of 1,142 were arrested, 15 of them, German liaison officers directly responsible to Adolf Hitler, were expelled, 37 others were charged with high treason, the rest were cooled in jail for a couple of days, then released.

"While I do not charge the German Government with any such intention, the danger exists that irresponsible elements might march into Austria from Bavaria. If that happened we would have Czechoslovak and Jugoslav troops marching in to protect the interests of the Little Entente (Hungary, Romania and Yugoslavia) and a virtual war with my poor country as the battlefield. That is what I fear." (Dollfuss's quote)

Patted on the back by representatives of half a dozen nations, little Millimetternich-Dollfuss flew to Paris then returned to Vienna with a real prize in his pocket, a US$29,975,000 League of Nations loan. Back home in time to hear of a new grenading, this time upon a squad of police, Chancellor Dollfuss felt powerful enough to order the dissolution of the Nazi party throughout Austria; which he promptly did."

Some explanation of the press article is mandatory. Engelbert Dollfuss was a small man – in size only. He was only about 154 centimeters (about five feet) tall. Because of his height he was refused entry into the army but after vehemently insisting and trying different enlisting offices, he was allowed to enlist. He distinguished himself in battle with his leadership skills earning many medals and decorations. After the war he entered government service. In his most recent position prior to becoming the coalition choice for chancellor, he was the Minister of Agriculture where he initiated a number of reforms that increased agricultural production during the depression and helped earn money from agricultural exports. As with any leader, the press always plays up and makes fun of any unusual physical characteristic. For Dollfuss it was his height. When he dissolved parliament and became a pseudo-dictator, the press labeled him "Mini-Metternich" or simply "the small Metternich" (after Crown Prince Metternich, the autocratic chancellor of Austria from 1833-1848 who re-established Austria as a major political force in Europe). Dollfuss did not mind the analogy to Metternich – but he never liked the "mini" pseudonym or the constant jokes on his height.

"Austrian Leaders"

Postcard showing the diminutive Chancellor Dollfuss (front) with (from left to right) Vice-Chancellor Schuschnigg, General Stefan, Cardinal Innitzer, Prince Starenheim (in uniform), Cabinet Minister Stockinger, and General Fey. (Source: Author's Personal Collection)

So, in June 1933 the attempted Nazi coup was suppressed and the Nazi Party was outlawed. While many Nazi Party members fled to Germany, quite a number remained in Austria and secretly continued to support the Nazi Party where they continued to use violence to disrupt the Dollfuss government. They became "underground Nazis"

The government tried to improve the economy but instead it worsened as the conditions in Europe were still very poor and the Nazis continued to use violence to undermine the government. This came to a head in 1934 with two separate and unrelated events.

Dollfuss's first crisis was the result of a battle between the two paramilitary units of the two major political parties in February 1934 that almost erupted into a full civil war. The Christian Social Party had its own military group called the Heimwehr, which was incorporated into the National Front Army but was maintained as a separate elite unit reporting directly to Dolfuss. The Social Democrat military group was called the Schutzbund. The constant friction between the two political parties erupted into an armed confrontation when Dollfuss became the dictator. The army of the National Front was much stronger and better equipped than the Schutzbund and easily defeated them. The last Schutzbund stronghold was a group of apartment buildings that were heavily defended. Rather than storm the complex which would have resulted in heavy casualties on both sides, Dollfuss ordered that artillery be used if they did not surrender. They did not surrender. The resultant artillery fire did the job but many civilians – men, women and children were killed and wounded as a result of the indiscriminate bombardment. While many were taken to hospitals in the other districts, the main hospital was the best place for the more seriously injured and the overflow patients that the other hospitals could not treat. The hospital could not accommodate all of them and some of the injured died from the lack of care. The public outcry permanently damaged Dollfuss' image and resulted in a move to expand the hospital.

The easiest solution was to relocate the morgue, which the hospital had been trying to do for years and use the space to expand but it was not until the Social Democrat uprising occurred that sufficient money was set aside for the new morgue and the expansion of the hospital. A special ad hoc committee was set up to resolve the problem. I was assigned as the official representative for the morgue. We had monthly meetings but the relocation efforts were not going well. The problem was that there was no suitable space in the first district big enough and available for the morgue. Moreover, as soon as the residents of the neighborhoods in any other district found out that the committee was considering relocating the morgue into their neighborhood they protested in masse. They contacted their parliamentary representatives, marched around the morgue carrying signs and spoke to every building and land owner to not sell out to the morgue. The project languished until one day in April when there was a fire that destroyed a group of old wooden houses in the fourth district. Rather than rebuild them the owners were willing to sell the property to the city for the morgue at a price that would allow them to rebuild better houses elsewhere and charge higher rents. It looked as if we were finally making some progress.

This project was the direct responsibility of the Minister of Social Welfare. He would send the Deputy Minister with his suggestions if he was not able to personally attend, which was most of the time. Since the Deputy Minister was not the Minister he did not have the power to approve anything we suggested. It was also sometimes difficult to distinguish between what he was asking for and what were the requests of the Minister. Often, after we had decided on something, the Minister would overrule us a few days later. After a while it became obvious that to avoid unnecessary work, he had to be there. We asked that he attend every meeting emphasizing the need for his leadership and our willingness to schedule the meetings to meet his availability. He accepted. So, as of June 25th we decided to meet at the Chancellery on a bi-weekly basis. His preference was Wednesday which also worked for us. Given the work schedules of the Minister and the committee members, we decided to meet at 11 AM and work through lunch. The Minister would order lunch which he paid from his budget. Attendance was just about 100 percent for every meeting. There is something about a free lunch that negated other commitments. I also liked that time because I could watch the changing of the Chancellery guard which took place precisely at 12:50. I had never seen the ceremony before I became a member of this committee. It was impressive.

Our scheduled meeting on Wednesday, July 25, 1934 was almost canceled. It was summer and half of Vienna was on holiday. President Miklas was in Carinthia, Southern Austria. The vice chancellor was in Lido, Italy. Chancellor Dollfuss had scheduled the last cabinet meeting before the summer recess on Tuesday, July 24th but a number of the Ministers that were still in Vienna couldn't make it that day so it was postponed to the 25th. We had just received the estimates on the cost for the new morgue from three contractors in sealed envelopes. We were going to open them and evaluate each estimate at our meeting on the 25th. Were it not for the importance of moving forward on this matter our meeting would have been canceled but the Minister was leaving for his vacation the day after the Cabinet meeting. I called the morgue to let them know that I would be gone for most of the day.

Everything seemed to be going very well. We started on time at 11 AM and had a general discussion on the procedures we would use to evaluate the bids. Lunch was brought in at noon. At 12:15 the Minister was called out of the meeting to attend to some critical problem so we also took a break and finished eating. The Minister still had not returned when we finished eating. It was now a little after 12:45. I walked over to the window and looked down at the courtyard just in time to see the guards march in for the ceremonial changing of the guard ceremony. However, this time there was an added attraction. Right behind them were about eight trucks loaded with police and soldiers. I asked the other committee members if they were aware of the change in the ceremony. They were not so most of them joined me at the window. As the men started to get out of the trucks my forensic training took over and I started to notice details that the others were missing.

I called all of the other committee members to the window. "Look, this is strange," I said, "the soldiers and police are in trucks owned by a local company. They are not military vehicles. And the police are in the same trucks as the soldiers. This is very unusual." As they got out of the trucks I said, "Look, some of the soldiers do not have guns and others have mismatched uniforms. Something is very wrong here."

I was right. As soon as they got out of the truck some of them trained their rifles on the guards and took them prisoner taking their rifles. The others rushed into the building. We could hear shouts and screams as they went from office to office and ordered everyone out. This was happening very fast. We looked at each other and realized that we had no option. We were to become prisoners of these men.

About one minute later, they burst into the room and ordered everyone out into the hall. "We are soldiers of the SS Standarte 89 and we have come to liberate Austria from the cruel dictatorship of Dollfuss. Do as you are told and you will not be harmed. Heil Hitler!" Those two last words said it all. We were caught in the middle of a second Nazi attempt to seize the government and make Austria a Nazi country. We were herded downstairs into a large room in the basement. There were about 60 of us in the room. We were told that more people were being held in other rooms in the basement on the other side of the Chancellery.

Our guards were quite talkative. As far as they knew their coup was successful. They took control of the building without firing a shot. They told us that there were more than 150 of them involved in the coup in Vienna and hundreds more in other cities. In the Chancellery group there were about seventy of them, supported by some Nazi members of the Vienna police. Additional men were taking over the radio station and the telephone exchange. Under Dollfuss, the press and the radio was totally controlled by the government. He had closed all private radio stations so now there was only one radio station in the city. Our captor mentioned that as soon as Dollfuss and the cabinet were captured there would be a signal sent to the radio which would broadcast to the Nazis to take over the governments of the major cities throughout the country.

The guards were smiling and congratulating one another and repeatedly telling everyone not to worry that no harm would come to them. All of a sudden two shots rang out. We did not hear anyone scream, only the two shots. "Some fool must have resisted!" one of the guards said. Since there were no other shots heard it seemed as if he was right.

Someone came in and said that Dollfuss had been shot but that he was only wounded. The radio station had been captured. The signal that the chancellor was captured had been phoned to the radio station and they were now broadcasting the message to start the coup in the other cities.

Three of the Nazi police officers came downstairs with a radio to where we were being held and turned it on. The broadcast repeatedly said that Dollfuss and the Cabinet had resigned and that a new government had been formed under Anton Rintelen, a well-known former Cabinet Minister currently the Austrian Ambassador to Italy – and a staunch supporter of the National Socialist movement. The man who carried the radio into the room disconnected it and said that he was bringing it to the other rooms where more hostages were being held so they could hear the broadcast. We were told again by our jubilant guards that no one would be harmed, that the government was in transition and as soon as Rintelen arrived and appointed a new Cabinet we would be released. This alleviated the fears of the hostages. We had been confined to the room but were now allowed to go to the bathroom which was much appreciated. For some that were not supporters of the Dollfuss regime, there was a sigh of relief and some overt happiness. For the few Jews in the rooms there was fear and dread. Their worst nightmare had occurred. The Nazis had gained control of the government. For most, however, there was sadness and concern. Most of the people there were government workers that now wondered if they would have a job under the new regime. Whether they supported Dollfuss or not they respected him and what he was trying to accomplish.

I now took the time to look at the faces of the soldiers and policemen guarding us. To my amazement, I recognized two of the policemen. They were indeed real police officers. While I knew that many Nazis had clandestinely infiltrated the police force, this was the first time that they came out in the open. One of the police officers that I knew saw me staring at him. At first he was going to come over to yell at me for staring at him but as he approached he recognized me and extended his hand. Instinctively I grasped his hand and shook it. He was very excited and shook my hand quite vigorously. "Congratulations Michael, you are a witness to history!" He told the other members of the coup in the room who I was. Two other police officers, one I knew and another that I did not know, came over and also shook my hand – but much less enthusiastically.

About forty five minutes later, one of the soldiers came into the room and reported that the building was being surrounded by the Heimwehr; the government-controlled paramilitary group that reported directly to General Fey whom we learned was also a prisoner in the Chancellery. Evidently, just before the coup, General Fey must have secretly called the Heimwehr before being captured. The troops had just arrived and had surrounded the Nazis in the Chancellery. The Heimwehr outnumbered the Nazis and were much better armed. They obviously decided to wait for orders before attacking and risking the lives of the hostages because there were no shots being fired.

People now poured into the streets from stores and businesses. Sirens could be heard throughout the city. Additional police and army units were also responding to the crisis. Police cars were lined up forming a barrier around the Chancellery to hold back the crowds that were now approaching to find out what was happening. The Heimwehr were completely in charge and the police followed their orders. Armored regular army units started to roll in about forty minutes later. They formed a secondary barrier behind the police cars and set up machine guns that pointed at both the Chancellery and at the crowds in case there were additional Nazi attackers in the crowd.

All of a sudden conditions changed. Some men in army uniforms that were obviously not real soldiers told our guards that something was wrong. The radio station was no longer broadcasting. The Nazi leader of the coup, Fridolin Glass, never arrived at the Chancellery and they did not know where he was. Moreover, the coup leaders could not find Rintelen. He was staying at the Imperial Hotel and was supposed to come to the Chancellery before the announcement had been made on the radio but he too had not arrived. Their joy dampened considerably. They were now clearly worried.

We were left with the original guards. Hours passed without any word of what was happening. Finally, someone came in and said that the coup had failed. The government had found out about the plot from an informer apparently just before it occurred. Dollfuss had ordered all of the cabinet ministers to leave the Chancellery about thirty minutes before the Nazis arrived which was why the Minister we were meeting with was called out of the meeting and did not return. Only Dollfuss and some of his aides stayed, including General Fey who commanded the Heimwehr that had surrounded the building. As soon as he learned of the plot he had called the Brigade Commander who was on maneuvers just a few kilometers outside of the city which is why they were able to arrive fully armed so soon. The radio station was recaptured after some fierce fighting but, unbeknownst to them and to most people, was that Dollfuss had prepared for such an event as this. After the failed Nazi coup in 1933 he set up a secret substation in an adjoining building with the ability to cut the transmissions from the main radio station in case it was captured. Within twenty minutes of the capture of the main radio station, the lines were cut and the broadcast was terminated. Meanwhile, Rintelen was being detained at his hotel pending an investigation of his role in the coup based on the radio broadcast identifying him as the head of the new government. For some reason he did not expect the coup to move as quickly as it did so he did not leave the hotel before the broadcast was made announcing that he was the head of the new government. Once this was announced, he was detained by the guards assigned to protect him at the hotel. The cabinet members that left the Chancellery before the coup met in the Ministry of Defense building along with key military and political figures and set up a new temporary government under Kurt von Schuschnigg, another Minister. He was now the acting chancellor empowered to deal with the situation. His first act was to open a line of communication with the Nazi leadership in the Chancellery so he sent an army officer, under a white flag of truce, with a message letting the Nazis know that the temporary government was willing to negotiate by phone. The telephone exchange was recaptured without a fight. The Nazis controlling the Chancellery agreed so a phone line was opened for negotiations. At this point they were positive that the coup had failed and they were now only interested in getting out alive. As the leaders of the SS Standarte 89 were negotiating with the government, it looked like that they would be allowed to leave the

Chancellery for Germany without being arrested if they gave up and no one was killed.

All of a sudden, the police officer that knew me ran into the room. He asked if there was a doctor in the room. There was no doctor. He came up to me asking that I come with him immediately. As we ran upstairs to the Corner Room, he told me that President Dollfuss had been seriously wounded and had lost a lot of blood. He would surely die if left unattended. We ran upstairs to the room where Dollfuss had been shot. Dollfuss was on a couch with his head resting on some chair cushions. He was very pale and listless. He was not moving. He had indeed lost a lot of blood. There had to be at least two liters of blood on the floor beside him. This was about 25 percent of the blood in the human body. As I knelt over him with two other Nazis, I looked at his eyes. The pupils were dilated and unresponsive. I knew that he was not going to make it. He died in less than three minutes as I helplessly tried to stop the bleeding. His last words were, "Lads, you are so good to me. Why aren't the others like you? May the Lord forgive them. I only wanted peace. Give my regards to my wife and children."

The room was silent. As I started to get up I noticed that Dollfuss's wounds were not fatal. One bullet hit him in the side of his neck passing through without hitting any major vein or artery. The other bullet also hit him in the neck but traveled down his body exiting on his right side. Since he was unarmed it was obvious that he had been purposely shot with the intent to kill him. From the wounds I deduced that the first bullet caused him to lose his balance and fall forward. In his stooped over position the second bullet entered his neck and exited through his right side. Neither bullet severed any vital organ, artery or vein. They were not fatal if properly treated. He slowly bled to death while the negotiations were being carried out. With some simple first aid, the bleeding could have been either stopped or at least slowed down substantially but left unattended and untreated, he just slowly bled to death while everyone ignored his pleas for help. The police officer that shook my hand and told me about the coup, came over to me and confided that Dollfuss repeatedly asked for a doctor and then a priest when he realized that they were not going to get a doctor for him. All of Dollfuss's requests were refused so there was no doubt in my mind that they purposely let him bleed to death. I must admit that I had not realized how short he was even though his diminutive height led to many jokes about him. Even when he made public appearances, he seemed taller. His diminutive height and thin body was definitely a contributing factor in his bleeding to death. He had less blood than a larger man.

Another few hours passed. I was not permitted to return to the rest of the hostages since I knew that Dollfuss was dead. In fact, only the people in the Corner Room knew that he was dead. Rudolf Messinger was the police officer that initially recognized me and had me brought to the Corner Room. He took me to the side of the room and explained the situation in detail. I do not know why he did it but he did. The coup was code-named Operation Summer Festival. He told me that it was country wide with groups ready in every major city waiting for the radio broadcast that the Chancellery and the government officials had been captured and that a new government had been formed. At that point the armed revolt was to begin in the major cities. However, the broadcasts stopped after fifteen minutes. There were no radio transmissions at all after that so the leaders in the other cities feared that the radio station had been recaptured and the coup put down so they just waited for additional confirmation. He pointed to the two men in the room that were jointly in command of the Nazis assigned to take over the Chancellery. Franz Holzweber was in charge of the Chancellery military operation. He was one of four group leaders reporting to Fridolin Glass, the leader of the entire coup in Vienna. The other group leader with him was Otto Planetta. His responsibility was to seize Dollfuss, Miklas, and the cabinet ministers and hold them hostage. It was Planetta who shot Dollfuss. Both leaders were dressed in a Captain's uniform which was the highest officer uniform that they were able to get. Two other group leaders were responsible for the takeover of the radio station and the telephone exchange.

I was treated quite well now. Even though I was not part of the coup and not a Nazi, my assistance with Dollfuss and the fact that the two police officers knew me and vouched for me was enough to have me treated almost like one of the conspirators. I was permitted to go to the bathroom to wash the blood off of my hands without an escort. I promptly returned to the corner room when I finished washing. I stood in a corner out of the way. I could see from the activities that there were many issues. There were heated discussions between Planetta and Holzweber about the course of action to take.

Holzweber called Messinger and two other police officers over to him. They were instructed to get General Fey, the commander of the Heimwehr brigade that was surrounding the Chancellery, and bring him to the balcony. Holzweber and Planetta left the room. They returned about thirty minutes later. Messinger came over to me and told me that they had Fey address his troops from the balcony telling them that everyone was safe and that they should not attack. He was forced to make the announcement at gunpoint with Messinger and another officer laying on the floor holding on to Fey's ankles so he would not jump off of the balcony. The Heimwehr moved back about 30 meters but kept their guns trained on the Chancellery. As far as they were concerned, General Fey was a prisoner and was no longer their direct commander but they did not want to risk the lives of the hostages so they waited for orders from the new government.

Another hour or two passed. Negotiations by telephone continued. Holzweber finally addressed the men in the room. "Comrades, Operation Summer Festival has failed. The radio station has been recaptured. Communications are being restored. A new government has been sworn in and is in full control. Unbeknownst to us, there was a secret second radio transmitter that was set up just in case something like this occurred. Within the hour the main radio station was shut down and transmission started a few hours ago at the secret station refuting the takeover and that the government was not under our control. We have been promised safe conduct out of Austria if we lay own our weapons and surrender. I have accepted the offer. Comrades, lay down your weapons and follow me."

With that, they put down their guns and left the room. I, along with the two Dollfuss aides in the room, stayed in the room. When they left, we rushed to another room and looked out of the window. About ten army trucks were lined up in front of the building. The Nazis exited the building in single file and boarded the trucks, about seven men to a truck. There were army vehicles with machine guns mounted on them and motorcycles interspersed with the trucks as well as in front of and behind the column. When they were all loaded the column of about twenty-five vehicles drove off. We watched them as they left. The Heimwehr, the police and members of the provisional government ran into the building. One of Dollfuss's aides went downstairs to meet them. He led them to the Corner Room. It was only then that they realized that Dollfuss was dead. They were never told that he was dead. They were repeatedly told that he was only wounded.

The room was now filling up with senior army officers and government officials. One of the aides told the people entering that I was called in to try to save Dollfuss's life but it was too late. I was identified as working in the morgue. One of the Cabinet Ministers came up to me and asked about Dollfuss's wounds. I told him that the wounds were not fatal and that he could have been saved with prompt medical attention which was refused so Dollfuss had slowly bled to death. I was asked if I was absolutely sure to which I mentioned that in addition to working in the morgue I had a medical degree. He asked for my name. When I mentioned my name many of the policemen asked if I was related to Markus Baumann the Coroner at the morgue who was well-known to them. I replied that he was my father which elevated my status immediately. The other aide also mentioned that when I was called in to try to save Dollfuss he had already lost too much blood and had died within a few minutes of my attempt to stop the bleeding. Many of the people in the room came over to me and thanked me for trying to save his life. I gave a detailed statement to the police including Dollfuss' last words and asked if I could leave. My clothes were bloodstained and I wanted to change. There was no objection. As I walked to the door, Kurt von Schuschnigg came over to me and also thanked me for trying to save Dollfuss's life. He walked with me into the hallway and asked for the details. Even though he knew that I had just given a detailed report to the police he wanted to hear them personally. I spent about twenty minutes with him giving him as much detail as possible including repeating the remarks of the police officer Messinger that the leaders not only refused medical attention but that they also refused his dying request to bring in a priest. I also told him Dollfuss's dying words. Based on what I told him he immediately countermanded the order to allow the participants in the coup to leave Austria. They had not negotiated in good faith. The safe conduct out of the country was contingent on no one being killed. When they agreed and surrendered they knew that Dollfuss was dead. The trucks were diverted to a nearby military base to await further orders.

I remembered what my father had told me about publicity and getting my picture in the newspaper. Since I did resemble my father if my picture was published with my name spelled with the double "n" and it was reported that I came from Judendorf it could lead to our exposure. Before von Schuschnigg left I asked him to see that my name was not mentioned in any public information release as I wanted to avoid all publicity. He said that he would take care of it. I also asked him if he could arrange for an unobserved exit for me from the building. He asked one of his aides and a senior army officer to find one of the Chancellery guards and have me taken out of the back of the building without being seen by the press. A security guard was found. The four of us, with the guard leading, went through some rooms and corridors until we reached a small door at the back of the building. The guard unlocked the door and peered out. There were police and soldiers but no reporters. As the guard stood by the door, the army officer and the aide went out with me and explained to the officer in charge of that area that I was a doctor and had tried to save the life of Dollfuss. He told the officer that I did not want to see the press. He stared at me and my bloodstained clothes and said that he understood. He let me pass asking if I wanted an escort to wherever I was going. I politely declined. As I started to walk away I realized why he was staring at me so closely. I had momentarily forgotten that there was blood on my clothes which was not too conducive to making my way through the crowd and hailing a taxi. I decided to accept the officer's offer and had a police car take me to the back of the morgue.

I walked around to the side of the morgue where there was a small door that was always locked. I entered with one of the keys that I always had with me. Luckily, no one was around. They had all left the morgue to see what was happening. I went to the locker room where I kept a change of clothes. I washed up and changed clothes. I took the bloody clothes and burned them in the incinerator and went home.

Early the next morning I went to my desk and waited for the rest of the shift to arrive. The subject of conversation for the entire day was the attempted coup and the death of Dollfuss. When I was asked where I was at the time, since they knew that I was at the Chancellery, I told them that I was held in the basement with the other hostages and then set free after the Nazis surrendered. The newspapers covered the assassination in great detail describing the battle to gain control of the radio station. While no one was killed there were many wounded during the battle to re-take the radio station.

Photograph showing a wounded Nazi being taken out of the radio station after the coup failed. The radio station was shut down by the government ending the broadcasts which delayed uprisings in other cities. (Source: Author's Personal Collection)

We also learned that there was a second factor that killed the coup attempt. When President Miklas learned of the coup while he was in Corinthia he managed to reach Mussolini by phone and apprise him of the situation. Within minutes, Mussolini ordered his army units stationed at the Austrian border to mobilize and wait for further instructions. He sent telegrams to Hitler and Miklas telling them that he was ready to enter Austria and put down the rebellion at the request of Miklas or any of the leaders of the Austrian government. Hitler backed down and gave orders to end the revolt.

About a week later I received a letter from the wife of Dollfuss. She expressed her gratitude for my attempt to help her husband which she learned from Kurt von Schuschnigg. She enclosed the formal announcement of her husband's death which is colloquially called the "death card".

Gebet für persönliche Anliegen

O Gott! Du hast es gewollt, daß wir durch das Leben und Sterben des großen Bundes-kanzlers Dr. Engelbert Dollfuß ein Beispiel erhalten haben, das der Nachahmung wert ist. Er hat die Sorgen der heutigen Zeit zutiefst erkannt und bis zu einem blutigen Sterben verkostet. Er hat zum Verbessern der Zeitver-hältnisse den einzig sicheren Weg beschritten, den geraden Weg deiner und der Kirche Gebote und Lehre. Hilf uns durch seine Fürbitte, daß wir in unseren Anliegen deinen Willen stets erkennen, deine Hilfe zu unserem Wohle er-fahren. Wir empfehlen dir, o Gott, all die Anliegen der Kirche und des Vaterlandes, aber auch unsere eigenen Anliegen und Sorgen, besonders aber . . . . Hilf uns in Hinblick auf den Kreuzestod Jesu Christi und auf den Mär-tyrertod unseres Bundeskanzlers. Der du lebst und regierst von Ewigkeit zu Ewigkeit. Amen.

Mit kirchlicher Druckerlaubnis.
Apostolische Administratur Innsbruck.

Herausgeber: Kath. Aktion für Tirol. — Druck der Vereins-buchdruckerei A.-G., Innsbruck Maria-Theresien-Straße 40.

Death Card: Our Beloved Chancellor

Dollfuss was religious. His wife chose a picture of him praying while in uniform. A prayer is to the left. These were sent to friends and family when someone died. This was the tradition in Austria and Germany. (Source: Author's Personal Collection)

The Foreign Press Reported:

"Austrian Chancellor Dolfuss was assassinated by the Nazis in their failed July 25, 1934 attempt to take over the Austrian government."

Kurt von Schuschnigg was formally appointed chancellor by President Miklas. His first act was to try the Nazis that took part in the coup for murder and treason. Planetta and six other leaders were found guilty of treason and executed. Most of the others were sentenced to long prison terms. At my request, von Schuschnigg did not call me to testify. There was enough damning testimony from the participants. Many Nazi Party members fled to Germany. The Nazi Party was outlawed and its headquarters building seized.

For a while it looked as if the Nazis were gone for good. Jews throughout Austria were elated with some actually celebrating the executions. There was still a small but dedicated cadre of Nazis throughout the country that continued their political activities as underground Nazis.

Hitler, of course, denied that there was any direct involvement by the German government in this coup attempt. He called it a spontaneous revolt by concerned men of German descent that were disenchanted by the way Dollfuss was governing the country. He condemned the actions of SS Standarte 89 likening them to traitors to the National Socialist movement. However, documents were seized in Nazi Party headquarter buildings in various cities showing that the headquarters of the Nazi Party in Munich was financing the revolt. Moreover, the Munich Radio station announced that Dollfuss had resigned before the revolt had even started. Hitler had to re-assess his strategy for Austria. This bungled coup attempt set him back. World opinion was strongly against him. He knew he had to make amends. Austria would remain independent for the time being. Nazi terrorism essentially stopped along with their anti-Semitic propaganda and attacks on Jews. Jews had been given a reprieve. Mazel Tovs could be heard throughout the second district.

CHAPTER FOUR

A GOOD DEED

"The quicker humanity advances, the more important it is to be the one who deals the first blow."

"Oppression is the essence of power."

Ernst Kaltenbrunner, Head of the Austrian SS

Conditions for Jews in Vienna improved considerably after the ill-fated coup. The Nazis, under direct orders from Hitler, essentially stopped its attacks against the government and the Jews. The von Schuschnigg government openly courted Jewish financial support which was given quite generously. During the next eighteen months diplomatic relations with Germany improved substantially. In February 1936 an agreement was reached in a meeting between von Schuschnigg and Hitler that Germany would respect the independence of Austria and not interfere in Austrian politics. In return, von Schuschnigg agreed to remove the ban on the National Socialist Party and to release all party members still in prison as long as they were not serving time for a capital offense. While many Jews were not happy with this new situation, they still supported von Schuschnigg. While there were some isolated attacks on Jews by some now-legal Nazi Party members they were very infrequent and no one was seriously injured. Apparently, the Nazis were going to keep their word to abandon violence and work within the established Austrian political framework. Captain Josef Leopold, the new head of the Austrian Nazi Party, even had some meetings with Cabinet officials and von Schuschnigg to re-emphasize his commitment to peaceful coexistence.

One of the many things that I learned from my father was that I had to do better than everyone else at my level to ensure my position.

To be exemplary was actually not difficult. Most people with civil service jobs did the minimum amount of work required. If they dealt with the public they used their position, even if it wasn't important, to bestow upon themselves an air of importance. For example, Heinrich, one of the workers at the morgue with whom my father became very friendly, was in charge of the department that provided copies of death certificates to people that needed them for deceased family members. These were mostly for legal reasons such as a claim on an estate. The records filing system at the morgue was actually very good. If he wanted, Heinrich could have provided copies of any death certificate the same day. But this would have required him to get up, go to the filing room in the basement, look for the proper file, get the certificate, make a copy, give it to the person and return the original to its proper place in the filing system. Alternatively, he could have asked one of the two records clerks to do it and make the copy but the two records clerks were much lazier than Heinrich. They had their own routine which included when to file new death certificates, when to make duplicate copies of death certificates for people that came into the office, when to answer requests for duplicate copies that came by mail or telegram, etc. There was also lunch, which somehow always seemed to take more time than was actually allotted, and a few coffee and bathroom breaks during the day. The two records clerks, Hilda and Lena, were in their mid-fifties who had been working there for more than 15 years. Their patterns were set, they had tenure and were not about to disrupt their routine, especially if it meant working harder. So, if Heinrich wanted to search for a death certificate, make the copy and re-file the original neither of them cared as it was one less thing that one of them had to do. Heinrich did not care to disrupt his routine either. So whenever anyone wanted a copy of a death certificate the process took two to three days or even longer.

I singled out Heinrich for a reason. We became great friends after the German annexation of Austria due to a procedural change that I suggested which I will explain later.

One rainy night in August 1937, two seemingly unrelated deaths occurred that enhanced my future position in Austria. It also wound up saving the lives of many Jewish men and their families – and it came from a violently vitriolic anti-Semitic Nazi.

The first death was that of a vagrant, a homeless man that had been hit by a truck as he was running across the street from Donaulände Park. The man ran across the street from the park apparently without looking. The truck tried to stop but skidded on the wet surface and slammed into the man sending him flying about 50 feet from where the truck finally came to a stop. The vagrant was killed and his body was pretty well mangled. He was brought to the morgue at around 6 PM. The second was a teenage boy of about seventeen years old that was found in the same park. The boy's body was reported directly to me by an officer that Mischa sent to the morgue. My friend Mischa was a patrol officer who fortuitously happened to be on duty that night. As you might expect from his nickname, he was Jewish. The park was on his beat and he had been called to the scene by a woman walking her dog in the park who had discovered the body around 7:30. As soon as she saw it she screamed and ran out of the park. Mischa was near the entrance when she ran out. After calming her down to the best extent possible, he persuaded her to take him to the spot where she discovered the body. He asked her to call the police station and tell them about it as he started to probe around the boy's body. There was a teenage boy lying on the ground with a single bullet wound to the head. The gun was in his hand and there was no evidence of foul play. The rain had made the ground muddy and the only footprints at the scene were from the boy, the women and her dog and his own. The obvious cause of death to the boy was a self-inflicted bullet wound to the head – obviously a suicide. There was a note but much of it was illegible due to the rain. The boy had his wallet and jewelry which further supported the suicide premise rather than a robbery. A quick look at his identity card identified him as Johann Kaltenbrunner. This was the same surname as the head of security for the Austrian Nazi Party, Ernst Kaltenbrunner. His ring had a family crest on it which further supported that the dead boy could be his son. Mischa decided to take the initiative. He picked up the gun and the note and put them in his pocket along with the boy's wallet and ring. He emptied out the boy's pockets and took the money, keys and everything else. Two more policemen arrived at the scene. He sent one of them to get me telling him to first try the morgue and then my apartment if I was not at the morgue and the other he had stand about 30 feet away to keep any people away from the body. Since it was raining and it was now nine o'clock at night no one came to the scene but the other policeman did exactly what he was told without giving it a second thought. I happened to be working late that night due to the late arrival of the homeless man at six o'clock that had been killed by the truck so I was there when the policeman sent by Mischa arrived to bring me to the park. As soon as the officer told me that Mischa wanted me to come to the park to see a dead body, I stopped working on the vagrant and left with the officer. I asked one of the ambulance drivers, Hyman, to drive the ambulance and we drove to the park following the police car. He parked the ambulance at the entrance next to the police car and waited in the ambulance. The police officer brought me to where Mischa was waiting. Mischa asked him to wait with the other officer.

Mischa showed me the boy's wallet and ring with the family crest and told me that he believed that he was the son of Ernst Kaltenbrunner. I agreed. I told Mischa to accompany the body to the morgue and that he should ride alone in the ambulance with the body. I gave him a key to the back door of the morgue. Since it was raining only two more policemen had showed up at the park. He told them to remain at the scene without telling them anything specific other than to cordon off the area and went to the morgue with the body in the ambulance. Upon arrival, he brought the boy's body in through the back door using the key I had given him. I stayed and inspected the scene which Mischa had cordoned off and fully agreed with his conclusion that it was a suicide. I returned to the morgue in the police car that brought me to the park arriving about thirty minutes after Mischa. I confirmed the address. He was indeed the son of Ernst Kaltenbrunner. I thought about the body of the homeless man that had been brought in earlier. My mind was really working hard that night. I devised a plan which I told to Mischa. He thought it over and agreed.

Ernst Kaltenbrunner was a ruthless man who would stop at nothing to achieve his goals. He was arrogant, proud and he was vehemently anti-Semitic. He joined the Austrian Nazi party in 1927 and was committed to Hitler. When the Nuremberg racial laws were passed in Germany (so-called because they were announced at a Nazi Party rally in Nuremberg), he used his influence to rid the Austrian Army of Jewish officers. Even though he was not in the army, there were enough Nazi sympathizers in the army that he could control. There was no doubt in his mind that Germany would take over Austria, preferably without bloodshed. But if it came down to fighting he did not want any Jewish officers in command since they were the most likely to resist and order the men under their command to fight. He had his Nazi cohorts in the army ask the few Jewish officers to resign under severe threats. If they refused they planted incriminating evidence on them or in their homes and have them arrested, sentenced and thrown into jail. After two Jewish officers were disgraced and thrown into jail because of the false evidence, the rest realized that resigning was the best (and only) thing to do. The other Gentile officers did nothing to support the wrongly accused Jews. They did not like them either and welcomed the opportunity to get rid of them, especially when some of their friends were promoted to take the place of the Jewish officers. Within three months there were no Jewish officers in any branch of the armed forces.

I left the morgue using the Chief Coroner's car which was parked in the front of the morgue. The keys were in his office. I drove to the Kaltenbrunner home, which was a very large house located in a very fashionable suburb. He was from Linz but had a second home in Vienna which he used when he was needed for Nazi party business here. It was well guarded so I could not just drive in. I told the guard that I had to see Herr Kaltenbrunner on an important matter on official business from the Coroner's Office. It was now eleven thirty. Kaltenbrunner had already gone to bed but I insisted that he be awakened. While the guards pressed for a better explanation I remained steadfast in my refusal to disclose anything other than it was very personal and of the utmost importance and could absolutely not wait until morning. After about twenty minutes of arguing, cajoling and pleading, the guard called the house and woke him. To say that he was extremely angry when he found out that it was only someone from the morgue was an understatement but I convinced him that what I had to say was very personal and private. He looked at me, disheveled and wet, examined my credentials and concluded that I was not a threat to him or his family. Still, he was a bit reluctant to have the guards leave. I leaned over to him near his ear and told him that my visit was regarding his son, Johann, and that we really needed to be alone. After being searched for the fourth time, he dismissed the two guards that accompanied me into the house and we went into his study. I was impressed. The study was an enormous room filled with books of all shapes and sizes neatly arrayed in the built-in mahogany bookcases. There was a large table to one side and a beautiful carved mahogany desk on the other side. There was a lectern by the desk which I assumed was for private meetings held in the library. The windows and the glass doors leading the garden were adorned with lace curtains and tapestries. A picture of Adolf Hitler was centered above the mantle. There was also a large bronze bust of Hitler on the mantle.

We stood by the table as he demanded to know impatiently what this was all about. I told him that the body of a boy that I believed was his son was in the morgue. He had shot and killed himself in the park and left a note. I showed him his son's wallet, ring and watch. He almost collapsed but managed to restrain himself, holding on to the table. I told him that I had not told anyone about this, not even my superiors. He stood silently for a few minutes and asked why I had gone to such great lengths to come to his house and tell him this and keep it secret. I told him that I thought it best to see how he wanted to handle this. He asked me what I meant.

I told him that only I and a close friend on the police force who found the body knew that it was his son and that it was a suicide. Given the high profile of the family, I wanted to give him an option. I could report this as it really happened or we could destroy the letter, which was totally illegible anyway and I could report that an unidentified teenage boy had been found murdered in the park. I also told him that the body of an unidentified homeless man who had been hit by a truck crossing the street on the other side of the park had been brought into the morgue a couple of hours before the discovery of his son's body. Given this situation, I told him that I could plant the gun, ring, watch and wallet on the homeless man and let it be inferred that he robbed and shot your son in the park when he resisted the robbery.

I could also fill in the death certificate indicating that the time of death was earlier so it could be attributed to the vagrant. I told him that the obvious conclusion would be that your son was murdered during a robbery and that the homeless man was the murderer. This would save the family from considerable anguish and embarrassment that occurs with a suicide. Only the three of us would ever know. This way his son would be buried in the family mausoleum in the church cemetery with the full church rites, which would not be accorded for a suicide, and he would not have any disgrace associated with his death. There would be no adverse publicity – only sympathy.

The general sat down. He was silent for about three minutes ."Are you sure no one else knows about this?" he asked. "Absolutely!" I replied. "Then let's do it! What should I do now?" he asked. "Nothing," I replied. "I will take care of everything. I will report receiving an unidentified body of a teenage boy. I will put your son's ring, watch and wallet on the dead vagrant and make the discovery that the items in his possession belonged to the unidentified teenage boy and further discover that he was your son. The officer who brought in your son's body is a close personal friend. He is waiting for me at the morgue under strict instructions not to talk to anyone until I get back. I will deduce that the dead boy was your son from the items we found on the vagrant. I will notify my superiors and let them handle it. I know that they will immediately take charge and push me aside. Something this important, with the guaranteed press coverage, is an opportunity that they will surely covet. They will make all of the statements and handle all of the press interviews. They will come to you with the news of your son's murder and the fact that they deduced that the vagrant was the killer and that they had solved this horrible crime. You and your wife will be asked to identify the body."

"So, what's in this for you? Do you want money?" he asked. "No, I do not want any money. I do not want anything at all. This is not blackmail. I respect your commitment and dedication to the National Socialist Party. I just want to do my part to help. I wanted to give you this chance for an alternative way to deal with this horrible situation. I did not want anything to deter you from your work or give aid or ammunition to the enemies that I know that someone in your position must have."

He thanked me profusely, grabbing my hand and shaking it almost violently. He burned the suicide letter. "If he only knew that I was Jewish!" I thought to myself as I left the study but before I did I turned and said, "By the way, the officer who found the body is a Jew, but I can vouch for him." Kaltenbrunner did not say anything.

When I returned to the morgue I explained that Kaltenbrunner had agreed. The way things were going in Germany, Austria and the rest of Europe it was clearly good to have a high-ranking friend in the Nazi Party. As an added precaution, Mischa had a great idea. He placed the gun in the hand of the vagrant whom we wheeled over to Kaltenbrunner's son and shot a second bullet into his chest right above the heart thus dispelling all doubt that this was indeed a murder. A person cannot kill himself twice. Mischa again stood guard over both bodies.

I left the morgue and went to the home of Gephardt Schröder, the Coroner to whom I reported. He was quite angry when he saw me but was very appreciative when I explained the situation. He got dressed and we both went to the home of Otto Krüger, the Chief Medical Examiner. It was now close to two AM. He too was initially very angry at being awakened but Gephardt explained that an unidentified body of a young boy with two bullet wounds, one to the head and one to the chest, was found in Donaulände Park. He added that the body of a vagrant was accidentally killed crossing Untere Donaulände was also in the morgue. He had the wallet and jewelry of Johann Kaltenbrunner in his possession and a gun that had two shots fired. Otto sat down and listened attentively. We told him that we thought the dead boy was most likely the son of Ernst Kaltenbrunner. When I also added that I had only told Gephardt and we both agreed to not say anything to anyone else before we spoke to him to seek his advice his demeanor changed. He smiled (actually it was more of a self-centered smirk). He knew the importance of this and the opportunity it afforded him with the press, with Kaltenbrunner and with the Nazi Party. He also knew that he owed me something in return for bringing him this opportunity.

He quickly dressed and we went to the morgue. I showed them both bodies. Mischa showed him the gun, ring and wallet that were found on the vagrant's body, hidden in his under pants. The vagrant smelled so bad when he was killed that no one really touched him let alone looked in his undergarments for anything. Otto was satisfied. He told Mischa to inform his superiors in the police department. About an hour later the Chief of Police, who had also been awakened by the officer on duty due to the importance of the case, arrived with the district one police captain. After a preliminary investigation they all agreed that Johann Kaltenbrunner, the son of Ernst Kaltenbrunner had been tragically murdered in Donaulände Park during the night by the vagrant. The Chief of Police decided that he would go with the district captain, Otto and Gephardt to the Kaltenbrunner home to notify the family. I waited at the morgue with Mischa.

Ernst Kaltenbrunner had gone back to bed as if nothing happened. He had already sworn the guards to secrecy to say that no one had come to his home that night. They, of course, did not know the subject matter of my visit anyway but he was not taking any chances. He had told his wife when he returned to bed that it was just some important party business. This was not an abnormal occurrence.

Two police cars with sirens blaring and red lights flashing drove to Kaltenbrunner's house. The guards on duty thought they were there to arrest Kaltenbrunner and were almost considering firing on the police cars. Luckily, they decided against it. One of the police officers explained the situation. The guard called the house but they were already up as the sirens woke them. It was now 6:15 in the morning.

Ernst Kaltenbrunner came to the door and acted genuinely shocked when he was told that his son Johann had been murdered. His wife fainted and had to be revived with smelling salts. They dressed and went to the morgue accompanied by their oldest son, Karl, who was home visiting from university.

By now, word of the crime had been leaked to the press. They came to the morgue. The top police officers, my boss and his boss took the credit for solving the crime. Ernst and his wife, Elisabeth, went into the morgue which now had an entourage of the police, press, Nazi party members, etc.

The press began taking pictures of my boss with the Chief Medical Examiner and the police chief (the Kaltenbrunners refused to be photographed) and interviewing them when they arrived at the morgue. Mischa was in the holding room standing guard so the press could not get in to see the body in case some snuck into the morgue. Surprisingly, no one questioned the time gap between when the bodies were brought in, when the victim was identified and when they were called in. Instead, they focused on the importance of the crime and that it had been solved within hours of occurring. The fact that they had nothing to do with solving the crime was immaterial. They lined up to take credit for the quick resolution of the crime. By now the morgue was a zoo. The word was out now to the public. Literally, hundreds of people, mostly Nazi supporters, were gathered outside in the rain wanting to know if the rumors of the murder of Ernst Kaltenbrunner's son were true. Additional members of the press, including some from the international press corps, were also there. The press had to wait outside by my orders until my boss gave the word to allow them to come into the morgue where the Chief Medical Examiner and the Chief of Police gave the official story of the murder that was quickly solved by the combined efforts of the morgue and the police.

Gephardt and Otto came into the holding room with Ernst, his wife and their eldest son. She again fainted at the sight of her dead son. The positive identification was made and the family retired for the requisite period of mourning, leaving from one of the side doors to avoid the press. Public sympathy was enormous. The official story was that Johann had been out on a date with his girlfriend (which was true) and had evidently cut across the park instead of walking around it to the bus stop when he was obviously accosted by the vagrant with a gun. They surmised that Johann must have resisted and moved toward the vagrant when the vagrant fired twice with the first bullet hitting him in the chest and the second bullet hitting him in the side of his head as he spun around from the force of the first bullet. The vagrant proceeded to rob him. He probably panicked when he heard the woman walking her dog so he ran across the street without looking and was hit by the truck that killed him. The press had a field day. For more than a week there were articles on his son and his lost potential of service to the country. Hundreds of people came to pay their respects at the funeral parlor. There were articles in the press on Ernst Kaltenbrunner and the Nazi party. There were articles on the homeless and the safety in parks and other public places. Many homeless men were rounded up and thrown into jail while they were investigated for potential criminal tendencies. Some homeless men were dumped at the edge of the city and told never to come back. Some people saw it as a conspiracy against the Nazi Party in Austria which led to various theories and finger pointing. Luckily, the vagrant was not Jewish.

About three weeks later there was a knock on the door of my office late one afternoon. It was Ernst Kaltenbrunner. He had come to personally thank me again for what I did for him and his family. As he said, words could not express his gratitude. He again offered me any form of remuneration that I wanted but I again refused. I gave him the pistol that Mischa had stolen from the police evidence room the next day. We correctly thought that it might be a pistol belonging to the family, which it indeed was. As there would not be a trial no one even noticed that the gun had disappeared. When Mischa put some evidence from another crime into the security room, he just went over and took the pistol. As he looked at the pistol he realized that two shots had been fired from the gun. Perhaps realized is not the right word. He knew that there were two bullet wounds in his son's head and chest but it didn't sink in until that very moment: how could that be since it would have been impossible for his son to take a second shot after shooting himself in the head? I told him what we did to dispel any thought that this was a murder and hoped that he would not be offended. If we left the body with only one shot to the side of the head someone could conceivably theorize about suicide and a possible cover up – but with two fatal shots, one in the head and one in the chest, there could be no doubt that it was murder. There was a pensive moment as he got up and clasped my hand with both of his hands, thanked me again, and left.

His parting words were "If ever you need anything that I can do for you, please do not hesitate to ask. I am truly in your debt." These were words that I surely would remember and take advantage of, should there be a need.

Needless to say, we capitalized on it!

CHAPTER FIVE

A LETTER TO THE FUEHRER

"The best defense is a good offense"

> Carl von Clausewitz, Prussian major-general
> and military theorist.

On September 18, 1937 my father died of complications from pneumonia. He had been sick for about ten days with his condition worsening daily. By now, Hitler was in full power in Germany with an increasing interest in Austria. Since he came to power in 1933, Jews were openly persecuted and urged to leave Germany – but without any assets or money. The Nazi Party was legal in Austria and they were getting stronger. I do not know exactly what I was thinking but I decided to write a letter to Hitler during my period of mourning. Perhaps I was influenced by the Kaltenbrunner cover up and his parting words. Perhaps it was influenced by the trip my father and I made to Munich when he was invited to speak at the seminar. In any case I wrote the following letter:

October 3, 1937

Dear Fuehrer,

I am sure that you will not remember my father and me but I was in Munich with my father, Markus, many years ago. My father took me to the Hofbrauhaus. I will never forget that night. It was April 20. You were there celebrating your birthday with your comrades. You and my father share the same birth date so it was an unexpected surprise for both of us. We mentioned the coincidence and were immediately invited to join the group and were treated to a couple of rounds of beer. My father and I were brought over to your table, where we were introduced to you and we offered a toast in your honor. I clearly remember the enthusiasm, the camaraderie, the focus of your group with your brown uniforms and august style. He was very impressed with you and your beliefs and as a Volksdeutsch he wished you every success. I believe he also made a donation to the party.

He recently died. On his deathbed he recalled this story and for a few minutes I could see the tears well up in his eyes and the pride he felt of having personally met you. He also regretted that he would not live long enough to see Austria and Germany become one nation as was its destiny with you as the leader.

I know that you are very busy and that you may not even get to read this letter but I just wanted to share the moment of an old dying man and what you have meant to him after so many years. Thank you from the bottom of my heart.

Sieg Heil,

Michael Baumann

Assistant Mortician

City Morgue, Vienna

I read and reread the letter. I started to laugh and was going to tear it up. Instead, I mailed it special delivery to him in Berlin.

Chapter Six

"May God protect Austria!"

"As I stood at the grave of my predecessor, Chancellor Dollfuss, the situation was very clear to me. I knew that in order to save Austrian independence I had to embark on a course of appeasement. This meant that everything had to be avoided which would give Germany a pretext for intervention and that everything had to be done to secure in some way Hitler's toleration of the status quo."

> Kurt von Schuschnigg, Chancellor of Austria, spoken at the funeral of Chancellor Dolfuss who was assassinated by the Nazis (from his book Austrian Requiem)

In 1938 there were about 185,000 Jews in Vienna which was about eight percent of the population. However, Jews dominated many professions and businesses. To put things in perspective, Austria was awarded four Nobel Prizes in medicine. Three of the four doctors were Jewish. In fact, more than one-half of the doctors and dentists in Vienna were Jewish along with more than sixty percent of the lawyers. A large proportion of university professors were Jewish and a disproportionate number of students attending universities and medical schools were Jewish. This led to a strong undercurrent of anti-Semitism which flared up publicly at times, especially at the Vienna University.

To deal with many of the issues related to Jews in Vienna there was a special Jewish organization called the Israelische Kultusgemeinde (IKG), the Israelite (Jewish) Community Organization. It was located in District 1 on Seitenstettengasse. Adjacent to the office was a small synagogue that shared the same façade. The IKG had many functions such as combating anti-Semitism, caring for the elderly and indigent, establishing religious school curricula, and maintaining all of the records of Jewish births, deaths, marriages, etc. There was an elected Board of Directors that ran the IKG. All Jews that wished to be a member of the IKG paid a tax based on their income. This allowed them to vote in the election of the Board. The IKG was apolitical. It did not participate in politics by nominating Jewish candidates or supporting specific non-Jewish candidates. However, it would openly campaign against candidates that were violently anti-Semitic. There were three main political parties in Austria:

- The Christian Social Party which was essentially a Catholic-based political movement that was openly anti-Semitic and had specific anti-Semitic platforms

- The Pan-German Party which was also openly anti-Semitic. There were a number of different smaller German parties including the National Socialists (Nazis) that were violently anti-Semitic. Their main goal was unification with Germany

- The Social Democrat Party which did not have any anti-Semitic platforms and did not form coalitions with the violently anti-Semitic factions. As one might expect it was this group that most Jews supported – not that they were that friendly to Jews either

Vienna was not only an important center for the Jewish community in Europe the city also had a very important role in Nazi history.

Adolf Hitler was born in Braunau, Austria on April 20, 1889. His family moved to Linz where he spent most of his youth. He moved to Vienna from Linz in 1908. He was nineteen years old and an aspiring painter. He tried to get into the Academy of Arts but was refused admission twice. He was not successful as an artist. He tried to earn his living by painting scenes from postcards and selling the paintings to merchants and tourists, but they did not sell well. In 1909 he ran out of money, lost his apartment and had to go to a homeless shelter. In 1910 he became a housepainter and was able to make enough money to leave the shelter to live in a house for poor working men. He lived in Vienna until 1913 when he moved to Munich after inheriting some money from his father's estate. Years later, Hitler said that he became a vehement anti-Semitic and a fanatic Jew-hater during his time in Vienna. Jews were the most prosperous part of the community. They dominated the professions. They kept to themselves and did not share their wealth. Many dressed in long black coats and black hats and had long sideburns. They didn't even speak German; they had their own language, Yiddish. Because of the way these Jews dressed and the different language that they spoke, he concluded that Jews were a separate and distinct race and not just a religion. This is reinforced in Mein Kampf (1924), where he specifically mentions that "his transition from opposing anti-Semitism on religious grounds to supporting it on racial grounds came from having seen these orthodox Jews (in Vienna)."

This might be a good time to mention another important aspect of Hitler's beliefs. This centered on the esteem he held for individuals that contributed to the ideals adopted by the National Socialist Party platforms. One of these was the fifteenth century theologian, Martin Luther. Martin Luther was born on November 10, 1483 in Eisleben, Germany. Luther was a German monk, theologian, and church reformer. He is also considered to be the founder of Protestantism.

Luther challenged the authority of the Pope by teaching that the Bible was the sole source of religious authority and that the priests and the church were there to promote this tenet. According to Luther, salvation was attainable only by faith in Jesus as the messiah, a faith unmediated by the church. These ideas helped to inspire the Protestant Reformation. Luther's translation of the Bible into a more common, readable German language made it more understandable to ordinary people, which had a tremendous impact on the German church and on German culture. His hymns inspired the development of congregational singing which was adopted by many other religions. His marriage to Katharina von Bora set a model for the practice of clerical marriage within Protestantism, which became the basis of King Henry the Eighth's split with Rome over his divorce from his first wife and his remarriage to Anne Boleyn.

Luther was also known for his writings against the Jews. At first, he was particularly anxious to get the support of the Jewish community for his movement. He thought that they would convert and join him based on conversations with some of the Jewish leaders but he either misinterpreted their conversations or they just appeased him by telling him what he wanted to hear. In any case, they did not convert. After this setback, he became strongly anti-Semitic and published a treatise entitled, *On the Jews and their Lies*. His statements that Jews' homes should be destroyed, their synagogues burned, money confiscated, and their liberty curtailed, were revered by Hitler.

In Mein Kampf, Hitler calls him a great warrior, a true statesman and a great reformer comparing him to two of his other heroes, Richard Wagner the composer who was openly anti-Semitic, and whose works glorified the Germanic people, and Frederick the Great, the emperor that unified Germany in 1722.

During the 1920s, taking advantage of the chaos in Germany, Hitler quickly built up a fanatic following and gained voter support as he blamed the Jews and the Communists for the economic disaster in Germany. He promised to restore Germany to its rightful place as an economic giant and world leader. He was believed. Once in power, Hitler started building up the army, navy and air force creating many jobs. While much of this was done covertly, England and France had spies that informed them of this build up even if they did not know the full extent. This was forbidden under the Treaty of Versailles, yet they did nothing.

The League of Nations that was set up after the First World War to resolve international problems was totally useless. They couldn't agree on anything plus the United States congress voted against joining so it was not even a member. The United States foreign policy of the post-World War I period was isolationism. Domestic and, to some extent regional issues in the Americas, were all it cared to deal with politically. As he had no respect for the League of Nations, following Japan's lead, Germany withdrew from the League of Nations on October 21, 1933.

Hitler supported Generalissimo Franco, the fascist leader in Spain, in the Civil War that began in 1936. This was the testing ground for the German army and air force that helped Franco win. This was clearly against the Treaty of Versailles. England and France again did nothing. Hitler marched into the Rhineland in 1936. This was also in direct violation of the Treaty of Versailles. England and France did nothing.

At this point Hitler was pretty sure that he had carte blanche to totally disregard the Treaty of Versailles, provided he did it in steps with some time in between each step to assess the reaction of England and France, the two main countries that enforced the Treaty. Under this scenario, Hitler chose Austria as next conquest.

A key tenet of the Nazis was anti-Semitism. This became a main platform in Austria. The von Schuschnigg government was not popular since it bordered on fascism and was dictatorial but it was not overtly anti-Semitic so he had the open support of the Jewish businesses and general Jewish populace. The Austrian economy was still a disaster while the economy of Germany was strongly recovering under Hitler. The combination of economic recovery and anti-Semitism that National Socialism espoused was growing increasingly popular throughout Austria. It was the Jews not the Austrians that were to blame for all of the country's problems. Part of the economic recovery in Germany was due to eliminating the power of the Jews. Once they lost control, the country could again have unrestrained economic growth with the people, not just the Jewish hierarchy, reaping the rewards. He described the von Schuschnigg government as a force working together with Jews and acting as their police force. Von Schuschnigg was supporting the economic stranglehold that the Jews had in Austria and they in turn were supporting him financially. These accusations coupled with the lack of economic recovery in Austria attracted many member to the Nazi Party. By 1936 their ranks increased substantially particularly with young men and women between 18 and 25 and university students comprising more than 50 percent of the membership.

When my father came to Vienna in 1921 life was reasonably good for Jewish people with steady incomes. For a brief moment he toyed with the idea of not hiding the fact that he was Jewish but since he had gone to all of the trouble to establish his Gentile background and recognizing that conditions for the Jewish community could change at the whim of the rulers as had often occurred in the past, he decided to keep to his plan. At that time the thought that Hitler would become a threat was not even considered. In fact, my father knew nothing about him at all when he arrived in Vienna. When he arrived the Christian Social Party was in power and they were openly anti-Semitic. This reinforced his decision to remain Gentile.

When he started at the morgue it did not take him too long to assess the politics of the hierarchy there. The Chief Coroner was openly anti-Semitic. When my father needed anything done such as moving a body, getting the area cleaned up after an autopsy or getting an ambulance driver, the Chief Coroner would tell him loudly, "Get one of the lazy Jews to do it. They need to do some work for a change instead of sitting around on their hynees (Jewish colloquial for asses) and getting paid."

Violence against Jews in Vienna was increasing. Jews that were outspoken about the Nazis were in constant danger. The arts and entertainment scene in Vienna had many Jews who openly ridiculed Hitler and the Nazi Party. One of the top Jewish comedians used the stage name "Moishe Pipik" which freely translated from Yiddish means Moses Bellybutton. My father did not know the exact origin of the name but over time it became a satire word for a stupid person who caused accidents without ever getting hurt or someone who did stupid things that made everyone laugh and that often wore mismatched clothes. In other words someone that stood out in a crowd – but for all the wrong reasons. Moishe Pipik, whose real name was Yehudi Abromovitz, was very popular, even with non-Jews. In addition to his jokes, he had an uncanny talent in that he could mimic the voices and personal habits of many famous people – other actors, politicians, royalty, etc. He could imitate Hitler so well that if you closed your eyes you would swear that you were in Hitler's presence. Hitler, as you might imagine, was not very popular with the Jews of Vienna as well as with many other political groups so he told many Hitler jokes.

Sometimes Moishe would put on a small false mustache, comb his hair in the Hitler fashion, put on a jacket with a swastika and make a mock Hitler speech mimicking every motion and nuance that Hitler used during his speeches. After delivering a nonsensical diatribe he clicked his heels, raised his arm and shouted, "Heil Me!"

Before Hitler became chancellor, his comedy was tolerated by the pro-Nazis in Vienna. They felt that he was too public a figure to be adequately dealt with but after Hitler became chancellor it became a seething issue in the Austrian Nazi Party. At first there were just warnings, then there were threats. He ignored them. One night as he was going home from one of his performances he was surrounded by a group of about ten young Nazi Party members who proceeded to beat him with clubs and their fists. They kicked him when he fell to the ground. They turned him on his back and pulled up his shirt. One of the boys took out a small pocket knife and tried to cut out his bellybutton but it was too recessed so he just mutilated it. He stood up and loudly said to others as well as to the small crowd that had gathered when they heard his screams but could do nothing but watch since the young Nazis had large wooden clubs that they waved menacingly at the small crowd of mostly Jewish people, "Now, you are Moishe Neinpipik (Moishe no bellybutton)!" Another youth took the knife from his hand, knelt down and carved a small swastika just above his bellybutton saying, as he stood up, "Even better, now you are Moishe Nazi Pipik!" They ran away. The entire event took less than twenty minutes, way too short for any police response – even if they had decided to intervene.

Moishe was beaten so badly that he was hospitalized for a month. His arms and his legs were broken as was his jaw. It took him another three months at home to recuperate. For the rest of his life, he walked with a limp and never regained full control of his left hand. It took another two months for him to be able to mimic people and return to the stage, but he did learn his lesson. He never told another Hitler joke or mimicked him or any other Nazi in any of his performances. He received a standing ovation as he came on stage for his first performance. Everyone stood up, clapped vigorously and shouted words of encouragement. Well, almost everyone stood and clapped. There was one exception – one table where four young men with swastika armbands were sitting. Even though wearing the swastika armband was illegal, they put it on after they sat down knowing that no one would complain lest they get beaten. At every performance there was at least one table where four young people, sometimes with young women, would buy their tickets and then, once at the table, put on their swastika armbands.Sometimes they would disrupt the performance if they did not like a particular joke or skit but for the most part they just sat and watched as a constant reminder that Moishe, or for that matter, any performer, better watch very carefully what they say and do while on stage.

SUBCHAPTER – Jews for Hitler:
The National Socialist Jewish League (A digression)

"If you can't beat them, join them"

Origin questionable

Not all Jews were rich or even well-off. Many could not afford to attend a university or to even finish high school. In fact, about one-third of the Jews in Vienna were poor, especially the large number of post-war immigrants from Galicia, Poland. Regardless of your status in the Jewish community you followed the events in Germany with respect to Jews on a daily basis. It was clear that the Nazis hated Jews but the Nazi focus was on rich Jews that dominated the financial, business, commercial, legal and educational world. It was rich Jews that had to sell their assets in Germany at very low values. It was rich Jews that were forced to emigrate. It was rich Jews that were the subject of all of Hitler's speeches. There were still many Jews living in Germany that had jobs. Rich, selfish Jews were clearly the targets. This gave rise to one of the most bizarre Jewish groups to be formed in Vienna – or for that matter anywhere in Europe – the "Jewish Youth for Hitler" movement.

There were many Viennese Jews that resented the success of the "rich Jews" just as much as the non-Jews and the Nazis did. They, too, saw the rich Hassidic Jews that dressed differently, kept to themselves and shunned other Jews. They certainly didn't share their success with other Jews. They would only hire Hassidic Jews to work for them. Even the successful Jews that were not Hassidic did not help other Jews. In fact, as soon as they became successful, they moved out of the predominantly Jewish second district to other parts of the city. They often ignored their former friends if they happened to meet on the street or at a public event as if they were ashamed that they came from this background. These successful Jews had the best seats at the theater and concerts and joined professional societies. All of this was beyond the reach of many other Jews.

There were some Jews that considered themselves to be avant-garde philosophers and part of a new wave of Jewish intellectuals even though they could not afford to go to a university. Their prospects for success were nil. At first, a few small groups of these Jews, mainly young men and women between the ages of 18 and 23, met at bars and coffee houses in the second district in the evening with no specific agenda. As they discussed the situation in Austria and Germany and the Jewish issue, surprisingly a number of them agreed with the Nazis. In their minds it wasn't a Jewish issue it was an issue of rich selfish Jews and it was these rich selfish Jews that were denigrating the rest of them. Sometimes these discussions got out of hand and fights broke out between opposing sides. When the police were called to the scene and they listened to both sides, they invariably let the pro-Nazi side go free and arrested the anti-Nazi side. If there were any damages, only the anti-Nazi side had to pay for them. One time, one of the policemen saluted them with, "Heil Hitler!" This totally reinforced their belief that there was a place for them in the Nazi movement. Soon, by word of mouth, these individuals or groups that thought the same got together to discuss the possible role that they could play in the Nazi Party. They did this secretly since they knew that their parents, family members and most of their friends would not understand. In addition, they believed that the union with Germany was inevitable. It was just a matter of time. Many genuinely believed that if they could establish their place with the Nazis that their friends and family would realize that they were right and embrace them and their decision. It was just a matter of time.

So, on November 17, 1937 the Jewish Youth for Hitler movement was formed. There were about 80 young men and women at the initial meeting where they elected Ezra Koppelman the President, Helmut Stein the Vice President and Cynda Rabinovitz the Secretary/ Treasurer. Ezra volunteered to establish contact with the Nazi Party to explore the possibility of becoming party members, or at least auxiliary members. This was clearly a dangerous task. The Jugend (Hitler Youth) were constantly attacking Jews in the street and many of them were always at the party headquarters. They guarded the door along with some of the adult Nazis. Anyone not known to them had to explain why they wanted to get into the building.

Ezra took up a collection from the members at the initial meeting and at the next two meetings. At the third meeting there were over 150 interested Jews, still mostly young men and women without good jobs, that were dissatisfied enough with their current status to try something different – and you could not get more different than joining a pro-Nazi Jewish group. By now, Ezra had collected almost 1,000 Marks.

The next morning he went to the Nazi Party headquarters on Teinfaltstrasse. He was, of course, stopped at the door but when he said that he was from the outlying city of Wiener Neustadt with a contribution for the party, which he proudly showed to the guards, he was escorted directly to the office of Captain Josef Leopold who was the head of the Nazi Party in Vienna. So far, so good!

While he had rehearsed over and over again what he was going to say, he froze in the presence of Leopold. He knew that he was standing in front of a virulent anti-Semitic person. Ezra did not expect to be taken directly to him. He thought he would be taken to some lower level party functionary that would be perhaps more open and receptive to his offer. Ezra debated between telling him the real reason he was there or making up some story about the Weiner Nuestadt Nazi Youth Group and getting out of there as soon as possible. It was obvious to Leopold that something was on Ezra's mind since he did not immediately return the salute. At first he just attributed it to the fact that the young man standing before him was so impressed to be meeting him that he was speechless. Top ranking Nazis always had a superiority complex and Captain Leopold was the epitome of this. He patiently waited for some response from Ezra but after about a minute of awkward silence he got up from his desk and walked to Ezra, putting his hand on his shoulder to calm him down. By now Ezra was shivering as if it were freezing in the office.

Finally, he blurted out that he had come to make a contribution to the Nazi Party. He held out the envelope with the money. Leopold took it and thanked him and told him to sit down on the couch in his office. Ezra sat down on one end and Leopold sat next to him. Ezra finally regained his composure and started the conversation blurting out. "Is there any role that a Jew could have in the National Socialist Movement?"

Captain Leopold was taken aback by the question. No one had ever asked him this before. Rather than respond directly, he asked, "Why would you ask such a question? Our Fuehrer has made it clear that the Jews are the root cause of our problems and have no place in our society."

Ezra the started to explain some of the things that the group had discussed without initially saying that he was Jewish. He explained that there were some Jews who believed that it was the rich Jews that were the real enemies and that they discriminated against less fortunate Jews just as much as they discriminated against non-Jews. Many of these less fortunate Jews hated the rich ones, especially the ones that wore their own style of clothes and had the long sideburns and beards. He became a bit philosophical and related the old adage that "the enemy of my enemy is my friend".

Leopold was clearly intrigued by this line of conversation. He had never thought about it. To him all Jews were despicable. Yet, he knew that in Germany there were certain Jews that had special skills that continued in their jobs. There was even a name for them, "useful Jews". He also knew that Jews married to Aryans were allowed to work and live in relative peace. He sat there for about three minutes before responding. "I guess under special circumstances there could be a place for Jews – but certainly not within the Nazi Party." He again asked Ezra why he was asking these questions. At this point Ezra either had to tell him the true reason he was there or simply say that he was asking a rhetorical question and leave. He decided on the former recognizing that this was clearly the only opportunity he would have to test their theory.

"I am not really from Wiener Neustadt. I live in Vienna. There are a number of young men and women that are Jewish that believe that it is the rich Jews that have alienated themselves from society by taking advantage of others. Many share the same dislike for these rich Jews that won't even help their fellow Jews. They believe that there could be a place for Jews that were not part of this group when Germany takes over Austria. They believe that this is inevitable and believe that they could do better under a German government than they are doing now, especially if there is a place for them in the New Order."

Ezra stopped short of saying that he was one of those people and that he was Jewish but he could see from Leopold's face that he realized that he was talking to a Jew in his office. Captain Leopold immediately jumped up from the couch and walked back to his desk and sat down behind it. Ezra could clearly see that he was perplexed by the situation and he knew that he had to talk fast to continue the conversation or be thrown out of his office and probably beaten.

Ezra stood up, walked over to the desk and stood directly in front of Leopold looking at him squarely eye-to-eye and continued, "Please, sir, hear me out. Just as there are good Aryans and bad Aryans, there clearly must be some good Jews amongst the bad Jews. Just as not all Aryans embrace National Socialism; not all Jews embrace Judaism. Many Jews recognizing the false dogmas of Judaism have converted to Catholicism. Many Aryans have married Jews. Clearly, there is a lot of confusion and doubt on this issue. Many Jews believe that Adolf Hitler through National Socialism is the only way to come out of the economic disaster that we are all enduring. We want the same things as you – better jobs, better working conditions and freedom from the oppression that these rich Jews have over us. We, too, have been oppressed, stifled by the Global Jewish Conspiracy. These Jews show no mercy or compassion to us. They do not associate with us. We are in different worlds."

He paused to catch his breath and continued, "Our fathers fought in the war alongside our German brothers. Many lost their lives for the common cause. Many of our fathers received medals for bravery, for saving the lives of both Jewish and non-Jewish soldiers. As a soldier you know that there is no religious differentiation on the battlefield. Once in uniform we are all equal targets for the enemy."

Again he paused, "For thousands of years Jews have lived in many countries and while we have never really been accepted as equals by our fellow countrymen, we have been allowed to live among them. Life has not always been easy. There have been many pogroms and persecutions but here in Austria, for the past one hundred years, Jews have been accepted. Many of us are content here and we would like to continue to be a part of society at some level. We know that there are still Jews living and working in Germany, making a positive contribution to the German economy. We know this just as you know this. Surely, there must be a place for us, especially if we help in realizing the objectives of the Nazi Party in Austria – and in unifying our two countries."

Ezra sat down in the chair in front of the desk, "That is all I have to say. We are ready and willing to work for Hitler and National Socialism. I hope that you will see some merit in this."

Captain Leopold listened attentively to Ezra's remarks. When Ezra was finished he just sat at his desk obviously in deep thought about what should be his next course of action. In order to understand what course of action he decided upon, it is important to understand the man who was the leader of the Nazi Party in Austria.

As within any political party there are different factions with different beliefs and methodologies. So it was within the Austrian Nazi Party. Initially, in the early 1930s, there were two distinct political factions. One believed in the tenets of National Socialism along party doctrines. They were mostly middle-class professionals, blue collar workers and shop keepers over the age of thirty. The other, consisting primarily of younger people in universities and in various professions or university graduates that could not find jobs in their chosen profession, gave their allegiance directly and only to Adolf Hitler whom they believed was the personification of the Nazi Party. The latter group became the dominant voice in the party. Hitler's speeches appealed to the young more than the old. But there was one common view – that Austria and Germany should become one country. Here again, there were two distinct views on how this should be accomplished. One faction believed in evolutionary methods (political negotiation) while the other believed in revolutionary methods (violence). To the latter group, time was of the essence. Austria was a mess which needed to be fixed as soon as possible. Berlin supported both views. Officially, it was evolutionary but there were no objections to civil disobedience. In fact, civil disobedience worked for the Nazis in Germany. Whenever 'peaceful demonstrations' of German National Socialists were suppressed and demonstrators were arrested, it became a battle cry for Hitler. The 1934 attempted coup where Dollfuss was assassinated was done with the tacit approval of Berlin. When the coup failed Hitler feigned regret, disavowed any knowledge or support of the failed coup and recalled the head of the Nazi Party, Theodor Habicht, replacing him with Captain Josef Leopold. He also recalled the German Ambassador von Rath and replaced him with Franz von Papen, a mild-mannered aristocratic man that was clearly in the 'evolutionary' camp. Captain Josef Leopold was also an evolutionary. Hitler wanted an evolutionary to be in control, but someone who would follow orders without question so if he needed something done outside the law, there would be someone in charge who would do whatever was asked. Captain Leopold was that man. He had served 26 months in prison for his subversive Nazi activities against the Austrian government. As a result, he was greatly admired and respected by party members in Austria and Berlin. He inspired his followers with his acumen, quick wit, strong convictions and leadership. He marched alongside his followers in demonstrations, gave fiery speeches but stopped short of overt violent acts. Once back in control there was some strong opposition to his evolutionary policies by the revolutionary elements. There were still some well orchestrated acts of sabotage against the government and against Jews by those that believed in revolutionary methods. His inability to control these factions led to constant friction between von Papen and various other Austrian and German Nazi Party members that believed in evolution. At times it was so bad that Leopold flew to Berlin to personally speak to Goering, Himmler and, if he could get an audience, to Hitler, to whom he was fanatically loyal – and Hitler knew it. He was radical, outspoken and a strong individualist – and extremely ambitious. He saw himself as the Nazi leader of Austria reporting directly to Hitler once Austria became a part of Germany. After all, wasn't he the most ardent and loyal Hitler Nazi in the country that constantly risked imprisonment to champion the Nazi cause? In February he moved against the revolutionaries in a manner similar to the way that Hitler dealt with Ernst Röhm – assassination. He ousted the most overt radicals from the party. Three of the most outspoken leaders met with fatal accidents the same night. As this was not officially sanctioned, his prestige dropped considerably within the Nazi party in Austria and Berlin. He also knew this and had to do something to reinstate his position.

He got up from behind his desk and walked over to the window looking outside at the city with his back towards Ezra. It was obvious to Ezra that he was considering a number of alternatives. Various scenarios raced through Leopold's mind. Should he shoot this Jew now and put him out of his misery? Should he just throw him out of his office? Should he consider his offer and work with Jews? If so, what would the rest of the party think? They would probably have him committed to an asylum. Yet, what a coup if he could get Jews to support Hitler! It would surely be a first! He was never a conformist which was why he had so much friction with other party members. Once he developed this rationale, he decided on a course of action as he asked Ezra to wait in the next room and instructed his secretary, Helga, to send everyone waiting to see him away, cancel all of his appointments for the day and not to let anyone into his office. He instructed her to get Himmler on the phone with the utmost urgency tracking him down wherever he might be. Helga cleared the waiting room making up an excuse of stomach illness, not very serious but enough to cause considerable discomfort. She instructed the guards at the door to turn away every one whether or not they had an appointment instructing those that had appointments to call Helga in the morning to reschedule their appointment. While some protested and tried to enter his office anyway, they were held back by the guards. Helga returned to her desk and called Himmler saying that it was an emergency

This was Leopold's lucky day! Himmler was in his office and agreed to take the call. Leopold carefully explained the situation. Unbelievable as it may sound, he had a young Jew in his office that was part of a Jewish group in Vienna, primarily of young men and women that wanted to work for Hitler – and, perhaps, become some auxiliary part of the Nazi Party once they proved their value. At first, Himmler thought it was a joke. "Okay! Okay! Now tell me why you really called. Trouble with von Papen again?"

"No! No! I am really serious. I, too, thought at first it was a joke. But now I am convinced. There is a Jew boy in my office that says he has a group of Jew friends that feel as alien to the rich Jews that run the economy as we do – and for all of the same reasons. They have no love for them. They are not treated well by them. They feel that the only opportunity that they will have to better themselves is under German leadership – not as equals, of course, but under some acceptable level that would have them better off than they are now. When he first told me that he was a Jew and started to explain the reason for his visit to my office I had the immediate urge to take out my pistol and shoot him on the spot but as I listened I realized that he was serious and perhaps they could be of some use. I have never heard of anything like this and wanted to get your advice on what to do about this situation."

There was about two minutes of silence. "Are you still on the line, Herr Himmler?" Himmler finally responded, "Yes! Yes! I am thinking about this. I, too, have never come across anything like this before. I will call you back within the hour. Hold the Jew boy there and say nothing to anyone. Do not leave the office until you hear from me."

Without saying anything to Ezra, he instructed Helga to screen all telephone calls. Only calls from Berlin and his wife were to be given to him. About ninety minutes later, the phone rang. It startled Leopold who was now sitting at his desk doing some paperwork. He jumped up almost knocking the glass of water that was near the phone off of the desk. "Heil Hitler!" was the first words out of his mouth as he picked up the phone. "Heil Hitler yourself! What time are you coming home for dinner tonight?" his wife responded. "Oh, it's only you! I was expecting an important call from Berlin."

That was really not the correct response and she let him know that she did not appreciate being categorized as 'only you'. He apologized and said that he was waiting for an extremely important call from Berlin and, depending upon the call, would let her know what time he was coming home for dinner. He abruptly hung up only realizing after the fact that his wife would not take kindly to his ending the conversation in that abrupt manner – but he had more important things to worry about.

Another twenty minutes passed. The phone rang and again his opening words were, "Heil Hitler!" This time it was Himmler's secretary who asked him to hold for Himmler. Himmler got on the phone and proceeded to let him know that this unusual situation was discussed with Goebbels, Goering and Hitler. They unanimously agreed to "allow these Jews to be an ex-officio group within the party with the potential for auxiliary membership after three years of exemplary service to the Fatherland. They would be directed under the command of a special Propaganda Ministry officer reporting directly to Goebbels who would be coming to Vienna from Berlin. We will decide how and when to use these Jews and he will implement it. They will not wear any uniforms but will be permitted to wear special armbands that will have a Jewish star and a Swastika on it. Someone here will prepare an appropriate design for the armband. At this point they will not be allowed to wear a party pin. They, of course, must salute Hitler and take an oath to our Fuehrer." After some additional discussion, Himmler commended him. He told him that the Fuehrer was extremely interested in this situation which was actually in line with some ideas he had about treating Jews that had served the Fatherland different from the other Jews. Hitler was continuously aware of world opinion and had received much criticism about his policies towards Jews in Germany. There was no doubt in his mind that Austria would become a part of Germany. He just had to wait for the right time. Having Jews support his efforts would clearly enhance his position. Himmler must have commended him five times during the course of the conversation. Plaudits came not only from Himmler personally but, as Himmler told him, also from Goebbels, Goering and Hitler. As far as Leopold was concerned this was his assurance that he would be the head of Nazi Austria when the time came. He was restored. He was elated!

In a very different mood, he went into the next room and asked Ezra to join him in his office even offering him some refreshments to the point of not taking no for an answer. He did not say anything else at the time. He called Helga and told her to bring in some beer, cheese and fruit. A few minutes later she came in with a tray of cheese and fruit along with various beverages on a cart and wheeled it over to the table near the other window. She placed the tray on the table and set up it with linen napkins and silver utensils.

Leopold invited Ezra to the table and as they sat down facing each other, he began by telling Ezra that he had brought this to the attention of Berlin and that he had just been informed by Himmler that Adolf Hitler as well as Goebbels and Goering were excited about this opportunity to show the world that Jews, under the proper circumstances, could be an integral part of the New Order. They spent a good hour discussing the terms and conditions all of which seemed reasonable and perfectly acceptable to Ezra.

When they finished, he got up and escorted Ezra to the front door. "This is the first time that I have sat at the same table to eat with a Jew." At the door Ezra turned and saluted, "Heil Hitler!" Without a moment's hesitation Leopold responded, "Heil Hitler!"

Two happy people emerged from the meeting that day and each knew that they had some difficult work ahead of them to make this work. Leopold could bide his time and wait for the arrival of the special officer from Berlin before letting anyone know about this but Ezra had to inform the group and set up the protocols to work with the Nazis. Moreover, they had to consider various personal items as they emerged into the public domain. Many of the members of the group would be ostracized by other Jews and most likely even their own families. Those that had jobs with Jewish firms could lose them. Moreover, they needed to expand and attract more members.

With this in play, Leopold decided to stop all party-led attacks on Jews and Jewish establishments. This time he really meant it. There was too much at stake for him personally. He followed this up by sending a message to Ezra summoning him to a remote café at 10 PM just when the café closed and he knew it would be deserted. The café shuttered its doors but allowed the two to stay and talk. Leopold told Ezra that he was going to restrain party members from all attacks on Jews. He decided to do this to demonstrate that Ezra's new relationship with the Nazis was already reaping a benefit. "Perhaps this could be used to attract more members?" he replied, making sure that he emphasized that this was a temporary situation and that he could not restrain the acts of violence forever against those Jews that deserved it. The way he described it, the Austrian Nazi Party never planned or condoned these attacks. They were the personal actions of some party members that had to strike out at Jewish tyranny. Regardless of whether Ezra believed him or not, he had clearly accomplished something for the entire Jewish community which he emphasized at least five times during his speech to the group the next evening. Captain Leopold told Ezra that he had the support of the Nazi Party but not to publicly acknowledge it yet but that he could infer this in announcing the respite of attacks on Jews during this period of assimilation which he could use to attract more members. During the course of the next few weeks a number of things happened.

Captain Franz Schüller from the Propaganda Ministry arrived from Berlin to interface with the Jewish group. He had a twenty page written document prepared by a committee that Goebbels personally headed on how to use the Jews, how to treat them within the Austrian Nazi Party and various propaganda items such as leaflets, posters and official statements for the Jews to use when they were being interviewed by the press, participating in demonstrations and just going about their normal daily business. After much controversy, an armband had been designed. It was a light blue armband with a solid yellow Jewish star flanked by two larger black swastikas, one on each side of the star. Inside the solid Jewish star was a small black swastika in the center. The official name of the group became the National Socialist Jewish League (NSJL). The letters were also on the armband. Ezra was given the rank of Juden Obergruppenfuehrer (Jewish Senior Group Leader).

On December 9, 1937 press releases were sent to newspapers throughout Austria and Germany as well as to the foreign press announcing the formation of the National Socialist Jewish League. Members informed their families, friends, bosses and co-workers that they had formed and joined a pro-Nazi Jewish organization that had been sanctioned by Berlin. They also told everyone that there would not be any acts of violence against any Jew for the time being.

In spite of this, as expected, most were ostracized, disowned, cursed and scorned by mostly everyone they knew. While a few recanted and quit, most stayed the course. Every member had a story about the reactions of those whom they told ranging from passive to violent responses but if I had to choose one word to describe the collective responses it would be disbelief.

The foreign press coverage was phenomenal. Almost every paper in Europe and the United States printed the story. Reporters descended on the Nazi Party office. Ezra was on hand to answer questions using the material that had been prepared for him. Hitler was extremely pleased as was Leopold. He was back in favor with Berlin – thanks to a Jew!

While the group lost a few members, many more came forth, especially when there were no attacks on Jews as Ezra said. The Nazis were willing to wait to see who their enemies were and who their friends were among the Jews. This had a strong impact on the discontented and disenchanted Jews. It was a clear signal that what they have been told about all Jews being enemies of the Nazis was not correct. They had once again been lied to by the wealthy corrupt Jews that owned the newspapers who wanted to discourage any independent thinking. More than 200 young Jewish men and women joined the group by the end of the month with about 250 more joining in the ensuing three weeks.

The first official meeting of the group was set for a Friday night, for obvious reasons. A large meeting hall in the second district was rented for the occasion. It was lavishly catered with ham and pork being among the meats served conspicuously accompanied by a pig's head as the centerpiece. Four official Nazi photographers from Berlin were present. Reporters were there from different Viennese newspapers No reporters came from Jewish-owned newspapers – they boycotted the event. Reporters and photographers from the foreign press were given prominent places in the meeting hall. Euphoria reigned at the initial meeting. Captain Schüller was eloquent. He repeated over and over again that Hitler personally conveyed his congratulations to the group and would be watching their progress – along with Goebbels, Goering, Hess, and Himmler.

"As we speak, their eyes are upon us. This will be a lesson to the world that we are only against the Global Jewish Conspiracy that has robbed Germany of its rightful place in the world. It will show the world that these Jews even discriminate against other Jews. Their only God is gold. Their covenant is greed. They are usurers that take advantage of the misfortune of others. They have no code of ethics. Their greed and oppression knows no boundaries or borders. As soon as they are rooted out of society the world will be a better place. In time, they will envy you (pointing to the new young Jewish Nazis). They will watch history unfold while you will be unfolding history. Austria will again be united with Germany. It is our destiny. Our Fuehrer has ordained it. One day all German people of Europe will be united with the Fatherland. The rich Jews and the Communists have interfered with Germanic destiny for far too long. They will not be welcome here and will migrate to the countries that they dominate. But, as I stand here and welcome you to our cause, let me also be clear about my position. You have taken a personal decision, the correct decision, to join us. This is an individual decision. Your friends and family will not get a free ride when we are one country. If they want to be a part of the New Order, they must join with us before the union. So, your first task is to convince them that we are the only choice and that Adolf Hitler is the true Messiah. I am not asking anyone to renounce their religion. Our Fuehrer has never asked that of anyone. Many of us, like me, are Lutherans. Many are Catholics and Protestants. His only requirement is that he be placed above your religious beliefs. You cannot have two Masters, two Gods – at least here on Earth. In the afterlife, you are free to do as you wish but while you are alive here on Earth your mind, heart and soul must belong to our Fuehrer. So it is now with great pride that I will administer the oath of allegiance to our Fuehrer. If you are not prepared to take this oath, leave now."

He paused and looked around. Everyone seated also looked around. Not one person got up to leave. With that, he left the stage and walked over to the table on the floor level and picked up a bible. He specifically mentioned that it was the Old Testament as he walked around the table and stood in front of the group. Without him saying anything, the group stood up in unison. Captain Schüller extended his right arm in the typical Heil Hitler position. Everyone standing did the same.

"Repeat after me: **I swear by God this sacred oath**: (pause/response) **I will render unconditional obedience to Adolf Hitler, the Fuehrer of the German Reich and people** (pause/response) **and will be ready to give my life at any time for this oath** (response)."

"Please be seated. By the power given to me by our Fuehrer I now welcome you as members of the National Socialist Jewish League. I will be in charge. I cannot stress how important this is for your people. All of Germany, no, all of the world, will be watching you as will our Fuehrer, Adolf Hitler. You will obey any order without question given by me or by Captain Leopold and his staff just as any soldier obeys his superiors – for this is what you are, soldiers in fight for the supremacy of our Fuehrer and the Fatherland. Is this understood?"

A thunderous "Ja!" echoed through the meeting hall. Captain Schüller smiled as he invited Captain Leopold to make some remarks and close the meeting. As he started to turn to sit down, Ezra shouted, "Heil Hitler!" The rest of the group, now formally the National Socialist Jewish League, immediately did the same, shouting "Heil Hitler!" Captain Schüller stopped his turn and faced the group. He smiled as he raised his hand and returned the salute, "Heil Hitler!" as did Captain Leopold and the rest of the Austrian Nazi Party members present.

Leopold reiterated the welcoming remarks of Captain Schüller. He distributed the armbands which everyone put on. As each member received the armband from one of the party members there was the usual "Heil Hitler!" salute. Once this was done, forms were distributed to each member requiring them to list where they lived, all of their family members, where they worked and whether the owner of the establishments where they worked was a Jew.

The League had some very specific tasks:

- Participate in all demonstrations and political rallies wearing their armbands. They were given some training on marching together as a unit.

- Recruit more Jews. This consisted of two types of members. Jews that were interested in joining the party that had positions of importance in companies, in government or in any area deemed important to the Nazis (e.g., working at the telephone exchange or the railroad system) would be secret members that would be spies and pass any information that they thought was important to the party. Jews that were in mundane jobs or jobless, that had little influence would join as open members and would participate in public events.

- Raise money for the party within the Jewish community. This was tantamount to extortion. Wearing their armbands they would visit various Jewish-owned shops and businesses with a notebook in their hands politely asking for a donation letting it be known that if they did not make a contribution that they could not guarantee that the establishment would not be vandalized. Almost every business made a contribution. Those that didn't had their windows and doors broken within a day or two. They did not refuse a second time.

- Prepare a list of wealthy and prominent Jews in Vienna along with the shops and businesses that they own. While much of this information already existed in the IKG it was good to have a backup in case someone destroyed the IKG files.

- Form similar Leagues in other major Austrian cities.

A month later the League had more than 600 open members of which more than 80 percent were young men between the ages of seventeen and twenty-two and fifteen percent were women between the ages of twenty three and twenty five. The rest were older. They also had 37 secret members that acted as spies in various Jewish companies and government agencies. Although they tried, they could not get any member of the IKG to join as a secret member nor did they form a similar group in any other Austrian city.

Now, you might ask how I became aware of this group and all of these details. Well, Ezra Koppelman, the leader of the group was the son of Hyman Koppelman, one of our ambulance drivers. Hymie, as he liked to be called, and I got along very well. He had four children and his wife was not very healthy. She had a problem delivering her fourth child and was no longer able to have any more children. Her medication and doctor bills were a burden and as a result Hymie let it be known that he was available 24 hours a day, seven days a week in case anyone needed a driver. He needed the extra money. I used him exclusively at night and weekends since he was extremely reliable and trustworthy. He never disappointed me, was always punctual and could be relied on to keep anything confidential that was asked of him. He was the ambulance driver that I used the night when Kaltenbrunner's son committed suicide. When Ezra first told his father about his plan to try to join the Nazi Party, he was very skeptical and upset. Violent arguments occurred every night which had a further debilitating impact on his wife. If it were not for the poor health of his wife and the money that Ezra contributed to the household, he would have thrown him out of the house that night. Instead he came in early the next morning and asked for my advice telling me the whole story in detail. I recommended that he just let Ezra do what he wants. He should not condone it nor should he try to stop him. At this point it seemed to me that Ezra was resolved to join whether or not he obtained parental consent so the choice was either to accept it and live with it or possibly lose him. Moreover, from what he said the impact of their constant fighting was very bad for his wife. He should just express his disappointment and disapproval and wait.

We discussed this for about an hour before Hymie finally acquiesced. That night he talked it over with Ezra mentioning that he had discussed the situation with me and what I had recommended. The next morning, I received a personal visit from Ezra thanking me for interceding and recommending the course of action that his father took. I was surprised at his visit and his presence. He was well-dressed, very neat and stood erect, looking me in my eyes as we spoke. He was quite articulate and had a good command of the language. Had he not have had to quit school to go to work to supplement his father's income there was no doubt in my mind that he would have been very successful in whatever profession he selected. Instead, he was a low paid sales clerk at Schiffer's Department Store. We discussed his interest in the Nazis and I could easily understand his train of thought. He had nothing now. He had a long-time girlfriend but couldn't afford to take her anyplace nice, let alone get engaged and marry her. All of his money, little as it was, went to the family. He was the oldest and quit school in his senior year of high school to get a job. His younger brother, Benjamin, was now a senior in high school and was faced with the same dilemma. His salary and his father's salary were not keeping up with inflation and the cost his mother's medical treatments. Ezra bowed his head and sadly said that he had approached his manager, Asher Birnbaum, at the store for a raise or promotion or just to be able to work more hours but he was refused. When he asked if he could talk to the owner, Mr. Schiffer, who was also Jewish, he was told by the manager that "just because you are a Jew doesn't mean that you can see him. He has no time for the likes of you. You should be glad that you have a job under the current conditions in Vienna. If you need help, go to the Jewish Charity. They will give you some soup."

Ezra was taken aback by this. The manager had no reason to talk down to him in this manner. When he mentioned this to some of his friends, many of them had similar stories. That's when he started talking about the Nazis and how life could not be any worse under their rule. In fact, if Hitler could improve the economy of Austria by even half as much as he did in Germany there would clearly be more opportunities in Vienna for betterment. He stood there for a few seconds waiting to see my reaction. Unfortunately, I could see the logic in what he said even though I did not believe it. I could not see any life for a Jew under the Nazis or any government that was so overtly anti-Semitic. That was why my father came to Vienna and hid the fact that we were Jewish – and why I continued with the deception. However, I could not stand there and debate the subject. I also did not want to say anything negative about the Nazis that could possibly get back to them so I just shook his hand, wished him luck and accompanied him to the front door of the morgue.

Throughout 1937, with the Nazi party now legal and the economy of Austria still in the doldrums, party membership increased substantially – primarily in the larger cities and still with a disproportionate amount of young adults and teenagers. The party had both publicly visible and secret members. The secret members were spies in critical places such as the police and military hierarchy, in government ministry offices and with key industrialists. While no one the staff that worked for von Schuschnigg was a Nazi spy, some of the staff of his closest friends and government officials were secret Nazi spies. Every move he made was dutifully reported to Berlin – sometimes even before he could inform his cabinet.

The Austrian Hitler Youth Organization (Hitler Jugend) was officially recognized as a legal entity. This allowed them to march in parades and participate in all demonstrations. With the continuing economic problems in Austria compared to the strong economic recovery in Germany, many young men and women in universities embraced National Socialism as the panacea for all of their future concerns. Many graduates could not find decent jobs so those that were not party member while studying became post-graduate members. While attacks on Jews stopped in the city, acts on Jews continued at the Vienna University with one addition – members of the National Socialist Jewish League now participated in the demonstrations. About one hundred Jewish students that did not come from rich families and did not have good prospects for jobs after graduation, joined the League. They were not attacked. The police rarely interfered. Even the rector of the university was taken aback by this new element of Jews demonstrating against Jews.

Under these conditions I started to get concerned. Even though my Jewish identity was hidden there were some potential points of discovery. For example, I used a Jewish doctor so my name was in his records. Suppose the Nazis were successful and took control of Austria. Under these circumstances they could investigate all of the patients of Jewish doctors. All they had to do was ask each male patient to drop his pants to see if he was circumcised. I did not want to be discovered in this manner. I believed that all Jewish men pretending to be Gentiles used Jewish doctors since any physical examination would reveal their circumcised penis, so I was sure that there were others like me. I set up an appointment with Doctor Nussbaum, my personal physician, and explained my concern. He understood perfectly and told me that there were others like me pretending to be Gentile. Some had approached him with the same concern and he had given them all of their records and deleted their names from every record and file in his possession. He would now do the same for me.

He decided to contact the others that were in similar circumstances that had not yet made this request. As I was leaving I turned back to him and asked if he could tell me the names of these other patients. I thought it would be beneficial if we got together to see if there was anything that we could do to protect one another. While he refused to give me any names due to doctor-patient privilege, he offered, with my permission, to contact them and give them my name. If they were interested they could contact me. He would not even tell me how many men were in the same situation due to his professional ethics.

Within three days I received calls from five men that had been referred by Doctor Nussbaum. We decided to meet at the house of one of the men on the idea of setting up some sort of relationship. My apartment was too small.

We had our first meeting on Friday, December 8, 1937 under the pretext of playing cards. We did not play any cards. Instead, we introduced ourselves to each other. There were six of us in this group and we all had false papers hiding the fact that we were Jewish. The other five were:

- Wilhelm Roebling was a doctor. He was married with two children, a boy Helmut who was fourteen years old and a girl Helga who was twelve years old. His Jewish wife also had false papers as did their children. He had a very unique situation in that he never had his son circumcised as he was living as a non-Jew for more than eighteen years. We were meeting in his house. As far as his children knew, they were Catholic. His parents were dead and her parents also had false papers.

- Kurt Schultz was an owner of a chain of office supply stores. He was the oldest in our group. His wife was also Jewish and was from Berlin. Her family had left Germany in 1933 for the United States. They had three children two boys, Kurt and Wolfgang, ages twenty one and twenty three and a girl, Magda, twenty. They all had false papers. His oldest boy was engaged to a girl from a known Jewish family. His youngest was attending college in the United States and was not likely to return in the current environment. His children knew that they were Jewish and both boys had been circumcised.

- Klaus Frühling was a civil engineer who worked for the City of Vienna. He was not married.

- Hermann Schmidt was a lawyer. He was married to a Gentile whose family had helped him establish his non-Jewish identity. They had met in Salzburg when he successfully defended her father from a ruinous lawsuit that would have left him bankrupt. Her father was totally open-minded and welcomed him in the family but recognizing the strong undercurrent of anti-Semitism increasing in the country had immediately suggested that he become a Gentile and set up a practice in Vienna. He was very rich and influential in Salzburg and was able to set up Hermann's new religious identity with an excellent set of real documents – the best that money could buy. They had one child a girl nine years old. She did not know that her father was Jewish.

- Friedrich Steiermann was a dentist. He was married and his wife was not Jewish. She obviously knew he was Jewish and kept the secret from her family. They did not have any children by choice.

Doctor Nussbaum told us that there were more but they had elected to keep their secret – even from us. We decided that we would meet every Friday night for a weekly card game. We chose Friday night since this was the start to the Jewish Sabbath and Jews were supposed to be praying in the synagogue at that time, not playing cards.

I decided to also switch dentists and every other Jewish service provider that I used as we all did. While these service providers did not know I was Jewish, they all understood perfectly. Many mentioned that they planned to leave Austria as soon as they could since I was not the first Gentile to stop using their services. However, unlike most, I was nice enough to come to them and explain the situation. Most of their patients or clients either just stopped coming or sent nasty letters denigrating them and telling them that they should send all records immediately to their new service provider. Many of them did not pay their bills.

At our third card game Klaus recommended that we actually play cards so he asked what card games we knew. We all knew five-card draw poker and five card stud poker. That was about it. Klaus taught us a couple of additional poker games and we started to play poker. Klaus's rationale was that if we ever were questioned on where we were on a Friday night and we said that we were playing poker with a group of friends, we needed to know what poker games we played, who won and who lost for consistency in case corroboration was needed. It was a reasonable suggestion so we played cards every Friday night but the main purpose of the card game was to discuss the economic, social and political situations since they were tightly interwoven. We also discussed the plight of the Jews in Vienna. With the National Socialist movement in Austria still gaining power and as their ranks continued to increase we were very worried. Attacks against Jews increased with impunity. Violence continued against the von Schuschnigg government as well. Hitler was threatening to take over the country which von Schuschnigg was adamantly against. Finally, he had enough. On January 26, 1938, von Schuschnigg ordered the police to raid all of the Nazi headquarters in every major city. In the Vienna office there was evidence of their organized violence and corruption. In addition, there was a plan for the Nazi takeover of the Austrian government prepared by the second highest ranking Nazi in Austria, Dr. Leopold Tavs. This became known as the Tavs Report. The police arrested many of the party's leaders and he again banned the party from all political activity. Hitler was infuriated that such incriminating evidence was carelessly left in the office. Captain Leopold was ordered to Berlin as was Ambassador von Papen. We and I'm sure all Jews and were elated – with one notable exception – the National Socialist Jewish League.

We spent more time after this talking more about the economic and political scene and less time on the plight of the Jews since we thought that von Schuschnigg's ban of the Nazi party eliminated them as a significant threat. We celebrated. Unfortunately, our elation was short-lived. Less than one month later, on Sunday, February 12, von Schuschnigg was summoned to Berchtesgaden to meet with

Hitler. From what we learned from the rumor mill, von Schuschnigg was looking forward to the meeting. It would be one chancellor to another – a chance to finally clear the air. He was expecting another agreement similar to the February 1936 Agreement where Hitler re-affirmed Austrian independence in return for the release of imprisoned Nazis and the reinstatement of the Nazi Party. With the ban on the party and the evidence obtained in the raids, von Schuschnigg felt that he had the upper hand and he would tell Hitler in no uncertain terms that Austria will remain an independent country as guaranteed by the Treaty of Versailles.

Wilhelm found out on Monday from one of his patients who was one of von Schuschnigg's aides that as soon as von Schuschnigg was led into the meeting room, Hitler launched a tirade that lasted for a full twenty minutes. He demanded that the Nazi Party be reinstated and be allowed to participate in all political activities; that all imprisoned Nazis be released, that they be allowed to wear the Swastika publicly and salute each other with "Heil Hitler!" and that two people be appointed to von Schuschnigg's cabinet with one of the key positions, Minister of the Interior, going to Dr. Seyss-Inquart. The Minister of the Interior was one of the most important positions on the Cabinet as it controlled the police force. The second appointment was to go to Edmund Glaise-Horstenau. If von Schuschnigg did not comply by Wednesday, February 16, Germany would invade Austria. He refused to even discuss Austrian independence. In fact there was no discussion, only demands. The chancellor was in a quandary. There was no way he wanted to have a war that would spill Austrian and German blood plus he knew that the Austrian army was no match for the German army. He promised to promote Hitler's demands to President Miklas. He had no other recourse. On their way out, one of his aides slipped in the snow and twisted his ankle. He was the one that came to Wilhelm the following day.

Wilhelm called us that night and we decided to have an impromptu card game the following night. We prepared ourselves for the worst. We believed that von Schuschnigg and Miklas would capitulate to Hitler's demands. His popularity with the people was at an all-time low. He was a dictator as was Hitler but he was ineffective when it came to restoring economic growth. He knew that key positions in the army and police had been infiltrated by underground Nazis but he did not know the extent of the infiltration. He was not even sure if the army would fight. So, in our minds it was no longer if Hitler would annex Austria, it was just when he would do it.

On Wednesday, February 16, 1938 von Schuschnigg and Miklas acquiesced to Hitler's demands. The ban on all political parties, including the Nazi Party, was lifted. Dr. Seyss-Inquart was named Minister of the Interior and a diehard Austrian Nazi, Edmund Glaise-Horstenau was appointed Minister-at-Large meaning that he was on the Cabinet and could vote but had no specific area of responsibility. On February 19, all Nazi prisoners were released from prison. Perhaps the most amazing fact about this development to us was that Dr. Seyss-Inquart was not a member of the Nazi Party. While he believed in most of the doctrines, including anti-Semitism, he had many personal differences with party members, especially the revolutionary ones so he elected not to join the party but openly supported National Socialism. It is believed that this was a prime factor in von Schuschnigg and Miklas agreeing to appoint him to such an important cabinet position. They believed that Dr. Seyss-Inquart was a man of principles and could be trusted. They also knew Glaise-Horstenau and believed the same of him even though he was an outright Nazi but one of moderation.

On February 24, we were glued to the radio as von Schuschnigg explained the situation and proclaimed that he would not agree to any more Nazi demands, that Austria will remain independent and that all Germans living in Austria will have their rights fully protected. He reiterated that Austria had done all that it could do and would not make any more concessions.

On March 8, von Schuschnigg unilaterally decided to schedule a plebiscite (vote) on Sunday, March 13 on whether Austria should remain independent or be annexed into Germany. This would show Hitler and the world that the Austrian people wanted to remain independent and that he was acting on their behalf. He told Seyss-Inquart about the plebiscite in the morning and asked him not to tell anyone. This was a test to see if Seyss-Inquart could be trusted. He knew that if he hadn't heard anything from Berlin by that afternoon that Seyss-Inquart had not said anything. He did not receive any communication from Berlin that afternoon. Seyss-Inquart was apparently a man of his word. He informed some of his staff and key supporters later that afternoon. By morning, however, his decision to hold the plebiscite was known in Berlin. Goering found out about it that night from the secretary of Guido Zernatto, the Secretary General of the Fatherland Front. She was a Nazi spy. Goering placed a call to von Schuschnigg but he wisely decided not to accept the call as he left Vienna to go to Innsbruck.

On Wednesday, March 9 von Schuschnigg arrived in Innsbruck for a political function and publicized that he would be speaking at 8 PM on the radio. At 8 PM he announced that there would be a plebiscite vote on whether the people of Austria want to remain independent or become a part of Germany and lose all autonomy. He had not even notified all of his Cabinet Ministers. They learned about it from his broadcast as did everyone else including President Miklas. By far, this was the best speech that von Schuschnigg ever made. It was strong, emotional, patriotic and clearly from his heart. I was with some friends in a local bar. As he spoke all of us stared at the radio as if we were able to see him standing at the microphone in Innsbruck. He spoke slowly and seemed to carefully craft each sentence to emphasize his position. He ended by an emphatic plea and with a quote from a famous Austrian patriot, Andreas Hofer, who rallied thousands of Austrians to fight Napoleon with, "Austrians, say yes to Austria! Men, the time has come!"

Three of the people listening in the bar stood up and cheered. They looked around afterward and sheepishly sat down feeling a little bit embarrassed but one of the wives stood up and said that we should all be on our feet after such a speech. We all stood up and there was a moment of silence. The rest of the evening was spent discussing the speech and whether we would help promote the plebiscite. We left it that each of us would decide and let our conscience be our guide on the appropriate action. I opted to do nothing. All I needed was to have some confrontation with the Nazis and be discovered as a Jew. On my way home I thought about Hofer and his rallying cry remembering that he was defeated by Napoleon. I hoped that this would not be a repeat.

Hitler and Goering also listened to his speech. Hitler was furious but Goering was more pragmatic. He simply said, "We will see about that (holding the plebiscite)." Even before von Schuschnigg had finished his speech a messenger was dispatched from Berlin to Vienna to deliver another ultimatum to von Schuschnigg. The messenger was a portly Nazi by the name of Odilo Globocnik. By the time von Schuschnigg returned to his office, Globocnik and Seyss-Inquart were already waiting for him. Hitler's ultimatum was very specific:

- Cancel the plebiscite

- Disband the existing Cabinet and form a new Cabinet with National Socialists having at least two-thirds of the new Cabinet.

- Resign immediately and appoint Seyss-Inquart to replace him as chancellor.

He made it clear that the army was massed near the border and was prepared to move up to the border as a prelude to an invasion. Hitler made it clear that he would attack Austria if his demands were not met.

On March 10 von Schuschnigg had still not decided what to do. He had already secretly ordered ballots to be printed. They only had "Ja" (yes) on them for independence. Anyone that wanted to vote for annexation had to bring their own ballot with a "Nein" (no) on them. The voting would be in the open and not by secret ballot so everyone at the polls could see how you voted. Moreover, he set the voting age at 24 and older since the largest age group supporting Hitler was between 18 and 23. This was actually allowable according to the constitution. Unfortunately for Schuschnigg, there were no secrets. His government had numerous spies who, by the end of the day, informed Goering and Hitler of his plans and activities as soon as they were decided.

Hitler was furious at von Schuschnigg for the third (and last) time. He conferred with Goering and they agreed to close the border and send troops to the Austrian border with the lead being taken by the Austrian Legion of Nazi Exiles. They called von Schuschnigg and in no uncertain terms ordered him to stop the plebiscite or they would invade Austria that night. Since von Schuschnigg did not want war. He informed Hitler that he would cancel the plebiscite. They gave him until 2 PM to resign and hand the government over to Seyss-Inquart or Austria would be invaded.

After much soul-searching, at 3:30 in the afternoon of Friday, March 11, 1938 von Schuschnigg resigned. He did not want to "spill any German blood". He ordered all Austrian troops to withdraw from the border and not to resist the Nazi army. He disbanded the Cabinet and recommended to President Miklas that Dr. Seyss-Inquart be appointed chancellor. Miklas refused to appoint him. Miklas looked for an alternate candidate but no one he approached wanted the position. Meanwhile, Hitler seeing the reticence of Miklas ordered troops to cross the border in the morning and ordered the Nazi Party in Vienna and other major cities to seize control of all government buildings and communications in the morning as well. In the cities where the Nazi movement was particularly strong, the Nazis didn't wait for morning. By nightfall, most buildings were under Nazi control or under Nazi siege in six major cities.

Rumors were rife. Given the state of affairs, a group of about fifteen of us decided to stay and listen to the radio in the cafeteria of the morgue. We sat staring at the radio. Hours passed. Nazis were running around, trying to seize control of key buildings and services and we surely would not want to run into them or any of the other political groups. In a last ditch effort to counter the Nazi takeover, von Schuschnigg legalized the Communist, Trade Unionist and Christian Democrat parties that had been banned since 1934 and gave them permission to demonstrate publicly – and they did – often with clashes with the Nazis throughout the city. No streets were safe tonight.

At 7:45 there was announcement that von Schuschnigg would speak in five minutes. We moved even closer to the radio even though we could hear everything very well from where we were sitting.

At 7:50 a different von Schuschnigg started to speak. It was clearly not the same man who a few days ago delivered such a powerful speech. He was subdued and morose. He started to explain in detail the behind-the-scene threatening political machinations that had developed since March 8, just three days ago. He spoke of the impending invasion by Germany and that he had decided to have the troops withdraw and not fight. His specific words were, "we are resolved that, on no account, and not even at this grave hour, shall German blood be spilled." He announced his resignation and that of the cabinet. As Seyss-Inquart still had not been confirmed by President Miklas he could not say who would be his replacement. He finished his broadcast with **"May God protect Austria!"**

We sat around the table for another hour or so discussing what the impact of annexation would mean. Most comments were actually quite positive. The economy of Austria was a disaster while Germany was booming. What did we have to lose?

After hearing von Schuschnigg's speech and seeing no viable recourse Miklas knew there was no alternative. Just before midnight he appointed Dr. Seyss-Inquart as chancellor. He had held out for ten hours. This was duly noted by Hitler.

The next morning, in a well-orchestrated plan, Seyss-Inquart reportedly sent a telegram to Berlin requesting that German troops enter Austria to maintain order in the country. The telegram had been prepared in Berlin two days before. Seyss-Inquart was just the messenger. In fact, there are some that believe that the telegram was never really sent but that it was miraculously received in Berlin that day.

The Nazis took to the streets.

Marching along with them was the National Socialist Jewish League.

CHAPTER SEVEN

AUSTRIA DISAPPEARS

"We will root out the causes of the poverty and despair that has kept Austria lagging behind the Reich. Those that have caused these problems, the Jews and the Communists will quickly learn that they have no place in the New Order. Their days of cheating and stealing are over."

Adolf Hitler, Vienna,

March 15, 1938 (Speech excerpt)

Saturday, March 12: Bodies started to arrive at the morgue at around 10 AM. I was finishing some paperwork when the first ones arrived. I had been busy working since 7 AM in the basement as we were going to expand and add additional cold storage facilities and another laboratory. At ten o'clock Otto came down to the basement. "Have you heard the news? The Nazis have crossed the border at Braunau and are on their way to Vienna as we speak! Most of the staff has taken to the streets to welcome them. There are rumors that Hitler is also coming today. I forgot you were down here until just now." I had not heard about any of this due to my self-imposed confinement but before I could comment he added, "By the way, there are two dead Jews in the holding room." I went into the holding room where the bodies of the two dead Jews were lying on two tables.

The first one I looked at was an older, well-dressed Jewish man who had hung himself. I thought nothing of it. The suicide of a Jewish businessman in Vienna was not uncommon. Two or three Jews typically committed suicide each month due to the extremely poor business conditions as they faced bankruptcy and ruin. The second was another man who evidently fell or was pushed off of a building or some other high place which could have either been a suicide or a murder. From his identification papers and last name he also was identified as being Jewish. Since just about everyone had left the morgue to await the arrival of the Nazis, I decided that I would process them now before going out with the rest of the staff to wait for the Nazis to arrive in Vienna. I should have left then. My mistake. Fifteen minutes later two ambulances arrived with four more suicides – all Jews. There was a family of three that died of a lethal injection administered by the father and one man with an apparent self-inflicted gunshot wound to the head. Before the attendants could unload the ambulance, another one came in with three more bodies. During the next three hours, fifteen more bodies were brought to the morgue. All were Jews and all were suicides and they were from different districts although most were from the second district. The attendants from the last ambulance with four bodies just left them at the entrance and went back out to get more. I asked Hans, one of my assistants to get a group of secretaries together to call their relatives. All of suicides had their identification papers on them. As the distraught family members of the deceased showed up they were led into a large waiting area. There were not enough seats so most had to stand and wait. I decided that I would go to the waiting room and explain the procedure to them. Before I could even go to the waiting room, one of the coroners came out of his office and looked at the many bodies. He turned to me, not realizing that they were all Jewish, and asked, "So many deaths at one time? Was there a major accident? What was the cause of death for all of these people?" I turned to him and said one word – "Anschluss!"

But, this was just the beginning!

On the morning of Saturday, March 12, 1938, the German army marched triumphantly into Austria – unopposed. In fact, they were welcomed by most of the population, even by Austrians of non-German descent. Tens of thousands of men, women and children lined the streets and highways waving Nazi flags, raising their right arm and yelling, "Heil Hitler!" Clearly, many people, whether they were outright Nazis or not, believed that Austria was going to have better times under Hitler. The radio kept broadcasting that von

Schuschnigg resigned and had been replaced with Dr. Arthur Seyss-Inquart.

On Sunday, March 13, preparations were being made for the triumphant visit to Vienna by Adolf Hitler, the Savior of Austria. That day, Dr. Seyss-Inquart joined the Nazi Party with membership number 7,467,338. Now that he was the chancellor of Nazi-controlled Austria he decided that he should finally become a party member. This was done quietly in a private ceremony in his office but the news was made public shortly thereafter.

Vienna was going all out for Hitler. All of a sudden flags and banners, some of which were fifteen meters long, miraculously materialized out of nowhere and were hung all along the route that Hitler would be traveling from Linz to the Imperial Hotel where he would spend the night before speaking at a mass rally on Tuesday.

As I was walking to the morgue I saw a crowd at the street corner. I went over to look. There were a group of Nazi brown shirts, the SD, overseeing about a dozen Jews that were on their knees scrubbing the street and the sidewalk with their coats and jackets. Two young Jewish boys were carrying water from a hydrant to the SD sergeant who would sometimes pour the water over the kneeling Jews. The Sergeant would occasionally make some comments ridiculing the Jews:

"It's time for your annual bath."

"Even with this pure Viennese water you are still filthy Jews!"

"Who says the Jews have no place in the New Order? I have found a place for them."

"Hurry up, you filthy Jews we have many more streets to clean!"

One of the SD officers kicked an older man who was exhausted and started to falter. In doing so he got some water on his boot. He turned to a young Jewish man immediately to his left and ordered him to clean his boot. The young man wiped the boot with his dirty coat making it worse. The soldier was furious and struck him a few times. An elderly lady from the crowd took pity on the young man and gave him a clean handkerchief. The Sergeant scowled at her but given her age he allowed her to give the handkerchief to the young man provided that when he was done that she take it back and put it in her purse. She agreed without a moment's hesitation. The Captain turned to the crowd pointing at the young man and said, "See, you can train them – as long as you don't spare the rod!" One of the onlookers paraphrased a famous proverb, "Spare the rod, spoil the Jew!" Everyone laughed. This was not an isolated incident. It was being repeated throughout Vienna based on the remarks of Goebbels. "Jews need to be put in their place! They need to be shown that their elevated status is a thing of the past. They must be taught humility for their past transgressions. Their thievery will no longer be tolerated!"

I stayed for about ten minutes staring in disbelief. Vienna was a city of culture. How could people allow this to happen? I looked around. With the exception of a few elderly people not only were the people allowing this abuse they were abetting it. They cheered the SD. They cursed the Jews. Some spat at them or in the street so they had to clean it up. There was no doubt in my mind that I had misjudged Viennese hatred for the Jews. I slowly walked to the morgue quite depressed. What I didn't realize was that this was relatively tame compared to what was going to happen to the Jewish community during the next few days.

To legitimatize the bloodless takeover, Hitler officially rescheduled the plebiscite where the people would decide whether or not Austria should become a part of Germany. On March 13th he appointed Josef Bürckel, the Gauleiter (regional leader) of the Saar, as the Gauleiter of Austria with the task of setting up the plebiscite which was scheduled for Sunday, April 10. He was simultaneously given the responsibility of integrating Austria into Germany. Austria became Ostmark, a province of Germany. Independent Austria ceased to exist.

I spent much of Saturday night attending to the suicides that had come in throughout the day and evening. As there was not enough room in the waiting rooms and other public areas to accommodate all of the tearful sobbing family members, we cordoned off an area outside the morgue and asked that only two family members come inside to identify and claim the body. We were lucky enough to find three policemen to help us with the crowd. Most policemen did not want to have anything to do with helping Jews so I suspected that they were Jewish but did not ask. To put this in perspective, when one of the relatives of a family of four that had committed suicide went to their apartment to get some of their personal belongings there was a sign at the entrance to the building and on the doors of the other Jewish apartments, "Dear Jews, why not follow the great example set by your neighbors in apartment 3D?"

I estimated that there were more than one hundred bereaved people waiting to claim the bodies. While we tried to get as many bodies out of the morgue as quickly as possible, it was not easy. The families had to arrange for the private funeral homes that they used to send a hearse. Many used the same funeral home so while they had a few hearses they did not have enough to accommodate this amount of deaths at one time. Many families had to wait for the hearses to come back after dropping off the previous body; some had to wait for three or four round trips. Between supervising the releases and preparing the paperwork, I was too exhausted to go home so at 3 AM I went to my room in the basement and tried to sleep. I only slept for about three hours.

I was awakened at about 6:30 AM on Sunday. Another group of dead Jews arrived. This was another story. These were Jews that had obviously been beaten to death or killed in some other manner. They had all been murdered. It was not a quick death. Most had no identification at all. They had no jewelry, no wallet, nothing. Everything had been stolen, obviously by whoever killed them. Some were brought in by relatives and some by the ambulances. When they were brought in by the ambulances they were all just summarily dumped at the back receiving door of the morgue. Many of the drivers made vicious anti-Semitic comments to the attendants at the door, two of whom were Jewish.

"Here are some more dirty Jews!"

"We are bringing them here because we do not want these filthy Jews littering the streets of the city with the Fuehrer here!"

"Finally, here is a good Jew!"

"Dead Jews and Hitler! What a great combination!"

As the day progressed and more bodies were brought in, I was able to piece together the events of the previous night. With Anschluss and the arrival of Hitler with his openly anti-Semitic remarks about Jews having no place in the New Order, pent up Austrian anti-Semitism was unleashed and given a free rein. Mobs of people, especially the Hitler Jugend, randomly entered Leopoldstadt, the second district with the largest number of Jews and randomly attacked Jews on the street where they were robbed and beaten. Jews were pulled off of busses and trams then robbed and beaten. Jewish stores were looted with the owners and all Jewish customers robbed and beaten. Homes were invaded with the same results. The police stood by and did nothing. To single out the Hitler Jugend and members of the Nazi Party would be an understatement. Groups of workers, shopkeepers, housewives, teachers, people that you would think would not harm a fly, Catholics, Lutherans all participated in the attacks. Most of the Jews were badly beaten but some were killed – especially if they put up any resistance in the street or in their shops. One grocery store owner who resisted was thrown through his plate glass window and pelted with cans of food until he was dead – as was a Jewish woman customer in the shop at the time that protested. Age was not a deterrent. Teenagers and children were also attacked and while no children were killed, many were badly beaten. The hospitals were full of victims. We received twenty-four bodies by 7:30 AM.

People began coming to the morgue at 8 AM. The violence had subsided with daylight. Night gives courage to mobs. When their sons, fathers and other family members did not come home those at home thought the worst. Some members of the family went to the local hospitals and some came to the morgue. Some family members had gone to the shops that they owned and when they saw the destruction and the amount of blood they came directly to the morgue. My assistant, Emil, classified each unidentified body by sex, approximate age, color of hair and eyes, height and weight and grouped them together by sex. He also looked for anything that would help identify them such as birthmarks and scars. The storage bins were already filled with the suicides from the day before so he turned two basement storage rooms and the garage into makeshift morgues. There were not enough tables and gurneys so many of the bodies were lying on the floor covered with sheets. He had first left the heads uncovered but some were so badly beaten that anyone walking through that area to find their own missing family member would be sickened by the massive facial destruction. So, he had the bodies with their faces badly beaten totally covered with the information lying on top of the body. The basement storage rooms had the men and the garage had the women.

By the time the relatives were allowed entry into the makeshift morgues, each sheet was thoroughly blood-stained but there were not enough sheets to replace them and Emil was worried that this was just the beginning of the violence. He was right.

The violence during the next two nights continued and spread to other districts. There were no Jews on the street or on any public conveyance. No Jewish shop was open so the mobs broke into many of the closed shops and looted them. Jews were not safe at home either. More than three thousand apartments and private houses were invaded with beatings and robberies occurring in all of them. There was not one piece of furniture left in some apartments. Everything was either stolen or smashed into pieces. All that the family had left was the clothes that they were wearing. Some had every pocket ripped off so even their last coin was taken. Watches, rings, earrings were all taken. In some cases the earrings were ripped off the ears of the women wearing them.

Late Monday afternoon, March 14, Hitler made a triumphant entrance into Vienna. As he rode through the city in his motorcade, he was greeted as the conquering hero. In the interim, between Saturday and Monday the city was transformed into a living Hell for Jews. The violence had toned down only with respect to the number of murders. Evidently, the authorities were warning against murder but still some bodies arrived at the morgue. I was again told that they were only from Jews that fought back when they were robbed and injured one or more of the attackers.

On Tuesday, March 15, around 11 AM, Gustav came into the autopsy room and asked if I was going to the rally. "We should get there early. Hitler will be speaking at 2 o'clock. He is staying at the Hotel Imperial. He arrived last night." Being Jewish I had no desire to go. However, I could see by his excitement that he was really expecting me to go with him. The only plausible answer was to be enthusiastic. "Yes, of course! I wouldn't miss it! But what about work?" Gustav replied, "Everyone is let off for the afternoon. The dead can wait!" On the way out Gustav invited five more coworkers, all of whom wholeheartedly accepted. None of the Jewish workers had showed up at the morgue for the past two days.

So off we went, seven of us from the morgue. Berta commented that it was auspicious since seven was a lucky number. We arrived at Heldenplatz at around noon. Already there were tens of thousands of people waiting with more streaming in every minute. Considering that the rally was not starting for another two hours I was amazed at the number of people already there – and of the extravagance of the event. Long Nazi banners hung from every building. There were Nazi flags on every lamppost. A bandstand had been erected and a military band was playing patriotic songs and selected works from Austrian and German composers. SS, SD, HJ (Hitler Jugend), army and police manned wooden barriers erected to hold back the crowd from the Hofburg where Hitler was going to speak. Food stands had been set up giving away free pretzels, wursts and beer. Souvenir vendors sold all sorts of Nazi material from small flags to lapel pins to balloons with swastikas on them. Toy cars, planes and tanks with Nazi emblems were available for young boys and nurse dolls with swastikas on their uniforms were available for young girls. The Hitler Jugend were distributing leaflets extolling Nazi virtues and accomplishments, emphasizing that Austria was an integral and necessary part of Germany. They simultaneously denigrated the Jews. Alongside of them, wearing their special armbands were members of the National Socialist Jewish League. While they did not yell out any anti-Semitic epithets they loudly yelled, "Heil Hitler!" Everybody was greeting each other with Heil Hitlers as were the Hitler Jugend when they handed a leaflet to each person in the crowd. People were smiling. People were exuberant. People were happy. This was clearly the beginning of prosperity and the elimination of the economic dominance of the Jews. Without a doubt the second most talked about subject was the Jews. The first was Hitler and the good things that he will do economically.

The total control that Hitler had was beyond belief. It was him and him alone that was responsible for the economic recovery of Germany. It was him and him alone that would restore the economy of Austria. It was him and him alone that would finally put the Jews in their place. Everyone owed their full and complete allegiance to him – not the Nazi party or the Nazi government – and certainly not to God although he stopped short of saying this at the time.

At first I just stood there with my colleagues not saying anything while they were enthusiastically yelling Heil Hitler and talking about the "New Order". Oskar noticed my reticence and asked if I was feeling alright. "A tooth ache," I responded. "Well," he said, "just make sure you do not go to a Jew dentist!" He disappeared for a couple of minutes and came back with two large beers. "Here, this will help" he said as he gave me one of them. I quickly realized that saying nothing made me stand out among my coworkers so I decided to wholeheartedly participate in the rally. I thanked Oskar and quickly drank the beer. I waited a few minutes began shouting, "Heil Hitler!" and other such nonsense – but I refused to yell out anything anti-Semitic. Oskar turned to me and said, "Now, that's more like it!" I replied that the beer did the trick and perhaps he should leave the morgue and take over the practice of one of the "Jew dentists". He laughed and told the others in our group what I said. They all laughed and agreed. For the rest of the day he was addressed as "Herr Doctor Oskar."

The speeches began shortly after 2 PM. The new Nazi Mayor, Hermann Neubacher, gave the opening remarks. He began by extolling the benefits that Hitler had brought to Germany and that Austria would follow that same path. He concluded by turning to Hitler, looking at him squarely in the face with his arm outstretched in salute saying, "Vienna and its people are yours to command." He stepped aside.

Seyss-Inquart, the new chancellor followed. His remarks were even more ingratiating. Goebbels was next. He was much more pragmatic and was the first to speak vehemently against the Jews. "They have no place in a Free German Society. For too long they have controlled and subverted the government of Austria. Their days of control are over." Each time he mentioned the demise of the Jews, the crowd roared. I knew that there was always an undercurrent of anti-Semitism in Vienna but I had no idea how virulent it was and how much wide-spread support there was for the expulsion of Jews from the social and economic life of the city and the country until now. I was now very glad that I had asked Dr. Nussbaum and the other Jewish service providers to destroy my records.

Hitler stepped up to the microphone on the balcony. The roar of the crowd was spontaneous, tumultuous, deafening. He waited. Even when the crowd finally quieted down after almost ten minutes of shouting, he waited. He waited for another two full minutes while the crowd remained silent eagerly watching him, waiting for him to speak. He started low and slow. He thanked the people for their support of him and the tenets of National Socialism. "No matter what your party affiliation was before today, you have a place in the New Order. There is room for Social Democrat and Christian Social Party members in the National Socialist Party. The Catholic religion will not be tampered with. There is, and always has been, a peaceful coexistence between church and state. This will continue. There will be a new economic rebirth of Austria. It has already begun and will continue. We will root out the causes of the poverty and despair that has kept Austria lagging behind the Reich. Those that have caused these problems, the Jews and the Communists will quickly learn that they have no place in the New Order. Their days of cheating and stealing are over."

At this point the cheers of the crowd were so overwhelming that Hitler had to stop talking for almost five minutes. When the cheers finally subsided enough for him to continue he again waited for two full minutes before speaking. He made an interesting analogy,

"Vienna is a pearl! I will place it in a setting worthy of a pearl! Rest assured that Vienna will be an important part of the Reich. We have so much in common with our similar language, culture and love of fine music and the arts. These will flourish under my care. I am Austria's son. I am coming home to the place of my birth. Do not doubt for a moment that I do not hold Vienna in the highest esteem. Remember this when you go to vote next month." The crowd went wild. We had a contest to see could yell Heil Hitler! the loudest. Oskar won but I was told that I was a close second.

Goebbels took the podium again. "Today we Germans proclaim that this day will be remembered as the day preceding the creation of a new greater Germany that will astonish the rest of the world and set an example of a new economic standard, one where every German will be free to work and raise his family. Our commitment is for a better life for you and your children and their children. The yoke of Jewish oppression will be lifted. Today we dedicate ourselves to our Fuehrer, Adolf Hitler, in body and soul. Let us pray."

He bowed his head. The crowd, thousands upon thousands of people immediately grew silent. They bowed their heads. Many had tears in their eyes – as Oskar had. I took out a handkerchief and pretended to dry my eyes. There was no doubt in my mind on the propaganda mastery of Goebbels. He had no use for religion. His God was Hitler – but he knew how to manipulate the crowd. There were many Christians who worried about the Nazi policies against religion. After all, Austria was a Christian country with the Christian Democrats the former leading political party. This prayer brought a new wave of comfort to them. Here was Goebbels one of the top three men in the Nazi government leading a prayer. Clearly, he supported the right to be religious and pray freely. Yes, the Nazis were really tolerant and the rumors about religion having no place in the New Order were false. Everyone prayed in Vienna and in every other city, town and village throughout Austria. The speeches were broadcast throughout the country with loudspeakers set up in every public square and park so those without a radio would not miss Hitler's speech.

All of a sudden the sound of airplanes could be heard. Low at first but increasing in loudness until it was almost deafening. Everyone looked up. There must have been at least two hundred German planes – bombers, fighters, cargo planes, and troop transports. It was awesome. It took almost twenty minutes for the planes to fade completely out of sight into the clouds. The sound of their engines lingered on for another five or six minutes. It was effective. If anyone doubted the power of the Third Reich their doubts no longer existed.

Just about the time the sound from the last plane dissipated it was replaced by music from the military band. What followed was, without a doubt, the most impressive parade and show of military strength in the history of Austria. It was led by the Austrian Legion (of Exiled Nazis). They were followed by all types of military vehicles and a few thousand soldiers – SA, SD, SS – then came the Hitler Jugend grouped by age range so they increased in height as the groups progressed with the youngest first followed by the mid-range and then the eldest. Between the troops and the vehicles in special flatbed trucks were the "Heroes of the 1934 attempted coup". Many of these "heroes" had fled to Germany. Some that had not left had been imprisoned by the von Schuschnigg regime and were now free. Some had remained in Austria and became underground Nazis. Military bands were interspersed between all of these groups. There must have been one hundred Nazi flag bearers. The procession lasted for almost two hours. Finally, some mounted Vienna police paraded by. There must have been fifty horses. Right behind them, bringing up the rear so to speak, was the National Socialist Jewish League. About 300 of them were asked to participate in the parade. Their position in the parade was specific – right behind the horses – and their manure. Some people cheered the Jews and others booed. The overall procession and the speeches whipped the crowd into frenzy. Goebbels and Hitler had won Austria. The voting the next month would only be a formality. They knew it. We knew it. The Jews knew it.

We continued celebrating until well after midnight. Every bar and Konditerei (coffee house) was packed. Our group was subdued although quite a few of the other groups decided to go into the Jewish quarter to break into stores and homes to rob and beat up Jews. I staggered home around 1 AM.

On the third day, the violence stopped. Under the direct orders of Goering, Gauleiter Bürckell ordered a full regiment of SS soldiers into the city with the heaviest concentration in Leopoldstadt. This was not done to protect the Jews. It was done to protect their property. These were assets that eventually would belong to the Third Reich just as had occurred in Germany in the early 1930s. These mobs were not stealing from the Jews, they were stealing from the Nazis and destroying Nazi property. Something had to be done to protect German assets. Jews on the street could still be attacked but they should not be robbed. The police and SS were so instructed and they arrested many people caught robbing Jews but they did not have enough soldiers to cover every street.

With Anschluss two things immediately happened. One was the creation of jobs for thousands of unemployed Austrians; the second was the persecution of the entire Jewish population of Austria – which also had a very strong positive economic affect on the non-Jewish population of Austria and Vienna in particular. There was even a special name for the mass attacks – Blitzverfolgung (lightening persecution).

In the weeks following Hitler's entry into Vienna and the setting up of the Seyss-Inquart government, massive public works programs began. Construction started on new roads, factories and housing. Just outside of Linz the construction began on a new steel mill, appropriately named the Hermann Goering Steel Mill. It was going to be the largest and most modern steel mill in Europe.

Foreclosures on farms were stopped and arrangements made for the payment of the debts. Many farms were returned to their former owners. Food was distributed to the poor and unemployment benefits were restored to those that had lost them under the von Schuschnigg government. This provided food and money until these people could be hired to work on one of the many new projects underway. Jews were summarily dismissed from many jobs and immediately replaced with non-Jews regardless of their qualifications. SS and SD stood outside Jewish stores "urging" non-Jews not to shop there. With very few exceptions, they were heeded. One woman did not listen. The SS soldiers blocked her exit, confiscated her purchases, gave them to passers-by and forced her to sit in the window of the store for the rest of the day with a large sign around her neck letting everyone know that passed by, that she was a Jew-lover and it was people like her that perpetuated the power of the Jews.

In some Jewish-owned stores that provided services such as tailor shops and shoe repair stores, SS soldiers accompanied non-Jewish customers into the store to pick up items that were left there.

They were forbidden to pay for the items and for those that had prepaid they forced the owner to give them their money back. On the way out, they were advised not to bring any more items there. When a Jewish customer came in to get their cleaned clothes the SS soldiers would inspect the work by taking the cleaned items out of the bag and wiping the floor with each item before allowing the Jewish customer to leave saying that now the clothes were fit for Jews to wear. Sometimes they would tear the pockets off and say "Now that you have no pockets you will have to carry your money in your mouth or up your ass." Jewish customers were often robbed of money and jewelry by the soldiers either on the way in or on the way out in total disregard of Bürckel's directive. In non-Jewish stores, whatever a Jewish customer bought was seized by the police or soldiers as they left the store and given away to non-Jews walking by. When one non-Jewish woman who had just received some of the merchandise that was seized from a Jewish customer stayed to wait for the next Jewish customer to get more free things, the soldier glared at the woman and told her, "Don't behave like a Jew! You have enough! Let someone else get something!" She quickly left.

It took five days to empty the morgue of dead Jews. It would have taken longer but there was an SS directive to get rid of the dead Jews by the end of the week. We worked around the clock. Of the 77 dead Jews brought into the morgue that were murdered that week, 71 were claimed by their families. Six remained unidentified when the SS deadline came so they were loaded into a dump truck that the SS provided to get them out of the morgue. We did not know where the truck took them. We did take photographs of them in case a relative or friend showed up. This was a good idea. The following week three of them were identified by family members. They did not live in Vienna. They were here on business and were not immediately missed. Only when they did not return home as scheduled did the families begin to worry and came to Vienna to find them. I tried to help them locate the bodies but ran into a stone wall. No one at the police station, SS office or any cemetery would tell us what happened to the bodies. I wisely decided not to pursue this any further. I found out later that when one of the relatives persevered and went to the police station to complain he was severely beaten and warned not to return or else he would find out where they were taken by joining them.

While most of the suicides were Jews there was one notable exception. On the evening of March 16 two bodies were brought into the morgue in an ambulance accompanied by two high-ranking Nazi SS officers. I was on duty and was called to the waiting room. The officers informed me that they had brought in the bodies of ex-General Emil Fey and his son. They had both shot themselves in the head. The officers wanted me to examine the body, confirm that they were suicides and immediately issue death certificates. I complied without asking any questions. They thanked me, saluted and left. A few minutes later Emil Fey's wife entered the morgue and enquired about the bodies of her husband and son. I took her to the holding room. She looked at them and started to cry. I could see from her red eyes that she had been crying earlier. She kissed her son on the head and her husband on his lips making the sign of the cross after each kiss. I quietly walked out of the room and left her alone with the two bodies. About forty-five minutes later she came out of the holding room and asked for me. An attendant brought her to my office. I offered her a seat and she sat down. "He was hounded to death, you know. They just would not let him alone." She said in a broken voice. She just had to tell someone and I was the only one immediately available.

"The day after the Nazis marched into Austria, the SS came to our house and told my husband not to leave the house – he was under house arrest. They had a list, you know. Their spies made a list of all of the people that opposed them. My husband was near the top. He had thwarted the 1934 coup attempt with his Heimwehr Brigade. As a result the Nazi leaders were executed and hundreds were thrown into prison. Luckily, they did not shut off our phone service. Our son was at the Military Academy and came home as soon as we told him about the house arrest. The next day my husband tried to get in touch with von Schuschnigg and Miklos but they were being detained as well. Finally, he reached an old army friend whom he knew was pro-Nazi and had been promoted. His friendship with my husband was very strong and he decided to tell my husband the truth. He was going to put on trial for the murder of Chancellor Dolfuss and for blaming the Nazis for the assassination. The witnesses would either be persuaded to change their story or they would disappear. For the next few days the house was continuously searched with many of our personal things taken or broken. Our bank account was frozen and all visitors were forbidden. This evening Emil and my son shot themselves so they would not be put on trial."

She sat there silently for another ten minutes abruptly got up, thanked me and told me that a relative would come for the bodies once they were released by the SS. Two days later the bodies were released. I notified her. The bodies were picked up by two male relatives that evening.

I had been very busy attending to the dead bodies being brought to the morgue so did not have an opportunity to talk to Hymie about his safety during the three-night pogrom that occurred following Hitler's speech. Knowing that he would be working late to make some extra money I made it a point to ask him to come to see me when everyone else had left for the night. His job was one of the few that Jews were allowed to keep – at least for the time being. We had to fill out special forms allowing him to continue working but he stayed home during while the anti-Semitic riots were occurring. I called him at home.

At about 10:30 PM he came to see me. I stopped what I was doing and asked him how he and his family were doing under the circumstances. He lived in the second district which was the prime target for the roaming bands of anti-Semites that were wantonly beating up and robbing Jews in the street and invading homes and stores. He said that he had been "spared" saying the word spared with great emphasis. The building he lived in was invaded by a mob and every apartment where the occupants were Jewish, they were beaten and robbed – except his and two others in the building. Their sons, as was Ezra, were members of the National Socialist Jewish League. As soon as they heard the commotion and realized what was happening they stood outside of their apartments wearing their armbands holding out their identification cards and the black club they were given upon joining. As the looters approached each one loudly shouted, "Heil Hitler!" and stood sideways so the armband with the swastikas and Jewish star was clearly visible to the looters. The mob stopped, looked at the young men standing there with their armbands and looked at each other. The apparent leader stood at attention and saluted back quickly leading the group to the next apartment. It seems that this was the situation through the entire three-day period. Only one League member's apartment was invaded because he was not home at the time.

"I guess it was a good decision for him to joint the League." I said. Hymie replied, "Well, at first, as you know, I was doubtful. There was often friction between the League members and everyone else in the Nazi party. The Hitler Jugend would sometimes insult them until it led to a fight. They would accidently spill something on them. Some of the Jugend would knock into them in the hall – nothing serious or very harmful, but just enough to throw them off balance. Most of the time, their complaints were ignored. Every once in a while one of the older party members would jokingly admonish the Jugend, 'Please don't be so cruel to our young Jews or else they may not like us any more.' Or 'Don't hit them in the face, they have to march with us tomorrow and we do not want them to look bad, do we?' There was something happening like this almost every week. A few of the members quit but when they did their apartments were invaded and they were all robbed and beaten up as 'traitors to Jews and Nazis that had no place in either world'. As bad as it was, it was sporadic and no one was really injured. Some of the older Nazis actually liked the idea of having Jews against Jews. They often interceded on their behalf protecting them from the Jugend. But there were some real benefits. When one of the League members was fired for joining the Jewish League, the Nazis visited his boss and threatened to blow up the establishment if he was not rehired – and at a higher salary. This is exactly what happened to Ezra. Schiffer closed the department store as soon as the widespread looting occurred. After the robberies stopped he re-opened. His store was not looted because it had its own well-armed security force. When it re-opened, Ezra went back to work and went to the locker room to change into his uniform. Everybody working there has a locker where they keep the store uniform. Ezra brought some National Socialist Jewish League membership applications to the store with him and told the people on the shift how he and the other League members were spared as they confronted the mobs. His actions were reported to the manager, Asher Birnbaum, who fired Ezra on the spot. He went to the Nazi Party headquarters that morning and told Captain Leopold what happened. Captain Leopold immediately informed Schüller. Schüller organized a response. He asked Karl Kreutzer, a long-term party member and one of the members that was openly supportive of the Jewish League, to help him. They conferred. Karl left and returned within the hour with his wife and two children, fourteen and nine years old. They went to Schiffer's Department Store along with four young men from the Hitler Jugend. At the store Karl went to the children's department and asked many questions on the quality of the clothing, what materials they contained since his children were sensitive to certain products. The salesman could not answer all of his questions. He had to ask the manager, Mr. Birnbaum. Normally, Mr. Birnbaum did not leave his office for security reasons but when he was told that a family of four wanted to ask him some questions he came out to see them. As soon as he walked over to meet them, three Hitler Jugend members grabbed him and pulled him into the changing room. Karl and the fourth HJ member held the salesman. In the changing room the three youths took out a knife and held it to his throat. They simply gave him a choice: rehire Ezra with a raise and a promotion or lose an ear. Ezra was rehired and a new position was created for him, Assistant Manager for Men's Clothing. This was not an isolated occurrence. If any League member applied for a job, the Nazis would visit the prospective employer and make sure that the League member was hired. Most of the time, the bosses acquiesced even if they were not Jewish. While they were forbidden to hire Jews, hiring Jewish League members was allowed. The few hold-outs that refused to hire them were dealt with accordingly. A small fire was set in a refuse can in front of their store at night with the message that the next fire would be in the store. Windows were broken with the threat of in-store violence that would cause much more damage. The bosses and owners were told not say anything about the threats. They were to say that they were being hired 'because they were in the National Social Jewish League that embraced the Fuehrer and the Nazi ideology'. In any case, all League members soon had jobs. This was actually set up in Berlin. Goebbels wanted to set an example that Jews could have a place in the New Order to encourage more Jews to join the League. It worked to some extent. By February 1, 1938 there were 814 members of the National Socialist Jewish League, including my son Benjamin, Ezra's younger brother."

"So," I said, "it looks like Ezra made the correct choice, right?" "I don't know. I just don't know. I guess we will have to wait and see." Hymie replied as he left the room.

About five days after Anschluss, the Gestapo moved into Vienna in full force. They took over the luxurious Metropole Hotel on Morzinplatz in the first district. This was one of the largest and most modern hotels in the city that had just installed a state-of-the-art telephone system. It occupied one square block in the heart of the first district. The back basement of the hotel was converted into a prison. Prisoners were brought in through a special back door. Very few emerged alive unless they told the Gestapo everything that they knew and agreed to become a Gestapo informer. This was one the main reasons why the Gestapo arrests were mostly done secretly. They did not want to let the friends and family of the person arrested know that he had been arrested in case they became a Gestapo informant. If the arrest of the person was known and he turned up a few hours later unharmed it was obvious that he talked and was now a Gestapo informer. A second reason was that if his co-conspirators knew that someone they worked with was arrested, they would hide and warn others. The vast network of informers was a major reason why organized resistance was kept to a minimum.

Postcard: The luxurious Hotel Metropole, headquarters for the Gestapo in Vienna. It was destroyed by Allied bombs and was not rebuilt. (Source: Author's Personal Collection)

Between March 15th and April 9th there were massive political rallies, demonstrations and parades. Prominently featured in all of the parades was the National Socialist Jewish League. They marched with the Nazis in their own section wearing white shirts, black pants, black shoes and their blue armband with the Jewish star and swastikas. They were filmed and photographed. These pictures were released to the foreign press saying that the acts of violence against the Jews were spontaneous outbursts from the citizens of Vienna and not in any way orchestrated by the Nazi Party. There was a place for Jews under the Nazi regime. All they had to do was to embrace Hitler and National Socialism just as these young Jewish men and women did. This was very effective in disowning the Nazis from the anti-Semitic violence of the first few days following the Nazi entry into Austria. Goebbels used the Jewish League over and over again to make his point – there was a place for the right type of Jew in Germany.

In spite of this, Nazi anti-Semitic rhetoric accelerated. On March 30th full page ads appeared in all of the Vienna newspapers promoting a new exhibition that would come to Vienna in the summer. It was entitled "Der Ewige Jude" (The Eternal Jew). The exhibition traced the origins of the Jews from biblical times to the present day. Starting with the Hittites and the Babylonians, the insidious Jewish Golden Conspiracy and Zionism were exposed along with its racial defilation. Currently in Munich, the exhibition was a resounding success attracting hundreds of thousands of attendees from all over Germany and neighboring countries. The exact date and venue of the exhibition coming to Vienna would be forthcoming.

The Nazi propaganda machine now moved into full gear promoting the plebiscite everywhere. Every piece of mail was cancelled with a special plebiscite cancellation reminding people to vote yes (Ja!) on April 10.

Letter envelope cancelled with the special postmark: Ein Volk, Ein Reich, Ein Fuehrer (One people, One Germany, One Leader) and Wien (Vienna) around the date of the plebiscite, 10 April 1938. (Source: Author's Personal Collection)

It was now Sunday April 3. The plebiscite vote was seven days away. This Sunday was important for sports. There was a soccer game between the top Austrian team and the top Italian team in the afternoon. It was sold out. As we could not get tickets, we decided to meet at a local bar and listen to the game together. Gustav set it up. We were going to have lunch first and adjourn to the bar. There were four of us from the morgue. Fritz and I arrived at noon and got a table. Otto arrived next. About fifteen minutes later Gustav walked in with a bouncing gait and an ear-to-ear smile. "Guess What? I have four tickets to the game!" "Really?" Fritz replied thinking that Gustav was kidding as he was often prone to do. "No, I'm serious!" he loudly replied holding out four tickets still grinning. "How in the world did you get them?" Fritz asked.

"There is this guy I know. He's a Jew. He buys a lot of tickets and resells them at a profit. It's a great business as long as you have the money." Fritz replied, "That's why the Jews are in control. They have the money to do these things." Gustav continued, "Well, I have been buying from him for a long time and I always wait until about one hour before a game and see if he has any tickets left. If he does he discounts them so I only pay about 25% more than the cost.

Normally, he charges double – and sometimes, even triple. This time he had eight tickets left so I bought four." Fritz interjected, "You should have bought all eight. I know some guys who would still pay double to get some tickets." All of a sudden, Gustav scowled at him. His voice changed and he angrily replied, "Do I look Jewish to you? I do not go around making money off of friends – or friends of friends. This is a Jewish thing. That is just one of the things that separates us from these damn Jews." Fritz apologized and it was quickly forgotten.

We paid him for our tickets, left the restaurant and went to the stadium. As we entered the stadium we were handed flyers advertising the forthcoming Ewige Jude exhibition. The flyer again emphasized that the path of Global Jewry from the Hittites and the Babylonians would be a major feature of the exhibition. The stadium was packed. People were standing in the walkways and entrances to each section. We were very lucky; our seats were in the second row right by the announcer's small raised platform. The band was seated to his right and did not block our view. There were four empty seats in the row in front of us. Gustav saw them and remarked, "I guess the Jew didn't find any last minute customers for the four remaining seats. See, the Jew would rather see them go to waste than sell them for the price that he actually paid for them without making a profit. That's a Jew for you!"

Both teams entered the field and reached their designated places standing at attention facing us. First, the Italian National Anthem was played as everyone in the stadium stood up. There was no singer just the music was played. There was a brief pause before the band played the next anthem. We were all waiting to see how this would be handled. The Austrian and the German National Anthems had the exact same music but the words were different. The band started to play and was accompanied by a famous opera singer. He sang the Austrian words. Some stood in silence and some sang along with the singer. We looked at each other. Gustav started to sing so we all joined in. When it was over, I turned to my companions and mentioned that I was surprised that they sang the Austrian words and not the German words. We sat down in anticipation of a hotly contested match. As we waited, the crowd grew silent and started to stand up as Dr. Josef Goebbels came to the podium. This was totally unexpected. No advance notice was given about his attending the game but he was just the appetizer. He took the microphone in his hands and said a few words of welcome. There was some applause and he waited for the applause to die down before serving the main course. He turned to the left and nodded his head. All of a sudden a large banner was unfurled. It was the theme of the "Der Ewige Jude" exhibition in Munich. The German title was written in Yiddish script.

Postcard from the Munich Eternal Jew (Der Ewige Jude) Exposition showing a stereotypical Jew with gold in one hand, a whip in the other with a map of Germany under his arm with the hammer and sickle symbol of Communism (Russia) on it. (Source: Author's Personal Collection)

The exhibit opened in Munich in 1937. It was so successful that it was decided to send it to other German cities. It opened in Vienna in August 1938.

Without turning to acknowledge that the banner had been unfurled, Goebbels announced, "Fellow Germans, it gives me great pleasure to introduce our Fuehrer, Adolf Hitler! Heil Hitler!"

The crowd went wild as Hitler approached the podium. They stood up and cheered with some standing on the seats to get a better view. Goebbels waited for him to reach the podium and again loudly re-iterated, "Heil Hitler!" The crowd roared their response, "Heil Hitler!" It was deafening.

Hitler just stood there saying nothing as Goebbels returned to his seat. Hitler waited for the cheers of the crowd to die down. We could see his face clearly as he turned his head to view the different sections of the stadium. He was clearly ecstatic at the reception he was receiving. Finally, after five minutes he held up his hand as a signal for the crowd to be quiet as he realized the crowd had no immediate intention of quieting down. Then he stepped up to the microphone, asked everyone to sit down. He had to repeat the request for everyone to sit down three times before everyone sat down. They were just too excited and wanted to get a better view of the Fuehrer. He spoke very slowly enunciating every syllable:

"Are there any Babylonians in the stadium? If so, raise your hands." There was silence as people looked around at each other, puzzled at the question. Hitler waited for two minutes. The stadium was silent.

"Are there any Hittites in the stadium? If so raise your hands." Again silence. People were taken aback and did not know what he was talking about. After another long pause, he continued,

"Are there any Jews in the stadium? If so, raise your hands – and do not lie about it or I will have any Jew not admitting being Jewish arrested." About 15 percent of the people reluctantly raised their hands. Now it was his turn to be silent as everyone looked around at the Jews raising their hands. Hitler continued, "Now, stand up!"

The Jews stood up as the crowd started to yell out obscenities. There were four Jews right in front of us in the first row. He made them stand for almost five minutes so everybody could look at them and see where they were located. They were clearly very worried and some were visibly shaking.

"Now, sit down!"

They sat down. I could see that they were afraid not knowing what would happen to them.

"Now, you may ask, what do all of these peoples that I have mentioned have in common? I will tell you. They are all thousands of years old, they are all mentioned in the Bible but only the Jew has survived. All of these other races have disappeared just as the dinosaurs and other creatures that have outlived their usefulness. Yet, the Jew remains. How has this happened? I will show you."

He paused. All of the Jews were visibly worried. The four in front of us anxiously looked around expecting to be attacked. Hitler continued, "How many of you knew that you were sitting next to a Jew? Do not raise your hand if you came in with a Jew. I just want to know how many of you, without prior knowledge, knew you were sitting next to a Jew?"

People looked around at the Jews. Since the Jews raised their hands and stood up, everyone in the stadium now knew who they were. No one raised their hands. Hitler rephrased the question. "How many of you did NOT know you were sitting next to a Jew?" Just about every non-Jewish person raised their hands.

"Now you know how they survived! They hide among us. They try to become one of us. They dress like us. They talk like us. They come to soccer games like us. They do everything possible to fool us but the reality is that they are Jews. They cheat us. They steal from us. They prevent us from prospering. In Vienna, the Jews control the newspapers. They control the professions blocking the employment of non-Jews. They control the universities. My fellow Germans, how long will you put up with this Jewish conspiracy? How long will you be in their shadow? How much longer must the economy of Austria suffer at the hands of these Jews? In seven days you can change this. In seven days you can show the world that Austria will not put up with this Jewish hegemony any longer. In seven days you can take your place in the booming German economy. Vote yes for unification with Germany! Vote yes for Austria!"

The applause was thunderous. People were screaming. People were jumping up and down. Now phase two began. Hitler Youth groups had been watching when Hitler asked for a show of Jewish hands and had them stand. While he was speaking, these groups positioned themselves around many of the Jews that had raised their hands. As the crowd was shouting Hitler stepped back and Goebbels returned to the podium. He raised his hand and yelled, "Heil Hitler!" As the audience responded, he nodded and the HJ groups moved into place. They pulled the men from their seats and threw them down the steps kicking them as they rolled down. Some went up to the men, women and children in the middle and upper rows, pulled them into the aisles, opened cans of paint that they had brought with them and, using paint brushes, splattered yellow paint on their clothes, on their head, in their faces and on their arms and hands as they tried to shield their faces. The crowd roared their approval. The four Jewish men sitting in front of us in the first row were thrown onto the field, as were many others sitting in the first few rows which were the most expensive seats. They were chased by the Hitler Youth carrying thin long sticks hitting them in the legs and buttocks as they ran for the exits which were blocked so they had to run around the field as they were being chased and hit with the sticks. The crowd roared their approval as they spurred the Jugend to hit them harder. They pushed the painted men, women and children to the exits and told them to get out of the stadium. They did not hit them but did push them along. The Jews on the field were herded to a single exit and told never to come to a sporting event again. Within twenty five minutes it was over. There was not one known Jew left in the stadium. The crowd was wild – yelling, screaming, applauding, and laughing. Goebbels took the microphone again. The crowd quieted down when he asked for their attention.

"My fellow Germans, I declare this stadium to be Judenfrei!" Again, there was a tumultuous response from the crowd. When the noise started to die down he added. "Now imagine a Judenfrei Austria! It is within your power to do this in seven days. Vote Yes! Heil Hitler!" Yet another outburst of approval! On Goebbels's next signal the band played the anthem and the same opera singer sang the German version, "Deutschland, Deutschland Über Alles." This time, just about everyone in the stadium stood up and sang including the four of us. Most had their arms raised as we did. When we finished singing the anthem, free beer and pretzels were generously dispensed. We each drank four beers as we watched the game. Hitler must have left sometime before or during the game. We did not see him or Goebbels again that day.

To complete the day's success, the German team won the game but all the newspapers' front-page headlines in large, bold type the next day read:

Austria 7, Jews 0

Seven more days to the plebiscite Hitler's speech was printed word for word along with photographs, a detailed description of the crowd's tumultuous cheers and Goebbels's final statement declaring that the stadium was Judenfrei and that Austria would be next. The score of the game:

Germany 2, Italy 1

The great climax to a great day was headlined in bold on the back page in smaller type. After this incident Jews wisely no longer attended any sports event. This didn't really matter because in a few months the Nazis issued an ordinance prohibiting Jews from attending sporting events anyway.

During the next week the public was bombarded with leaflets, newspaper ads, posters with volunteers handing out flyers promoting the plebiscite. The Jewish League was prominent in this activity, especially in the second district which had the highest population of Jews.

On Sunday, April 10th, Plebiscite Day, I got out of bed around 7 AM and proceeded to the polls at 8 AM. The lines were long but moved quickly. This was to be a secret ballot but it was anything but secret. There were voting booths with curtains around them. Inside were two boxes for ballots. One was for yes votes and the other was for no votes. On the table next to the place where you were given your ballot after you showed your identity card and were verified as a legally registered voter, were another two boxes – one for yes and one for no. Even the ballots were designed to emphasize the Yes (Ja) vote. The ballot had the following text:

Plebiscite and Greater German Congress

Ballot

Are you in favor of the March 13, 1938 union **between Austria and Germany** and do you support the Fuehrer, **Adolf Hitler?**

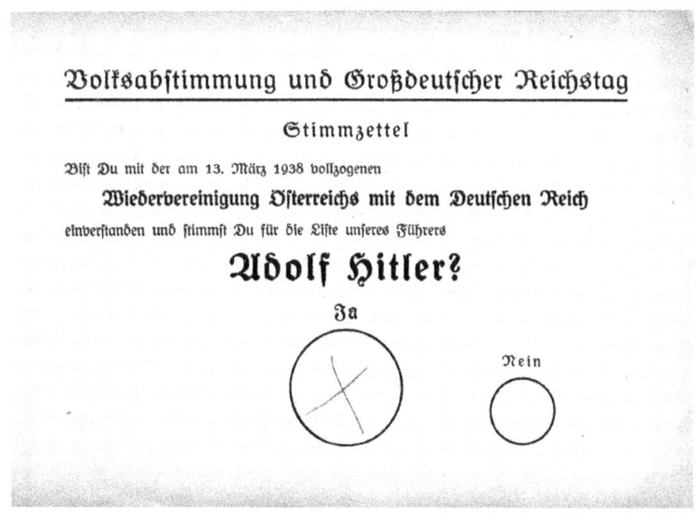

Ballot with the large Ja (Yes) which was how this person voted. The ballot is dated March 13, 1938 which was when Hitler declared the Austria was annexed into Germany. This "legalized" the invasion. (Source: Author's Personal Collection)

The vote was 99.7% in favor of unification (Anschluss). Jews and other "undesirables" were not permitted to vote. While this was supposed to be a secret ballot, an armed Nazi soldier asked each voter if they "preferred to vote openly to show their support for Hitler". Very few voters refused. The names and addresses of all voters that chose to vote in secret were taken down when they left the voting area regardless of how they said they voted. They were not treated favorably after that.

As soon as you were given your large ballot with the large Ja, a large, well-armed SD or SS officer asked if you really needed to go to the booth, "Since it was obvious that you were going to vote yes, why not do it here at the table so everyone could see your open support for Anschluss?" Without saying anything I marked the yes circle on my ballot and put it into the yes box for everyone to see. Immediately, the SS officer looked me in the eye, saluted and said, "Heil Hitler!" Caught up in the moment, I screamed back, "Heil Hitler!" It was so loud that it actually startled the officer – and the rest of the people in the room. For a brief moment everything stopped. The SS officer quickly regained his composure and nodded approval. The rest of the people resumed their activities. When I reached the door I turned again and shouted, "Heil Hitler!" Those sitting down at the tables stood up as everyone turned towards me and replied. "Heil Hitler! Heil Hitler! Heil Hitler!" I left the polling place thinking to myself that I had either done the stupidest or smartest thing that a Jew in hiding could do. I decided that it was more smart than stupid and laughed to myself all the way home.

The "secret ballot" process continued all day. I found out that anyone that elected to go into the booth to actually exercise their right for a secret ballot had their name taken down when they left – even if they said that they voted yes. It was assumed that you were going to vote no if you voted in the booth so even if you voted yes, it was believed that you only voted yes as an afterthought because you reconsidered after seeing the soldier standing there. The SD and SS soldiers on duty were told to respect the sanctity of the voting process and not to open the boxes in the booths or on the tables. Goebbels did not want anything negative about the voting to be reported in the foreign press that were invited to the polls. He knew that they were going to win. Why taint the results with any irregularities?

Cardinal Innitzer had publicly come out in support of Hitler and Anschluss after meeting with Hitler and getting assurances about the sanctity of the church. His open support was not received favorably by the Vatican. He arrived at the opening of the polls as was requested by Hitler. He was brought to the front of the line and was photographed as he posed for the cameras first by allowing them to photograph him marking an "x" in the Ja circle on the ballot and then putting it into the Ja box on the table. A special edition of the pro-Nazi Vienna paper, Volkischer Beobachter (The People's Observer), was printed within the hour showing him voting yes and distributed for free to everyone waiting in line or heading to the polls, to people in stores and businesses, and at homes throughout the city. Planes were standing by at the airport to deliver these special editions to every major city in the country. By noon every significant city in the country had the free special edition showing the support of the Catholic Church and the Cardinal's statement supporting Hitler.

By 11 PM the vote had been tallied. An overwhelming 99.7 percent of the eligible voters voted for Anschluss. In Vienna more than 15 percent of the people had been excluded from voting. No Jew was permitted to vote nor were Communists and others deemed undesirables such as gypsies, people with criminal records, etc. In recapping the plebiscite there was no doubt what would be the outcome. Hitler actively campaigned for it along with most high-ranking party leaders such as Himmler, Goebbels and Goering – and, of course, Josef Bürckel. The two major promises repeated over and over again were an improved economy and the elimination of the power of the Jews. He delivered what he promised. There were more than 400,000 unemployed Austrians on March 12 when the Nazis marched into the country. With the firing of Jews and von Schuschnigg supporters, and the public works programs, more than 100,000 unemployed Austrians now had jobs by April 10, the day of the Plebiscite. More than 80,000 of these jobs had been created in Vienna during the first three weeks following Anschluss. Jews had been dismissed from all government jobs with their jobs given to non-Jews. In addition, Jewish stores were boycotted so sales in non-Jewish stores increased substantially. Arguably, there were some irregularities in the voting process with the exclusion of the Jews and Communists but the fact remains that Hitler's support was overwhelming. Hiring continued. By the end of the year unemployment dropped to less than 100,000 and within eighteen months unemployment was around 32,000. Jews, Communists and von Schuschnigg supporters that lost their jobs were not included in the statistics. They were non-persons.

Life started to become a bit more normal for me after the Plebiscite. Fatal attacks against Jews diminished as the Gestapo and SS protected Jewish assets and Jews in the street, especially Hassidic Jews that were quite recognizable because of the way they dressed. That is until Saturday, April 23 when twelve bodies were brought to the morgue at around 3 PM. It was Passover and many Jews were going to pray at their synagogue wearing their nice clothes. Evidently, this disturbed quite a number of Hitler Youth and other Nazis especially those in the police department. Random attacks began again. A large group of Jewish men, women and children above the age of ten in the second district were forced from nearby synagogues during their prayers and marched to the Prater amusement park where they were forced to crawl around on all fours and eat grass making animal sounds while they crawled around. Having them imitate pigs was the most prevalent animal selected. If they didn't eat enough grass one of the Hitler Youth members would stand on their hands until they ate more grass. Afterwards, many were strapped onto the roller coaster cars – not inside them, with some upside down. The roller coaster was run at full speed causing all of them to vomit. Actually, those that were strapped to the roller coaster cars were the lucky ones. All of the other Jews that were not strapped to the roller coaster got sick with twelve of them dying of heart failure and poisoning due to eating the grass. The ones strapped to the roller coaster vomited up all of the grass. In addition to this incident, many rich and famous Jews were attacked in the street or at their place of business. Others were arrested by the regular police and beaten before being released. The SS and Gestapo allowed these things to happen as long as Jewish property was not damaged and the Jews were not robbed. For the most part this was the case. However, there were a few select exceptions.

For example, a Nazi mob attacked the owner of a Jewish cabaret, Felix Grünbaum, and the Director of the Scala Theater, Rudolf Beer. They were beaten to death with clubs and their wallets and jewelry were taken. Some Jewish store owners and former politicians were also severely beaten with some dying. When the bodies of Grünbaum and Beer were brought to the morgue they were unrecognizable. I had no idea who they were until a few hours later when some witnesses showed up at the morgue under the cover of darkness and identified the bodies based on the clothes that they were wearing at the time of the attack. I called their families and released their bodies immediately to them. I decided to stay through the night since more relatives of the missing Jews from the synagogues that had the members taken to Prater Park were now showing up to claim the bodies. Twelve Jews (seven men, three women and two children) died that day from eating grass. Ten prominent Jews were beaten to death.

I released all of the bodies to the grieving families. By morning all of the bodies had been claimed. I was angry so I filled out a report that twelve Jewish people had died from being forced to eat grass and ten more had been beaten to death by Nazi mobs. I handed it to the Chief Coroner in the morning. He looked at it and looked up at me. He tore up the report and directed me to rewrite the report stating that 22 Jews committed suicide as part of the Jewish Passover ritual in atonement for the Jews slaying the first born of Egypt. Like most Austrians, he had become a good Nazi.

CHAPTER EIGHT

LIFE GOES ON – FOR MOST

"While millions of established Germans were unemployed and in misery, immigrant Jews acquired fantastic riches in a few years - not by honest work, but by usury, swindling, and fraud."

From The Eternal Jew exhibition; Vienna, August 1938

The Nuremburg laws were put into place in May under the specific orders of Dr. Seyss-Inquart and the newly appointed Gauleiter of Vienna, Odilo Globocnik.

If ever there was a man born to be a Nazi, it was Odilo Globocnik. He was a real piece of work. He had no conscience. His hatred for Jews was only outdone by his blind obedience to Hitler and his love for money and the finer things in life that money could buy. He lived well. He ate and drank well. He enjoyed the company of women and, with power came the means to fund it all. He would have made a perfect "before and after" poster advertisement for the benefits of being a Nazi. The "before" picture would be a relatively thin morose man who had failed in business while the "after" picture would show a portly, self-confident, arrogant man who had found his niche in the Nazi movement. His nickname, "Globus" was derived from his last name combined with his rotund shape. On May 24, 1938 Odilo Globocnik was named Gauleiter of Vienna reporting to Bürckel.

Odilo was born in Trieste, Italy. When he was thirteen, his family moved to Klagenfurt which is a city in the province of Corinthia in Southern Austria. His parents were virulent anti-Semitics, especially his mother who taught him that Austria would be better off without the Jews and that if you did something against them it was not a criminal act. He had been a construction worker, or, as he liked to put it when he joined the Nazi party, a "building tradesman". In

1930 he went to a meeting of the National Socialist Labor Party (NSDAP). He immediately saw his opportunity and joined the party. He was a loud, boisterous man and attended all public functions, often getting into fights with the authorities trying to break up the group. He had no problem assaulting anyone who got in the way of the public demonstrations but somehow always managed to escape before arrests were made. He also had a knack for organizing the people in the demonstrations to maximize their effectiveness. Being in the forefront of the demonstrations and avoiding capture caught the eye of the Nazi party leaders in Vienna. He also knew his place and blindly followed any order from a superior party member. He was assigned to a group responsible for disseminating propaganda and supplies such as guns and explosives to the more fanatic party members that were not afraid to use them. He also was involved with the funding many of the activities of the party. He was very good at that and went out of his way to get the best prices for the things he bought. The savings he generated from his astute buying he shared between himself and the party. He liked to party and was fun to be with. He had a good sense of humor and he paid for the drinks with the money he made from the results of his astute buying practices. In fact, he always spent whatever money he made so he was in constant need of more money so he worked that much harder to get it. He definitely was not lazy and his energy was contagious. If he needed any help or asked someone to do him a favor he was never refused. His leadership abilities were now catching the attention of the senior party members in Germany. If they wanted to stage a demonstration all they had to do was ask Odilo and he would muster a hundred or more party members and friends some of whom didn't even belong to the Nazi party because there would always be free beer after the demonstration courtesy of him and the party. He had truly found his calling.

In 1931 he was placed in charge of setting up and implementing a courier and intelligence network in Vienna and to disseminate money from Germany to the NSDAP offices throughout Austria. He even convinced one of the bishops in Vienna, Bishop Klagenfurt, to help distribute the propaganda and weapons that would eventually undermine the Austrian government and pave the way for Austria's annexation by Germany. His steadfast devotion and ability to organize now caught the attention of Himmler who personally helped him in his career. Odilo rose fast in the party with Himmler's support. He continued his outspoken criticism of the Austrian government and the Jews. In 1933 he was finally arrested at one of the demonstrations that had gotten particularly violent. He claimed that he wasn't even at the demonstration and that the police were persecuting him for his NSDAP affiliation. The witnesses at the demonstration developed amnesia and many other people attested that he was somewhere else so he was released for lack of evidence. He demanded, and received, an apology from the authorities. His legal battle and the subsequent apology from the authorities made the front page of all of the Vienna newspapers. Membership applications for the NSDAP increased by more than 50 percent during the next three months that was directly attributed to Odilo's publicity. This further impressed the Nazi hierarchy. Himmler had evidently brought this to the attention of Hitler because at the recommendation of Austrian Gauleiter Bürckel, Odilo was confirmed by Hitler as the Deputy Gauleiter for all of Austria and Gauleiter of Vienna. He had just turned twenty-nine becoming the youngest man to attain this position. He was arrested three more times between 1933 and 1935 and spent a little over a year in prison in two separate sentences. In prison he created a Gestapo-like Aryan organization that created chaos at his command. Many of the guards supported him. He set up a system where Jewish prisoners had to bring cigarettes and other items to Odilo and his group to avoid being beaten. His prison group increased substantially. When the prison members were released they joined the Nazi party and followed his orders without question including illegal actions. So, even in jail, his exploits on behalf of the party were watched by senior party officials. On September 1, 1934, between prison terms, he joined the SS (number 292776).

Odilo as Gauleiter of Vienna, had total control of the city and the suburbs. The expression "power corrupts" is a fitting description of Odilo. As his authority increased, he became less charismatic and more demanding. While he still was very good in accomplishing the tasks set out for him by Berlin, he had changed. He no longer had to ask anyone to do something; he told them. He was gruff, relentless and uncompromising. He used whatever tactics were necessary to accomplish his task, and continued to take his personal commissions from all financial transactions. Since his orders came from Bürckel who reported directly to Hitler, he felt that everyone in Austria was subservient to him. He demanded obedience to his requests and would often not give his staff in Vienna or his superiors Germany information on his activities. He was doing too many things and rather than ask for assistance, which he felt might be considered as a sign of weakness, he decided to do everything himself. The added stress took its toll as he talked down to people. He did not make many friends in the party or in the SS as the Gauleiter of Vienna. In fact, after a time, his enemies outweighed his friends. They grew suspicious of his lifestyle and found many improprieties in his business conduct. Finally, some of the higher-ranking members of the party complained directly to Goering who went to Hitler. After a brief investigation, on January 30, 1939 Odilo was removed as Gauleiter of Vienna. It looked bad for Odilo but Himmler personally interceded and all charges against him were dropped. Odilo's career had apparently come to an abrupt end but he decided to enlist in the Waffen SS as a non-commissioned officer in March. His penchant for leadership and getting things done proved invaluable. He had learned a valuable lesson on how not to deal with people. He reverted to his former self. His men followed his orders enthusiastically without question as he was more personable. His experience as Gauleiter of Vienna enhanced his public speaking and his ability to quickly assess any problem and find a solution. On September 1, 1939 Germany invaded Poland. Odilo served with exemplary distinction. The men under his command were among the most aggressive in the SS taking the most prisoners and capturing the most territory compared to any other similar detachment in the SS. Again, he was noticed by Himmler and the SS hierarchy. He was back in power but in Poland not Austria – but that's another story – and not a nice one.

Now that I have provided this background on Odilo, you need to know what a Gauleiter is. In 1925 the Nazi party was re-organized by Hitler. Germany and countries where there were large German populations were divided into regions or Gaus, which was an old German word. Each of these Gaus had a leader (leiter) personally appointed by Hitler and answerable only to him. There were 15 Gaus inside and outside of Germany before Anschluss. Josef Bürckel had been the Gauleiter of the Saar region before being chosen to be the Gauleiter of Austria and the liaison between Germany and Austria for the Anschluss (annexation). Gauleiters were the supreme commanders of their territories. All other Nazi groups were subservient as were all appointed government officials.

Austria, which had nine provinces before the Anschluss, was re-apportioned into seven Gaus, each with a Gauleiter. For each Gau, Bürckel chose an Austrian Nazi. As such, the appearance was that Austria was being governed by Austrians rather than by Germans. There were many Austrians that were worried that Austria would be totally under leaders brought in from Germany which would eliminate any Austrian autonomy. They did not want to become just another province of Germany with all decisions made in Berlin. He correctly judged this concern and avoided any confrontation by making these appointments. At the end of the day, however, absolute rule from Berlin was what resulted anyway since the Gauleiters owed their primary allegiance to Hitler and to no one else. Austria was totally absorbed into Germany and Vienna became subservient to Berlin.

Vienna was a very important city. Vienna essentially controlled Austria. All important political decisions for the entire country were made in Vienna oftentimes without regard or consideration for the other provinces. It was the cultural center of Austria and also had the largest Jewish population. Jews had a disproportionate place in the economic, cultural and political scene relative to their population. As such, there was substantial animosity between all of the provinces and Vienna. Hitler recognized this and used it to his advantage. The message was clear: support him and the provinces would have a much higher degree of autonomy with much less dependence on Vienna – and he would get rid of the Jews.

Immediately, the Nazi statistical control system was put in place. Everyone was required to prove their race. Forms were distributed throughout Austria. The "Forms of Proof" (Prüfungsergebnis) had to be filled out, verified and submitted for filing. The form had four categories pure blooded Aryan (Deutschblütig), Quarter-Jew

(Mischling 2.Gradeo), half-Jew (Mischling 1.Gradeo) and full Jew (Jude). The back had information on the parents and grandparents of the person. Everyone had to bring proof of the race of their parents and grandparents to the Central Information Office where the documents were verified and the form was stamped with their classification indicated.

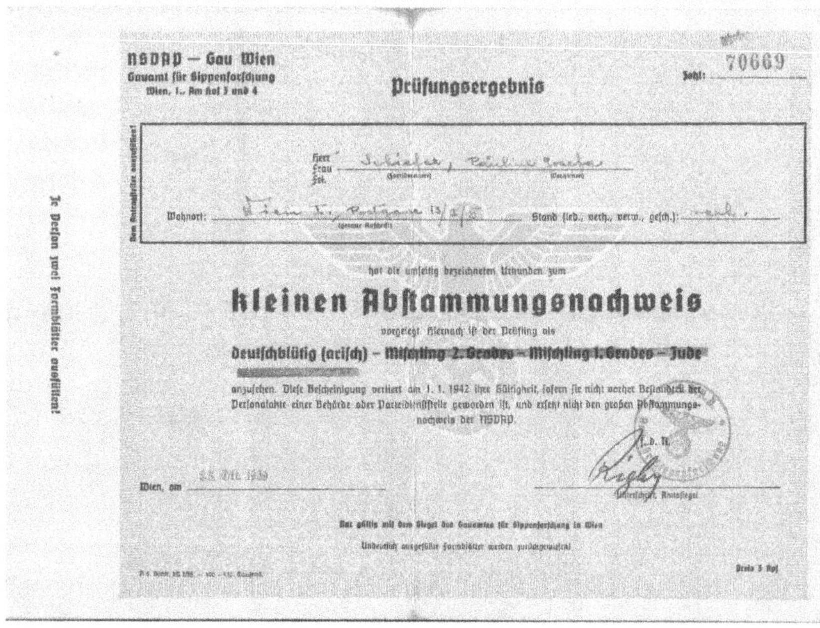

Front of the form for the proof of one's bloodline (Prüfungsergebnis). This form was filed on October 25, 1939 for a woman of full German blood which was verified (stamped and signed) (Source: Author's Personal Collection)

Documents such as this were used in most Nazi occupied countries to identify Jews. This form has the classification for Jews (crossed out) as set forth in the Nuremburg Laws:

- Mischling 2. Gradeo (Mixed blood second class): one-quarter Jewish (one grandparent was Jewish)

- Mischling 1. Gradeo (Mixed blood first class): one half Jewish (one parent or two grandparents were Jewish)

- Jude (Jewish): Full Jew (both parents or three grandparents were Jewish)

As soon as the provisional government was in place under Odilo and Bürckel, Jews were fired from government jobs, discharged from the army, and dismissed from the police force. Jewish teachers had to resign and Jewish students were barred from attending the University of Vienna and other universities. Beatings occurred with increasing frequency. Jews were stopped on the street and made to clean the street or the public urinals. Hassidic and orthodox Jews that dressed in their typical black coats and black hats with their peyos (long sideburns) were favorite targets. Their sideburns and beards were cut off and sometimes they were even set on fire. Their black coats were painted with many obscene things such as male genitals and obscene words. It was not good to be a Jew.

As previously mentioned, Adolf Hitler was born in Austria. A second infamous Austrian Nazi had a major role in the extermination of Jews. His name was Adolf Eichmann. Although he was born in Germany, he grew up in Linz. At the time of Anschluss, he was a Second Lieutenant in the Jewish section of the SD and he was given the responsibility to find "a Solution to the Jewish Problem" in Vienna. This should not be confused with the "Final Solution" where Jews were to be exterminated. He set up his headquarters in the Rothschild Palace at 20 Prinz Eugen Strasse in the third district. He first ordered an audit of Jewish assets. On April 28 an edict was issued that all Jews with assets above 7,500 Schillings (US$2,000) were required to fill out a special asset declaration form. All Jews also had to register by filling out another form that had their names, addresses, and dates of birth for all family members in the household. In May, the Austrian Schilling was replaced by the German Reichsmark at the exchange rate of 2 Reichsmarks for 3 shillings.

To avoid international controversy, on June 4 Eichmann allowed Sigmund Freud, who was 82 years old, to leave Vienna. He was allowed to leave after many international agencies and well-known people requested his release. The Nazis estimated that the value of his assets were about 95,000 Reichmarks so they assessed an exit tax of one-third of the total value in cash, which he did not have. Marie

Bonaparte paid the 31,350 Reichsmark exit fee and he was allowed to leave with most of his possessions including his antiquities collection with more than 5,000 pieces, most of his furniture and personal possessions and his extensive library. His office/home building on Grabbengasse was divided into six apartments and rented to six families. In addition to his wife and daughter the Nazis allowed his doctor and maid to also leave with him. His four elderly sisters elected to remain in Vienna. One died in Theresienstadt and three in Treblinka. He had to sign a letter stating that he was not ill-treated by the Nazis. Similarly, Jews known internationally in the fields of literature, science and entertainment were allowed to leave under similar conditions.

The plight of the Jews being systematically persecuted and exiled from Germany and Austria drew international attention. From July 6 to July 14 President Franklin Delano Roosevelt convened a conference of 32 countries in Evian, a resort city in France, to address the Jewish persecution and refugee issue. The net result was that not one country modified its legislated quota to allow more Jews into their respective countries, including the United States. This became a strong propaganda point for Hitler who asked, "Why should Germany be singled out as not wanting Jews when no other country wanted them either?" He was more than willing to send them to any country that wanted them.

On August 2, 1938 another round of anti-Semitism and acts against Jews in Vienna began. It was initiated by the opening of The Eternal Jew (Der Ewige Jude) Exhibit in the Northwest Train Station. Gauleiter Globocnik personally presided at the opening. This exhibit first opened in Munich in 1937. It was now in Vienna. Its popularity was enormous due to a mass advertising campaign making it the "in thing to see" for everyone. More than seven thousand people attended the opening ceremony. In the first hour alone, about two thousand people walked through the exhibit. By the end of the day more than ten thousand people had viewed the exhibit which consisted of hundreds of items denigrating the Jews as a race. A special film was shown on the Jewish menace. When it closed on September 30 more than 350,000 people had visited the exhibit (more attendees than Munich). If you do the math almost 40,000 people per week

(5,500 people per day) lined up to see the exhibit. Everyone at the morgue went. At first, I decided not to go but this became impossible as every weekend I would be asked if I had gone. When I said no, I was looked at as if something was wrong with me. So, on Saturday September 3, I stood in line for more than two hours and visited the exhibit. The exhibit took up three floors in the station with more than 600 items on exhibit and the anti-Semitic movie. I spent three hours at the exhibit.

Souvenir post card showing the Der Ewige Jude (Eternal Jew) Exhibition at the Northwest train station in the second district of Vienna that opened in August 1938. Many visitors left the exhibit and roamed the city attacking and robbing Jews on the street with some store and home invasions also occurring. (Source: Author's Personal Collection)

More than 350,000 Viennese people lined up and waited for up to four hours to see the exhibit which featured more than 600 items portraying Jews in the worst possible fashion. A special anti-Semitic movie was also shown.

The exhibit started with the origins of the Jews that traced Jews back to the Hittites and showed stone reliefs of facial profiles of Hittites carved in stone that had big noses. I immediately remembered Hitler's question at the soccer game, "Were there any Hittites in the stadium?" From there the history of the Jews was presented showing every negative thing possible. There were gross caricatures of Jews taking advantage of, cheating and stealing from anyone who wasn't Jewish in everyday situations and violating Aryan women.

During the exposition Austrians not even in the Nazi party stepped up their harassment of Jews as did the Nazi Party members. Groups of Jews were stopped on their way to the synagogue and lined up on the street against shops owned by Jews. Children were given eggs and rotten fruit and vegetables to throw at them while adults watched and laughed. Sometimes, some of the adults also threw the eggs and rotten produce. Some of the soldiers brought little toy shovels with them which they gave to the children. These shovels were used to pick up dog shit and horse manure from the street and fling it at the Jews. The soldiers that instigated these acts rarely threw anything. Sometimes they would make the Jewish men and boys drop their pants and shorts and bend over so the target became their bare asses. Only males were selected for this ultimate embarrassment. The Nazis correctly felt that denigrating women and young children could create some sympathy for them, which they did not want to happen. After the supply of eggs and rotten produce ran out, the Jews were forced to clean the sidewalks of the mess that they made. They even had to clean the shovels which they were forced to wipe off on their clothing and then sometimes forced to lick them until they were clean. Any resistance was met by the swift kick or the rifle butt of the soldiers organizing the degradation. Once, after the pelting was finished, the soldiers invited the crowd to go in and clean out the shelves of a Jewish-owned store even though this was forbidden. When the Gestapo arrested four of these soldiers for court martial and possible imprisonment, they claimed that they were so pleased with the "spontaneous enthusiasm" of the crowd that they were caught up in the fervor, especially seeing all of the goods in the store for which the Jews were overcharging. The corporal that was the highest ranking soldier was demoted and all were sentenced to one year in jail. This was a clear message that the assets of the Jews belonged to the government. While there were some isolated cases of looting, no policeman or soldier was involved after the sentencing of the soldiers.

After the exhibit opened, many Gentiles renewed their courage and just walked over to a Jewish neighbor's store or apartment and ordered them out saying that they were authorized to take control of it (which was not true). Sometimes they came with a few friends and family members to enforce the takeover which was referred to as "wild" Aryanization. The Aryanization process set up by Eichmann was not open to the public. More than 5,000 apartments and small businesses were seized in this manner until Eichmann stopped it. He let it be known that this was not going to be tolerated. After this was announced any Jew could report the unauthorized seizure of an apartment or personal property to the SS and the perpetrators would be arrested, sent to prison or a concentration camp and the items returned to the Jews. What made matters even worse was that the people that seized the Jewish businesses illegally through wild Aryanization before the edict was issued had no idea on how to operate them and soon they were bankrupt. One Nazi estimate put the amount of these failures as high as 65 percent. This further infuriated Eichmann as he requested that a list of all of these businesses obtained during the wild Aryanization be developed. These businesses were among the first to be confiscated under the legal Aryanization program. If the Jew that owned the business could be located, he would be given the money that Eichmann's accounting group determined was the "fair market value for a Jew."

The Ewige Jude (Eternal Jew) Exhibit was carefully planned to coincide with another series of restrictions for Jews. After the exhibit opened there were very few protests about Jewish discrimination. In addition, about 15,000 Jews from the other cities in Austria were forcibly moved to Vienna, all into the second district. The Nazis wanted to concentrate the Jews in one area. This policy continued. Whenever Jews had to give up their homes and apartments in other districts, they could only relocate to the second district. The IKG had to find places for them to live. This often required existing families to have to share their houses and apartments with total strangers. Here again, the idea was to create very poor living conditions to encourage Jews to emigrate.

On August 26, 1938 the Zentralstelle fur Judische Auswanderung (Central Office for Jewish Emigration) was established by Gauleiter

Josef Bürckel based on the recommendation of Adolf Eichmann to facilitate the mass emigration of Jews. Eichmann was appointed to head the Zentralstelle and was given a free hand in setting the policy. He immediately sent for Dr. Josef Löwenherz, the former Executive Director of the disbanded Israelische Kultusgemeinde (IKG) to implement a plan to expedite emigration. When the elderly man was shown into his office, Eichmann walked up to him, looked up and down at him and slapped him hard in the face, almost knocking him down in the process. Reeling from the blow, the shocked man asked why Eichmann had hit him to which Eichmann replied, "Because I can!" He followed his explanation by telling him that he had the power to do anything to the Jews in Austria that he wanted. Their lives were in his hands and it was up to Dr. Löwenherz and the IKG to help him get rid of the Jews in Austria – either to other countries or to concentration camps. The choice was his.

Eichmann did two things that greatly enhanced his career. The first was to consolidate the entire emigration procedure into one office at the Zentralstelle. This was actually the suggestion of Dr. Löwenherz, who, when Eichmann complained that not enough Jews were leaving Vienna, explained that a Jew had to go to ten or more different offices to get the documents and get them stamped, pay the taxes, etc. First, they had to line up at the police station to get the form to get the permit to emigrate. Then they had to fill it out and go to another place to get it stamped indicating that it was properly filled out. This allowed them to go to another office to determine the amount of money that they owed in taxes and other fees. After that had to get the money and go to another office to get the form that they needed to pay the taxes and fees. Once they paid the taxes and fees they received a receipt that was used at yet another office to get the form that showed that they had no other assets. If they did, additional taxes were required to be paid. Finally, when they no longer had anything of value, they went to another office for the exit permit.

The person or family also needed an entry permit from the country that was going to take them. Once that was obtained they had to report to another office to get the exit permit approved. Sometimes, additional fees were imposed to get the exit visa which required yet another form and a return visit to finally get the exit visa which often had only a four to eight week window to emigrate. If they could not leave within that time period they had to repeat many of the steps again. At each juncture of the process they had to wait on lines that sometimes stretched for blocks. The line started to form at 4 AM. While they waited they were targets for Hitler Youth and other gangs that would hit them and force them to do menial tasks. They were not robbed just humiliated and made to suffer minor injuries. Sometimes the SD would take the first 100 or so people on line and order them to go home just when the office opened. This was often repeated during the day. After waiting four or five hours on line as they approached the office entrance entire groups of Jews were just ordered off the line. Any protest or attempt to explain was met with violence. No one standing in line was allowed to have an open umbrella when it rained. If they opened one it was taken away and destroyed. Many times the same thing was done with hats and kerchiefs when it rained. God forbid that any Jew that stood on line in winter was wearing a fur coat or a coat with a fur collar. The coat was taken and they were forced to remain on line without any coat. They were not allowed to leave the line. The cold was unbearable. Many Jews that finally got the paperwork completed could not get all of the travel arrangements and entry documents in time before the expiration date so they had to repeat the process.

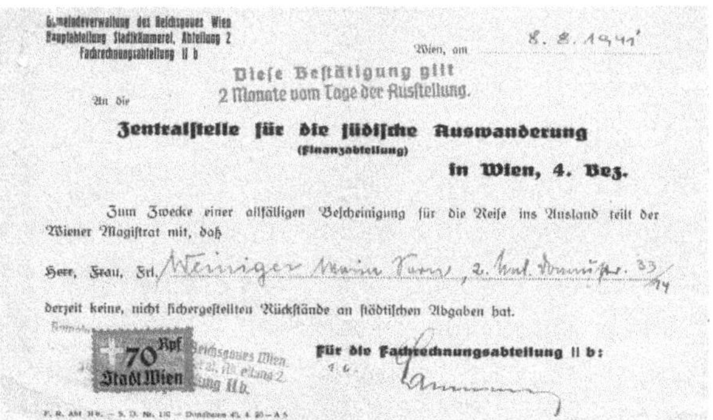

Original form from the Finance Department of the Central Office for the Jewish Emigration, Vienna dated August 8, 1941 stating that Fraulein Weiniger did not have any additional assets and could therefore be allowed to emigrate. This permission expired two months from the date of issue. (Source: Author's Personal Collection)

This was but one of a series of documents needed by Jews to get their exit visa to leave Austria. They also had to have a document of acceptance in the country of immigration.

Löwenherz suggested the one-stop emigration office. He assured Eichmann that most Jews wanted to leave Austria just as much as he wanted them to leave and this would expedite emigration. Eichmann took his suggestion and implemented it. By doing this in one office with fewer forms and with hardly any red tape or bureaucracy, emigration increased tenfold. To facilitate this, he re-opened the IKG and had Löwenherz re-instated as the Executive Director. He now also had full control of the process and could administer it with many more people at a much lower cost since the IKG did not get paid for their services. Within one month there were more than 700 people working on Jewish emigration. By year-end more than 1,000 people were employed to facilitate emigration. As a result emigration exceeded 5,000 Jews per month with some months up to 8,000.

The second thing that Eichmann did was to maximize the money he could extort from Jews to allow them to emigrate. Initially, he would force wealthy Jews to leave the country and confiscate their homes and businesses including all of their cash, works of art, and jewelry as the price for emigration. However, there were many Jews that were not rich so he instituted the practice that Jews should get additional money from friends and relatives abroad to get their exit visas. If a Jew worked for a foreign company, the exit taxes were even higher. In most cases the companies paid the higher taxes. Sometimes a company did not want to pay the higher tax which Eichmann used as a propaganda tool publicly stating that the performance of these Jews was so bad that the companies they worked for didn't want them. Most relented and paid. In addition, he ordered Löwenherz to raise money from many of the Jewish organizations and non-Jewish charitable groups abroad for Jewish emigration. To set the tone, he ordered about 20,000 of the wealthier Jews to leave the country. These were owners of banks, newspapers, large businesses, etc. They left penniless. From the declaration forms there were about 36,000 Jewish-owned businesses. These were confiscated and mostly sold to Nazi party members at exceptionally low prices. This was performed under a special law called the "Aryanization of Jewish Property."

The combination of seizing all the wealth of Viennese Jews plus all of the foreign money pouring into the country for their emigration generated hundreds of thousands of Reichsmarks per month. He was a financial hero – and was getting rid of thousands of Jews without sending them to ghettos and concentration camps, where they would still have to be fed and guarded.

We continued to have our weekly card games but there was nothing much that we could do. Any overt action on out part would raise suspicions and could lead to us being discovered as Jews in hiding which meant instant death or deportment to a concentration camp with all of our assets confiscated.

Some Jews knew that they were not going to be able to emigrate and decided to disappear. About 800 went into hiding with the help of non-Jewish friends (according to an estimate made by the IKG). The actual number was 942 according to a Nazi audit made against the declaration forms submitted. The Nazis were great at keeping records. In 1934 there were approximately 191,000 Jews in Austria. This dropped to 185,000 by 1938. 6,400 Jews had left Austria. The data is shown below for the nine provinces:

Location	1934	1938
Vienna	176,034	169,978
Lower Austria	7,716	8,010
Burgenland	3,632	3,220
Styria	2,195	2,028
Upper Austria	966	980
Tyrol	365	346
Carinthia	259	257
Salzburg	239	189
Vorarlberg	42	18
Total	191,448	185,026

Source: Rosenkranz, Verfolgung, 311

The Aryanization of Jewish businesses increased. Jews accounted for about 10 percent of Vienna's population. However, their influence in Vienna was disproportionate to their numbers. For example, three quarters of the newspapers, banks, textile manufacturing and other factories were owned by Jews. More than 250,000 Viennese Gentiles worked for Jews in these places alone. Thousands of others worked for Jews in many retail and service enterprises. This led to a high level of animosity among the majority of the population. It would be wrong to say that everyone working for Jews disliked them. Many were quite happy and loyal. With the high level of unemployment in the country many owed their existence to these firms – and many were grateful and content. When the Aryanization program began under Eichmann, the SS enlisted the help of the local police. Mischa was among those asked to help. Mischa provided this account of the typical Aryanization procedure:

The owners were forced to sign over the ownership of the asset to a private firm or individual that was often a front for the SS for a fraction of its value. In many cases it was in exchange for their exit visa but in some cases it was just forced on the Jewish owners. This was typically done on Saturday so the Jew could not go to pray. On Monday morning the SS, the local police and the new owner would call all of the workers together and announce that there were going to be some changes for the betterment of the German worker. For example, at the Ankar Bakery, where Mischa was present, an SS officer that was very adept in public speaking started the meeting.

"Heil Hitler!"

"Heil Hitler!" the workers enthusiastically responded.

"Thank you! Now, here you have been working for Jews. How much money do you think the Jew who owns this factory makes each month?" No one ventured a guess. "Well, I will tell you. He makes more than 300,000 Schillings per month." Gasps of shock and disbelief echoed throughout the factory floor. "As of today, this ends. You will no longer be exploited by these mongrels. The despicable Jew and his family have decided to leave Austria where they are not welcome to go to another country that puts up with this Jewish domination. In return they have sold the factory to a good Aryan Austrian (pointing to the new owner standing beside him). Now, of course, you want to know what this means for you. The new owner, of course will have to pay off the loan but, even with this, he is going to raise everyone's salary by 5 percent effective today. The time of Jewish exploitation of the German worker has ended."

There was an instantaneous euphoria that swept the workers as they cheered and saluted. Heil Hitlers resounded throughout the factory floor. Whether they liked or disliked their Jewish owner was immaterial. They were going to get a raise that they never would have received otherwise. They believed the highly inflated monthly income figure that was told to them and most now really believed that they had been exploited by the Jewish owner. If anyone did not believe what they were told they said nothing. They knew that to do so would have resulted in instantaneous dismissal and possibly even arrest. The new owner did not have a higher payroll cost. These firms employed Jewish workers that were immediately fired. Not all of them were replaced so the payroll cost was actually lower than before the Aryanization.

This was repeated countless times whenever a Jewish factory or business was Aryanized. The level of support was phenomenal. This was even more pronounced in the professional sector. More than half of the lawyers, doctors, dentists and college professors in Vienna were Jewish. When the Jewish professionals were forbidden to have non-Jewish clients, the number of clients and income of non-Jewish professionals increased substantially. They were as elated as were the workers in the Aryanized businesses. In universities, those that were promoted when the Jewish professors were expelled were similarly elated. In addition, more non-Jewish students were now admitted to fill the void created by the expulsion of Jewish students. These students were now guaranteed that they would have a good future that would have gone to a Jew had it not been for the Nazis.

Support for Jewish rights dwindled – not that they were very strong in the first place. Anything that could be done to get Jews to leave the country would be to everyone's benefit. More people now willingly participated in the denigration of Jews. Forcing Jews out of the apartments and homes that they obtained by cheating Gentiles became a good thing. Many Viennese turned out to jeer at the Jews being escorted to their new quarters, which was either a squalid apartment that Gentiles did not want to live in or a room rented from another Jewish family. Escorts were a must. The tide of public opinion had turned so strongly against them that they were not safe moving to another residence alone. Individual families moving were often attacked and robbed of everything that they had with them including the clothes that they were wearing since there were often valuables sewn into the linings of their garments. These gangs, which became known as "der Heuschrecke" (the locusts) for obvious reasons, were vicious in their assaults often beating up old and young alike. Of course, no one came to the aid of the Jews during the attack. Well, almost no one. There was one time that I knew about when a young man tried to intercede when a gang attacked a Jewish family but he too was severely beaten, robbed and stripped. The word spread.

However, when word of these attacks came to the attention of Eichmann, he immediately interceded and ordered the SS to escort and protect families being relocated. He even contacted the heads of the Jewish community and the rabbis and told them that the SS would provide a secure escort and they were to notify them in advance of anyone moving. Here again, this was not done from the goodness of his heart. As far as he was concerned everything of value from these Jews would eventually belong to the Nazis. Robbing these families was essentially robbing the German government. He was just protecting German assets. However, the initial attacks had a very good psychological impact. Recognizing that they had to place themselves under the protection of the SS in order to be safe and also recognizing the groundswell of anti-Semitic sentiment against them, many Jews that were hesitant and many that said that they would not leave, now decided to leave Austria – at whatever the cost.

Eichmann's program of having Jews raise money from other Jews, Jewish organizations and non-Jewish charities exceeded even his expectations. In the first six months he raised more than 500,000 Reichsmarks for the Nazi coffers from these sources. He was a star. Moreover, using the one-step office process emigration accelerated and was ahead of schedule. With both rich and poor emigrating, the Nazis became "equal opportunity deporters".

We also contributed secretly to those families that could not raise sufficient money to obtain their exit visas. As we did not personally know that many Jews we provided funds on the recommendation of Dr. Nussbaum. He decided to help families with two or more children as his first priority that had obtained the requisite entry permit from a country in order to emigrate but did not have enough money to pay for all of the exit costs. He worked with the IKG on this. They made a list of families that fit into this category along with the amount of money they needed to fully pay their exit costs. Those that had the least to raise were put on the top of the list and those with the most on the bottom. This way we could maximize the value of the money. We also had to be careful in the amount of money we withdrew from the bank lest it become suspicious. We did not want any enquiries from the authorities as to what we were doing with sudden large withdrawals. The black market was flourishing and it was tolerated to a certain extent but the amounts of money that we needed could probably implicate us on the supply side rather than the buy side of the black market. We had no defensible use for the money and we did not want to deplete our own cash reserves in case we needed the money ourselves. Still, we managed to funnel another few thousand Marks per month for emigration.

To enhance the revenue Eichmann continued to increase the price of emigration. Based on the financial worth of the wealthy Jew, he would set a price that was at least 25 percent higher than the total value of their assets – just in case they had any assets left after the legal Aryanization. Emigration applicants were told to contact friends and relatives in Vienna and abroad for the balance. External-based income increased even more in the second six months of emigration. He became the "Financial Wizard of the Jewish Solution." He was now given absolute power by Himmler over the Jews with orders that even officers of superior rank were to obey him on any Jewish matter.

At 9 AM on October 14 I received a call. It was Hymie Koppelman, the Jewish ambulance driver that had been fired a few months after Anschluss. "Michael, I need help! I will understand if you refuse but as I have no one else to ask. The Gestapo is after us and we will be deported to Dachau as soon as they find us. Ezra has already been deported. They are after Benjamin and the rest of us. We fled our apartment last night and stayed with a relative but they cannot hide us forever. We thought that we could try to escape to Croatia where we have some family but are at a loss on how to get there. Knowing your ability to solve problems I thought that I would at least ask for your help. If you are willing to help us I will explain everything when we meet."

I thought it over for about five seconds. I knew that I had to help him. I suggested that they hide during the day and come to the morgue using a back door that I would unlock at around 9PM when there was no one in that area. He agreed.

At 8:30 I unlocked the door and waited for them. Precisely at 9 they entered the morgue. I locked the door and took them downstairs to the makeshift dormitory that I used when I stayed overnight. They each had a small traveling bag with them that obviously contained everything of value that they owned.

"This is all that we could take. It is not much but it will have to do," Hymie said with a heavy sorrowful voice. "Ezra was arrested last night and deported to Dachau along with all of the Jewish Nazi League. Benjamin narrowly escaped and we are sure that when they find out that he is missing they will come for him and us. As you know, Ezra and his League of Jews for Hitler actively campaigned for Hitler before the plebiscite. In spite of being treated badly by the Hitler Jugend and many of the SD and police, they came out and urged everyone to vote yes. They marched. They spoke at rallies. They gave out flyers. They did whatever was asked of them. Well, you know that the plebiscite was a triumph for Hitler with more than 99 percent voting yes. Ezra and the group felt that they clearly showed the Nazis that there was a place for them in the united Germany. For about three weeks they heard nothing. Every time that Ezra approached Captain Leopold he was told to wait until the new person in charge of the Jews in Vienna was appointed. As you know, Captain Adolf Eichmann was appointed to that position. Another couple of weeks passed without any contact from the Nazi Party. About a week ago Captain Leopold contacted Ezra and told him that Eichmann wanted to personally thank the group and make a speech. Last night was the meeting. Almost every member of the group was there. Ezra asked Benjamin to go up to the spotlight platform to turn on the spotlight if Eichmann wanted it on. Benjamin climbed up the series of ladders to the platform which was hidden in the rafters of the building and he waited for the signal."

Benjamin now took over, "At 8 PM Eichmann arrived with Schüller, Leopold and some SS soldiers. He took center stage. Ezra greeted him with 'Heil Hitler!' but Eichmann did not return the salute. Ezra was a bit dismayed but continued with the introductory remarks and gave the podium to Eichmann. As he walked to the podium the group stood up and applauded. Once at the podium he raised his hand to quiet the audience. They thought that he was going to give the salute so they stopped clapping and yelled as loud as they could, 'Heil Hitler!' which again was not returned. Eichmann began by saying. 'Now here's what I want you to do. I want you to make a list of all of the Jews that have money, jewels and other valuables hidden away as well as all of the Jews that have transferred property that they own to Gentile friends to hide their ownership. I also want you to find as many Jews as possible that are hiding and who is hiding them. Finally, make a list of all of the Jews pretending to be Gentiles.' He paused and looked at Ezra, 'How soon can you do this?' he asked."

Benjamin paused for a moment to take a sip of water, "Ezra was surprised at these requests. They were outcasts amongst the Jewish community. No one trusted them. There was no way that they could get this information. Ezra told this to Eichmann, who said, 'Well if this is the case you are no longer of any use to me. With that he raised his hand and about two dozen SS soldiers entered the room and blocked all of the exits. He yelled at the group, 'You Jews would sell your mothers to live. You think that you can infiltrate the Nazi Party and bring it down from within? You may have fooled the Austrians but you do not fool me for a second. There are trucks outside. Leave the building in an orderly fashion, turn in your wallets, identification cards and all your money and jewelry. Do not hold anything back or you will be severely punished. Get in the trucks quickly. I have prepared a new home for you in Dachau'. Ezra was shocked and he tried to approach Eichmann but as soon as he got up an SS soldier hit him in the back with his rifle knocking him down. He kicked him for good measure and told the others on stage to carry the Jew traitor to the truck. In less than ten minutes the room was empty. After a brief search of the adjacent rooms, the Nazis left. I watched this from the spotlight platform. I waited almost two hours before climbing down and leaving the building after making sure that there was no one around. I quickly went home and told my father what had happened. The Nazis had a list of all of the League members and their families. There was no doubt in his mind that they would make a list of those that were not at the meeting based on the identity cards they collected from the members they had deported so we decided to leave our apartment that night."

Hymie now continued, "We packed some things and went to my brother's apartment a few blocks away. We discussed our options all night and decided to leave Vienna and go to Zagreb where we have some family but we are at a loss on how to leave the city undetected and get to the border. The border is well patrolled and we do not have passports or entry visas. That is when I thought of you."

I decided on the spot to help them. I asked if they could get a man that he trusted who knew how to drive to come to the morgue that night. He called his brother who immediately came to the morgue. Meanwhile, I filled out some papers and took some bandages from the storeroom and some blood from the blood storeroom. I bandaged his wife's head and sprinkled some of the blood around the bandage. Benjamin and his sister were going to be the family members allowed to accompany her. I took a driver's uniform from the locker room and had his brother put it on. I had Hymie put on an attendant's uniform and gave him the papers. They were for the transfer of a patient from Vienna to the hospital in Bratislava. This included a temporary emergency visa given to the hospitals expressly for the transfer of emergency patients and their immediate family. There was a Jewish community there that I believed could help them get to Zagreb. Bratislava was only 70 kilometers from Vienna while Zagreb was more than 150 kilometers. There was not enough time for a round trip to Zagreb plus it would be difficult to explain why an ambulance would travel that far for an emergency. Bratislava was the only option. I also filled out another form identifying Doctor Fenstov, a specialist in head injuries at the Bratislava Hospital, who was to going to perform emergency surgery on his wife. I did not think that the border guards would call Doctor Fenstov to confirm this at such a late hour. He was a legitimate doctor there with a specialty in head trauma. If they called the hospital they would confirm that he was on staff there and was in charge of the head trauma section.

I went to the front office and took the keys to one of the ambulances parked in the back of the morgue and gave them to his brother. They drove off with the sirens blasting and red lights flashing at 10:40. I waited anxiously in the morgue.

At 4:37 in the morning his brother drove up to the back of the morgue and parked the ambulance and entered through the back door. I had given him a spare key as I did not want to leave it unlocked. He was smiling as he entered the basement room where I was staying. The trip had absolutely no problem at all. They were stopped at the border leaving Austria and on the other side. They showed the papers to the guards who opened the back door, saw the woman with the bloody bandages, the IV and her sobbing children. They promptly closed the door and let them pass. They drove to Bratislava and turned off the siren and the flashing lights when they reached the city. They asked for directions to the main synagogue and woke up the caretaker that lived adjacent to the synagogue. Luckily, there was a sign on his house indicating him as the caretaker. After hearing their story he let them come into his house and said he would introduce them to the rabbi in the morning. The caretaker saw no problem in getting them to Zagreb. The trip back to Vienna was also uneventful. The border guards just waved him through without stopping. I returned the uniforms and the keys as he got dressed. He spent the next two hours in the storeroom with me. We were too excited to sleep so we just had some coffee and talked about the deteriorating conditions for Jews. He thanked me a number of times saying that it was not often these days that some one that was not Jewish would help Jews, especially in this manner that could result in prison or worse. At 7 AM he left saying that my action had restored his faith in people - that there still were some decent people left in Vienna. I never saw him again.

It only took one day for the word to get out that the entire Jewish League had been sent to Dachau. When he was sure that the deportations were known Eichmann told the IKG to spread the message, "This is what we do with our Jew-friends! Imagine what will happen to you Jews if you stay behind in Vienna. Raise the money! Pay your taxes and exit fees! Get out while you can!"

One will never know how much of an impact this had on the remaining Jews, but within eighteen months more than 100,000 Jews left Austria. For those that are interested the Nazis kept detailed records of where these Viennese Jewish emigrants went, possibly so they could get them back again later when they conquered the world:

Country	Jews
England	31,050
Switzerland	5,800
France/Belgium/Holland *	4,800
Czechoslovakia*	4,100
Subtotal Europe	**45,750**
United States	29,942
Palestine	15,200
Shanghai	6,220
Other Asia	970
Argentina	1,690
South Africa	1,125
Australia	1,050
Bolivia	940
Total	**102,887**

*recaptured

Most of the Jews that went to Czechoslovakia left for other countries as soon as possible knowing that Czechoslovakia would be the next target for Hitler so less than 15 percent were recaptured. The table was actually incorrect. More than 20,000 Jews went to Shanghai. This was reportedly downplayed due to the decision of the Japanese occupying Shanghai not to persecute Jews despite protests by Himmler.

One day, about six weeks of the enactment of the Nuremberg Laws, there was a knock on my office door at the morgue. Two German SS officers were standing there. My heart sank to my stomach, my knees weakened and I could hardly get up from the chair.

"Michael Baumann?"

"Yes?"

"I am Colonel Orloff Stryker and with me is Captain Hans Kaupfner. We have something for you. Heil Hitler!"

"Heil Hitler!" I replied. They handed me a letter. With a noticeably shaking hand, I opened the letter. Some co-workers had gathered around my office looking in with a mixture of fear and curiosity. "Why are these German SS officers here? Was Michael being arrested? What did he do?"

I read the letter silently to myself still very visibly shaking.

Berchtesgaden

December 17, 1938

Dear Michael:

Thank you for sharing that intimate moment between you and your father with me. With all that is going on I often forget about those times when we were struggling for recognition and success. Your letter brought back fond memories of my time in Munich and of my tribulations in Vienna.

With respect,

Adolf Hitler

I read the handwritten and hand-signed letter out loud, showed it to everyone and told the officers and the growing crowd of on looking co-workers of my original letter to the Fuehrer. The officers wrote my name in their books. I did the same with their names – you never know when you could use a name in vain. They saluted, turned and left.

To say that my stature at the morgue changed after that day would be an understatement. Essentially, I could walk on water. Whatever I wanted or needed was mine for the asking. In fact, a few of the secretaries that would not even give me the time of day before this were now eager to make my acquaintance. Little did I know at the time how valuable this letter would be for my future endeavors. About five weeks later I was promoted to Assistant Coroner when an opening came up but still retained all of my duties as a mortician since morticians were scarce. There was no doubt in my mind that the letter from the Fuehrer brought me that promotion as I did not have the tenure. Moreover, I was soon invited to join the Nazi party, which unlike my father, I did. I wore my purchased Nazi Party pin every day. Another benefit from the promotion was that I now had my own office, even though it was very small. This afforded me much more privacy which also became extremely important for my work.

I decided to re-decorate my office as soon as I moved in. I took out all of the filing cabinets that lined the right wall and had them brought to a basement storage room. That made my office look much larger than before. In the center of the wall right behind my chair I hung a large profile picture of Adolf Hitler facing left. On the left side in the direction that the profile faced, in an over-sized ornate frame, I hung the letter from Hitler with some patriotic ribbons at the top of the frame. On the right side, in a smaller frame, I hung the letter from Cardinal Piffl that I received after the college debate. To the right of the Cardinal's letter I hung a large silver crucifix that I bought from an antique store. I spent one whole week's salary on it. It was really elaborate and in its own right was complemented by most of the people coming into my office. I, of course, told them that it had been in my family for decades. I hung the pictures such that when I stood against the wall and faced the picture of Hitler our noses were at the same level.

This overall situation was truly amazing. What made it amazing was the fact that the letter was a pure fabrication. While we did go to Munich for the convention, we never went to the beer hall, and, being Jewish, we would never have introduced ourselves to Adolf Hitler and his viciously anti-Semitic adherents. In fact, if we went to that beer hall and were discovered to be Jewish, we probably would not have gotten out alive. I must confess that I do not even know what possessed me to write such a letter and actually send it to Hitler. I was even more amazed that among the thousands of letters that Hitler must receive that mine would be singled out and brought to his attention – and that he would write a personal reply, especially since it was almost one year later.

We were all glad that Wilhelm was a "Gentile Aryan" doctor who could treat us. At this point, given the circumstances for Jews in Vienna, Dr. Nussbaum sent a messenger to tell us that given the rapidly deteriorating conditions for Jews in Vienna, some other Jewish families that he had been treating that were also passing as Gentiles that originally declined to establish contact with us had changed their minds. They felt that it would be good to have some true friends and contacts in case there were problems with their identity. There were eight families that asked him to establish contact with us during the next few weeks.

We each took responsibility for notifying two of these families. However, we decided against expanding the card game group. They would be invited to contribute financially to our work but not get directly involved. We really wanted to limit exposing our group to discovery if one of them were picked up and tortured. We immediately contacted them using a special letter that Dr. Nussbaum addressed to each one. We did not tell them our real names only that we existed as a small group. We set up a post office box so if they wanted to contribute financially to the work we were doing they could do it anonymously. Most of the families were quite well-off and were more than willing to help as much as possible. We were now able to expand our food and medicine supply which was given to the IKG ostensibly through the Red Cross as well as help more families emigrate.

Some of these families also knew one or two additional Jewish men or families that had established themselves as Gentiles with false identity papers a long time ago. Overall, between Dr. Nussbaum's and their lists, we now knew thirteen Jewish families passing themselves off as Gentiles. We decided that we would never meet in a group and that none of the thirteen families would know any other family in the group that they did not already know. Secrecy and security were our utmost concerns.

Random attacks on Jews accelerated, particularly on public transportation. Jews should not be allowed on buses, trains or in taxis. They should walk. This was the attitude of a number of ad hoc groups that randomly attacked and robbed Jews. It was not unusual for them to stop a bus or a taxi and ask for identification. Anyone with a beard that looked Jewish or with the stereo-typed Jewish nose or with a Jewish name was beaten and robbed unless a policeman or SS soldier was there but it got totally out of hand. In one incident two Greek Orthodox priests were on a bus when it was stopped. They were in Vienna for a religious seminar. They were not that fluent in German but spoke enough to get by. But before they could explain who they were, they were dragged off of the bus and beaten. It was only when the group proceeded to rob them that they saw the large crucifix on each of them and fled. The priests were badly beaten and required hospitalization. Quite a number of Viennese of Italian descent and Italian tourists were also mistaken for Jews due to their large noses and were robbed and beaten. One was the relative of the Italian ambassador which caused considerable amount of bad publicity. The third incident was particularly damaging.

Hitler was aware of the hatred between Arabs and Jews. With the vast oil reserves in the Middle East he courted Arab support. They had no love for the English and the French that were occupying and controlling much of the land. Hitler sent special envoys to see if they would join him in his crusade to exterminate Jews and defeat England. One of his staunchest supporters was the Grand Mufti of Jerusalem, Haj Mohammed Effendi Amin el-Husseini. He visited Berlin many times and recruited more than 20,000 Moslem men into the Waffen SS. His goal was to unite the Arab leaders in the Middle East to rise up against the British and kill all the Jews that were increasingly coming into Jerusalem. A secret meeting was held in Berlin in 1941 with the envoys of three major countries chaired by the Mufti. It looked like they would reach an agreement. On the way back home, some of them stopped in Vienna for a few days of sightseeing. That was a mistake. Four of them were on a train speaking Arabic. Some of the passengers thought that they were speaking Hebrew. At the next stop some of the passengers asked the conductor to stop the train as there were Jews aboard. They called over some Hitler Jugend that were riding on the train. Unfortunately for them, they did not speak German. The Hitler Jugend told them to pull down their pants. They refused. The Jugend started to beat them with the clubs that they carried and pulled down their pants when they fell to the floor.

Being Moslems, they had circumcised penises. To the Jugend, they were Jews riding the subway when it was forbidden. They continued beating the men until some policemen arrived. All four men were badly beaten, required hospitalization and sustained permanent injuries. The incident resulted in the Arab leaders deciding not to join Hitler and fight on the Nazi side. This was a devastating blow to Hitler who was furious.

As bad as these three incidents were, it was good for Jews. A formal protest was lodged by the church in the case of the priests and from the Italian ambassador for the many Italian citizens attacked. Hitler was furious about the Middle Eastern men's beatings. He went after Goebbels since the Hitler Jugend reported to him. Himmler was also admonished for not protecting Jews in Vienna as well as for still having so many there. With the strong pressure from Berlin, Gauleiter Bürckel directed the Gestapo, the SS and the police to double their efforts and arrest any person or group caught attacking and robbing Jews. They printed this warning in all of the newspapers. They rode the buses and trains in plain clothes. A large number of arrests were made with particularly long prison sentences and fines. They were widely publicized which substantially reduced but did not totally eliminate the beatings and robberies. In addition, if a Jew knew his attackers he could report them and they would be arrested. This included neighbors that broke into their homes and stole their possessions. This, too, was publicized.

Being a known Jew in Vienna was a nightmare. You lived in constant fear of attack. You were not even safe in your own home. Every knock on the door was a cause of concern. Men and women had to go to work, which, by now, was mostly forced labor for menial tasks for which they received little to no pay. Jews still had to buy food and other items. Children had to go to school. The elderly had to go to their doctors. Even if you were not attacked you were often made to do ridiculous demeaning things. This ranged from street cleaning, to exercising, to carrying heavy stones from one place to another and back again, shoveling snow after a snowstorm, etc. While severe beatings were unusual minor beatings and punches to the groin and face were common as was soiling their clothes. It was particularly bad when it rained as Jews were often forced to roll around in puddles until they were soaking wet and dirty. In addition, the SS, SD or Gestapo could arrest a Jew for no reason, which they sometimes did. In these instances, severe beatings were commonplace. Every time Jews left their homes they were targets. Case-in-point:

There was one SS officer from the German town of Beverungen. He would stop a bearded Jew, preferably a rabbi, and order him to the nearest barber shop and have him sit down in one of the chairs. He ordered the barber to shave him – but only on one-half of his face. The other half stayed unshaven. Once this was done, the SS officer paid the barber for one half of a shave and ordered the half-shaven Jew out of the barber shop and released him to go about his business. He was the subject of ridicule where ever he went until he got home where he would have to shave the rest of his face. Sometimes some Hitler Jugend would stop him and parade him around the area so everybody could see the "half-shaven Jew". When the officer was asked how he got the idea to do this, he replied that his town issued notgeld showing a barber giving a Jew only half a shave with the text.

Anti-Semitic notgeld (emergency money) from the city of Beverungen showing a barber only shaving half the face of a Jew. David was slang for a Jew. (Source: Author's Personal Collection)

Text:

"Oh, David, what on earth to do?

They've only shaved half of you.

No, it really isn't very funny,

Today you can't make any money.

It's your turn to see how it goes,

Now you're the one led by the nose."

(Now you're the one being cheated)

Many more Jews now tried even harder to emigrate. Life for a Jew was Hell on Earth!

One evening at the weekly card game, Karl came in with a large box. "Presents!" he exclaimed. He opened the box. Inside were smaller glossy white gift boxes. In each box, wrapped in delicate white paper was a crucifix. They were simple in their design. There were no jewels in them but they were made out of silver. Two days ago he had seen a group of SD soldiers randomly stopping pedestrians in the street and asking for their identification. They would take the Jews and form a group where they had them draw a Jewish star on the sidewalk in chalk and have them rub it off. They would repeat this for hours. Karl noticed that the SD did not stop anyone wearing a visible cross hanging from their neck. That's when he got the idea so he went to the Catholic bookstore next to Stephansdom and bought a box of crucifixes. He told the manager that he was going to give them out as prizes in the summer camp that he owned which pleased the manager immensely. He was given a very large discount for them.

We wholeheartedly commended Karl for his observation and quick action. Yet, we sat there pensively for a few moments contemplating our action. Even though we were in hiding, we were Jewish. Should we wear such an outright symbol of Catholicism? We all decided to do it and to have our family members also wear one. Karl had bought enough crucifixes for every family member in our group and for the thirteen other families as well. During the next few days, we distributed the crucifixes and were not surprised when we learned that everyone decided to wear them. In fact, most were already wearing them as they had the same thought years ago. Not being discovered was tantamount to any other consideration. In the Spanish Inquisition, many Jews openly renounced their religion and wore crosses until they were able to leave Spain. Once free they reverted back to Judaism. The rabbis of the time thoroughly endorsed this subterfuge.

You may remember Heinrich, who was in charge of the death certificates in the Records Department. With the annexation came the Nuremberg Laws. When the Nuremberg Laws were applied to the Jews of Austria it became critically important for everyone else to prove that they were not even part-Jewish. The Nuremberg Laws classified many non-Aryans as Untermenschen (sub-humans) with Jews being on top of the list. Jews were specifically defined as follows:

- Full Jew: two Jewish parents or three or four Jewish grandparents

- Mischling (mixed breed)

- Mischling First Degree: Half-Jewish (one Jewish parent or two Jewish Grandparents)

- Mischling Second Degree: One-quarter Jewish (one Jewish grandparent)

- Conversion to Christianity did not make you non-Jewish, since this was a racial issue not a religious issue. Being Jewish solely depended upon your parents and grandparents. Many children of converted Jews that were raised as Christians and that never even thought of themselves as Jewish (or even knew that they were Jewish since their parents never told them) woke up one morning and found out that they were Jewish and either had to emigrate with their Jewish parents or were deported to ghettos and concentration camps when their time came. They were immediately ostracized when their "true identity" was revealed and were expelled from their schools with the known Jews shortly after Anschluss

- Conversion to Judaism makes you Jewish. This anomaly transcended the racial issue as it was felt that you were a traitor to the Aryan race by converting to Judaism thereby ceding your racial birthright

- One Jewish great grandparent made you one eighth Jewish which, under the proper circumstances as determined by a Nazi Review Board could make you completely non-Jewish. But it was better to not even have a Jewish great grandparent. You were tainted.

People had to prove that they were not Jewish or even partly Jewish going back at least two generations with three being even better. Copies of birth and death certificates not only for a person's parents but for their grandparents and, if they really wanted to establish their Aryan ancestry, from their great grandparents, were needed especially if there was any doubt. Doubt about being Jewish was caused in a number of ways. First, if a person "looked" Jewish. The Nazis had many studies comparing the physical characteristics of Jews and non-Jews, particularly the size and shape of the nose so, anyone with a particularly large, wide nose made the person and his family suspect. A second doubt was raised if the family name was on a list of typical and atypical Jewish family names including the one "n" versus the "double n". As it was relatively simple to add an "n" to a last name, families with the double "n" were also investigated with more scrutiny. The burden of proof was on the family so they had to prove that they were not Jewish. Even if the male was not circumcised he had to prove that he was not of Jewish descent. Many Jews had converted to Catholicism decades ago and had stopped circumcising their sons. A third case was if someone denounced you as being partly Jewish. Some non-Jews coveted the possessions and businesses of their friends and neighbors so they denounced the owner to the authorities in the hope that those they denounced could not prove their Aryan heritage. In addition, anyone with an important job or starting a new job had to prove that they were not even partly Jewish. All professionals such as doctors, dentists, teachers and lawyers had to prove that they weren't Jewish "since Jews permeated these professions at exceedingly high rates and would clearly publicly deny being Jewish to continue lying, cheating and stealing from Aryans." This became even more important when a law was enacted where Jewish doctors were only allowed to treat Jewish patients. Jewish doctors had to clearly identify themselves as being Jewish under penalty of deportation to a concentration camp.

The large label was pasted on the door and the small one by the doorbell indicating that the doctor was Jewish and could only treat Jews. (Source: Author's Personal Collection)

When Anschluss occurred I was living in an apartment in the fourth district and commuting to the morgue, which was in the first district, by bus. To minimize being challenged and potentially being discovered as being Jewish, I moved into an apartment in the first district which was within walking distance to the morgue. It was much more money than I could really afford but it was literally a life-or-death situation. My mother helped me with the rent which was somewhat embarrassing but necessary. My apartment was just across the street from a large shoe store. I decided to buy a pair of comfortable walking shoes for the eight-block walk to the morgue from my apartment. My first visit after work was not successful. I have a wide foot and the shoes that they had were a bit too tight. Fritz, the son of the owner took care of me. Rather than lose the sale, he volunteered to go to some other shoe stores with whom they had a relationship and see if he could get some better-fitting shoes.

I agreed and returned the next day. He was successful and brought out four pairs of shoes, three black and one brown, in different styles. I bought a very comfortable pair of black shoes. I returned the next day after work and asked if he still had the brown shoes. As he had already returned the shoes to the other stores, he asked me to return the next day and I bought the second pair. He mentioned that he had not seen me in the store before so I told him that I had just moved into neighborhood and lived across the street. "Where?" he asked. I told him and found out that we were neighbors. They lived in the building adjoining my building. Coincidently, Fritz walked to school at the same time that I walked to the morgue, precisely at 7:30. We would often meet and walk together for about five blocks until he turned to go to his school and I kept walking straight to the morgue.

Fritz was sixteen years old and an honors high school student. He had a great singing voice and was a lead member of the Stephansdom church choir. He had been a member of the Catholic Youth Organization and spent many hours in charitable work. His father owned the shoe store for more than twenty years and his mother worked there as well. He had a younger sister, Greta, who was fourteen and was also a member of the choir and had also been a member of the Catholic Youth Organization. The family worshipped together every Sunday for as long as he could remember. They were devout Catholics. Initially the Nazis tolerated the Catholic Church but over time, they started to persecute the clergy and members of the Catholic Youth Organization. After being warned about his participation in the Youth Organization and the consequences that it could have on his family, he and his sister quit the organization. This was duly noted by the Nazis and one of his friends at school who was in the Hitler Jugend who invited him to join the Jugend, which he was seriously considering. In addition to waiting on customers after school, he picked up supplies and delivered shoes to customers using a motorbike belonging to the business. While he had some Jewish friends, they were not close. In fact, he was glad when they were forbidden to attend high school. They were always acting superior and were at the top of the class. His math teacher was Jewish and they did not get along at all. He was particularly happy to see him go. Sometimes he would participate with his friends when they ridiculed

Jewish students and forced them to do stupid things such as crawl to their next class, or try to walk balancing their school books on their head stopping to pick them up whenever they fell or were pushed off by another student. He did not participate in any rough stuff such as hitting them, knocking them down, throwing things at them or robbing them. He felt that these things went too far according to his Catholic teachings. Once, however, he did pour a bottle of ink on a Jewish boy who stood up and loudly corrected and embarrassed him in front of all of the other students. He took out the bottle of ink from his school bag, walked over to the boy who was now sitting down, and poured it over his head. The rest of the class laughed and applauded. The teacher smiled and ignored the incident refusing to let the Jewish boy leave the classroom to clean himself up. In fact, she made him stay after class to clean up the desk, seat and floor since he had allowed the ink to mess up these areas.

He had a girlfriend who was also Catholic. They were in the choir together and started to go out after the first few practices. Their parents became close friends after Fritz started to date her.

I enjoyed our walk together but was not particularly concerned when I did not see him for a couple of days but after almost a week. I thought that he might be sick and decided to ask about him on the weekend if he did not show up on Friday. He didn't so I made a mental note to ask his parents about him on Saturday. However, when I returned home that night I immediately knew that something was wrong. Fritz was standing in front of my apartment. He snuck into the building when another tenant opened the locked outer door. His face was thinner and he was very nervous. He jumped every time someone made a noise.

"Do you have a few minutes?" he asked. I, of course, said yes. "Would you like to come in to talk?" Before I even finished the sentence he nodded yes. When we entered the apartment he went over to the window and looked out, obviously to see if anyone saw him. I asked him how long he had been waiting for me since it was late. He told me that he had been waiting for almost five hours. He turned around from the window and told me what had happened.

"On Monday, after school, I arrived at the shoe store and was surprised to see some Gestapo and SS soldiers in front of and inside the store. My parents were against the wall with my younger sister, who was visibly upset and crying. One of the Gestapo men was yelling at them but I could not hear what he was yelling. At first, one of the SS soldiers refused to let me into the store but when I said that they were my parents, the SS soldier grabbed me by the shoulder and forced me into the store. I dropped my schoolbag and was going to pick it up but the soldier would not let me get it. He kicked the bag away and shouted. 'Get over there, you dirty Jew!' and threw me against the wall with my parents. What in the world was this soldier talking about? I thought. I am not Jewish. I started to explain that there must be some mistake but before I could finish the sentence the soldier slapped me in the face and told me to shut up. I looked at my father and saw that his lip was bleeding and his face was bruised. My mother and sister were crying. My father tried to say something but was hit from behind in the back with the rifle butt of one of the SS soldiers, 'Shut up, you filthy Jew!'

I leaned against the wall and did not understand what was going on. I still believed that this was some awful mistake. My parents were Catholic not Jewish. I watched in disbelief as the Gestapo confiscated all of the money in the cash register and all of the cash and jewelry that we had including the class ring that I had just received as a graduating senior. A couple of the soldiers helped themselves to some shoes. A truck pulled up outside the store. We were herded into the truck as the soldiers pushed us and even struck me, my mother and my father to get us to move faster. I still could not believe what was happening but now realized that this was not the time or the place to say anything. As I got into the truck I saw people that were standing outside watching the proceedings rush into the store to take the shoes that were now fair game to the crowd as they were told that the owners were Jewish. One of the soldiers rode off with our motor bike. The Gestapo purposely kept the truck parked there for about 15 minutes as we watched every single shoe being taken from the store. When the store was devoid of shoes people were even taking the furniture and fixtures. It was a total loss. The truck finally pulled away.

In the truck, my father was not allowed to say anything. My mother and sister were still crying. After twenty minutes we reached a former gymnasium in the second district. It was guarded by SS soldiers. We were forced out of the truck and into the gymnasium. There were thirty or forty people waiting in the hallway. They had all been abused in some manner – bruises, torn clothes, bloody lips and noses. Some were holding their arms, chest and stomach in obvious pain. We stood in the hallway for almost two hours before we were called into another room still forbidden to talk. Seated at a desk were two SS officers, a woman stenographer and a clerk. Two armed SS soldiers stood at the entrance and another at the other door in the back of the room. We were forced to line up facing the table.

'So, you thought you could hide by pretending to be Catholic? A Jew is still a filthy, stinking Jew on the inside. You may have fooled everyone you know on your outside appearance but the truth comes out in the end.'

I was taken aback by this accusation. We were not Jewish. I am not Jewish. I was not circumcised. I am Catholic. My father is a devout Catholic. How could they make these accusations?

The SS officer looked at me standing there confused and in disbelief. 'So you didn't even know that your parents were Jews, did you?' he said. He looked at my father and yelled, 'Drop your pants! Show your children your penis! Show them that you are a Jew!'

My father hesitated. He just stood there. One of the SS soldiers came over from the door and slammed the rifle into the back of his legs knocking him to the floor. 'Don't make me tell you again! Take down your pants before I have them ripped from your body!' With that, still lying on the floor, my father pulled down his pants around his ankles. The SS soldier kicked him to get him to turn around so he was facing us. I saw that he had a circumcised penis. I could not believe my eyes. He was Jewish! I was Jewish!

With his pants still down around his ankles he was forced to stand up. He instinctively covered his pubic area with his hands. 'I don't blame you for hiding that piece of shit penis you have. You are even a disgrace to your fellow Jews. At least they do not try to hide their Jewishness.'

He looked down at the paper he had on the table and asked how long my father was pretending to be Catholic. My father responded that he had converted to Catholicism in 1918 right after the war. They had not believed in or practiced Judaism for a long time and decided to convert. They went through the required church procedure and they no longer considered themselves to be Jewish from that time on. When I was born they did not have me circumcised because they were no longer Jewish. They never told me or my sister that they had been Jewish and had converted. They saw no point in doing so. As far as they were concerned they were legitimate Catholics.

The SS officer in charge was quite disturbed by my father's explanation. 'A Jew is a Jew no matter what form he takes. Some try to hide amongst us pretending to be Aryans. Some try to hide amongst other mongrel races. As out Fuehrer has said time and time again, Jews are not a religious order. They are an unclean race of degenerates that undermine our very existence. They are part of a global conspiracy that tries to infiltrate every aspect of our society. You have tried to infiltrate the Catholic Church but when we trace your ancestry it is clear that you are Jews. You are going to be taken to your house. You will have fifteen minutes to pack some personal belongings. Some soldiers will accompany you to make sure you only pack personal items and do not try to pack any money, jewelry and other such items that you have stolen from the people around you. These items you will turn over to the soldiers. Make sure you take all of your valuables out of their secret hiding places. If we search the house after you have left and find anything you will be severely punished. You will be sent to Poland to a city especially set up for Jews. There you will be among your own kind. Now pull up your pants and hide that abomination of a penis!' With that we were again herded onto a truck and driven home. We were given precisely fifteen minutes to pack clothing, toiletries and personal items such as family pictures. We were only allowed to pack one small suitcase each. We were carefully watched and my parents had to give all of their jewelry, silver items, or anything that could be valuable to the SS. My father also had to give the SS officer his personal and business bankbooks and sign a form authorizing the SS to take over the accounts, the business, his apartment and the lease to his store.

I tried to be strong and comfort my sister and parents but they were dazed and distraught by the events of the day. Suddenly, I realized I would never see my friends again. Then it came to me! Would they even be my friends now that I am Jewish? I believed that I would never know the real answer but thought that they would still be my friends since I had not really changed. I am still the same person today that I was yesterday. As we were being led out of the house I saw Rolf and Stefan, two of my classmates and lifelong friends standing in the street. Rolf lived two houses down the street and Stefan lived across the street. As I passed by them I waved to them. They both spat on the ground and yelled that I was a 'dirty Jew and should be ashamed of myself for trying to fool them'. Now I did not have to think about the loyalty of my friends. I was now a Jew! I had no friends! Once back in the truck we were told that we were going to be staying at the gymnasium with the other lying Jews until our transportation to Poland could be arranged. We had no money, no store, no income and probably no longer any Gentile friends."

Fritz asked if there was any type of work at the morgue that he could do to earn some money. His family had nothing. They were staying at the gymnasium but since their transportation to Poland was not going to occur for another week or two and they were not being fed, two of them were allowed to come and go freely. The other two had to stay in the gymnasium to ensure that they would return. All of the people there were in the same situation. They had converted to Christianity but were discovered to be Jewish. Some of the families had Jewish grandparents that had converted and they did not even know it. The Nazis had confiscated the records of the churches and they were systematically going through the records looking for these religious conversions, which is how they found out about his parents. What made matters worse was that his parents did not have any Jewish friends. There were Jewish customers but none of them were friends. After this exposure, his parents contacted all of their Gentile friends for help. More than 90 percent did not want anything to do with them. They were hostile, denigrated them and either slammed the door in their face if they came to the apartment or just walked away from them if the encounter was in the street. About 10 percent were sympathetic of which about one half gave them some money but asked not to be contacted again. Fritz's girlfriend also shunned him. She had been humiliated at school by the other students for going out with a Jew even though she didn't know it at the time. Some boys offered to show her a real Aryan penis but she kept on saying that they never had sex. They believed her but really enjoyed the innuendos.

I told him that there was nothing available at the morgue and offered him some money. At first he refused telling me that he had come to ask for work not charity. I insisted telling him to think about his family and not his pride. He reluctantly accepted with tears welling up in his eyes. I asked if they had gone to any of the Jewish organizations for help but he said that his father had not since they had shunned Judaism for more than twenty years. I suggested he contact the church and see what they could do for them. He had not considered that but thought that it was a good idea. There were many families in the same predicament. Perhaps the church could do something. He turned and left. I never saw him again but on my lunch break I happened to meet a Jewish former employee in the morgue on the street and told him of the family's plight. He was not surprised. The Nazis were even crueler to Jews that had converted to Christianity. The Nazis believed that this was part of the Global Jewish Conspiracy to dominate the world by infiltrating every aspect of Aryan life. He quoted something he read in the anti-Semitic German newspaper, Die Stürmer: "Beware of the hidden Jew! The hidden Jew is our worst enemy. He uses all of his cunning to deceive us, cheat us and make us complacent until they are ready to strike. We must ferret them out and expose them for what they are. Until this has been accomplished, none of us are safe in our homes, in our schools and in our businesses."

My father had built a solid, well-documented background and the Nazis knew that all civil servants had to have a background check. Moreover, with the letter from Hitler, which was prominently displayed in my office, and the occasional mention of Colonel Stryker and Captain Kaupfner, anyone sent to check on me because my last name had the double n, simply accepted my credentials without checking them at the source. The German system was very thorough and they assumed that the Austrian system was as thorough

– a misconception that was clearly in my favor. I had the backup documentation anyway so I was not too worried especially since my father told me that the Baumann families of Bruck were Aryan and had been Catholic for generations. In small towns where there were no synagogues, there were no records of who was Jewish. I slept easier knowing this.

By now it was evident that Hitler had no use for the Catholic Church. He had to be the supreme God, not Jesus Christ. Moreover, they accepted Jews as long as they professed their love of Christ. The position of the Nazis was evident in a popular souvenir postcard showing how the Nazis were cleansing Austria of those that have caused the prolonged poor economic conditions that plagued the country.

Postcard: Mander s'ischt Zeit!

Now is the Time (to get out)!

The enemies of Germany are fleeing in front of the Nazis. They are: a Jew carrying his money box, a politician (wearing the red and white Austrian colors), a trade union member (boy), a capitalist (well-dressed businessman looking back), and a priest. (Source: Author's Personal Collection)

The need for duplicate copies of death and old birth certificates increased ten-fold for those that had to prove their Aryan ancestry. The building in which the central morgue was located was the repository for all the official death certificates of Vienna as well as the pre-1910 birth certificates as there was no room for them in the hospital. Heinrich was allowed to hire some more people to handle the increased requests for copies which, for some strange reason, consisted entirely of members of his family. This type of job ordinarily required passing a civil service exam but due to the urgency of so many people having to obtain duplicate records, the city government waived this procedure to expedite the process. This was a very good waiver for Heinrich, or should I say for his family, because there was no way on Earth that any of them would have passed the civil service exam – even if they had been given the answers in advance. Having said that, while most of the regular civil service employees were not speed demons, Heinrich's relatives made them look like speed demons. Being hired by Heinrich brought a sense of security to them not shared by the workers in other departments so they were exceptionally slow which was compensated for by their gross incompetence. They often misfiled the new death certificates or the ones that were being re-filed after copies were made. They often copied the wrong death certificates for the person requesting them who had to wait another few days to get the right ones – and even then there was no guarantee that the second attempt would be any better than the first. This was particularly bad for people with a common surname since there would be so many certificates to search through before finding the correct one. Some of Heinrich's relatives refused to even search for the certificates for people with common surnames. The backlog increased so it could now take up to seven working days for someone to get copies of old birth and all death certificates, particularly if they needed a few of them.

Once or twice a month Heinrich and I would go out to lunch. No matter how heavy his workload was, he would always find the time to go to lunch with me. Our lunches were not on any set schedule because I would only go when I had time and since most days were very busy under the Nazis, I just did not have that much time. So, when the occasion arose, we would go. One such day I went to his office

I was amazed at the crowd of people that were waiting there. Some were quite calm and some were very anxious. The anxious ones were fidgeting while sitting or were pacing back-and-forth like a caged animal. They were obviously under some pressure to prove that they were not Jewish and they were in a hurry. One of these people in a hurry, a man in his forties who had the misfortune of having a large nose, was at the window pleading for a copy of his family's death certificates as soon as possible as he was a candidate for a new job at a prestigious company and the only issue to get him into the first round of candidates was the Jewish question. Unfortunately for him, he was pleading with Gretchen, one of Heinrich's less-than-average intelligent relatives which she compensated for with arrogance. Needless to say, the man's request fell on deaf ears.

As we walked to lunch I thought of something that could get really get me in good with Heinrich and perhaps access to all of the documents. Heinrich always needed money. His wife liked to wear nice clothes and he had two children in a private school as his wife insisted that this was necessary. She also worked to help pay for these extras but even with both of them working, their expenses always seemed to run ahead of their income. One of the reasons that Heinrich particularly liked going to lunch with me was because he knew that at least every other lunch, he could borrow some money from me, which every once in a while he paid some back just to re-establish his credit. This lunch was most likely going to be a borrowing lunch since he had gone for about two months without borrowing anything from me. Besides I always paid for lunch. As we were eating I suggested a plan to Heinrich how he could make some extra money – perhaps a lot of extra money. He stopped eating, which alone was a miracle. He became all ears, as the saying goes. I told him that he could take advantage of the need of the people requiring copies of death certificates that were in a hurry by expediting the process of giving these people copies of the death certificates within 24 hours, perhaps even the same day – as long as they were willing to pay extra for it. For example, I mentioned the man at Gretchen's window who anxiously needed copies of some death certificates for a job requirement. "Suppose you set up a system where for a small fee that person could get next-day or even same-day service? I am absolutely sure that the man would have paid three, four or even five Marks per certificate to get them the next day and perhaps possibly more to get them that same day. If he needed five certificates, which was not unusual, you could get twenty to thirty Marks just for doing your normal job a little faster." I even suggested re-allocating the work using the two experienced women, Hilda and Lena, for this on a dedicated, shared profit basis and perhaps hiring one or two very experienced clerical people to assist them as needed. I suggested using Hilda and Lena for a number of reasons including getting them on his side so they would not say anything to anyone else and capitalizing on their knowledge and efficiency which, albeit slow, was much better than any of his relatives. I was pretty sure that they would welcome the extra money as well. Heinrich jumped at the idea. He thought it was absolutely brilliant. I know he really liked it because for the first time ever he opted not to have dessert and coffee. Moreover, he even forgot to ask for another loan. He was in a hurry to get back and implement my suggestion. I went even further offering my advice on setting up the system and the recommending two experienced people to help him whom I knew and trusted which he accepted. He knew by this time that the relatives he hired were pretty bad and would not be able to perform well in this situation. So, I also skipped dessert and coffee. First, we got Hilda and Lena on board. They loved the idea and jumped at the chance to make some extra money as I had expected. Heinrich mentioned that I had suggested that they hire two new employees if the plan was successful. They really liked this idea of having two new people work for them for three reasons. First, they did not think much of Heinrich's relatives (and that is putting it mildly), second it gave them the stature of being a supervisor and third they would not have to work too hard. I already had two Jewish women in mind for this job. Heinrich told me to let the two women that I had in mind know that there could be a job opening in his department. One additional thing that the German annexation brought with an improved economy was inflation. Prices were increasing much faster under German rule than under Austrian rule. So as soon as it was agreed, Hilda, Lena, Heinrich and I met to develop the "rapid service" plan. First, I suggested that they set up a special window called Expedited Service with an explanation and rate schedule. For example, for up to three birth or death certificates the charge would be five Marks for same day service and three Marks for next day service. Each additional copy would be three Marks for same day service and two Marks for next day service. So if someone needed six copies and wanted same day service, they paid fifteen Marks for the first three certificates and nine Marks for the last three certificates which came to twenty four Marks. This was not an inconsequential sum of money especially if they had twenty or thirty people per day requiring this service. They thought that perhaps this was too high but I explained that if it was too low that too many people might want the service and you might not be able to handle the requests. Besides, they could always lower the fee later if it was too high and not successful. We set a target of implementing this value-added service for the following Monday. Over the weekend we all came into the office and posted the notices announcing this new service throughout the waiting room. A special window was set aside for this service. Heinrich's youngest daughter made some signs enlisting some of her fellow students during the week so they would be ready by Saturday. She was studying art at the private school she attended and did a very nice job that even included a swastika and eagle at the top and bottom of each sign to make them look official. She also designed some special forms that people would fill out indicating how many certificates they needed and allowing them to calculate the amount they had to pay for the special service. We duplicated the forms. The response was overwhelming. On the first day, twenty-seven people took advantage of the service (fourteen opted for same day service with the rest opting for next day service). Hilda and Lena ran ragged trying to fulfill all of the orders – but they did it. Overall, they took in more than three hundred Marks. The second and third days were even better. They split the proceeds amongst themselves as I declined to take a share when offered and they did not insist too much after I refused. Heinrich took a larger share than the two women. At the end of the third day, Heinrich burst into my office highly excited and elated. He could not contain himself as he thanked me over and over again. He asked me how soon I could get the new people to start work. I told him that I would have them there tomorrow. I called up the two women that were from Jewish families passing themselves off as Gentiles. I had already asked them the previous week if they were interested in working, which was answered positively. They reported to Heinrich the next morning and were immediately put to work. They were very good – and very fast. They were very respectful towards Hilda and Lena complementing them at every opportunity. Hilda and Lena could relax and supervise. It was a win-win situation. The two new women were not supposed to share anything in this windfall which they had agreed to in order to get the job. However, the plan was so successful that Hilda, Lena and Heinrich decided to give the two new women some extra money to maintain their efficiency and loyalty. They were all ecstatic – and on the road to becoming quite well-to-do. By the end of the second week, they each had made almost a month's salary.

Now, while I liked Heinrich and was happy to help him I really had an ulterior motive. The two women that I placed there, Silvia and Bette, now had access to all of the original death certificates, and the storeroom with all of the old birth certificates that were pre-1910. Now, when we needed to create a false identity for someone we could actually provide them with an original death certificate instead of a copy which could be falsified as well as some original birth certificates for their older deceased family members. An original birth and death certificate had a large circular embossed (stamped in the paper) seal that was stamped on a round gold circular stamp that was pasted on the lower left corner of the birth certificate. When someone was born or when they died two official originals were prepared. One was kept on file and the other given to the family. The replacement copies had a small embossed seal on the lower right side of the birth certificate and a red rectangular pasted stamp with the word "duplicate." When we needed to establish the identity of someone, Silvia and Bette would make a copy of the original death or birth certificate and replace the original certificate with the copy. They smuggled the originals out during their lunch break. We had developed a transfer process just in case they were searched on the way out of the building or in the street. Each would have a large purse with a hidden area between the lining and the wall of the purse. They would go to lunch and switch matching purses in the lady's room of the restaurant with another woman working for us. Actually, you might say that we were creating real false identities.

Three days later, Heinrich came to my office out of breath as he obviously was running (another miracle) to let me know how the rapid service operation was going. To say he was ecstatic was an understatement. He told me how much they were earning and that they could hardly keep up with the demand. I countered by saying that he should raise the rates to lighten the load without necessarily reducing the income. That was readily accepted as "another great Baumann idea" so he decided on the spot to add another two Marks for each type of service. On his way out he turned and thanked me again. "Are you sure you do not have any Jewish blood in you? This is such a great scheme!"

CHAPTER NINE

EXTENSION OF LIFE

"No doubt Jews aren't a lovable people; I don't care about them myself; but that is not sufficient to explain the Pogrom."

> From a private letter by Neville Chamberlain, Prime Minister of England, July 30, 1939 regarding Kristallnacht.

On November 9, 1938 a two-day pandemic wave of anti-Semitic terrorism swept through Germany and Austria coordinated and led by the SS. I was working late that night so I had already decided that I would spend the night in the storeroom rather than risk being challenged on my way home. I did not realize what was going on until the next day.

The action against Jews that night was carefully orchestrated by Joseph Goebbels with Heinrich Himmler having responsibility for implementation. It had been planned for months and had Hitler's and Goering's approval. It was specifically set on these dates which was the fifteenth anniversary of the failed Nazi Putsch of 1923 (November 9) and the birthday of Martin Luther (November 10) but the excuse given was the coincidental shooting of Ernst von Rath, a low-level German diplomat in Paris by a young Polish Jew on November 7 who died on the morning of November 9.

This coincidental assassination needs an explanation. Ten days earlier, on October 28, about 17,000 Polish Jews living in Germany were deported without warning to the Polish border and left there without food, water or shelter. Among them was the family of Herschel Grynszpan, a student living in Paris. He found out about it from a friend of the family. He had evidently met von Rath previously because he went to the German embassy and asked for him by name.

He was told that von Rath was attending some function where he was making a speech. He went there but was refused admittance. Returning to the embassy, he waited for von Rath to return. When von Rath returned he implored von Rath to intercede and help his parents. When von Rath refused, they argued and Herschel pulled out a pistol and shot him. Herschel was subdued and arrested.

Rath never regained consciousness. He died two days later on November 9. Goebbels took full advantage of the situation condemning the assassination as a plot by the Global Jewish Conspiracy to assassinate Nazi leaders. With the police instructed not to interfere, the orders were given that Jewish businesses and synagogues were to be systematically vandalized per the plan already developed. Almost every single identified Jewish store throughout the major cities in Germany and Austria had their windows smashed. Synagogues were looted, set on fire and allowed to burn down without any interference from the fire brigade. When they were called to a synagogue fire it was just to ensure that the fire did not spread to adjacent buildings. In Vienna, all but two synagogues were totally destroyed. One was the Vienna Synagogue which was located at Seitenstettengasse. It was built between 1824 and 1826 in a residential neighborhood in the first district. At the time it was built there was a law in Vienna that only churches could be built as "free standing" structures so the synagogue was attached to other buildings with a similar style. Since it was built touching adjacent buildings and was close to a landmark church, there was no way that the fire could be controlled without totally destroying the entire city block. One of the adjacent buildings was the Jewish administration office, the Israelitischen Kultusgemeinde (IKG) but all of the other buildings around the corners were private businesses and residences. Instead, the synagogue was forcibly entered and completely vandalized with everything of value stolen and everything else destroyed.

In Vienna, more than four thousand Jewish shops were looted and more than two thousand Jewish homes were invaded and looted during the two-day pogrom. Many residents were forced out of their apartments just with the clothes that they were wearing and told that the invaders now lived there and they were being evicted. Beatings were commonplace but not one Jewish girl or woman was known to have been raped. Sexual intercourse between Aryans and Jews had been outlawed by the Nuremberg Laws. Some women were almost raped but when one of the members of the mob reminded the would-be rapists about the Nuremberg Laws, they stopped. The Nuremberg Laws were rigorously enforced. In Linz, a few soldiers raped some Jewish women. The Gestapo found out about it and arrested two of the soldiers who were subsequently sentenced to four years in prison for violating the Nuremberg Laws.

About 6,000 Jews in Vienna were arrested that night of which about one half of them were sent to the Dachau concentration camp in Bavaria. All of those sent to Dachau were killed or forced into slave labor never to return home. This night became known as Kristallnacht or "night of the broken glass" due to the breaking of the windows of almost every identified Jewish-owned store in Germany, of which Austria was now an integral part. The Jewish community throughout Germany was notified that they had to pay more than 2 billion Reichsmarks for the damages they caused.

Since Kristallnacht had been well-planned and instructions distributed to every city well before von Rath was shot, there were lists of Jews to be arrested that were also prepared in advance. There were lists with the addresses of every synagogue in Germany and Austria. There were lists of Jewish shops. Still, many people to his day still believe the spontaneous reaction to the von Rath assassination rationale for the action.

Surprisingly, Kristallnacht created a major rift within the Nazi hierarchy. Goering personally interceded. He was outraged. Even more important was that Hitler was also outraged – even more so than Goering. Goering had no objection to the acts of violence against the Jews. He didn't care about the synagogues being burnt down. He didn't care about Jews being beaten up with some sent to concentration camps. However, he vehemently objected to the wanton destruction and theft of goods and property from Jewish businesses and residences that would have been confiscated by the government rather than destroyed or stolen by uncontrolled mobs of people. The loss to the government was enormous. Moreover, German insurance companies were liable to pay for most of the damage to commercial and residential property. When Himmler countered by saying that the Jews would pay for the damage it just didn't fly. Goering responded by saying that they would have gotten this wealth anyway and that there was absolutely no excuse for the magnitude of the loss. Goebbels agreed saying that he never intended that the property loss was to spread beyond the destruction of the synagogues and the breaking of the windows as was specified in his instructions. The target was supposed to be the Jews not their property. He emphasized that this was what Hitler was thinking when he agreed to the action. Goering was much more powerful than Himmler. With Goebbels now distancing himself from the immense property loss, Himmler was alone and clearly in trouble. On the spot, he agreed to moderate his policy and control the actions of the mobs and the SS. He now fully realized that this was the property of the Third Reich and could not be allowed to fall into private hands. Goebbels also agreed to tone down the violent aspects of his anti-Semitic propaganda. Humiliation of the Jews was still allowed as long as there was no property stolen or damaged.

Hitler was also angry that it had gotten so out of hand that the foreign press was reporting it very negatively. The idea was supposed to be that the people had enough of the Jews and were showing their indignation by spontaneously burning synagogues and damaging stores by breaking the windows – not by looting them with mobs roving the streets and randomly attacking Jews in the streets and breaking into their homes and beating people. Arrests were planned in Vienna to emphasize the need for more Jewish emigration so the lists were carefully drawn up by Eichmann in advance. Eichmann focused on selected lawyers, doctors, store owners and business men with a few troublesome activist Jews and a couple of young rabbis thrown in for good measure. Here again the SD, the SS and the Gestapo overreacted and arrested many Jews not on the list. They were freed during the next two days but those on the list were sent to Dachau never to be seen again. This reinforced the message that any Jew that could leave the country should leave the country as soon as possible which was why mostly upper class Jews from large families and single men and women with good jobs but not much tangible wealth were targeted.

The net result of the internal dispute amongst the Nazi hierarchy was that the quality of life for Jews and Jewish business owners in Vienna actually improved after Kristallnacht. The number of murdered Jews being brought to the morgue dropped to only two or three per week. Still, a Jew walking the streets of Vienna was a target. A Jewish life had little to no value. A case in point:

One afternoon the bodies of two Jewish men, each with their pants drawn down to their ankles, were brought to the morgue. One had no visible injury while the other had the top of his head blown off – but it appeared that it had been blown off from the inside out. I was told of the incident by the ambulance driver that brought them in who said,

"A group of SS soldiers and an officer were in a bar yesterday when an SD officer came in to show them a new pistol that he had received from a relative in the United States. It was a 38 Special used by the New York City police force. Immediately, there was a heated discussion on which pistol was more powerful, the German Luger or the 38 Special. Specifically, which one had more killing power? They decided to put it to the test betting on which gun was more powerful. They went outside and rounded up a group of Jewish men that were walking on the street. They selected four that were about the same height and weight and let the rest go. They asked each one their age, weight and height. Their height was of particular importance. They were looking for tall Jews. Two were very close on all three statistics so they let the other two go. The two young men that were selected were 33 and 35 years old. Each weighed close to 70 kilograms (about 155 pounds) and were almost equal in height – a little less than two meters (about six feet) tall. They led the two men into the alley next to the bar and had them drop their pants and bend over ninety degrees so their upper torsos were parallel to the ground. The SS officer with the luger and the SD officer with the 38 special approached the men from behind and inserted the barrel of the gun just about one centimeter into the asshole of each Jew. They looked up at the rest of the soldiers watching and fired. The bullet from the German Luger apparently lodged in the skull of one of them since it remained in the body while the bullet from the 38 Special went through the other man's spine and skull into the wall that he was leaning against blowing off almost half of the top of his scalp. They stood for a few minutes and examined the bodies and returned to the bar for some more drinks after wiping the barrels of the pistols on the dead men's shirts. They were not that happy that the American pistol was more powerful except, of course, for the owner of the 38 Special as he did not have to pay for any drinks for the rest of the day. The bodies remained in the alley unnoticed for the entire night. The owner of a neighboring store that used the alley to take out his garbage discovered the bodies the next morning and notified the police who in turn notified us."

The police had been called so they questioned the bar owner who told them the story. The police, in turn, told the story to the ambulance driver. The men were not robbed. They had their money and jewelry. This was not a robbery this was merely a weapons test. We were able to notify each man's family. They had been worried sick but had already prepared themselves for the worst. When a Jew did not come home at night without calling, the family knew that he was either in a hospital, had been arrested or was dead. In many cases, there was very little likelihood that they would ever see the missing family member alive again.

On November 15, 1938 Jewish children were formally expelled from all schools and the "Decree on the Exclusion of Jews from Cultural Life" was enacted. Jews were not allowed to attend plays, movies, concerts, sporting events, or any public exhibition. With the passage of these two decrees a series of additional measures were included:

- Jews had to surrender of all precious metals, typically gold and silver, to the government

- Government, military and civil service pensions to Jews were eliminated

- Stocks, bonds, jewelry, art works and similar convertible valuables could be transferred or sold only to the government

- Jews could no longer keep pigeons as they could be used to send messages

- Jews could no longer get or keep a drivers license

- All radios were to be surrendered to the authorities

- Tenant laws/leases were no longer applicable to Jews. As such, they no longer had rights to the apartments and houses they rented and could be forced out at a moments notice with some exceptions.

On December 3, the Aryanization of all remaining Jewish assets began in Vienna – but in a much more orderly "legal" fashion to keep everything intact with some concessions given such as exit permits to make it appear more voluntary and legitimate to the international community. Until the war actually started Hitler was very cognizant of the power of the press and international opinion. He did not want to be challenged for his actions by a united Allied coalition that could include America. America had the largest Jewish population in the world and he believed that the "Jewish element" was so strong that they could possibly force the government to change its isolationist policy and support England and France in any action against Germany. This he had to avoid.

Even with Himmler's directive, each week at least three Jewish men and older boys were brought to the morgue. In some cases the identification of the bodies was not possible due to the severe facial beatings and the removal of all of their valuables. Many of the men and boys were brought in with their pants off or around their ankles. While some Jewish men had forged identity papers or did not look Jewish if there was any suspicion that they were Jewish they would be asked to drop their pants. Often, without provocation, a group of Hitler Youth would walk up to a man if he looked Jewish, take him into an alley or into a secluded doorway and have him drop his pants even though they did not have the authority to do this. You could have the best forged papers but you could not hide your circumcised penis. Any least bit hesitation was met with violence that could result in a severe beating, especially if the person was found to be Jewish.

Any Jew killed by the Gestapo or the SS went unpunished. For example, one SS Sergeant was particularly barbaric. His name was Hans Joerdl. His stated goal was to kill one Jew a day when he was on duty and he liked to do it at around 1 PM right after he had eaten lunch when the streets were crowded with people still going to or returning from lunch. As he would often tell his cohorts, "There is nothing as satisfying as killing a Jew for dessert." He would have four or five SS soldiers with him and randomly select one or more Jews by setting up a mini-roadblock on the sidewalk and inspecting the papers of people walking in the street. Sometimes he would see some Jews dressed in their black coats with their paises (long sideburns) and stop them. He would order them to drop their pants. If they did not move fast enough he would shoot one of them in the foot or in the thigh and laugh while they tried to pull down their pants after being shot in the leg and limping around. Sometimes he would shoot the person next to the one that he ordered to drop his pants if that person didn't move fast enough. He would kill the person that was slowest in dropping his pants or kill the Jew who initially hesitated for causing him to shoot the other Jew. Once when a Hassidic family of five was stopped he ordered the youngest son, who was about nine years old, to drop his pants. The young boy was embarrassed and hesitated so he shot and killed his older sister blaming the boy. "See what you have done, Jew-boy, you have killed your sister!"

One of his favorite ways to decide who was to die was to have the group perform some tedious exercise or bit of work. Whoever lasted the longest would be the winner and as a prize the winner would be executed. "Can't have any fit Jews around!" he would laugh as he rewarded the winner. Sometimes he ordered the survivors to piss on the slain Jew. Fearful and embarrassed they could not readily piss. They had to stand there until they could piss while everyone was watching. Some stood for one or two hours before they were able to relieve themselves and were constantly hit in the stomach or sides near their kidneys to expedite the process. After they pissed they could leave but the last one was beaten again for "keeping everyone waiting". Once a woman walked by and saw that her husband was one of the men standing there with his penis out trying to piss on the dead body. Without thinking she ran to him. This delighted the sergeant who ordered her to stand behind him, wrap her arms around his waist and shake his penis up and down and sideways to help him piss. They cracked jokes and made other obscene comments until he was able to piss.

Sometimes, some male had not declared that he was Jewish so when he was ordered to drop his pants he panicked and ran. He was typically shot in the back and killed as he was running away. The SS thought it great fun to humiliate private Austrian citizens particularly if they were not members of the Nazi Party. They seldom bothered older people or anyone with children. A favorite target of a particular group of SS soldiers was a young couple obviously out on a date. They would question them, take them aside and have the boy drop his pants asking his date to look at his exposed penis and examine it to make sure it wasn't circumcised. They would always make snide comments about it. Once, I was told that a young man actually got aroused and got an erection during the inspection so they asked his girlfriend to jerk him off "to see if it really worked" while they laughed. In spite of the ridicule, he climaxed. His obviously embarrassed girlfriend had to pull up his pants and tuck his limp wet penis into his underpants as she pulled them up. Once a non-Jewish youth visiting from Italy who did not speak German panicked and ran when he was ordered to drop his pants. He was also shot in the back and killed but his death was blamed on a robbery and his family was told that the police had killed the robber, who was a Jew. All of his personal property was recovered from the Jew and returned to the family with an official apology for "still having these criminal Jewish elements" in Vienna. Jewish males that had not declared that they were Jewish that dropped their pants when ordered were almost always shot on the spot or directly in the genitals and lay in the street until they bled to death. This gave rise to an expression that having a circumcised penis was "a dead giveaway!" I doubt that anyone who uses this expression today knows its origin.

I traveled to work early in the morning when it was still dark outside since very few people, including Nazis, were up and about and tried not to leave the morgue after 7 PM to go home. If it was after 7 PM I would sleep in the morgue in one of the small storerooms in the basement where I hid a sleeping bag, some clothes and toiletries. The Nazis would sometimes set up random checkpoints during the morning rush hour to check identities but they rarely set them up between 5 PM and 7 PM. This was an informal situation where a group of SD or SS would just stop people walking in the street and ask to see their papers. The rationale was that workers would not mind too much if they were a little late getting to work since they could tell their bosses that they were delayed at an SS or Gestapo checkpoint but they would mind being late after work when they were going home for dinner which was their own time. After all, the original name of the party was the National Socialist Worker's Party so they had the worker's best interest at heart. Once the curfew for Jews was set at 8 PM they randomly stopped people at night to make sure that they were not Jews violating the curfew. As long as the streets were crowded during the day I felt safe since I was a party member and had all of the correct papers. I was occasionally stopped for a spot check during the day but was never detained and was never asked to drop my pants. I always yelled Heil Hitler and proudly held the lapel of my jacket or collar of my shirt out with my other hand showing the pin in case they didn't notice as I gave them my papers. My salute was always enthusiastically returned. Most of the time, the soldier apologized and didn't even ask to see any identification. When I did go home late for some special reason that warranted the risk, I took back alleys and other shortcuts to get to my apartment fearing that if I was stopped at night I could be put to the ultimate test – the dropping of my pants. I even thought about gluing my extra foreskin to the head of my penis but I painfully remembered the results of my attempts to do this when I was eight years old.

In spite of all these precautions I was seen in the alley one cold night in late December by a soldier who was a bit drunk and had stopped in the alley to relieve himself while the others in his group waited at the other end of the alley. I did not see him in the dark back doorway of one of the businesses there relieving himself so I proceeded down the alley. When he saw me, he turned towards me and immediately asked what I was doing. I told him that this was a short cut to my home. He called to the others. They suspected that I was a Jew trying to avoid being caught by taking the back alleys at night. They did not ask for any identification and would not listen as I told them that I was a party member, since they said that anyone could buy a pin, even a Jew. They just decided on the ultimate test as they ordered me to drop my pants. It was very cold that night and as I dropped my pants the head of my penis shriveled up into the extra fold of foreskin that the Mohel left on me. One of the Germans shined the light from a flashlight down at my penis. To both of our surprise it appeared as if I was not circumcised. He turned off the light and told me to go home which I did – but not before going into a lighted doorway on a deserted street and pulling out my penis again. Sure enough, the ultra cold weather caused the head of my penis to withdraw under the extra fold of foreskin. It was totally hidden. Looking from the bottom of my penis and pulling the foreskin back a bit, I could clearly see the circumcision scar but without manually retracting it, it looked uncircumcised. I quickly went home thinking that I was indeed lucky that I was stopped in the winter and not the summer and that the Mohel missed the mark. In any case, I now started to rethink about ways to cover the head of my penis with the extra flesh left on by the Mohel. Even though my first experience at eight years old was a painful disaster, pain is much better than death. I again tried all forms of glue but they either did not hold or gave me a horrible rash or would tear my flesh if I happened to get sexually excited. I even thought of using surgical thread to sew the skin but realized that it would not work as I would have to stitch the flesh directly to the head of my penis which would be extremely painful and would surely get infected. I also thought of the damage an erection would do to any stitches as well as to my penis. This occupied my thoughts for much of the day and night and started to interfere with my sleep. I knew I had to come up with a solution. In the meantime, I vowed never to go out late at night again.

January 5, 1939 is a date that I will never forget. I was working the night shift. It was late that Friday night about two weeks after the alley incident. It was still snowing hard when they were brought in at 11:14 PM. Five students on their way back to their university in Salzburg after the Christmas holidays were in a car that crashed. The driver was evidently in a hurry and was speeding. He was apparently not drunk as I could not detect any alcohol on his breath or body nor did the police report finding any liquor bottles in the car. Due to the speed that the car was traveling at the time, it skidded off of the slippery road on a sharp curve, turned over and caught fire after careening off of a tree. All five students were killed as they were trapped in the burning car. There were two girls and three boys.

Due to the fire the bodies of the students were burned extensively. The burns covered about seventy percent of their bodies – with one notable exception. Two of the male students had urinated in fear at the time of impact so their genital areas were not burned. I opened their pants to confirm my initial observation. So here I was looking at two perfect penises highlighted amid the charred flesh of their burned bodies. I thought to myself that the only part of the burnt body that was not destroyed was the part we Jews could use the most. That's when I got the idea as I focused on the unburned penises. Was there a way to benefit from this odd occurrence? Could I remove their penises and somehow adapt one of them to cover my penis like a glove or apply it in some other fashion such as wrapping it around my penis like a scarf? It was worth a try.

I took a scalpel and proceeded with some highly unorthodox surgery. With the first one, I slit the skin from underneath and pulled the skin off of the penis. It got messy at the head of the penis and had some thin spots but it was whole. For the second I just cut off the entire penis and scooped out the internal meat. I covered the area back up with their pants, took some embalming fluid and poured it over the pubic area of both students and ignited it. Now these corpses were burned on about 90 percent of their bodies and no one could easily see that two of the boys had no penises (assuming anyone would even look for them anyway). This turned out to be the case. The families all opted for cremation or a closed casket funeral on the advice of the funeral parlors.

The penis is a muscle with many blood vessels. It is the pumping of blood into the penis that causes the expansion of the blood vessels that in turn causes the erection. The penis itself is highly elastic due to this feat of nature. I believed that this interwoven set of blood vessels was not too easy to remove which was why I first tried to slit and skin the first one. With the second technique, scooping out the insides, the walls of the penis stayed much stronger compared to slitting and skinning. I first tried the slit penis wrapping it around my penis but it was too loose and could not be easily tied on to my penis. After a few attempts, I put it under the hood, covered it with embalming fluid and incinerated it. I slipped the other whole hollow uncircumcised penis that I had cut off over mine. It easily stretched to cover mine completely. I attached it at the base with a string but that didn't work so I attached it with some of the glue that did not give me a rash. Looking in the mirror, I was pleasantly surprised. It looked like the real thing. You could not tell that it was not my penis – and it obviously proved that I was not circumcised no matter from which angle you looked. I made one further modification in that I cut some of my pubic hair and pasted it around the base of the attached penis. This effectively hid the glue line so it really looked like my own penis. It changed my life.

I could now travel freely day and night. I did not have to sleep in the storeroom anymore although I still kept some clothes and toiletries there. I could go home at night as late as I wanted. I could go to a restaurant for dinner without worrying about being discovered as a Jew. I had renewed confidence. I was even more outspoken at work due to the extra confidence my new penis gave me. I am sure that Freud would have some psychological explanation of this phenomenon but as he had fled Vienna some time ago I was not able to ask him.

Having a penis covered with another penis had some serious inconveniences. First, you could not urinate too well through it. In fact, you really couldn't urinate at all. At first I tried to align my penis opening with the opening of the attached penis but this did not work well. Even when I made the hole on the attached penis bigger it did not work well at all. While some urine came out of the opening on the attached penis most did not so the attached penis swelled up like a balloon from the trapped liquid. I had to cut a hole at the base of the penis to let the trapped urine drain out as I squeezed it. This worked much better but was very messy, took a long time to drain completely and I had to squeeze it a number of times to get all of the urine out. This clearly could not be done standing up at a urinal in a public restroom. The only way to urinate with the false penis was sitting down in a stall and either totally removing the attached penis or by sitting and squeezing out any urine that would not freely drain from the hole at the bottom. Still a bit messy and time consuming but effective. The best way was to remove it completely while in the stall, urinate and re-attach it when finished. I tried this process a couple of times using a knife to cut along the glue line. This reduced the length of the attached penis so after a little more than one week it was too short to adequately cover my own penis. Once, in a restaurant bathroom, while using the knife to carefully cut the false penis at the glue line, a man, obviously in dire need, burst into the adjacent bathroom stall shoving the door open with great force and banging it against my stall. It startled me so much that I cut myself rather severely. It took almost fifteen minutes for the bleeding to stop. The waiter came into the bathroom after about ten minutes to see what the problem was. I told him that I had an upset stomach. When I finally stopped the bleeding and returned to the table, I asked for the check even though I had not finished my meal. The waiter called over the manager who was very concerned that the dinner had caused the problem. He was prepared to not have me pay for the meal but I told him that I had just started a new, strong medication and was warned that it could cause an upset stomach so I insisted on paying the bill. When I got home I dressed the wound better and resolved to again look for an alternative to cutting off the false penis with a regular knife lest I emasculate myself as I was doing to the dead males.

Pulling the penis cover off without cutting it was painful and damaged it at the glue line. I tried using a solvent to loosen the glue but it took too long, was messy, gave me a rash and interfered with the application of new glue if any of the solvent was not totally washed away. Cutting was really the only option. I just had to remain calm and avoid a repeat cutting accident which meant that whenever someone entered the bathroom I would stop cutting the penis until I heard what he was doing. I started looking around the city for the smallest knife that I could find. After about three days of searching I found one in a hobby shop that was used to carve intricate details on the balsa wood used to make model airplanes. The knife was made in Switzerland and was quite expensive for its size but the blade was adjustable and fit into a case. It was absolutely perfect. I went to every hobby store in the city and bought one or two of these knives from each store that carried this particular knife. By the end of the week I had nine of them.

I also had to control my sexual feelings. One strong erection and either the cover would split apart or would just separate from the glued ends, which was often painful and looked like a hat on my erect penis. The latter was not too bad as I could re-attach it when my erection went down but with my luck I could get my identity challenged at that very moment. Dropping my pants at that time would have been the end of me. So now I decided to carry a spare penis cover just in case the one I had on split apart or was damaged at the glue line when separated from the base by an erection or by a faulty removal.

There was also an issue of time. The false penis would discolor from the residual urine or crack and lose its flexibility over time. The attached penis would only last about three weeks at the most before deteriorating or discoloring to the point of being useless or becoming too short from the repeated cutting and re-attaching. Every time I removed the penis cover, I left a small piece attached to my body. It was almost impossible to cut it off exactly at the glue line without the risk of cutting my skin so the cut was actually made a little above the glue line. To decrease the frequency of urinating I changed my eating and drinking habits. First I gave up coffee and tea in the morning. I also gave up beer unless I was with people that were drinking but I drank very slowly so I had only one beer for every two or three that they drank. I would also wait until the last possible moment before urinating. This practice did not actually last too long. It was just too uncomfortable and sometimes painful. A couple of times I held it in for so long that I had trouble urinating when I finally did decide to go to the bathroom and became worried that if I could not urinate on my own that I would have to be taken to a hospital which would have blown my cover, so to speak.

I also had an issue on preserving the spare penis covers. If I just left them out exposed to the air or in a jar with air in it, they would dry out and get brittle. If I stored them in water they would swell and distort. They could not be used at all and I really needed to have a supply of spare covers. I tried all sorts of preserving methods from soaking it in saltwater, alcohol, embalming fluid and other chemicals. While some extended the shelf life of the penis cover, they would also result in strong discoloration and odors. Having a brown or orange penis with a white body was not good even if it wasn't circumcised. After much trial and error I developed the technique of heating the penis in mineral oil for about two minutes and using some cosmetic cream for women's skin that I rubbed on the inside and outside of the cover until the cream was absorbed in the skin. This worked! This extended the shelf life of the penis cover to more than six weeks. Even with this extended time period it became quite evident that I would need to get a continuous supply of uncircumcised penises to maintain my ruse since the length would be too short after multiple removals. Luckily, for this purpose, size did not matter as long as it was from a fully developed male. Of course, the longer the penis the longer it lasted since it took longer to get to a size too small to re-attach from the repeated cutting.

Where, you might ask, did the supply of these penises come from? I was a mortician at the city morgue – need I say more? I had two types of available bodies. The first was from any unclaimed body which, unfortunately, did not happen too often. The second was from a poor family. They could not afford a private funeral home so when I offered to prepare the body for burial for a very low fee they gladly accepted and were very appreciative. As a result I had access to the body. Right before I embalmed the body I removed the penis. After embalming I dressed the body in the burial clothes provided by the family. Most of the time, I did this at night when I was alone in the room. If the embalming was done during the day when there was a chance of someone coming into the room, I would wait until night to get the penis. The embalming process did not affect the penis. If another mortician embalmed the body and it was left in the morgue overnight, I would sneak in at night and remove the penis. I can assure you that not one relative, friend or lover of the deceased asked to see the dead man's penis once they were in the coffin and dressed for burial. My low-cost body preparation was spread by word-of-mouth and I started to get requests from many people as soon as someone died. Instead of having the body sent to a private funeral parlor, they would have the body sent to the morgue after calling me to see if it was okay. At first, this was very good for me since it assured that I would have a steady stream of penises but what I did not think of when I was offering my services was that half of the people that died were women and that many of the males that were brought in were too old or too young to have acceptable penises. My extra-curricular work at the morgue tripled so I was working late almost every night.

Finally, it became so bad that I had to tell many people that I could not do it – but I would screen the calls and still offer my services for men that died between eighteen and sixty. Hopefully, no one would notice this restriction which could cause some people to possibly think that I was engaging in some type of homosexual necrophilia.

My apartment became a storage depot for removed penises. I would treat them as soon as I got home and was still experimenting with different storage techniques to see if I could extend the shelf life even further. I tried refrigeration, immersion in brine; airtight containers, under vacuum, etc. until finding the optimum method which was storing the treated penis in a mixture of mineral and sunflower oil. I had all sorts of chemicals and equipment at my disposal at the morgue so I had a miniature chemical laboratory hidden in my bedroom closet and a free-standing bureau in which I built a secret compartment. I worked on this late at night near an open window to minimize the chemical smell that could waft into the hallway. Even in the dead of winter I had to work with the window open wearing a heavy coat. I hoped that there was never a fire in the building or any reason to have my apartment searched. I also worried about a robbery so I added two more locks on the door and bars on the windows that could be opened from the inside.

Conditions for Jews further deteriorated in 1939. Wealthy Jews were still able to buy their way out of Austria but they also had to pay for poor Jews to emigrate with them. Many middle-class Jews were able to get money from relatives living abroad or from the various Jewish agencies in Switzerland or Palestine to be able to pay for themselves and some of the others. In addition, each émigré had to have entry papers from the country to which they were going to emigrate. To do this they had to have a sponsor. Most rich Jews had little difficulty in getting sponsors. Many middle-class Jews had relatives living abroad that could sponsor them. Some Jews that worked for international companies such as AT&T would have their company sponsor them. Poor Jews had a problem. Many wanted to leave but could not get sponsors. Many of them took courses to learn other professions and crafts such as becoming a plumber, electrician, carpenter, seamstress, etc. Having a skill that could result in immediate employment in the new host country significantly increased the chance of having an entry permit issued by the requisite government agency.

The Nazis knew approximately how much money each Jewish family had since they had to fill out the forms some months ago listing their wealth. Recognizing that the Jews did not really declare everything that they owned they always set a higher price than the reported assets depending upon the specific circumstances for each family. If the Jew owned a business, it was assumed that the larger the business, the larger the lie about how much wealth they had undeclared. Here again, some Jews actually were truthful in listing their assets so they now were penalized since the Nazis believed that they were lying and had much more hidden away. It was not good to be an "honest Jew" since that term did not exist in Nazi belief. Once the Nazis knew which Jews had relatives in the United States it further increased the price for them to leave the country. After all, the United States was the richest country in the world as were their Jews so they could pay more.

About 8,000 Jews were now leaving Austria each month. But for those that did not make the list because they had no money, no sponsors, and no exit permits or decided to stay for personal reasons, conditions further deteriorated. Beatings and humiliations occurred daily throughout the city whenever Jews were going to and from work or going shopping for food and other necessities. Jews living as Gentiles in Aryan neighborhoods were much safer but were still afraid of the penis test.

I still met with my five Jewish friends that had false identity papers and were pretending to be Gentile every Friday night without mentioning the procedure but now I felt it was time to reveal my secret for their safety and the safety of their families. I had accelerated the penis removals and brought ten spare penises to the meeting. I also had perfected the procedures for urinating, removal and reattachment, etc. On February 14, 1939 just about five weeks after removing the first two penises I decided to give the card group the opportunity to truly become Gentile. It was at the apartment of Karl for our weekly card game when I abruptly stood up from the table and dropped my pants. "What do think of this? Does it make me look Gentile?"

They all stared in amazement. One even asked if I was really Jewish or was I a spy getting ready to turn them in. I assured them that I was Jewish and explained what I had been doing for the past five weeks and took out one of the spares and laid it down on the table. They stared at it in disbelief. "Touch it!" I said, "It doesn't bite!" No one ventured to touch it as they sat and stared at it. After a minute or two of abject silence, Wilhelm took a pencil and poked it. It rolled across the table towards Friedrich, who reeled back defensively. We all laughed. It broke the awkward silence. I reached into my briefcase under the table and pulled out a small jar of the other nine uncircumcised penises from my briefcase.

"Alright, who wants to become a Gentile first?" I walked across the room to the couch and opened the jar of penises and took out the tubes of glue and the small knives that I had brought with me. There was some initial hesitation. Grown men do not show their penises to other men unless they are homosexual. They were all noticeably embarrassed as they looked at each other waiting to see who would be the first to drop his pants. Kurt was the first. He finally stood up, walked over to me and with his back to the others, dropped his pants. "Be gentle!" he jokingly said, "It's my first time with a man!"

That broke the ice as they all lined up and, in turn, dropped their pants to get "fitted". One of the men, I think it was Hermann, commented that the cover made his penis longer. He actually said that it extended his penis. From that time on we decided to refer to it as the "extension". The rest of the evening was spent on learning how to care for their new body part – what to do and what not to do, how to take showers, how to piss and how to try to avoid getting an erection (applying pain to the body) and how to repair the damage caused by an erection if you couldn't control yourself and, if possible, to remove the extension in time to avoid damage. I explained the need to carry the small special knife, a tube of glue and a spare extension in case the one they were wearing was damaged or destroyed. A key point was that if it was discovered that they were Jewish by some other method that they had to destroy the extensions, preferably by setting it and the spare they were carrying, on fire. The glue was flammable so if they had the time, they were told to take off the extension and the spare, squirt the glue all over them and set them on fire. So they also had to carry matches or a cigarette lighter, which meant that they also had to carry cigarettes, cigars or a pipe. I also emphasized that secrecy was of the essence. If they told one person too many who was arrested, tortured and forced to talk about Jews in hiding, not only would they be arrested and tortured but we all would as well. Torture betrays the best of us. It went without saying that we hoped that none of us ever were arrested. We agreed that we would never act independently on revealing that we had these extensions other than to our immediate families.

Kurt had a great idea. Since we had to carry the spare extension and a small tube of glue Kurt thought of a way to conceal these items just in case one of us was searched. He was a smoker so he took out a pack of cigarettes and said that he could modify the package to create a hidden compartment to store the spare extension and the small tube of glue. Cigarettes could be taken from one end of the pack. The other half of the pack would hold the spare extension and the small tube of glue which could be only be accessed from the bottom. The best way to hide this was to have a leather cigarette case in which the entire pack of cigarettes would fit. This would also justify the matches or a lighter. This was a great idea so we spent the rest of the evening watching Kurt modify six of the cigarette packs that Karl had in his apartment. In the morning, Karl visited a few cigarette stores and bought twelve leather cigarette cases, two for each of us. From then on, Karl's cigarette brand became the standard for everyone. This was a great idea since street searches for contraband were conducted once in a while and it would be difficult to explain why we were carrying a penis in our pocket without being arrested as a sexual deviant that had probably just murdered someone and cut off their penis.

Once they were all fitted we began talking about the extensions and what a brilliant thing it was. One thing led to another. We decided that we would try to help as many of the people that we knew that were posing as non-Jews as possible. At first I was hesitant. I just finished telling them about the need for secrecy and now we were completely reversing our position but the more I thought about it the more I realized that it was the right thing to do. After all, wasn't I taking the same risk by sharing my procedure with the five of them and their families? At this point, however, our only consideration was to help only those Jews who already had forged papers and were not known to be Jews. We made a list of all of these families and how many males were in the family. We identified eighteen males in the thirteen families pretending to be Gentiles. We discussed each family in great detail. We wanted to make sure that we were all comfortable in revealing our secret to them. We could not find any reason not to provide extensions to any of them. We now had our work cut out for us.

During the next two weeks we visited the Jewish families and introduced them to the extension. To say that each one was overjoyed by the revelation would be an understatement. They were, of course, also sworn to secrecy. They were not told anything about the origin of the extensions and the identity of anyone else. Luckily, none of the male children in any of the families were under twelve years old. They were old enough to realize the gravity of the situation so they could be trusted with the extension. They were still restricted from sports in case the extension was to fall off. They were not currently participating in sports due to their having a circumcised penis so it did not add any additional restriction to their daily activities but we had to emphasize this in case they felt that having the extension would now allow them to participate in sports. We made them take an oath in front of their parents that they would not participate in sports or in any activity that could result in damage to the extension or exposure. We emphasized sex as well. They understood perfectly.

This placed an enormous burden on me. To adequately supply eighteen males with their own extension and a spare required thirty-six Gentile penises. Until then I was able to get one penis out of about twenty dead male bodies. Most of the bodies brought in were claimed by their families and brought to private mortuaries for embalming. As I mentioned the supply of penises came primarily from indigent men whose families could not afford private mortuaries, from unclaimed bodies or from the embalming that I was doing for poor families. In addition, I was competing with the medical schools that always needed cadavers for their students. I could not send a penis-less cadaver to a medical school. I obviously had to extend my supply base. Getting access to private mortuaries was the only way to ensure a steady supply. To do this I recruited three of the young men from the families that we had selected to get the extensions. Two were about nineteen and had no jobs since they had been worried about being discovered as Jews. They had been university students but dropped out when it became too dangerous for them to continue to go to school lest they be discovered to be Jewish. The other one was twenty two and had a job as a salesman in a department store which was very easy to give up. I gave them a crash course in anatomy and brought them to the morgue at night to teach them about embalming and the other aspects of working with dead people. While finding this distasteful, they realized the importance of it and excelled at it. Within two weeks they were ready. I secured some false papers for them attesting that they had been medical school drop-outs for family reasons and they each applied to work at a different large private funeral home that had their own mortuary. As private mortuaries were always understaffed in this area (for some reason not many men wanted this type of job) all three were immediately hired during their first interview. Moreover, they all volunteered to work late at night and on weekends which brought them strong favor with the existing workers who could now go home on time and did not have to work as many weekends as well as with the owners, who could actually take on more business. Since this was a salaried position, the workers did not make any extra money working nights and weekends nor did any of the existing workers lose any income if they did less work. This was another win-win situation. They were vey popular and were given complete unsupervised access to the mortuary. This was exactly what we needed. It gave them private, after-hours access to many dead male Gentile bodies. We were now able to obtain ten to fifteen uncircumcised penises a week selecting only the largest penises. At first, they were very worried that they would be discovered but after a couple of weeks they realized that what I told them was true – no one asks to see the penis of a deceased loved one once they were embalmed and dressed for burial.

One thing I can tell you. Regardless of what you may hear from a woman, to us size does matter. It was impossible to fit a well-endowed male with a penis from a smaller less-endowed male. There was a limit to a penis' elasticity.

Even with the three men working at the private funeral parlors, I continued to emasculate as many as four deceased Gentile males prior to their burial each month. It almost seemed that it was becoming a hobby. I could just see myself in a conversation if the subject of hobbies came up at work.

So, Anton, what do you collect?

I collect stamps, mainly from Europe

And you, Hans?

I collect coins

And you, Michael?

I collect uncircumcised penises. Care to try one on?

I had created the "Extension of Life"

CHAPTER TEN

EXPANSION

"And whoever saves a life, it is considered as if he saved an entire world."

> The Talmud, a Jewish book of learning (also the inscription engraved in the ring given to Oskar Schindler by those he saved, Schindler's List)

To reinforce the need to emigrate, the persecutions became endemic. As I mentioned, dead Jewish males were still being brought into the morgue daily. Jews were still leaving Austria at high rates. As many as 4,000 Jews per month were leaving in the second half of 1939. The two key factors were that they received their entry permit to a country that would accept them and that they also received their exit permits after paying their back taxes which meant that they had nothing left and were leaving the country destitute. They were meticulously searched at the border to make sure they had not hidden anything of value. If anything was found it was confiscated and they could be held up at the border for days with every bit of luggage and clothing examined or they could be sent back to Vienna. This was at the discretion of the officer in charge.

On October 11, 1939 deportations of Jews from Vienna to ghettos and concentration camps formally began with the deportation of 1,500 Jews to the Nisko Ghetto in Poland. Using lists that were at the IKG office the Nazis selected the people and had the IKG notify them to show up at the IKG headquarters at 9 AM for relocation to the east. They were to bring one suitcase for each person. This was the first and last time that the Nazis selected the Jews for deportation. They randomly selected one family from different buildings. All subsequent lists were the responsibility of the IKG.

At the appointed hour most were already there. Only a few were late. They were kept waiting all day. At 6PM the trucks arrived to take them away. This was again done to emphasize the need to emigrate. It worked. Emigration increased.

In early November we decided to expand the "program" to help known Jewish men and their families escape from Austria. We knew that there were many Jews that could not get exit visas since they did not have a sponsor in another country. However, we couldn't just provide extensions to known Jews and transform them into Gentiles and have them continue living and working in the city. They were known to be Jews. Having them just disappear was not a problem. Jews disappeared every day. Just relocating them to another district under a new name was too risky. What if some one they knew recognized them? We decided that the only way that this would work was if we were able to get them to leave Austria illegally. Jews could not travel out of Vienna. Any Jew caught outside the city was returned to Vienna, sent to a concentration camp or simply shot on the spot. It was up to the arresting officer to decide. If they were caught at the border trying to get out of Austria they were often able to bribe the guards to be returned to Vienna. Most of the guards did this because they realized that the Jew would try again and that if he was caught again they would receive another bribe. This actually happened a number of times. One young Jewish man whom we helped by giving him money tried four times to cross the border into Croatia illegally. He was caught and returned three times. He mentioned that he now knew the names of the guards and some of their personal life. When he did not come back the fourth time we assumed that he had made it – or he was dead. The former was confirmed about two weeks later when his family received a post card from him from Zagreb.

We decided to implement the escape plan. We would take one or two known Jewish families, fit the males with the extensions just in case they were stopped on their trip and provide false identification and travel documents to smuggle them out of Austria into Switzerland. While Switzerland was far away, it was the safest place being a neutral country with most people very sympathetic to the plight of the Jews. Once across the border we felt that they would be allowed to remain in the country if discovered. In addition, most of the Jewish relief organizations had offices there. There were some other reasons as well. First, very few people wanted to go to Czechoslovakia, Hungary, Poland or Yugoslavia as they were totally different environments culturally and linguistically. Once there they had no one to turn to. Even though there were Jews in the bigger cities they did not know them and did not feel comfortable with them. In addition, essentially all of the Jews illegally leaving Vienna could not travel across Austria so they tried to cross the border into these countries. As a result the border was more heavily guarded on both sides. None of these countries wanted more Jews. At least in Switzerland they spoke German and we could provide some contacts there. After only a few minutes of discussion we unanimously agreed that Switzerland was the only real option.

We also decided on Switzerland even though these other countries were closer due to our belief that these other countries would either be conquered by Hitler or would join him. As we found out later, we were right. Yugoslavia had been created by the Allies after the First World War. It consisted of a number of ethnic areas that wanted to be independent. Hitler recognized that and for their collaboration they were made independent countries. Yugoslavia was split into Croatia, Serbia and Slovenia as independent pro-Nazi countries. The pro-Nazi Croatian (Ustasa) fascist government set up a concentration camp at Jasenovac which was a complex of several sub-camps, in close proximity to each other, on the bank of the Sava River, about 100 km south of Zagreb. The women's camp of Stara Gradiska, which was farther away, also belonged to the complex. Most of the Austrian Jews that escaped to Croatia were arrested without warning and sent to Jasenovac where not one survived. Arrests, murders and deportations occurred in Serbia and, to a lesser extent, in Slovenia. When we found this out we were extremely happy that we had decided on Switzerland as the only viable country.

To facilitate the escape, we decided to set up an underground escape system modeled after the Negro slave escape route set up before the American Civil War. The American system provided food and shelter for the runaway slaves along a secret route in safe houses as they were transported to the North where they would be free. The Swiss border was about 450 kilometers (285 miles) from Vienna. The roads and rail system were very good. By road, the trip would take about 16 hours in good weather. Heavy traffic congestion could add up to four hours to the trip. Since there were often random searches, particularly late at night to catch smugglers we decided that travel would only be during the day. Our next step was to find people in each identified city that would help us. Meanwhile, we would only use the trains, which was a bit riskier due to the number of stops and the close contact the escapees would have with their fellow passengers. We were not sure how comfortable they would be on the train in the presence of the other passengers so if they appeared very nervous or said something wrong in response to innocent conversation, they could be discovered. We did not want to send any families with small children on the train for security reasons.

Eight cities were selected based on conversations with the many Jews that were forced to move to Vienna from those cities. Without revealing our intentions, we had Dr. Nussbaum ask his patients about any people they trusted in those cities. He also asked three other doctors that he trusted to do the same. Two weeks later we had a list of three or four people in each city. Three of the safe houses were in cities were near the Swiss border where we planned to cross, Three were on the roads to these cities, and two were just outside Vienna in different directions. We traveled to the cities on the list each weekend and through discrete conversations with the suggested people mentioning who had given us their name and why we were there, we were able to set up the network. All of the people that agreed to help us were close personal friends or had sons or daughters married to a Jew. They were all very willing to work with us recognizing the risk that they were taking.

With the safe houses in each city set up, we formulated our escape program. The only way the program would work was if the selected person, couple or family would agree to flee the country relatively quickly, within a few days of being selected, and not say anything about their leaving to anyone else, be it family or friends. They had to essentially suddenly disappear as if they had been deported by the Nazis to a concentration camp. We would spread rumors that this had occurred.

We simultaneously still tried to find Jewish families that had false papers that were able to live undetected as Gentiles. Dr. Nussbaum contacted all of the other Jewish doctors to see if they had any patients that were pretending to be Gentiles and were able to get two more names. We also decided to try to find as many Jews as possible that were in hiding. Some Viennese people hid Jews from the Nazis in secret rooms in their houses or businesses. With finding the Jews being hidden by Gentiles, however, we had competition. One thing the Nazis were very good at was to get local people to work for them. So the Nazis were able to find a few Jews and many non-Jews who would work for them as informants in return for special consideration. For Jews it was a "guarantee" that they and their families would not be deported to a concentration camp. Non-Jews were paid a bounty for each Jew and person hiding a Jew that they found. They became "Jew-hunters". We knew about this and were able to identify some of them through Mischa. However, we knew that there were many others that Mischa could not identify as he had no access to other precincts' records. We knew that we had to be very careful in the selection process so we devised the following set of rules:

- Jewish men in hiding or men not known to be Jewish by the authorities whom we found out about, investigated and trusted would be given the extension so they could emerge from hiding. We would provide documents that showed that they were Gentiles living in another city and had just come to Vienna to find a better job. We would provide both original and forged identity papers to prove that they were not Jewish. We would get jobs for them so they would be able to live openly as Gentiles.

- If the authorities knew that a man was Jewish there would not be any point in providing the extension unless he and his family agreed to flee the country within a couple of days. We would arrange for their trip out of Austria to Switzerland.

- If they were Orthodox Jews and dressed accordingly, they would not be given the opportunity to escape.

- No Communists would be selected.

- If a person in the family had an alcohol or drug abuse problem the family would not be selected as the risk was too high. This information we hoped would come from their family doctors.

- If anyone in the family were even remotely suspected to be cooperating in any form with the Nazis, they were not to be offered the opportunity to escape.

- No one would be told of the extension until the eve of their departure.

To manage the program, we decided to set up independent groups around the city headed by men that we trusted implicitly. Each group would only know who was in their group and have no contact with anyone from another group. A group would have no more than three members and would be responsible for finding hiding Jews and conducting the investigation to see if they were trustworthy along with our help as needed.

Friedrich, the dentist, was responsible for setting up the central information database and the forgery center where we would prepare the false documents along with providing some real ones. He enlisted five people. Three were Jewish and two were not. The two non-Jewish men were his patients. They were Swiss and they were anti-Nazi. Friedrich learned this from their office conversations before and after Anschluss. Friedrich would subtly steer the conversation to how the person felt about the unification of Austria with Germany to all of his foreign patients. There were mixed responses. Some were decidedly for it and Friedrich vehemently agreed. Some were non committal as was Friedrich. A small minority were openly against it. In these instances Friedrich said nothing. There have been instances where someone was actually working for the Nazis trying to ferret out anyone not fully supporting the Nazis. Of that small minority against it, most were Swiss with the remainder being from Central Europe. Not that Austrians openly admitted that they did not fully support the Nazis – at least to him. Only a few did not believe in the persecution of Jews. Abel Schwechter was one of them. He was Swiss. What made him particularly attractive to Friedrich was his unique talent. He was an engraver and artist for the Austrian mint which, of course, was why Friedrich had singled him out to join us.

At work he had access to all sorts of printing and engraving supplies. He was also able to copy signatures perfectly. Anton Fischer was also chosen for his unique position. He worked for the Ministry of Communications as an electrical engineer and was very good at fixing broken radios, transmitters and all sorts of electrical equipment. He had access to walkie-talkies and wire tapping equipment, some of which he managed to smuggle out of the Ministry for our use. He also had access to all of the non-secret files stored there. Goebbels chose the Ministry of Communications building to be the Ministry of Information and Propaganda headquarters for Austria and for the Eastern territories of Bohemia and Moravia, Hungary, and Czechoslovakia due to the communications capability which he started to build up as soon the country was annexed. It also became the central records center for all Nazi officers in the country. As such Anton was able to obtain dossiers on all of the German officers and other important Nazis stationed in Austria or being transferred to Austria.

I was never to be identified nor was the source of the extension to be revealed. The recipients were never told that it was a real penis from a dead Gentile. They were told that it was artificially made from a ram. Secrecy was also maintained to fullest extent possible. While most accepted the explanation some knew or suspected otherwise but said nothing. Their facial expressions gave their thoughts away when they were given the "ram" explanation. Five of the men and two of their sons that we initially fitted with extensions agreed to be group leaders in their districts. These seven districts covered more than 95 percent of the Jews living in the city. They worked with one or two other known Jews in their district. Each of us in the card group was responsible for being the sole contact with one or two of the group leaders.

For Jews in hiding that elected to emerge from hiding and for Jews that were pretending to be Gentile, we had to train them on the art of applying the extension and the other requisite items such as urinating. The best way to do this was to have someone wearing the extension go to the house of the new recipient, show the males what it looked like and perform the miraculous religious conversion.

So, we began a program of house calls for extension installation and maintenance.

Supplying forged papers was relatively easy since we had the help of Abel Schwechter, our Swiss group member that was the engraver at the mint. There were two basic needs. One was an identity card and the other was the Ahnenpass which was a booklet containing the person's family history (family tree) going back at least three generations showing that there were no Jews. Getting an Ahnenpass was actually quite easy. You could buy them in many stores. You filled out the form and had it notarized providing copies of certain items such as birth and baptism certificates. Once verified you were declared to be a pure Aryan as long as you did not have any Jews in your family going back at least two generations with three or four generations of history even better. A pure Aryan could trace his lineage back to their Great, Great Grandparents without having any Jews. In reality, most people could not document their lineage beyond their Great Grandparents with many not even being able to go that far back.

Most of the birth and baptism certificates from small cities, towns and villages were very simple forms and were easily duplicated and forged. In addition, the two women that we placed in Heinrich's employ at the records office were able to get us actual death and pre-1910 birth certificates for family members for the people we fitted. Jews in hiding were the easiest since we could give them the actual family names of Gentiles that had a long history of living and dying in Vienna. Forging the identity card (kennkarte) was much more difficult at first. They were produced on special paper with an oilcloth cover that was even harder to duplicate. There were various hand stamps in them but these were easy for Abel to duplicate. The only difference between a Jewish identity card and passport from an Aryan/non-Jewish identity card and passport was that all Jewish identity cards had a large black printed "J" on the cover and the passport (Reisepass) had a large red "J" stamped on the first page. Some time later the regular name of the person had to have "Sara" for a woman and "Israel" for a man written as their middle name. This included anything that a Jewish person wrote (letters, return addresses) and legal forms. Failure to do this was punishable by imprisonment and possibly death.

Identity card (Kennkarte) and passport (Reisepass) with the J for Jew (Jude). (Source: Author's Personal Collection)

Our first attempts at forging the identity cards were not that good. However, that did not last long. I soon realized that in addition to having access to deceased people, I also had access to their personal belongings in many instances, which, of course, included identity cards, passports, pictures and a myriad of personal effects. Depending upon the person and how they died I could easily take some things. Once we had the originals it was very easy to substitute the picture of the deceased with the person of our choice. Some of the people that were brought into the morgue were victims of violent crime or accidents so it was easy just to take what I needed as if the documents were not there when they were brought into the morgue. Often a robber would take all of the valuables and not take personal items of identification so if they were arrested they could not be directly tied to the victim of the just-completed theft. Sometimes, I was called to the home of a murder, suicide or death where there was no family doctor available where I could manage to take some of the things

I needed. During the day I had to compete with the other medical examiners to go to the scene but when it was late at night I had a clear field to go to the death scene since no one else wanted to go. I let it be known that I was available at any time during the night to go to the scene of a crime or to someone's house if they died at home. Here again, I scored points with my co-workers. As I was the only unmarried person on the coroner's staff I used that as the reason for volunteering. All the rest were married and had children. They were often called during the night to go to a crime scene. Now, with me volunteering, they were hardly called at all. I also told them that I did not sleep too much at night anyway which was a result of my attending school during the day and having a full time job at night. Between traveling to school, to my job and back home and doing the homework, I had very little time to sleep. After six years of following this regimen I was able to function with much less sleep than most. They were extremely appreciative and as a result would honor any request that I made during working hours.

If a person died at home the opportunity to get documents and personal effects was the best. Whenever a body was discovered at the deceased's home where a family doctor was not in attendance, a Coroner or an Assistant Coroner had to go to the place of death to certify that the death was from natural causes before the body could be moved. It was often very easy for me to take the documents.

We also decided to set up an entire infrastructure to facilitate our rescue efforts. As most of us were of above average income with some being quite wealthy, money was not a problem. We purchased or rented the following properties:

- A dry-cleaning store where we set up our forgery operation. We staffed the store with some of the Jews in hiding that we fitted with the extension that wanted to emerge from hiding. This gave them a job and started them on a new life. The dry cleaning store was a good front to obtain all of the necessary chemicals that we needed. All of the items we needed such as ink could be openly purchased. Moreover, the cleaning fluids masked the smell of the printing inks and other chemicals that we used

- Three rented safe houses which were large apartments in commercial areas where very few people lived. They were used to hold the families prior to their departure

- Two cars and two small vans

- A furniture store that had two large moving vans which we fitted with a secret compartment by installing a folding wall about two-thirds from the backdoor. When not in use the wall could be removed. When it was needed it was easily and quickly fitted onto some special hinges on the inside walls of the van. The closed compartment could hold up to eight people fairly comfortably

- Two garages near the furniture store in which we parked one car and one van. We also used these garages to store food, clothing, and other supplies

On November 23, 1939 all Jews were required to wear a large yellow six-pointed star of David on the left breast area of all their outer garments upon penalty of arrest and even death. The IKG was given responsibility for preparing and distributing the stars. This made Jews obvious targets for ridicule, robbery, beatings and persecution whenever they were outside. Life was now extremely difficult and dangerous. Before this was enacted most Jews could blend in with the general population and were not obvious targets for gangs and vicious anti-Semites unless they were Hassidic Jews or "looked Jewish" and were asked to see their identity cards. Jews now lived in constant fear. They could be followed home and have their home robbed and be beaten in the process, especially if they resisted. They could be waylaid on the street but the robbers could be apprehended by the Gestapo and their many agents so it was better to wait until they were home.

To find Jews that would be willing to flee the country, we asked our trusted friends in the Jewish agency, the IKG, as they were required by the Nazis to maintain this information and set up deportation schedules, to help us. They selected individuals, couples and families that they felt could not emigrate on their own but were trying. We gave them a short list of the information we needed such as if they had children, lived with other family members in the same building, etc. We also tried to find out who were their family doctors so Dr. Nussbaum could find out if there were any health problems. We knew that the doctors would not talk to us but felt that they would talk to Dr. Nussbaum. Due to safety issues, we initially avoided families with very old and very young family members and families that had relatives living in the same apartment building or where there were family members that were ill or required special medication. We set the minimum age at twelve years old until we could be sure that the escape system worked. We did not set an upper age limit as long as they were ambulatory and alert. Our preferred candidates were professionals or craftsmen that we felt could find jobs in any country where they were finally relocated but this was not a rigid criterion. We tried to rescue people according to our schedule but over time we often had to move quickly based on the deportation schedule set by the Nazis.

After we did a background check on the family, we would have one of the IKG members approach them at home and ask them to consider fleeing the country with their immediate family. If the answer was positive and they agreed to our conditions, one of us would contact them. Since we decided not to reveal the extension until the eve of their departure, we had to rely on the power of persuasion to convince them to take the risk. We never identified ourselves by name and did not tell them that we were Jews in hiding. Our most useful cover story was that we were working with the Swiss Red Cross. We gave the person three days in which to really decide if they wanted to escape asking them not to discuss our visit with anyone else. Surprisingly, quite a number of people elected to stay in Vienna. They did not want to leave other family members behind, particularly if there were very young or very old family members that were excluded from our escape program. Many times we could not find out about all of their family members. Some just did not want to take the risk since being caught. This slowed down the process since we wound up wasting a week or two in the background check and in waiting for their negative decision.

Once the person agreed we told them to get ready for a departure within one week. They should quietly sell any assets and possessions of value that they still had converting them into cash or jewelry.

This was usually minimal since the Nazis had already aryanized businesses, property and houses. What little money they had was spent for food and other necessities to live. Some had fur coats, pianos, silverware, etc. but when they tried to sell it to non-Jews they were only given about 10 to 20 percent of its value. Most other Jews were in the same situation so they could not purchase these items so we decided to buy their assets at close to full value. They were not permitted to sell any furniture or do anything overtly noticeable that could signal their plan to leave. Many Jews were selling their possessions in order to live so as long as they were realistic in what they sold there was no overt suspicion.

On the appointed day, all family members would leave their home at their normal times. They brought all of their valuables with them in purses, backpacks, briefcases, attaché cases, schoolbags, etc. All of the family members would go to a special address in the downtown area where they would be met by one of the group members and taken by car or van to a safe house. We would photograph all of them and provide false identity cards and other personal documents. We also provided false travel documents. We could prepare a complete forged set of papers in about four hours after receiving the photographs. With two people working on this we could easily create new identities for a family of four overnight.

For the first few months we managed to help about thirty known Jewish men and their families escape to Switzerland using cars and trains. Luckily, not one was challenged. We actually thought of not even bothering to fit them with penises when we received messages from the Swiss people helping them that three of the families said that they felt so safe with the extensions on that they showed no fear or hesitation when they had to show their papers at the various check points along the trip. They each commented that they probably would not have acted so confidently without the extension due to the fear of being discovered. Based on these comments we never again questioned whether or not we should provide each male with an extension. Once in Switzerland they had to give the extensions to our Swiss contacts that destroyed them.

Kurt remarked one night at the card game that if we ever decided to go commercial with the extensions, he had just the ad campaign for the Vienna newspapers: "Jewish? Lacking confidence? Afraid to go out at night? Purchase a penis extension! It will change your attitude – and your life." While we laughed at the joke we knew that this really was very serious – a matter of life or death.

With war, further restrictions were placed on Jews with the express purpose of creating ghetto-like conditions without the typical ghetto wall. Food rationing was soon instituted and there was a list of foods that Jews could not openly purchase. In addition, Jews were only allowed to go food shopping between noon and 1 PM. By that time most of the food that they could buy was already bought by non-Jews so what was left was often spoiled. Sometimes, Jews were stopped on the street and not allowed to continue until after 1 PM so they could not even get to a store to buy any food. Jews would often have to take circuitous routes to the stores since many were stopped on direct routes by people watching them go to the store. When one elderly woman complained that they had nothing to eat, one of the Hitler Youth suggested that she go down to Prater Park and eat grass. He even offered to escort her there saying that if she behaved herself in the park he would see to it that she got to ride the roller coaster. He was one of the boys that participated in the previous park incident and was quite proud of it. His companions applauded the idea. She kept quiet and did not say another word. They kept her standing there until 2 PM.

In addition, Jews were now not allowed to receive any food, clothing or anything of value from other people in Vienna and from abroad. To enforce this, there were Jew-watchers. They lived in the apartment building and were usually the janitors. They kept track of the Jews entering and leaving, who visited them and would confiscate packages mailed or delivered to them since it was illegal for Jews to get items of value. This often included inspecting their mail for similar reasons.

Deportations resumed in November. There were two methods that the Nazis used to select the Jews for deportation. The first and main method was to have the Jewish agency (IKG) prepare the list, notify the people on the list and have them report to the various embarkation points set up throughout the city. There were books that had lists (hausliste) developed for every building in Vienna that had Jews living in them. As Jews were deported or if they emigrated, their names were crossed off of the list.

List of Jewish tenants (Hausliste) living in an apartment house on Lessinggasse (Lessing Street) in the second district. The tenants whose names were crossed out either emigrated or had been deported (source: IKG, Vienna)

Some of these embarkation points were Jewish schools, the burnt out shells of the synagogues destroyed on Kristallnacht, former

Jewish social clubs, gymnasiums or at the IKG building. The penalty for not reporting was very severe. Instead of being sent to a ghetto you were sent directly to a concentration camp. However, you could appeal their deportation decision by having your employer state that your job was a "position of critical importance" or having your doctor attest that you were too sick to travel (which would sometimes require corroboration by a Gentile doctor appointed by the Nazis to confirm the infirmity).

Sometimes an "important" Jew would protest. One such man was Mordecai Gottlieb. When he reported for deportation he loudly protested. He had an important job with a German-owned firm. He was not fired as most other Jews had been fired because his skills were needed. He told the SS officers loudly that he was very important and there would be consequences if he was deported. His loud tirade was watched by the other Jews in line for deportation as well as well as the other SS officers in the room. The SS officer at the desk was not sure what to do. He had Mordecai wait in the back of the room. When Mordecai reached the back he turned around and he could see that the SS officer at the desk was arguing with his superior, an SS Captain. After a few minutes the Captain came over to Mordecai and asked about his health as everyone in the large room watched. Mordecai told him that his health was perfect. The Captain asked Mordecai some questions. Mordecai was single, lived alone, worked for the Krupps Company as a production scheduler for a steel foundry in Vienna and was well-respected at the company. The Captain took out a penlight that he had in his pocket and shined it in Mordecai's eyes to watch the pupils dilate. He shined the light in each ear. He asked Mordecai to stick out his tongue. As he shined the light into his mouth he punched Mordecai in the jaw with a powerful uppercut causing Mordecai to bite off his tongue. Mordecai screamed in pain as the blood gushed into and out of his mouth. He collapsed to the floor screaming. Now, get on the train. No Jew is as important as you say that you are, especially now without the tongue that you used to arrogantly talk back to an SS officer. With that, he ordered three of the Jewish men that had already been processed to drag the screaming Mordecai to the train. As he was being carried on the train, the captain told another man to pick up the severed tongue and put it in his pocket. "When you get to the resettlement camp you give the tongue to him and see if can have it scheduled to be sewn back on!" That was the last time anyone heard from him.

The second deportation selection method was where the Nazis would select specific apartments to raid and herd the people that lived in those apartments into trucks for deportation. This was initially done during the day but sometime later during the night to minimize the visibility of the action and to take advantage of the lighter traffic at night in the city as well as to be sure that all family members would be home. All Jews had a curfew that initially required them to be at home by 8PM. This was later moved to 6PM and finally, towards the end of the deportations, to 4PM. The target residences were selected randomly so as not to provide any warning to their victims but once selected the date and time for each building was recorded in a special ledger at the SS and police headquarters. Each Monday the entire week's schedule was listed in this ledger. Here again, Mischa proved to be invaluable. When the Nazis were setting up the program they asked for volunteers from the police force to assist them. The SS, who were in charge of the program needed police officers that knew each district, especially the second district which had the highest concentration of Jews. Mischa volunteered and was readily accepted because of his outstanding record and knowledge of the second district as he used to live there as he would say, "Before it became infested with Jews." This also gave him access to the ledger.

Since we knew in advance which buildings were going to be hit, we concentrated our efforts on those buildings first, starting with those that would be hit on Thursday. We did not have enough time to set up escapes for the buildings that were going to be hit before Thursday. We had a couple of members of the IKG working with us. Using the list of all the residents in the targeted buildings they selected those that met our criteria for further investigation. Where there was any doubt, we passed on them. Since we only had two of the specially modified moving vans and since each van could take up to eight people in the false compartment, we could take sixteen people at a time. Surprisingly, even with the mounting oppressive conditions, the increasingly stringent restrictions and the deportations, not all of the families that we offered the opportunity to escape accepted the offer – for the same reasons as before. Even if they were deported they would be together with friends and other family members wherever they would be sent. Many thought that the place that they were going to be deported to would have better conditions than where they currently lived. Only about 40 percent of those offered accepted the opportunity to escape at this time. Another part of the problem was that we could not let them know that their building would be hit that week. They would surely ask how we knew, which we could not. The risk of the Nazis finding out that we obviously had a spy in their system was too great.

In all of the ghettos throughout Europe the Nazis used Jews to carry out their orders. A Jewish council, usually of elders, was set up and, surprisingly, so was a Jewish police force that reported directly to the SS in charge of the ghetto. They had uniforms, special badges for each ghetto, and clubs. They lived apart from and better than the rest of the people in the ghetto. Given the deplorable conditions in the ghetto there were always more volunteers than places on the special ghetto Jewish police force. The more brutal you were, the more secure was your position on the ghetto police force. Anyone not getting immediate cooperation from the Jews he was ordering to do things was a prime candidate for replacement. In some cases, the Jewish police were more brutal than the SS, which greatly amused the SS. While Vienna was not a ghetto in the strictest sense of the definition since it had no walls and Jews could travel freely within the city, there was still an attempt to build a Jewish police force to help with the deportations. The SS let it be known that they were forming a Judische Polizei. They expected a large response given how badly conditions in Vienna had become, the number of Jews in Vienna and the results of similar offers in the other ghettos. They were sorely disappointed. After two weeks of recruiting in every district only six Jews volunteered. All were either criminals or had some mental disorder. While they were disappointed they at least had six members of the Vienna Jewish Police Force, the Jüdischer Ordnungsdienst (JURO). They appointed Wilhelm Reisz as the Police Chief. He was a good-looking, well-educated young man from a religious family but was not very close to them since he had married a Gentile and they strongly disapproved of the marriage to the point of disowning him. He was also mentally unstable, prone to violence, and uncontrollable, sometimes violent, outbreaks. Some of his family members had committed suicide immediately after Anschluss and his brother had been beaten to death right before his eyes by a mob. One would have thought that this would have made him vehemently anti-Nazi. Instead it made him anti-Semitic. In his mind he believed that if his parents were not Jewish none of this would have happened. Moreover, if they were not Jewish his marriage would have been perfectly acceptable to his parents – and to her parents, who also disapproved of their marriage. He took out his anger on the Jews of Vienna. If someone did not move fast enough, if he thought that someone was looking at him in an "evil manner", if someone did not answer a question correctly without hesitation, he would start hitting that person with his club. It did not matter if it was someone young or old, man or woman or child, ill or pregnant. He would sometimes start beating them so violently that his own men had to restrain him. His reputation for cruelty spread amongst the Jewish community and the SS. He was feared much more than the SS and when he approached a family that looked as if they were wealthy (or had been wealthy) based on the clothes that they were wearing, he would demand some jewels or money that he believed they were hiding. If they had anything, they would immediately turn all or part of it over to him. If they did not have anything or pretended that they didn't in order to save what little wealth they had for their next destination, he would beat one of the family members. Those that were pretending not to have anything quickly relented and gave him something. The beating stopped. Those that didn't have anything could do nothing but helplessly watch as a family member was savagely beaten to unconsciousness. He would use the money and the jewels, which he pawned, to host drinking parties with his masters, the SS. As far as we knew, he was the only Jew in Vienna treated almost as an equal with the SS. He was a "drinking buddy."

By the end of December 1939 more than 110,000 Jews had left Austria. At this point there were still about 75,000 Jews left in Vienna. We had our work cut out for us.

CHAPTER ELEVEN

EMIGRATE OR ELSE!

"Vienna cannot be conquered with bayonets, only with music."

"Every boy who dies at the front, dies for Mozart."

Baldur von Schirach, Gauleiter of Vienna, 1940-1945

Continuing with the policy of encouraging wealthy Jews to emigrate out of Austria, the Nazis periodically deported a small number of poor Jews and rabbis during 1940 to various ghettos such as Theresienstadt, Nisko, Lublin and Lodz. They were not deported directly to concentration camps. There were a number of reasons for this. The first was that at the time of deportation, concentration camps were not yet death camps; this change occurred later so the death camps were not yet built. Second, they allowed correspondence between the people sent to the ghetto and the people remaining in Vienna. There were shortages in the ghetto so most of the correspondence was related to the sending of money, food, clothing and other living necessities from people in Vienna to the deportees. Jews could not openly receive anything from other Jews and certainly not from Gentiles while in Vienna but they could when in the ghetto to where they were deported. Mail to Jews in Vienna was checked and anything of value was confiscated. Even deliveries by messengers were intercepted at the residence of a Jew by the Jew-watcher and confiscated. Theoretically, these items were supposed to be turned in to the authorities but none of the Jew-watchers did it. The authorities turned a blind eye to this practice since they couldn't really enforce it and it made the Jew-watcher much more resolute and efficient in intercepting these packages if he could keep them. In the ghetto, Jews could receive packages that were sent by Jewish and non-Jewish friends, family and former business associates (yes, there still were some Gentiles that openly helped Jews). Conditions in the ghettos were believed to be somewhat better than in Vienna with respect to being allowed more freedom and they were not beaten in the streets. Conditions were still bad enough to provide the incentive for most of the remaining Jews that had emigration options to emigrate. More than 70 percent of those that could afford to leave the country left. Obtaining the entry visa to another country was the major problem. In the United States you could get tentative approval to be on the list for acceptance but had to wait until the quota for the next year opened. This letter of acceptance kept many Jews from being deported.

While the countries at the Evian Conference refused to increase their quota to allow more Jews into their respective countries, one country stands out for its willingness to help Jews in Vienna – China. This was solely due to one man, Dr. Ho-feng who was the Consul General of China in Vienna from 1938 to 1940. During this period, he issued about 30,000 visas allowing Jews to leave Vienna. The stated destination on the exit visa was Shanghai where a German enclave had existed since the 1920s. However, once the person left Vienna, they were free to go anyplace they desired. All the Nazis cared about was that they had the proper visas. Of the 30,000 émigrés, about 25,000 did go to Shanghai. The rest went to other countries.

Finally, there was some good news and some not-so-good news. On April 1, 1940 the Chinese government officially notified the Jewish Relief Committee that Jews could freely come to Shanghai without much formality. Entry visas would not be required. Every application would be accepted as soon as it was received as long as the fees were paid. That was the good news. The not-so-good news was that conditions there became worse than in Vienna as time progressed. Initially, conditions were actually very good. The Jews had complete autonomy and set up a mini-Vienna. There were restaurants, shops, Konditerei, medical centers, etc. Unfortunately, the émigrés boasted about this in the postcards and letters that they wrote home. These were read by the Nazis who placed strong pressure on the Japanese government that was occupying Shanghai. The Japanese immediately placed many restrictions on the Jewish community, limited the space that they could live in and sometimes curtailed water and power to the community. Within a few months conditions there were no better than Vienna. However, the Japanese refused to arrest them or limit immigration. They were making money on the immigration just as the Nazis were making money on the emigration. After these actions, there were very few jobs and living conditions were poor with extremely poor sanitation, very different food (forget kosher), electricity not always available, no running water in some apartments, and overcrowding. The Japanese refused to expand the area so arriving Jews often had to move in with strangers. Part of the increasing employment problem was because most of the Jews that could afford to emigrate there were doctors, lawyers, dentists and other higher educated people. They had no trade skills plus the language barrier was unbelievable. Chinese was nothing whatsoever like Yiddish or German. They couldn't read the signs, the newspapers, etc. Language schools were set up but the difficulty in learning Chinese resulted in most of the people dropping out. The trip was also arduous. Those that could afford it went by ship. This required multiple transfers and was expensive. Those that couldn't afford it went by land to the trans-Siberian railroad terminal in Moscow and took the four or five-day train ride to Vladivostok and by land to Shanghai. This could take two or three weeks. In spite of this some twenty-five thousand Jews that might never have survived the deportations and death camps elected to go to Shanghai – a wise decision in spite of the hardships.

Himmler and Goebbels were still not satisfied. Himmler sent a special representative to Tokyo to pressure them to kill the Jews. One of the proposed plans was that they would provide ships for the Jews and once the ships were at sea they would evacuate the crews and sink the ships. Other options including setting up Dachau-style concentration camps or just sending over their special execution squads, the Einsatzgruppen. All were refused. The Japanese government informed the Nazis that these Jews would be treated as displaced refugees (stateless people) and accorded political asylum and they would continue to allow immigration. Some years later, we believed that the reason for this policy was based on an event some forty years earlier. In 1903, a Japanese delegation went to various countries to raise money for military supplies. War with Russia was imminent and the Japanese needed guns, ammunition and especially naval supplies such as mines and torpedoes. They could build ships but did not have the factories for the naval supplies. At that time Japan was not considered to be a serious power so not one country or financial institution decided to lend them the money – until the delegation arrived in New York. They met with a coalition of banks and were turned down. However, some of the bankers were Jewish. They asked the delegation to meet with them in two days. In two days, the Japanese delegation met with a different group of bankers and industrialists. They were all Jewish. They had decided that Russia and Communism was the enemy of Judaism and agreed to help Japan stop Russia. They secretly loaned them more than they required. Japan was able to purchase what they needed. On February 8, 1904, just before Japan formally declared war on Russia, they launched a surprise attack on the Russian fleet in Port Arthur, China and won a decisive victory which was followed by additional naval and land successes. They won the war – and they evidently did not forget the help from the Jewish community.

In July 1940, Gauleiter Josef Bürckel was transferred to another country. This move was primarily due to the dissatisfaction that Hitler had with him. It was not based on his administrative performance, which was excellent. It was based on his lack of assimilation into Viennese culture and the animosity that the Viennese had towards him. He lacked the diplomacy and the cultural acumen to get the people of Vienna to support him. He totally ignored cultural development. The arts were deteriorating and this was not on Bürckel's agenda. He couldn't care less – and it showed. Reports about his lack of cultural assimilation were sent to Himmler, Goering and Hitler indicating that the Viennese people, some of whom were staunch supporters of Anschluss, were losing their enthusiasm for National Socialism and Hitler. They just expected more based on Hitler's speeches. In his place Baldur von Schirach was appointed as the new Gauleiter of Vienna. We immediately compiled a dossier on him.

Baldur von Schirach joined the Nazi party in 1925. He was an ardent believer in the party doctrines and was a very good public speaker and leader. He followed Hitler with unquestioning loyalty. In 1929 he was appointed as the leader of the National Socialist Student's Union. His oratory skills and rationale for explaining that the problems of the country were caused by others, especially the Jews, were very impressive on young minds. Quite a number of students joined the Nazi party and Nazi social clubs sprung up across the country in many high schools and universities. With the economy in chaos, inflation rampant, and the prospects for jobs after graduation nil, the students saw a much brighter future in National Socialism. Von Schirach did so well during the first two years leading the Student's Union that, in 1931, he was made Reichs Youth Leader of the Nazi Party with full control of the recruitment and indoctrination of all students of every age. This included the Hitler Jugend, the special Hitler youth organization that had young boys and teenagers as members replete with brown uniforms and formal training in summer camps and after school. When Hitler was appointed chancellor in 1933, von Schirach was made the Reichs Youth Leader for Germany. He now made participation in the Hitler Jugend (HJ) and other youth organizations mandatory and included more intense training programs that would prepare them for military service. The top performers were invited to join the prestigious SS when they reached conscription age. This created strong competitive positioning in the HJ to be the best. The children were indoctrinated towards Hitler to the point that they became spies for the Third Reich and often turned in family members and family friends that said anything negative about National Socialism or made jokes about Hitler. They were taught to vehemently hate Jews as the source of all problems in the world and that they were sub-humans not worthy of any pity or compassion. They were exposed to this rhetoric every day.

Baldur von Schirach also had some other attributes that Hitler thought would make him perfect for the job. He was a poet. Two books of his poems had been published. They were mostly about the glory of Germany and the German youth. He also came from an aristocratic family and considered himself a patron of the arts. He thoroughly enjoyed classical music and the theater and he knew most of the people in the arts in Berlin and Hamburg. He also had an interest in fashion design. He was perfect for Vienna.

Based on these qualifications, Baldur von Schirach was appointed Gauleiter of Vienna and Reich Defense Minister for the southern region of Austria. Essentially, he was the power in Vienna with the mayor and all other elected and appointed officials subordinate to his absolute control. Von Schirach's prime directive was to improve the cultural situation in Vienna to reinforce the promises Hitler made on March 15, 1938. While Vienna was still to be subordinate to Germany namely Berlin and Hamburg, the cultural capitals of Germany, Vienna should at least be a close third. Part of the problem was that many of the actors, playwrights, musicians, orchestra directors and composers were Jewish and had been summarily dismissed with Anschluss. Moreover, at least one-half of the audiences attending concerts and plays were Jewish due to their disproportionate wealth. They also donated money to support the arts. One of von Schirach's personal prime objectives was to remedy this and restore the cultural life of Vienna which he did with a passion.

When von Schirach arrived, deportations had already begun so at this point he was really just overseeing the operation that was being commanded by Adolf Eichmann. One of the first things he did was to meet with Eichmann and get apprised of the situation. He did not change anything that Eichmann was doing and reasserted Eichmann's mandate to lead the effort with his full support. Jews were initially being deported to ghettos at a low rate as Eichmann was still extorting money from wealthy Jews and from foreign donations so that they could leave the country and take some of the poorer Jews with them. From a financial standpoint this was still very successful. Baldur decided to use some of this money to revitalize the arts and to pay for leading conductors, actors and playwrights to come to Vienna to perform and, for some, to live. He also lowered ticket prices and increased salaries that were independent of ticket sales so while box office receipts declined, performer and support staff salaries increased. Theater attendance tripled overnight.

On October 2, 1940 von Schirach was called to Berlin for a special meeting of Gauleiters and Reichs Governors of the occupied territories. In attendance was Hitler, Himmler, Eichmann, Bürckel, von Schirach, Frank (Gauleiter of Poland which was renamed the General Gouvernment), and many other Gauleiters and officials. At the meeting each Gauleiter reported on the number of Jews resident in the ghettos in their jurisdiction. Von Schirach reported that Vienna still had about 60,000 Jews living in Vienna. Hitler was not pleased with the progress of any of the Gauleiters but was particularly angry that Vienna still had so many Jews since he had a particular animosity for Viennese Jews from the time he lived there. On December 2 von Schirach received a letter letting him telling him that Hitler had decided to deport all 60,000 Jews to Poland as a top priority. Vienna was a central city with many administrative functions. There was a housing shortage and the second district, where most of the remaining Jews were now concentrated, was prime property. Getting rid of the Jews would alleviate most of the shortage. He directed Gauleiter Hans Frank to take these Jews and resettle them in Poland in existing ghettos and work camps and to create new ones as needed. He mandated von Schirach to have Vienna Judenfrei by the end of the next year. This set the rate of deportations and emigrations at 5,000 per month.

We learned about the Nazi deportation plans from Anton Fischer, the Swiss member of our group that worked in the Ministry of Communications. The members of the SS and SD talked openly about all of this in the cafeteria where Anton often ate lunch with them and after work where he often went to the beer hall with them as well. He almost always treated and therefore was always in demand as the SS and SD officers liked to drink more than their budget could support. The more they drank, the more they talked. Moreover, there was no attempt by von Schirach to keep this confidential. He had weekly staff meetings where he informed his staff of all developments. He appointed various people to take charge of these mundane tasks. He spent most of his time on the cultural issues and could not be bothered with administrative issues. This was also to our benefit. At the December 12th staff meeting Adolf Eichmann spoke to the group and outlined the plan for the deportation of the Jews. His plan was to deport the requisite 5,000 Jews per month to have Vienna cleared of Jews by the following Christmas using the railway system. Himmler was going to secure special Jewish transit railcars for the deportations. Emigrations would still be encouraged and those with prospects of emigrating within the year were to be spared from deportation until the very end. Unfortunately for him and fortunately for us, this schedule was not realized.

Between Anton in the Ministry and Mischa in the Central Police Station, we had a great intelligence operation. We accelerated our plans.

Many Jews were now destitute, even formerly wealthy ones were now very poor. Many were still waiting for their permits. If they wanted to go to the United States they had a long wait. The quota for 1941 had been met and now the soonest anyone could get an entry permit was for 1942, more than thirteen months away plus there were more Jews applying for entry into the United States than the 1942 quota would allow so many would have to wait until 1943. Most that were left had already been systematically robbed of their assets, their cash and jewelry and anything else of value. Between having to voluntarily give them up or from home invasions, their wealth had disappeared. To make matters worse, any Jew that had some form of property or had worked as a professional or manager was assessed back taxes that were due even if they had been paid. These back taxes had to be paid before the exit visa could be obtained. When the tax was paid, a special tax paid receipt called an "Unbedenklichkeit" was issued along with the exit permit. This was obviously done to force the last drop of assets out of the departing Jews. Many of the Jews sold everything that they had to raise enough money to pay the back taxes. Most of the money raised to help them pay their back taxes and exit fee now came from foreign donations and from friends and family in the country where they were going to emigrate. It was usually not enough so they had to beg or borrow the difference from whoever was left in Vienna. Here we were able to help.

Using Dr. Nussbaum and the IKG we arranged for money to be secretly given to those that needed it to leave the country. They were never told where it came from. Dr. Nussbaum would give the money to the IKG and one of the workers would give the money to the family after asking them to come to the IKG office.

We only gave the money to Dr. Nussbaum who we trusted implicitly. We did not want to take a chance with anyone else. If the Nazis found out they would rationalize that a Jewish doctor would certainly have the money to pay for these Jews to leave. If confronted, he would give them all of the unspent money that he had hidden. We gave him an additional 15,000 marks which he could give up or use as a bribe.

He was finally discovered as being the source of the money when one of the men that received the money at the IKG office was stopped and searched by a Gestapo agent as he was almost running home to tell his family the news. The agent was suspicious and stopped him. He found the envelope with the money. Under threat of torture, he identified the IKG person who gave him the money who, in turn, identified Dr. Nussbaum. Two Gestapo agents came to his office and asked him if he was giving money to Jews so they could pay their taxes. He immediately confessed and gave whatever cash he had on hand plus the 15,000 Reichsmarks in the envelope that we provided expressly for this situation to the Gestapo. They took everything and, surprisingly, left without arresting him but did admonish him to stop doing it. Given the smiles that the Gestapo men had he thought that were going to keep the money which was why they did not arrest him. This turned out not to be the case. Two days later there was a knock on his door. He opened it and was surprised to see the same two Gestapo agents there that had confiscated the money. He thought that they had come back to arrest and deport him or to see if there was any more money, which he did not have. He started to tremble but before he could ask them why they were there one of them stuck out his hand holding all of the money that they had taken from him a few days earlier, including the envelope with the 15,000 Marks. The Gestapo agent told Dr. Nussbaum that Eichmann himself had directed them to return the money after they had reported it. They did not arrest him because they wanted to get orders from their superiors on how they should proceed. Eichmann told them that the money would come to the Nazis anyway but if it helped rid Vienna of more Jews in the process it was a good thing. They didn't care where he got the money and they certainly did not want to stop the flow. As such, Dr. Nussbaum was essentially given a green light to continue what he was doing. We increased our contributions quite thankful for the way it worked out.

Dr. Nussbaum was one of the last Jews deported from Vienna (directly to Auschwitz) due to this activity. We continued this for as long as emigration was open. It stopped for a while when the war started on September 1, 1939 when the Nazis invaded Poland. This terminated emigrations to England and France as they declared war on Germany a few days later. All of a sudden, emigration resumed in February at the request of the American embassy. They were not involved in the war. It was a new year so the quota was open again for Austria but there were many more Jews in Vienna than the quota allowed. Even though most of the Jews leaving Vienna in 1940 were not permitted to go to the United States due to the quota limit, there were enough Viennese Jews with relatives there that could send them money or arrange exit visas to other countries that would accept them such as South Africa, Colombia and Uruguay which also agreed to continue taking Jews as they were also not in the war. Shanghai continued to be open without restriction but, based on the recent letters received from those that had emigrated there, conditions had deteriorated so much and work opportunities were so limited that many only chose this as a last resort. Still, it was better than being deported to a ghetto so emigration to Shanghai continued, although at a substantially reduced rate.

In addition to the direct aid, we devised a method to help some families smuggle what little wealth they had left out of the country. This was Wilhelm's idea. He got the idea while washing up after surgery. There were a few small wet pieces of soap left on the sink. He picked them up and squeezed them together to form a larger piece. They were very pliable and formed whatever shape he wanted. He took a coin out of his pocket and pressed it into the center of the soap and folded the edges around it. It was totally hidden. He carefully wrapped the soap and carried it to his locker. He changed into his street clothes and left the hospital carrying the wrapped soap in his pocket. By the time he got home the soap had dried and hardened.

At the next Friday night card game, when it was time to ante, he took out the piece of soap and threw it on the table saying, "I'm in!" We started to laugh but we could see that he was serious. Friedrich finally remarked, "At least you could put in a whole bar, this piece is hardly worth the ante." Wilhelm answered, "Oh, but it is. In fact it is worth more than the ante." With that he pulled the soap apart revealing the hidden coin. We were speechless. Wilhelm told us how he came to do this and was thinking that we could use bars of soap to hide jewels for the Jews that had them and were willing to risk smuggling them out of the country. Toiletries were among the few things that Jews were allowed to take out of the country. We thought that this was an excellent idea. Klaus Frühling, who was a civil engineer for the city of Vienna, volunteered to set up the system.

The next day, Klaus visited two soap factories to learn the art of soap making or, actually soap re-making. On the pretext of examining plant effluent, he was given a tour of each plant. His focus was on how they recycled scraps, remnants and off-quality soap to make sure that they were not going into the Danube River. He found out that all of the scrap was simply put back into a large vat. The scraps were heated to 80 degrees centigrade so they melted. The molten soap left the tank through a heated pipe at the bottom where it was sent to a larger vat with newly prepared soap and mixed in with the new soap. From the large vat through another heated pipe the molten soap flowed into a dispensing pipe which was perpendicular to the outlet pipe and was about one half meter long. About every ten centimeters there was a hole. The soap flowed out of the hole into molds that were on a conveyor belt. The molds were filled and they cooled as they traveled down the belt and dropped out of the mold at the end of the belt. Scrap soap was scraped off of the belt as it returned to be refilled. The scrap soap fell into a bin where someone periodically emptied it into the vat. There was very little waste. Klaus gave each plant a letter saying that they were not polluting the river and that they were operating safely. On his way out he asked the owner if he could purchase a mold as a souvenir of his visit. Both owners gave him a mold at no charge. We now had a mold from two different branded soap companies. We could make bars of soap with the company designs and names on them.

Klaus took over a section of a garage and bought some electric heaters, thermostats and pots. He set up his operation. It was actually quite simple. He would purchase bars of soap, put them in the pot and heat the pot up to the desired temperature so the soap melted. Using a soup ladle, he would take some of the molten soap and fill the molds about halfway to the top. As soon as this was done he would place some jewels, preferably diamonds, on top of the soap and immediately pour the rest of the soap on top to fill the mold.

Once cooled, you could not see that anything was inside. We found that it was better to use jewels than gold coins due to the weight of the gold coins which made the bars of soap too heavy. Once we perfected the process we told Dr. Nussbaum and he carefully spread the word selectively to only the most trustworthy of his associates. We were even able to facilitate the purchase of diamonds in the black market sometimes in exchange for other valuables, particularly bulky ones such as silver candelabra, fur coats and heavy jewelry. While most wealthy Jews had all of their overt assets confiscated, some managed to secrete some money, jewelry and other valuables that were mostly kept for them by some trusted non-Jewish friends, hidden in their apartments or hidden in their former businesses which they were able to get after they were closed for the day. Some were still able to get money from former associates, especially when they told them that they were leaving the country. We also provided some money.

Selected families, once they were granted their exit visa and paid all of their taxes, brought their jewels to Dr. Nussbaum who, in turn, gave them to someone else to give to us. We were able to return the bars of soap the following morning. As an added precaution, we took a wet cloth and rubbed the soap to give it a "used" look. We were afraid that if the bar was new, one of the guards could confiscate it for their personal use but no self-respecting Nazi would use a bar of soap that had already been used by a Jew. We tried to restrict it to one bar of soap per family member, which was why we suggested that they convert their remaining wealth into diamonds. While emigration was allowed we must have processed more than two hundred diamond-laden bars of soap. Not one was discovered. One family of four that had five bars of soap was asked by one of the border guards why they had so much soap but before the father could answer, the guard's partner said, "Because they are dirty Jews, but all of the soap in the world won't wash away their filth." The other guard laughed and let them pass.

The Jews were not the only ones persecuted after the Anschluss. The Catholics were next, especially the clergy. While Hitler made promises about not tampering with the church, those promises were also lies. There could only be one Supreme Being in Germany and that could only be Adolf Hitler. There were periodic marches and demonstrations by the Catholic Youth Organization. This came to a head about six months after the Anschluss. As actions against the church accelerated, Cardinal Innitzer gave a sermon on October 7, 1938 that spoke out against the Nazi actions such as closing seminaries and arresting outspoken young priests. He said, "There is a cross over Austria but it is not the cross of Christ." He was referring specifically to the Nazi swastika which was called a Hakenkreuz (hooked cross). He went on with some more diatribes against the Nazis. On October 8 more than 8,000 young Catholics marched in a parade that culminated at St. Stephen's Cathedral that affirmed that Jesus Christ was where Christians owed their primary allegiance by carrying large banners with "Jesus Christ is our Fuehrer!" This caused a confrontation with the Hitler Jugend that quickly led to fighting. This resulted in the police being called. As one might expect only Catholics were arrested. The next night a large Nazi mob broke into Cardinal Innitzer's residence that was across the street from the cathedral wreaking havoc. Luckily, he was not there. Icons and crosses were destroyed, paintings and tapestries were slashed and a young priest that tried to stop the mob was thrown out of a second-floor window that injured him severely. He died a few weeks later. This led to protests in churches throughout the country which caused the Nazis to relent a little – at least publicly. They continued to arrest and torture the Catholic Youth leaders, some of whom would just disappear on their way home at night. They also continued to close seminaries and parochial schools.

Catholic demonstrations were largely ignored in most of the rural cities but were no longer tolerated in Vienna. As the Nazis had done with the police and army, they had some of their members join the various Christian and Catholic Youth Groups. Once they learned through these spies where and when a demonstration was to occur, the SS mobilized the Hitler Jugend to disrupt the peaceful marches turning them into riots that the police had to quell. The police still only arrested members of the Catholic Youth Organization. Those from influential families were released unharmed the next morning. That same morning the Gestapo told their parents that if they wanted to retain their status they had better control their own children and stop them from demonstrating. Most of them complied under parental mandates in order to preserve the family's standing – and safety. They knew that the Nazis would arrest their parents or siblings and beat them or fine them a large sum of money if they continued. These tactics effectively reduced the ranks of the Catholic Youth Organization and the number of demonstrations. It was also a wake-up call for Cardinal Innitzer. He was now resolutely anti-Nazi and helped Jews that converted to Catholicism escape from Austria since they were now reclassified as Jews.

The morgue was busier than ever. In addition to the normal deaths there were Jewish suicides and the random Jews that were killed for fun or because they resisted something that an SS, SD or SA soldier asked him to do and now Jews that were dying of malnutrition and disease. Some of the Jews would rather die than submit to the degradation thrust upon them by the Nazis – and the Nazis were happy to oblige. At this point we were still allowed to keep all of the bodies in the same area. A few months later there was a directive that Jewish bodies could not be kept in the same room as Aryans. This was later extended to include gypsies. We had to set up a makeshift morgue in one of the large basement rooms that had no facilities to preserve the body in refrigerated compartments.

After five days, if the body was not claimed it was disposed of in a local crematorium as was mandated by the Nazis and the ashes thrown into the garbage. We took pictures of them before cremation and listed any scar or other physical characteristic on the back of the photograph. For deportations, the Nazis just rounded up Jews and detained them for one or two days mistreating them constantly during their incarceration to extort hidden wealth before sending them to a ghetto or to Dachau. A few were also sent to Mauthausen Concentration Camp just outside of Linz when it opened. When someone was missing overnight the family would go down to the IKG the next day and try to find out where their loved were. This was futile since the Nazis never gave any of this type of information to the IKG. The morgue was always the last stop in their search. Jews could not get tattoos for religious reasons so if someone who had been beaten to death was brought in with a tattoo we immediately knew that he had been mistaken for a Jew. A quick look at his penis confirmed our assumption. Having the relatives come and identify a loved one was a heart rendering scene. The screams, the cries, the fainting were too painful for many of us to bear. However, there was a sizeable minority of my co-workers that relished at the sight. They hated the Jews so much that the death of a Jew was justified and the rest better get out of Austria lest the next time it is one of them that are in the morgue on the table. They were quite open with their beliefs. Some would purposely come into the room saying, "Save your tears. You will surely need them again and again unless you get out of Austria." or "If you don't leave it is one of you that will next be on the slab." The message was clear.

Chapter Twelve

Head Over Heels – A (really) Close Encounter

"Sexual relations outside marriage between Jews and nationals of German or kindred blood are forbidden."

Law for the Protection of German Blood and German Honor, September 15, 1935 (The Nuremberg Laws), Section II

Sometimes passion rules! And so it was with Johann Schmidt, the oldest son of Helmut Schmidt, on the eve of his departure to Switzerland with his family. They were passing themselves off as non-Jews and had false identity cards but were worried that they could be identified as Jews if they were ever confronted by the Nazis and asked to drop their pants. We did not know about them until they spoke to an IKG member at his home. They had relatives in Canada and were anxious to leave Austria but could not legally apply for a permit as they were not known to be Jewish. Even when we told Helmut Schmidt about the extension and how it could allow him to protect his false identity he told us that his decision to leave Austria was final. Johann, who was eighteen, his younger brother Hans, who was fourteen, and their father Helmut, were fitted with new penis extensions prior to going to bed in the safe house the night before they were to leave for Switzerland. All of the forged travel documents had been delivered to the safe house and their route out of Austria was set. However, Johann had a girl friend that he felt compelled to see one more time before leaving. So around 11:30 when the rest of the family was asleep he snuck out of the safe house using the back door that opened into the alley and went to see his girl friend taking a tram to get there. He felt that with the extension he could travel freely within the city because if he was stopped he had a Gentile penis. His girlfriend worked at a bar as a waitress and typically worked until midnight. They had been going together for about five months and they were in love. They had never "gone all the way" and she had no idea that he was Jewish. The fact that he was Jewish was the only reason that he had not tried to have intercourse even though he wanted to do it many times. He knew that he had to restrain himself that he could not take the chance that she would see his circumcised penis and realize that he was a Jew – at least until he felt he could really trust her. However, his decision to wait changed on the eve of his departure. He did not know her father but suspected that if her father found that he was Jewish that he would end the relationship immediately and perhaps even turn him in to the authorities to be sure the relationship ended. Johann's father had been using forged papers for the family for a long time. He was a well-respected businessman that no one suspected of being Jewish so Johann surely couldn't risk the safety of his entire family through a sexual indiscretion. However, his reluctance to go all the way was well-received by his girlfriend. With working in a bar, every man she had gone out with thought that she was "easy" and tried to have sex with her by at least the second date if not on the first. Sometimes the encounters were ugly with name calling and, on one occasion she was even hit by her date. As such, she felt that it was love and respect that kept Johann from doing anything before they were married or before that they really knew each other very well and were both ready which intensified her love (and passion) for him. In fact, she was more of the aggressor on their last date and it was Johann that was restrained but now he felt that he could remove the extension at just the right moment and proceed to have sex with her. If she saw his penis afterwards, saw that he was Jewish (and resented it), told anyone and there was an investigation, they would be long gone before he could be found. He viewed this also as a test of her true love for him if she found out. He decided that he would not voluntarily tell her lest she panic on the spot and cause a problem. Moreover, this was clearly his last opportunity.

Johann went into the bar and sat at one of the tables near the door. She was very surprised and very happy to see him. He waited for her to finish work and on the way to her apartment he grabbed her hand and held it. She smiled at him. It was a perfect night – good weather, clear sky, stars. About one block from her apartment, he told her that he and his family were leaving tomorrow as his father had just been promoted and transferred to a job in Germany due to the sudden death of a senior manager in his company in a car accident and he was needed there right away. They would of course come back and get their possessions later. She was shocked and heart-broken. He consoled her as best as possible, told her that she could come visit him and that he would come back to visit her as often as possible. One thing led to another and they slipped into the cellar of her apartment building where she lived with her parents. The door was always locked but she had a key. There were some rooms there that were used for storage and one of them had some furniture stored in it. It started out slowly with some kissing and rubbing when all of a sudden she unloosened his pants and pulled them down. He realized that in his haste to leave the safe house, he did not put a belt on his pants. It took him completely by surprise. It was a bit awkward so they lost their balance and they fell to the floor with her on top of him. He rose to the occasion and she just mounted him before he could even think about what was going on. It took him a much longer time to climax than Gretchen. In fact, she had about three orgasms before he really started to lose his fear, feel good and climax. He was pinned down with her on top of him so there was also a feeble attempt at a second time before she got off of him.

Johann went to another area in the cellar to urinate. As he looked down he realized that his new penis extension was gone. His first thought was that he had dropped it on the floor during his initial moments of passion but a quick search revealed that it was nowhere to be found. "Where could it be?" he asked himself still searching the floor. Now he quickly realized where it was; it was inside of her. Now the real problem was how to get it back. Gretchen was already fully dressed, tired and ready to go upstairs and go to bed but what a smile she had. She came over and was telling him how much she enjoyed their lovemaking; how he was the best ever, among other things. Johann heard none of this. He was too engrossed with his new problem.

His mind was in the panic mode. What a disaster! What would happen when it fell out? How could he explain that he needed the spare that his father was holding for them? What if he was stopped on the way home since he didn't bring his spare? It would mean certain death for him. He had to do something – and it had to be quick.

As she continued to extol his virtues, he grabbed her by the arm and kissed her passionately. "Before you go, I have to try something that one of my friends told me about. You must let me," he pleaded. Without further adieu, he grabbed her, gently laid her down on a table that was in the room, lifted up her skirt, pulled down her panties and began a session of oral sex. At first she protested but as he proceeded her protests turned to moans of pleasure. He had never done this before and was not sure at first if he was doing it right. But when he heard her moan in pleasure he knew that it was good enough. As he continued he probed inside her vagina with his fingers, and he probed, and he probed. Occasionally, she would let out a little yelp of pain as his fingernails scratched against the wall of her vagina. He would apologize saying that this was his first time and continue probing. However, the recovery process was not going so well. It was obviously stuck up in her vagina at a greater distance than the length of his fingers (which made sense since his erection was much longer than his fingers). All of a sudden he remembered that he had a pencil in his back pocket that he brought with him to write down his new address should she have asked. He took out the pencil and resumed his probing with the blunt end. In a few seconds, he found the object of his quest. Now the trick was to get it out and not to push it further in. He carefully probed until he believed that he found the opening of the penis cover. He gently inserted the pencil then pushed up so the penis cover was touching the wall of her vagina. The fact that she was shaking from pleasure and having orgasms did not help the procedure. However, his perseverance paid off and he was able to get it far enough out to grab it with his fingers. The entire process distended her vagina to the point it resembled a gynecological examination but she was too rapt to feel anything.

He put the penis cover in his pocket, ended the oral sex session and helped her up. She could hardly stand, let alone walk. They had to wait about ten minutes for her to get her strength and composure back. He went into the other room and put the penis cover back on. It was now a really loose fit as he did not bring any glue with him so used some string that was tied around a package being stored in the room and hoped that he would not get stopped on the way home – but at least he had it on. He walked her to the front door where she kissed him again and spoke of her undying love for him and could not wait to visit him in Germany or for him to come visit her.

When he reached the safe house without being spotted and snuck back inside through the back door he questioned his judgment about this whole incident. Was it really worth it to have put him and his family in mortal danger for a couple of hours of sexual pleasure? "Yes! Yes! Yes!" He said aloud in bed as he turned and fell asleep.

A week later he sent her a letter from Switzerland telling her the whole story. He was Jewish and had been pretending to be a Gentile and that his father had decided to leave Austria in fear for their safety. He professed his love for her and apologized for not telling her that night. Since he was not sure if she would accept him as a Jew, he could not risk the safety of his family. He invited her to come to Switzerland and, if she could forgive him, to marry him and go with the family to Canada. A week later a letter arrived. She was very angry that he did not tell her the truth and she was not sure if she ever could forgive him for not trusting her. That being said, she accepted his proposal of marriage and would be in Switzerland by the end of the week. She added in a post script that she knew exactly how he felt. She decided not to tell her parents that she was going to marry a Jew.

CHAPTER THIRTEEN

BETRAYAL

"The Germans make good Nazis but lousy anti-Semites. The Austrians make lousy Nazis, but what first-class anti-Semites they are!"

Alfred Polgar, Jewish writer who was born in Leopoldstadt and immigrated to the United States in 1938 where he became a film critic in Hollywood

Unfortunately, before and during the war there were a number of people, regardless of religion, ethnicity, and nationality that would do anything to stay alive even at the expense of others or would look to profit from another person's misfortune.

Remember Mischa, my co-conspirator in the Kaltenbrunner cover-up? Well, as I mentioned earlier he was Jewish and many of his fellow officers at the precinct knew that he was Jewish. However, he was very popular with his fellow officers. More than once he had risked his life and saved some of them. So, when Germany annexed Austria and the dismissal of Jews began, I went to General Kaltenbrunner with a request for special consideration for Mischa. I wanted Mischa to be transferred to another precinct in the city and all records of him being Jewish expunged and replaced with non-Jewish credentials. I must admit that I expected all sorts of belligerence on the part of Kaltenbrunner, even to the point of not even being allowed to see him as he was now in charge of the SS. However, as soon as his adjutant informed him that I was there I was given preferential entry ahead of all of the other people waiting. He was very cordial and shook my hand with both of his hands as if we were old friends when the adjutant brought me in, actually coming over to me rather than waiting for me to come to his desk (after, of course, the Heil Hitler! salute, which I returned). When the adjutant left, he again expressed his gratitude about how everything was handled. I asked about his wife and how she was doing. He said that she took it very hard and was inconsolable for many months before coming to grips with it and moving on. He told me that all during this time he kept thinking about how bad it would have been and the resultant guilt that she would have felt or the blame that she would have placed on herself and on him that probably would never have gone away if she knew that he committed suicide and was not murdered in a robbery. He thanked me for asking and simply asked what he could do for me (as opposed to what I wanted from him). I told him about Mischa and before I could even finish making my request, it was being done. At this point I found out something totally unbelievable. The Nuremberg Laws of 1935 had an escape clause. Under Article 7 of the Nuremberg Law, Hitler could remove the Mischling and Jewish status of a person by aryanizing him. Applications for special treatment were presented to him by some high-ranking Nazi with an explanation. Whether he personally reviewed each application or not I do not know, but I did find out from Kaltenbrunner that hundreds of half-Jews and quarter Jews plus a few full Jews were aryanized by Hitler and served in the Luftwaffe and the Wehrmacht. It should not have surprised me. Hitler considered himself above God and therefore with his power of life or death, a Jew-to-Aryan conversion was certainly within his domain. A special document was prepared called the Deutschblütigkeitserklärung (German Blood Declaration). This was an official document that converted Jews to Aryans on a racial basis. He showed the Wehrmacht form to me. It read as follows:

I approve that __________ may serve in the ______. At the same time I declare that ________is of equal status with German-blooded persons with respect to German racial laws with all of the consequent rights and obligations.

(Signed)

Fuehrer and Supreme Commander: *Adolf Hitler*

Commander and Chief of the Wehrmacht: *Wilhelm Keitel*

Secretary of State and Head of the Reich Chancellery: *Hans Heinrich Lammers*

Two days later the document arrived by special messenger with Kaltenbrunner's title and signature as head of the SS in place of Keitel's signature. Mischa was promoted to detective, transferred to another precinct, and given a new Aryan name. He became Ernst Köppner (but I continued to refer to him as Mischa). In addition to the Blood Certificate, new official documents on original forms were created for him one of which was a hospital medical record of his circumcision as a result of having paraphimosis, a condition where the foreskin of the penis does not retract leading to infections that are ultimately treated by surgically removing the foreskin. The Nazis had a solution to every problem. Luckily, he was not married so it was much less complicated to have him disappear as a Jew and resurface somewhere else as a Gentile. Kaltenbrunner also wrote a personal note that he had been on a secret assignment for the SS pretending to be Jewish due to his paraphimosis, and anything that Detective Ernst Köppner needed was to be accorded to him. Furthermore, if they had any issues they should bring them to his personal attention. Mischa chose the main headquarters police station in District One.

Mischa adapted well as a detective in the new precinct. Not only did he fit right in, he used his innate sense of humor to reinforce his new pro-Nazi, anti-Semitic Aryan identity. The police, many of whom had been underground Nazis were vehemently anti-Semitic. They either ignored Jewish persecution or joined in sometimes even teaching children how to humiliate Jewish children – the younger the better. For example, there was one police officer that stood outside different schools in the eighth district in the morning and asked the children if they were Jewish. The first few times the Jewish children, being innocent, answered truthfully and said that they were Jewish. The officer would tell them to step aside. When there were three or four of them he would make examples of them in front of the non-Jewish children. The officer would take the first child and ask to see their homework or notebook or lesson book and tear one of them up along with their homework. For the other two or three Jewish children he would have the non-Jewish children do the same things. Children can be very cruel to each other especially when led by an adult of authority. Many of the children were hearing virulent anti-Semitic comments at home, in the street and in school so this was just reinforcing what their parents, teachers and other adults were saying over and over again. Most also thought it was great fun. The Jewish children, who were invariably crying, were not allowed to go home after their humiliation. They were forced to go to class where the teachers would ridicule them further for not having their homework or for the bad way in which they treated school property when their books were destroyed or just for being Jewish. It was worse when it rained. Not only were their school books or homework destroyed, they were knocked down and forced to roll in muddy puddles until all of their clothes were wet and muddy. They had to sit in school the whole day in that condition crying incessantly. There were no longer any Jewish teachers at the schools. They had been dismissed shortly after Anschluss. Most of the remaining teachers either supported the persecution or were too afraid to do anything. Word gets around quickly. At one school, an older female teacher, a devout Christian, tried to help one of her young pupils, a small petite, eight year old Jewish girl with long black hair, who was being forced to roll around in the mud under the direct supervision of that policeman. The officer called her a Jew-lover and knocked her down into the muddy water and kicked the muddy water all over her from head to toe. She was told to go home and rethink her "love for Jews". Similar incidents occurred sporadically until Jewish children were no longer allowed to go to school although by that time many families no longer sent their children to those public schools.

Mischa avoided these types of acts but did want to seem in the least bit pro-Jewish. He used his humor instead. For example, he was talking with a group of fellow officers one morning when he spied a cockroach scurrying across the room about two meters away from the group. He ran over and stepped on it hard. His sudden movement and the loud crunching sound of the cockroach's skeletal collapse startled the other officers so they stopped what they were doing. All eyes were on Mischa as he took his foot off of the squashed cockroach and looked down. He frowned and knelt down talking to the dead roach, he apologized, "I'm sorry Herr Roach. I thought you were a Jew!" Of course, the men laughed and repeated the story to every other officer in the precinct. Many who were not there came up to him later that day and complemented him on his wit saying that they were going to say this the next time they stepped on a bug. The story made its rounds.

On another occasion, in the locker room after completing his shift, he asked the officers there if they knew the difference between how a Jew wipes his ass compared to a normal person. Of course, no one knew so Mischa proceeded to demonstrate. He brought out a box of toilet tissues from the bathroom and placed it by his side as he sat down on the bench.

"First, the normal person," he said. He took a sheet of toilet paper and pretended to wipe his ass. He discarded the paper under the bench. He repeated this three more times, each time discarding the used toilet tissue and taking a new one. "Now, the Jew." First he made sounds of farts with his hand to his mouth. Many, many farts. "Jews breath in a lot of hot air through their big noses which turns to gas," he said to the laughing crowd of officers, which now numbered more than thirty. Mischa took a sheet of toilet tissue and used it but instead of discarding it, he took it back up and held it in front of him just below his knees. He folded the sheet in half. He simulated another wiping of his ass and repeated the process folding the paper in quarters. He did this procedure five times until the size of the paper was just about the size of a small postage stamp. Finally, he discarded the well-used toilet paper after inspecting it to be sure he used every last bit of clean space. The men started to laugh when Mischa made the second fold. By the time he made the fifth fold the group was laughing hysterically. There was no doubt that they were going to repeat this many times during the course of the next few days. On one occasion instead of throwing the multi-folded paper away he put it back into his wallet and said in a Jewish accent, "Vy trow it avay ven it can be vashed und used von more time?" Mischa left no doubt as to where he stood on the Jewish issue.

Mischa helped us many times but there was one particular incident of significance worth mentioning. We were in the process of arranging the escape of the Herman family. They were being hidden from the Nazis by a longtime Gentile friend that owned a chain of clothing stores. They were being hidden in a medium sized back room in one of the larger stores in the eleventh district (Simmering) which had one of the lowest Jewish populations in Vienna. There was no toilet and there were no windows. The owner of the store had hidden the door to the room with a tall wooden shelf with shirts on the shelves that could be easily moved to reveal the door.

The Isaac Herman family consisted of six people: a father, a mother, a grandfather, two sons, 16 and 14 years old, and one daughter, 12 years old. The grandmother had died some years before. The conditions were very bad in the room where they had to stay during the day. They could leave the room to use the bathroom and walk around in the store after closing as the inside of the store could not be seen from the street. Food would be hidden in a small compartment in the store which they could get at night. Getting enough food was a major problem. The store owner could not afford to feed a family of six without going into his savings, which were not that much due to the poor business conditions and buying so much food was a clear indication that he was hiding Jews. Isaac discussed the situation with his friend and decided to flee the country illegally. We found out about the situation from the IKG when the friend took a chance and went to the IKG on Isaac's behalf.. Isaac's neighbors knew that they were Jewish. Twice one of the neighbors forced their way into his apartment and took things. One neighbor extorted some money from them so he would not come in and take things. He no longer had a job so it was only a matter of time before they were penniless. When stopped in the street and it was learned that his name was Isaac he was beaten and robbed. Rather than wait for more bad things to occur he decided to go underground with his family. They also had an uncle, his wife and a male cousin, 19 years old who were known Jews that he asked if they wanted to flee with him. All told there were nine people that wanted to flee – six males and three females. His uncle lived in the thirteenth district which also had a very small Jewish population.

There were 21 districts in Vienna. Seven of them had sizeable Jewish populations with the first, second and ninth districts having the most. Each of these seven districts had one of our secret groups operating in them. We also had one group responsible for all of the other districts. This was located in the fifteenth district (Fünfhaus). They were responsible for checking out the families in their district to make sure that they were trustworthy and had no family members that could pose any problems during the escape (too old, too young, too ill, etc.). We usually only handled families in one district at a time. In this case, the uncle his wife and their cousin was being handled by the group in the ninth district. The background check of the Herman family was thorough and complete with the uncle and cousin accepted on the recommendation of the Herman family without a background check. Since each group in each district operated independently and secretly, there was no way for the group in the ninth district to contact the group in the other district to check the background of the uncle and cousin and, frankly, they didn't really see the need. In fact, they did not even mention that the uncle lived in another district. As far as we knew, they all lived in the same district and had all been verified. However, if they had told us everything and we had checked it out, they would have been told that the uncle was a suspected collaborator with the Nazis. He was actually biding his time as to when to turn in the Herman family for the reward. He did not need the money right now and knew from past experience that every two or three months the reward for turning in hidden Jews was increased but there was no doubt in his mind that he would turn them in for the reward when he needed the money. When Isaac came to him and told him of the planned escape and the Jewish network, his face lit up. Isaac could see how happy he was and he also smiled. He was glad that he thought of including his uncle in their plans. Of course, the uncle had other thoughts in his mind which caused him to smile. Imagine the reward and the recognition that he would receive in exposing a Jewish escape network. There could be twenty or more Jews involved. He simultaneously reflected on his great strategy to delay turning them in. The wait was well worth it. No wonder he was so happy!

Three days before the planned escape, Isaac and the uncle were brought to our safe house at 828 Fruehlingstrasse, which was a walk-up apartment located on top of a dry goods store. The store closed promptly at 7 PM every night which made it easy for us to facilitate the movement of people there at night. It was a largely commercial area so there were not too many people living on the block and it had a back entrance that led to a back alley that paralleled the main street which was used for deliveries to and from the many stores that lined the street. We had rented three of these types of apartments in different parts of the city that would afford us privacy and that provided alternative entrances and exits. So three days before the escape, they were brought to the safe house, shown the layout of the rooms, informed of the plan and shown various escape routes should the hiding place be compromised. Originally, the families were not given the specific address of the safe house and they were brought to the safe house in the back of a van that did not afford any view of the outside streets. However, we soon realized that the people had to know where they were being taken so they could at least know the neighborhood and better understand the potential escape routes if needed. They had to collect all of their valuables and personal items during the next three days without raising any suspicions. Only things that could be easily carried and preferably hidden in their luggage should be brought. We provided luggage and briefcases with false bottoms and removable linings to hide money, jewelry, documents, etc. They would bring their valuables to the apartment where they would be re-packed in the special luggage. All of this had to be hidden because of the border inspection process. If the border guards saw so many valuables they would know that they were fleeing the country. All of the escapes we arranged were on the pretext of vacations or business trips in Switzerland. We had entire itineraries printed up along with round trip train tickets, reservations in hotels or correspondence with friendly non-Jewish families in Switzerland pretending to be their relatives and saying how they are waiting for them to visit. All of the arrangements were openly made with reputable travel agencies. The fact that these families never returned was never an issue since travel agencies do not monitor the return trips of their clients, they just issue the tickets and hotel vouchers. At this session we also answered any questions that they asked. At every session some male asked about the "penis test". It was not unusual for the Nazis to ask to see the penises of travelers at the border crossing if they suspected someone of being Jewish. At this point, we allowed the group leader, at their own personal discretion, to let the men know something about the penis extension. It was not a detailed explanation; they were not shown a penis extension on any of the men there nor shown any unworn example or told where they came from. They were only told that each male would be fitted with a false penis (we never used the word extension) that would pass any inspection. No more information was given.

So, at the initial meeting they were told that they would be picked up and brought back to this apartment in three days to re-pack their luggage and be taken by truck from Vienna to a small railway station where we had connections to board the train to Switzerland. They would also be given false travel papers – and they would be given the false penis that would enable them to pass as Gentiles. We also familiarized them with the neighborhood showing them some maps and escape routes in case of a problem.

The next day, the uncle went to his contact at the local police station. He told him everything about this secret underground Jewish escape organization including the location of the safe house and the story of the false penis that would be given to them on the night of the escape that would make them look like Gentiles enabling them to pass any inspection at any border checkpoint. This false penis story immediately piqued the interest of his police contact who reported this to the main police station in district one. The uncle was taken to the district one police station where he was brought to the precinct captain. He repeated the story giving even more detail about the escape plan except this time he called it an extra penis. The police officers looked at each other with a sly grin. This was a chance to break up a major secret Jewish escape organization and to learn about a new procedure that the Jews had developed – the extra penis. They could see their promotions ahead of them. Because of the potential magnitude of the operation they immediately notified the SS. The uncle could not reveal any details whatsoever on the extra penis. So as the story made its rounds throughout the police station most of the other officers had doubts. It did lead to number of new jokes about Jews having two penises. It was all over the station. Everyone was laughing. However, there was one officer, a detective named Mischa, who did not laugh. He knew that it was no joke. He was able to get all of the details about the informant from one of his friends. He immediately left the station and contacted me. I in turn contacted the group leader and informed him of the security breach and the name of the informant.

We put our heads together and, surprisingly, quickly developed an alternate plan that had three components. The first component was that we would pick up both families on the appointed night. The Herman family would be taken to another safe house. The uncle's family would be brought to the original safe house at around 10:30 PM.

The second component capitalized on the fact that there was a reward for turning in hidden Jews. Anyone that reported Jews masquerading as Gentiles would get 500 Marks per Jew. Similarly, if anyone reported the hiding place of Jews and the people that were hiding them would also get 500 Marks per person for the Jews and for the people hiding them. There were a number of people who became Jew-hunters and took advantage of this financial opportunity. They worked in small groups and they did their own investigations on anyone they suspected of hiding Jews. There were many techniques that they used including watching for people buying extra food and medical supplies, prior known associations with Jews in business, heavy activity at night, etc. Once a person was suspected of hiding Jews, their entire family would be watched 24 hours per day by these informants. We decided to use this to our advantage.

The third component was based on the perceived behavior of the Nazis. They would most likely wait until the entire group could be caught rather than just arrest the Jews when they showed up at the safe house.

On the day of the escape, we sent two teenage boys into a store known to be owned by a Jew-hunter, Otto Klink. They picked out some merchandise and when they were at the register they just started loudly talking about the people that they saw sneaking around the apartment down the street from them above the dry goods store at night and how it was suspicious and how they wondered if they were crooks or something. Otto picked up on their conversation immediately. He asked them about the apartment which they offered to show him. He went with them. The boys mentioned that they never saw anyone there during the day, only at night and that they always covered the windows when they turned on the light or used flashlights and sometimes a truck came by at night or early in the morning and they all got into it and drove away. They also mentioned that some people had been brought there last night but had left a few hours later. This was enough for Otto. He made some calls to his friends and decided that they would stake out the apartment that night. There were eight of them in his group and they decided to set up two shifts of four people. One shift would watch from 7 PM to 1 AM and the other shift from 1 AM to 7 AM. Two men would watch the front and two men would watch the back from two parked vans belonging to the business. As soon as the suspected Jews arrived one of the men watching the entrance where they arrived would let the other two know and would also go to the store which was only a few blocks away to get the other four.

Based on the magnitude of the operation, the Nazis had started their surveillance the day before and were using other apartments and stores for their surveillance totally out of sight while Otto's two-man groups were in the back of two vans which they drove to the safe house around 6 PM. They parked one of the vans in the street just about five meters from the front door. The other they parked in the alley where they could see the back door and anyone approaching. Their arrival was duly noted by the Nazi surveillance teams who thought that they were part of the escape plot when they drove up, parked the vans outside the apartment and climbed over the seat and hid in the back.

That night, a dark blue van came and picked up the uncle, his wife and their son at 10 PM at their home with their luggage. They were driven to the back of the apartment and told to go up the stairs and enter the apartment through the unlocked door and start re-packing. They were reminded not to turn on any lights except in the back room with the door closed. If they needed to leave the room for any reason they should close the light first before opening the door. After re-packing they should just wait until the others came which might take a few hours. They were given a flashlight which they were instructed not to use until they reached the top of the stairs and entered the apartment. They were watched by many eyes as they went up the stairs and entered the apartment.

The blue van was seen by the Nazis hiding at each end of the alley. The van waited until they reached the top of the stairs and entered the apartment before driving away. Given the situation we had devised a particularly ingenious escape plan for the blue van. The blue van had false license plates from Salzburg and a broken taillight which were duly noted by the Nazis when they entered the alley. After the driver dropped off the uncle and his family he drove halfway down the alley with his lights off and pulled into one of delivery bays of Fritz's bakery located further down the alley and parked the van. There were two other blue vans of the same make and model as the one we used which was precisely why we used this particular van that night. Fritz changed the Salzburg license plates to Vienna license plates, fixed the broken taillight and attached two signs, one on each side of the van that said Fritz's Bakery that we made beforehand. This part of the alley could not be seen from any of the places where the Nazis were hiding. Fritz left the van parked there then crawled unseen across the alley in the dark, jumped over a fence to the other side of the street and waited in the driveway of a store. About five minutes later a car pulled into the driveway. He jumped into the back seat of the car. They drove off without being noticed. Meanwhile, the Nazis were waiting for the dark blue van with Salzburg plates and a broken taillight to leave the alley so they could arrest the occupants a few blocks from the alley. Since it didn't leave the alley they just thought that it was waiting a little further down the alley and did not give it too much thought at the time. They would get it later. We did this because we had been told by Mischa that the Nazis would radio ahead to pick up the vehicle after it drove away and was far enough from the apartment that the arrests could not be seen or heard if there were gunshots by the people in the apartment.

For the Nazis, this was a big operation. The uncle had told them that there would be a family of at least six Jews there trying to escape and at least one senior member of the escape team that knew the entire operation as well as the drivers of the escape vehicles and the vehicles that brought them to the apartment. Once they had the family they could force them to reveal who had been hiding them. Moreover, they would be given the extra penises at the safe house which was of particular interest to the Nazis. The Nazis were looking at potentially twenty or thirty arrests and a chance to break up the biggest Jew-smuggling ring in the city. Overall, there were about twenty police officers, five SS officers, and about forty SS soldiers hidden in the various stores and buildings across the street from the apartment and at each end of the alley with additional men and vehicles in a two block radius around the apartment. Their headquarters was a drug store directly across the street where they set up a command post with radios and other equipment the day before. At a moment's notice they could seal the area trapping everyone inside. Most of the SS soldiers at the site would be used for supporting gunfire if needed. At the signal, the police would make the raid with an SS officer and some of the SS soldiers. Overall, they did not expect any trouble. They had conducted many such raids and never had to fire a shot. The Jews usually just gave up. But, as this was supposed to be set up by a large well-organized underground Jewish group, they decided not to take any chances so they came in force with instructions to shoot to kill if there was any armed resistance.

Both surveillance teams noted the arrival of the uncle and his family. Otto sent for the other four men at the store. Two entered each van observed by the watching Nazis and then they waited…and waited…and waited for the truck to arrive to take the occupants of the apartment out of the city. By 6 AM Otto concluded that perhaps the truck might not come until the next night or perhaps during the day when the street was crowded. They obviously could not keep their vans parked there without being noticed. Otto made the decision. They would enter the apartment now through the back door so as not to create a disturbance that would arouse any neighbors that could call the police. They would quietly capture all the Jews that were there, turn them in leaving half of their group in the apartment to wait for the escape vehicle or more Jews to be brought there. They left the vans. Two from the van parked in the street stood at the front door while the other two went to the back door joining the four that were already there. Five of them, including Otto, went up the back stairs. One waited downstairs. They had four pistols between them and all of them had small heavy clubs and flashlights. Otto gave one pistol to the two men watching the front door, kept one and gave the other two guns to two of his companions, one of whom was standing in the alley guarding the back door. Their movement was duly noted by the SS. They slowly climbed up the stairs and opened the back door which was unlocked. The rooms were dark since the uncle was told not to put on any light. They turned on their flashlights and entered the apartment. The uncle heard them enter and thought that they were the rest of the group. He shut the light in the back room and went out to meet them loudly complaining about why they had left him alone for so long. Otto took his tirade as an attack. He and his men immediately clubbed the uncle viciously. The uncle let out a loud scream and tried to shield himself from the ensuing blows before falling unconscious to the floor bleeding profusely from his head and face as they still continued to beat him. The wife also screamed – but just out of fear, not from being beaten – as they were in the other room with the door closed they did not know what exactly what was going on. The wife just screamed when she heard her husband scream. The men ran into the room where the screams came from, opened the door and pointed their flashlights at the wife and son who surrendered without any harm coming to them. They were told to go into the main room and lay down on the floor while they searched the back room and the rest of the apartment. When the men searched the rest of the apartment they were very disappointed that there were no other Jews there. One of the men went downstairs and let in the other two members of the group that were waiting out front. At that point the Nazis mobilized. They thought that Otto's group was the escape team. They could not hear the screams of the uncle as he was being beaten so did not expect anything out of the ordinary. They moved en masse up the alley to the back staircase and to the front door simultaneously. The man watching the back stairs had one of the guns. As it was dark he did not clearly see the SS uniforms as they ran to the stairs shouting. He thought that it was the Jews coming to pick up the uncle and his family and that they had seen his group go into the apartment so they were attacking them to rescue the family. He panicked and opened fire shooting the first policeman leading the group twice, once in the chest and once in the head, killing him instantly and wounding two others. His shots were returned and he was killed instantly. Conditions worsened. All of the soldiers and police upon hearing the shots started shooting into the windows of the apartment from the roofs and windows of the buildings across the street. In the ensuing firefight, all of Otto's men in the apartment were either killed or wounded. The uncle had been beaten very badly and would never regain consciousness. The wife and his son were not hurt since they were lying on the floor when the shooting started and now they were still on the floor but with two of Otto's men lying dead on top of them. It was all over in about ten minutes. The soldiers even fired at the two vans parked in the street and alley in which Otto's men had been hiding lest there be some unseen gunmen hiding in them. Both vans were completely destroyed with the one parked out front in the street catching fire and exploding a few minutes later.

The few residents of the street upon hearing the shots and the explosion came out to see what was happening. Soon the fire department showed up since someone reported the burning van.

Now came the hard part – trying to figure out exactly what was going on. They turned on the light and laid out the bodies. At first they thought that Otto's gang was the Jewish escape group that was going to smuggle the hiding Jews out of the country. The captain decided to check the men to get the extra penises so he asked one of the policemen to pull down the pants of all of the dead males and examine the penis of each man. He refused. He was asked again but he still refused. There was no way he was going to touch a Jewish penis with his bare hands. His fellow officers were not helping. They were making all sorts of snide remarks such as "See if you can arouse them!" and "Get them hard!" and "Watch out for the piss! They can piss even when they're dead, you know!" which strengthened his refusal. Finally, another policeman stepped forward with a handkerchief in his hand and thoroughly examined each man's penis. He saw that none of Otto's men were Jewish and that it really was their original penis since it didn't pull off. The man who had been beaten half-to-death was indeed a Jew with a circumcised penis. Seven out of the eight men had uncircumcised penises as did the one shot in the alley. They could not find an "extra penis" either in their possession, on their bodies or in the apartment. They decided that this was a non-Jewish gang that smuggled Jews out of Austria for money – until one of the police officers recognized Otto as the person that was the informant. Now they were completely baffled. Moreover, the dark blue van with the Salzburg license plate and the broken taillight that had dropped the Jews off in the alley had apparently disappeared from the face of the Earth since they could not find it when they searched the alley. They concluded that it had escaped in the confusion even though the soldiers at each end of the alley swore that the van never passed them. The only Jews in the apartment were the uncle and his family and he was the collaborator that had informed the police about the escape plot. Otto's two wounded men were in no condition to talk. With Otto and the uncle dead they never received a plausible explanation. The talk about a mass escape, a secret Jewish underground organization and false penises was assumed to be a total fabrication or misunderstanding of the uncle. Later that morning one of our group members went to Fritz's Bakery just before they opened and simply drove our delivery van out of the delivery bay right past the Germans without anyone thinking anything about it.

The two wounded police officers recovered and were back on their beat a few months later. One of Otto's wounded team members died and the other recovered but swore he knew absolutely nothing. He was just asked to be there that night. The uncle's wife and son were arrested and deported to Dachau. The Herman family was successfully transported out of the city from another safe house on the other side of Vienna that very same evening. This was without any incident since all attention was focused on the SS operation on Fruehlingstrasse.

Every once in a while one of the policemen who participated in the muddled events of that night would walk down the street as part of his routine patrolling, stop and look at the apartment wondering what had really happened that night.

CHAPTER FOURTEEN

CAROL

"Just who is and who is not a Jew is something that I determine for myself."

> Karl Lueger, anti-Semitic Christian Social Mayor of Vienna, 1897-1910, when questioned about his friendly association with Jews.

As soon as Hitler came to power in 1933 he authorized a census to determine the Jewish population of Europe. The census estimated that there were 9.5 million Jews in Europe with the following breakdown:

Country	Jews	Country	Jews		Country	Jews
Poland*	3,000,000	Lithuania*	155,000		Sweden*	6,500
Russia**	2,525,000	Greece*	100,000		Denmark*	6,000
Romania*	980,000	Latvia*	95,000		Estonia*	5,000
Gemany*	565,000	Yugoslavia*	70,000		Spain	4,000
Hungary*	445,000	Belgium*	60,000		Ireland	3,600
Czech.*	357,000	Turkey	56,000		Luxemburg*	2,200
England	300,000	Bulgaria*	50,000		Finland	1,800
Austria*	250,000	Italy*	48,000		Norway*	1,500
France*	225,000	Switzerland	18,000		Portugal	1,000
Holland*	160,000	Danzig*	9,200		Albania	200
					Total	9,500,000
**only 70% under Nazi control			*under Nazi control:			8,458,000

Before the war, the Nazis set up concentration camps for political prisoners, criminals, gypsies and Jews that they thought could cause trouble. These camps, such as Dachau and Oranienburg, were located in Germany. As the war progressed Germany was faced with the problem of a rapidly increasing Jewish population with each victory. This was unacceptable to Hitler and had to be addressed. The first approach was to set up ghettos.

In 1516 Venice passed a law that no Jew could live in the city. They converted a former walled iron foundry complex that was formerly owned by the Ghetto family into dwellings. Jews not able to move into this area had to live outside the city. In addition, every Jew doing business in Venice had to wear a yellow coat. Yellow was associated with the prostitutes of the city so it was chosen for its obvious denigrating association. This was the reason that the Nazis chose yellow for the color of the Star of David that Jews had to wear. To put things in perspective, Jews were not the only ethnic group singled out for exclusion in Venice at that time. Turkish merchants and their families had to live in the palazzo area known as the Fondaco dei Turchi. Other outsiders were similarly treated but the Jews were treated the worst as they were locked in the "ghetto" at night. Moreover, it was overcrowded and lacked proper sanitary conditions but it was livable and there were never any restrictions on the amount of food or anything else that could be bought by the Jews.

The Nazis created ghettos to isolate the Jews in many cities in Europe. The largest and most infamous were Lodz, Lublin and Warsaw in Poland and Theresienstadt in Czechoslovakia. However, in Vienna, they decided not to create a special, isolated ghetto. The policy at the time was to encourage as many Jews as possible to emigrate. This worked in Germany where the government was able to confiscate all of their assets in return for emigrating.

Leopoldstadt, the second district, had the highest concentration of Jews. This district is a large island (19 square kilometers) surrounded by the Danube Canal on the east, west and south and the Danube River on the north. Due to its historically high Jewish population and the matzoh factories that were located there, the island was given the nickname, "Mazzesinsel" (Matzoh Island). This district is also well-known because it is where the big Prater Amusement Park with the giant Ferris wheel is located. In addition, many Jews lived in other districts.

A wall was usually built around a ghetto but as the second district was an island surrounded by water on all sides and there were still many Gentiles living there as well they decided not to set up a ghetto as long as they could get Jews to emigrate.

In 1937 the population of the second district was about 70,000 people with a Jewish population of about 27,000 (38 percent). At the height of its occupancy the number of people in the district was about 195,000 with all of the increase being Jews that had to relocate there when they were forced out of their residences in other districts and had no other place to live. Here again it is important to emphasize that travel in and out of Leopoldstadt was completely open. There was no barbed wire, there were no electrified fences, and there were no guard houses on any of the many bridges connecting the island to the rest of the city.

The Nazis used the Jewish Council (IKG) to assign people to the various apartments and carry out all orders imposed upon the Jews in Vienna. Non-Jewish residents in the second district could volunteer to give up their apartments for incoming Jews. The non-Jewish residents of this area that volunteered could take over the residence of one of the Jewish families that had to relocate there. A special relocation exchange service was set up to do this. Wherever possible, they gave the non-Jewish resident a bigger and better apartment than the one that they had to give up to encourage more non-Jewish residents to volunteer to exchange their apartments. Since the number of Jews forced to move into the district was far more than the number of non-Jewish volunteers, there was a larger number of nicer Jewish residences available so invariably all of the volunteers were upgraded. If the rent was higher in the new apartment, the Jews vacating were assessed a fee for the difference. The Nazis, of course, kept the best homes and apartments for themselves and their pro-Nazi supporters. Essentially all of the relocated volunteers were quite pleased with the change. None of the Jewish families voluntarily moved. They were forcibly displaced, especially when their tenant rights were revoked. They could be forced out by any Gentile that wanted the apartment as long as the district authorities approved. The Jewish family could fight this forced extradition in court – at least in the beginning, but, as time passed, they lost more and more of their rights. Still, Jews with special jobs and skills were often allowed to keep their apartments with the support of their employer. While many Gentiles in the second district took advantage of the upgraded relocation opportunity, many did not as they had businesses there (some of which they illegally took over from Jews), had a large close-knit family within a small radius, had children in school with many friends, or owned the apartment buildings. Overall, only about 25 percent of the Gentiles living in the second district volunteered to relocate out of the district. One thing that the remaining Gentiles did try to do was to make the apartment where they lived "Judenfrei". When the Jews lost their tenant rights and they were a minority in a particular building the landlord would evict them as long as they had another tenant ready to rent the apartment, which was often a problem. Very few Gentiles wanted to move into the second district with all of its Jews so essentially all of the apartment evictions were from other districts. Sometimes the Jews would offer a much higher rent to stay there or would fight the eviction in court which could be done for the first year or two. Eviction could be also denied on health reasons, occupation reasons or if they worked at the IKG. To accommodate evicted Jews from other districts or other cities, many residents were forced to allow other Jews to share their apartment for which they received some payment.

Our group had decided that any thought of us leaving the country was out of the question if we could help the Jews in Vienna by providing food and medical supplies and money to help them emigrate. At that point we did not think about trying to smuggle known Jews illegally out of Austria since the Nazis were strongly encouraging legal emigration. However, as conditions worsened and the emigrations began to be restricted, we decided to see if there were ways to get known Jews living in Vienna out of Austria illegally. Also, since the safety of the Jews being hidden by Gentiles was tenuous (they could be turned in by the many Jew-hunters and informants) we placed a high priority on finding them and helping them get out of the country or, if they chose to stay, become a bona-fide Gentile with the help of the extension, false papers and a job which we could provide. We also had to prepare forged documents for the people that we were helping to escape and we would likely not have too much advanced warning of who and how many people we would have at a time so the preparation of the forged papers had to be done after they agreed to flee. We did not want to have them wait for any extended period at any of the safe houses where the risk of discovery would be great so we tried to prepare their documents before the night of their escape.

At the morgue I redoubled my efforts to get the real documents such as identity cards, passports, etc. from the deceased. Wilhelm came up with a great idea. Whenever someone died of old age or a sickness at their homes I created a "toxic environment". When I arrived at the scene I would immediately tell everyone present that I suspected that the person had died from a communicable disease. Once they heard this, there was a rush out the door by everyone in the house or apartment, which was cordoned off. To play it safe I or Wilhelm would inoculate all of the police and any other person at the scene that were "exposed" to the body to prevent them from getting the disease. No one ever questioned how come I happened to have the antidote with me. They were just glad to get the inoculation. Not one of the inoculated policemen or other people got sick so I was actually looked upon as some kind of medical hero. Once everybody left the house or apartment I could search the place and take whatever I felt could be used by the escapees. When the body was removed and I left, no one tried to enter the apartment due to the quarantine notices that were conspicuously placed on all of the doors and windows, not even relatives or thieves. Even after I declared the residence safe, the relatives were wary and just came to get valuables such as jewelry and money, which I never took. If they could not find some of the photographs or documents that they wanted to keep they assumed that they were taken by the authorities, lost, accidentally destroyed or thrown out by the deceased. Only once was I surprised by a family member of a recently deceased elderly person as I was taking the box of collected documents and photographs to my car. It was a private house with a tree-lined walkway to the street that did not allow you to see anyone on the street so I waited until it was late to minimize being seen. As I walked out the front door around 8 PM I met a young woman who had entered the walkway. We were both startled. When she saw the box I was carrying she thought that I was a robber but I quickly identified myself as the Assistant Coroner and told her that the woman who lived there, Elsa Schmidt, had died due to a potentially contagious illness and that I was taking some personal items out at the request of some family members. As I was telling her this I reached into my pocket and pulled out my identification card. The young woman told me that Elsa was her great aunt and she was just coming to check on her as she had not been feeling too well. She had been away from Vienna on business and had just returned. She was very distraught and did not question why I was doing this so late at night. I inoculated her, gave her the box and left her there. I never heard from her again but I did get a note from Elsa Schmidt's older sister thanking me for taking the trouble to get the valuable mementos from her sister's home and giving them to her niece who in turn gave them to her. She added that if some other family members had taken them that she would never have received anything and they really meant a lot to her. I noted down her address thinking that perhaps in time I would again take possession of these items adding the older sister's possessions as well when she died.

Things were going extraordinarily well until one day my life irrevocably changed - again. And it was fate that interceded.

I met Carol at the hospital when her father died. I was visiting a friend at the hospital across the hall and happened to be there when he died. He had been sick for quite some time so his death was not unexpected. He died of a disease that we now call pancreatic cancer that was further complicated by pneumonia. He died in the hospital and was surrounded by his family when he died. Aside from being absolutely gorgeous, Carol was also very calm and took charge of the situation without any overt emotional outburst. She consoled her mother and older sister who were crying loudly and uncontrollably and quietly told the other family members what to do. Klaus and his wife should take Aunt Freda and Uncle Johann home. Cousin Friedrich should go with her and help her select the casket and make the funeral arrangements. Adolf, her brother, should take their mother and sister home and prepare the home for visitors. She gave them a book on Mozart to take home with them that she evidently was reading while they were waiting. Cousins Wilhelm, Dieter and Gretchen should go shopping for food, beer and wine to bring to the house. I was impressed and smitten. I just had to get to know her better.

I came over and introduced myself offering to do anything to make the situation as easy as possible. She thanked me and asked about the procedure for releasing the body, getting the death certificate, etc. I offered to help her get everything she needed and expedited all of the release papers so she could arrange for her father's body to be picked up early the next morning and brought to the funeral parlor. I wanted to ask her where she worked and what she did but didn't at that point. This was not the time and place for this type of tête-à-tête so I told her that I could either send the official death documents to her office, her home or to her mother's home when they were ready in a few days. She opted for her office not wanting her mother to receive them in her distraught state so I was able to get the name of the company for whom she worked and the office address. I worked late that evening and finalized all of the documents. Two days later I personally delivered the documents to her office mentioning that it was on my way to the morgue. She thanked me, we spoke for a few minutes and I left. Again, I did not think that this was the time or the place to express my feelings and try to set up a date but I did ask her if she had a business card. She did not have her own business card so she wrote down the phone number on a piece of paper.

Carol Freundlich worked for a large law firm as a legal assistant. She was also going to law school at night with plans to become a civil lawyer. Perhaps this explained why she was so articulate, calm and rationale following the death of her father. The law firm was in the Hartmann Building in the center of the city about ten blocks from the morgue. There were many law firms in that building which included the law firm in which Hermann Schmidt, one of my card game members, worked. I paid him a visit and asked if he knew Carol (he did not) or the firm for whom she worked (he did).

Now, as I have mentioned, we had an intelligence network in each district that we used to check out every Jewish family member whom we were going to help escape. I decided to bend the rules a little and use this network to find out as much as possible about Carol.

Carol was 28 years old and was graduated from Vienna University with a Bachelor of Arts degree cum laude seven years ago. She was an active sorority member and had a few boyfriends at the university but none were apparently serious. She had one serious relationship with a lawyer who worked for the same firm but it ended abruptly and badly. I could not find out the reason or which one actually broke off the relationship. That was about two years ago. She occasionally dated but again nothing appeared serious. She liked classical music, tennis, swimming and jogged every morning in Augarten Park between six and seven AM. She was not a member of the Nazi party nor was she a sympathizer. One of her best friends at the university, Esther Kaufman, was Jewish and she despised the way that her friend was treated. She was almost arrested trying to help Esther but one of her teachers interceded on her behalf and the police just took down her name but did not arrest her. She was very close to her family and spent almost every Sunday with them after going to church. She was a Lutheran. She was also very generous. Whenever her brother, sister, parents or relatives needed something she would help them. She was well paid as a legal assistant and was more than happy to help her family whenever possible. Due to the network that we had in place, I was able to get all of his information within six days.

I was not athletic so meeting her on a tennis court or while jogging was out of the question. As I was not intending to take any law courses I decided to use classical music as an approach. I went to the library and took out a few books on classical music. For about two weeks all I did with my free time was to listen to classical music and write down notes describing the music, the composer and any critic's review. After this two week crash course, I was ready to accidentally meet her. I waited in the lobby of her building while Hermann went to the floor on which she worked and waited out of sight until she came out of the office to go to lunch. I had pointed her out the day before from a doorway hidden from view. He followed her into the elevator which was always crowded at lunch time getting into the elevator last so he was blocking the door and had to be one of the first people out of the elevator. Meanwhile, I was downstairs in the lobby watching every elevator that came down knowing that she would be on the one with Hermann. Eventually, the elevator with

Hermann and Carol came to the lobby. I acted as if I was just waiting for him to go to lunch. I went up to him. As he left the elevator, I came up to him, shook his hand and started to talk to him. All of a sudden I turned to Carol and stopped talking. God she was beautiful! I thought to myself. After a very brief awkward moment I said, "Carol? Is it you?" She, of course replied, "Yes! It is me." I asked about her family and how they were doing. She replied that all things considered, everyone was doing okay and again thanked me for my help. I introduced her to Hermann and asked if she would like to join us for lunch. Unfortunately, she had something that she had to do but she said perhaps another time. This is a typical, polite response – but I was not about to dismiss it. I asked her about lunch tomorrow (busy) and Friday (also busy). I was going to give up after the third invitation as I thought that she just wasn't interested in me at all when she said that she would be available for lunch Monday or Tuesday of the following week. My heart skipped a beat as I chose Monday.

We met for lunch the following Monday. I waited in the lobby of her building. She came down promptly at 12:15 and we walked to the restaurant. I chose a very nice medium-sized restaurant – not too expensive or ostentatious, as I didn't want to seem overly eager to impress her. She commented that this was one of her favorite restaurants which made me quite happy. We were seated at a table towards the back and in the corner which was what I had requested when I made the reservation. While ordinarily she did not drink at lunch she decided to have a glass of white wine with me. We ordered the special dishes that they had prepared for the day and began to talk. We discussed our jobs but I was careful not too get into too much detail about my job as it was clearly not a pleasant mealtime conversational subject so I steered the conversation more to what she did. I also used the opportunity to talk about classical music. I was a bit nervous with my new-found subject matter and got some things confused. She politely corrected me a few times and rather than play the music fool any longer I confessed that I did a cram course in classical music to impress her and find a subject of common interest to break the ice. She asked how I knew that she was interested in classical music. I hadn't counted on the conversation going this way and I clearly couldn't say that I had her investigated. Suddenly, I remembered the Mozart book at the hospital and said that I assumed it since she was reading about Mozart at the hospital. She smiled and told me that she was very impressed. First that I noticed the Mozart book and second that I went to all of this trouble to match the conversation with her interests. Most of the other men she dated just talked about themselves. We spent the next half hour discussing what I listened to and how I liked it. She invited me to a classical music concert that was going to be at the Music Hall in two weeks. I accepted with the proviso that we go out the coming weekend. She accepted. I was elated and couldn't think of anything but her for the rest of the day – and the night. And for the next couple of days as well.

Spiriting Jewish families out of the second district was impossible at night after the curfew was established as there were too many informants watching the buildings. Our efforts were restricted to helping only those that were leaving their homes during the day, preferably going to other districts where the likelihood of their being watched was lower since it was an established daily routine. We concentrated on single men and women or young married couples without children. Once we established contact and they agreed to leave the country, we set the plan in motion. They could not bring any large personal belongings with them or sell anything that they owned except items that Jews were selling every day such as silverware, art, etc. A few of them still had some money and jewelry but many did not. So now we also had to provide clothing and amenities to the people we were helping to escape. On the appointed day of their departure, we would have them feign illness and tell their employer that they might not be at work for the next couple of days so they would not be immediately missed. We always set Thursday as the escape day so there would be four days before they had to go back to work. When they did not return to work on the following Monday, the reactions were mixed. Some employers attributed it to "Jewish laziness"; others just assumed that they were too sick to work and waited well into the week before making an enquiry. Some thought that they had been deported and gave it no more thought. Unfortunately, some of the people we helped escape had relatively important jobs in the companies in which they worked. As they were not paid much money and had special skills, replacing them with non-Jews would incur a significant expense and a long learning period. So, when these Jews did not show up for work the next week they were reported missing to the authorities. Initially, the authorities did not do anything. After all, who cared if some Jew did not go to work? However, after receiving four of these "missing Jew" reports at the second district police station, they decided to investigate. They went to the registered address of these Jews in the district and found that each of them was indeed missing, along with their spouse if they were married. They were no longer in their apartments, the food had spoiled and all small personal items such as pictures were missing from their frames. Moreover, none of their neighbors had seen them for days. At that point the police informed the Gestapo. Now it became a Gestapo matter so some Gestapo men went to the apartments where the missing Jews lived. Intensely forceful and brutal questioning of the Jews that lived in the same apartment revealed that they had escaped in some sort of underground network. It seemed that the escapees had told some of the people the night before they left not to expect them back as they were going to flee the country. Some talked about this special underground network that would help them get out of the country. This information was told to their neighbors, in spite of our warnings, for the best of intentions. As they were not going to come back they wanted their friends and neighbors to share their possessions including their dated ration cards which they left behind. Food was scarce and to take the ration cards with them, they thought, would be criminal. While the neighbors were sworn to secrecy, they readily told everything under the intense questioning of the Gestapo. From interviews with the employers of these Jews, the Gestapo also learned that all of the disappearances occurred on a Thursday and that all of the escaped Jews had pretended to be sick at work on that Thursday, with most leaving work early. They also realized that all of the missing Jews were either single or married without children.

Once the existence of the underground Jewish escape network was uncovered, unbeknownst to us, the Gestapo brought in the SS and together they set up a large number of surveillance teams that followed about seventy Jews that were single or married without children that had good jobs and were potential escape risks. They were not sure if the local police were involved so they decided to make it a secret operation. About 200 SS soldiers and about fifty Gestapo agents were used for this special task force. To staff this major operation they sent for about 150 SS soldiers from neighboring cities whom they had dress in plain clothes. They did not want to take a chance that even one of them would be recognized by someone during the day even though they were dressed in plain clothes. Their surveillance paid off.

Ernst Goldfarb and his wife Elsa had been approached and had agreed to flee the country. Ernst was a senior bookkeeper at a paper factory in the industrial zone. Elsa was a legal assistant for one of the law firms that were involved in the Aryanization of Jewish assets. Her knowledge of Yiddish and of Jewish customs proved invaluable to the law firm. Since these assets were secretly co-owned by the SS she was of high importance. Ernst was twenty-seven years old and Elsa was twenty-four years old. They had been married for almost four years and had decided not to have any children until they could save enough money to buy a small house. On the appointed Thursday, Ernst and Elsa started coughing and complaining about being sick at their respective jobs at about noon. They both left early. Elsa left at noon and Ernst at 12:15. Both Ernst and Elsa were among the seventy Jews under secret surveillance. He was followed to the address we gave him. His wife was already there and she had also been followed. Once the plainclothes SS officers saw each other and that both Ernst and Elsa were there together, they knew that this was going to be it. One of the undercover officers called the SS headquarters from a phone in the shop across the street and two unmarked cars with plainclothes SS officers and Gestapo agents came in a matter of minutes. A few minutes later, one of our cars pulled up into the driveway at the side of the store. Ernst and Elsa were taken to one of the safe houses. The two SS cars followed them. They changed positions every three blocks so our driver would not get suspicious.

The car pulled up into the alley behind our safe house at 148 Edelhofgasse. Ernst and Elsa got out of the car and entered the safe house through the back door. One of the cars with the SS men stayed at the safe house and the other followed Max. Unfortunately, Max also had some supplies for the forgery operation in the car so he went to the cleaning store after dropping Ernst and his wife off at the safe house. It was late in the afternoon so he just pulled up to the back door delivered the supplies and drove home. All of this was watched by the SS officers following him who noted the address of the cleaning store and continued following him home.

Meanwhile, one of the SS soldiers in the car watching the apartment called and sent for more reinforcements. About twenty more SS soldiers and Gestapo agents in plainclothes took up positions in the stores and businesses around the apartment. Later that night, under the cover of darkness, additional SS soldiers in uniform arrived and took up positions in the alley and set up a perimeter in a two-block circle around the apartment. At 11:30 Rolf and Karl, who were the drivers assigned to pick up Ernst and Elsa, went to the safe house to fit Ernst with the penis extension and take them to a train station outside of Vienna to go to Switzerland with the false papers that we had prepared. They drove up and parked the van in the alley. Rolf went upstairs and Karl stayed by the van we were using that night. Karl used this opportunity to relieve himself. He walked across the alley over to some bushes. As he was urinating he noticed a shadow in the alley about 100 feet away. He started to look around and saw someone watching the alley from the window of the house directly opposite the safe house. He quickly realized that they were in trouble. Without indicating that he saw them, he zipped up and slowly walked across the alley and up the stairs. When Karl closed the door behind him he ran to Rolf and told him that he thought that they were being watched. Rolf went into one of the darkened front rooms and peered out the window. Sure enough he could see someone watching their building from the apartment across the street. Luckily, he had not gotten to the part where he showed Ernst the extension so he went to the kitchen and burned all of the penis extensions using the glue from the tubes in the sink, scooped up the ashes, rolled up the tube and flushed the tube down the toilet. While he was doing this, Karl was on the phone talking to Meyer. They had not planned for anything like this. At first they thought about blocking the street with a truck once the van with Ernst and Elsa had passed so they could get away but realized that it would put more of them in danger as they could be caught and since the Nazis had radios, a description of the van with Ernst and Elsa in it would most likely have already been radioed ahead. They decided that they would bring Ernst and Elsa to the van and drive away as if nothing was wrong hoping at least that they would be followed rather than be arrested on the spot. If they were able to drive away Karl would try to find a way to let them out of the van without being seen or to try to suddenly speed up and lose anyone following him. The Nazis had indeed decided to follow them to capture more of the escape team. The van ambled slowly out of the neighborhood and slowly continued towards the outskirts of the city. Rolf could see other cars starting to follow him. Meanwhile, Meyer called Max and told him what was happening. Max and his wife quickly packed what they could and left the building from the back entrance to a car that we had sent to get them. Meyer also notified all of the employees at the cleaning store not to go to work the next day.

When the van left the safe house the SS swarmed in and searched it as well as all of the adjacent stores and apartments but found nothing. They simultaneously decided to raid the cleaning store where they found our forgery operation. No one was working there at the time. We never kept any records of the employees so they were safe but we lost everything else.

Karl knew Vienna very well so he knew some special streets that could afford him an opportunity to let Rolf, Ernst and Elsa get out of the van without being seen by their pursuers. The Nazis were not very close behind. As they turned the corner of Hofmanngasse which had many row houses with high hedges he briefly stopped as Ernst, Elsa and Rolf jumped out of the van and went into the garden of the first row house with high hedges without a fence where they hid behind the hedges. Karl quickly sped up the block before slowing down to the speed that he was driving for the past twenty minutes. When the Nazis turned the corner, the van was at the same distance it had previously been so they suspected nothing. When the Nazis passed, Rolf took Ernst and Elsa to another safe house by taxi. Meanwhile, Karl reached the outskirts of Vienna and pulled into a gas station. He parked the van by one of the pumps. He asked the attendant to fill up the gas tank and walked around the other side of the gas station to the bathroom and started running. He ran about two kilometers and took a taxi to the train station. At the station he took a train to the main station where he boarded a bus and got off about four blocks before his normal stop. He walked to his home. We never knew how long the Nazis sat there before checking the van and seeing it was empty and realizing that they had all escaped.

While this was a setback for our operation at least no one was captured or hurt. Even though we did not have any records of the workers at the cleaning store, we gave them the option of leaving the country or continuing to work for the network at a new location that we would set up as soon as possible. They all elected to stay. Unfortunately, we lost our forgery operation and all of the supplies which were scarce. We had to find another place as soon as possible. We had taken the precaution of hiding all of the documents and stamps in a false ceiling panel just in case something like this happened. This was a daily procedure. Luckily, they were not discovered and we were able to get them a week later.

Our operation the following week was not so lucky. We still didn't realize that the safety of the entire system had been compromised. When they were questioned, Ernst and Elsa admitted that they told a number of people that they lived with about the operation and that they would be leaving the country that Thursday. They also wanted to make sure that everything of value that they left behind would be used by others. We attributed the close call to an informant amongst those that they had told so we saw no reason to terminate the operation.

The next week it was the turn of Mikhail and Florenz Shöenbrunner. Mikhail was the chief accountant at a food packaging factory that had a large contract supplying the army. Mikhail was under SS surveillance. Florenz was a highly skilled heart surgeon working at the main hospital. While she was not permitted to operate, she served as an advisor during operations. She was also being watched. Again, they both feigned illness and left early on Thursday. They too went to a predetermined address and were observed together by the surveillance officers. They were brought to a safe house at 231 Strudhofgasse. Again, the car picking them up and dropping them off was followed but Fritz was using his personal car so he drove it back to his home rather than to the garage where we kept the vehicles and supplies. That night, it was Johann and Nicolas who were driving.

They pulled up to the safe house with Johann entering the apartment. This time the Nazis were not going to take any chances that they would lose them. They closed in. As there was not much cover, Nicolas saw them coming and pulled the pistol out from his belt and started firing. He wounded one of the soldiers before being cut down in a hail of bullets. Johann heard the shots and quickly removed his extension and his spare along with the extensions he had brought for Mikhail. He placed them in the sink squirted the glue over them and ignited it. He threw the tube into the fire as well. The Nazis ordered them out: "Raus! Raus! Juden Raus!"

Johann gave Mikhail the option of him and his wife surrendering but Johann decided that he would not surrender and be subjected to torture and perhaps break and reveal the names of his accomplices. Mikhail and Florenz briefly talked it over and came to the conclusion that they too would be tortured but since they had no names to give that they most likely be horribly tortured until they died. They decided not to surrender. While they were deciding, Johann called Fritz and told him what was happening. Fritz immediately packed his valuables and went to the roof of his building. All of buildings on the block were adjoined so he climbed over a small wall to the next building and then again to the next and the next. He entered the corner building whose entrance was on the other side of the block from the entrance to his building. When he reached the street he hailed a taxi and went to a safe house.

Johann only had the six bullets in his pistol. Mikhail looked at Johann and nodded, holding his wife's head cradled in his arms. Johann placed the pistol about two inches from Florenz's head and fired. Without allowing Mikhail time to look down he raised the pistol and shot him in the head as well. It was basically one continuous motion. The Nazis realized that they were shooting themselves and stormed the apartment. Johann went to the door and fired two shots down the stairs hitting two of the soldiers rushing up to the apartment put the pistol into his mouth and pulled the trigger using the last bullet in the pistol.

When they were brought to the morgue I instantly recognized him. As soon as it was clear I opened the pants of all of the males.

Since Nicolas was shot outside he still had the attachment which I quickly removed. I had just finished removing it when the SS captain in charge of the operation came in. "What are you doing?" he yelled. "Just determining whether they are Jews or not because sometimes some non-Jews help them but these are all Jews. You know, of course, that there is a bounty for every Jew turned in dead or alive. We have four Jews here at 500 Marks per Jew. That makes 2,000 Marks. Are you here to pick up the certification papers to collect the bounty?" It did not take him too long to pick up on this. "Uh, uh, yes that is why I am here." I went over to my desk and put the extension in the same drawer that had the forms. I filled out one of the forms and gave it to him. I saluted, "Heil Hitler!" He grabbed it, smiled, saluted, turned and quickly left. I never saw him again as I am sure he did not want to be identified as having taken the form and cashing it in since I am also sure that he decided not to share the money with the any of the other participants in the raid. As soon as he left I took the extension out of the drawer and the one in the pack of cigarettes, walked over to the hooded area, squirted some embalming fluid on it and set them on fire.

With this second incident we decided to suspend our operations until we figured out what was happening. We again enlisted the aid of Mischa. The next day he went over to the SS headquarters. On the pretext of delivering a report he spoke to a couple of the SS soldiers that he had worked with in the past. He just casually mentioned that he heard about the raid that took place last night to one of his SS friends. He confirmed it and introduced him to a few of the SS soldiers that had participated in the raid. They proudly started telling him about the roles they had in the raid. Most just talked about the events of that night, but one mentioned that he couldn't wait for the next one because "next time we would do it differently. We are learning with each experience". Mischa asked what he meant and that's when he was told about this clandestine SS and Gestapo surveillance program. Mischa stayed there another hour, gathering information before coming to the morgue to tell me about the SS operation. We immediately terminated our activities.

Yet another thing happened to make life even more miserable for Jews – and more difficult for us. Jews now had to wear a large yellow star.

CHAPTER FIFTEEN

WAR

"Now that all the relevant documents are being made public we shall stand at the bar of history knowing that the responsibility for this terrible catastrophe lies on the shoulders of one man, the German Chancellor, who has not hesitated to plunge the world into misery in order to serve his own senseless ambitions..."

> British Prime Minister Neville Chamberlain's speech to the House of Commons just hours after Hitler's troops invaded Poland.

On September 1, 1939 Germany invaded Poland. A few days later after Germany refused to leave Poland, England and France declared war on Germany. Reportedly, Hitler was surprised. He did not expect England and France to come to the aid of Poland just as they let him annex Austria and Czechoslovakia. Russia and Germany had signed a non-aggression pact a few months earlier, so Russia stayed neutral. In return, Russia took a part of Poland and forcibly took control of Estonia, Lithuania and Latvia with Hitler's blessing. Hitler only had to fight the war on one front – the Western Front.

The French were ready for him. In anticipation of just such a scenario they had built the impenetrable Maginot Line, a solid network of artillery guns, concrete pill boxes, anti-tank blocks and other fortifications on the French border facing Germany that could easily defend the country against a frontal attack from Germany. The Germans had other plans none of which included a frontal attack against the Maginot Line. Instead, the German army overran Belgium and Holland in a few days in May 1940 at a very high speed using heavy armor and war planes combined with heavy infantry. This gave rise to a new war term, "blitzkrieg" (lightening war). They used their air force (Luftwaffe), which was under the command of Hermann Goering, to totally destroy Rotterdam in what was the first example of "carpet bombing" even though the city offered no resistance. This was purposely done to demonstrate the futility of resisting the German army. It worked as city after city surrendered without a fight. The British army stationed in Belgium was routed and had to retreat to Dunkirk. With their backs to the sea, the Nazis knew that the British army was doomed. Goering decided to bypass the British army and continue the Blitzkrieg into France deciding that the Luftwaffe and reserve ground troops would finish off the British army later while the armored divisions with their crack infantry attacked France before the French had a chance to reinforce the Belgian border. After all, the British were surrounded on three sides with their backs to the sea and were obviously at the mercy of the German army so they laid siege to the British waiting for the Luftwaffe and Wehrmacht to be free to coordinate the attack after taking France. But the British seized the opportunity to make the largest evacuation in history. Mobilizing everything that could possibly float, an armada of hundreds of naval vessels, private ships, yachts and small boats sailed across the English Channel over a period of nine days from May 26 through June 4, 1940 and rescued more than 218 thousand British soldiers and 120 thousand French soldiers. The codename for this massive rescue effort was "Operation Dynamo" so named because the rescue operation was conceived and implemented in the room that contained the electricity generator (dynamo) in the cellar of Dover Castle, the headquarters of the British Navy. If you do the math it is about 36,500 soldiers per day or about 1,600 soldiers per hour. It was surprising that the commander of the German reserve army besieging the British did not consider that such an evacuation could be possible so he did not monitor the situation and recognize it as a mass evacuation. He was not even admonished for his lapse of intelligence. The war in France was quick and with a minimum of loss of German lives, planes and armored vehicles. It was a complete rout. After the evacuation, the British newspaper headlines read "Disaster turned to Triumph" – but it was no triumph.

The French army was routed. Even though they had concentrated most of their forces on the Belgium border, their outdated tanks and planes were no match for the modern mechanized German army and the large air force with its superior fighters and high capacity bombers. The Belgian border stretched for almost 500 kilometers. Since the French did not know exactly where the German army would attack, they had to spread their forces thinly along the border. By the time that the specific points of attack were known, the German army had broken through the lines of defense before they could be reinforced. All the French could do was to slowly retreat fighting as they retreated. The French formerly surrendered a few weeks later and an armistice was signed on June 20, 1940. Hitler had conquered Western Europe in nine months; only England remained. Paris was declared an open city and was spared from aerial attack. Hitler came to Paris for the surrender ceremony and a triumphant tour of the city. The surrender ceremony was held in the same railcar in Versailles that was used for the unconditional surrender of Germany at the end of the First World War. The railcar was sent to Berlin after the signing ceremony. France was divided into two parts one of which was not to be occupied by Nazi soldiers. This was called the French State (Etat Français) instead of the French Republic (Republique Français). The capital was set up in the city of Vichy which was about 310 km from Paris. Vichy was selected as the capital for a number of reasons. It had the best and most modern telephone exchange system in the country that had been installed in 1935. Using this exchange, telephone calls could be quickly made to any point in Europe or around the world. Vichy also had the second largest number of hotel rooms in France after Paris and a very large opera house which could be used as a makeshift parliament. This French State was also referred to as Vichy France and was headed by a French Nazi supporter, Marshal Philippe Pétain. He was also strongly anti-Semitic.

We followed these events incredulously. Never, in our wildest imagination did we dream that the war would progress so swiftly with such a dramatic set of victories for the Nazis. From our standpoint, the war seemed over and we thought that perhaps it was time for all of us to leave Austria. However, with the way the war was going we were not sure where we should go. We were not even sure that Hitler would respect the neutrality of Switzerland since he obviously didn't with Belgium and Holland or Scandinavia. So we decided that we were much better off staying where we were since we were not suspected of being Jewish. We stopped all of our escape activities deeming it too dangerous under the present set of circumstances.

At one of the card sessions as we commiserated amongst ourselves, Friedrich got angry, stood up at the card table and loudly said, "Look at what the British did at Dunkirk! Totally surrounded with their backs to the sea they engineered the rescue of more than 300 thousand soldiers. We have not even engineered the escape of one person for the past three months!"

I must admit, I was taken aback at his sudden outburst. Friedrich was the quietest person in the group. He did not speak much and he never raised his voice. I guess when something is important enough it can change a person's demeanor. We felt very embarrassed. Friedrich was right! Here we were sitting in a warm room with plenty of food and in good health because we decided to lie about our Jewish heritage while many of our fellow Jews much less fortunate than us were trapped in Vienna facing possible starvation, disease and death or deportation. We unanimously decided to reactivate our rescue operation. Wilhelm asked if we should assign a codename to this renewed effort since it seemed to work for the British. We briefly discussed this before we realized that he was joking.

Conditions for Jews in Vienna deteriorated even more after the war began. Emigration stopped since all of the countries in Western Europe that were accepting Jews were either at war with Germany or had been conquered. Most Jews had already been stripped of their money and anything of value through the various taxes and laws imposed upon them. Deportations from Vienna were actually reduced since the rail cars used for taking Jews from Vienna to the Ghettos in Poland were redirected to the conquered countries that had much larger Jewish populations that were being deported or were needed to supply the extended German army.

During the winter some entrepreneurial boys started a business based on Jewish deportations. It did not start out as a business. A group of young Hitler Youth members that happened to live near the Aspang train station, which was the main embarking station for Jews being deported to the ghettos in Czechoslovakia and Poland, were having a snowball fight one afternoon when a truckload of Jews being deported stopped at a traffic light near the station. Open trucks were used because the SS could cram more Jews in an open truck than in a closed truck. Besides, an open truck afforded no protection from the weather so the SS liked the idea of driving down the street at a high speed with the harsh, icy wind blowing on the group of huddled Jews. Once the tailgate was closed, two SS men rode in the truck cabin and a car followed behind to make sure no Jew jumped out of the truck. Actually, no one even tried to escape at that point. There were entire families together and at that time, most of the deportees believed that they were just being resettled in a place that had better conditions than they had in Vienna. The usual transport caravan was about eight to twelve trucks. There was a traffic light on the main street at the entrance to the station where the trucks had to make a left turn. All of the trucks could not pass through the intersection during one green light, especially since they had to wait for opposing traffic to pass, so some had to stop when the light turned red and wait for the next green light to continue.

As usual, some of the trucks were stopped at the traffic light that day. One of the Hitler Youth saw the truck and immediately realized that the people in the back were Jews. He yelled to his friends, "Juden! Juden!" and started throwing snowballs at them. His friends joined in. They ran closer to the truck and threw the snowballs as hard as they could. Clearly their intention was to inflict injury. They cursed at the Jews as they threw the snowballs. The Jews were tightly packed in the back of the open truck. They were totally exposed. Some of them could not even raise their hands to defend themselves against the snowball onslaught since their hands were tightly wedged against the collective bodies. While it only lasted less than a minute, a few people were hurt with some bleeding. The SS in the car rolled down the windows and congratulated the boys as they drove off. The boys were elated. They told their friends.

Deportations were occurring three or four days per week. So, on the following day there were now about fifteen Hitler Youth lined up along the road just before the traffic light. Each had an arsenal of snowballs that they had prepared in advance. As soon as the trucks were spotted they lined up along both sides of the divided road with some on the median and some on the opposite sidewalk. The truck drivers saw the boys lined up along the street and slowed down almost to a crawl to afford the maximum time to the boys. They started to throw their snowballs. Purposely, some drivers waited for the light to turn red which afforded the boys even more time and the ability to consolidate their attack forming almost a semi-circle around the three trucks left at the light throwing with deadly accuracy at the screaming, shivering helpless passengers. Their screams attracted some adult passersby but instead of doing anything to help they just watched until one young man asked if he could have some snowballs to throw. The first boy he asked said no as did the second. With the third boy he took out some coins and offered to buy some of his snowballs. The third boy happily sold the man the rest of his snowballs. By the time the light changed, all of the snowballs had been thrown. Many of the Jews, particularly those standing around the perimeter of the truck facing outward were hurt. As for the boys, they couldn't care less if it was a man, woman or child at the perimeter. They threw the snowballs at them without any mercy.

There were no deportations the next day. So, the boys, now numbering about twenty, were disappointed and loudly cursed the Jews for not being there. The crowd of adults, which was larger than the day before, was also disappointed and joined in the cursing. "What a waste!" one of the boys remarked. "Look at all of the snowballs we made that we cannot use". "No problem," another responded, "We can use them tomorrow." The next day, the same young man who had paid for the snowballs the day before, approached the group and asked if he could buy one of the piles of snowballs. He offered to pay one Mark for the pile. The boy whose pile the man had pointed to gladly accepted. This gave some of the other boys an idea. One of the boys that had obvious leadership abilities faced the crowd of onlookers and asked if anyone else would like to but a pile of snowballs for three Marks. About six hands went up. When the trucks came by the number of snowball throwers had almost doubled from the number two days ago. The impact on the Jews was devastating. More than twenty were injured with two seriously bleeding from head injuries. The guards at the station didn't care as long as the Jews could be loaded onto the trains. They allowed anyone with medical training to help the injured but not all of the caravans had someone with medical training.

The next day the boys agreed to come early to make piles of snowballs and offer them for sale – but at a higher price. They prepared some cardboard signs the night before that read, "Pelt the Jews! five Marks per pile!" About fifteen people, including a couple of women and girls, bought snowballs. At three o'clock the trucks rolled by and slowed down from the higher speeds that they used to get to the station. There were now about thirty snowball throwers lined up along the street and at the traffic light on both sides of the street forming a gauntlet. Those in the trucks at the light were bombarded for about two minutes with the snowballs.

For those of you that are familiar with snowfalls, you know that for the first day or so after the snowfall the snow is relatively soft and fluffy but by the third and subsequent days, much of the snow turns into ice. Since Vienna was not a very cold city, many days were above freezing which abetted the conversion of snow into ice. By the fourth day ice balls were being thrown – not snowballs. The injuries increased fivefold with four or five having some quite serious eye injuries. However, with so many people, now numbering more than fifty, it got way out of hand. Many of the people had really lousy aim so some of the ice balls hit and cracked the windshields and side windows of the trucks. One SS officer was hit with flying glass which went into his eye when his side window was shattered by an ice ball. The cracked window and windshields took a couple of trucks out of service and slowed down the deportations. When the officer in charge of the deportations learned about the damaged trucks and the SS officer's eye injury, he ordered the police to intervene and stop the snowball throwing. No arrests were to be made but the snowball throwing was to be stopped. From then on, there were no more organized snowball throwing incidents but every once in a while one or two of the Hitler Youth boys would throw some snowballs at the passing trucks as they walked across the street.

It had been almost four months now since we had managed to help anyone escape. All of our activity was helping a few Jews in hiding emerge from hiding with the help of the extension and false identities that we created for them. Most of these were based on real documents obtained from Heinrich's office. We found eleven Jews (six men and five women) in hiding and managed to get real jobs for them and they in turn volunteered to help us when we needed them. We still provided food and medicine to the IKG for their soup kitchens and hospitals and continued to give them money for other activities. They were now feeding around ten thousand people per month. Providing food, clothing and, for that matter, anything of value to Jews by Gentiles was forbidden so we were risking our lives in doing this. Even though the IKG was being watched, some police officers accepted money to look the other way. We never used Jewish people to deliver the food and medicine lest the police turn them in for the reward. Instead, we used some friends and sympathizers most of whom were Swiss that volunteered for the task. Vienna had a small Swiss community many of whom were abhorred at the treatment of the Jews. The police just believed that they were doing this on their own for humanitarian reasons. After all, the Red Cross was a Swiss organization. Turning them in was not an issue since there was no reward for Swiss Jew-lovers plus they were making good money by looking the other way. They did not suspect that Jews were really behind the humanitarian operation. We also believed that the Gestapo and the SS knew what was going on but they did not want hundreds of people dying every day from starvation or disease so they allowed the additional food and medicine. Hundreds of deaths would have been "too public."

At one of the card sessions, we were talking about the food and medicine relief operation and how easy it was to bribe the police. That's when Wilhelm had an idea. It was really wild. The only way Jews were able to leave the district after curfew without scrutiny was when they were picked up in a raid by the SS and deported to a ghetto or a concentration camp. This was an SS operation that was always unannounced and sudden. We knew from our intelligence that the deportations were on hold due to the trains being used in other countries. This was not made public nor was it revealed outside of the SS headquarters. As such, the police had no idea why the deportations had stopped or when they would resume. "Suppose," Wilhelm said, "we were able to get some SS uniforms, weapons and an SS truck and enter a district to collect and deport Jews? We could get them out of the country once we had them and they wouldn't even be missed." At first, everyone laughed but when we saw he was serious we stopped laughing. "How in the world could we mount such a bold operation?" Klaus asked. His answer was "corruption". Wilhelm mentioned how easy it was to bribe some of the guards at any checkpoint at the border and the police that allowed food to be provided to the IKG so it would stand to reason that others could also be bribed. He said we only needed three things: SS uniforms, weapons and an SS truck. Again, everyone laughed but again we realized that he was quite serious so we set about figuring out how we could do it.

Getting an SS truck depended upon finding some guards that we could bribe that had guard duty at one of the many motor pools and truck depots scattered around the city. The SS did not do motor pool guard duty as it was beneath them so they had the regular army do it. The SS did not treat the army guards with respect. They would come in to get vehicles whenever they wanted gruffly ordering the guards to open and close the gate, hurry up with the paperwork, etc. Often they didn't even bother with the paperwork. As a result, there was strong animosity among the army soldiers on guard towards the SS. We knew this. We capitalized on it. We made a list of the SS motor pools and watched them for two weeks to see which one had the lowest number of night shift guards and found that SS Group Seven, located in the ninth district, only had two regular army soldiers on duty during the night and on weekends. We asked Mischa if he could find out the names of the guards assigned to the motor pool. By now, Mischa had developed a small network of SS and Wehrmacht friends that were his drinking buddies. He asked one of them about borrowing a truck for a special police operation in the ninth district and asked for the names of the guards. He received the list the next day. We asked Mischa to do a cursory background check on all of the army guards that were assigned to this motor pool and selected two from the same shift. One was Karl Huber. He was from Essen and was married with three small children. They were not doing too well since he had a better paying job before he was drafted into the army so he certainly could use some extra money. Selecting him had another strong positive. He would most likely send most, if not all, of the money to his family so no one in Vienna would see him with any extra money. The second soldier was Dietrich Fischer. He was from Hamburg, was overweight and was not married. He liked to gamble, was not a heavy drinker and frequently used the services of prostitutes. No one would notice if he increased his sexual activity or if all of a sudden he had some extra money which they would attribute to a lucky night at the card table. Moreover, they were both on duty for alternate weekend nights. We decided to meet with both of them. We chose one of the local bars and spoke to each one individually. We told each one that we were smugglers and had great connections at the Swiss border and that we could bring in quite a lot of contraband that was not available in Vienna because of the war. Our problem was delivering the smuggled goods throughout the city once we brought the goods here. We wanted to borrow an SS truck for the weekend to make local deliveries. No one would question what an SS truck was doing with the boxes in which we repacked the goods. Both of the guards were eager to participate in the smuggling scheme – but not only for the money. They really wanted to do something against the arrogant SS soldiers that treated them so badly.

Getting the uniforms was actually easier than we expected. There were a number of locked warehouses at the railroad stations that had military supplies. The guards never entered the locked warehouses as they made their rounds as they never imagined that anyone would want to steal these supplies let alone be able to remove them without being seen. There was just a small group of guards at the main gate that occasionally patrolled the area when they felt like it. A few days after successfully enlisting Dietrich and Karl, we held an impromptu meeting at lunchtime bringing sandwiches to accompany our discussion. We needed eight men. Six would be used for each rescue and there would be two backup men. We asked for volunteers from our network to be SS soldiers. We would need the SS uniforms of a Captain, a Lieutenant and six regular soldiers with a complete spare set so we needed sixteen uniforms. We picked men that were about the same size to minimize the need for stealing too many different size uniforms. We managed to succeed and only needed three different sizes. While this was going on, Mischa formed a small task force to inspect the warehouses on the pretext of theft prevention. He was able to identify the warehouse where uniforms were stored. During his inspection, while the rest of his team was in the compound, Mischa drove around the area and selected a spot that could not easily be seen from any guard post. He tied a blue ribbon onto the fence at the best spot. His report confirmed that theft was highly unlikely due to the excellent security at the warehouses.

We were able to break into this warehouse and during the course of two nights take what we needed out of the boxes. It was surprisingly simple. The day before the break in Mischa drew a little map showing where he had tied a small blue ribbon and the location of the warehouse with the uniforms. At 1 AM we went directly to that area and easily found the spot with the small blue ribbon which we removed. We cut two-thirds of the wires holding the chain link fence to the post creating an opening through which we could easily pass through. After we got in we secured the fence back to the post with some flexible wire. The area was well lit but since no one was really watching we were able to sneak into the warehouse. Thinking ahead, we added one more person to our team – a glazier. We broke one of the window panes, reached in and unlocked the window. As we went about our business the glazier did his. He carefully removed a matching window pane from an upper-level window and replaced it with a new one. It was very difficult to spot it once he splayed on some mud. He replaced the broken pane with the one from upstairs. It was a perfect match. He put all of the broken pieces of glass into a canvas bag. He also took off the hasp on the lock, moved it up about three centimeters so it wouldn't lock and re-secured it to the window with some putty. Once this was done, the window could be pushed open even though it looked like it was locked from the inside. We took only one of each item (one pair of pants, one shirt, one pair of socks, one pair of boots, etc.) per box and resealed the box which is why it took two nights to accomplish our task. We decided to use this procedure so when the boxes were taken from the warehouse to be used whoever opened the box would just think that there was a miscount from the factory since only one of the items were missing. We decided not to take entire boxes of the clothes since they could be missed on an inventory check that was conducted once per month. We knew that if we did it in this manner without raising any suspicion that we would have a virtually endless supply of uniforms. Kurt always had a warped sense of humor. As we were taking the boots he would trade one left boot for one right boot so there would be at least one pair of boots per box with two left foot and two right foot pairs of boots. He did this about ten times on each night. There would be twenty soldiers in the field who would get mismatched boots that they could not wear. Each night when we left the warehouse we would reattach the metal wires to re-connect the fence to the post just in case anyone patrolled the perimeter during the day. Using this procedure, you could not tell that the fence had been disconnected from the post.

Getting two Luger pistols, which were only used by officers, was actually the easiest part of our quest. Mischa simply took them from the police evidence room. Whenever a weapon was recovered from the scene of a crime, it was kept in this room. As you might expect, there were some crimes committed by SS officers. They were rarely prosecuted but the pistols that were used and left at the scene of the crime were put into the storage room without even registering them or the date and time that they were brought in. There was never any attempt to trace them to their owners and their owners never claimed them lest they wind up being charged with the crime. Most of these were crimes of passion. Sometimes a husband or father would catch the officer with his wife or daughter, attack them in a fit of rage and be wounded or killed in the ensuing struggle. Some left the pistols there in their haste to leave. Mischa went to the precinct early with his holster empty, entered the evidence room, took one of the Lugers and simply put it into his holster for the day. In two days we had two Lugers. No one knew they were missing.

The most difficult thing to get was the four rifles and two submachine guns that the SS soldiers always carried during the raids. We tried everything that we could think of to get the guns in Vienna to no avail. All weapons were under heavy guard and always well inside a military post. We decided to look elsewhere. In every country conquered by the Nazis there was a strong resistance movement. Unfortunately, there was no real organized armed resistance movement in Austria but France had a very large underground resistance movement engaged in kidnappings, assassinations and sabotage. Since Lyon was one of the known centers of the French resistance, we asked some of our Swiss friends if they had any trusted friends or family there. We chose Swiss friends since they spoke German. A few gave us the names but they did not know if they knew anyone in the resistance. We would have to establish contact with the resistance through them if they had the contact or on our own if they didn't. The next question was who would go? I volunteered. I had a plan. In my capacity as a mortician and Assistant Coroner I could suggest to the SS that I travel to France to visit other morgues on the pretext of information gathering. The Germans were really keen on statistics. So I called Col. Stryker and proposed setting up a system to see how many Jews were being killed and sent to the various morgues in France. This system could be extended to other countries. Col. Stryker thought it was an excellent idea. In this manner they would know how many Jews were no longer available for deportation. They often wasted time looking for some Jews only to find out that they were already dead. So I was given written orders and a special travel permit to Lyon and another that allowed me to travel freely within all of France. These documents formed the basis of much of our future smuggling work. The Nazis typically changed travel permits every three months so whenever we learned that a new form had been issued, I set up another trip to France. Moreover, these particular permits could be filled in to allow unrestricted travel to any city in any occupied country.

On Friday I drove to our new forgery operation so they could make copies of the documents. Once they copied them, I drove to the garage on Thurngasse and switched cars with one that was specially modified for this trip.

I left Vienna very early Saturday morning and I arrived in Lyon by late Sunday evening. I checked into my hotel and went to the SS headquarters in the third arrondissement early the next morning. The purpose of my visit had been sent by telegram the week prior with explicit instructions that I was to be given full cooperation. This was dutifully extended to me. I was given a car and a driver and carte blanche to do whatever I wanted. One thing I learned from this trip was that anything to do with the "Jewish Problem" was given a very high priority by the express authorization of Himmler. I was driven to the main city morgue which was located in the second arrondissement. It took about twenty minutes to get there. Using an interpreter, I spent the day at the morgue discussing procedures and the data program that I was going to set up. I distributed the special bilingual forms that I had prepared and set up some classes for the next day. When I returned to the hotel I dismissed the driver and told him to come back at eight the next morning. I went out and proceeded to call on the contacts provided by our Swiss friends. I had thought about calling them first but was not sure of the security of the phone lines. I was able to visit two families the first night but they had no contacts with the resistance.

The next day I was back at the central morgue giving classes on how to fill out the forms and how to code them so they could be put into a central filing system that would be maintained in Lyon with a weekly summary sent to me in Vienna which I would forward to Berlin. It was a slow process since everything I said had to be translated. I also asked them to review all of the deaths of Jews for the past six months and tabulate them on the forms. They groaned audibly at this request. I needed no translation to understand their response. We had set up two days for the training of coroners in Lyon and three days for the coroners located in the other major cities in France where there were Jews. Here again, notification of my visit had been sent in advance with instructions to come to Lyon on selected dates for the instruction. Overall, about 120 coroners were ordered to Lyon for this assignment. This gave me five nights in which to contact all of the families on the list. On the third night I got lucky. One of the families had a son who was in the resistance. He was no longer living at home and they did not have an easy way to contact him but they would try through some of his friends. That night his father went to some of his son's closest friends and asked them to get a message to his son. Two days went by. It was now Friday and I was scheduled to return to Vienna on Saturday morning. At about 4 PM a message was delivered to my hotel from the father of the young man that had joined the resistance inviting me to join a Doctor Jacques Montreaux for dinner at the Auberge restaurant at 8 PM. I picked up the message when I returned to my hotel at 7 PM. It was walking distance from the hotel.

At 8 PM I went to the restaurant and asked for the table of Doctor Jacques Montreaux. I was brought to his table. He was about seventy years old well dressed with totally white hair and a white goatee. A black cane with a bronze metal top in the shape of a duck was near the table. He introduced himself in fluent German as Doctor Montreaux without getting up and explained that he was sent because he was a doctor which could be helpful in explaining our dinner together as we could be discussing the work that brought me to Lyon. We ate and spoke for about two hours but I could see that he wasn't entirely convinced that I was legitimate. I had a very high clearance in the Nazi party. I had a car and a driver which was only given to Nazi collaborators of high authority. He was not about to compromise the resistance by helping me without being absolutely sure. I suggested that he wait about one minute and follow me into the bathroom. While puzzled by the strange request, he agreed. I went into the bathroom and removed the extension from my penis. I waited in one of the stalls until he entered. We were the only two men in the bathroom. I opened the stall with my pants down and pointed to my penis. He reeled back in disgust not realizing what I was doing until I said, "Look, I am circumcised! I am Jewish!" He moved closer and looked. There was no doubt that I had a circumcised penis and that it was an old scar from birth. My credibility was now solid. He went back to the table, sat down and waited. I re-attached the extension and returned to the table. We both laughed about the "proof". Over coffee I asked what he would have done if I was indeed a Nazi spy and we had captured him. He reached into his jacket pocket and took out a small capsule. It was cyanide. He told me that he was prepared to use it rather than get captured which is why someone of his age was sent to meet with me. I found out later that he was 78 and was not in the best of health. I explained that I needed eight rifles and two submachine guns that were used by the SS. He was pretty sure that the resistance had or could acquire the weapons. He left and told me to stay in the hotel until I was contacted. I returned to the hotel at 11 PM and stayed up until about 3 AM waiting for a call or some message that never came. I dozed off to sleep on the chair.

At 6 AM there was a knock on my hotel door. I went to the door and asked who it was. "Room service!" At first I was going to tell him that it must be a mistake since I didn't order anything. Then I realized that this could be the contact that I was waiting for. I opened the door. A hotel waiter rolled in a cart with my breakfast on it. He handed me a map with the road I should take out of Lyon. There was a small city, Belfort, about 10 kilometers off of the main highway and about 8 kilometers from the border. I was instructed to stop there to get gas at the gas station at the south entrance to the city and tell the attendant to check under the hood because I was hearing "a noise that sounded like a sick cat". I was to use those exact words. He added that someone there spoke German. That was all I was told. As the waiter left the room he turned to me, smiled and said, "By the way there is no bacon on the breakfast tray!"

I checked out of the hotel as soon as I finished my breakfast and proceeded along the route laid out on the map. I am sure they chose this isolated route to be sure that I was coming alone. I am also quite positive that they had the switchboard monitored to make sure I did not make any telephone calls. In any case, about three hours later I arrived in Belfort and drove to the designated gas station. For a small village, the gas station was busy. There were seven cars getting gas three of which were driven by German soldiers. I told the German-speaking attendant that I wanted him to check under the hood because I was hearing a noise that sounded like a sick cat. The attendant opened the hood to check determine the cause of the noise. He said that I had a problem with one of my belts and that it should be replaced. I agreed and backed the car into the only bay of the garage as requested. The attendant opened the hood. At that point the son of the family that put me in contact with the resistance came out dressed as a car mechanic and asked where I wanted the guns to be placed. The car had a special hiding place. The rear seat was hollowed out and the seat top was attached to the bottom by a set of screws. With the hood up, the inside of the car was blocked from view. I showed him the screws. We unscrewed them together and lifted the seat top from the bottom. The space was more than enough to hold the guns. We wrapped each gun in some old sheets and rolled them up in an old piece of carpet that was in the office. This was to have the guns fit tightly in the compartment so there would not be any noise when I was on the road. The wrapping and loading of the guns and ammunition took about twenty minutes. The changing of the belt took another fifteen minutes. After all, it was the reason that my car was in the bay. I paid for the gas and the belt and continued on my trip. At each border crossing and checkpoint I just showed my travel pass and was waived through without any search.

When I returned to Vienna I went directly to the warehouse on Thurngasse. We unloaded the guns from the car. I took my own car and went home. About a week later I turned in my report quantifying the number of dead Jews processed by nineteen morgues in the major French cities. The SS was very surprised and pleased with the numbers. They did not know that the number was that high. They were obviously doing a great job. They proudly forwarded a copy of my report to the SS headquarters in Berlin, which, in turn, was sent directly to Heinrich Himmler. My name became well-known at the SS headquarters in Berlin but not only because of this report. One of Hitler's photographers at Berchtesgaden was Ernst Baumann. He distinguished (or rather extinguished) himself by taking some intimate pictures of Eva Braun, Hitler's mistress, and getting transferred to the Russian Front when an outraged Hitler saw the photos. When asked "if I was related to the former photographer at Berchtesgaden, Ernst Baumann who was transferred to the Russian Front," I immediately said yes. I figured that if he was at the Russian Front there would be no way that he could deny it. After I learned about Ernst Baumann it came to me. Most likely it was the Baumann name that resulted in the letter I sent about my father's death reaching Hitler while he was in Berchtesgaden. Ernst Baumann was still in favor with Hitler at that time.

Two days later our card group met to set up our plan. We had decided that we would go on Friday night and that we would take sixteen people at a time since our two moving vans held eight people each in the special compartments. We contacted the IKG and they gave us the name of Hyman Sztein. He and his wife had told the IKG that they wanted to leave Austria but did not have the means. We told him of our plan and that he should select 14 other people that lived in his building that we would come for in a mock SS raid. We gave him the criteria for the selection process: families he trusted that he felt would be willing to leave under these circumstances, none with small children or health problems, etc. He was only to let his wife know that the raid was a ruse so she could help in the selection process. She knew much more about the neighbors than he did. We took this precaution because we were afraid that if the selected people knew the truth they would tell others and instead of 16 we would have dozens of people clamoring to get on the truck. While we realized that it would be an extremely frightening experience we made it a mandatory condition. He and his wife cautiously and casually brought up the subject of escape to the people he thought would want to leave and selected fourteen of them. Two days later, he gave us a list of the people that would be taken with him and his wife. These were people without much family left in Vienna that had been turned down for entry permits for the United States or were planning to go to England before war broke out. We told him to try to be as sure as possible about the people he selected. Once we "deported" them there would be no recourse. We could not bring them back to the building. He reconfirmed his selection.

At 7 PM on Friday night Jacob and Fritz went to the depot and took the truck from the motor pool. They gave the guards half of the money when they picked up the truck and told them that they would get the other half when they returned it on Sunday night. The chosen SS imposters met at the furniture warehouse and changed into their uniforms, took their weapons, got into the truck and drove into the second district. The truck pulled up in front of 144 Haidgasse where Hyman lived with his wife. The SS soldiers and the officers ran up the stairs to each designated apartment and took out the people on the list. They screamed and cried but did not resist. They were given fifteen minutes to gather their belongings, which was the standard time allowed during these deportations. This gave them a chance to take their valuables such as jewelry, money, pictures, etc. in the one suitcase which was also the standard. They were loaded onto the trucks. As they drove out they could see many people peering out of their windows watching the deportation. The whole operation took just under 50 minutes.

The truck proceeded directly to the garage on Thurngasse where we had the moving vans. As soon as the guards got off and we unloaded the sixteen people from the truck we told them that we were not Nazis but fellow Jews that were going to help them escape from Austria into Switzerland. At first they did not believe it but when Hyman confirmed it their tears of fear turned to tears of joy. Many asked to use the bathroom, which had a shower, to clean up. Out of fear, some had relieved themselves in their pants or dresses. They changed clothes and were told of the plan. They would be fed and they would be put into the hidden compartment of the special furniture moving vans with eight people per compartment in the morning. Since the Nazis raided the forgery factory we did not have the capability to produce any forged documents to allow anyone to leave using the trains and buses. Our new forgery operation still lacked much of the supplies needed to prepare false identity cards and travel permits. So, for now, we had to rely solely on the moving vans. Once they were in their respective vans, the false panel would be closed and the van would be immediately loaded with furniture. They would be driven to the Swiss border and into Switzerland. The journey would take one or two days depending upon the traffic and road conditions. We had safe houses along the route so they would not have to stay in the vans overnight if they chose to leave the van for the night. If there was a heavy rain or snow storm, we would either stop at a safe house or proceed very slowly at the discretion of the driver and the passengers so it could possibly require a third day to complete the trip. While they were concealed in the van they had to be very quiet. We showed them the sedatives and the other drugs that should be administered to anyone that was getting claustrophobic lest they panic, start screaming and give everyone away. For this type of operation we decided not to give the men extensions since if they were caught they would be recognized as escaping Jews even if they did have the extension. In fact, we felt it would be more dangerous to fit the men with extensions since capture would definitely result in the Nazis discovering the extensions.

The next day, Saturday, at 6 AM both of the moving vans pulled out of the garage and took different roads out of the city. The SS truck remained parked in the garage. The vans had no trouble leaving Vienna. There were only one or two patrols on the roads at that early hour and they had no reason to suspect anything. The vans proceeded to the Swiss border along separate routes without incident. The roads were relatively empty, driving conditions were good and the people confined in the van did not made any noise. At midnight, about five kilometers from the border, the two vans met at Feldkirch and waited until morning. The drivers spoke to the people and made sure that they were alright and that they could stay in the compartment overnight. They all said yes. Their spirits were high, knowing that the next morning they would be in Switzerland. We picked Feldkirch because we had heard that this was the easiest place to cross into Switzerland with much less attention to formalities. The vans waited until 8 AM as there would be many cars and trucks crossing the border at that time. There was a very strong commercial business between the two countries which was enhanced by the war. Merchandise very scarce in Austria and Germany due to the war was much more readily available in Switzerland so the trade was quite brisk, if you had the money. The two vans were allowed to leave Austria and enter Switzerland with only a cursory examination of their documents and without even having to open the back of the van for inspection. They proceeded separately to the warehouse we rented in Chur, a small town near the border. Each van was unloaded so the eight people could finally get out of the compartment. They had been confined in that small compartment for more than 24 hours and were quite happy to get out and to be safe in Switzerland. One of the young couples, ardent Zionists, started singing the Hatikvah, the Jewish national anthem. All of the others joined in. The drivers did not. They did not know the words.

The drivers went to various stores in the city and purchased many of the scarce items that could easily be resold at a substantial profit. The vans, again fully loaded with the same furniture in the front two-thirds of the van and food, wine, special apparel such as nylon stockings, silk blouses and Swiss watches in the false compartment returned to the border. One of the vans was stopped at the border and told to pull over to the inspection zone as this was a random procedure. A quick look inside confirmed that there was the furniture that was listed on the manifest and they were released. Our plan was really quite simple as we never really delivered any furniture. We just moved it back and forth between Vienna and Switzerland. Outbound we smuggled the Jewish cargo to Switzerland and inbound we smuggled contraband goods back to Vienna. We entered and left Switzerland through different cities so as not to raise suspicion.

As the war progressed this reverse smuggling became such a lucrative business that the profits we made offset all of the costs incurred in the bribes, rents, food and clothing needed to sustain our network. In fact, we started to send vans across the border without any Jewish people in them to bring back these precious items and we contracted with one of the large distributors in Munich to market the goods in major German cities offering a more than adequate commission for his service. Even simple household goods like pots and pans became best sellers once the Allies started to bomb the major German factories and cities. Factories that used to make pots and pans were converted to produce war materials which intensified the shortages for pots, pans and many other items. Our most lucrative product was shoes. The shoe shortage was unbelievable as every shoe factory in Germany was converted to make army and SS boots. Italian shoes, especially ladies fashion shoes, would sell for at least ten times what we paid for them. One time we had a request from a rich industrialist in Berlin. He wanted men's and women's shoes for his daughter's wedding. At first we thought that he just wanted shoes for the bridal party but he wanted shoes for the entire guest list. He had asked each guest to select their shoes from an Italian catalog. He really wanted to impress them – and he did – all 320 of them – all at exorbitant prices. He sent his order to the shoe company and had them delivered to the city in Switzerland that we designated. We picked them up and delivered them without any problem.

Whenever we had a load of goods for our distributor in Munich we would go directly to Salzburg from the Swiss border and then to Munich. From Munich we would drive back through Salzburg and return to Vienna.

I would travel bimonthly to Lyon and once or twice to Paris and Vichy ostensibly to confer with my morgue colleagues in France to check on the data system that I had set up. In reality, it was to buy the various solvents, paper and inks needed for our new forgery operation as well as for some champagne and wine. I also used this opportunity a couple of times to have dinner with Colonel Kaupfner, the SS officer that delivered the letter from the Fuehrer to me. He had been promoted and was now in charge of the SS in Innsbruck. He was a connoisseur of wine so I always selected some rare wines for him. He was most appreciative. We became good friends.

CHAPTER SIXTEEN

IMPERSONATING A JEW

"The best political weapon is the weapon of terror. Cruelty commands respect. Men may hate us. But, we don't ask for their love; only for their fear."

Heinrich Himmler, Head of the Gestapo

Carol lived alone downtown close to her office. She moved there about three months after getting the job. Her parents lived in the suburban area of Favoriten. The commute to work from her parent's house took more than one hour in the morning. She typically worked until 7 or 8 at night. While the commute time was only about 40 minutes at that time, she did not like to wait alone at the bus stop at night, especially when it was very cold, as the buses ran infrequently at that hour. As she did not want to drive, the best thing was to live closer to her job. Her apartment was seven blocks from the office along a main shopping street which was crowded every night so she felt safe walking home alone.

I resolved not even to try to have sex until I knew her very well and trusted her, so to speak, with my life, which was the case when I would let her see my circumcised penis. She was a devout Lutheran and a virgin. I do not know why I mention this together in one sentence. I did not know enough about the Lutheran religion to know if pre-marital sex was as much of a taboo as it was in the Catholic religion but the facts were that she was a virgin and she was a Lutheran. I knew that she was a virgin because she told me. It was after our third date when I started to get carried away. She had invited me in to show me her apartment and I, being male, interpreted this as an invitation to see more than just her apartment. I was really turned on and was willing to risk discovery so I took made some strong sexual advances which she politely repulsed twice. I took the hint and mellowed. I apologized. She accepted. We spent about three hours just talking about all sorts of stuff. It was during this conversation that she told me she was still a virgin. I told her that I was not. I steered the conversation towards the Nazis and the Jews. That is when she told me about her best friend at the university, Esther Kaufman, who was Jewish. Esther was humiliated many times and was finally expelled for being Jewish as were some of her favorite teachers. She deplored the way the Nazis were treating the Jews and that said that if she could find a way to help them without jeopardizing her job and her family, she would do it. At first I was not sure if she really meant it or was just saying it to sound more humane. After an hour of talking about it I could see that she was really genuinely sorry that she could not do more to help. I felt that it would only be a matter of time when I felt I could let her know that I was Jewish.

After that night I did not push sex. There is no doubt that she appreciated it and it was really in my best interest anyway. We really hit it off after that. We started to see each other every weekend with dinner at least twice during the week.

Carol and I continued to get more serious. On October 10th I proposed to her and she accepted. Until that time I had not met her mother as she lived out of the city and we just never really took the time as there always seemed to be something going on in the city and I must admit I was quite nervous to see her again as the only time that I had met her briefly was when her husband had died. I was afraid that it might bring back sad memories and perhaps cast me in a bad light. Now, we had to make the obligatory trip to meet her. She called her mother that night and told her that I had proposed and that she had accepted. Her mother and the rest of her immediate family already knew all about me. Carol had told them about me after our third date. I occasionally was mentioned in the press which impressed her mother, who told Carol's aunts, uncles and cousins. We set the visit for the following weekend.

Two days later, about 6 PM there was a knock on Carol's door. She looked through the peephole and saw that it was Esther. She opened the door. Esther threw herself into Carol's arms, "They killed him! They just killed him!" She just about collapsed. Carol didn't know what to do. She held her for what must have been five or ten minutes before she was able to speak.

She and her father were at a store just a few blocks away. They were returning to their home when they were stopped by a group of SS soldiers. They started to molest her. Her father protested. One of the SS soldiers threw him to the floor and continued to grab her breasts. Her father got up and pulled the soldier away from her when another soldier simply drew his pistol and shot him in the head. They laughed and just walked off. He died in her arms in a few seconds. As he died he looked at Esther and tried to say something but he died before he could utter a word. People just looked at them. No one offered to help. He had been shot in front of a grocery store. The owner of the store came out an ordered Esther to get "that dead old Jew" away from the store as it was interfering with business. She just stayed on the ground cradling her dead father's head in her hands, oblivious to anything as she was in a state of shock. The owner went back into the store and got three employees. One grabbed Esther and the two others kicked her father's body off the sidewalk into the street. She snapped out of her state of shock and started screaming at the men, hitting and kicking them. One punched her in the stomach. She doubled up in pain and fell to the sidewalk. About five minutes later the police arrived. She started to tell them what happened. They couldn't care less. What was another dead Jew to them? They stayed there until a truck came. They loaded her father into the back of the truck. When she tried to get into the truck they just threw her to the ground and drove off. She was just left there on the ground. When she got up, she walked over to one of the policemen standing by the patrol car that had responded to the call by the store owner and wanted to know where they were taking her father the policeman slapped her and told her to shut up. He also drove off. She didn't know what to do. She knew from a former classmate where Carol lived so she made her way to Carol's apartment.

Carol called me. I could tell that she was very upset. She couldn't talk on the phone. I rushed over to her apartment. Esther was sitting on the couch staring straight ahead. Her face was blank, void of emotion. Carol told me what happened. I called Wilhelm and he came over and gave her a sedative. I calmed Carol down and stayed with her until about two in the morning. Esther was sleeping and was going to stay the night. She could not leave anyway since Jews were not permitted outside of their homes at night due to the curfew. She woke up once or twice and screamed then fell back to sleep. The sedative kept her immobile for another six hours. Carol called in sick the next day and stayed with her. I left to try to find out where they had taken her father as he had not been brought to the morgue.

I had a description of her father from Carol based on what Esther had told her and I called Mischa and asked if he could find out where the body was taken. Since the incident occurred in the center of the city, it was under the jurisdiction of his precinct so he was able to track down the men that retrieved the body. What he found out amazed and disturbed both of us. The truck drivers were part of a private service contracted by the government. They could do whatever they wanted with any dead Jew that they picked up and had three options. The first was to bring the body to the morgue. This was typically avoided since they had to fill out forms and wait until they were submitted, reviewed and the body was accepted. If it was a busy night, they could wait two or three hours. The second was to sell the body to one of the medical schools. If the body could not be sold it was simply thrown into the city garbage dump which was the third option. The body would be covered by the next day's garbage and, since it was a Jew, nobody in authority cared. Since her father was old, they could not sell the body. It was not that there wasn't a market for old bodies it was that there were just too many old bodies available so there was a surplus. After two or three tries, the men dumped the body in the garbage dump. I went to the garbage dump to try to find the body but it had already been covered up by the previous day's garbage. I obviously did not tell this to Carol. I just told her that I could not find out where they took his body.

Later that afternoon, when Mischa returned to the precinct the two men from the truck wanted to know why he was so interested in the body. They were told that Mischa was asking questions about the dead old Jew. Rather than answer directly, he raised his voice and demanded to know what interest was it of theirs to question him. That was another trait that set Mischa apart from many others. He could think instantaneously and use the system to turn the tables on the people asking him questions that he did not want to answer. They immediately backed down and stammered an explanation which was that they just wanted to know if Mischa was thinking to selling Jewish bodies to medical schools. They went on to say that if he needed some extra money perhaps he would be interested in an arrangement that they had with another detective in the second district. This piqued Mischa's interest and he told them to continue.

They had a special deal with Detective Hans Gruber. Mischa knew of him but did not know him personally. The drivers knew the people in charge of obtaining cadavers at two medical schools. They developed an arrangement with them in that if there was a need for a particular type of body, say a young girl or boy or even a baby, they would pass this information to Hans who would go and kill some Jew to supply the needed body. Sometimes, Hans had to kill an entire family to get the children or the baby. They would dispose of any unsalable body in the dump and no one would ever know what happened to them. They shared the proceeds fifty-fifty. They asked Mischa if he would also be interested in a similar arrangement.

Mischa clenched his teeth and made a fist with both of his hands with such force that his fingernails almost broke the skin in each palm as he contained his shock and disgust. Calmly, he told them that it was certainly an interesting idea and that he would think about it. That evening, just before I left for the day, Mischa came to the morgue and told me about his conversation. We both quickly concluded that we had to do something about it. Until now we were always on the defensive. This called for drastic action. We were determined to put a stop to this. I called the others and told them the story asking for ideas for our next Friday night session.

When Esther finally woke up and regained her composure she started to grasp the reality of the situation. Then she realized that her mother knew nothing about what had happened. She must be worried sick since she and her father did not return home last night. She was in poor health which is why they had not left the country. Esther tried to walk but was not able. The shock, the punch to the stomach and the sedative were still taxing her system. Carol offered to go to their apartment in the second district where she lived to let her mother know what happened. This was very dangerous and Esther advised her not to do it saying that we could find another way. Carol would not listen. Carol took Esther's identity card which had her address and went to the second district. She took the bus and got off close to Esther's apartment. As she got off the bus she saw two SS soldiers forcing some Jews to wash the street. Rather than pass by this disturbing scene, she abruptly turned around and started to walk in the other direction. That was not a good thing to do. She was seen doing this by a couple of Hitler Jugend who were staring at her since she was quite beautiful. Suspecting that she was Jewish since she made such an abrupt about-face, they stopped her and asked for identity card. Carol started to protest when one of the boys grabbed her purse and looked inside. He pulled out Esther's identity card. It did not look much like Carol so the boy asked if her name was Esther Kaufman. She did not want to say that she had Esther's identity card because Esther was at her apartment. They could accuse her of hiding a Jew for which the penalty was death plus they would surely execute Esther for giving her identity card to her and hiding in her apartment. She told them that it was a very bad picture but that it was her. Regardless of what she said she was in serious trouble. She was not wearing the yellow star. That was grounds for immediate deportation or even death. She hadn't thought about that until one of the boys asked her why she was out in the street without the star. Now she was really frightened. There was no good way to get out of the situation. She decided that she better tell the truth and suffer the consequences. Perhaps, they would be lenient given the circumstances. As she was thinking about how to tell the truth one of the boys had gone over to one of the SS soldiers and told him that they had found a Jew walking in the street without the yellow star. Two SS soldiers came over to her. She started to tell them the truth when one of them hit her in the jaw knocking her unconscious.

When she came to she realized that she was in some prison. They immediately noticed that her picture did not match the picture of Esther on the ID card. When they searched her purse they found her real identity card. They asked her how she got Esther's card, why she was pretending to be Esther, and what was she doing in Leopoldstadt. Since she had some money in her purse they thought that was she bringing them money or was part of a plot to help Jews escape. She denied any wrongdoing and said that Esther was an old schoolmate and she had dropped the card in the park when they met for lunch. Now, she was just trying to return it to her and see Esther's mother whom she had known for a long time. They didn't believe her. First of all, Jews were not allowed to go to the park (Carol had forgotten about this). They started to beat her and ask her who she was working with in this plot. She kept on denying that there was a plot. For some reason she finally asked one of the guards to contact me. At first he did not pay any attention to her but when she mentioned that I worked at the morgue he recognized my name. He asked how she knew me. She said that we were engaged to be married. He had no sympathy for Jews or Jew-lovers but realized when he heard my name and that we were engaged that he needed to contact me as soon as possible due to my strong connections in the Nazi party. He told the other officer with him who Carol said she was and that he was to send for a doctor to take care of her. I was called at the morgue and told that Carol had been arrested and was being held at the prison in the Gestapo headquarters. I dropped what I was doing and rushed to the Gestapo headquarters at the Hotel Metropole. When I arrived I asked for Corporal Hoffmann, the officer who had called me. He took me into one of the interrogation rooms and brought Carol in. She was badly bruised and could hardly walk but was bandaged so I knew that they had given her some medical treatment since she had mentioned my name. A Captain came in but before I could say anything he informed me that Carol was under arrest for a number of charges including impersonating a Jew. I asked him if there was such a charge as I never heard of anyone trying to impersonate a Jew. Usually, it was the other way around with a Jew trying to impersonate someone who wasn't Jewish. The Captain just glared at me and said, "Now there is such a charge!" He turned and left. I was permitted to stay another ten minutes and ordered to leave. I told Carol that I would not rest until she was released. I told the Corporal that Carol was my fiancée and that she was an idealist and, while clearly in the wrong, that she was not part of any plot and that I would take it very personal if any harm came to her. I mentioned a few of my SS contacts. He told me that he would personally watch out for her. I took down his name and serial number. I also demanded to see the Captain again. The Captain returned quite angry that I summoned him but before he could say anything I angrily said that I was on my way to see Col. Stryker and that if any additional harm came to her I would make it a personal crusade to use my influence to exact revenge on him. I took out a small pad and asked for his full name and serial number. He was clearly taken aback by my outburst. He thought for a second and told me that he was SS Captain Kaspar Neumann serial number 1334765. I moved to within a few inches of his face, looked directly into his eyes and loudly said, "Heil Hitler!" He responded, but much less enthusiastically.

I immediately called Col. Stryker but he was in Berlin. I called every other SS officer I knew but they were reluctant to get involved with the Gestapo on anything "Jewish" other than arresting or killing them. As a last resort, I called Ernst Kaltenbrunner for an appointment. Without a moment's hesitation he agreed to see me immediately. I told him the whole story. He agreed to intercede and personally called Captain Neumann. When he hung up he actually snickered and said out loud, "Imagine, being arrested for impersonating a Jew!"

I returned to the Gestapo headquarters. Carol had now been locked up for 28 hours. Captain Neumann personally escorted her out and apologized to her and me for the mistake. He also said that if I had told him that I was a friend of General Kaltenbrunner he would have released her immediately. Carol was released to my custody and I took her home in a taxi. She was almost in shock and in a lot of pain. She was totally silent on the way to her apartment. I did not press it. When she got there Esther rushed to the door. She was sick with worry. She did not know what to do. She couldn't leave the apartment as she no longer had her identity card. She was shocked and very sorry to see Carol in such condition since she immediately realized that she had caused this to happen to her best friend. Unfortunately, the Gestapo kept Esther's identification card when they arrested Carol so she still couldn't risk going back home. I offered to get a message to her mother. Carol looked at me and before she could say anything, I just said, "Don't ask." And I left. As I left, Wilhelm arrived to look after both of them. I had called him from the Gestapo headquarters before they released Carol.

I called Matthias, the group leader in Leopoldstadt and asked him to get a message to Carol's mother. He contacted someone he knew who promised that he would tell her mother what happened.

The next morning Matthias was contacted by that person and given the bad news. When Carol was arrested they took Esther's identification card from her and went to the apartment looking for Esther. When her mother said that she did not know where she or her husband was, they beat her until she was unconscious. She died a couple of hours later. Matthias came over to the morgue and told me the story. He could have called but decided to tell me in person. I sat in disbelief and went to Carol's apartment and broke the news to Carol and Esther. Esther collapsed. Carol did her best to comfort her but to no avail. I sent for Wilhelm who again sedated her and left. When she was sound asleep, Carol came over to me and asked how I knew the top Nazi SS general in Vienna well enough to get her released and find out about her mother. She thought that I must be working for the Nazis to do all of this. In fact, she thought that I must secretly be a high ranking Nazi. I just said that I was a Nazi party member due to my job and that I had to work with many Nazis especially Gestapo and SS officers, including General Kaltenbrunner, who interceded for her on my behalf. She did not believe me. She got angry and started yelling at me. In her mind no one not working directly for the Nazis could do and know these things. Unfortunately, she was right. It was now or never. I had to tell her the truth. I tried to embrace her but she shook me off. "Okay," I said, "I will tell you everything. Come and sit down on the couch." She walked over to the couch and sat down. I could see that she was still in considerable pain. Her face was still swollen where she had been hit and she was holding her left side.

"First, let me begin by saying that I love you and I trust you enough to place my life in your hands." I waited for a response but she just stared at me still very angry. I paused and finally blurted out, "I am Jewish. I have been pretending to be a Gentile, a Catholic, since my parents came to Vienna when I was thirteen years old. I belong to a group of similarly hiding Jews and we have managed to infiltrate the Nazi system with astounding success. This has given us access to high-level Nazis in the SS and Gestapo, including General

Kaltenbrunner. It was through his relationship that I managed to get you released."

She just looked at me and got even angrier. "How dare you say that you are Jewish! I do not believe a word that you say! Get out of my apartment!"

I grabbed her and insisted and told her that I could prove it but to do so would be very embarrassing. She insisted so I dropped my pants and pointed to my penis, which was covered with the extension that I was about to remove. Before I could do it she saw my uncircumcised penis and ran to the door, opened it and ordered me out. I waddled over to her, my pants around my ankles which restricted my stride, stood directly in front of her and pulled of the extension quickly, which caused me quite a bit of pain. I leaned forward and grabbed her and again showed her my penis and the extension which I held out in my open hand. She stood there with her mouth wide open. It was an awkward ten to fifteen seconds. I finally broke the silence by asking her to please close the door. She didn't move so I waddled over and shut the door. She went to the couch and sat down. I pulled my pants back up, walked over to the couch and sat down beside her. For the next hour I told her everything including all about the extension, Kaltenbrunner's son's suicide, and the work that we were doing. She listened attentively asking a few questions now and then. When I finished, repeating that she now had my life in her hands, she looked at me in a totally different light. She sat there silently for the next five or so minutes. I respectfully said nothing but did not move away from her. She leaned over to me and whispered, "Could I see it again?" I knew exactly what she was talking about. I undid my zipper and took out my penis. There was some blood at the base of my penis which happened when I abruptly pulled the extension off. She saw the blood and asked if it hurt. I replied that it hurt a little. She immediately got up, went to the bathroom and came out with a small bowl of water and an antiseptic. She started to clean the abraded area around the base of my penis. As she wiped around it, it got hard. With a sense of urgency that I never knew existed in her, she undressed and we proceeded to make love for the first time on the couch, in spite of her pain. We could not go into the bedroom because Esther was sleeping there. We finished and dressed thankful that Esther did not wake up. Carol asked if she could help us. I told her that she could but for now we had to do something with Esther.

I stayed the night and we carefully made love two more times on the couch before we drifted off to sleep. In the morning, we both called in sick and we waited for Esther to wake up. At about 10:30 she awoke. At first she did not realize where she was and she screamed but when she saw Carol it all came back to her. I told her that we could get her out of the country. I briefly described the escape system and the work that we were doing. She refused. As long as there was one Jewish person living in Vienna that could be saved she would not leave. She asked if she could join the group. She was fluent in French, German, Italian and Yiddish. Surely we could find a use for her linguistic skills, she said. At that point I confided that I was one of the leaders of the group to which Carol replied that she had just about reached that conclusion due to the things that I was able to do once I told her about our activities.

The next day she dyed her hair dark black. I brought a camera and took some pictures of her for the false papers that she would need to live in Vienna. Since she spoke French we decided to have her be the niece of Hans Mueller, one of the Swiss families that were helping us in Lyon. We also had to get her a French identity card. Hans was contacted and readily agreed to help. I gave him the name of the man who helped me with the guns. Hans contacted him and was able to get a real identity card of a girl that reasonably matched Esther from the description that I provided. Esther became Rene Dubois, the French niece of Hans Mueller, who came to work in Vienna from Lyon.

One of our group members, Mikhail, worked in a leather tanning factory and was able to get her a job in the head office because of her language skills. Esther had spent two years in Paris as an exchange student in high school so she had a very good French accent. The head office never bothered to check her references since she was referred by Mikhail and had the proper identity card. This turned out to be fantastic. Since the company shipped leather to France, Germany, Italy, and Switzerland she had access to the truck travel permits within Ostmark (Austria) and to enter these countries as well. The leather factory had been owned by a Jewish family for many years but was aryanized in May 1938. The entire family that owned the factory was among the first contingent of 20,000 Jewish emigrants. The former owners went to the United States where they had relatives in return for selling the business. The new owner was Joachim Braun who had worked there for about eight years as the office manager. He had been an early secret member of the Austrian Nazi Party. Actually, he was only a part owner – the visible owner. One half of the profits went to the SS, the silent partners, who owned the other 50 percent of the company. This, of course, was never made public, but was a boon to us. Their ownership meant that the special transit permits were never questioned and the vans were hardly ever searched. Most of the time, the vans were waived through the border checkpoints because they were on "the list". This was a secret list of SS-owned assets in Austria that was given to the border posts. There was a tacit understanding that these trucks were not to be stopped and searched. The only time they were searched was when there was a high security alert and even then the search was cursory. Often, the SS used the trucks from the various former Jewish assets to do a little smuggling between SS officers stationed in other countries. Most notable was the smuggling of wine, cognac, champagne and food delicacies from France and Italy. It isn't as if the SS couldn't bring these products back and forth themselves, it was the quantity and the disposition of the items. Many SS officers had a lucrative business reselling these products to local merchants and officers of the other military groups. Esther was able to get some blank travel forms for us to copy and she was able to borrow the rubber stamps which we were able to duplicate and return to her the next morning. Unfortunately, the forms were sequentially numbered so we were not able to keep them but our copies were really great. You could not tell them from the originals. We used the same range of serial numbers so should a border guard ever ask for confirmation of a shipment by calling the head office, at least the serial number would show up in their records. This was relatively safe since the factories shipped direct using the forms sent to them by the head office. It took up to eight weeks before the used travel permit with the border stamps were sent back to the headquarters from the factory so if the headquarters were called to confirm the shipment all they would know was that it was a valid travel permit number. They always approved any calls coming in from the border guards, which was not very frequently. Whenever we used a false travel document and the copy was returned to the head office, we would give Esther the number and she would watch for it, intercept it and destroy it before anyone there could file it and notice that there were two bills of lading with the same number. Once, when she missed taking the copy she was able to go to the file and pull the original one so the forged copy was not detected as it was filed instead of the original.

Carol was the liaison between Esther and the group. They would often go out to lunch or have breakfast together which gave Esther the opportunity to give Carol anything new as well as any pertinent information that she learned at the company headquarters. Of particular importance was when new travel permit forms were issued. For security reasons, the Nazis would make some changes periodically to the forms at certain unannounced intervals. As soon as the new forms or a new stamp was issued, Esther would pass them to Carol. The copies were made overnight. One of our Swiss friends owned a coffee shop downtown near the tanning company's head office which we used as a drop zone. Esther stopped at the coffee shop every morning so should she ever be followed as a routine security check, which was often the case for foreign workers, it would be part of her daily routine. She was able to pick up the item the next morning. Because of this procedure, Esther came to the office early every morning to establish this routine so when she had to return something that she had taken the night before there would not be anyone in her office to see her put back the item. Once in a while someone else was also in early so she would ask that person to please get something for her. When she was alone was able to put the item back. Luckily, this did not happen too often. The new owner of the business sometimes came in early as well but his office was down the hall and he could not see what she was doing. He did notice that she was always there early. Because she came in early, she was able to reduce the backlog of paperwork that had accumulated. This was also noticed. About three months after being hired, she was given a raise and a promotion for her outstanding work. This gave her access to even more of the things that we needed.

We also realized that we had another potential problem based on Carol's arrest. Suppose one of the members of our network was captured, taken to the Gestapo headquarters prison and was subjected to torture. We might not find out about it until it was too late and we were compromised. We put our heads together one night at our weekly card game but could not come up with a solution. At about ten o'clock Wilhelm received a telephone call, got up and excused himself. He had a critically sick patient in the hospital and the hospital called that his temperature had increased and asked if he could come to the hospital to check on him. As he got up to leave, Friedrich had a great idea. If we could get Wilhelm or one of our other doctors (we had two others that were now living with our extensions) to become the doctor for the Gestapo headquarters prison, we could learn of anyone's arrest sooner rather than later. Furthermore, if they called Wilhelm before or during the torture it would reduce the possibility of exposure. The Nazis would typically torture a person then call in a doctor to fix them up enough to keep them alive for more torture. Doctor Fritz Lehmann was their current doctor. He was about fifty-five and was an early member of the Austrian Nazi Party. He was one of the underground Nazis. As were most of the early joiners, he was virulently ant-Semitic and a fanatic supporter of the Nazi party. He had no compassion for the people being tortured – even if they were eventually proven to be innocent. His rationale was that if you were even suspected of being an enemy of the state, there must be some truth in it so while the person may be innocent of the specific charge that resulted in their arrest, they were most likely guilty of something else. "Either you are with us or against us!" he would often say so even being neutral was not acceptable.

On my advice, most of our group had joined the Nazi Party in 1939 about ten months after Anschluss shortly after they were fitted with the extension. Our first task was to eliminate Dr. Lehmann so we put him under twenty-four-hour surveillance. We also investigated his past to see if there was some scandal that we could use against him. Unfortunately, he was clean. He led an exemplary Nazi life. Too bad for him as it meant we had to physically eliminate him either through death or injury. On the night of November 12th during a heavy rainstorm, Doctor Lehmann's car was hit broadside by a fully-loaded coal truck traveling at high speed through a red light. He was killed immediately upon impact. The driver of the coal truck fled the scene. The coal truck did not have any identification on it and the license plate was issued to a company that was no longer in business. Obviously, the authorities concluded, the truck was part of a coal smuggling operation.

The following morning after the body was brought to the morgue I called the Gestapo headquarters and asked to speak to someone in charge. I informed the operator of the reason for my call. After about three minutes, Colonel Lange answered the phone. I had never met him. I identified myself and informed him of the death of Doctor Lehmann using his Gestapo medical identification card as the reason that I knew that he was working for the Gestapo. Colonel Lange, who was a close friend of the doctor, personally came down to the morgue to view the body. I had also notified the doctor's family first so they were already there. I was with the family, consoling them as best as I could, when Colonel Lange arrived. He also consoled the family, embracing the doctor's wife. After about fifteen minutes, he came over to me and asked to view the body. I took him into the back room, uncovered the body. He stared at the dead doctor for a minute and we went into my office. He saw the framed letter from Hitler on the wall. He was impressed. We started talking and I dropped a few names such as Kaltenbrunner, Kaupfner and Stryker. He knew Kaupfner very well so we talked about him for a while. After a few minutes I bought up the issue of Doctor Lehmann's replacement. Colonel Lange said he had not yet even thought about it. I suggested Wilhelm who was a close personal friend of mine and a member of the Nazi Party. Colonel Lange agreed to see Wilhelm at 3PM on Wednesday since he had some prior commitments until then. This was great as it gave us an opportunity to do a background check on Colonel Lange.

We mobilized our intelligence network and quickly found out that Colonel Lange was fifty-two years old and had been a member of the Nazi Party in Austria since 1926. He was married and had two boys, 18 and 21. Both of the boys lived at home. His 21-year-old son was finishing college and was going to enlist in the SS when he graduated. One of their favorite pastimes was hunting. The three of them went hunting whenever they could as the boys grew up. He had hunting trophies in his office and at his home. He also liked fishing but both of his sons found it too boring so they rarely went fishing with him, unless it was to another country that they had not yet visited. He particularly liked scotch whiskey, a habit he picked up while on a family fishing trip in Scotland before the war. Luckily, Wilhelm had done some hunting so they could at least talk about hunting. We quickly went to the various taxidermy shops around the city and bought a deer and boar head. We were lucky enough to get an eighteen-point buck's head. We brought them to Wilhelm's office and mounted them on the wall making it a point to tell Wilhelm about the eighteen-point buck which was a really good trophy. One of the group members, an ardent hunter, gave Wilhelm a crash course in the finer points of hunting such as a list of places to hunt and what to hunt for at these places.

Wilhelm showed up promptly at 3 PM on Thursday. He was shown into Colonel Lange's office. After some preliminary talk Wilhelm steered the conversation to hunting referring to the trophies that Lange had on the wall. Immediately, that became the topic of discussion. Wilhelm casually mentioned that he had shot an eighteen-point buck and had the trophy mounted in his office. Colonel Lange had a sixteen-point buck at home which was his pride and joy trophy. Col. Lange asked if he could see it. Of course, Wilhelm said yes. They left his office at about 3:30 and went downstairs. Colonel Lange's car and driver were waiting downstairs. They got in and went to Wilhelm's office. On the way, Wilhelm mentioned that the one thing that he wanted to try but never got around to, was fishing. Colonel Lange's ears perked up on that piece of information. Colonel Lange told Wilhelm that he liked fishing very much as it was the only time that he really had a chance to relax and do nothing. His sons preferred hunting so they did not do much fishing together. Perhaps, Colonel Lange thought, Wilhelm would join him next weekend for fishing. He asked. Wilhelm accepted. When they arrived at Wilhelm's office and went in Colonel Lange looked at the buck. He pulled a chair over to it and stood on it to get a better view. He counted the points. Sure enough, there were eighteen points. As he left, Colonel Lange turned to Wilhelm and confirmed 5 AM on Sunday for the fishing trip. Wilhelm was retained on the spot, subject, of course, to a thorough background check, which he passed without any problem.

Wilhelm went to the Hotel Metropole, the Gestapo headquarters, on the following Monday. He arrived before Colonel Lange and waited in the lobby. Colonel Lange arrived about one hour late. He apologized for being late and for only catching three small fish between the two of them the day before. Wilhelm dismissed the second apology saying that he enjoyed the trip and the company. The poor fish catch was offset by the consumption of almost one bottle of double malt scotch, four bottles of beer and some wursts and bread. Wilhelm had made sure that the Colonel had most of the scotch which we provided from our smuggling operation. We chose one of the best and most expensive brands of scotch. Wilhelm brought two bottles with him making sure that the Colonel took one full bottle home with him.

Colonel Lange personally introduced Wilhelm to the rest of his staff and escorted him downstairs to have his ID tag made. He even waited while Wilhelm was fingerprinted and photographed. He gave Wilhelm a tour of the headquarters and the prison. There were about twenty cells in the basement and three torture rooms plus some additional cells on some other floors but these were reserved for special prisoners such as Kurt von Schuschnigg, the former chancellor of Austria. The torture rooms were located among the cells so that the prisoners could hear the screams of the people being tortured. Pinned to the walls in each torture chamber were ears, noses, tongues, fingers, toes, testicles and uncircumcised penises. Some eyes were kept in a jar of water on a table in the middle of the room. Each prisoner was shown these things when they were brought into the room asking them if they had a preferred body part that they wanted to contribute to the display. This was very effective as a number of prisoners opted to tell everything rather than be subjected to such torture.

There were nine prisoners in the cells. Most were in pretty bad shape. The average lifespan for a prisoner was about one week. Very few of the prisoners were ever released unharmed if there was even shred of doubt about their involvement in some clandestine anti-Nazi activity. If, after one week of intense torture, the prisoner did not tell them what they wanted to know they concluded that the prisoner really didn't know anything and could release them but many times, rather than take any chances they shot the prisoner anyway. Only if the prisoner was cooperative without torture, or at the onset of torture, and once they corroborated the information would they either let him or her go – provided that they became an informer for them – or, if not, execute them. Being arrested by the Gestapo was a death sentence if they were brought to the Hotel Metropole prison and did not cooperate. Six were political prisoners, members of groups that were opposed to Nazi rule. The other three were gypsies that had just been captured. The Gestapo wanted to know where the rest of their group was hiding.

Wilhelm tended to the torture victims. All during this time he was watched by one of the guards. Many of the people he was fixing up begged to be killed. It broke his heart not being able to help any of them.

Unlike his predecessor Doctor Lehmann, Wilhelm decided not to wait until he was called in to treat a tortured prisoner. By the time he was called in it could be too late. The physical and mental torture that a person could stand varied by individual. He could not take a chance that one of our group members was captured and forced to talk before Wilhelm was called in to revive him. To enable this plan, Wilhelm made it a point to become closer to Colonel Lange. They went fishing together at every opportunity. Wilhelm provided Colonel Lange with scotch and other scarce items that were particularly welcomed by his wife. It wasn't long until Wilhelm was invited to Colonel Lange's home to meet his wife and two sons. During one of the dinners, which were usually held on a Saturday night, Helmut, Colonel Lange's youngest son casually mentioned that he had always wanted to go hunting with a crossbow. The next week two top-of-the-line professional Swiss crossbows were delivered to Helmut compliments of Wilhelm. That weekend Colonel Lange and Helmut went hunting together for the first time in about six months. Colonel Lange's wife, Wilhelmina, and Wilhelm's wife, Frieda, also became great friends. Frieda knew all about her husband's activities and was eager to help him solidify his relationship with Colonel Lange. They even joked about the coincidence of their names Wilhelm and Wilhelmina. Wilhelmina liked to sew. Frieda used our network to contact the Jewish refugee community in Shanghai through the Swiss Jewish Refugee Association. In five weeks a shipment of the finest silk arrived from Shanghai which Frieda gave to Wilhelmina. Wilhelmina was ecstatic. This high quality silk was impossible to get for the past three years.

Wilhelm and Colonel Lange went to lunch at least two times per month. Colonel Lange was a member at the Jockey Club and recommended Wilhelm. Unlike me, Wilhelm accepted as in his position being known publicly was a benefit. With Wilhelm being at the Gestapo headquarters two or three times per week he was well-known to the other SS and Gestapo members. Wilhelm made it clear to them that if they ever needed something from him or from Colonel Lange that he could help them with, he would be only too pleased to intercede. About one week after his offer, one of the SS officers hesitantly approached him. His son, a Lieutenant in the army, was going to be transferred to the Russian Front. Casualties there were very high. About one in three soldiers were wounded and one in four killed. The Russians had launched a major counter-offensive during the winter and the German army was retreating. Wilhelm took his name down and promised to see what he could do. Wilhelm sought our advice on this matter at the weekly card game. While he could go to Colonel Lange and ask for the soldier's son not to be transferred to the Russian Front it could put Colonel Lange in a precarious position if he tried to intercede and was questioned by the Wehrmacht he really couldn't say, "because his father asked him to intercede." Obviously, many such requests were being received and it was a strong bone of contention within the army hierarchy. Klaus came up with a brilliant idea. The second district was becoming increasingly depopulated as more Jews were being deported. Many suspected that deportation meant death not relocation to a better place. Suppose rumors of a planned Jewish uprising in Vienna began to circulate in the SS and Gestapo headquarters. We knew that no such threat existed so we started it focusing on Leopoldstadt which had the highest concentration of Jews that were still interspersed with Gentiles. An uprising there would be a disaster. Soon, it reached the top officers. Klaus had also suggested that Wilhelm hint to Col. Lange that they should create a special tactical force of regular soldiers to periodically sweep through Leopoldstadt to make impromptu searches for weapons. The SS were stretched too thin for this and they were always associated with deportations. If truckloads of SS soldiers entered Leopoldstadt, it could accelerate an uprising and would clearly drive the rebels into hiding.

The next day, at lunch, Wilhelm asked Colonel Lange if there was any truth to the rumors he was hearing that the Jews were planning a major uprising that could result in the total destruction of many buildings and the death of many German civilians and soldiers. Colonel Lange confirmed the rumors but added that at this time they were only rumors. "Too bad that you do not have a special containment squad," Wilhelm said. "That could be the difference between a successful uprising and a stifled rebellion." Colonel Lange asked Wilhelm to explain his statement. "Suppose you set up a non-SS squad to perform perfunctory random raids whose only goal was to search for weapons. These should only be regular army and not the SS since the SS was associated with the deportations." Colonel Lange thought that this was an excellent idea. Wilhelm casually mentioned that he had just met Lieutenant Oskar Stueben who was the son of SS Captain Otto Stueben the other day and thought that he would be a good candidate for this duty as he seemed to be very energetic with strong initiative. Without a moment's hesitation, Colonel Lange said he would take care of it. When he returned to his office he immediately called Col. Huber who was Lieutenant Stueben's commanding officer in the Wehrmacht whom he knew and suggested setting up a Tactical Search Squad. Col. Huber was well aware of the rumors. He really liked the idea and commended Colonel Lange for it, telling him to proceed with full speed to set it up under his personal authorization. The next day, under special orders authorized by Col. Huber and Colonel Lange, a special search squad was set up under the command of Lieutenant Stueben. He was given permission to select seven other soldiers for this duty. Not surprisingly all of the selected team members were related to the SS and the Gestapo staff at the Gestapo headquarters. He was thanked profusely by the SS and Gestapo whose sons he saved. Seizing the opportunity, he mentioned that it would really help him plan his schedule if he knew when any new prisoners were brought in before they were even interrogated. Given his elevated status, it became an actual written procedure at the prisoner registration office. As soon as any new prisoner was admitted Wilhelm was to be called and given a full description of the prisoner or prisoners before they were interrogated. This was one of the smartest moves that we ever made. By the way, we knew for a fact that the Jewish community in Vienna did not have any weapons stockpiled and that they had absolutely no intention to revolt. This was going to be the proverbial "wild goose chase" whose only purpose was to keep the selected soldiers out of the Russian Front. After nine unsuccessful raids where nothing was turned up, Wilhelm came to me and said that if they did not find anything soon there was a risk of the special squad being disbanded and being sent to the Russian Front after all. I contacted Klaus and we managed to smuggle some arms into Leopoldstadt. On the next raid, eight rifles, seven handguns, four homemade bombs, and two hand grenades were found in one of the buildings from which the Jews had already been deported. These were all taken from the immense SS and police property rooms of items confiscated from other raids and from our own small arsenal. A special report was written by Colonel Lange and sent to Huber and Kaltenbrunner who forwarded to directly to Himmler. Himmler commended Huber who commended Lange, who commended Otto and also called Wilhelm and thanked him for the idea. It had obviously saved many German lives.

CHAPTER SEVENTEEN

THE "PROGRAM"

"The construction of a lunatic asylum costs 6 million Marks. How many houses at 15,000 Marks each could have been built for this amount?"

German Primary School Mathematic
Book Problem

"Can you tell how long it took for someone to die?"

That was the opening remark of Col. Stryker as he abruptly entered my office. It even preceded the customary "Heil Hitler!" He again repeated his question as I raised my head obviously startled at his unexpected abrupt intrusion and the odd question. "Can you tell how long it took for someone to die?" He repeated.

I responded by saying that I really didn't know. I needed more information as to the cause of death, the condition of the body, how the body was preserved, etc. If the body was weeks or even days old, these conditions could have a significant bearing. I told him that most of the time we could tell approximately when they had died but I never had been asked to determine how long it took for someone to die. There were some instances when someone had died due to injuries sustained during an accident. Here the death was not immediate so they may have died on the way to the hospital but the length of time from when the crash occurred and when the person died was not accurately recorded. The only accurate timeline in this case was when the ambulance arrived at the scene of the accident and when the person died in the ambulance or at the hospital. So, again, I said that I really didn't know if it could be done.

He ignored what I said and continued talking. "These are new bodies. Fresh bodies. From yesterday." He replied. "So, can you tell?"

I again replied that I really didn't know. I would have to see the bodies before I could even make an educated guess. I assumed that he was talking about some crime scene where perhaps the time of death was critically important to a suspect's alibi. I reiterated that I would have to see the bodies. That was a mistake! Unfortunately, at the time I didn't realize it.

Col. Stryker replied, "Good. Take whatever you need to perform multiple autopsies" as he pulled me by my arm out of my office. Without giving me time to adequately arrange for someone to cover for me, I gathered what I needed and just managed to let one of my co-workers know that I was leaving as I walked down the hallway and out the door. He escorted me to a large black car, with two swastika-adorned flags attached to the front bumpers, which was waiting outside the morgue. There were two motorcycles standing by and as we entered the car, the motorcycles revved up their engines. The driver was an SS Lieutenant, which was unusual, and there was another SS Lieutenant seated next to him. We drove off with the motorcycle escort preceding us. For the first ten minutes Col. Stryker did not say anything. I wisely decided not to ask. He turned to me after the ten minute period of silence and said that what he was about to tell me was to be held in the strictest confidence. He explained that in Germany there was a program initiated by the Fuehrer to protect Aryan purity, the bloodline of the German people. It was code-named Aktion T-4 (named after the address of the program's headquarters on Tiergartenstrasse 4 in Berlin). It was a top-secret program to eliminate contaminated elements from society. He stopped at that point and looked at me waiting for my reaction. I did not even begin to understand what he was talking about so I simply said, "Please go on," which he did. He continued explaining the T-4 program proudly stating that he was in command for all of Austria for this important project.

The T-4 program would eliminate physically and mentally deficient people so they could not reproduce and were no longer a burden on society or their families that had to care for them. The mental institutions were overcrowded with these degenerate people who had no hope of ever becoming normal and leading normal lives. "Some do not even realize that they were alive," he added. They were such a burden on their families that he was sure that many of them would want them out of the way so they could get on with their lives and no longer be distracted by these expensive burdens. I sat there for a few minutes trying to decipher what he was talking about. Then it hit me. It was evident that he was talking about killing these people but they were not really people to the Nazis that had no value to society. They were disposable - and the Nazis were going to accelerate the disposal process. I sat in disbelief saying nothing as I realized that the Nazi government, Hitler specifically, had put in motion a program to murder helpless individuals that were clearly no threat to the security of the country. In the Aryan mind, racial purity was of the essence and it justified the strongest of measures such as this program. After all, wasn't the elimination of Jews a race purification issue?

I tried to hide my shock. I was not successful. Col Stryker saw the expression on my face and gave me some time to compose myself. After a minute or two, I asked him what the exact purpose of our trip was.

"Well," he said, "the program has been active in Germany for more than one year. We have been experimenting with different ways to eliminate them. We have tried injections which work quickly but many of the doctors and nurses administering them had strong issues with it. They were revolted at the idea of killing these patients for whom they had been caring. They had moral and ethical problems, especially if they were religious. Some had nightmares, some threatened to tell the newspapers, politicians and the family members of the people they were killing. They often refused to sign the death certificates attesting that they died from natural causes. Most just simply refused to do it. Moreover, we couldn't control the secrecy as everyone at the institution quickly learned about the situation if not directly from the staff chosen to administer the injections, then from the unexplained disappearances of the patients. Early on we decided that we did not want to shoot them since the body would clearly show that they did not die of natural causes when we released the body to the family. We eventually decided to take them from the institutions to a central place to have soldiers shoot them and that all of the bodies would be cremated immediately after they were shot so it no longer mattered how we killed them. Here again, there were problems with the soldiers that had to shoot the victims, especially if the victim looked at them when they were being shot – or if it were a child." He paused to catch his breath and continued, "It's not like killing a Jew, you know! Many soldiers refused and there was no way that the medical staff would shoot them. So, we've been experimenting with other methods that would not involve anyone directly looking at them while eliminating them."

He continued, "To this end we have set up a collection point in Vienna at the Wagner von Jauregg Mental Hospital, which is also known as Am Steinhof. From there, the selected patients are transported to Hartheim, a small city outside of Linz where there is a larger mental institution. They are transported by a special bus with the windows painted so no one could see them inside the bus. At Hartheim we have built a large, enclosed building away from the hospital where we put them in as soon as they arrive, close the door and pump in carbon monoxide from a series of trucks lined up outside with their exhaust pipes extended into the building. After they are dead they are cremated in the special large crematorium that was built expressly for this purpose next to the building. This also minimizes the number of people that know what is going on and it allows us to eliminate many more patients at a time. After they are killed, they are cremated and the ashes are collected and sent to their families along with a death certificate listing some fictitious cause of death. The problem is that there are too many of these degenerate people in Austria and the building is so large that it takes too much time for them to die so we are having trouble maintaining our schedule. From the time the first busload arrives in Hartheim and we have enough busloads of these inmates so we can fill the building, gas them, which can take more than eight hours to ensure they are all dead, until we take the bodies to the crematorium, it can take ten more hours. While this is going on, more buses arrive and we do not have any place to put them once the building is full so they stay on the bus and they shit and they piss and they vomit on the bus so it has to be thoroughly cleaned before it can be used again. Some refuse to get out of the bus so the guard has to go into to this filthy bus and force them out. The guard and his uniform are covered with all of their filth by the time he forces them out of the bus. Those guards protest vehemently to their superiors about doing this type of work which again compromises secrecy. It's quite a mess. You can see the problems that we have. So we have been looking for alternatives."

He stopped to gauge my reaction. I just stared blankly at him trying to understand the rationale that could justify such an abhorrent action. He continued, "One method that is now being tested is gassing them in transit. We have modified a number of small vans by running the exhaust pipe into the compartment where the people are being transported. This would pump carbon monoxide into the compartment from the engine as it drives which kills the people during the ride. The Austrian firm, Sauer, is producing these special vans for us. Under the pretext of transferring them to another, specially modified institution that could offer them better care, we would pick them up from various hospitals and institutions in Eastern Austria take them to Am Steinhof. Once there we selected some for the special test and put them in these specially modified vans. At first we were going to drive them to Hartheim but our task was to determine how quickly the various gasses work so we decided just to load them in the van and drive around the outskirts of the city. We assumed that they were dead when the kicking, screaming and banging on the sides of the compartment stopped for five minutes but we really didn't know if they were all dead. This took about thirty or forty minutes. To be absolutely sure, we decided to drive around for at least one hour. We assumed that they all would be dead when the van returned to Am Steinhof so the van could go directly to the crematorium which streamlined the process. However, in at least two of these tests not all of the people died even after one hour in the back of the van. There were pockets of air on the floor under some of the bodies that kept one or two of them alive. When the door was opened and they were being unloaded at the crematorium they regained consciousness and started to struggle and scream and vomit. The staff were taken aback and had to call the soldiers over to shoot them. Some refused. This created a big problem."

I asked what he meant by various gasses. He told me that at the T-4 headquarters someone got the idea of trying potent poison gases in these vans that would be pumped in alone or, to save money, would be introduced with the carbon monoxide exhaust fumes. He added, "and I am proud to say, Vienna has been selected as the testing place for this project." They decided that they did not want to conduct the tests in Germany as there were already too many rumors so they selected Eastern Austria. They did not tell him why they made this decision and Col Stryker did not ask. He was too happy to have been selected for this important project – and naturally, he thought of me to help him.

He continued with his explanation. "Last week we received four vans that have been specially equipped for these tests. They had some special insulation around the passenger compartment to deaden the sound but it was not completely soundproof. The exhaust pipe extends along the side of the van to the roof. There is a special compartment mounted on the roof. We can insert a canister of gas into the compartment on the roof, open the valve and mix it with the exhaust gas or we can just pump only the poison gas into the van by not hooking up the exhaust pipe. There is a heavy mesh screen across the entire top of the inner compartment. This spreads the gas and prevents the occupants from blocking the incoming gas. We found that when we just piped the gas directly into the van simply by extending the pipe into the compartment from the side or up from the bottom, once in a while one of the imbeciles inside would realize what was happening and stuff clothing inside the pipe to block the incoming gas. This would mess up the engine stopping the vehicle. It would sometimes take the drivers an hour to figure out which one of them had enough sense to block the pipe. Even after we tied up that patient, some of the others that had seen what he had done did the same thing – sort of a 'monkey see, monkey do' situation. So now we are more sophisticated but we still did not know how long it actually took all of them to die. This is why you are here. We have completed the first round of tests. We used two vans with the exhaust gas mixed with two different poison gases and two with each poison gas alone.

We drove around for more than two hours which is long enough to make sure that they were all dead so we would really like to know how long it took them to die in each van."

He turned to me and looking directly into my eyes said, "Given your experience at the morgue, your obvious commitment to the Third Reich and since I had met you when I delivered the letter from our Fuehrer, I knew that you would be the logical choice for this. Am I correct?"

By now I regained my composure and fully understood the "program". I quickly realized that I had no option and that I was clearly the right person for the job. I replied that he could count on me and that I was proud to be able to serve the Fatherland. He, of course, again emphatically mentioned that I should not speak of this to anyone. I agreed thinking to myself that this would be the last thing I would want anybody who knew me to know.

We arrived at Am Steinhof, which is in district 7. It had been a busy weekend. The four vans were loaded on Sunday and were driven around the area for about one hour. Col. Stryker further explained, "We put six patients in each van. An older man and an older woman, a man and a woman between 30 and 40 years old and two children one that was less than 10 years old and a teenager. This would give us a good cross-section from which to select the most efficient gas if the rates of dying were different. We also put some mattresses and bedding in the van to take up space so it would simulate a crowded compartment when the van was full. This also reduced the amount of good air in the van to expedite the process. About a kilometer from the institution, the vans were driven off of the road into a secluded area. The driver and the officer accompanying him attached a rubber hose from the exhaust pipe into the inlet valve going into the passenger compartment on the two vans selected for the poison gas/exhaust mixture. The two types of poison gas were introduced into the four vans and off they drove. These vans have a separate driver's compartment lest there be some gas leakage from the passenger compartment into the driver compartment. We installed a microphone in each van so the driver and his partner could listen to the screams and choking of the dying patients. It had an on-off switch so they did not have to listen to the passengers all of the time rationalizing that some might not want to hear the first ten or twenty minutes of the screams. A couple of the drivers mentioned that they listened attentively with one or two betting on how long it would take for them to stop screaming. The point was to wait until there were absolutely no discernable sounds coming from the compartment. They recorded the time but continued driving around for another thirty minutes or forty just to be sure. We did not want to have any of them alive when the van returned. So, as you can see, the timing of death is approximate and I need a more accurate time to optimize the process. Gasoline is in short supply, you know."

In a makeshift morgue in the basement of the Am Steinhof guarded by four SS soldiers with machines guns outside each of the two entrance doors were four long tables with six bodies on each one. The bodies were positioned sideways on the table so their feet dangled from the table. Each body was covered with a separate white sheet. At the foot of each table was a clipboard with the name of the gas used, the starting time when the gas was turned on after the hose was connected to the compartment, the time when they no longer heard any noise and the time when the back door was opened. The medical records of each of the victims were also there.

There is an inherent will to live – whether you are mentally sound or not. So it was with the mentally retarded people that had been selected for liquidation. This was painfully apparent when I removed the sheet from the first table. It is still painful to remember and describe the bodies. They were grotesquely contorted. They had banged, clawed, kicked and tried everything that they could do with their frail bodies to get out of the van. Their hands and heads were bloody. At least two of them had fingernails broken or pulled out. From the head injuries of two of them it was apparent that they banged their heads repeatedly at what must have been the door. Their clothes were disheveled and torn, surely the result of one of them pulling another from the door so he could try to get out. One of the young children, who could not have been more than ten years old, was evidently knocked to the floor and trampled in the panic. I am sure that they yelled and screamed until the gas was strong enough to render them listless before they became unconscious and slowly died as their respiration decreased commensurate with their becoming unconscious. They had urinated, defecated and thrown up. They were also discolored. Carbon monoxide replaces the oxygen in the blood causing asphyxiation. In the process the skin turns blue/black. I looked at the chart on the first table. The gas used was a combination of carbon monoxide from the exhaust and a poison gas called mustard gas that was banned by the Geneva Convention in the First World War. It raised painful blisters on the skin of those exposed to it. It burned the lungs of those that breathed it. It was a painful death that was not very quick. This was evident when we looked at the bodies on the other tables and compared them. Clearly, this combination was the worst. All of the bodies on the other tables were in some grotesquely contorted mangled condition. There were just varying degrees of contortion. These were the worst. The blisters were obviously very painful. The facial contortions were commensurate with the obvious pain. Those killed with only the mustard gas were less contorted but clearly died in agony. The carbon monoxide exhaust diluted the mustard gas prolonging their agony hence the higher degree of contortion.

I am no stranger to death. I have seen dead bodies and pieces of bodies from accidents. I have seen decomposed bodies brought in days and weeks after death with a stench so unbearable that it was difficult to perform the autopsy without getting sick. I have seen accidents where you could not be sure which body part belonged to which victim. This was different - very, very different. I could not hide my revulsion. Neither could Col. Stryker. We both actually had to leave the room and walk outside to regain our composure. The specially selected Am Steinhof staff members were a bit taken aback to see us react that way. While they didn't say anything directly to our faces I am sure that they spoke of our reaction amongst themselves after we left.

Outside Col. Stryker turned to me and said that he could not believe what he saw. It is one thing to remotely do what you are told but it was another thing to actually see the results firsthand. It was very simple to follow the logic of not wanting mentally deficient people as a burden to society and contaminating the purity of the Aryan race. It is easy to sign an order from the confines of an office and move on to other things. The firsthand viewing of the bodies put this in a totally different perspective. At this point he was not sure that this was the best solution – not that he had a better one. At first I thought he had much more compassion than I had thought he had and was condemning the killing of these people but as he continued it was not the program he was condemning, it was the method used. He turned to me and said, "See, now you we why we need a better way to kill these degenerates so they die completely and more quickly. We are working to provide a humane service with these tests – so some must suffer for the benefit of those that will follow but we should at least try to minimize the time and improve the condition of the bodies and the impact that it would have on those unloading them for cremation. Even I reacted poorly to these bodies!"

That statement totally sobered me up. I regained my composure as my revulsion switched from the bodies to him. Here was a perfect example of the Nazi indoctrination that pervaded the SS. These helpless people were sub-human so eliminating them was justified – it should just be done more efficiently to minimize the impact that their misshapen bodies would have on the medical staff, workers and soldiers that would have to work with the corpses. This incident put the SS in perspective in my mind. I could now easily understand why the SS was put in charge of the extermination of the Jews and other undesirables and why the concentration camps were run by the SS.

I recounted a bit of what I remembered about them. The SS, or Schutzstaffel (protective squadron), was an elite special unit formed in 1926 that was comprised of men with very strong personal commitments to Adolf Hitler and the Nazi ideology, particularly in the purity of the Aryan race and the need to protect this purity at all costs. Initially, it was set up as small protective group assigned as Hitler's personal bodyguards. They were fanatical in their beliefs and loyalty and would do anything to maintain their status as being in the elite SS. The SS did not have much importance in the Nazi party hierarchy until a small man of slight build took it over in January 1929. His name was Heinrich Himmler. He transformed it into a powerful elite military unit that was both respected and feared.

They were clearly the hard line fanatics of the Nazi regime that would unquestionably do whatever was asked of them. Furthermore, they believed wholeheartedly in what they were doing. After the war many SS concentration camp guards claimed that they were just following orders and couldn't protest lest they be condemned but after gauging Col. Stryker's response I would not accept this excuse. They truly believed in what they were doing and that whoever was identified as subhuman was not worthy of any pity.

I returned to the make-shift morgue after about fifteen minutes. Col. Stryker elected to remain outside. Three workers from the sanitarium worked with me as we went from table to table to try to determine how long it took for the people in each van to die. We did blood tests and took tissue samples in addition to performing the normal autopsies. I looked at the samples under a microscope. The results were inconclusive. We could not discern any timing differences between the victims. However, we did notice that the victims on Table One and Table Two were the most contorted and messed up (mustard gas with and without exhaust fumes). The bodies on Table Three were less contorted with those on Table Four being the least contorted. They had evidently died quicker than the rest because the gas must have been more powerful to render them unconscious quicker. Their clothing was almost intact and their faces were not as contorted. We looked at the chart. The Table Four bodies had been exposed to 100 percent Zyclon B, which I later learned was hydrogen cyanide. It was not mixed with the exhaust as was the case with the victims on Table Three. Thus, we reached the conclusion that 100 percent Zyclon B was the quickest method – and the least disturbing for the victims hence it would be the least disturbing for the people involved in disposing the bodies.

The staff took pictures of the people on the table after the autopsies. They had already taken pictures of the bodies when they opened the van for the first time and after they had placed the bodies on the tables. I instructed them to take close-ups of the faces of each group to illustrate my conclusions. In spite of the lack of quantitative results, they were quite satisfied with the observed qualitative results and they whole-heartedly agreed with my conclusions, especially with the photographs as back up. They decided to report that "while each individual gas or mixture of the gas with the exhaust fumes accomplished the job and they all died, the use of Zyclon B alone was clearly the best option as it left them in a much better appearance that would more closely simulate death by natural causes should the body have to be given back to the family. Moreover, the condition of the bodies would be more acceptable to the staff assigned to their ultimate disposal."

After the report was written and I signed off on it, I was allowed to leave the make-shift morgue with the proviso from the doctor in charge not to mention anything about the program to anyone. Col. Stryker was with me and he reiterated his complete trust in me and mentioned the personal letter that I had from the Fuehrer. That was good enough.

Before we left the doctor in charge took us on a tour of the facility which included a visit to a small, locked storage building outside of the facility. There were two guards at the door. This was where the various gases that were being tested were stored. He inspected the labels on each canister until he found the hydrogen cyanide. I was shown one of these canisters of the poison. I expected that it would be a large gas canister but it wasn't. It was in a circular air-tight metal container that looked like a small can of paint. I was told that the contents of the canister were solid crystals that were transformed into the poison gas when exposed to air. All the person had to do was to unscrew the cover on the top of the van, dump the crystals into the special metal mesh holder that extended down into the van and screw the cover back on. The air inside the van would cause the gas to form. This was a fairly rapid process. The label read: ZYCLON B GIFTGAS. As a souvenir, the head of the project actually gave me a label from the poison gas canister saying, "For now, you can't say anything but one day the world will surely be a better place and you can proudly display it to show that you were part of the program to purify the German bloodline. Heil Hitler!"

Actual label (reduced size) from a can of Zyklon B hydrogen cyanide poison gas (Giftgas). The can contained the solid white crystals that reacted with the air creating the poison gas. (Source: Author's Personal Collection)

The crystals were poured into vents in the ceiling of the gas chambers which were designed to look like showers. It took twenty to thirty minutes to be sure that everyone inside was dead. The bodies were removed by special Jewish work teams (Sonderkommandos). Gold fillings were removed from the dead bodies, long hair was shorn and all other items were collected (eye glasses, rings, watches, etc.) before the bodies were sent to the ovens.

On the way back, Col. Stryker gave a ride to Captain Strauss who was going to be in charge of the Western half of Austria for this program reporting to Col. Stryker. The three of us sat in the back with the same two lieutenants that had driven up with us sharing the front seat. Seated in the back I listened as the two of them discussed the program. They decided that the best way to proceed with the program would be to first eliminate the mentally disturbed and physically deformed Jews and other undesirables in the institutions and use them to confirm my conclusion. They also had a discussion which they felt was decidedly humorous on how you could tell a deformed or mentally deranged Jew from all the rest of the Jews since they were all obviously deformed and mentally deranged and by rights, they all belonged in an institution and be treated to a ride in these special vans. They laughed as they discussed this. I looked away so they would not see the revulsion in my face. Captain Strauss asked whether or not homosexuals should also be included in the program since they were not presently in institutions. Col. Stryker thought that this was a very good question and wrote it down in his little pad saying that he would contact Berlin to find out.

Col. Stryker accompanied me to the morgue the next day and told my boss that I had been on a special assignment for the Third Reich the day before and that there should not be any questions asked of me. There were no questions asked but I could see a mixture of jealousy and animosity in my boss's eyes that I had been chosen for the secret assignment rather than him – and that he was not even allowed to know anything about it. It also reinforced my job security.

I did not sleep at night for the rest of the week. At work I was like a zombie. All I could think about was the program. I was mentally searching for a way to try to stop it – or at least delay it. I decided that I needed more information.

I called Col. Stryker on Monday saying that I wanted to find out more about the status of the "program". He was curious as to why I was calling on this particular top secret matter but rather than discuss this on the phone he asked that I come to his office. The SS had taken over a former Ministry building for their headquarters. This was located in the first district. The security at the headquarters was very tight. I was first stopped at an outer barrier and asked to state my business. He saw my Nazi party pin but did not say anything. The guard called Col. Stryker's office to confirm my appointment. I was told to proceed to the reception area inside the building. There were two guards armed with sub-machine guns at the front door that watched me approach and enter. I signed in at the reception desk in the lobby on the ground floor, was given a badge to wear while I was in the building after I surrendered my identity card which was to be held until I left the building when I would exchange my visitor's badge back for my identity card. I waited about fifteen minutes until Col. Stryker's secretary came to escort me to his office. I waited another twenty minutes in his waiting room before he came out to greet me. He apologized for my wait and ushered me into his office after the obligatory exchanges of Heil Hitler.

Before I even sat down he wanted to know why I wanted more information. I had thought about this before I called. I said that if there were going to be more tests I needed to know if I or anyone else from my staff would have to perform additional autopsies on these people and would we have to issue death certificates, which would obviously need to have the real cause of death changed to one of natural causes. In most cases, as was done in Germany, the families of the people were given their ashes and the death certificate which stated the cause of death at the institution. However, at Am Steinhoff, there were weekly family visits for most of the patients. The relatives would immediately find out that they were no longer at the institution and the staff would have to tell them about the transfer. The relatives would most certainly try to track the people down. He sat there for a few moments thinking about what I had asked. He admitted that certainly he had not thought about it. "Yes," he mentioned, "there would certainly be more tests". Then he raised his voice and almost to a point of anger said, "Do not refer to them as people. They are not people. They are mistakes. They are blemishes on the face of the Earth that should have been destroyed at birth."

I was taken aback but said nothing. He calmed down and said that some more tests were scheduled for this weekend using different amounts of the hydrogen cyanide gas, different sized mesh screens and with more degenerates per van. He had not thought about the selection process but now decided that those patients that had weekly family visits should be among the last to go.

I also suggested that recording equipment be added to the vans which could be a decisive method to determine when the people...uh.... subjects, died rather than just relying on the drivers' observations. Col. Stryker stood up. "What an excellent suggestion!"

He thought that it was such a good suggestion that he immediately called Captain Strauss and asked that he join us. Captain Strauss arrived in less than five minutes carrying a briefcase with the data from the first round of tests since Col. Stryker told him that I was there and that we were discussing methodology. We stood up and again said the obligatory Heil Hitlers as Captain Strauss entered the room. Col. Stryker turned to me and asked that I repeat my questions and suggestion on using recording equipment. Captain Strauss also thought that they were very important questions and also really liked the recording suggestion. He admitted that he had been so engrossed in the methods to kill them that he had not considered the aftermath of his actions. Surely their relatives would have to be notified and would have to be provided with a cause of death and a death certificate and they would most likely want to claim the body for burial so they had to have a reason why the body was cremated. He really felt that the suggestion of setting up recording equipment was absolutely superb. They decided that this was important enough to send immediately to Berlin. They looked at each other and said that my visit was very opportune. There was something else that they needed my services for that went beyond the gas victims. Captain Strauss filled me in on what was happening. They basically decided that hydrogen cyanide would be used and that they had defined the timetable and other pertinent aspects but they had some other problems. He took out a piece of paper from his briefcase and handed it to me. It had the following text:

- There were about three hundred thousand institutionalized inmates throughout Austria and Germany according to a detailed study and approximately six thousand more that were cared for at their homes based on the records that were taken from doctors throughout the country.

- Lethal injections would be used on those inmates that could not be moved. They would secretly have one staff member that was thoroughly committed to Hitler's beliefs at each institution working for them. At night, that staff member would sneak into the room of the intended victim and inject him with air to cause an embolism or inject him with some medication that he was allergic to or inject him with a powerful poison that was difficult to detect. In the morning, when it was discovered that the patient was dead it would be attributed to natural causes.

- Lists had to be drawn up and timetables had to be prepared for those institutionalized in Ostmark (Austria). In the interim, tests were to be made on the optimum concentration of gas to be used along with determining the best ways to disperse the gas in the van.

- Home care patients would be last since it would be more difficult to explain why they suddenly had to be institutionalized and they would probably have to wait for some time to pass until they could justify death by natural causes. There was one exception to this – Jews. From the medical records forcibly obtained from the Jewish doctors they knew where these home-care Jews lived and since they didn't care what the families thought, they were prepared to include them in the first batch – along with their families if necessary.

They had not yet received any information as to the exact date when the mass transfer program would begin but they were ordered to start the tests. Captain Strauss was already compiling a list of all potential inmates in Vienna institutions. Physical handicaps that qualified for the list were carefully and meticulously described in detail. It covered primarily birth defects as opposed to people that lost their limbs or were otherwise crippled in an accident or were wounded in the 1918 war. Comatose patients regardless of the cause were included on the list for immediate injection. The list included what is known today as Down syndrome, autism, cerebral palsy, debilitating birth defects, dwarfism and many others.

Captain Strauss stood up, came over to me and thanked me for my "obvious commitment to the program and my loyalty to the Third Reich and to the Fuehrer." Heil Hitlers were exchanged again as he turned and left Col. Stryker's office.

We sat down again and Col. Stryker reiterated Captain Strauss' plaudits to me for asking such relevant questions and taking such a concerned interest in ensuring the success of the program. We sat there for another ten to fifteen minutes talking about a variety of unimportant subjects. As I stood up to leave, Col. Stryker asked if I was married to which I replied that I was not. "No matter," he said and mentioned that he and his wife periodically entertained and wanted to know if I would be interested in coming to one of these dinner or post-event parties. I replied that I would be "most honored". He smiled and shook my hand and we saluted, "Heil Hitler!"

Just before I was ready to leave I asked about the origin of the T-4 program. Col. Stryker turned around and walked over to a file cabinet in the right corner of the room. He took out a key from his pocket and unlocked it. He opened the top drawer and pulled out a file and brought it over to the desk.

"In a way, I also have a letter from our Fuehrer," he said and with that pulled out a letter that was hand-signed by Hitler that said:

"Reich Leader Bouhler and Dr. Brandt are charged with the responsibility for expanding the authority of physicians, to be designated by name, to the end that patients considered incurable according to the best available human judgment of their state of health, can be granted a mercy death [Gnadentod]."

"You are hereby charged with the responsibility for this program in Ostmark."

(Signed) **Adolf Hitler**

He added that Hitler had wanted to do this for quite some time to protect the German bloodline and reduce the burden on the state as well as on the families of these beings that had a "life unworthy of living" that should be terminated. The program was started as soon as the war started. At first it was only for adults but was soon expanded to include children. Resources would be scarce so war would more or less justify it and the war would make it less obvious that this secret program was being carried out, perhaps even justifying it the minds of the people.

Col. Stryker went on to say that in October (1939), he was invited to attend a meeting in Berlin convened by Dr. Brandt who was Hitler's personal physician. Dr. Brandt began the meeting by reading a letter. It was from the parents of Gerhard Kretschmer who lived near Leipzig. They had just birthed a horribly deformed baby boy in May who the doctors said would not be able to do anything for himself ever and would probably die in his childhood. The parents pleaded with the doctor to terminate the life of their newborn child but the doctor refused. The parents decided to go directly to the highest authority in the country, Adolf Hitler. Through some friends who had access to one of his inner circle, they sent a letter in which they described the situation and begged Hitler for permission to have their newborn son mercifully put to death. Hitler agreed and authorized it. It was a turning point in his thinking about these patients who were burdens to society and a threat to Aryan racial purity. Shortly thereafter he charged Dr. Brandt to set up the "Reich Committee for the Scientific Registering of Serious Hereditary and Congenital Illnesses" to address the issue. Thus, the program was started. Even though some doctors in Germany supported the program, very few wanted to actually participate in the executions. Many were willing to issue false death certificates but did not want to know any details. The committee collected the records from all institutions and, in some cities, from doctor's confidential records of their impaired patients in home-care programs. These were tabulated and life or death decisions were made from these records without the decision makers ever seeing the patient. Of course, all Jewish patients were to be eliminated regardless of their condition.

Dr. Brandt went on to say that the program was already in place for conquered countries. Special killing squads known as Einsatzkommandos, which were mainly responsible for killing Jews, were already charged to kill all patients in mental institutions in Poland. About 17,000 patients had already been shot to death. If any nurse or doctor protested they were also shot. Of course, he mentioned, we can't do that here so secrecy has to be maintained and we must use subterfuge to accomplish our goals. He concluded by saying, "Gentlemen, the future of Aryan racial purity is in our hands. The Fuehrer is counting on us. Heil Hitler!" And with that he received a standing ovation from the attendees.

I could see how proud he was to be heading up this important program. Various subcommittees were set up and he was personally charged with determining the best method and type of gas to use.

He put the file back in the cabinet, locked it and personally escorted me to the reception desk. Everyone rose and saluted as soon as they saw him. They returned my identity card for the visitor's badge and remained standing as Col. Stryker and I spoke for another minute or two before I left. As I left, the two guards at the front door that had noticed the attention that I was being given by Col. Stryker, saluted me as I passed by them they saluted me. I did not bother to salute back. The two guards at the barricade watched as I left the building and, after seeing the two guards at the entrance salute me, they too saluted. This time I returned the salute and went back to the morgue realizing two things. The first was that if secrecy was the utmost of importance and that this could be the key weakness in the program. The second was the way the SS respected authority. The two guards at the barricade had absolutely no idea who I was but when they saw the two guards at the entrance salute me, they surmised that I must be very important and worthy of their salute. They had not saluted me on the way in. My thoughts turned to what could I do to expose the program and let people know that this was going to happen.

There was, however, a short-term thing that I could quickly do and that was to warn Jewish families with mentally disturbed or physically impaired family members that were being cared for in institutions or at home that they needed to remove and hide them if at all possible. We enlisted our former personal doctor, Dr. Nussbaum.

Without going into too much detail, Dr. Nussbaum let every Jewish doctor know that their mentally and physically impaired family members were in danger of being killed if they stayed in their respective homes, hospitals or institutions. Unfortunately, not much was accomplished by this. Some of the families did not believe what they were told. It was too barbaric for such a civilized society. Others had little choice because their family member was totally dysfunctional and they had no way to care for them if they were even able to have them moved from an institution to the home of another friend or family member. Overall, maybe five or six institutionalized family members were taken from their respective institutions and sent to live with relatives. I learned later that three of them had been tracked down by the SS and returned to their former institutions from which they were taken and killed.

Families that had physically or mentally disabled family members living at home fared much better. Many of the families were able to send their affected family members to relatives while others were able to hide them with friends and neighbors for the next week or two. Once they were hidden, Dr. Nussbaum gave me their names and I prepared false death certificates for them using a false signature. When the SS came they were told that the person had died and were shown the death certificate. The SS accepted it, crossed them off of the list and wrote deceased next to their name. Two or three days after the SS left, the family member was returned home and kept hidden in the apartment or house. The SS never returned for them.

On my next trip to Am Steinhof I slipped into one of the offices and stole some letterhead stationary and envelopes. I had Wilhelm type an account of what was going on with these children and adults and send it to the newspapers and the churches. I asked him to do it since he could include some medical terms to make it more convincing that it was someone from the Am Steinhof medical staff that had written the letter. I found out later that I was not alone in this. Throughout Germany people with a conscience that were involved in the program also leaked this information to the press and churches. There was an uproar throughout Germany. On August 24, 1941 Adolf Hitler formally ended the T-4 Aktion program. However, on August 30 and August 31, all of the remaining Jewish patients were deported to concentration camps where none survived. Child euthanasia secretly continued through 1945 and selected adult euthanasia secretly resumed in August 1942. Overall, it is estimated that approximately two hundred thousand men, women and children were put to death in Germany and Austria as a result of the T-4 program.

While Col. Stryker had mentioned inviting me to attend one of his social events, the formal invitation never came. In retrospect I realized that it was just one of those polite niceties that you say to someone at a moment when, at a loss for words, you try to make that person feel more important than the person really is. It had just that effect. It elevated my self-esteem. I felt that I was truly liked and respected, even if it was by someone that I detested. In my mind I began to picture what it would be like to attend one of his dinner parties which I am sure would have included a number of important

Nazis. Perhaps Ernst Kaltenbrunner would be there. I would bet that he would have been shocked to see me there – or perhaps just pleasantly surprised. My imagination ran wild. Perhaps Gauleiter Bürckel would be there and, upon me being introduced to him, he would complement me on my "commitment and support of the third Reich" as I am sure he would know of my work. If Col. Stryker hadn't mentioned it, I surely would have brought up the personal letter that I had received from the Fuehrer. Maybe, I thought, I should bring the letter with me in case someone there wanted to see it. All me grandiose musings were in vain. An invitation never came.

What happened next was even more unlikely.

About two weeks after my visit to his office, Col Stryker came to see me with Captain Strauss. It was about 3 PM. Because of my apparent interest and the relevant questions that I had asked he felt compelled to tell me that he had received an answer. Actually, it was more than an answer, it was an accolade. While they had addressed the notification issue they had not thought about recording the deaths in the vans. He had been the first to make this suggestion which was deemed important enough to tell Himmler who really liked the idea. Moreover, they liked the word "subjects" that Col. Stryker highlighted with quotation marks and had used in his questions. He was personally notified of this first by a telephone call from Dr Karl Brandt, the mastermind behind the T-4 Aktion program, which was followed by a letter a copy of which was also sent to General Kaltenbrunner, his superior officer. He stared sheepishly down at his lap and admitted that he had not said that I had asked the questions and made the recording suggestion but he quickly regained his composure and assured me that he was not really trying to hide it. He just didn't think that it would get such an overwhelming positive response from those overseeing the program and saw no reason to say that someone else had suggested it. I must confess, I told him, that I too would never have thought that the questions warranted such a response but that I was truly happy that it worked out so well for him and congratulated him. There were some problems with the system that my suggestions would help solve. For example, when they cremated the people and scooped up the ashes they had no idea to whom some of the personal items such as rings and bracelets belonged to that were taken from the bodies prior to cremation. As a result some were sent to the wrong families and some were kept by the workers removing the items so when the families asked for them they were nowhere to be found. Moreover, the people that filled out the death certificates simply used set reasons such as acute appendicitis as the cause of death. However, a couple of the people whose death was attributed to appendicitis had already had their appendix removed. So, with implementing my suggestions, it placed the overall responsibility for death certificates, etc. into the hands of one qualified coroner or mortician in the geographic area that would review the patient's medical records and select a more realistic cause of death. That person would be responsible for building a team to work in the program under their direct supervision. In Vienna, Col. Stryker proudly stated, that I was the clear choice. He said that Captain Strauss fully agreed. So, despite my revulsion, I was drafted into the program.

"Come, we must have a drink and celebrate!" he said with a broad genuine smile after giving me the good news.

"But it's only two thirty," I said, quite surprised by the offer.

"So what," he replied, "where does it say that friends cannot have a drink in the afternoon?"

I went into my boss's office with Col. Stryker and Captain Strauss and told him that I had some important confidential business. He had not acknowledged my entry into his office and did not even look up when I spoke to him until he heard that I was leaving early. He looked up and was surely going to say something when he saw the two SS officers. His demeanor quickly changed as he stopped what he was doing and stood up to greet us. I introduced him to Col. Stryker first who shook his hand after exchanging Heil Hitlers. That was a good sign. Normally, SS officers did not shake hands with civilians but because he was my superior, he condescended to do so. I introduced him to Captain Strauss who was standing near the open door. I was, of course, excused for the rest of the day. As we exited, Col. Stryker turned to him and told him that I may be called upon from time to time to provide special assistance to the SS in a matter of state security. My boss knew enough not to ask for any additional information. He just smiled politely and affirmed that I and the entire staff at the morgue, including him, were at the complete disposition of the SS. Col. Stryker smugly smiled. He was used to this kind of response – but it always made him feel good to hear it again, especially in front of me. We left and went to a nearby bar and had quite a number of drinks together. I was feeling no pain when we left the bar around ten o'clock and I wasn't sure that I could make it home on my own. Waiting outside the bar was Col. Stryker's private car. I got into the car, very relieved. Col Stryker had the driver drop him off first at his office as he still had some things to take care of. He instructed the driver to take us both home. I deferred to having Captain Strauss dropped off first.

The next morning was not too pleasant. I got up with a very bad headache and was a little nauseous. I thought of either going to work late or not even going in at all saying that my involvement with the special SS project had extended into the next day. I decided not to do this and managed to get to work on time. This turned out to be a very wise decision.

I still had my headache when I arrived at the office. I took some aspirins and turned around to get some water from the table against the wall. As I looked up, I realized that I had the letter from Cardinal Piffl on the other side of Hitler's portrait along with the silver crucifix. With the Catholics now considered unfriendly by the Third Reich and subject to attack I realized that I needed to take them down and replace it with something more appropriate. I replaced the letter with my Nazi Party membership certificate but could not find anything in my office to replace the crucifix. I left the space empty for now.

At 11AM, Captain Strauss came to the morgue and told me that we would be having lunch. I asked if Col. Stryker would be joining us. He mentioned that Col. Stryker would meet us at the restaurant as he had not gone to the office in the morning since he had to attend to some private business.

When you elevate someone who had no importance in civilian life to a position of importance in the military it invariably changes him. As a civilian there was no doubt in my mind that Captain Strauss would have politely asked if I wanted to go to lunch with him. As an

SS officer he just told me that we were going to have lunch. It was obviously an honor for a civilian to be asked to have lunch with high-ranking SS officers so it was inconceivable that his offer would be turned down. So, his invitation was "Let's go to lunch!" with "now" being understood without him having to say it.

We got into his car and went across town to a very well-known and expensive restaurant. I had never been there and I mentioned that to him along with the rave reviews that I had heard for the restaurant. I knew that this was exactly what he wanted to hear. After all, what good is being important if you couldn't flaunt it? Col. Stryker was already there waiting at the bar in a room just outside the main dining room. We joined him for a drink before going into the restaurant.

We were greeted at the entrance to the restaurant by the Maitre'd who welcomed him by name and showed us to a table strategically located in the center entryway into the restaurant where everyone entering the restaurant could see us. This was Col. Stryker's regular table and while he did not always come to have lunch there whenever he did show up this table was his – even if someone else was eating there when he walked in. The unfortunate people eating at the table were abruptly moved to another table unless they were someone of equal or higher importance. With luck, there would be another table available at the time but once or twice the people had to wait ten or fifteen minutes for another table to become available before they could finish their meal. While there were surely some initial protests by the displaced diners as soon as the Maitre'd pointed to Col. Stryker and told them to complain to him, their protests died. If it was very inconvenient, the restaurant just made the meal complementary along with an equally complementary bottle of wine which was always a well-received compensation.

Today was a lucky day – at least for some diner. The table was not occupied since we arrived early. We sat down and he updated me on the program. They had identified sixty four subjects that would be used to complete the tests during the next few weeks. The basement room that had been used for the makeshift morgue would be transformed into a real morgue. Whatever I needed was going to be provided to me under a special order signed by Col. Stryker.

I had carte blanche. There was also a special letter addressed to my boss at the morgue excusing me from work for the next two weeks to undertake this special task and not to ask any questions. Occasionally, there was a brief interruption as some high-ranking officer or government official came into the restaurant and came over to say hello to Col. Stryker. He loved this attention and every once in a while would furtively glance my way to see my reaction when a particularly important person stopped by. I acted impressed and mentioned this to him on the way out. It was exactly what he wanted to hear.

While I was setting up the morgue I interfaced with Captain Strauss on a daily basis. I saw that he rarely asked anyone for anything – he just ordered everyone to do whatever he wanted. If their response was not quick enough he raised his voice and shouted at them. At that point they jumped. I was really beginning to understand the machinations of the SS and why they were so fanatic and proud to be in the SS. They acted like and were treated like they were just one level below God although I think that some of them thought they transcended God's position – at least on Earth.

I typically worked late every night on installing a fully operational morgue. In five days the job was done even with signs showing people how to get there from the main entrance and with the title of Coroner in gold letters on the frosted glass top of the heavy wooden door that led from the hallway to the morgue. Captain Strauss was ecstatic. He had been told by the head of the sanitarium that it would probably take more than ten days to install a fully operational morgue so he had allowed two full weeks for the job just in case it took longer than estimated. This was what he had reported to Berlin and why the program was not going to start until the following week. He now had the distinct pleasure of informing his superiors that the morgue was ready nine days ahead of schedule and that he was ready to implement the program. I didn't know this or I would have realized the implications that by finishing the work ahead of schedule that I was actually accelerating the program. No one had told me that they had told Berlin that it would take two weeks to complete. I was working at a quicker pace than I normally worked at as I wanted to finish and return to my job as soon as possible. Moreover, being under constant scrutiny, I had absolutely no thought of slowing down. I now got very depressed and did not sleep at all that night. However, I got a reprieve. Since all of the paperwork, personnel and equipment had been set up to start the following week it would be too difficult to change it so they decided to keep to the original schedule. Still, I didn't sleep too well for the next few days even though I kept telling myself that if I didn't do it, someone else would have done it. Then I realized what I was telling myself. I was excusing my actions. I was rationalizing my cooperation with the Nazis. This turned out to be one of the two main excuses after the war by many Nazis with the first being that, "I was only following orders."

On Saturday night we celebrated. There was a group of about ten of us from Am Steinhof and from Captain Strauss's office including Col. Stryker. We got totally smashed which didn't really matter since the program was not starting for a few more days so we had a few days to recover.

I had no secrets from the card group and had kept them informed of the progress of the T-4 program. I also expressed my grief in building the morgue ahead of schedule. The group consoled me by saying that if I had not been involved, I could not have warned the Jewish families and saved the lives of their invalid family members. Moreover, I would not have been able to have Wilhelm send the anonymous letters to the press and to select people in the government thereby attempting to stop the program. Clearly, I was doing more good than bad. They re-emphasized that when I later informed them that finishing the morgue ahead of schedule did not move up the start date of the program. "See God understood and was on your side!" Karl remarked.

While all of this was going on, Austria and Vienna prospered. Unemployment virtually disappeared. Professionals had so many clients that they couldn't handle all of them, especially the incompetent ones. Newly graduated university students had multiple job offers according to their grade point average. More Gentiles owned businesses and stores even if they were also incompetent. More Gentiles were accepted in the universities that included students many from cities outside of Vienna and were therefore assured of a good life upon graduation. Taxes were higher, there were some shortages of goods but this was minor compared to conditions before Anschluss. Jews were still used for forced labor with little to no pay and there was no end to the tasks that had to be done from shoveling snow to building roads to digging ditches to harvesting fruit and vegetables.

Throughout 1941 decrees were passed to further limit Jewish life. Jews were excluded from:

- using public transportation

- keeping pets

- using a barber or beauty shop

- having a typewriter (had to be turned in)

- having electrical appliances (had to be turned in)

- having furs or woolen clothing (had to be turned in)

Anyone caught with forbidden items faced deportation. Life became increasingly harsh.

Another key project of Anschluss was to make Vienna a major trading port for the Balkan countries and countries to the east. The port was expanded and tremendous warehouses were built both at the port and at the train stations. A few of these were as large as a soccer field. Expediency was the driver. Initially, there were not any separate barriers in the warehouse. At first, there were just large square areas delineated by black paint that were numbered by aisle and row. Merchants, traders, shipping agents and others involved in importing and exporting goods leased as many of these squares as they needed. There were guards after hours in each warehouse for security. It was up to the lessees to erect a fence, which was typically a six-foot chain link fence or a cinder block wall. Some had barbed wire on top but most did not. Once each company had enclosed their areas the guards were removed and a central guard station was set up with routine patrols of the warehouse area with occasional patrols entering the locked warehouses. As such, the warehouse had 24 hour security. Special buildings were built for very expensive items. These too were built by the lessees. This system was very successful. There was a long waiting list of customers and as soon as one was finished it was filled up with merchandise within three weeks with the only delay being how fast they could erect the chain link fences or the cinderblock walls. Chain link fences were in short supply and now had to be imported from France and Italy to meet demand.

In addition, secret factories to manufacture war materials were set up throughout Austria mostly around large cities but not within them. The massive Hermann Goering Steel mill was being built just outside of Linz. Due to the labor shortage caused by the war, prisoners of war and Jews from ghettos and concentration camps had to be used.

Vienna was treated differently. There were no war material factories built within the city limits and the suburbs. The closest was a warplane factory and chemical plant in Wiener Neustadt which was about 50 kilometers south of Vienna. However, there were six refineries in and around Vienna that had been built well before annexation. Rail lines were expanded and intercity bus service was vastly improved. Roads were widened and repaved. Travel throughout Austria and Germany was shortened considerably. Moreover, car sales boomed. Hitler had ordered the industry to develop a car that was affordable to all working people. The result was the Volkswagen (people's car) and it was immensely popular. It was small, economical and low cost. A larger model would soon be available for larger families as well as a minivan for very large families. Hitler and the Nazis were loved by all. Well, almost all.

CHAPTER EIGHTEEN

RETRIBUTION

"And if any mischief follow, then thou shalt give life for life, Eye for eye, tooth for tooth, hand for hand, foot for foot..."

Exodus 21: 23, 24

Between Wilhelm's contacts at the Gestapo, Anton Fischer's position at the Ministry of Information and Mischa's position in the Central Police Station and my camaraderie with the SS, we had developed quite an intricate information network.

One day, Mischa learned that there was going to be a raid on a group of gypsies hiding in a partially constructed apartment building in the seventh district just on the outskirts of the city. They were heavily armed. The police and SS knew that they would not give up without a fight. Before proceeding in an operation of this type where they expected armed resistance, the police would send some plainclothes policemen into the adjacent buildings just before the raid telling the tenants to gather downstairs and be ready to leave the building immediately upon being told to evacuate. There were only two apartment buildings next to the building that the gypsies occupied one on each side. There were a few stores directly across the street. Behind the building were a number of vacant lots where construction had started for some new apartment buildings. Construction had stopped due to the war. This empty back space was used by the gypsies to enter and leave the building at night without being seen. Were it not from a captured gypsy who revealed their location under torture, they would not have been discovered.

Mischa volunteered to help and was put in charge of tenant evacuation in one of the adjacent buildings. He selected eight policemen one of whom was Hans Joerdl, the police sergeant who was now a detective that killed one Jew a day and another was Detective Hans Gruber who killed Jews to sell their dead bodies to medical schools. The nine policemen were divided into three groups. Mischa paired himself with both Hanses. They went into one of the buildings that was next to the target building. Another three went to the building on the other side to the left and the third group of two detectives went to the stores. The evacuation procedure started about thirty minutes before the attack. At the same time the streets were blockaded at a safe distance from the target building so the gypsies could not see what was happening. While the buildings and stores were being cleared soldiers would go to the roof of each building and wait. The main attack would appear to be coming from the open field in the back. Armored vehicles would be brought in which would draw the gypsies to the back of the building. Once the attack started, soldiers would attack from the street. Based on the tortured gypsy's information, there were about 75 men and their families hiding in the large building. Four floors of the building had been constructed with the framework of the rest of the building constructed. There were no windows – only the empty spaces. The entire ground floor was boarded up. The structure afforded many places from which to defend the building from attack. This was not going to be easy.

Mischa and the two Hanses entered the building at 2:30, knocked on all of the doors and told the occupants to assemble in the hallway entrance to the building. Soldiers simultaneously entered the building and waited for a signal before going to the roof. At precisely 2:50 the occupants were to leave the building from back and side doors so they could not be seen from the target building and proceed directly to the blockade barrier. The detectives would lead them to the barrier. At 2:50, just at the moment of departure Mischa turned to his partners claiming that he had heard some noises from one of the apartments above. He told the residents to leave signaling for one of the soldiers to lead them to safety. Mischa asked his partners to accompany him upstairs to check out the noise. They started to bang on the apartment doors again. Meanwhile, the attack began as heavily armed police and SS soldiers, backed up by an armored vehicle attacked the building. As expected, there was heavy resistance. They could hear the gunfire and the sound of exploding grenades and cannon fire from the armored vehicle. Bottles of flaming gasoline were thrown at the armored vehicles but fell short.

They reached the top floor of the building without finding any tenants. As they proceeded back down the stairs Mischa stopped on the third floor where there was a window facing the target building. He looked out of the side window. There wasn't any fighting in the alley between the two buildings as he had expected but there was gunfire from the roof which was being returned by the gypsies. He called to both men and told them that some gypsies were in the alley and that they were trying to enter their building. They both came to the window. As they both looked out of the window, he stepped back a few meters and pulled his pistol out of his holster and pointed it at them. They didn't see any gypsies. As soon as each one turned around to let him know that they didn't see anyone, Mischa fired directly into their faces hitting them almost squarely between the eyes. This was accomplished in a few seconds. They both died instantly.

The fighting continued for about forty minutes more. By that time most of the armed gypsies had been killed or wounded. The rest surrendered. They were all lined up against the wall – the men were shot; the women and children were loaded into two transport trucks that had been waiting. After this was done Mischa sadly reported the death of his fellow detectives, Hans Joerdl and Hans Gruber. The head of the operation, an SS Captain and a few others followed him to the place where they had been shot. As one of the officers bent down to look more closely Mischa quickly asked the captain if it would not be better to first call the coroner's office to get an official analysis of the accidental shooting to be absolutely sure that it came from the gypsies and not from the soldiers. Mischa mentioned that he intended to recommend them for a police medal and wanted an official report. The captain agreed and stationed a guard there to be sure no one touched the bodies. Mischa went into one of the apartments that had a telephone and called me. I had been apprised of the situation so I made sure that I was on duty.

I arrived at the building and was taken to the area where the detectives had been shot. I also asked to see the building where the gypsies were hiding. With great precision I measured distances between the gypsy building and the one in which the detectives had been shot and took some pictures. I repeated this from the area where the detectives were shot. An SS Lieutenant accompanied me while an SS captain waited for the results from his vehicle parked in front of the building as he completed his paperwork. I could see that he was anxious to hear my report. I approached him and told him that there was no doubt in my mind that the bullets had been fired by one of the gypsies even to the point of potentially identifying the type of gun that was used. With his permission I was able to view the confiscated weapons and take the suspect gun with me for further tests. The captain was, of course, very relieved with my conclusion. The last thing he wanted on his record that some one from his group had fired wildly resulting in the death of two Vienna police detectives. An ambulance came and took their bodies to the morgue. Their families were notified. A few days later there was a large public funeral honoring them as heroes who gave their lives for the Fatherland. They were both awarded the Police Service Medal posthumously.

About three days later the body of a truck driver was brought to the morgue. He was a victim of a hit and run driver. He was one of the drivers working with Hans Gruber in the killing of Jews to sell their bodies. A week later, the other driver was killed in an attempted robbery. No one noticed the coincidental death of the three men. We had some concern that one of the people involved with their business at one of the medical schools might say something but in order to say anything they would have to reveal their part in the business. We rightly concluded that nothing would be said. We also thought about doing something with the body buyers at the two schools but decided that if they had any brains at all that they would rationalize that the three deaths were not just a coincidence and that they would not try to enlist anyone else as a replacement. Just to be safe we monitored cadaver deliveries at the two schools.

We were still making a substantial profit on our black-market smuggling of scarce goods from Italy and Switzerland. The government initiated a major crackdown on price gouging, profiteering and black-market activities. We were essentially immune. We had gradually brought more and more SS and Gestapo hierarchy into the profit-sharing mode. Even von Schirach turned a deaf ear. He was used to lavish entertainment that lasted throughout the war. He entertained just about anyone that came to Vienna of any importance – no matter how slight. He also gave lavish parties and dinners to the people involved in the arts. After all, he was appointed Gauleiter on Vienna for the express purpose of fostering the arts. There were new operas, new symphonies and perhaps his greatest coup, convincing Richard Strauss to move to Vienna. The Gauleiter was now our best customer. To service his specific requirements, we expanded our smuggling operation to include France. To this end we enlisted the French resistance that would steal or purchase the items, especially champagne and wine and smuggle the contraband to Switzerland where we had already developed a transportation network and set of storage depots. We employed many of the Jews that were living there, some of which we had smuggled into the country, until they were able to immigrate to other countries. Those that had no place to go had a secure job with us throughout the war.

Richard Strauss was recognizably the greatest living composer in Germany and was a world-renowned composer as well. He was 79 when he moved to Vienna with his entire family. His relocation to Vienna was welcomed by the Nazis in Berlin. His son had married a Jew. Given his status, this was tolerated by the Nazis but with many restrictions placed on his son's two children. They could not attend school, go to concerts, go to any playground, etc. In fact, other than the composer and his wife, the rest of the family was under house arrest. With very few exceptions, they could not go out of their house. Recognizing this, von Schirach personally flew to Berlin and with the approval of the Nazi hierarchy, went to Strauss and offered to bring him and his family to Vienna where he would compose special symphonies and other works for the Vienna Philharmonic Orchestra. In return, he and his family would have complete freedom to move about in Vienna and for the children to attend school, go to the playground, etc. He even offered to build a house for him which Strauss could design. Strauss accepted. So, at 79, Richard Strauss and his family relocated to Vienna in the house specially built for him (NB: this is now the Dutch Embassy in Vienna). A car was placed at his disposal with drivers available 24 hours per day. He was also supplied with more than enough food for his family including many luxury items not even available in Germany. We now included him on our preferred customer list.

In spite of the large share of the profits given to the Gestapo and the SS and the special discounts we gave to anything earmarked for von Schirach and Strauss, we still managed to keep about 20 percent. In other words, we parceled out 80 percent of the profits. Initially there was some opposition within our card group but Wilhelm said it best, "twenty percent with full immunity is better than prison or death!" We agreed. It was one of the best decisions we made as a group.

Having the SS and Gestapo on our side was also a significant benefit. We could, and often did, eliminate the competition. We didn't worry about the small-time black marketers but as soon as some group became too large and well-organized where prices started to fall, we would report them to the Gestapo. They would be arrested, sent to prison and prices would increase. We did not report every group to the Gestapo, just the ones that were run by Nazi party members and known anti-Semitic individuals. Not everyone in Austria belonged to the Nazi party so we felt that anyone not belonging to the party and not openly hurting Jews (we checked) was also fighting the Nazis. If they made a profit along the way, so be it. After all, that was what we were doing.

As the war progressed and the tide turned so the Nazis were losing, our biggest problem was finding products to ship to Switzerland to justify the vans crossing the border. Sending empty vans to Switzerland was a sure sign that we were smuggling contraband back to Austria. We had to maintain a two-way flow of goods. One problem was that with more and more war factories being destroyed by Allied bombing in Germany, many new factories to replace them were needed in Austria. The easiest way to do it was to retool an existing factory to produce needed war items. One of the first factories to be converted to producing war products was the mattress factory. Furniture factories were next, and so on. The production of non-essential goods decreased by more than 85 percent between May 1943 and January 1944.

CHAPTER NINETEEN

PISTON RINGS

"Demoralize the enemy from within by surprise, terror, sabotage, assassination. This is the war of the future."

Adolf Hitler

With deportation a key directive, we decided to increase our escape activities. The schedule was to deport about 7,500 Jews per month but the box car and train shortage would only provide transportation for about 5,000 per month at most. In reality, only enough special box cars to transport about 2,500 Jews per month were really available due to troop and supply train schedules. There were no trucks available at all. They were in demand for the war. In fact, in 1944, the Nazis offered to free one million Jews in return for 10,000 trucks from the Allied forces. The Nazis had just marched into Budapest. Hungary had about one million Jews of which 460,000 were in Budapest. The war on the Russian Front was going very badly. There were not enough trucks to bring in supplies or to evacuate wounded troops. On April 24, 1944 Adolf Eichmann went to Budapest and met with one of the leading Jewish community members, Joel Brandt. On May 17, with the offer in writing, Brandt was allowed to leave Hungary to go to Aleppo, Syria for a meeting with Moshe Shertok of the Jewish Agency of Palestine. The answer was no. The Agency had approached the British Government and was turned down. The United States and Russia also informed them that they would not negotiate with the Nazis.

We decided to take a lesson from Hitler's statement – sabotage. We recognized that anyone caught in this endeavor would be tortured and could be "persuaded" to reveal our network we still decided to risk it. By the way, when any form of sabotage was currently done in occupied Holland, the worker executions were ordered by none-other than Dr. Seyss-Inquart, the former Gauleiter of Vienna who was now the Gauleiter of Holland.

We decided that we had to put as many trains as possible out of commission. We thought about blowing up the railroad tracks but we did not have any experience with explosives. With our luck we would have blown ourselves up. Besides, railroad tracks are easily repaired and we certainly couldn't blow up or derail any trains with innocent people on them. We focused on sabotaging the equipment. Just how we were going to do it was a mystery to us. We didn't know anything about trains.

On November 18 Dieter Schultz, the leader of our group in the ninth district, was arrested. It happened in one of the stupidest accidents related to the extension. Dieter was an active member of the Nazi Party, which helped him in his business. His wife hated the Nazis and detested going to any Nazi Party social events so Dieter always went to these functions alone. Dieter liked to drink and would often come home late at night quite inebriated. This would often lead to intense arguments with his wife. Dieter was attending a party awards dinner when he went to the bathroom after drinking a few beers, actually, quite a few beers and many shots of schnapps. Dieter was a little bit too inebriated – perhaps much more than usual and he bumped into at least one of the attendees and a wall as he staggered to the bathroom. He went into a stall, locked the door, sat down, removed the extension and urinated. When he finished urinating he stood up a bit shaky, re-attached the extension and zipped up his fly albeit with some difficulty. He left the stall and staggered back to the private room. Unfortunately, he got the extension caught on the zipper (which was why he had so much difficulty zipping up) so it was actually hanging outside of his pants held on to his pants by the zipper. He walked about halfway to his table when one the wives noticed the extension sticking out of his pants. She gasped and grabbed her husband by the shoulder. Her husband turned around and looked. He started laughing and pointing to Dieter. Others looked as well. At first everyone laughed thinking that it was a joke. Actually, everything would have been fine if Dieter quickly thought about it and pretended that it was indeed a joke. Instead, in his inebriated state, he panicked as he looked down and saw at what everyone was laughing. He rushed over to one of the SS officers and wrested his pistol away and threatened the rest of the people at the party. Still, many thought that this was a joke until the SS officer walked up to him to get his gun back. Dieter fired hitting him in the stomach. The other men tackled him and brought him down. In the ensuing struggle, the extension was torn off and was kicked across the room. Fortunately, no one paid any attention to the extension as Dieter continued to struggle. He was arrested and brought to the Gestapo headquarters prison. At this point the fact that he was Jewish had not yet been discovered. As far as the other people at the party were concerned Dieter was drunk, was playing some sort of practical joke and had just gone crazy. Unfortunately, it was an SS officer whom he shot which was why he was taken to the Gestapo headquarters and not to the regular municipal jail. In the struggle, Dieter's arm was broken as they wrested the gun from him. It took three men to finally get the gun away from him. He released it only after they broke his arm.

As soon as he was processed, which was a little before 11 PM, Wilhelm was called and told that they had just arrested a party member that was drunk and had gone crazy at a party dinner. The prisoner had a broken arm. Wilhelm asked for some details: name, approximate age, where the arm was broken, etc. When he heard the prisoner's name, he paled. He knew Dieter. Wilhelm quickly dressed and went to the prison. As he was leaving home he turned, went back, and picked up a pack of cigarettes which he put into his medical bag. Since it was late and Dieter was a party member who was injured, he was kept in one of the waiting rooms until Wilhelm arrived. There were no thoughts of interrogation at that time since Dieter was essentially unconscious from the drinking and the subsequent injuries that he sustained in the struggle to get the gun. Wilhelm arrived at 11:45 and asked to see the prisoner. He was admitted to the waiting room where Dieter was being held. He dismissed the guard who returned to his post. He was now alone with Dieter. Before doing anything he went to a room at the end of the hall. This was the listening room. Every prison cell, waiting room and interrogation room had hidden microphones in them. He was shown this room on his initial tour with the explanation about how some prisoners would resist torture but when they went back to their cells they would sometimes discuss the information openly amongst themselves. These types of conversations often took place in the waiting rooms as well. As he was told by the guard, "It is amazing how stupid these people are. They sometimes tell us more than we even thought about asking them when they are alone together. Once we play back the recording they can no longer protest their innocence so they tell us everything." He entered the room and made sure that the microphone in Dieter's room was not turned on. Since every room was labeled he easily saw that the microphone was not on.

He went back to the room and woke up Dieter. Dieter looked around, realized where he was and panicked. He hadn't fully sobered up but he realized the mess he was in. Dieter told Wilhelm what happened and said that he had no idea what happened to the extension. He told Wilhelm that he didn't think he could survive the torture and that Wilhelm had to help him escape. Wilhelm told Dieter that he was sure that he would not be subjected to torture as he was a party member and that this would just be attributed to a drunken episode. He was clearly not an enemy of the state. Moreover, would try to have him released by noon at the latest on a medical discharge. Dieter just had to remain calm, tell them that he didn't remember anything about the night before and appear highly apologetic but Dieter did not believe him. He had shot an SS officer; there was no way he would be released in the morning. Wilhelm started to reset Dieter's broken arm. Dieter yelled out in pain a number of times and again re-iterated that he could not hold up under any torture. Wilhelm assured him that he would stay with him and attribute his actions to an alcohol intolerance problem and that he probably would not even be interrogated. He told Dieter that he brought a spare extension just in case he did not have his spare with him so no one would discover that he was Jewish. Dieter was now mumbling incoherently and was getting louder. He again apologized to Wilhelm for losing the extension. It was a good thing that he was alone with Dieter as his ranting would surely have raised suspicions. Wilhelm tried to get Dieter to put on the spare extension he had brought but Dieter was still too uncoordinated and he was worried. Suppose he had to urinate and he was watched by a guard? His uncircumcised penis would be discovered. With his broken arm he would have problems re-attaching the extension even if he wasn't being watched. Dieter said over and over again that he would be watched and that he could not go to the bathroom, take off the extension and put it back on, especially if he had to go more than once. No matter what Wilhelm said, Dieter was too scared to listen. He had to go the bathroom so Wilhelm went with him and waited outside. Between the pain from the arm and his unsteady state he decided to urinate standing up since he was not wearing the extension. He went to the bathroom, wet his trouser leg and came out in an even higher state of duress. It took more than fifteen minutes before Wilhelm managed to calm him down. He asked Wilhelm if he could give him something for the pain from resetting the broken arm and some additional pills to take in case he was interrogated. Wilhelm agreed to give Dieter a pill to kill the pain telling him that it would last about twelve hours so he would not feel any pain even if they started to torture him as part of the interrogation process. Wilhelm reiterated that he really did not expect the Nazis to torture him in the morning since he was a party member and they did not suspect him of being Jewish. He handed him three pills, one to take now and two just in case they wore off. However, he told Dieter that if they forcibly interrogated him he had to pretend that it was very painful and he had to scream very loudly so they would not know that Wilhelm had given him a painkiller. Dieter said he would do this. Wilhelm gave Dieter precise instructions on what to tell the Gestapo and the SS in the morning. Essentially, it was that he (Dieter) had too much too drink and collapsed against the SS officer. As the officer pushed him away he inadvertently grabbed the gun from his holster and in the ensuing struggle, the gun accidently went off wounding the officer in the stomach. That was all he remembered. Dieter still was not that confident. He was totally distraught. Wilhelm got a glass of water. Dieter took one of the pain pills and put the other two in his pants pocket. They continued talking about the release procedure. Dieter started to cough. He stood up looking at Wilhelm and started to say something as he collapsed. One minute later Dieter was dead. Wilhelm looked down at Dieter and said aloud, "You are right, there is no doubt that you would tell everything that you know." He called out to the guards. Two came in response. He told them that the prisoner was dead. He had taken a poison pill that was evidently hidden in his clothes. Wilhelm demanded to know who had who searched him when he was brought in. The two guards admitted that they did not search him as they had no idea that he was a suicide risk. After all, he was a party member who just had too much to drink. The guard looked through his pockets and found the other two pills and handed them to Wilhelm. "Cyanide!" he exclaimed and looked at the guard in an angry manner. Wilhelm could see that they were extremely worried and did not know what to do. Wilhelm suggested a solution. He would say that the cause of death was an embolism to the brain which caused him to go crazy in the first place and shoot the SS officer at the meeting. The guards were to say that after they put the prisoner in the waiting room he collapsed so they called Wilhelm and that when Wilhelm arrived the prisoner was already dead. Wilhelm would arrange an early pick up from the morgue where he knew one of the Coroners and use his influence to have the death certificate confirm that Dieter had died from an embolism. He asked to see Dieter's personal effects and asked one of the guards to call me at home and asked the other guard to flush the two pills down the toilet. When the guards left the room, Wilhelm pocketed the special pack of cigarettes that Dieter had with the false compartment that held the spare extension and the tube of glue and replaced it with the regular pack that he had taken before he left for the hospital.

I was at home when the phone rang. The guard identified himself and asked me to hold the line as he went and brought Wilhelm to the phone. Wilhelm explained the situation in limited detail with some innuendos. While I didn't fully understand what he was talking about I did realize that something serious had happened as soon as he mentioned Dieter's name and that I had to come to the Gestapo headquarters immediately. When I arrived I was shown into the holding room and saw Dieter's body. Wilhelm said that a man by the name of Dieter Schultz, whom he pointed to, had gone crazy at a party dinner at the Blue Dolphin Restaurant. He had shot a guard and had committed suicide at the Gestapo headquarters. He explained that the guards were remiss in not searching him so they did not find the poison pills that the prisoner had hidden in his clothes. He added that they would get into very serious trouble about this in the morning.

Wilhelm went on to say that this could be avoided if I helped him, and the guards, by certifying the cause of death as an embolism, which he would put into his report. I, of course, agreed. He told the guards that I had agreed and that I would personally come back for the body at 6 AM before they finished their shift so no other guards had to be involved. The two guards breathed a sigh of relief and thanked Wilhelm and me profusely. Wilhelm went home and I went directly to the morgue since it was already 5 AM. I signed out for one of the morgue ambulances with a driver that I knew very well and arrived at the SS headquarters at 5:45 AM. We rolled in the gurney. The two guards put Dieter on the gurney and thanked me over and over again. I told them that I was glad to help. I filled out some forms and gave them to the guards. On the way back to the morgue, I had the ambulance driver stop at the Blue Dolphin but it was closed with no one around to open it. I was hoping that there would have been some one there cleaning the place but it was too early. I really wanted to get in and search the place for the lost extension before the cleaning people found it. When I returned to the morgue I immediately took Dieter's body into the autopsy room and performed an autopsy. I removed all traces of the poison in his stomach and opened his skull. I reported that I had found an embolism that had caused him to have a decreased oxygen supply to the brain. This confirmed the original diagnosis of Wilhelm. I also added that the alcohol had intensified the condition causing him to go crazy. I signed the autopsy report. I left the morgue and went to Dieter's house. It was now 10 AM. Dieter's wife answered the door. I could see that she was out of her mind with worry. At first she just started to tell me that Dieter had not returned home from the party dinner and she was really worried that something had happened to him or that he had been arrested. Before she could finish she stopped and realized that if I was there, there was a serious problem. I told her that Dieter was dead. She fell back onto the sofa almost collapsing rather than just sitting down as she looked up at me. I did not give her all of the details. I just told her that he had an embolism at the dinner that he had gone crazy from it and in the ensuing struggle, someone was shot and that Dieter had died at the Gestapo headquarters from the embolism. I added that his Jewish identity was not compromised so at least she did not have to worry about that. I further mentioned that his body was now in the morgue and that I would get his body released as soon as possible. I asked her to call one of her closest friends to come over to console her during this trying time. I left as soon as her friend arrived. Overall, once getting over the initial shock, his wife took the news pretty well. I guess that they had lived in fear of exposure for so long that she had mentally prepared herself for such a situation. On the way back to the morgue I again stopped by the Blue Dolphin. It was open and there were two men cleaning the party room. They had swept the floor which was pretty dirty. The pile of garbage was off to the side near the far wall. They left it there as they proceeded to straighten out the tables and chairs. I identified myself as being from the Coroner's office and told them of the shooting incident that had occurred last night. They were not aware of it but had noticed a spot of what looked like dried blood but did not give it a second thought. It was not the first time that they found dried blood on the floor after a party. They showed me where the spot was and had no objections to my looking around the restaurant. I walked around a bit before going to the pile of garbage. I kicked it a little and poked at it until I saw the extension which I picked up and put in my pocket. I walked around a little more, thanked them for their cooperation and left. I destroyed the extension as soon as I returned to the morgue. Later that day an SS officer came to the morgue which I had not anticipated. Since the incident involved the shooting of an SS officer there had to be an investigation. I showed him the body being careful to only reveal the body from the stomach up so he could not see Dieter's circumcised penis hoping that he would not ask for a complete view of the body. He didn't. I took him to my office. He immediately noticed the letter from Hitler. I had developed this technique of standing just to the left of the letter which was hung at the same level as my face when standing next to it. I had made an elaborate border around it so it was very noticeable. Whenever, I had someone new in my office, I would stand alongside it until they noticed it. He stared at it for about two minutes before turning to me and asking about the letter. I told him the story. He was impressed. I gave him a copy of the death certificate and asked if it would be okay to release the body to the family as promised. He had no reason to question the cause of death and certainly did not want to contradict someone who had a personal letter from Hitler. He co-signed the release forms and I immediately went to Dieter's body and took the spare extension from my package of cigarettes and attached it to Dieter's body just to be safe. I called Dieter's wife who called a couple of the men in Dieter's group. They came at 6 PM. While not really condoned in the Jewish religion, Dieter's wife agreed to have the body cremated to hide the fact that Dieter was Jewish should there be any further inquiry into the incident that could possibly result in exhumation. The next morning Dieter was cremated and his ashes were buried at night next to a fresh grave in the Jewish cemetery. The location was recorded so if this madness were ever to end favorably, his remains could be recovered so he could be given a proper Jewish burial. That was the least we could do for his wife who requested it. We asked her if she wanted to stay in Vienna or if she would prefer to leave. We gave her a week to think it over. She opted to leave with her two daughters. The next weekend we took them by train to Basel and arranged for them to be taken to England were she had an uncle. They had no trouble crossing the German border with the death certificate of her husband as the reason for leaving. From Basel they traveled to Milan where they were able to get a ship to Spain and then to Ireland. We had an arrangement with some Irish dissidents that we paid to smuggle Jews into Ireland and then into England as we often had no time to get the necessary entry permits into England. We replaced Dieter with Konrad Schaffer as the new head of the group. We also told each of the group leaders what had happened to Dieter with respect to the extension so they could tell their members to be extremely careful when they were out drinking. We obviously did not mention the real cause of Dieter's death.

To extend the deportation schedule we decided to learn all we could about the rail system to see if there was anything that we could do to slow down deportations from the occupied countries through Vienna and directly from Vienna as well. Mischa was already providing as much information on the SS raids as was possible.

We first compiled a list of the key civilians that had responsibility for train traffic in and out of Vienna. We were lucky, there were three Austrians of Swiss heritage working in key positions. We compiled dossiers on all three and found two that we thought would be sympathetic to our cause. We eliminated one since he was a member of the Nazi Party. We used our existing Swiss friends we were working with us to make some enquiries and contact the other two men. As we did not know the two men directly, we took a risk that even if they did not help us that they would not say anything. The first man identified, Bertrand Graber, was responsible for coordinating trains in and out of the Sudbahnhof, one of the two train stations used for trains transporting Jews. The other, Gaston Tanner was a railroad engineer but since the annexation, he also worked in the central terminal maintenance office. One of his duties was to monitor the inventory of spare parts. Being an engineer he was the daytime shift supervisor since he knew all about engines. This proved extremely valuable. Both detested working for the Nazis. They knew about the deportations and the rumors of instant death at Auschwitz for the passengers. They had seen the trains packed with frightened, half-starved people crammed into the boxcars with no room to move.

We met with both of them separately one night after work in a local bar. They did not know it at the time but they had to agree to work for us on the spot. If they did not we had decided to shoot them when they left the bar as if they were robbery victims. We could not compromise our operation. Luckily, for them, both immediately agreed and were quite enthusiastic about it. Once they agreed we invited them to our next weekly card game where we discussed various options. There were a number of critical items that were in relatively short supply that could be depleted to the point of disrupting service. These included ball bearings, pistons, piston rings, certain wheels, and some throttle components.

Per Gaston's recommendation, we decided to focus on the pistons. Gaston explained how this worked. In a steam engine, the boiler, fueled by wood, oil, or coal, continuously boils water in an enclosed chamber creating high-pressure steam. The steam from the boiler is sent to the front end of the cylinder containing a piston. The high pressure steam pushes the piston down the cylinder. Attached to the piston is a coupling rod that turns the wheel around one half-turn. Once this is done the steam leave the cylinder through a vent. The steam escapes in a quick burst giving the engine its characteristic *choo* sound. At the same time, high pressure steam enters the back end of the cylinder. This pushes the piston back up the cylinder, pulling the engine wheels around another half turn. At the end of this stroke, the steam is released from the rear vent of the cylinder causing another *choo*. Each piston has a ring around it to maintain a seal so that all of the steam is used to move the piston which in turn moves the coupling rod that turns the wheel. If the ring does not fit tightly in the cylinder, it leaks so that all of the steam is not forced into the cylinder chamber and the power to the wheel decreases. As the space between the piston and the cylinder increases, the efficiency of the engine diminishes to the point of not fully turning the wheels. He suggested that we concentrate on the piston rings since they were the easiest piece of equipment to sabotage. All of the other parts were both too big and heavy or were so strong that they hardly ever wore out. There were a few things that he could do:

- Order the wrong size piston rings

- Damage the ones in the warehouse so they would fail when the train was en route

- Steal some of the existing rings to reduce the spare parts inventory

He decided to do all three. So, in early November, Gaston put his plan in motion. Every time that he visited any of the warehouses he took a few piston rings out of a box. He always left one or two rings in the box. Being an engineer, he had studied metallurgy and knew that there were certain things that you should not do to piston rings. The number one thing was not to subject them to high heat and freezing cold in succession as it would cause the pistons to become brittle and after a very short period, they would crack and fracture. The brittleness could not be detected even under close visual inspection. So Gaston would alternately place some of the metal piston rings in the kiln in the maintenance shop and immediately afterwards in a bucket of ice. He repeated this four or five times. He could treat six piston rings at one time in this manner about twice a week at the maintenance shop at night when no one was there. Once they were treated he replaced them in different boxes. He was careful to only put three or four of them in any single box. Moreover, he put a tiny white dot on the inside of each treated piston ring so he would know which ones were good and which ones were bad. By November 15th all of the bad piston rings were in place. Whenever a piston failed or whenever there was some maintenance needed on the engines used for deporting Jews he made it a point to be called. Sometimes, if he found out the date and time for a train to arrive at the station, he would be there waiting and schedule some unnecessary maintenance just so he could have the piston rings replaced. He would replace at least three of the good piston rings with defective ones. These trains were easily identified by the yellow Star of David painted on the side of the boxcars near the door. They were dedicated to the transport of Jews under the direct orders of Himmler and were given priority treatment and passage through the station. Typically, there were about fifteen boxcars to each train with each boxcar holding as many as eighty Jews.

Original postcard of soldiers responsible for loading Jews posing by boxcar number 14 with the yellow Jewish Star (upper left corner). Trains with these special rail cars had priority over any other train by the direct order of Himmler. (Source: Author's Personal Collection)

To further increase ring replacement Gaston adjusted the feeler gauges. This was a device that measured the clearance between the piston ring and the cylinder. If the gap was more than 0.08 millimeters the ring had to be replaced. Surprisingly, there were now even more piston rings that had to be replaced on the trains carrying Jews. In fact, piston ring failures and preventative maintenance replacements increased by about 40 percent. This worked so well that we decided to select trains not deporting Jews lest someone get suspicious that only the trains transporting Jews had piston ring failures. While we did not want to sabotage every train we did enough to cause congestion since the failure always occurred while the train was en route to its next destination from Vienna. This was done to freight trains, particularly those carrying military supplies to the Russian Front, and trains carrying any products from the occupied countries to Germany. In some cases the piston ring failed after a few hours and in some cases failure occurred a day or two after the train left the station. The failure was complete. The piston rings would fracture and essentially disintegrate in the cylinder or the blow-by (amount of steam leaking into the crankcase) would be so high that the train would slow to a crawl. Many times two piston rings would fail. If they both fractured, the steam could not be compressed so the train just stopped. This really caused a mess as no train could use the track while the disabled train was on the track. Since the train could barely move, the only option was to send a maintenance crew out to the train which could take up to six hours just to get there depending where the train had broken down. The crew would replace the piston rings in the field, which could take up to ten hours. Sometimes they used one of the defective piston rings so the problem repeated itself within twenty-four hours after the crew left. This went on for about three weeks before one of the senior managers decided to investigate why there were so many piston ring problems all of a sudden. He called a meeting of all the people involved in supply and maintenance which included Gaston and explained the situation. He needed some volunteers to investigate the rash of failures. Gaston was only too willing to help. Two other men volunteered to help one of which was Bertrand. They set up a schedule and went to the main maintenance warehouse the next afternoon. Gaston selected six piston rings from different boxes, all of which, of course, did not have the small white dot so he knew that they had not been mistreated. Not surprisingly, the extensive laboratory tests showed all six of them to be in perfect condition. Gaston suggested that perhaps it was the quality of the metal being used since the war caused so many shortages that all of the alloying components were compromised. The laboratory agreed that this was a possible explanation and informed the Station Master that they were going to visit the manufacturers. The investigation ended as abruptly as it started.

As this was going on, Gaston continued removing some spare piston rings from the store rooms in the other train stations and slowed down the replacement procedure. He would stay late one or two nights a week and misfile the request forms or just destroy them. Sometimes he would write a seven that looked like a nine or a one, so the wrong size piston ring was delivered. If he was lucky, he could intercept a shipment for the other stations at the receiving dock and substitute a box of new piston rings with a box that had some treated pistons. In this way the trains would break down leaving other stations that would be traced back to different maintenance shops and piston ring plants. This ruse worked very well and slowed the rail system considerably. About one in four trains passing through Vienna would have piston ring failures which delayed the deportations throughout Europe. Even if the failure did not occur with the trains going to the death camps they failed on the return trip. Trains returning from the Russia Front with wounded soldiers were never given bad piston rings. In fact, they would be inspected to make sure that they did not have any defective piston rings.

Due to the slowdown, there were nights where there were no SS incursions into any district to arrest and deport Jews. Mischa would let us know which nights there was nothing scheduled so we would use our truck and pick up as many as sixteen people at a time. This in itself was unusual. Typically, when the SS came for deportations they would bring five or six trucks and take out two or three buildings. Once when our SS officer was asked by two policemen on patrol why there was only one truck he said that this was a special situation in that this truck would go directly to Poland since there were no trains available. He added that even if they were able to rid Vienna of only one single Jew wasn't it worth it? They wholeheartedly agreed. We also decided to get a second SS truck each weekend in case we had a problem with one of them.

We were able to make twelve raids during November 1941 and September 1942 when Vienna was actually totally void of any deportable Jewish people. There were still some Jews with special jobs, the Jews working at the IKG, Mischlings and Jews married to Gentiles that were excluded from the list of deportable Jews – at least now. Of the sixteen trips to Switzerland, thirteen were uneventful. Three had problems.

Trip number seven was not a lucky seven. The van left the city at eleven PM with Gunter driving and Ambros in the passenger seat. About forty-five minutes outside of Vienna it started to rain. It was not a particularly heavy rain but it was enough to make the road slippery. Gunter did not compensate for the slippery road by slowing down nor did he go any faster than usual. He just maintained his normal speed, which was really not very fast. He was about 10 km from St. Florian when he reached a section of the highway with a few curves. As the van was rounding one of these curves curve, a car that was coming from the opposite direction at a high speed veered into his lane. Gunter could not pull the van over to the side of the road quick enough and the van collided with the car. The car was knocked off the road and into a ditch on the other side of the road. The van careened into a tree. Ambros was thrown partially through the windscreen. He was badly hurt, bleeding and unconscious. The high wheel of the cab prevented Gunter from going through the windscreen. He was not badly hurt but was a little disoriented. The driver of the other car was seriously hurt. He was the only occupant in the car. He was unconscious and was slumped over the steering wheel. He was bleeding from the mouth and nose where he hit his face on the steering wheel. He reeked of alcohol. There were no other cars on that section of the road at the time of the accident but after about five minutes two cars came by and stopped to give aid. One had a single man and the other had two men. About ten minutes later a third car – a man with his wife and one child also stopped. All of the other cars that now passed just slowed down to look but did not stop since they saw that three cars had already stopped.

From the moment of impact the eight people in the van started screaming. They were trapped and worried that they would be burned alive if the van caught fire. They could smell the petrol leaking from the damaged gas tank. Actually, the petrol was not from the gas tank. It was from one of the five-gallon cans on the side of the van that hit the tree. One of them had been punctured and had drained completely onto the ground where the rain washed most of the gasoline into a ditch. This posed no threat. There was no danger of the van catching on fire but they did not know this so they were screaming and pounding on the walls of the van begging to be let out. The drivers of the three cars that stopped to help heard the screams of the eight people trapped inside the van. The back door was locked which surprised them. They ran to the cab and saw Gunter slumped over the wheel. They carefully took him down from the cab. He was semi-awake and held his right side. They saw Ambros half-through the windscreen and were going to take him out of the cab but the screams of the trapped people distracted them and they decided to help them get out of the van. One of the drivers ran back to his car and took the jack handle from the jack in his trunk and ran back to the van. Together they pried the lock off of the door forced open the back of the van. To their surprise the van was filled with furniture. They walked around the van looking for another door but didn't find anything. One of the drivers of the car went over to Gunter. Even though he was still woozy he heard the screams of the eight people trapped in the van. He managed to get up, regained his composure and, with the help of the man who came over to him, walk to the compartment of the van. He knew he had a major decision to make to explain the screaming people inside the van. He obviously couldn't leave the people locked in the van and wait for the police to come. He had to tell the men that had stopped to help what was going on. First, he went under the van and opened the hidden trap door and told the people inside that there was no danger and that they were working to get them out but they had to be quiet. He asked if anyone was hurt. Other than a few bruises, no one was hurt. We required that all of the people in the van lay down while the van was moving. There were always extra blankets to protect the people just for occasions such as this but this was the first time that an accident actually happened.

Gunter turned to the men and told them that there were eight people, two Jewish families that were being smuggled out of Austria to save their lives as they were gong to be deported to a concentration camp where they would be killed. He looked at Ambros, bleeding and unconscious with half of his body through the windscreen and walked over to the other car and saw that the driver was also seriously injured, reeked of alcohol and needed medical attention. He asked for their help. The men looked at each other and three agreed to help unload the furniture to let the people out. The man with his wife and child did not want to risk his life for some Jews but he did agree to notify the police about the accident and get medical help without telling them about the Jews. Gunter thanked him but just to be safe he noted the license plate number and told the driver that there would be a problem if he did tell the authorities about the hidden Jews. The driver reiterated his promise just to report the accident and not to say anything about the Jews. While the three men were unloading the van, Gunter went over to Ambros. Gunter tried to take him out of the cab but his chest hurt too much. He knew that he had some broken ribs. The other men stopped unloading and took Ambros over to the side of the road and wrapped him a couple of the drop cloths used to protect the furniture in transit. They did the same to the driver of the other car who was badly hurt. They placed him in a position where he could not see the van if he regained consciousness. Once the two injured men were taken care of, they continued to unload the van as quickly as possible just throwing the furniture out of the van on to some drop cloths spread out on the ground. They were able to do this in about twenty-five minutes. Furniture was strewn haphazardly all around the van with some still inside. A few pieces were broken as they hit the ground. Lighter pieces were thrown into the grassy area that was away from the road. The boxes of clothing, household goods and personal items were kept in the van. Soon enough furniture had been removed to open the false compartment. Just then another car came by and stopped, one of the men went over before the driver got out and told him that everything was under control and thanked them for stopping. He also said that the police and already been notified and were on their way to help so they need not stop in the next city and inform them. Gunter thanked him for his quick thinking.

Gunter went into the van. They unlatched the door and the people got out. He confirmed that other than a few bruises no one was hurt. He asked the men for one more favor. Could they load some of the furniture back on the van before leaving? He explained that he was going to take the false door off of its hinges and put it down on the floor of the van. He needed to have some of the furniture put back into the van on top of the door to hide the fact that there was a false compartment. The men understood and proceeded to put back some of the lighter items, the upholstered furniture and all of the appliances. Gunter took the eight people and their possessions about two hundred yards from the accident into a grove of trees and told them to wait out of sight and not make a sound. About two-thirds of the van was loaded when he came back. He thanked the three men and again asked them not to say anything, even to their families or else it could result in the arrest and death of the two families. He offered to pay them some money but they refused. They agreed not to say anything to anyone and drove off. Gunter went to the spot where the eight people were waiting and moved them farther away from the accident site and told them not to move from there and that he would have someone come get them the next day as soon as possible. He added that they would know it was a friend if he was whistling. He also brought over some chairs for them to sit on. There was no cover so they were all wet but at least they were not hurt.

Another hour passed. A police car and an ambulance pulled up to the accident. The police officer questioned Gunter. Gunter told them that the other car had swerved onto his side of the road, hit him and that he was forced off of the road. The skid marks of the two vehicles confirmed this. They also smelled the alcohol on the other driver. The ambulance attendants took the driver from the car that was in the ditch and Ambros to the hospital in St. Florian. The ambulance attendants said that the driver of the other car and Ambros would recover. A second police car, also with only one policeman arrived. After Gunter gave the police the information, another ambulance arrived to take him to the hospital. The officer in the first police car agreed to stay there to watch the van and the furniture strewn all over.

As soon as Gunter reached the hospital he called his wife, Marta, from the nurse's station and told her what had happened telling her that he was okay but Ambros was in the hospital severely injured, the van was badly damaged and the furniture was partially strewn about the road. His wife asked about the special package to which Gunter replied that it was no longer on the van and that it would be good if someone came from Vienna to pick it up as soon as possible. He had put it in a grove of trees about 200 yards southeast of the wreck and that he would be back home before she could whistle the wedding march. He repeated the whistling statement two more times during the conversation. His wife got the message. The doctors insisted that Gunter, who had some lacerations along with three cracked ribs, stay the night. Gunter agreed on condition that he was put into the same room as Ambros.

Ambros had been heavily sedated. His face and head was bandaged and he had broken his right arm as he raised it to instinctively protect himself as he went through the windscreen. This saved his life but he still sustained some severe head injuries. His clothes were piled neatly on a chair in the room. Gunter looked under his gown, the extension was still firmly attached and had obviously had not raised any suspicion. However, as soon as he urinated there would be a problem so Gunter decided to remove the extension which he hid under his own mattress along with the pistol that he brought from the van. He also hid the spare extension and the tube of glue that was in the pack of cigarettes under his mattress. In the worst-case scenario Ambros would be discovered to be a Jew and would be taken away by the SS. If this occurred, Gunter was prepared to kill him and flee the hospital. The best-case scenario was that his "Jewishness" would not be discovered before the rescue team came from Vienna. Ambros was given a sedative and he drifted off to sleep.

Marta called Kurt at four AM since he was the direct contact for Gunter and told him word for word what Gunter had told her. Kurt called me. I, in turn called Frank and Helmut who immediately went to the garage and took out another moving van but without the compartment door. They would use the compartment door in the other van. A car with Franz and Johann accompanied them. They left for the accident scene just as the sun was rising. They were stopped by a police patrol car that was suspicious of a van going so fast at that hour of the morning but Helmut told the police about the accident and that they were going to see if they could salvage any of the furniture. The policeman went to his car and called the police in St. Florian who confirmed their story. The van was allowed to proceed but was told to slow down lest they wind up in the same situation; the roads were still slippery.

I also immediately called Wilhelm and told him that Gunter had some broken ribs but otherwise was not seriously hurt. Ambros had severe head injuries and was unconscious. They were both in the hospital at St. Florian. We assumed that Ambros had removed the extension. With Ambros unconscious, there was a real threat that a doctor or a nurse would see his uncircumcised penis and report him as a Jew. Wilhelm called one of his doctor friends at home that worked at the St. Florian Hospital and told him that one of the drivers of his neighbor's moving company had been badly hurt in an accident. He had sustained some severe head injuries and was in the hospital. Because of the nature of the injuries Wilhelm asked if he could arrange for injured man to be transferred to Vienna where he would receive better care due to the head injury specialists that were in residence at the Vienna Hospital. His friend agreed and went to the hospital to start the transfer process. Wilhelm quickly went to the Vienna Hospital and signed out for an ambulance and a driver and sped to St. Florian.

The car and the replacement van reached the accident site in about three hours. The wreckage was in plain sight and every car and truck slowed down as they passed the wreckage. Helmut went over to the police car and thanked the officer for watching and protecting the contents of the van and told him that he was there with the other moving van to load the furniture. The officer had been there from about four AM and was glad to be relieved. He returned to St. Florian. Franz and Johann got out of the car with a backpack containing food, water, first aid supplies and medicine. After a few minutes Franz started to whistle the wedding march as he walked. Five more minutes passed. The group heard him whistling and came out of the places from where they were hiding. He gave them the food and water. He bandaged the minor wounds of the two injured people. They were cold and wet but otherwise okay. No one needed any medicine. After eating and drinking they walked to the replacement van and got in.

The false compartment door taken from the damaged van was closed. The furniture was loaded back onto the van. The replacement van went to a safe house in Gmunden where they left the two families until new arrangements could be made to take them to Switzerland. Meanwhile, Wilhelm and the ambulance reached the hospital. Gunter was still sleeping. He gently awakened him. Gunter got out of bed and walked over to Ambros and lifted the sheet. Evidently, Ambos' circumcised penis was not noticed. Wilhelm went to the office to complete the paperwork for the transfer while Gunter got dressed and removed the hidden items from under the mattress. On the way out one of the nurses approached Wilhelm and whispered in his ear that Ambros was Jewish. Wilhelm acted surprised. "Are you sure?" he asked. She replied that she had tended to his urinating that morning and had seen his circumcised penis which she kept secret from the other hospital staff. She had many Jewish doctor and nurse friends that had been fired because they were Jewish. She had no love for the Nazis. She also made sure that she was the only nurse tending to both men in the room. Once in a while God does indeed smile upon us.

Gunter asked Wilhelm if he could ride back with Ambros. Wilhelm replied that of course he could. The ambulance arrived in Vienna at about seven PM. When the ambulance pulled into the hospital bay, Wilhelm arranged for a private room for Ambros with two private nurses to take personal care of him. He selected the two nurses. One was about sixty years old and was openly critical of the Nazi administration. Her son was a priest and had been treated badly by the Nazis whom she often referred to as damned heretics. The second had a Jewish husband and was treated poorly by the other staff members. Wilhelm told them that Ambros was an old friend of the family, that he was Jewish and that he was hiding from the Nazis. While this was indeed a risk, he had to trust somebody on the staff with this information since any one of the staff could easily discover that Ambros was Jewish as soon as they saw his penis. They both agreed to help. Wilhelm asked a close friend who was a specialist in head injuries to examine Ambros. Luckily, Ambros only had a concussion that would heal without surgery in about a week. His other injuries would also heal without surgery. Wilhelm personally took care of Ambros during the week along with the two nurses. After a week in the hospital, Ambros was released. He had permanent scars as a result of the accident. After Ambros was released Wilhelm gave 1,000 Marks to each nurse. Both of them initially refused to take the money but Wilhelm absolutely insisted. He knew that they could both use the money. They accepted and thanked him.

We arranged to have the van towed back to Vienna but the engine was beyond repair. It was a total loss. We now only had two vans so we purchased another van.

Trip number ten was the second problem. As usual we sent the two moving vans out on different routes to Switzerland. The van driven by Bernhard and Konrad was headed to Switzerland through Innsbruck. About 50 km from Innsbruck it started to rain so they decided that they would stop at a safe house in Innsbruck and continue the next day. They did not want a repeat of trip number seven. When they arrived in Tratzberg they had to leave the main highway. There was some road construction so the van had to make a detour on a narrow stretch of road. The rain had made the unlit road very slippery and even though Bernhard was driving very slowly he skidded off of the road into the unpaved shoulder which was a puddle of mud. The weight of the van and its contents was just too much. It got mired in the mud and could not move forward or backward. The few cars on the road just drove by them without stopping since they were not blocking the road and they did not realize that it was stuck in the mud. They just assumed the driver had pulled over to rest or to wait for the rain to stop. Bernhard and Konrad got out of the van to assess the situation. Bernhard opened the trap door and told the eight passengers (three men, three women and two children, 13 and 15 years old) that the van was stuck in the mud and that they were going to try to get it free. He told them to continue to lie down on the floor and not be afraid if the van were to rock back and forth and if he gunned the engine.

Bernhard and Konrad tried everything that they could think of. They collected some branches from nearby trees and try to make a footing but the wheels just crushed the branches without moving or if it did move, it only went a few centimeters until it again became mired in the mud. They took out some of the furniture hiding it behind the van so it could not be seen by passing cars and tried the same thing with the same results. The van was still too heavy for either of them to push and they were both in their sixties so had limited strength. For about two more hours they tried and tried without any success. In fact, it looked worse after their efforts than before. Just when they passed the two hour mark, the police arrived. They were on their usual patrol and saw the mired van. There were two local Tratzberg police officers in the car. They radioed for another car to come to the scene. They quickly assessed the situation and at first suggested that they just leave the van there for the night and return in the morning or afternoon when it stopped raining with a tow truck to pull it out of the mud. The contents of the van would most likely have to be fully emptied as they believed that the tow truck winch would not be able to extricate it with the furniture in it. Bernhard and Konrad told the police that there were some valuable pieces of furniture in it and they just couldn't leave it unguarded for the rest of the night and that they were on a tight schedule. The police understood and left Bernhard and Konrad sitting in the cab and said that they would call out a tow truck. It was now four AM. They closed the detour to all trucks to avoid a similar occurrence. At 6 AM a work crew came out and created a temporary bypass along the main road so no more traffic was diverted to the muddy detour.

At 9AM the police returned with a tow truck. As they were pulling up, Konrad went to the trap door and told the people what was going on and that they had to be very quiet. The tow truck driver assessed the situation and tried to free the van with the winch but, as the police officers had suspected, the fully loaded van was just too heavy. They asked Bernhard if they could wait until they could get some men from the town to help unload the van. Bernhard knew that the more people that became involved the more difficult it would be to get away without their cargo being discovered. They were really in a dilemma. It could take days for the ground to dry sufficiently to move the van. The tow truck driver suggested an alternative but it would be expensive. He could drive one of them to a lumber yard in the area to get some plywood construction boards and some beams. The plywood would be laid on top of the beams to create a path that could support the van. It was about four meters from where the van was stuck to the hard portion of the unpaved road. They would have to buy the lumber and the boards which they could easily do this since each van carried a few thousand Marks in case they needed to bribe a policeman or official along the way. They opted for the most expedient solution which was to buy the lumber and boards. While Bernhard was talking to the men, Konrad walked around the van bending down as if inspecting it for damage. When he reached the trap door he again informed the people of the situation. The eight people had now been in the van for more than eight hours. The two children started to get cranky and whine. Bernhard told them to give the children the sedatives. The parents complied and the two children soon drifted off to sleep.

Bernhard left with the tow truck and went into town to get the wood. The police car stayed with Konrad who opted to sit in the police car while they waited. Another few hours passed. It was 5 PM and the rain had not yet stopped when the truck with Bernhard, two men from the lumber company, who agreed to help for some money, arrived along with the tow truck. Bernhard told Konrad that he had called us from the lumber company and informed us of the delay and that he believed that they had the situation under control. Bernhard had bought much more plywood than was needed because he had no idea whether one or two layers were needed to support the weight of the van in order to free it and get it back onto the road. There was one bit of luck. The lumber yard also had railroad ties so he bought a dozen of them as well. The men took the railroad ties and made a pathway to the road. The plywood boards were laid on top of them. Since he had bought so many boards they laid them out in two layers. A couple of the railroad ties were also placed in front of the back wheels along. The two officers stayed in the police car while all of this was being done. After the makeshift wooden road was finished, Bernhard sent the two men from the lumberyard back with the unused plywood. They wanted to stay and watch the operation but their boss had told them to return as soon as possible. As he told them in front of Bernhard, he politely reminded of this and they left.

The tow truck driver turned on the winch with Konrad at the wheel. It was now 10 PM. After a few minutes they were able to get the van out of the mud. It rocked violently back and forth during the procedure until it was free, Konrad had to jam on the brakes to stop the van once it was free. The people inside the compartment were jostled severely by this sudden violent motion. Even though they were told to lie down they were not so they screamed in pain from hitting the back and front of the compartment and the two children awakened and started to cry. Unfortunately, this was heard by the tow truck driver who returned to the front of the van to unlatch the winch. He jumped back, startled by the screams and crying. He started to yell at Konrad demanding to know what was going on. The two policemen that were watching the operation saw the commotion and got out of their car and came over to them. The adults by now recovered and calmed down. They held the children down covering their mouths so their stifled moans could not be heard outside. The tow truck driver told the police that he heard people screaming and crying inside the van. Bernhard and Konrad both laughed and said that the driver was just hearing things but the driver insisted. The police didn't believe him but as he was so insistent they opened the back door and shined their flashlights into it. They saw that there was no one inside and called the tow truck driver over to see. Bernhard pointed to the radio and said that it must have been the radio that they heard. With this explanation he too thought that his ears were playing tricks on him. Just then one of the children bit the hand of her mother that was stifling her crying. She bit very hard and the mother yelled as the girl started loudly crying. The sound carried through the empty van like an echo chamber. The police heard it and immediately withdrew their pistols and told Bernhard and Konrad to raise their hands. One officer went inside moving and throwing out some of the furniture so he could get to the front. With his flashlight he discovered the latches holding the compartment door in place. He banged on the door. One of the people inside opened the door. He saw the eight people inside. The coats that were on the floor had the yellow stars so he now knew that Bernhard and Konrad were smuggling Jews out of the country. He ordered everyone out of the van and told them to stand on the side of the van that could not be seen from the road. He ordered them to raise their hands. The tow truck driver spat at the Jewish families and started to call them names. Bernhard and Konrad were also ordered to stand with them. Konrad grabbed his chest and started to fall down. "He's having a heart attack!" Bernhard screamed as he knelt down to help him. As he helped Konrad he took a pistol out that was hidden in his boot and shot the two policemen killing one of them instantly and wounding the other. The two policemen were caught by surprise and did not have any time to shoot back. Without a moment's hesitation, Konrad turned and shot the tow truck driver in the back as he immediately started to run away when the officers were shot. The tow truck driver fell as Konrad shot the wounded police officer again killing him. He walked over to the tow truck driver and shot him again in the head. The people were screaming but Bernhard quickly went over to them and quieted them down. They had to act fast. The four men re-loaded all of the furniture into the van leaving the back third empty. The compartment door was not reattached. The three bodies were loaded into the back of the van. The eight people were told to get in the back. That took some doing since the women at first refused to get in with the dead men. Only after Bernhard threatened them and their children did they agree. They drove the tow truck and police car into the field using the makeshift wooden road but as soon as each vehicle cleared the plywood they were mired in the mud. The vehicles were visible from the road but as there was no longer any traffic on the detour, they believed that they could get away before they were discovered. Bernhard and Konrad got into the van and drove to the safe house in Innsbruck.

They arrived in one hour and forty minutes. Originally, the plan was to drop the eight people off at the back of a clothing store which was the safe house in Innsbruck but as it was now late at night the store was closed. Since they knew the home address of the contact, Bernhard drove within two blocks of his house and briefly stopped to let Konrad out before driving away. They decided that Bernhard would drive around the neighborhood and return to this corner in fifteen minutes. Konrad walked over to Franz Stiller's house. He went around back and knocked on the door. After a few minutes Franz came to the door. Although they had never met, Franz immediately knew who Konrad was. The van was now 24 hours late and Franz was worried. Our policy was never to contact anyone at one of our safe houses by phone just in case it was tapped so Franz knew nothing about the problem. Konrad quickly explained the situation sparing no details. Franz got dressed. They left from the back door and went to the corner. In a few minutes the van pulled up and Franz got in. They decided that they could not wait until morning to unload the passengers. The police could have found the abandoned car and tow truck by now and started searching for the missing officers and tow truck driver. The police knew that they were there to help a mired moving van loaded with furniture. The van arrived at the store at about 1:30 AM. The street was deserted as they pulled up in front of the store. Konrad and Bernhard quickly jumped out of the cab as Franz rushed to the door and unlocked it. They went to the back and opened the door. The eight people were hurriedly ushered out of the van visibly distraught. Konrad and Bernhard helped them with their possessions. They ran into the store. Bernhard and Konrad dropped everything on the floor, turned around and ran back to the van. They closed the back door, got in and drove away. Timing is everything. Just as they turned the corner a police car making its nightly rounds turned onto the street where the store was located from the far corner. The van was already out of sight when the police made the turn onto the quiet, deserted street.

Bernhard, with Konrad following in Franz's car, drove towards the mountains in the opposite direction from their return route to Vienna. On the way they stopped at a gas station and purchased three ten-liter containers which they filled with gasoline. They also refueled the van and made sure that the spare tanks that were on the side of the van were full. They reached the mountains at about five AM. It was still dark when they took a little-used winding side road up the mountain. At daybreak they stopped on the road overlooking a sheer vertical drop. They got out, emptied the three cans of petrol in the cab and in back of the van making sure that the bodies were completely doused. With Bernhard at the wheel, Konrad lit the gasoline and closed the door. With the van on fire, Konrad put the gear into drive, released the brake, and jumped out of the cab lighting one of the ten-liter containers that was placed in the cab. The van careened down the mountain bouncing a few times before hitting bottom and exploding. The fire lit up the area but at that hour at that spot there was no one around. As soon as the van careened over the cliff, Konrad got into Franz's car. They drove back to Franz's store.

That morning the abandoned vehicles were discovered by the police. They suspected that the men had inadvertently stumbled upon a smuggling operation and had been kidnapped by the smugglers. This had happened once before with two police officers that had stopped a truck outside of Innsbruck that was smuggling wine and other luxuries from Milan to Munich. In addition to the two drivers, there were two armed men hidden in the truck that overcame the two policemen, and took them hostage for the remainder of the trip through Austria. At the German border they gave each officer a case of wine and released them. The MO fit as they pieced the events of the night together from the various witnesses: A large moving van carrying furniture was stuck in the mud. In order to get it out they sent for a tow truck which was not able to extricate the van. One of the drivers went to town and purchased plywood to be able to create a floor to make a road for the van to get free. All of this was clearly visible at the scene. It was obvious to them that when they unloaded the furniture the police and the tow truck driver saw the contraband and were taken hostage at gunpoint. This was further substantiated by the two men from the lumber company who had left before the contraband was discovered. Based on the past incident they radioed the information to the police headquarters in Salzburg who mobilized to intercept the smugglers and their captives at the border. The smugglers were not intercepted so the authorities just thought that they had crossed the border before the roadblocks were set up. After the second day when nothing was heard from the missing men a country wide alert was initiated. For the next two weeks every large vehicle crossing any border was meticulously checked. We were warned of this by Mischa so we suspended our operations during this period. The search intensity declined in the third week and was just about abandoned after the fourth week. About three months later, in the spring, a group of hikers came across the burned wreckage of the van in a ravine and discovered some charred bodies in the wreckage. The police were called in and they identified the bodies as the three missing men. Here again they thought that it was the work of contraband smugglers – a deal gone wrong.

We were now down to only one moving van again so we decided to purchase another moving van as soon as possible. We were able to get one from another furniture store which we quickly modified with the hinges and the false door.

Trip number sixteen, was the most devastating and it wound up being our last trip using the moving vans. The two vans left the city at two different exit points as was normal. Our drivers were instructed to go to the nearest safe house if it started to rain en route. We were now transporting lighter weight commercial goods. Mattresses and bedding were favorite products since they were bulky and could easily be moved so we set up a mattress and bedding business. We hired eight people all of whom were Jews that had been in hiding or pretending to be Gentile. They were not told any details of the operation.

The two vans left the city without any problem and proceeded independently to Gmunden where they met at the same safe house. There were the typical check points where vehicles were randomly stopped and questioned. The contents of the commercial vehicles were typically inspected but most of these were superficial. The first van to leave had no problems and arrived that evening in Innsbruck. The second van was stopped about 15 kilometers from Innsbruck at a military checkpoint. About twenty French prisoners of war had escaped and there was an intense search to recapture them. Martin and Fritz were the driver and passenger respectively. Martin was new. He was 67 years old and had retired just two months before the Anschluss after working thirty two years as an elementary school teacher in Weiner Neustadt. Upon retirement he moved to Vienna two days after the Anschluss and decided not to let anyone know that he was Jewish. He was related to one of our group members, which was how we found him. He was Ambros's replacement and this was his first time on the job. At the check point Martin was asked to pull over for some routine questions. Martin became very nervous as this was a military checkpoint. He stuttered and stammered when the soldier asked him some routine questions. This made him suspicious. He called over his superior who proceeded to question him more rigorously. Martin got worse. The first soldier walked around the cab and asked Fritz to get out so he could ask Fritz the same questions away from Martin to check to see if their answers agreed.

Martin was also ordered to get out. Martin almost fell over his own feet as he got down from the van. Martin started to fidget nervously. That was the soldier needed to see. He called over two more soldiers and they decided to unload the contents of the van to see if they were being coerced to hide some of the escaped prisoners or if they were black market smugglers. They had some other French prisoner of war laborers working near the check point so another soldier brought them over. With Fritz and Martin standing there and watching, the laborers started to unload the van. After about forty-five minutes all of the furniture was unloaded. The guards quickly noticed the false compartment door but found that it had no handle to open it. They banged on the door realizing that there had to be someone inside. When it was opened they were expecting to find some of the French prisoners of war but instead they found eight Jews. Martin panicked and ran from the soldier who was watching him. He was shot in the back and killed. Fritz wondered if he should do the same to avoid being tortured but the soldiers quickly restrained him.

This was now an SS and Gestapo matter. They called the SS in Innsbruck. We knew nothing of this back in Vienna. As soon as the SS arrived they started beating Fritz to get him to talk. Fritz said nothing. They continued to beat him until he was unconscious. They decided to take them back to Vienna. They put Fritz in the back seat car, still unconscious with three SS soldiers, two in front and one with him in the back. The eight Jews were put in the back of an SS truck. A third car followed the truck as they left for Vienna. The van was parked behind the checkpoint. As Fritz was unconscious and since he was old they didn't bother to hand cuff him. They had been on the road for about forty minutes. The guard in the back with him dozed off. Fritz came to and quickly assessed the situation. He was as good as dead so he used this opportunity to reach into a hidden pocket tucked in at the waist. He took out the cyanide pill, put it into his mouth and bit it. Death was instantaneous.

The two cars and the truck reached Vienna a few hours later where it was decided to take them to the Gestapo headquarters as they were better equipped to handle this sort of situation. The guard in the back seat thought that Fritz was sleeping but when he shook him to wake him up he saw that Fritz was dead. He knew that he was clearly in trouble for not thoroughly searching the prisoner and watching him while they were in the back seat together. He would face some severe disciplinary action. They herded the eight Jews into six cells. There was a family of four that they put into two cells separating the two children from their parents. The children immediately started crying. The other four adults were put into separate cells. They put Fritz's body in another cell. As per the written procedure they called Wilhelm and told him what had happened. Wilhelm stopped what he was doing called me at the morgue and rushed to the Gestapo headquarters.

As soon as I realized the gravity if the situation, I called Magda who was Stefan's wife and told her that we may have been compromised. She was told to evacuate the mattress store and garage. She told the employees what had happened. They were told to go home, gather their belongings and go to one of the other garages to wait until we could assess the situation. Only two employees, the accountant, Rutger Knoebel, and the owner, Helmut Finster, were on file with the authorities. They took all of the papers and files with them as they evacuated the building and went to their respective homes. This was actually a legitimate business with full-time and part-time employees for Jews that emerged from hiding. They called their wives and children to come home. They gathered their possessions and drove their cars to the safe house on Lerchenfelder Strasse.

As this was unfolding, Friedrich told Fritz's wife about her husband. She took it hard and accepted our offer to get her out of Austria. She was no longer safe in Vienna. We helped her pack just about everything of value in her apartment and brought it to one of the garages that evening. She could sort it out later. We prepared the necessary documents for her trip to Switzerland. The only problem was that she had nowhere to go. She did not know anyone in any other country. She agreed that she would stay in Geneva with some friends of ours until we could arrange something more permanent. As it worked out, the Swiss family she stayed with had three small children. She never had any children and became their nanny in return for their hospitality. They children loved her as she devoted just about every waking hour to their needs. It was a perfect match.

She stayed with them throughout the war electing not to return even after the war was over.

Initially, the SS was pre-occupied with the Jewish prisoners but when they were convinced that they did not know anything about the operation only that they were put on a truck as if they were being arrested by the SS. They were taken to a garage and were told that the SS soldiers were really Jewish men dressed in SS uniforms. They were split into two groups with each group being put inside a secret compartment in a large moving van and told what to do while they were in the compartment. The van was loaded and they left Vienna for the Swiss border. Since each prisoner including the children told the exact same story when each one was interrogated individually, the SS believed them. They gave full descriptions of the people in the garage that had helped them. The SS officer in charge called the check point where the van was still sitting and asked for the name of the company that owned the van. It coincided with the information in Fritz's wallet. Within fifteen minutes, they assembled two trucks and twenty SS soldiers and raided the store but they were too late. All people, records and paperwork were gone. They did get about forty mattresses.

That night they checked with the police that were on duty the night before and confirmed that a single SS truck had come and arrested some Jews that were going to be driven to Poland. In fact, they had asked about it. The officer took out his log. In the true German fashion for detail, he had recorded the time and license plate number of the truck even though he did not have to do it. The police traced the truck to the depot. The truck was not there nor was it signed out. They questioned the two guards on duty that night but they said that they knew nothing. Whether they were believed or not was a moot point. The extent of the problem was so dramatic that they were not taking any chances so they detained the two guards while they checked out their story. Detained is just short of a formal arrest and would not appear on either of the guard's record. They did a thorough background check and found nothing to suspect the guards of any wrongdoing. They were released the following day. They checked all of the other guards and also found nothing suspicious. The SS search was too close for comfort. Karl Huber and Dietrich Fischer were the two guards that we were bribing. They were not on duty when the interrogations began but were very concerned when they were told to report to the motor pool for questioning. They kept calm and were not suspected. The SS assumed that the truck was stolen but for all they knew it could have been missing for a long time as there had not been an inventory check for weeks. They checked the maintenance records and found that it had been more than three months since the truck had any recorded maintenance. Typically, a truck is checked every two months. In the course of their investigation, they uncovered two other similar incidents of mock raids. Based on this they concluded that the truck had been stolen some months ago by the Jews that were running the escape network. They took an inventory of every truck in the depot. One other truck was missing. We surmised that after this close call Karl and Dietrich would stop helping us. We did not contact them to find out. We had already decided to abandon this operation.

We were now faced with a number of problems:

- What could we do about the eight Jewish prisoners that were being held in the Gestapo headquarters prison?

- How could we recover Martin's body which was still at the check point before they discovered the extension on his penis and the cigarette pack with the spare extension and the tube of glue?

- How to do the same for Fritz's body and personal effects which were at the Gestapo headquarters?

- How could we intercept the second van that would be returning later today from its trip? The police had been alerted to look for any moving van from the same mattress company. We had already called the safe house in Hernals but they had already left for the return trip

- What to do with the other SS truck that was parked in our garage?

- What to do with the people from the mattress store?

- What to do with the people in the garage that helped the captured Jews? Their descriptions would surely be wrested out of the prisoners

To intercept our returning van, we sent out four cars each on a different main road to the city that the returning van would likely use. There were three men per car. The cars went about 5 kilometers out of the city and sat at the side of the road waiting for the van to pass by. One man watched for the van. He signaled the next man who held up a sign with the driver's full name. The third man sat in the car in case the sign did not work and he had to give chase. This worked. The van was spotted and flagged down. The drivers were told what happened and that it would not be safe to return to Vienna with the company name on the van. The driver turned the van around. He followed the car to the nearby city of Baden where there was a safe house. Once there the driver of the car, Michael, had the van wait in a rest area just outside of the city while he went to the safe house and asked Hermann Glover for help. He called a friend that owned an auto repair shop and told him that a friend of his had just bought a used moving van for his business and needed to have the old company name removed and the new company name put on it. After negotiating a price, Michael went with Anton, the driver of the car, to get the van and bring it to the garage. The old name was removed and the new name was put on, Anton's Clothing Store. The orange van was painted green. With Anton as the passenger, the van headed for Vienna where it entered the city after a cursory check at the special check point set up for this operation.

Getting to the body of Fritz was quite easy. When Wilhelm arrived he was immediately brought to the room where Fritz's body was being kept. He confirmed that Fritz had committed suicide by taking a cyanide pill. He asked to see Fritz's personal effects. Without even questioning why, one of the guards brought his effects to Wilhelm. He asked the guard if he wouldn't mind bringing him a cup of coffee. The guard left. As soon as he did, Wilhelm substituted a regular pack of the same brand of cigarettes for the one that Fritz had with the spare extension and the tube of glue. He also removed the extension from his body. Now that this was done he was ready to release the body to the morgue. He called over the officer in charge and showed him Fritz's uncircumcised penis confirming that he was indeed Jewish as the imprisoned Jews had said. Wilhelm told the SS Captain that he would take care of sending the body to the morgue. The Captain gave strict orders that the body was to be kept at the morgue in case they needed it for their investigation.

Since all of the records were taken from the store, there was no way for the SS to identify the workers. We simply re-assigned them to other businesses. We now had to worry about the people in the garage that were seen by the Jewish families.

One of the things that I had not yet mentioned was that one of our group members worked in the theatre. He was an actor which in itself was nice but not overly important. What was important was his relationship with one of the make-up artists. Oskar was handsome, single and a reasonably good actor. He had been seeing Frieda for the better part of a year when Anschluss occurred. For obvious reasons, she knew he was Jewish but she loved him so there was no way that she was going to tell anyone. If she was not already married, they would have married each other. She hated her husband. He drank too much, was mean to her, was too heavy and went out with other women – on a paid basis. She was Catholic and her parents would not allow any talk of divorce. Her husband's parents also did not condone divorce. However, they did sympathize with her and bent over backwards to do anything that she wanted or give her anything that she needed. While her affair with Oskar was kept secret, they actually told her that if she found another man it would be alright with them as long as she didn't divorce their son. Frieda's parents were not that liberal. They just told her to make the best of it. Oskar had confided to Frieda that he was a member of a clandestine group of Jewish men that were working to smuggle Jewish families out of Austria and asked if she would be willing to help if the need arose. Frieda was only too happy to help. She was not a fan of the Nazis. When they took over, they purged the theatre of all Jewish members, most of whom were her friends. We now needed her help.

We invited Oskar and Frieda to one of our Friday night card games. We explained that we had four families and Fritz's wife that we had to get out of Austria. They were the families of the people in the garage and the widow of Fritz. There were three men, five women and six children, four girls and two boys ranging in age from fourteen to nineteen. We showed her pictures of each person that we had just taken in the safe house – a front view and two side views. "No problem!" she immediately answered.

Saturday morning she stopped by the theatre with Oskar and picked up what she needed from the storeroom. She came in with a large pocket book that was stuffed with crumpled newspaper. Oskar kept the guard busy telling him jokes. Frieda simply took out the newspaper and replaced it with what she needed. They left the theatre and went to the safe house where the families were being kept. In five hours there were thirteen totally different people in the room. All of the men were given false beards or mustaches. All of the children and the mothers were now blonde – the true Aryan color. We took their pictures and affixed them to the false identity cards that we had prepared. They were all given well-known German surnames. All of the males were already wearing their extensions. On Sunday we took each family to a different station and they left for England going through Ireland. We had arranged a special deal with the Jewish Relief Agency in Liverpool to have them relocate there. About six weeks later we received word that the four packages had arrived safely in Ireland. We found out that it was easier to get escaping Jewish people in through Ireland rather than directly to England. The Irish immigration authorities were much more sympathetic to our plight than the English immigration authorities, especially when it was mentioned that their final destination was England. To a man, they would not take any payment for helping smuggle Jewish families into England. In fact, they were delighted to increase the Jewish population of England.

While this was being set up we were concerned about getting Martin's body from the checkpoint before his extension was discovered. The soldiers at the checkpoint were just waiting for orders on where to send the body. When the SS called to find out the name of the company on the van, the soldier on duty asked the caller where they wanted the body sent. The caller asked his superiors and they decided that they would send someone for it. As soon as he hung up, the SS Captain in charge contacted Wilhelm to ask him where he thought the body should be brought. Wilhelm suggested the Central Morgue where they had the facilities to store the body. That would also result in both bodies being kept at the same location. The Captain agreed. He sent a truck with two men to get the body. They brought the body to the morgue about seven hours later. I personally waited for the body to be brought in. As soon as it was in and I was alone with the body, I undressed him and saw that the extension was intact which I removed and destroyed. I covered the body and placed it in the cold cubicle. I also asked the driver if he had Martin's personal possessions, which he did. I asked to see them and was shown them without any hesitation. Wilhelm had told me to do this as he wanted me to switch the pack of cigarettes with the spare extension with a real pack. Unfortunately, the guard jut stood by and was watching me. I suggested that he get a cup of coffee for both of us but he said he did not want any coffee. I picked up his wallet and dropped it by the guard's feet. As the guard bent down to pick it up. I quickly switched the cigarette packs. I opened the wallet, took out Martin's identification card and entered the number on the death certificate. I replaced the card in the wallet. The guard put everything back in the bag and left for the SS headquarters. As soon as he left I destroyed the extensions and put the tube of glue into a drawer.

As for the SS truck still in our garage, we were lucky. Johann, who was working at the mattress store office, was coming home from his new job when he saw an SS truck parked outside a local bar. There were two SS soldier inside having some drinks and talking to two young women. Using a coin, he removed the license plates being careful not to be seen by anyone passing by. Once removed, he took a taxi to a store close to the garage where our SS truck was parked. He had the taxi wait for him and ran to the garage. He borrowed a screwdriver and removed the license plates from our truck and handed Rolf the license plates that he removed from the other SS truck as he ran out of the garage to the waiting taxi. Fifteen minutes later he was back at the bar. Ten minutes after that the bad license plates were on the truck. He went directly home afterwards. Rolf put the switched license plates on our truck. One less thing to worry about.

We racked our brains for the rest of the week trying to figure out how we could rescue the eight Jewish prisoners being held at the SS headquarters. We were not able to think of a plan. They were to be put on the next train deporting Jews from Vienna.

At 2 AM two days later I received a call from Bertrand Graber, he was our man from the South Station. The train with the eight Jews from the Gestapo prison and about 750 Jews from various districts in Vienna had broken down about 20 kilometers from Vienna. All of the piston rings had apparently sequentially failed. They were able to move the train to a siding before the piston rings failed completely. There was no spare engine to send to the stalled train. At first the SS was just going to keep the train on the siding with all of the Jews aboard but when they found out that it could be one or two days before another engine could be brought up, they decided that the train was clearly visible from the main road that was too close to some towns. If it were found out that they were keeping Jews in the cars without food, water and sanitary conditions it could create a serious problem so they decided to use trucks to bring the Jews back to Vienna. The key point behind this was that they were telling everyone in Vienna that the Jews were being re-settled in the East in large Jewish communities that would put them all together so they would be better off than being in Vienna or being the unwanted minority in the countries in which they were living. There they could work together on farms and in factories to help with the war effort. They had to show that the Jews were being well-treated to substantiate this ruse.

When I received the call from Gaston, I knew exactly what we were going to do. It was risky but it was worth it. I called Kurt and Wilhelm and they both agreed. We dressed four of the team in SS uniforms and they took the truck that now had different license plates out of the garage and drove down to the highway from the Sudbahnhof. Seven SS trucks were already on the highway. This was all that they could spare. Our truck just slipped in when a space became available. The 20-kilometer trip took two hours due to the traffic. As we thought, as soon as the trucks arrived at the train they were loaded with as many Jews as possible. Our truck waited about ten minutes before pulling up to one of the box cars. The two men in the cab stayed there. The two men in the back got out as the back was filled with Jews. They were able to get eighteen Jews sitting and standing into the back of the truck with a space at the end of each seat saved for the two guards. Moreover, in the confusion we were able to get two entire families, including one family with six children. Based on our experience many people refused to escape if they had family members still in Vienna or a family member that did not qualify for escape according to our rules (sick, too old, etc.). However, we felt that if we were able to get an entire family from the train they would more readily accept our offer to escape to Switzerland since they had already been separated from other family members, friends, etc. The gate was closed the flap was lowered and the truck returned to Vienna. The SS decided that to expedite the evacuation process, all of the luggage would be left on the train. The Jews were told to remember the number of the car from which they were leaving so when the train was repaired they could go to their respective rail cars and reclaim their luggage. No one spoke and there were no papers to sign or identification cards to show. The SS wanted this completed as quickly as possible. There were not as many trucks crowded together on the return trip so when the truck was about three kilometers from the second district it turned down Wallenstein Strasse and preceded to Markt Gasse where we had a safe house and a large garage. The two guards said nothing during the trip back and since the people in the truck already knew that they were being sent back to Vienna they did not say anything either. When the truck arrived at the garage of the safe house, the people were ordered out and only then they were told where they were and that they would be smuggled out of the country. The expressions on their faces and the sighs of relief were indescribable. A few kneeled down and prayed. Some rushed over to us and thanked us profusely. We believed that no one, at this point even thought about not accepting our offer of escape. We were wrong. Two of the people had family members in the other trucks and refused to leave them. We decided to take them to Vienna but they had to wait until we could arrange it. Meanwhile we turned the truck around immediately and it set out for another run. It was now dawn. It took almost three hours to get to the train as the morning traffic in the city had already started. When they finally arrived there was only one more box car that had Jews. As they were number four in line they weren't sure that they would be loaded. When they came to the last box car, there were twenty-four Jews left. At first the SS soldiers were going to divide the twenty four remaining Jews into two groups as there were two more trucks behind our truck. Thinking quickly, our driver, Kurt, laughingly told the guards that it would be good for the twenty four Jews to be put into one truck and packed together like sardines, "After all, they smelled like dead fish, they would soon be dead fish so why not treat them like dead fish?" The soldiers at the train and the drivers of the other trucks laughed and agreed. They forced the twenty-four remaining Jews into our truck. Some had to lie on top of each other. The guard informed the other truck drivers waiting that they would not be needed. Kurt made sure that the two trucks that were waiting behind him were gone before he left. He did not want any of the trucks following close behind him to see them go to a different part of the city instead of going to Leopoldstadt. Before arriving at the garage, Kurt pulled off of the road in a deserted area at the outskirts of Vienna and had all of the people get out of the truck. At first they thought that they were going to be shot and they started to cry and protest. Wilhelm quickly calmed them down saying that they were SS soldiers bribed by the IKG to help them escape from Austria. He asked how many of the twenty-four people wanted to escape. As Wilhelm rightly surmised based on the previous run, some of them had family members that had been taken back to Vienna in other trucks. Only nine people, two families of three, one married couple and one single man, decided to take the chance and believe the guards. The ones that wanted to flee stayed at the place they stopped along with Franz. The fifteen people that wanted to go back to be with friends and family re-boarded the truck and were driven to the Vienna station after being sworn to secrecy. On the way, Kurt picked up the two people that wanted to go back. Whether they told anyone about their experience we did not know. We did know that the Nazis did not find out about it since there was never any investigation. After dropping off the people at the station without any trouble, the truck returned to the place where Franz and the nine others were waiting and took them to the garage.

The truck pulled into the garage at four PM. The nine people got off of the truck. A few had some minor injuries but overall, everyone was okay. We now told them where they were and that we planned to smuggle them to Switzerland. Again, the same reaction – tears of joy, prayers, thank you after thank you. We now had twenty seven people to smuggle into Switzerland.

We found out later that the luggage left outside of the train was just thrown back into the rail cars. When the engine was repaired the people were returned to the cars and randomly reloaded back into the box cars. While there was a discrepancy between the original count and the number of people re-boarding the train there was no time to investigate it. As such, the new count was used and none of the people that we removed were even missed.

Conditions in Vienna for Jews were now deplorable. Four of the people we rescued were sick but Wilhelm had medicine so they all recovered. We also fed them. For most of them it was the first real meal that they had in months. We made make-shift beds in the two vans and on the floor of the garage for the twenty seven weary rescued people who just went to sleep exhausted from their ordeal.

We decided to risk discovery and wait a few days for the people to regain their strength and for the medicine to take affect on those that were sick. We also needed the time to prepare the false papers and passes needed to get them out of the country. We did not have enough food to feed twenty-seven people for any extended period of time and we knew that buying large quantities of food was a signal to the informants that some Jews were being hidden so we did the next best thing. We took the SS truck out the next night with six of our people dressed in SS uniforms and "raided" one of the large food stores across town. We took the precaution of smearing mud on the license plate so the numbers could not be read. The men loaded the truck mainly with non-perishable food. They did take some fresh fruit, vegetables and chocolate. Jews were not allowed to buy these items. We know that some people saw them but no one called the police lest they get into trouble with the SS. The believed the SS was on a raid looking for Jews or contraband or both. This was not unusual. The truck returned to the warehouse around midnight without being stopped. We had enough food to feed all of the people for at least three weeks. The fresh fruit and vegetables were especially savored as was the chocolate by the children.

We decided to use trains and cars traveling during the day to get the twenty-seven people to Switzerland as soon as they were able to travel and their forged papers were prepared since they were not known to be missing. As I mentioned, one of the families was quite large – there were six children ranging in age from six to seventeen. Getting a family of eight out of Austria into Switzerland would be difficult. They did not want to be separated in two cars and the children could be difficult during the long car ride. We had to use the train. The father, Samuel Goldfarb, had been in the Austrian army so he had some military training and was still in good physical condition. Wilhelm came up with a great idea. Samuel Goldfarb would become a returning war hero on holiday with his family as a reward for his gallant service to the Fatherland after being wounded and decorated on the Russian Front. He would be going to Switzerland where his wife's grandparents lived. There was only one catch. He would have to be shot in case he was challenged. There was another issue. He also had the true stereotypical face and features of a Jew. He was lean (as most Jews now were in Vienna), had a big nose, bushy eyebrows and big ears. This increased his chances of being checked in more detail. He recognized this and agreed to be wounded in action. We took him into the bathroom, closed the door, started the two moving van motors to cover the sound, muffled the pistol with a towel and shot him twice in the arm carefully aiming so the bullets would pass through the arm and not require surgery to remove them. Wilhelm immediately treated him and put his arm in a sling.

For the next two days we held classes for all of the escapees teaching them their new identities. We really had to work on Samuel's children so if they were questioned they would say their new name and the other facts that were part of their cover story. They also had to refrain from speaking Yiddish at all costs. This had to be hammered into the minds of the children over and over again. Luckily, we had much more time with Samuel's children since we had to wait a couple of weeks for his wounds to heal.

On the fourth day we sent the healthiest group out. There were twelve people in the group: two families of three and three couples without children. The seven men and boys were taken aside and fitted with the penis extensions. The youngest boy was fifteen so we believed that there would not be any problems with this large group. They were amazed at the extensions. They all understood why it had to be done. The two families of three would travel by car. We stole two cars at 4 AM being careful to make sure that both cars had their registration documents in them which we revised with the new names and addresses of the escapees. At 6 AM we asked that the two families get in the cars and close their eyes as they were driven from the garage to the outskirts of the city. The two drivers gave the keys to the two fathers and got into one of our own cars that followed them. The closed eyes were a precaution so they would not know the location of the garage. The two families of three drove to the Swiss border where they were met with some of our people who facilitated their entry into Switzerland. The other three couples were driven to two different train stations also with their eyes initially closed. We watched as the train pulled out from each station. Each of the families had been given the names of people in the respective cities in Switzerland to contact that would help them. No family had the same contact name in Switzerland for security purposes. There were no problems.

We waited two days before sending out the next group to make sure that everyone arrived safely at their appointed destinations. All through the day we received the calls from our Swiss friends giving us the good news. Only one person was challenged at the station, Leon Fuchs, who was traveling under the name of Oswald Schäfer. He was traveling with his wife. They did not have any children. Someone thought that they recognized him and that he could be Jewish. It was not a positive ID. Two conductors approached him and asked for his papers which he handed to one of them. The conductors were straight forward. They told him that another passenger thought that he recognized him and that he could be a Jew. They pointed to the passenger. Sure enough, Leon recognized the passenger but was smart enough not to show it. He had waited on him a couple of times in the restaurant where he had worked before Jews were fired. Luckily, it was a restaurant owned by a Gentile which was why the person pointing him out was not sure. He only knew that Leon was no longer employed there after the Anschluss and thought that he had been told that Leon was fired because he was Jewish. Rather than answer questions Leon immediately raised his voice and complained bitterly at being even considered being Jewish. He was highly insulted at such a slur. In the middle of the platform he dropped his pants in front of men, women and children to reveal his Gentile penis and he challenged the accusing passenger to do the same. The conductors apologized profusely as he pulled up his pants. No one else was challenged that day. The others just showed their papers and went on through the border check points. At the border, one of the conductors told the border guards the story of Leon and how he dropped his pants at the station pointing him out in the line as they told the story. The guards laughed and stood up when Leon came through the check point. One of them said, "Finally, an Austrian with balls!"

When they arrived in Switzerland each of them told their Swiss hosts that they were extremely self-confident during the border questioning due to the false penis that they were wearing especially after seeing how Leon handled the situation. The old adage of "the best defense was an offense" truly applied here.

The next day we repeated the process with the remaining people exclusive of the Goldfarb family.

The Weinstein family, traveling as the Schmidt family, also had a close call. Unfortunately, Mr. Weinstein also looked Jewish. He was a bit fat with the large nose that is often caricaturized in German cartoons and hairy eyebrows. While he was able to board the train without incident, quite a number of people were staring at him and talking amongst themselves and even to strangers sitting next to them. This was clearly seen by Mr. Weinstein and his wife. While he tried to reassure her, she was getting increasingly nervous and fidgety. This added fuel to the fire as the other passengers noticed her nervousness. Finally, at one of the stations a couple of passengers got off and brought back two soldiers that were at the station. After telling the conductor to hold the train, they came over to the Weinsteins.

Gruffly, they demanded to see their papers, which appeared in order but each soldier carefully examined the facial features of Mr. Weinstein. They started to ask him some questions when Mr. Weinstein took the initiative, "I know, I know, I look Jewish! I am from Italy. Italians also have big noses." And without hesitating for an instant he took a newspaper, opened it and held it between his waist and the rest of the passengers, unzipped his pants and pulled out his penis which, of course, had the extension. He thrust his pelvis forward at the guards. The two soldiers were taken aback by this and they jumped back almost falling on the passengers seated across the aisle. Both guards and a couple of the passengers that had an unrestrained view looked at the uncircumcised penis, which was held out for about fifteen seconds before being re-inserted back into his pants. There was an awkward silence as the soldiers looked at each other and at the man that brought them on the train. He was clearly embarrassed as could be seen from his reddened face. After another fifteen or twenty seconds, Mr. Weinstein asked, "Would you like me to take out my son's penis as well?" The soldiers said absolutely not and apologized for their gruff action. They left and as the train got underway a few of the passengers also apologized. Mr. Weinstein accepted their apologies mentioning that this was not the first time that this had happened and that he was sure that as long as he lived in Germany it would be repeated. With that he raised his arm and loudly said, "Heil Hitler!" Everyone within earshot that had followed the proceedings stood up and responded. Even those that knew nothing about the incident, stood up and gave the salute which traveled down the entire length of the car. Mr. Weinstein and the passengers close to him watched this procession of salutes travel down the car and laughed when it was over. "Now, you have a story to tell when you are asked, 'So how was your trip?' when you arrive at your destination." They all agreed and started to laugh again. When one of the passengers also added that they had gotten suspicious because his wife looked so upset, Mr. Weinstein quickly came up with the appropriate response, "She just found out this morning that she is pregnant – and it was not a planned pregnancy. But I was telling her that it was a divine intervention for the Fatherland needs more children. Still, she said, that it was easy for me to say since I wasn't the one who would get sick in the morning." With that everyone laughed and a couple of the women passengers sitting near us couldn't agree more. For the next half-hour the conversation was dominated by one heavy woman that said that she had three children and that men had no idea what they asked of their wives. As she aptly put it, "Nine minutes of pleasure for him, nine months of discomfort for me!" And then she added, "Sometimes it is even much less than nine minutes, the inconsiderate oaf!" Her husband, who was half of her girth just sat sheepishly next to her as he turned away to look out the window after she made the last comment, as his face had reddened considerably from the embarrassment of his wife revealing some very intimate details of their personal life. Everyone else, including the Weinsteins, laughed at length from her comments and his reaction. For the rest of the trip, all of the passengers talked incessantly about a wide range of subjects. When they reached the Swiss border it was as if they were all one big happy family. When the two border guards saw their camaraderie as they walked down to check their papers, they asked if they were members of the same family. One of the passengers told the guards the entire story, including the remarks made by the heavy woman and her thin husband. The guards also laughed after staring the Mr. Weinstein's nose. They just gave a cursory glance at the Weinsteins' papers and passed the train through to Switzerland.

Now it was the Goldfarb's turn. We tested the three young children and they had learned their lessons well. We even dressed up as SS officers for the interrogation. They knew their new names and addresses by heart and said them without any hesitation. As an added precaution Wilhelm gave Samuel's wife a mild sedative to give to the children as soon as they boarded the train.

Samuel was dressed as a corporal replete with some medals that included the Iron Cross First Class for bravery and the medal for being wounded in action, the Russian Campaign Medal and the coveted Order of the Eagle. In the certificate that accompanied the Order of the Eagle, the citation read that, "...even after being wounded he stayed at his position directing artillery fire with deadly accuracy against the attacking Russian armored division from a forward observation post where they were vastly outnumbered. He manned a machine gun to cover the withdrawal of the other soldiers that were with him, one of whom was wounded. In the course of this covering action he was wounded for the second time. He was responsible for killing more than forty Russian soldiers and destroying more than fifteen Russian armored vehicles." This was actually a real occurrence that was reported in the newspapers. We gave him the clipping. His new name corresponded to the soldier in the article.

While they were learning their new identities, we took pictures of everyone and prepared the false identity cards and travel documents. At Mischa's suggestion, we also acquired one additional item – the silver Mother's Medal.

One of the unique programs set up by the Nazis was the "motherhood" program to increase the Aryan population. The First World War had taken its toll on the German population, particularly men. There were a large number of unmarried women as a result and population growth had suffered. Hitler wanted to increase the birth rate, particularly of stereotypical Aryan-looking men and women. The program consisted of two segments. The first was to encourage all married couples to have as many children as possible. If a couple had four or more children the mother would be awarded a certificate and a motherhood medal. The "Cross of Honor of the German Mother" medal was created personally by Hitler on December 16, 1938. The medal was inscribed, "The Child Ennobles the Mother" and had a ribbon so it was worn around the neck of the mother. There were three levels. Mothers bearing four or five children were awarded the bronze medal. Mothers with six or seven children were awarded the silver medal and mothers with eight or more children received the gold medal. The couple also received a cash award for each child starting with the fourth child. The second segment was more selective. Young men and women eighteen and older that were blond, had blue eyes and were in good physical condition were singled out and invited to resorts with the express purpose of meeting and mating. This was part of the preservation and perpetuation of the ideal German Aryan look. Thousands of young men and women were encouraged to have premarital sex at these all-expense-paid resorts. All expenses for the pregnancy and birth were taken care of by the government. The women were given "salaries" during their pregnancies until they returned to their regular jobs. The children became wards of the state and were raised in special homes. If the couple wanted to get married, the wedding was also paid for by the government. About one in twenty couples decided to get married. Essentially all of these were Catholic couples. No statistics were kept on the post-war divorce rate of these couples. Since Samuel and his wife had six children, she was eligible for the Silver Mother's Cross.

With his wounded arm and all of his medals plus the silver mother's medal the family was treated like royalty. Every soldier and officer stood up and saluted them. They were upgraded to first class on the train without any charge and not one soldier, police officer or conductor even asked to see their papers. Samuel just said he and his family were going to Geneva for a vacation to see his wife's grandparents after returning wounded from the Russian Front. He showed the article to anyone that asked about the medals. The passengers took turns bringing him, his wife and their children food and drinks which they collectively purchased. We all yelled in joy when we learned that the Goldfarbs had arrived safely in Switzerland.

As 1941 drew to a close, we celebrated the New Year and our successes. It was a good year for more than 150 Jews that were now out of Austria due to our efforts but with the Nazis more resolute than ever to rid Vienna of its Jews we made a resolution to redouble our work to help as many Jewish people escape to freedom as we possibly could.

CHAPTER TWENTY

A PIPE DREAM

"Jews were shipped to the East in batches of 1,000. If the lists did not bring in enough Jews in time for the train departures, SS trucks grabbed them off of the streets until the quota was met. Brutality was fierce..."

The Setting of the Pearl, Thomas Weyr, Oxford University Press, 2005

By January 1, 1942 almost 35,000 Jewish people had been deported first to ghettos and then to concentration camps of which Auschwitz received the majority. That left about 25,000 Jewish people still in Vienna. We could no longer use the single truck ruse to go into Leopoldstadt and make a false raid.

In March, there was an outbreak of cholera in one particular area of Leopoldstadt that had a very high concentration of Jews. Ordinarily, the Nazis would have left this untreated but there were still Gentiles living there and German soldiers had to go inside to round up and load the Jews into trucks they had to quell the epidemic. They cordoned off the area, set up some checkpoints and asked for some volunteer doctors to go into that section of Leopoldstadt to treat the sick and stem the epidemic. Wilhelm and the two other Jewish doctors in hiding in our group volunteered – they were the only volunteers. None of the Gentile doctors wanted to have anything to do with saving Jews from a Cholera epidemic which could endanger their own lives. When Wilhelm volunteered Col. Lange was commended for having selected Wilhelm to be the doctor at the Gestapo headquarters. Col Lange mentioned this to Wilhelm also adding his own personal commendation. They still went fishing occasionally but it was Col. Lange that had to make excuses for not going as much as Wilhelm wanted due to his job. He was now given responsibility for all SS activities in the Vienna Gau which had been expanded after Anschluss. He ordered everyone to fully cooperate with Wilhelm. As Col. Lange said at a special joint SS/army/police meeting to discuss the situation, "Dr. Wilhelm Roebling is acting on my behalf. In this operation he has my rank. You are to do anything he asks without question. We want to remedy this situation and quickly as possible so we can continue to follow the orders of the Fuehrer and make Vienna Judenfrei. Is this clearly understood?" The group stood up and yelled their agreement, faced Wilhelm, raised their right hands and yelled Heil Hitler. Wilhelm was clearly in charge.

The cholera epidemic stopped the deportations from the second district. Wilhelm said it was best to quarantine all of the Jews in the second district since they were all potential carriers of the disease. Non-Jews outside of the quarantine zone could go about their regular business since they were not carriers like "the filthy Jews". With Wilhelm in charge we had free access to the area where we could smuggle in much needed food and medical supplies. Wilhelm and the other two doctors were given an office and conference room in the SS headquarters with a secretary and an SS Sergeant to act as a liaison to the other military and police groups helping the doctors. Col. Lange had picked the perfect man for this job. Although only a sergeant, he was so committed to the SS and felt so highly of himself that he acted as if he were a general. Tall, muscular, blond, with large blue eyes, Sergeant Karl Röwe was the epitome of the Aryan man – and he knew it. Given a centimeter of authority he stretched it to a kilometer. He would interrupt staff meetings, politely order officers of higher rank to do what he needed and bark loudly at anyone with a lower rank. He had no regard for protocol and he always got the job asked of him done quickly, efficiently and correctly. Wilhelm noticed this and used his characteristics to the full advantage of the task at hand and his hidden agenda to provide substantial aid to the Jewish population.

Wilhelm requested that two ambulances be set aside for their dedicated use and that these ambulances also have a green cross painted on each side as well as on the front and on the back. He directed the sergeant to issue a directive that these ambulances were to be given free and unchecked access and priority to wherever they were going and wherever they stopped. All possible assistance was to be accorded the driver and the doctor if one was with the driver without question. The sergeant lived up to his reputation. By 3 PM the next day all of this had been done. That evening, Wilhelm wrote a letter to Col. Lange with copies the Adolf Eichmann, Col. Stryker and even Himmler, who was personally watching the Vienna situation extolling the performance of Sergeant Röwe. He, of course, sent a copy to the sergeant. The next morning Sergeant Röwe came to Wilhelm's office thanking him for the letter. It was one of the few times that Wilhelm actually saw the sergeant smile. At this point, Wilhelm knew that the sergeant "would take a bullet for him" (as the saying goes).

Under our direct written orders lists of food and medical supplies were prepared, given to Sergeant Röwe who gave them to the ambulance drivers. He also commandeered two trucks to help with the food supplies. The ambulances would carry the medical supplies. All of the materials were delivered to the Kultusgemeinde building where we set up another office for Wilhelm and the other doctors. Menachem was responsible for distributing the food and medical supplies to the neediest of the people. Without a doubt we saved many lives – at least for the moment.

With Jews having to wear the large yellow star and all of the other restrictions placed upon them, we could not think of any safe way to identify groups of Jews that were willing to escape. We let it be known at the IKG that we were looking for ways to find Jews that were willing to risk their lives and escape.

We were still able to pass information through a few of the Jewish people that had special jobs and were allowed out of their district during the day. Jacob Goldblatt, who was a very good civil engineer and was still working for the city water works. Due to his knowledge of the system, he was one of the privileged "useful Jews" in Vienna. He had an idea. He had mentioned it to one of the members of the Kultusgemeinde, Mendel, whom he trusted, who happened to be the same person with whom we were working. His name was given to us and we contacted him at the waterworks under the guise of enlisting his help to combat the cholera epidemic. Cholera was spread by water as well as by direct human contact. He explained his plan which had nothing to do with the cholera epidemic but the water-borne nature of the epidemic provided a great cover.

The basements of some of the apartment buildings were well below the waterline of the Danube River. He believed that a tunnel could be dug from the basement of one of the apartment buildings close to the river creating an underwater passage to the river that perhaps a few good swimmers could use to escape from Leopoldstadt. He had even identified some buildings with deep basements that also had short distances to the river and across to the other river bank. With the proper tools he would be able to dig the tunnel. He went over the plan in minute detail including how to reinforce the tunnel so it would not collapse during excavation and when the water rushed in and flooded the basement. There were some other issues. The most important one was that everyone in the building had to be Jewish and had to agree to have the tunnel and to help build the tunnel even if some were not going to escape. All of those opting for escape would have to be reasonably good underwater swimmers. The interesting part of his plan was that everything would be done underwater. The only time the person had to actually swim underwater was between the basement wall and the riverbank immediately outside the wall. The person would carry a metal tube with him and once outside the tunnel he would use it to breathe so the person would actually walk underwater across the river to the other side. It was at this point that the person needed help. Once the person reached the other side there had to be some mechanism to get them safely out of the water and to safety. The exit from the river had to be done in a manner where no one on the other side could see the person get out of the river and get to a safe place. Another issue was that every apartment building had a non-Jewish janitor that watched the building, monitoring everything brought into the building as well as everyone entering and leaving. It would be very difficult to get the construction materials past him and he would surely hear the construction. It was a crazy plan but it intrigued us. We told him to let us think about it.

We invited him to our next card game where his plan was the single topic of discussion. He reviewed his plan and drew a diagram of the building and the river. Jacob estimated that the distance from the building to the river was about seven meters. There was a concrete retaining wall that was about one-half meter thick. Between the retaining wall and the building's thin basement wall was loose dirt. The plan was to dig a tunnel big enough for someone to swim or almost walk through it, reinforcing it as it was being dug, break through the wall and would flood the tunnel and the basement. The selection of the building was critical. It had to be big enough that it had at least one large basement room that was not being used that could be flooded without flooding the room where boilers were located. The room with the tunnel had to be made watertight so the water would not leak into any other room. Once the basement was flooded a reasonably good swimmer could swim through the tunnel come up for air and use the tube to breath while walking underwater to the other side. As the river had a fairly strong current, he suggested installing a strong rope across the river that could be used as a guideline and provide stability to the person walking across the river. However, he had no idea what the person would do once they got across. The swimmer had to carry a waterproof bag with clothes, money, etc., get out of the river undetected, dry and dress quickly and get to a close place of safety. From there the person would have to be transported out of the city and smuggled to a safe country. The more he thought about it the crazier he thought it was and had just about decided to abandon the idea when he decided to mention it to Mendel. He had an answer to every question we had. For example, Friedrich asked him how people would enter the room since it would be flooded and the door would be sealed. The answer was simple. A large hole would be made in the apartment directly above the flooded room. A hinged trap door would be built that would be hidden under a wall-to-wall carpet. A ladder or stairs would be built from the trap door to floor of the basement so people could climb down once the basement was flooded. That meant that the people living in that apartment had to agree to it but Jacob felt that this would not be a problem since everyone in the apartment building would have to agree to the plan anyway before anything was done. He estimated that the water level would be about three meters which still left about one to two meters of free space between the water and the ceiling of the room so there would not be any danger of the apartment flooding.

We spent the entire evening discussing various options. It was truly a unique idea. We asked why the tunnel had to be so big and how could it be reinforced to prevent collapsing. He felt that it would be very difficult to find good swimmers that could swim through a narrow tunnel. Moreover, in his plan, it was actually easier to reinforce a large tunnel rather than a small tunnel. The answer was doors. He would create a four-door section, two meters by two meters with one door as the floor, one door as the ceiling and two doors on each side. What we liked about him was that as soon as we suggested any change to his plan he would pause and think about it for a few minutes and come back with an answer either positive or negative but, if it was negative, he would propose an acceptable alternative. When we asked him where he would get all of the doors, he said that every apartment had closet doors. They were readily available so there was no need to build anything and they were uniform in width and length. We were also very much concerned whether the people who could not or did not want to take advantage of this opportunity that were living in the building. Would they risk their lives and spend the time to dig a tunnel so only a few people that lived there and some that didn't even live there could escape? It was one of the most frustrating evenings that we ever had. When we finally broke up we decided that we would implement the plan if we could figure out how to get the escapees out at the other side without being seen by anyone on the other side. We decided to purchase a small delivery truck with a canvas cover and an open back that would easily hold eight people and their belongings.

The next day Wilhelm told Jacob that we decided to do it. Jacob just sat there in disbelief as Wilhelm explained that they thought it was worth trying and that they believed they could solve the problem of getting the escapees out of the river and even out of Austria safely. We told him, without going into detail, that we could accommodate eight people at a time once or twice a week without going into any more detail and what would happen to the people after they crossed and why we restricted it to eight people at a time.

The plan basically consisted of the following steps:

- Select a building based on the recommendation of Jacob and checking the residents with the IKG.

- Enlist the support of the people living in the building by offering them the first opportunity to escape. Those electing not to escape would get food, money and would share the possessions of those leaving.

- Smuggle tools into the building.

- Build the tunnel using the doors in the apartments in the building to shore up the tunnel (bedroom doors, closet doors, etc.)

- Break through and flood the basement.

- Set up a training program for good swimmers.

- Tie a guideline from the underwater tunnel to the other side.

- Take the copper tubing from the plumbing in the apartment or from other sources and use it to breath while walking to the other side once the person left the tunnel.

- Create some sort of diversion to distract any people on the opposite side.

- Meet the escapees on the other side and get them to a secure location.

Simple! Wilhelm and Jacob walked around the island as Jacob showed him the possible buildings he had identified. He also selected these buildings because there were some trees and bushes close to the riverbank on the other that could provide some cover for the emerging swimmers. Wilhelm passed the information on to me. I contacted Dr. Nussbaum and he went to the IKG to get their recommendation. They selected two of the buildings that Jacob had identified where all of the tenants were Jewish. Jacob and Mendel went to the building of first choice and asked to meet with the heads of the families of the people living there that were given to us the IKG as being very trustworthy. It was a four story building with six apartments per floor. There were nineteen families living in the building with the rest being single men and women. He asked them if they wanted to risk an escape without giving any details. At first they thought it was a joke but when Mendel explained that there was a secret Swiss network helping Jewish people escape and get to Switzerland they quickly and unanimously agreed. After seeing their interest, he asked if they trusted everyone living there before proceeding any further. They thought again for a few minutes talking amongst themselves, taking a person-by-person inventory of the building. The building was 100 percent Jewish except for the janitor who was the assigned Jew-watcher for the building. He hated the fact that he was the only Gentile living in the building. His friends ridiculed him all the time asking him if he was going to turn into a Jew one night. "You know," someone would say, "that these Jews have strange powers. While you sleep they will get into your head and make you dream that being Jewish is good and when you wake up you will beg them to find someone to circumcise your penis." Or they would say when they were at the bar, "Hermann, could you pass the matzoh? Oh! Sorry, I meant pass the pretzels." As a result, he increasingly hated the Jews, refusing to fix anything that broke and, in some cases breaking things that worked well if it inconvenienced them. He would use his passkey when he knew an apartment was vacant and tamper with the plumbing so there were leaks – not big enough to cause flooding but enough to make the floor and surrounding areas wet. Sometimes he would insert something into the pipe to substantially reduce the flow of water into the bathroom. It was so bad that hardly anyone ever left their apartments unattended. Many of the apartments already had two or more families sharing the apartment so they would assign someone to be there all of the time. Those that were still lucky enough to live alone would have a neighbor watch the apartment when they were out. One time one neighbor hid in the closet and waited for the janitor to take apart the bathroom water pipe before emerging from the closet and loudly confronting the janitor who had to re-assemble the pipes under the careful watch of the neighbor after making up some lame excuse as to what he was doing there.

Jacob emphasized the need for secrecy and asked again if there were any people living there that were suspect. The nineteen men there looked at each other and thought for about another 30 seconds and collectively said that they trusted everyone living there. Jacob explained the plan in more detail including that the escapees would be met on the other side, be given false papers and smuggled to Switzerland.

He explained that they would dig a large tunnel to the river from the basement. This would flood part of the basement and provide an underwater passage from the apartment house to the river. A key point was that the tunnel had to be big enough for someone to be able to easily pass through almost erect since he would be underwater carrying their valuables and a long pipe. He explained that once the basement was flooded the only way to enter the room would be from an apartment directly above which would have a large hole cut in the floor with a ladder or stairs going down into the flooded room. The people who wanted to escape would be trained to walk and swim underwater and use the tubing to breathe so they could safely walk underwater to the other side where they would be met by the Swiss people.

Once everything was explained to the men it was their task to canvas all of the other tenants to get their agreement and to determine how many wanted to escape. After the initial approval they had group meetings with all of the tenants on the floor. Less than half of the people said that they would want escape in this manner but they all agreed to help. The extra money, food and the sharing of the possessions of those that left definitely helped. They even agreed to let people from other buildings escape once the ones from their building that wanted to escape had escaped. They also agreed that small children not be told anything as they could innocently say something to other children or adults in other buildings, or anyone else for that matter. This was important. The Nazis and the Jew-watchers would often approach small children giving them candy or bread with jam and ask them about what was going on with their families or in the building in which they lived. Once the family escaped they would be listed as having been deported so they would not be missed.

The timing could not have been better. With the cholera epidemic we had unrestricted access to the district which could be used to smuggle in the construction material. We used one of the ambulances to smuggle the tools and other materials into the building. The guards at the checkpoint didn't check the ambulances on the way in and certainly didn't check the ambulance on the way out since it was presumably bringing dead cholera victims out. The people in the house were able to dig the tunnel in seven days under the strict supervision of Jacob.

The Jew watcher in the building was Hermann Schulz. He lived alone in his apartment which was adjacent to the main entrance into the building. Nobody could go in or out without passing him when he was home. He stayed in his apartment most of the day and locked the building at night so anyone coming in or going out had to get him to open the door. He greatly appreciated the curfew on Jews since that meant they all had to be in their apartments by 8 PM. We needed to get him to leave the building during the construction period and preferably stay out until late at night. We came up with a rather unique plan. We decided to hire him. The plan was simple. We created a special job for him. We dressed one of our men, Fritz, in an SS officer's uniform and knocked on the door of his apartment during the day. Hermann asked if he was there to take Jews but when the SS officer said no, he immediately cowered. He had taken many packages addressed to Jews and kept them instead of handing them over to the authorities. Fritz noticed his reaction and calmly said, "Relax, it could be worse. I could have been from the Gestapo." For some reason Hermann did not see the humor in the joke so he just stood there staring more at the uniform than at Fritz. Fritz continued. "I am here for a good thing. We have been watching you and reading your reports. They are very good." Fritz asked him if he would be willing to work on a special project for the next ten days or so. He was to pretend to be a construction worker across the street from a formerly Jewish-owned department store in the fifth district and watch for suspicious activity. He would get paid 75 Marks per day. As soon as Fritz finished, Hermann said yes immediately. He could make more in one day than he did in one week as the janitor. Moreover, we would have someone take over his Jew-watching responsibility at the apartment so he would still get his Janitor's pay – and get to keep the packages as well.

Hermann reported to the construction site and was told that he was one of four people being enlisted for this project. The other three were from our group. Each day for the next ten days Hermann left his apartment at 7 AM and did not return until 9 or 10 PM. The shift actually ended at 6 PM but each night one of the three would invite the others out to a bar for some drinks which we knew Hermann would not refuse. Even when he offered to pay we insisted that he did not. After a boring day at work, since nothing really happened at the site and some drinks, Hermann would fall into a deep sleep as soon as he got home. Twice we had to wake him up in the morning to go to the department store. We made sure that one of us picked him up to take him to the department store each morning just in case something like this happened. We wanted to make sure that he was out of the apartment building each day. Each day the group would make a list of all of the people shopping there that looked suspicious, particularly anyone being dropped off or being picked up by a car. They took down the license plate number using binoculars which they gave to Hermann. He liked this aspect of the job. To make it more interesting we had one or two cars go to the store two or three times a week. Their license plate numbers were duly noted by Hermann as he saw a pattern clearly emerging which he duly noted in the daily report.

As soon as Hermann left the apartment building, work on the tunnel would begin. As one team worked on the tunnel another team removed the closet doors from the apartments of those wanting to escape and others that volunteered to give up their doors for such a worthy cause. The first to go were the closet doors. There were 24 apartments in the building. Each apartment had two closets so there were 48 doors. A section consisted of four doors forming a square. One door was used for the floor, one for the ceiling and two doors for the walls, one on each side. We were able to get some metal L-shaped braces so we were able to attach the wall and floor doors very firmly to the wall doors. Another group was responsible for waterproofing the room so no water leaked out when the room was flooded.

The construction was an engineering mini-marvel. Jacob had devised an interesting process. A door was laid down on the ground and two doors were nailed vertically to the top and bottom edges of the door. Another door was nailed across the two vertical doors at the top creating the four-door section. The L-shaped braces were nailed at the juncture of each door to reinforce the structure. As the tunnel was being excavated, the pre-fabricated section was pushed into the tunnel, centimeter by centimeter. This effectively prevented any cave-ins during digging. It took considerable effort to push the sections into the excavation. It would have been comical were it not so frustrating to have people lined up one behind the other pushing with all of their strength to slide the sections into the tunnel. While this was indeed frustrating and far from being comical (at least to those pushing), the procession of doors being brought down to the basement was truly comical. Four people brought each door down to the basement negotiating the narrow stairs with its sharp curves. Luckily, there were no accidents although there were a number of close calls when one of the people in the front missed a stair or lost their equilibrium as they made one of the sharp turns. It was also difficult to explain to the children why, all of a sudden, the closet doors disappeared. We decided to say that they were being repaired which seemed to satisfy them.

When they reached the thick cement retaining wall, they knew that they had reached the river. There was a gap of about eight inches between the fabricated door sections and the river retaining wall. This was filled this in with some cement which was also applied to all of the spaces between the doors. A few bags of cement had been brought in for this purpose. The cement was allowed to set overnight.

To prevent the water in the basement from leaking into the rest of the cellar, the room had to be waterproofed. There was only one door to the rest of the basement. First, some putty was jammed into the lock so it could not be opened which also sealed the lock. Then the entire door was caulked around the edges from the inside. Plaster was applied over the caulk as an added precaution. The tenant in the room directly above the basement room agreed to have the trap door. A ladder was attached to the ceiling of the room and a square trap door, which opened upwards into the apartment, was cut out. A wall-to-wall carpet was used to cover the trap door. It was obviously much more cumbersome to have to roll it up every time we had to enter the basement but a throw rug was too easily moved in case the room was searched by the janitor.

The following night everyone evacuated the basement except for Jacob and two men who were very good swimmers. As an added precaution a rope was tied around their waists. The wall was about one-half meter thick. Jacob drew lines up and down the wall and around the perimeter. These lines were about 40 centimeters apart and formed a grid. The purpose was to break the wall into smaller sections that could be taken away once they broke through. They chipped away all around the perimeter and in through the grid in until there was less than 30 centimeters of the wall thickness left. This took two more days. They broke the wall starting from the bottom using two large sledge hammers and some wedge-shaped spikes. The depth of the tunnel minimized the noise in the street. In less than an hour they broke through at the bottom and the water started to rush in around their legs. They broke down the rest of the wall as quickly as possible as more and more water rushed in and started to fill the basement. They could hardly stand due to the current that the water created churning by them. Suddenly, the entire wall gave way. Jacob and the two men were swept into the basement by the shear force of the water. Being good swimmers, they made it safely up the ladder aided by the other men pulling them by the rope around their waists. After resting for a few minutes, they swam back underwater and took the remaining pieces of the wall out of the tunnel and the sledge hammers piling them in one corner of the basement. This was to ensure that the tunnel was clear so no one would trip on the wall fragments. The basement filled with water in less than an hour. The waterline was about two meters below the first floor room just as Jacob calculated.

While the tunnel was being dug, we used our resources to get about thirty pieces of copper tubing. Copper was the preferred metal since lead pipes were much heavier. The pipe had to be at least two meters long corresponding to the depth of the river at its deepest point at that location.

Once the tunnel was completed and the basement was flooded it was time to install the guide rope across the river to stabilize the underwater walkers and lead them to other side at the precise spot where they would be retrieved. We enlisted the aid of the son of one of our group leaders who was a very good swimmer but more important, he could hold his breath for a longer time than most which made him ideal for this particular task. He was driven to the spot across from the building that had the best cover during another heavy rainstorm at 2 AM. As expected there was no one around. He was wearing his swimsuit under his clothes. He took off his clothes in the car and proceeded to the river bank with a small bag tied around his waist and jumped into the river. Inside the bag was everything that he needed to do the job. Using a hand operated drill with a bit especially designed to bore through wet concrete he drilled a small-bore hole about a meter below the waterline and inserted a large construction screw with an eyelet at the end. It was difficult to screw the eyelet into the concrete. Every minute or so he came up for air and went back underwater to screw in the eyelet. After about 90 minutes it was securely positioned in the wall. He packed it with special putty that would cure underwater as an added precaution. A rope was tied to the eyelet. He swam to the building with the rope. One of our non-Jewish helpers stood on the opposite bank in front of the building. Seeing our man, he swam underwater and found the tunnel. He easily swam through. The rope was attached to another eyelet at the entrance to the tunnel in the basement. The rope was far enough below the water line so it could not be seen from the surface and would not be cut by any passing boat. After completing the task, he came back to the car, dried off and got dressed. He arrived back home at 5 AM.

It was decided that the order for the people that wanted to escape would be by a lottery after they passed the swimming tests. The test was not that easy. The person had to swim from the ladder to the tunnel entrance holding the tubing and wearing a backpack with their valuables in it. When they reached the tunnel entrance they had to swim underwater back to the ladder. When they reached the ladder they had to stick their head above water with a minimum of splashing to get some air and, at the same time blow out all of the water in the tubing. Once the water was blown out of the tubing they had to re-submerge and walk around the perimeter of the basement breathing through the copper tubing before emerging again back at the ladder. The perimeter of the basement exceeded the distance between the retaining wall and the other bank of the river so if they could do that they were likely to succeed in crossing the river. This took a lot of practice but surprisingly almost one-half of the people passed the test within two days. A test run was set up at 8PM with the same boy that had attached the eyelet to the opposite wall. He entered the tunnel, stuck his head out of the water when he exited the tunnel, blew out the water from the tubing, re-submerged and walked across the bottom of the river using the guide rope. When he reached the other side, he re-submerged and returned to the basement. The process worked! Cheers resounded through the building.

Eight people were selected by lottery. Once selected, the person had the opportunity to go immediately or to wait until his entire family was selected. He was placed on the standby list and another person was chosen. In this manner families could leave together as soon as they all won the lottery. One person would leave every ten minutes to give the person ahead of them time to clear the tunnel and start walking across the river where the person would be met by our people. They were told to be very careful to not make any splashing noise that could alert anyone passing by at the time even though we planned to create a diversion. They would be met on the other side by one of our people. We also gave them an address about fifty meters from the river where they would wait to be picked up in case they strayed from the point where our team member was waiting or if the person had to leave the riverbank for any reason. In this case they were to get dressed as soon as possible after getting out of the water.

We chose Wednesday, April 16th at 2 AM for the first escape. This day was not selected for any particular reason it just happened to be the first day where they had finally selected the first eight qualified people to escape.

The eight people went to the apartment of Yosef Balinsky whose apartment had the trap door to the basement. They arrived at 9 PM and tried to get some sleep – but no one did. At 1:15 AM the trap door was opened. They had their valuables in the waterproof back pack and slung the bag over their shoulders once they went through the trap door..

As a signal when they were ready we agreed that a flashlight would be flashed twice from roof of the building. We would signal back using a flashlight once the diversion was set up. Precisely at 2 AM one of the tenants went to the roof and flashed the light twice.

For the diversion, we set a parked car on fire about 700 meters from the escape route with some extra gasoline in it. The car exploded and two of the cars adjacent to it caught fire. This worked well as all eyes were focused on the burning cars. Dogs in the apartments near the cars went wild barking loudly and continuously at the burning vehicles.

One by one they lined up. The first to leave was an ex-college student, Aaron Kimmelman. He swam to the tunnel entrance, turned and smiled at the others before diving underwater. He easily swam through the tunnel. He quickly stuck his head out of the water and paused for a second watch the burning cars. He took some deep breaths, blew out the water from the tube and walked to the other side of the river holding on the taut rope. He reached the other side where Klaus was waiting for him. As soon as the fire started, Klaus walked across the road to the river bank. The area was becoming very crowded as people ran to see the fire. No one noticed him kneel down and sit on the riverbank. He waited for the first escapee. He did not have to wait long. Aaron emerged from the water in about five minutes. Klaus helped him quickly get out of the water and gave him the towel that he had brought with him. Aaron dried himself quickly to the extent possible. Still partly wet, he dressed and walked across the street where he was met by Helmut who led him to the truck and returned to wait for the next one. We flashed a signal that the first swimmer was out of the water.

The second escapee was Moishe Apfelbaum. He made it across without incident. He was followed by his wife. The remaining five came across without incident. In about ninety-five minutes the eight people had traversed the river and successfully emerged into the waiting arms of our team members. No one had strayed due to the guide rope.

The fire lasted another ninety minutes before being extinguished by the fire company. This turned out to be a problem. The streets were so congested that it was impossible for our truck to get to the safe house that evening. We decided to wait until the morning. All of the escapees slept in the truck. They were exhausted. At 7 AM the truck pulled out of the alley. Some empty boxes were in the back of the truck so the people could not be seen by anyone looking into the truck.

It took about thirty minutes to get to the garage where the people got out as we started to make the arrangements for them to be smuggled out of the country. We gave them two days to rest and regain their strength. On Friday we hid them in the clothing van compartment and transported them to Bern without incident.

On Sunday, April 20th we had the second run. We chose this date for a very specific reason – it was Adolf Hitler's birthday. As a diversion, we held a party at one of the bars that lined the street across from the building. We started at around 9 PM. Wilhelm invited some SS and army officers that he knew that were available that Sunday to celebrate the Fuehrer's birthday party along with some other friends. There were at least 20 SS and army men there. He kept this as an all-male celebration so he could bring in a couple of strippers. The alcohol flowed freely. Of course, he constantly offered toasts to the Fuehrer's health which no respectful Nazi would refuse. Whenever a policeman on patrol passed by they would be invited to join the celebration. Not one refused. After all, it was the Fuehrer's birthday

We decided to schedule the escape at 10 PM which was much earlier than the previous escape but if we waited too long the party may have broken up before the escape. So, at 10 PM Wilhelm instigated a fight between one of the army officers and one of the SS officers. As I mentioned, there was always animosity between the two groups with the army resenting the "holier than thou" superior attitude of the SS. This quickly became a large brawl spilling out into the street and requiring the assistance of the local and the military police. The fight lasted more than thirty minutes before the regular and military police arrived. Most of the brawlers, those that were not either too drunk or injured, either fled the scene or returned to their patrolling, well away from the brawl. When the authorities arrived, it took another hour to restore order and take care of the drunken and injured soldiers. As soon as the brawl started the exodus began. Now, with much more confidence, the people crossed the river in less than six minutes each. The entire operation took seventy-three minutes.

The cholera epidemic was in its third week and was being effectively contained and remedied. New cases dropped to only one per day and were expected to decline to zero by the following week. This is exactly what happened. The next week there were no new cholera cases.

We were basking in glory and congratulating ourselves on our second successful run. Our elation was short-lived. Unfortunately for us, with the cholera epidemic successfully resolved the Nazis managed to get a few extra boxcars through the direct intervention of Himmler. The Nazis were now going to resume deporting scores of people on Saturday, the day after the Friday escape. Unfortunately, Mischa did not find out about this in advance. That Saturday evening about 10PM, eight SS trucks entered Leopoldstadt. Four of these went to the west side of the district and four of them stopped across the street from the apartment house with the tunnel. They shot two people that did not move fast enough as a warning to the others. They emptied out two buildings in less than thirty minutes beating up anyone that offered the least bit of resistance. Sometimes the soldiers would bang on the doors of the adjacent buildings and when the people got out the soldiers just laughed. Some yelled that this was good training for them so they could be more efficient next time when it was really their turn.

As the building across the street was being emptied, the people in the building with the tunnel panicked. Were they next? Would there be another raid this night? Sometimes the Nazis came back the same night since they were short of trucks they had to use them twice per night. Would they come tomorrow? They all knew that about 1,000 Jews were typically deported each time. Did the Nazis reach this goal yet? They knew that the next escape would not occur until the following Tuesday. There was a sudden urgency to escape among those that were left in the apartment building before the Nazis could return and take them. They were no longer behaving in a rationale manner as more than thirty- five people ran downstairs into Yosef's apartment, shoving him aside when he tried to restrain them, drawing back the rug taking the copper tubing that was stockpiled in his apartment and proceeding underwater, through the tunnel and starting to cross the river. When there was no more tubing some of the people decided to do it without any tubing. They were desperate. Some had never swum underwater before. Only eighteen of them had taken and passed the test so at least they knew what to do while the others knew the procedure but had not trained for it. They dove into the water and one after another swam to the other side and dove down to swim through the tunnel. Some didn't even make it through the tunnel, drowning midway in their panic which sped up their heartbeats and increased their breathing rate. They blocked the tunnel making it even more difficult for those that followed. Those that made it through the tunnel walked into each other; some tripped and dropped their pipe. Many that had the pipe had not practiced using it so they misjudged the height to the surface and the end of the tube went below the surface after they cleared the tunnel. They wound up breathing water instead of air. They had to swim to the surface splashing and yelling in panic as they coughed and gasped for air. Some were too afraid of drowning to go back underwater so they threw their tubes away and started to swim to the other side of the river. They made a lot of noise. The swimmers were immediately heard by passers-by. They pointed at the people in the river screaming at them which alerted just about everyone. The police on patrol immediately called for reinforcements. A detachment of SS that were on the way to another raid was diverted to the scene of the turmoil. Residents and Jews from adjacent buildings were now looking out of their windows to see what was happening. The SS immediately brought in special trucks with floodlights mounted on them. These trucks were stationed throughout the city in case there were air raids. The floodlights were lit and were trained on the river as the SS fired their rifles and submachine guns at the swimmers. They were all killed. With the floodlights focused on the area the tubes from those still underwater walking to them could be seen. The SS fired at the tubes destroying the tips forcing the swimmers to come up for air. They were cut down as soon as their heads emerged from the water. Anyone that made it to the other side was also shot as soon as they stuck their head above water. Those that decided to walk down the river to a safer spot from which to emerge were easily spotted by the tubes sticking out of the water so the SS also shot their tubes forcing them to come up for air. They were also shot as soon as their heads emerged from the water. About three people started back to the building as they saw the bullets trace fine lines in the water or saw the blood from the dead people already shot. They knew that if they showed their heads they would be killed so they slowly turned around and went back to the building. By now the police and the soldiers realized that the swimmers were coming from a building across the river and dispatched two squads of soldiers to the area to locate the specific apartment building. They saw two pipes move toward the building and suddenly disappear below the surface. They quickly realized which building they were returning to which was obviously their starting point. They trained the floodlights on the building. The soldiers on the other side ran to the entrance of the building and burst into the front door. They ran down to the basement but found nothing. It was dry. They approached the room that had been flooded but the door could not be opened as it had been sealed to prevent any leaks. They tried to kick the door open but could not so they took a fire axe and attacked the door at the hinges. After five or six shots the door burst open as the weight of the water broke the door into pieces flooding the rest of the basement carrying the soldiers with it. Three soldiers almost drowned in the flood. Two were injured as they were smashed against the walls. One was killed as he broke his neck on the opposite wall.

More soldiers were pouring into the building. They burst into all of the apartments on the first floor. They burst into Yosef's apartment just as another person was coming out of the trap door. Two others had just come through the trap door and were still dripping wet. They were killed on the spot as were the few people still in the apartment, including Yosef. That night everyone still in the building was herded outside and deported. The building was thoroughly searched the next day. Seven people in hiding were discovered and shot. Their bodies were dumped out of the window and lay in the street until a truck arrived to take them to some unknown place. They were not brought to the morgue.

The next morning, we heard the news about the incident from a messenger from the IKG. The eight escapees that were still in the garage broke down and cried when we told them about it. We decided to smuggle them out immediately that morning in the back of the one remaining van. While they were still crying we abruptly ordered them into the van, closed the door and loaded it with clothing on racks which we had purchased from various stores around the city a couple of months ago. At 11 AM the van left the city and went to our safe house in Baden just outside of Vienna until we could arrange to get them out of Austria. This was a wise decision. The SS headquarters was notified that morning. They came to the house with the tunnel and the flooded basement to see where everything had happened. As the SS did not know how many Jews were successful in getting away before this event, they clamped down on security. At noon they mandated the every vehicle leaving the city was to be thoroughly searched, especially trucks. Random truck searches were instituted throughout the city. Many had to be unloaded to make sure that Jews were not being hidden inside. After dropping them in Baden, the driver switched the bill of lading showing that a partial shipment of clothing was being sent from Innsbruck to Vienna. The van returned to Vienna from a different route but was not even questioned. All attention was focused on vehicles leaving the city not those entering the city.

The bodies from the building where the attempted escape occurred were taken directly out of the city to some mass grave. During those three days, all of the houses at the river's edge were systematically searched. Even though nothing was found in any other building at the river's edge, these buildings were among the first to have the residents deported. The tunnel in the house where the escape had occurred was sealed at the exit. The water was pumped out or the basement and some more bodies were found.

We waited two more weeks before transporting the eight people to Switzerland. During this period we prepared false documents for them. To be safe the three cars we used only made short trips to the next city where we had a safe house and then to the next. Finally, after five days, they reached the border. By then security was back to normal and they were able to get into Switzerland without a problem.

Between truck and box car shortages and the piston ring failures, deportations of Jews had slowed to around 1,500 per month. This was well behind schedule. Adolf Eichmann, who was now in Prague, personally interceded from his headquarters there but there was little more that he could do to supplement the shortage of boxcars and the mechanical problems of the locomotives. Trucks were even scarcer now so they could not be used to transport Jews directly to the ghettos. The one thing that he did notice after looking at the maintenance records was that all of the breakdowns were caused by defective piston rings. He ordered a complete replacement of every piston ring on every locomotive and every spare in stock. The head of the railroad administration took no chances. He sent for all of the spare piston rings from Munich, Stuttgart and other large cities in Germany that did not have any history of piston ring failure. As soon as they arrived, every piston ring on the engines was replaced and all of the existing spare piston rings in inventory were discarded. This, unfortunately, ended the piston ring failures. Deportations increased to about 2,800 per month after that. Due to Hitler's rage at still having Jews in Vienna he diverted some trains to Vienna even at the expense of the war effort. Making Vienna "Judenfrei" was his highest priority. At this rate they calculated that Vienna would be devoid of Jews by October. This narrowed our window of opportunity.

We continued our card games where we brainstormed possible escape plans. Wilhelm reiterated that at least we saved sixteen people. We had learned a valuable lesson. We could not trust a large group to remain calm during any situation that was life-threatening. He also mentioned that we would not have been able to set this up were it not for the cholera outbreak that stopped the deportations. Then it dawned on him. If there appeared to be another outbreak of a communicable disease perhaps more people could be freed. Wilhelm had chosen his words carefully by saying "appeared to be sick" and not really sick. Obviously, he wasn't thinking of actually infecting people with any serious disease – it just had to appear that way. He also remembered the way in which to do it. While he was in medical school his roommate was not prepared for a final exam so he ate some soap. He got very sick with vomiting, diarrhea, and a slight fever. He went to the school nurse who immediately called for an ambulance. At the hospital they pumped his stomach and gave him some injections to stop the vomiting and the diarrhea. He was excused from the exam until the following Monday. He crammed over the weekend and managed to pass.

We called Mischa the next day to see if he could find out where the Nazis were going to hit during the next week. He was able to get us the exact address of two target buildings and the time, 10:30 PM. Wilhelm sent word to the IKG who in turn sent word to the target buildings. The healthiest adults in the target buildings were to eat some soap at 8 PM. Based on the recommendation of the IKG we selected one of the buildings. Their selection was based on the number of people that they believed would be willing to escape. About thirty people in the building volunteered to eat soap which we told them would delay the deportations. True to form, exactly at 10:30 PM the Nazis came with their trucks and pulled up to the building. They burst through the ground floor doors and ran up the stairs yelling "Juden Raus! Juden Raus!" Most of the people opened the doors and said they were sick. At first the Nazis did not believe them but as they forced them out of bed they started throwing up and making in their pants with white foam coming out of their mouths. They really looked horrible. The sheer number of people afflicted caused the Nazis to run out of the building. Clearly there was some sort of plague that they did not want to contract. They left the area and called the SS headquarters who in turn called Wilhelm at home since they were aware of his role with the cholera epidemic. He immediately got dressed and went outside to wait for the car that would take him to the building. It arrived about fifteen minutes later and took him to the area. Fearful of contracting this new, unknown disease, the driver asked Wilhelm if he could park one block away from the building. Wilhelm, of course, said yes. The soldiers that were waiting for him also asked if they could remain with the parked car to which Wilhelm also agreed. They all thanked him profusely, adding that they hoped that Wilhelm would not tell anyone at the headquarters that they asked not to accompany him. Wilhelm told them that their secret was safe with him. He would not say anything to anyone.

Wilhelm walked to the buildings and once inside he treated the sick people giving them shots or oral emetic medicines to counteract the effects of eating the soap. After doing this he went back to the soldiers and reported that the people in the building had some type of disease that had he could not readily identify and that the only way to be sure was to have autopsies performed on the bodies. Some were already dead and he had to remove the bodies for immediate cremation and instructed the soldiers to contact only me at the morgue to avoid a city-wide panic. Secrecy was of the utmost importance. Wilhelm took a quick survey on how many wanted to try to escape from Austria that night. Here again, most of the tenants did not for all of the aforementioned reasons. Only twelve people agreed to leave. He sedated them. The rest were sworn to secrecy. I had Kurt and Rolf with me at the morgue waiting for the call. We put on protective clothing and drove two ambulances to the apartment buildings and collected the dead bodies loading two or three at a time on a gurney and throwing them into the ambulance. When they were loaded we took them to the morgue. No police or soldiers wanted to inspect the bodies in the ambulances as we had expected. Watching us load them into the ambulances with the protective clothing was more than enough proof for them. Wilhelm gave orders that no one was to enter the building which was greatly appreciated by the soldiers. He rode in the ambulance with me to the morgue. Wilhelm and I took the "dead" bodies out of the ambulance and down to the basement where he revived them. We smuggled them out of the morgue to a safe house that evening when they regained consciousness. Wilhelm went to the hospital and took out some medicines that could be used by the IKG for the many sick Jewish people that were denied these medicines. He returned to the building and "inoculated" all of the "sick people" telling the SS that they should wait a couple of days before resuming any deportations and that thy should not enter the buildings. They agreed instantaneously.

I filled out the death certificates confirming that it was a rare form of typhus and ordered the immediate cremation of the bodies at one of the local cemeteries. We had many unclaimed bodies of indigent and Jewish people that were due to be sent out for burial in unmarked graves in the section of a field set aside for this. Instead, I took those bodies to the crematorium and had them cremated as if they were the typhus victims. I collected their ashes and put them all together in one urn.

Wilhelm returned to his office at around 3 PM. He had a surprise visitor waiting for him in his office. He had been waiting for him for forty-five minutes. Wilhelm walked into his office. The SS officer rose and introduced himself, "I am Adolf Eichmann."

Wilhelm was shocked. He didn't know what to say but Eichmann did not give him much time. He said that he had heard that Wilhelm had gone into the disease-infested area and stopped a major cholera epidemic from spreading which would have really upset the deportation schedule and that he did this again with the recent disease. Eichmann asked how long before he could resume deporting Jews. Wilhelm told him that to play it safe so none of the SS soldiers got sick that he should wait at least ten days which was three more than the incubation period for the disease. He reluctantly agreed and gave orders that the deportations should stop until Wilhelm gave the clearance. However, he ordered that anyone that showed symptoms of the disease be executed immediately and their bodies, along with any that died from the disease on their own, be cremated as soon as they died or were executed. He asked to be driven to the morgue with Wilhelm but that no call was to be made letting the morgue know that he was coming. He often did that recognizing that the element of surprise always caught the person he was visiting off guard and gave him the equivalent of a home court advantage away from home.

They left for the morgue together. On the way, Eichmann complemented Wilhelm again for his quick and decisive action and the personal risk that he took in entering Leopoldstadt to resolve both medical problems. When they arrived at the morgue Wilhelm took him directly to my office and introduced him to me. I told him that I was honored to meet him as I had heard so much about him. He was very unemotional. He didn't thank me or engage in any small talk. He just asked to see the bodies. I told him that I had them immediately cremated for health reasons. I could see that he was disappointed but he knew that I was right. I did show him the urn with the ashes. He said nothing, turned and left with Wilhelm.

We were hoping to be able to use this ruse to smuggle more people out of the city but with his order to execute anyone showing any symptoms of the disease we could not continue. We were afraid that anyone getting sick for any reason might be executed as a safety measure. After all, as one SS officer so aptly said, "The world would not miss a healthy Jew, so eliminating a sick Jew was not an issue. It should be done just as you would swat a blood-sucking, disease-carrying mosquito since both are the same."

We spread the word that no one was to go to any hospital for an illness for the next few days and the remaining Jewish doctors agreed to visit anyone that got sick at their homes. After ten days Wilhelm declared the quarantine over.

At the next card game as we congratulated ourselves on the second epidemic ruse. Wilhelm remarked, "Twelve down, 24,988 more to go." We laughed but we knew it was no joke. Wilhelm got his point across – we still had a lot of work to do before we could really congratulate ourselves. We also knew that this was a one-time event. We could not take the risk of doing something like this again.

CHAPTER TWENTY ONE

WIEN IST JUDENFREI! (THE JEWS ARE GONE)

"In Germany, the Nazis first came for the Communists, and I didn't speak up because I wasn't a Communist. Then they came for the Jews, and I didn't speak up because I wasn't a Jew. Then they came for the trade unionists, and I didn't speak up because I wasn't a trade unionist. Then they came for the Catholics, but I didn't speak up because I was a protestant. Then they came for me, and by that time there was no one left to speak for me."

Reverend Martin Niemoeller, German Lutheran pastor, who was arrested by the Gestapo and sent to Dachau in 1938. He was freed by the allied forces in 1945

After the false epidemic we were hard pressed to come up with any ideas. In May, Hitler personally called von Schirach and demanded to know why there were still Jews in Vienna. He would not accept any excuse. After that call the deportation effort was intensified even more. Von Schirach demanded and received a few more rail cars but was not able to reroute any more trains. Trucks were still not available. He was able to increase the number of cars per engine. They took longer to get to their destination but the calculated "deported Jew per diem" was higher even though the trains were slower.

On September 9, 1942 Vienna had no more deportable Jewish people left. "Wien ist Judenfrei!" Von Schirach personally called Hitler to let him know.

In a final review they realized that that the IKG had a staff of almost 1,700 people and their families. The high number of people was necessary to administer the large Jewish population. With essentially every Jew now deported, they did not need such a large staff. On September 22, the IKG was dissolved and replaced with a Council of Elders. The staff was reduced to 334, which were used to monitor and interact with the non-deportable Jews in the city and to finish the paperwork that included listing the vacated apartments for rental to Gentiles. By the end of September, approximately 1,350 staff members and their families not selected to remain were deported to Theresienstadt.

About two weeks later the various houses where Jews lived were searched for the final time and the newspapers officially declared that Vienna was Judenfrei. Three weeks later all of the Jewish apartments were opened for occupancy to relieve the housing shortage that had been a problem in the city. Within one month they were fully occupied. Every trace of Judaism had been removed including all of the mezuzahs[1] that were attached to the door frames.

In reality, there were still more than eight thousand known Jews left in Vienna: the staff of the Council of Elders (334 plus their families estimated at 420 wives and children for a total of about 750), Jews married to Aryans (which were the majority numbering close to 5,000), Mischlings first class (about 2,000), Mischlings second class (about 500) and the 172 useful Jews and their families (about 200 wives and children for a total of around 370). Even being in one of these categories was no guarantee that you would not be deported – or attacked in the street. Breaking any rule or just at the whim of the SS or Gestapo, anyone could be deported. They lived in constant fear which was fully justified. By the end of the war they only numbered about 5,800. About one-quarter of them were deported or murdered in spite of their protected status.

With Vienna devoid of deportable Jews, about twenty of the network members decided to leave Austria with their families. While they all had extensions they still were worried that they could be discovered. They had all stayed and helped us so we made this a priority. Many of these families had younger boys ranging from eight to sixteen years old and they were really more worried about them being discovered as being Jewish than they were worried about themselves. Moreover, each boy was living a restricted life. They were not allowed to participate in any sports since there was a risk that the extension could fall off in the shower after practice or after a game. They wanted their children to resume the normal life that they had before Anschluss. Within two weeks they were all gone. Their exits were uneventful. With Vienna free of Jews, the security at the border checkpoints was relaxed considerably. No one was asked to show their penis to the guards as long as their papers were in order. After all, Vienna was Judenfrei.

Well almost Judenfrei. There were still about 900 Jews in hiding – the U-boat Jews. They were hunted by the Gestapo aided by the Jew-hunters.

We barely had enough people to watch the Jew-hunters that we had identified and carry out any other needed task. We used many of the non-working wives and children of those that elected to stay in Vienna to fill the void. The children proved to be our greatest asset. They would hang out or play near the stores of the leader of a known Jew-hunting group. Each group had a leader and his place of business became their headquarters. Sometimes one of our children became very friendly (as we requested) with the children of the head of the group which gave them access to the store and sometimes to dinner in their home. Two of the group leaders actually asked our children to work for them during one of the dinners. Both agreed and were treated like members of the family after they agreed. One of these relationships was very successful – for us. One afternoon Johann, the son of one of the group members was playing ball with Kurt, the son of one of the Jew-hunter group leaders when Kurt mentioned that they had a hot lead and were concentrating their surveillance on this family about six blocks from the store. Johann made sure that he was invited to dinner that night. Kurt Senior liked to talk about his Jew-hunting activities at dinner. It was a good source of extra income and he was proud to do his duty. He was a member of the Nazi party and was openly anti-Semitic. It seems that by chance one of their members had been following a woman home for a few days that had been routinely doing grocery shopping a few times a week. Her husband and their children never came into the store to do any shopping. This actually roused the suspicion of one of the clerks in the store that was on his payroll. This was not normal. Every large family shared at least some of the shopping and she was not doing enough shopping for a family of four. This anomaly interested him enough to mention it to the Kurt. This was a typical procedure. The informants would tell them of any suspicious person. The Jew-hunters would follow that person for a week or two to develop a profile of the family. This is what they did for this woman. They followed to and from her home every day. She was married and had two teenage children – a boy and a girl. They lived in a small private house on Neulerchenfelder Strasse. On the fifth day as the woman was returning from her shopping she dropped the bag of groceries that she was carrying as she tried to unlock the door. The bag contained some canned goods and two bottles of milk which made the bag heavier than normal. When the cans and bottles hit the ground there was a loud noise typical of heavy things falling and breaking. Unfortunately, someone opened the upstairs curtains and looked out after hearing the noise. However, there was not supposed to be anyone home. Her husband was at work and the two children were in school. He had seen them leave this morning. On the off chance that one of them had come home early, he waited for each child and her husband. They returned home at their normal time. He waited until they all went to sleep before leaving and went directly to Kurt's home and reported what he had seen. Based on this, Kurt set up twenty-four-hour surveillance on the entire family and on the house. This is what they were good at. They found out that each of the children and the father were all food shopping. They bought food from different stores every other day and they were clearly buying more food than a family of four needed. Moreover, every once in a while, someone would move a curtain from the side of the house and look out the window when no one was supposed to be home. They were now sure that they had discovered hidden Jews. Johann was not able to find out the address but did learn that they intended to raid the house the very next night and call the SS once the house was secure. The call would be made from the store once they got the word that the house was secured with all of the people captured.

Johann ran back home after dinner and told his father who called me. I immediately called Anton Fischer. He was our Swiss helper who worked for the Ministry of Information and was an expert in communications. We explained the situation. He came to the morgue after stopping at the Ministry of Communications building to check a piece of equipment that had been troublesome all week. In reality, he went to get some special equipment. He brought four walkie-talkies and some wire-tapping equipment. We used one of our cars to go to the store and also took one of the vans. Late that night, under the cover of darkness, Anton followed the telephone line from Kurt's store and climbed the telephone pole. He put a device on the line that diverted the phone calls to the van that they parked beside the telephone pole. We could now listen to and intercept every call made from the store. Another line went from the van into the general exchange line on the telephone pole.

By morning we were ready. It was Wednesday. Carol was in the van. She became the operator at the SS headquarters that would receive the call from Kurt's store. At 6AM three group members went to the garage on Lerchenfelder Strasse which was not too far from the store. They dressed in SS soldier uniforms. Rolf dressed in an SS officer's uniform and joined them in the garage. The truck was to be used to pick up the hidden Jews and their protecting family once they were captured by the group. We decided to be standing by for the whole day just in case they changed their plans. They didn't. At 9 PM the seven other members of the Jew-hunting group arrived in two cars. One of the men went into the store to stay by the phone while Kurt and the rest went to the house. They were followed by one of our cars. They drove to the house parking about one block away and walked to the house. One of our men following in the car also got out and followed the group. When he saw them surround the house, he used one of the walkie talkies that Anton provided to radio the information to us in the van. We now had the address. This was also the signal to turn on the device so all calls would come to the van.

At 9:15 the group took up their positions. Kurt was at the front door poised to ring the bell. One man was with him while two went around back and one stayed at each side of the house. The house was surrounded. Kurt rang the doorbell saying that he was collecting for the Winterhilfe Relief fund, which was a charitable organization that provided relief for soldiers and civilians during the cold winter. The father opened the door to contribute. Kurt pulled the man outside where one of the other men held a gun to his head and told him not to make a sound. Kurt and the other man quickly entered the house with the third man holding the gun to the father's head right behind them. They closed the door. We did not hear anything at all. At least we were glad that no shots were fired. They called in the men from the sides of the house and from the back about six minutes after they had entered the house. About five minutes later Kurt got into one of the cars and drove back to the store. Apparently, there was no phone at the house they raided Two minutes after he arrived, the call was made. Carol intercepted it, "Hello, SS headquarters"

"This is Kurt Schmidt. Can I speak to Captain Fischer?"

"I am sorry, he is in Salzburg. Would you like to speak to someone else?"

"Yes, can I speak to the officer in charge?"

"Yes, of course. It will be Captain Wesseling. One moment please."

Carol handed the phone to Wilhelm.

"Hello, this is Captain Wesseling. What can I do for you?"

"This is Kurt Schmidt. I am a friend of Captain Fischer but I understand that he is in Salzburg."

"Yes, he is."

"As I said I am his friend and we have worked together a number of times. I have been finding hidden Jews and turning them in. Tonight, we have found another family at 217 Neulerchenfelder Strasse. They have been hiding a family of five Jews. The family hiding them has four members so overall the catch is nine people"

"Fantastic! I will send a truck over right away. We happen to have a truck just a few blocks away from your location that I can contact. The officer will be Lt. Bloch. He will not have any paperwork with him but I have taken down all of the information. Why don't you come down to the SS headquarters on Friday? Captain Fischer will be returning Thursday night and it would be good for you to deal directly with him since you have the relationship with him."

Kurt agreed and returned to the house to wait for the truck. Anton dismantled the apparatus leaving no trace of his handiwork. About fifteen minutes later our truck, commanded by Rolf (Lt. Bloch) pulled up to the house. Two of our SS soldiers got out and supervised the loading of the nine people into the truck. One of our SS soldiers stayed at the house to prevent the looting by the Jew-hunters and subsequently by neighbors that usually followed these raids. Lt. Bloch told Kurt, after congratulating him, that they believed that this family was part of a group of families that were hiding Jews so they wanted to seal the house until an investigation team from SS headquarters came and searched the house. Lt. Bloch told them that after the search everything in the house was theirs and, if the search of the premises revealed other locations where Jews were hiding that Kurt would receive the additional bounty. Kurt couldn't have been happier. At 1,500 Marks per person, they were about to make almost 15,000 Marks for the night's work with the potential for thousands more from the contents of the house and perhaps even thousands more if other Jews were found.

We drove the truck to the safe house on Lerchenfelder Strasse across town which took about thirty minutes. The van arrived shortly thereafter. When the truck arrived the people were told to get out. The women and children had been crying when they got into the truck but had stopped after about fifteen minutes. Everyone was silent as they got out of the truck As they got out and looked around. They thought that they were in the garage of the SS headquarters or the Gestapo at the Hotel Metropole. We told them that we were Jewish and that they had been rescued and that we were going to get them to Switzerland. They didn't believe us at first thinking it was a trick to make them talk, not that they had anything to really say. Wilhelm took the men aside and, after removing the extension, showed them his circumcised penis and spoke some words in Yiddish. They now believed. In a few seconds there were nine happy faces. We did not tell them anything about the organization or our clandestine operation telling them not to ask any questions. Using the van, we took both men secretly back to the house at around midnight where they were able to pack all of their valuables and some clothing. We took them back to the garage and left the house unlocked with one of men in plainclothes inside.

The next morning he stood outside the house and told their neighbors as they were going to work that the house had been raided, that the families had been arrested for hiding Jews and that the house was not guarded or locked so they were welcome to take what they wanted. During the next few hours their neighbors went into the house and took everything that was in it.

The next morning, we convened an emergency session of the card members. We had to get forged papers for both families and get them out of the country preferably before they were missed. Second, we had to put an end to Kurt and his group which was actually part of our plan. The raid took place on Wednesday which is why we told Kurt to go to the SS headquarters on Friday. It gave us all of Thursday to do our stuff.

We started working on the forged documents immediately. This would take at least one full day to complete and we needed some time to acquaint the two families with their new identities and the care of their extensions. This would be accomplished by Friday night so the earliest that we could move them would be Saturday. Friday was the day that Kurt was going to go to the SS headquarters for his reward so, depending on how this went, security in and around Vienna could be very tight for the weekend and perhaps for the next few days as well. We decided that we would move the families on Friday night to a safe house in Baden, just outside of Vienna, until we could make the arrangements to get them to Switzerland.

Friedrich came up with a great addition to the scheme. On Thursday, Johann made sure that he was invited to Kurt's house for dinner. Kurt was very happy to invite him. He came right after school so he had his briefcase with him which was not unusual. What was unusual was the 25,000 Marks that he carried inside of it wrapped in brown paper. Kurt talked about the operation of the previous night all through dinner. He even opened a bottle of good wine to celebrate. Right after dinner Johann excused himself to go the bathroom. He stopped by his briefcase and took out the package of money and hid it in one of the hall closets inside an empty shoe box. He stayed for another hour after dinner still listening to Kurt describing the raid and the potential for a lot more money.

On early Friday morning we phoned an anonymous tip into the SS headquarters that Kurt Schmidt had found a family that was hiding Jews and had raided them on Wednesday night but instead of turning them in he accepted a bribe to let them go. The anonymous caller said he had recognized Kurt and gave them the address of his store. The SS wasted no time. About twenty SS soldiers and an officer went to Kurt's store early Friday morning. Kurt had just opened the store when the SS in two trucks and one car pulled up in front. "I was planning to go to your headquarters at around ten…." but before he could even finish the sentence he was pushed into the store. They immediately informed him that he was under suspicion of helping hidden Jews escape and that they were going to search his home and his store. Kurt told the officer that there obviously was a misunderstanding. He had indeed found a family of Jews on Wednesday night but they were turned in to the SS who picked them up in one of their trucks. Without answering they asked for his home address. One of the trucks went to his home. They told Kurt to shut up and that he should explain everything at the SS headquarters.

While a search of the store did not reveal anything out of the ordinary, the search of his house turned up the 25,000 Marks and a note that the rest of the money would be sent as soon as confirmation that the families had arrived safely in Switzerland. Kurt and his family were arrested. He readily named the other members of his group and they were all arrested. Kurt still believed that this was just a mistake although he had no idea why 25,000 Marks were found in his home. Still protesting his innocence, he asked for Captain Fischer who came to the cell right away. Kurt began by saying that they had made the raid on Wednesday when he was in Salzburg. Captain Fischer stopped Kurt immediately and said he was not in Salzburg on Wednesday that he never left Vienna and was on duty that night. Now Kurt was really puzzled. Kurt said that Captain Wesseling had told him that he was in Salzburg. Captain Fischer told him that they did not have a Captain Wesseling at the headquarters. Kurt did not know what to say. He said that he could prove it if they went to the house on Neulerchenfelder Strasse that had been sealed by the SS. Based on his prior relationship with Kurt, Captain Fischer agreed to take him to the house. When they arrived, all they found was an empty shell of a house. Even the plumbing fixtures had been removed. Captain Fischer lost all patience with Kurt and ordered that he be taken to the Gestapo prison. For the next twenty four hours Kurt and his group were subjected to intense torture. The six men each independently confirmed the raid and the capture of Jews and the family that was hiding them but said that Kurt took care of the details and must have called for some other friends to act as SS soldiers or he had bribed the SS soldiers. Kurt was taken out of his cell on Friday morning and executed behind the Gestapo headquarters. His body was released to his family the next day. The others were released as the Gestapo decided that they did not know anything about Kurt's plans and had been duped into helping him. Unfortunately for them the torture took its toll with each of them suffering severe problems that would last for as long as they lived. They gave up their Jew-hunting activities. No one knew what happened to the 25,000 Marks that was confiscated from Kurt's house.

On Monday afternoon we completed all of the arrangements to get them to Switzerland. All of the Jewish males were fitted with their extensions and both families were given cars. They drove all the way to Basel without any problems. Again security was pretty much relaxed and their papers were in order. This was the only time we were able to thwart a Jew-hunter and save the people.

In September I received a letter at the morgue from the Baumann family in Berlin. I looked at it quizzically before opening it. I did not remember any Baumann family from Berlin and wondered why I was receiving the letter. The only solution was to open it. Inside was the death card of Jüngling Franz Baumann who had been killed on the Russian Front on July 31, 1942. There was no accompanying note – just the death card. I stood there looking at it still wondering why this was sent to me. It took me a few minutes and I came to the conclusion that he was related to Hitler's former photographer. One of the SS officers must have given the family my name and address as a distant relative.

Death Card for Jüngling Franz Baumann who was killed in Russia (Russland) on July 31, 1942. He was 32 years old. Four million Germans were killed on the Russian Front. (Source: Author's Personal Collection)

This card was used by Michael Baumann to substantiate his ruse of being Aryan by claiming that this was his cousin that was killed defending Germany.

I took the card and showed it to my colleagues at the morgue. My beloved cousin had been killed on the Russian Front. The Director of the Morgue found out about it and came to my office. He said that I could have a few days off if I wanted to go to Berlin to visit the bereaved family as I mentioned that I had not seen them for more than ten years. At first I refused but he insisted, so I took a week off and used the time to get more supplies for our smuggling operation[1].

---

[1] a mezuzah is a small rectangular ornament attached to the door frame that contains a prayer in Hebrew blessing the house. Religious Jews kiss their hand and touch the mezuzah for good fortune and health as they enter.

CHAPTER TWENTY TWO
THE BEGINNING OF THE END

"I have no intention of shooting myself for that Austrian corporal."

Field Marshal Friedrich Paulus, Commander
of Stalingrad, upon his surrender.

It was now 1943. I had a short wave radio that I kept hidden in the morgue. These were illegal and the penalty for owning one was imprisonment or death but it was the only way to get the real news. In January it became evident that the German army was not invincible. The tide was turning in North Africa. On January 23 Tripoli was captured by Montgomery. In February Stalingrad fell to the Russians. The battle had been raging since August when the Nazi Sixth Army reached the city. Stalin ordered the army to hold on at all costs until reinforcements could be brought in to relieve them. The defenders knew that if Stalingrad fell, the rest of the country was doomed to defeat. They held on tenaciously with bitter street-to street, building-to-building fighting. Losses were extremely high on both sides. With the onset of winter both sides dug in. Now Russian snipers took their toll, especially targeting officers. Since the German army expected to take Stalingrad before the winter so they did not have any winter clothing or supplies. It was so cold that the planes and large cannons froze – as did many Nazi soldiers. The strategy of the Russian counter-attack, with more than one million soldiers, was to surround the army to cut off all of its supply lines. The commander of the army, General Friedrich Paulus realized that it was hopeless and asked Hitler for permission to retreat to save the remaining men before they were totally surrounded. Hitler refused. Instead, he promoted Paulus to Field Marshall. No German officer of this rank had ever surrendered. The implication was clear. If Paulus surrendered, he would shame himself and would become the highest-ranking German officer ever to be captured. Hitler believed that Paulus would either fight to the death or commit suicide. He was obviously wrong. Paulus surrendered on February 2, 1943 with more than 100,000 troops. The Germans lost more than 750,000 men with the Russians losing more than one million men. It was the bloodiest battle of the war and it was the first major defeat of a German army in the war. The German army never recovered.

Morale in the army and the SS was visibly affected. This gave us renewed strength and conviction. For the next few months there were attacks and counterattacks but the final result was that the Russians were defeating the Nazis and slowly pushing them back to the border. This continued for the first five months until the German Army knew that they had lost Russia. Hitler was never informed of this conclusion. Anyone doing so would have been immediately executed. Defeat was not an option that Hitler recognized.

On May 9 Wilhelm was summoned to Col. Stryker's office at around 10 AM. No reason was given. He accompanied the messenger, an SS Lieutenant, who came with a car. They drove to the SS headquarters in silence. He got out of the car and entered the building. Stryker's secretary was waiting downstairs so he skipped the formality of signing in. He thought that this was a negative since there was now no record of him having come to the SS headquarters. He was immediately brought into Col. Stryker's office. There were three other officers there. He knew Col Lange but not the other two. They stood up when he entered and saluted. He returned the salute. Col. Stryker began without introducing him to the two other officers, "Do you know what is happening in Warsaw?" Wilhelm replied that he didn't. Col. Stryker continued, "The Jews are revolting! They have killed many soldiers. The fighting is now in its fourth week and there are no signs that it will end soon. It is an intense house-to-house battle. Who would have thought that Jews could do this?" Then he stopped and looked at Wilhelm and said, "You did!" He stopped and looked at the other officers who were nodding in agreement. "We could have had the same situation right here in Vienna with far more casualties if it were not for your suggestion about setting up the tactical squad. I must admit that at first I was very skeptical. Jews fighting! Absurd! But after finding the first cache of weapons I changed my mind a little but I still believed that if the Jews did revolt it would be futile against us. Maybe they could hold out for a few hours, maybe for a day, but not much longer. The Warsaw rebellion shows that I was wrong. As always, you have shown your devotion and allegiance to the Fatherland through your work at the Gestapo headquarters, the cholera and Typhus epidemics and with this suggestion. We have decided to recommend you for the Citizen's Medal for Exemplary Service to the Third Reich."

With that the seated officers stood up, faced Wilhelm and saluted him. Afterwards, they came over, the two officers he did not know introduced themselves and they all took turns shaking his hand. Wilhelm was stunned to say the least. Col. Stryker went to his cabinet and took out a bottle of double malt scotch (a gift from Michael Baumann) and poured drinks for all of them. Refusal was not an option. "To the Fuehrer and the Fatherland!" Col. Stryker proudly exclaimed. Col. Lange repeated the toast. Another round. Again, refusal was not an option. This time they toasted Wilhelm, "To a true patriot!" After a third round Col. Stryker put the bottle back into the cabinet and closed the door. One of the officers commented on the quality of the scotch. It had been years since he had one this good. "A gift from a dear friend!" Stryker replied. After some more small talk, Wilhelm was escorted back down to the car that was still waiting for him. The Lieutenant drove him to his office and let him out in front of the office building. The driver hurriedly got out of the car and opened the door for him. Wilhelm turned and thanked him adding, "Heil Hitler!" The Lieutenant smiled as he returned the salute. People on the street stopped to see who this important Nazi was getting out of the car. One of the onlookers was a patient on her way to his office who came up to him and asked him what was happening. He proudly told her that he was going to be recommended for the Citizen's Medal for Service to the Fatherland. She congratulated him and they went upstairs to his office together. She made it a point to tell everyone in the waiting room about the honor that was going to be bestowed on their doctor. They in turn told every patient coming in afterwards. Every patient congratulated him and saluted at least once with some doing it twice, once on the way in and again on the way out. Wilhelm had never saluted Hitler so many times in a single day.

He told us the story at the next card game complaining that his arm was sore from so many Heil Hitlers. He later found out that the Warsaw rebellion lasted until May 16 for a total of 27 days. Officially, only 17 German soldiers were killed and 93 wounded but Col. Lange confided in Wilhelm that many more were killed but were not reported. They did not want anyone to really know how many German soldiers were really killed by Jews. One estimate Col. Lange heard from some friends in the SS in Poland placed the number of soldiers killed at 84 and another at 92 with more than 300 wounded. There were no statistics on how many of the wounded died later in the hospitals but some did. Given the news from the Russian Front and North Africa, the Warsaw rebellion was downplayed. It was never reported in any German newspaper.

From the short-wave radio we learned that the war was not going very well for the Nazis. There were additional defeats in Russia. This was followed by a series of Allied victories in North Africa. On May 13, the German and Italian armies surrendered. North Africa was in Allied hands. We were ecstatic.

On July 9 the Allies invaded Italy landing in Sicily. They took control of Sicily and proceeded to the mainland landing at Salerno. In a surprise move, the Italians arrested Mussolini and formed a new government that sought peace with the invading Allies. We were again ecstatic.

Our conversations at our card games now centered on how soon the war would be over. With the surrender of Italy, we were sure that the Allies would march north without any resistance in Italy and attack Austria on their way to attack Berlin, perhaps by September. While they would probably not attack Vienna since it is out of their direct path to Germany, it would at least require most of the troops to leave Vienna to defend Germany. We decided that we should see how we could facilitate the return of the deported Jews who would soon be released from the concentration camps and ghettos when Germany was defeated. Germany would be fighting the war on two fronts with the Russians coming in from the East and the Americans and the British coming in from the South. Friedrich suggested a bet of 10 Reichsmarks on how soon the Nazis would be defeated. We all agreed to participate and wrote down our estimate on a piece of paper. Friedrich tabulated the results. The range was four to nine months. Kurt was the most conservative with nine months. I was the most optimistic with four months. We were all pitifully wrong.

Suddenly, there was a dramatic turn of events in Italy. Rather than accept the surrender of Italy, Hitler sent thousands of soldiers and armored divisions into Italy. Moreover, in a daring raid led by a Nazi commando, Otto Skorzeny, Mussolini was rescued from an isolated mountain resort. Using gliders, the element of surprise resulted in Mussolini being rescued without firing a shot. Mussolini, with Hitler's support, re-established his fascist government in Northern Italy. The Allied advance bogged down due to the stiff Nazi resistance.

All bets were now off. The war was going to continue for much longer than any of us had thought. Still, the news from the Russian Front was positive as the Russians continued to advance, albeit very slowly, recapturing city after city as the German Army continued to retreat with both sides incurring heavy casualties. Hitler allowed these retreats as the army finally learned not to say "retreat". Instead, they were regrouping to concentrate their forces for a strong counterattack or withdrawing to set a trap for the over-extended Russians. There were some counterattacks but any ground that they won was soon recaptured by the Russians. The Russians outnumbered the Germans in men, airplanes, tanks and artillery.

We still held our Friday night card games but were not doing much. We continued to look for hidden Jews and we continued to interface with the Council of Elders. We were hesitant about offering our escape service to Jews married to Aryans and to Mischlings. While they were treated very badly, they fared much better than regular Jews. Their Aryan spouses or family members took care of them. They knew that these types of Jews were still living in Germany where they have been immune from deportation for ten years. Based on this, essentially no Jew classified in these categories felt threatened enough to risk his life and that of his family to leave the country illegally. In addition, we felt that we could not trust their Gentile spouse or the Gentile relatives of Mischlings. Our only real source of potential escapees was from the 334 remaining Jews and their families still working at the Council of Elders and the useful Jews. Here again, the candidates for escape at the Council were non-existent. They were all worried about the repercussions of an escape on those that they left behind. Many thought that they could still be of service to the remaining Jews in the city whether they were still there because they married an Aryan or if they were Mischlings. We were very frustrated at their lackadaisical attitude but we were in no position to challenge them.

As the year progressed all traces of Judaism were wiped out. All of the apartments in Leopoldstadt were now occupied by Gentiles. All of the stores and businesses that were formerly owned by Jews were now in the hands of Gentiles and were renamed. All Jewish names on streets, buildings and businesses were changed to proper Aryan names. There was even an order given that the holes on the doors of Jewish houses and apartments where there used to be a mezuzah[1] be filled in and painted so they could not be seen. The burnt out shells of the synagogues that were destroyed on Kristallnacht were to be torn down and replaced by new buildings. Jewish foods were to be removed from menus. Bagels were outlawed. Any work of art, book or play that was of Jewish origin was banned and burned. Jewish slang words were also banned. Phrases such as "This doesn't look kosher to me." or "I do not want to play cards, I'll just kibbutz (watch with the occasional offering of some unrequested advice)." or "She's just an old yenta (gossiper)." could result in an arrest and a fine if overheard by the police, SS or Gestapo. People pointed to each other when anyone used a Jewish word and jokingly threatened to report them to the police. Others just laughed and said we should continue using some of their words just to remember that they are not around to cheat us anymore. That was well-received by the people around him as they repeated forbidden words over and over again. Luckily, no policeman or Gestapo agent came into the place while this was going on. They could have been mistaken for a coven of Jews.

CHAPTER TWENTY THREE

NOUS SOMMES JUIFS (WE ARE JEWS)

"From this place, French Jews were deported to concentration camps and to death. Nearly 100,000 Jewish men, women and children were interned here before deportation to Auschwitz. Only 1,518 returned."

Selinger Monument inscription at Drancy, France

On the night of June 27, 1944 there was a major accident at the Sudbahnhof train station. Two trains were inadvertently switched to the same track at the same time around 11 PM. One of the trains was carrying wheat and other farm products heading into Germany through Hungary from the Balkans. The other train was transporting Jews from France to Auschwitz. Auschwitz was located in southern Poland outside of Krakow not very far from the Austrian border which was not very far from Vienna. One of the main train routes to Auschwitz was through Vienna and the trains were always routed through Vienna at night to minimize discovery. This train had about 800 Jews from France. The accident derailed both trains. About 160 of the Jews and about 20 of the guards were killed or injured. About 150 French Jews escaped right after the wreck. The rest of the Jews were either captured in the station by the guards that were always stationed there when this type of train pulled into the station as they attempted to flee or they just stayed in the station to help other Jews that were hurt. There would have been much fewer escaping but many of the guards on duty at the station left their posts to help the trapped and injured people rather than worry about any escapees. A few of the young Jewish men had the foresight to pick up the rifles from the dead or injured guards as well as from the guards that had left their posts and laid down their rifles in their rush to aid the victims. The escapees fanned out and ran as fast as they could. Some fled alone; others were with their families and still others formed makeshift alliances with some of the other prisoners and left as a group. These were the ones that picked up the rifles. One man took three hand grenades from one of the dead soldiers in addition to his rifle. Some Jews that were helping others escaped as soon as the medical teams arrived and freed them of their caretaking responsibilities. This brought the estimated number of escapees to about 170. The accident occurred at 11 PM so between that time and 1 AM the prisoners were fleeing the station. They did not speak German and very few residents of Vienna spoke French, not that many people were even out that late. Moreover, they were dressed differently and had the yellow Star of David on their coats. Overall, they were not too difficult to spot.

It was about 2:30 in the morning when I was called and told about the accident and of the many bodies being brought to the morgue. Before I left for the morgue I called in some additional staff and then I called Carol and Esther and told them to call some of the other members of the group to scour the area around the station. Esther spoke French so I asked her if she could let our people know how to say something to identify the searchers as friends. She told me that she would tell them to say, "Nous sommes amis! Nous vous aiderons!" (We are friends! We will help you!). Depending upon the circumstances they could also add at their discretion, "Nous sommes Juifs!" (We are Jews!).

Carol and Esther called everyone whose number they had and told them that there were escaped Jews from France loose in the city and they should try to find them before the Germans did and that a car or van was mandatory. They had each searcher write down the message, memorize it and destroy the written copy. She suggested that at least two people go together so one could stay in the car or van with the motor running to be ready to drive away as soon as the other one found any of the escaped French Jews.

I decided to go to the station instead of the morgue to oversee the removal of the bodies and assess the overall situation. I arrived at the station at about 3:30 and proceeded to count the dead people that were still at the scene. Injured soldiers were brought into the station to await medical treatment from the many hospitals that quickly mobilized when they learned of the accident. Injured Jews and their families were brought to an open area about 100 yards from the accident and were surrounded by soldiers specifically. They were not sent to any of the hospitals. I set up a task force of police and soldiers that removed the bodies and brought them to one of the large warehouses at the station. Dead soldiers were to be taken to the morgue once the ambulances were available as they were still being used to transport the injured soldiers. The Nazi officer in charge told me that the dead Jews were to be loaded into German transport trucks and sent to the morgue after all of the dead soldiers had been taken to the morgue. Once the procedure was set up to segregate the bodies and send them to the morgue, I returned to the morgue to oversee the arrivals.

The bodies of the soldiers continued until about 6:15. I noticed that there were two different types of dead German soldiers by their uniforms. One was the standard SS uniform as the SS was in charge of the Jewish deportations. The other uniform I had not seen before. It was also black but had some silver braiding and an insignia consisting of a skull and snakes. I asked one of the SS officers about it and he told me that this was the uniform of a special Jewish control unit called the Einsatzgruppen. He did not elaborate further and I did not ask.

Meanwhile, we mobilized. The cars and vans scoured the street all night and into the morning. They managed to find thirty-eight escapees – twenty-two men, eighteen women and eight children. Esther and Carol went out together and found a family of six. While none of us could speak French the message that Esther provided was enough so the escapees quickly realized that we wanted to help them and quickly got into the cars and vans. One of the men from our search party found two families huddled together in an alley. They started to yell and cry when he discovered them. The two fathers came forward as the rest of their families huddled together in fear saying something in French that he obviously did not understand. In duress, he forgot the French words so he actually dropped his pants and, turning around so they could not see what he was doing, pulled off the extension before turning around again and shining his flashlight down at his crotch to show the adults his circumcised penis shouting "Jude! Jude!" That may have been the only word they knew in German! It had the desired affect and they quieted down. There were seven of them so two trips were necessary to take them to the safe house. Gabriel waited with the family of three while the family of four made the first trip. He stood at the entrance of the alley while they waited about forty minutes for the car to return. Gabriel later commented that it was the longest forty minutes of his life.

As we agreed beforehand, all of them were taken to our garage on Nordbergstrasse which was our farthest facility from the station since we knew that the searches would focus on the immediate area. They took turns showering and devoured the food. Some did not even wait for the food to be heated. They were so starved that they ate the pre-cooked meat and vegetables cold.

At about 7:30 AM a very gruff and angry SS Captain came to the morgue. He was in charge of the train. His arm was in a sling and there were some bandages on his face. He was unbelievably rude. He was barking orders to the other SS soldiers who came with him to the morgue as well as to the ambulance drivers. He came over to me and asked if I was in charge. I responded positively. He introduced himself as Captain Oskar Hahn and told me that someone else would be in charge of the dead soldiers that were already there and that he would be in charge of the dead Jews when they started to arrive. He was delaying bringing their bodies to the morgue until all of the soldiers were there and until he could make the proper arrangements to handle the dead Jews. He told me that we needed to "process" the dead Jews as quickly as possible and get them out of Vienna. I told him that I was totally at his disposal would do whatever it took to help him not really understanding what he meant by the word "process" and saluted. This calmed him down a bit. I was thinking of our standard process of filling out a death certificate by identifying the victim and writing it on the certificate, listing cause of death, the date and tagging the foot of the body. This was absolutely not the "processing" that he had in mind. Without looking at me he left and came back about two hours later. It was now about 9 AM. He came up to me and pointed to some of the dead Jews being brought into the morgue and proceeded to tell me that I would have to set aside a room to process each body which consisted of stripping them, searching their clothing for valuables, doing a body cavity search for valuables and pulling all gold teeth out of their mouths. All things that could be used such as eyeglasses were to be placed in separate piles in a separate area including their shoes and clothing. Their hair was to be cut off if it was long. "We do not want to waste one part of these Jews, do we?" he said. I was stunned. I stood there with my mouth obviously open and said nothing. The Captain rightly read my shock and consternation. He grabbed my shoulder very hard and said that these Jews were only killed a day or two earlier than intended and that this was what was done at Auschwitz to Jews that could not work. This further increased my anguish. I had heard rumors about the death camps but thought that they were a bit over exaggerated. Clearly, we all knew that many people died there but we thought it was just like in the ghettos where they died from malnutrition, disease, attempted escapes, etc. According to what the Captain said, the people from the trains were immediately put to death as soon as they arrived – especially the children and old people that could not work.

I cannot describe my feelings at that time. Anger, hatred, shock, remorse for not having saved more people from deportation. It took me almost a full minute to come to my senses. It would have taken longer but the Captain again intervened and shook me. He told me to gather the staff. I do not know what came over me but I refused. He was in no state of mind to be rebuffed by someone like me. In one swift motion, he took out his pistol and struck me in the head with it causing me to drop to the floor. It was hard enough to draw blood but not hard enough to knock me out or cause any severe injury. He pointed the gun at my head and told me to do it, and to do it quickly. With a soldier accompanying me, I sent two of the secretaries around to the gather all of the mortuary staff in the lunchroom. I told the soldier that I was going to call the other morgues and that he should go to the lunchroom to supervise the group. With the soldier in the lunchroom I called the other morgues and told the person in charge what was happening describing the processing of the Jews in a very graphic manner but omitted that they would have been killed immediately upon arriving at Auschwitz. They were all shocked as well and clearly did not want to participate in this barbaric procedure. I told them to disconnect or disable the phone system in such a manner that it would take a few hours at the minimum to fix it and if necessary to send the entire mortuary staff home immediately. Only the office staff was to remain. They agreed that this was a good option. I found out later that they sent the designated staff home without telling them the real reason. I do not know what excuses they used. There were four mortuary staff members at home. I called them, explained the situation and told them not to answer the phone for the next twenty-four hours.

In fifteen minutes, all of the mortuary staff was in the lunchroom. Without going into too much detail I told them that for security reasons, the SS was going to take care of the dead Jews and that the SS ordered that they should immediately go home, preferably right from the lunchroom without even returning to their offices and not say anything to anybody about the situation. Again I emphasized the security issue and even told them that they should not even answer their phones until tomorrow morning. On their way out, for the third time I stressed the security and secrecy issue and said that I did not want to find out tomorrow that someone had been arrested for not following the explicit orders of the SS. The soldier just stood there in shock. He did not know what to say. He clearly did not want to point his gun at these people and order them to stay. He similarly did not want to point his rifle at me in front of all of these people. He did not have this level of authority so he just stood there as they left. It was over in less than four minutes. When the room was empty he pointed his rifle at me and escorted me back to the Captain. The Captain saw us enter with me under guard. The soldier explained what I had done. The Captain was livid. His face was white and then red as his anger swelled. He came over to me, pistol drawn. I thought that this was the end. He was no more than three inches away from my face yelling and screaming and asking me what in the world possessed me to do this. Before I could answer, the door swung open. In walked two senior SS officers and Baldur von Schirach, the Gauleiter of Vienna. He had just come from the train station and wanted to see how the situation was being handled at the morgue with so many bodies. He was visibly disturbed that this had happened and that it took him away from his regular duties, which I found out later, was to attend a dress rehearsal for a new play that was being produced under his auspices. The whole cast was waiting for him. The Captain immediately stood at attention and saluted, which was returned by the three men. The Captain proceeded to tell von Schirach what I had done and that the processing of the bodies would be delayed. This was not what von Schirach wanted to hear. He came over to me and asked why I had done this. I explained to him what "processing" the bodies entailed. He, too, was visibly shaken. He did not know of this processing technique. He oversaw the deportations but apparently did not fully comprehend what was happening to the re-settled Jews when they arrived at their final destination. He quickly regained his composure so I continued. I told him that I was thinking about security and public opinion. If we involved twenty or thirty morgue technicians from across the city in this type of operation, the word would surely get out about what was happening to deported Jews. The Jews still in ghettos in other countries could riot just as they did in Warsaw. The people of Austria could protest and cause political problems, the international press would surely pick this up and Jews all over the world would increase their contributions to the war effort. Von Schirach thought about it and totally agreed with me. He ordered the Captain to send for some soldiers from the train station particularly those from the Einsatzgruppen that he knew were on the train in the rear cars that were not heavily damaged. Most of them were not injured. One of the Colonels with him had never heard of this Einsatzgruppen. Without going into too much detail, von Schirach said that it was a special SS division created to deal with the Jewish problem and that they were being transported to the Russian Front via Poland to replace some of those that had been killed or wounded. The Captain that had hit me was ordered to personally go and get them. Von Schirach turned to me and thanked me. He said that I had made an extremely good decision. He noticed the big bruise and the dried blood on my head so I related the story to him. He told one of the Colonels to send the Captain to the Russian Front as soon as he had completed his work at the morgue. He considered the actions of the Captain to be more of a liability than an asset. Von Schirach asked for my name. When I told him he mentioned that he had heard about me and the work I had done for the SS and the T-4 program. Col. Stryker was a personal friend of his. We toured the facility. I made some suggestions about how we could set up the processing to maintain the utmost efficiency and secrecy, which included knocking down part of one wall in the back of the morgue so the trucks could be driven directly into the morgue rather than have the bodies wheeled out through the halls from the open garage bay where someone could possibly see what was happening. He thought that this was an excellent idea. He told one of the officers, Colonel Uwe Gaus to stay with me, that I was to be in charge of the operation and that he should see to it that everyone, including Captain Hahn, followed my orders. He and the other officer left the morgue to attend to important matters of state as he said when he was leaving. I asked Colonel Gaus to send message to the station not to bring any more dead Jews to the morgue until authorized.

There was an office of a large construction company about a kilometer from the morgue. I went there with Colonel Gaus. The owner of the construction company dropped everything to fulfill our request. In less than one hour, a ten man wrecking crew was called in from their nearest construction site with the necessary equipment and sent to the morgue. At my suggestion, they went to a neighboring garage at one of the commercial businesses in the area and took the door and all of the necessary hinges, etc. which they bolted onto the cement walls of the morgue. In less than one hour a large doorway was created in the concrete wall. The whole process, from the time we left the morgue to go to the office of the construction company to the time the job was finished was four hours and twelve minutes. I knew this because Colonel Gaus wrote it down. He was amazed but I just shrugged it off as if this was something I did all the time. Inwardly, I was just as amazed.

As the construction process was being completed, Captain Hahn arrived at the morgue with about twenty-five Einsatzgruppen soldiers. They were awesome in appearance with their dark black SS uniforms and the death's head insignia. Colonel Gaus took the Captain aside and updated him on the situation. The Captain turned white. He was now reporting to me. He came over to me and started to apologize but I cut him short and told him that his role was to be responsible for the unloading of the dead Jews. He was not to set foot in the morgue. I even told him that if he had to piss he should "find a corner in the street to piss!" We stationed one of the soldiers in the regular ambulance receiving bays and told him to divert all the civilian bodies that we normally would receive to the other morgues and that the ambulance drivers would have to put them in cold storage until they could be attended to on the following day. I called the other morgues and had them also use the ambulance drivers to put the bodies in cold storage since the mortuary staff had been sent home. We were ready and gave the word to start sending the dead Jews to the morgue.

Dead Jews started to arrive at the morgue at around 3PM. The next 12 hours were extremely hectic at the morgue; we had to process more than one hundred Jewish bodies and put them into the trucks provided for the removal of the bodies and their delivery to Auschwitz. The processing procedure was to identify each dead person to the extent possible and list their names on a special form provided by the SS but the main purpose of the form was really to count the number of bodies so they could determine how many were still captive and how many had escaped. Once listed, the bodies were taken into the next room where they were stripped and systematically searched by the Einsatzgruppen. One soldier was responsible for the extraction of the gold fillings and another for jewelry. These items were put in a separate box. After processing, the naked bodies were put on the carts and brought to the trucks directly from the processing room. The bodies were simply stacked naked in the truck one on top of another. The trucks were covered transport trucks with a large tailgate that folded down but did not have any flaps to close up the back. There was an open space between the tailgate and the top of the truck. Since the trucks would be traveling during the day, I did not want to take any chance that someone could see the bodies inside so I one of the office staff to take a soldier to the storeroom to get all of the body shrouds. He came back a few minutes later with a cart full of shrouds. I personally went with him to Captain Hahn telling him that it was his responsibility to attach the shrouds to the rear of the truck so no one could see the bodies inside. When he asked how he should do it, I told him that it was his responsibility to find a way and abruptly left him to solve the problem. Colonel Gaus was again amazed about how quickly and coolly I assessed the situation and came up with a solution. We had two Einsatzgruppen working to compile the list of names and descriptions of the bodies (gender, age, etc.), fourteen in the "processing" room and six unloading the incoming bodies and loading the naked bodies onto the trucks and two working with Captain Hahn to secure the shrouds to the backs of the trucks. Once this was done the dead bodies were loaded into the truck. They were simply thrown in stacked one upon one another. They were able to get about thirty bodies into the truck in this manner. I made the mistake of going out to the garage while they were loading the bodies into one of the trucks. I had to turn away in disgust. Two very large Einsatzgruppen soldiers were standing at the end of the truck. Two or three others, depending upon the size and weight of the dead Jew, lifted the bodies to the two men. Holding their hands and feet, they swung the body back and forth until they had the momentum to throw the body into the back of the truck and on top of the bodies already there. What made it worse was that they were all joking and laughing about it. It became a game. They would make snide comments on every single body that they threw into the truck. For example, as one young woman was thrown into the truck, one of the soldiers yelled, "Here's one less Jew baby factory to worry about!" Another one took a child that must have only been six or seven years old, swung him around and around by his foot and threw him into the truck as everyone yelled, "Goal!" I had to leave before I vomited.

The processing of the Jews finished around 5 AM. Just as I was ready to close down the operation, another large group of Jewish bodies were brought to the morgue. We found out from one of the soldiers that these were the wounded Jews. The Nazis had no intention of providing medical treatment so they shot and killed all of the wounded Jews – and any unhurt family member that protested or got in the way. They just waited until all of the other Jews that had not escaped had been moved to another train before killing the wounded ones. I was again horrified but hid my feelings as best I could.

They were also processed. The processing was finally completed at about 1 PM. With the exception of two soldiers, the Einsatzgruppen contingent was sent back to the station in the same trucks in which they came to the morgue. I told Captain Hahn to go with them, which he did. Colonel Gaus and I went into the processing room. I cannot describe how sick to my stomach I became when I entered the room. I could also see that Colonel Gaus was also disturbed. It is one thing to order someone to their death but it's another thing when you actually see what is being done to them – at least for some Nazis.

The floor around the work tables was covered with blood. There were individual piles of shoes, eyeglasses, empty wallets and purses (some women had slung the strap of their purse over their shoulder so as not to lose it), other clothing, etc. There were two boxes in the corner. One had the extracted gold teeth and the other had all of the other valuables taken from the bodies including jewelry, watches, French money, some loose diamonds, etc. All of their identity cards, photographs and personal papers were thrown in a trash bin. I looked at the two boxes realizing that this was the sum total of more than two hundred people whose fate would never be known by friends and family. Their existence had been wiped from the face of the Earth. We left the room without taking an inventory of the items. Neither of us wanted to do it even though I was told that it was standard procedure and that I should do it. I did, however, lock and cordon the room off so no one would enter and see what was inside stationing two remaining Einsatzgruppen soldiers at the door. Colonel Gaus turned to me, saluted and left, thanking me for my efforts. He was visibly shaken by the day's events as was I.

The next morning Colonel Gaus arrived at the morgue shortly after I arrived at 6 AM. I wanted to be early to wash down the room. At around 7 AM two SS soldiers with a Lieutenant came and collected the two boxes with the valuables. I had told them to come to the morgue before the regular staff arrived. They were a bit surprised that we did not have an inventory list but the Lieutenant did not say anything in front of Colonel Gaus. They taped and sealed each box and gave me a receipt for two boxes of confiscated Jewish property. They also brought two trucks to collect the clothes and other belongings including the waste bin with all of the photos and identity cards. Four SS soldiers carted these items to the trucks, gave me another receipt and drove off. Later that afternoon I had the construction company come back to rebuild the wall and return the door to the other company. I did not want to have to explain the makeshift opening to any of the staff. I cordoned off and locked the two rooms that we used until noon. As people returned to work I told them that the job had not yet been finished so they were not to use the two rooms. I was repeatedly asked about what was going on and repeatedly said that it was an SS security issue that I could not discuss but they were free to ask the SS. No one was interested (or stupid) enough to ask the SS.

That afternoon I also had another unannounced visit. It was from SS Brigadeführer Erich Naumann, commanding officer of Einsatzgruppen B. He was in Vienna on another matter and had heard about the wreck and my actions. He commended me for my decision to maintain the utmost secrecy on the transporting of Jews to Auschwitz where they would be killed and my decision to use the Einsatzgruppen soldiers for the "processing". They were new Austrian volunteers to the Einsatzgruppen and he felt that this was excellent training for them. As he put it, "If they can work on the Jewish bodies and see how they hide gold and jewelry that they were supposed to turn in, it will make shooting them much easier." In reality, the new Einsatzgruppen needed no such training. That's when I learned the full scope of these death squads. He described in detail how they rounded up Jews in Russia and forced them to dig big open pits. Then they were lined up at the edge and shot in the back of the head with each body falling on top of the previous one – men, women, children and babies. Some of the Einsatzgruppen shot them with their clothes on but he said that, "I make them undress because they always hide things in their clothes. It is so much easier to shoot them where they live than transport them to Auschwitz. This wreck is a perfect example of the problems that can arise by transporting them to these camps. The cost far out exceeds the gold fillings and it ties up trains that could be used for the army. If it was up to me these French Jews would have been shot in France." Thousands of Einsatzgruppen soldiers executed more than 1.5 million Jews throughout the Eastern occupied countries wiping out entire cities, towns and villages of their Jewish population. He stood up and took the special badge off of his uniform and held it in his hand. It was a skull with snakes. He gave it to me as a memento of his visit and the work that they were doing to rid the world of Jewish vermin that, "you can proudly show to your children and grandchildren" when you have them. He saluted and left not even noticing that I did not return his salute.

Original metal Einsatzgruppen insignia with the skull and the snakes. (Source: Author's Personal Collection)

Einsatzgruppen were special unit of soldiers that rounded up and executed Jews in Russia as the Nazi army advanced. Entire Jewish communities (men, women and children) were massacred mostly by having them undress and stand in front of large open pits where they were shot in the head by these soldiers. Overall, more than 1.5 million Jews were murdered by the Einsatzgruppen.

The police, SS and the army set up an intensive search for the escaped prisoners. They released a story that the escaped prisoners were members of the French Resistance, saboteurs and their families, so anyone helping them was to be arrested for treason which had a the death penalty. This was made very public. Within two days they had rounded up 89 of the escaped Jews. By now they believed that some of them had managed to get out of the city so the search was widened. Rewards were posted throughout the city and the surrounding areas. The SS also told all of their informants that had previously turned in Jews and the Jew-hunters that the escapees were really French Jews, swearing them to secrecy offering a bounty of 2,500 Marks per Jew. This action led to the capture of another 26 bringing the total recaptured to 115. There were still about 55 missing. The search intensified.

Most of the escapees were re-captured without a fight, particularly families with children and older people. Some were turned in by the citizens of Vienna when they saw the escapees or if the escapees happened to knock on their doors to get help. Whether they believed they were saboteurs or not is a moot point. The fact is that they turned them into the authorities rather than risk being shot. Essentially all of the people that escaped had immediately removed and discarded their outer garments that had the yellow star or at least ripped them off to avoid immediate identification. As such, they were not seen as Jews but as French people, which gave some credence to the Nazi story that they were convicted political prisoners and other enemies of the state and their families. But not all of them were re-captured without a fight.

Two of the small groups that had picked up the rifles of the dead guards or from the guards helping the injured, managed to elude capture for the first three days. One group of three men forced their way into the home of a family of four on Felberstrasse. They were arguing on what they should do and evidently finally decided to steal a car after waiting for three days assuming by then the search would be less intense so they could drive out of the city and possibly back to France. They managed to stay there undetected for the next two days but they did not let any of the family members leave the house for the two days to go to work or school. On the third day people from the father's job, sent someone to the house to find out why he was not answering the phone. He was working on an important project and it was not like him to behave in this manner. He had been sick many times before and had never let that stop him from doing his work, especially if other workers depended upon it to do their work.

He rang the bell and knocked on the door but no one answered. He decided to notify the police. He accompanied the policeman back to the house. They decided to enter from the backyard so they rang the bell of the neighbor immediately behind their house. There was no answer. They proceeded to the back of the house and climbed over the short fence. Quietly, they approached the house. While all of the shades were drawn they managed to find an opening in the kitchen window and looked in. They saw one of the French Jews with his rifle watching the mother prepare some food. Quickly, they climbed back over the fence and called for reinforcements.

About twenty minutes later, the house was surrounded and the police delivered an ultimatum for everyone in the house to come out. The three men had vowed not to be re-captured but they also did not want any harm to come to the family so they let them out. The family told the police that there were three French men in the house with rifles. After a second warning the police stormed the house. Four policemen were superficially wounded. Even when one of them ran out of bullets he kept the rifle high pretending to fire. All three were killed.

The second group also had rifles. There were four men and one woman. They had four rifles between them but also had the three hand grenades taken from one of the dead train guards. They ran away together and found themselves in the warehouse district not too far from the train station. After a few tries, they entered one of the very large warehouses through an unlocked side window which they promptly locked from the inside. They decided to hide there hoping that after a few days they could escape from the city. The warehouse contained furniture; clothes and household goods such as pots and pans; utensils and dishes; industrial equipment and spare parts; lubricants; and other commercial goods. There were two large delivery trucks parked inside but the keys were not in the warehouse office. They looked for places to hide.

There were some empty 200-liter drums that had been washed for refilling. The woman said that she would able to hide in one of them. She was about 150 centimeters (5 feet) tall and was very slender. She taught gym and ballet classes at a high school. The open bung hole provided enough air to breathe. They rolled the empty drums to the area where there were filled drums. She got into the drum. It was uncomfortable but she believed that she could stay inside for the day. They rolled the empty drum to the area where there were filled drums. Once she was inside the drums, the others moved some filled drums around them so to reach the ones where she was hiding someone would have to move five or six drums. The others looked for suitable hiding places as well. Three of them decided to go into a small crawl space above the second floor. It was very difficult to spot and could only be reached using a small ladder which the last man removed and hid in another part of the warehouse. After hiding the ladder the last man noticed a small room in a back corner of the warehouse. It was some sort of workroom that had a kiln with a chimney. It looked like the workroom and the kiln had not been used for quite some time. Using a flashlight he could see that the top of the chimney was blocked to prevent rain from coming in. This confirmed his initial belief that it was not being used. There were rungs inside so someone could climb up to inspect the bricks and repair any of them that were broken. He was able to easily fit in the chimney and wedge himself in if he heard anyone coming to the room.

As expected, the next morning the warehouse was thoroughly searched. As soon as the first person that worked there arrived there was a team of police and soldiers already waiting. They first looked at all the doors and windows for any sign of forced entry or holes that would give someone easy access. All of the windows were locked from the inside and there were no signs of forced entry at any door or window which they were told had been locked. They searched the warehouse and left.

At 7:30 the last person left the warehouse and locked it from the outside. The man from the incinerator came out first. When he was sure that everyone was gone for the night he went to the drums and removed the top covers to let the woman out. It was not a pleasant experience as she had to take care of her normal bodily functions in the contained environment. She decided not to hide there again. They brought the ladder to the crawlspace entrance and the other three climbed down. Luckily, there were some work clothes and a shower in the bathroom so they were able to wash up and change. They hid their old and soiled clothes in the crawlspace. There was some canned food in one of the boxes. After eating they talked about developing an escape plan. There was a map of Vienna and the surrounding areas with the warehouse clearly marked on it. Circles were drawn about every half centimeter indicating delivery zones. One centimeter equaled one kilometer. Evidently, some of the businesses charged people for delivery based on the distance from the warehouse since there were prices written on each ring. They looked around the warehouse for things that they could use in their escape. There were many things that would be useful such as clothes and food. They could use one of the trucks but there were two problems. The garage door was locked from the outside with the lock built into the door and with a large chain and padlock that was threaded through the door handles. There were no spare keys inside the warehouse for either lock which made sense since if the keys were lost having the spare keys inside the warehouse would be ridiculous. Obviously, all of the spare keys were kept at people's homes or in the main office which was directly across from the warehouse. They also had to locate the keys to the trucks which hopefully were in the office. They assessed their position. The four rifles had five bullets in each one. They had not taken any spare ammunition in their haste to escape but they did have the three hand grenades. There were some knives in the warehouse which could be used as weapons. The next night three of them hid in the crawlspace. It was vey cramped but they managed. The other two hid in the workroom chimney. They survived the second day without incident. The third night, however, was not good.

About 8:30 PM the owner of one of the businesses using the warehouse returned to check some inventory. He had looked at the delivery list at home and wasn't sure if they had enough of this item in stock. He had better check, he thought to himself because if they didn't have enough he could get more from the manufacturer the same day if he placed the order very early in the morning. He drove to the warehouse and parked in front of the office to get the key. He was about to enter through the front door but before he put the key in the door he saw some light at the crack between the door and the floor. At first he thought that the last person out had just forgotten to turn off the light but he thought he heard some voices. He listened at the door and he definitely heard voices but they were very faint and he could not hear what they were saying. He went over to one of the windows and quietly moved one of the boxes in the alley over to the window to take a look. He saw the five people there huddled around the table with the map open. He also saw their rifles. He quietly got down from the box and ran back to his car and drove to the police station reporting that the warehouse was being robbed. The police returned with him to the warehouse and went to the same window to see what was going on. They saw the five people. They also saw the rifles lying on the floor next to them and realized that they were some of the escaped Jews and not robbers. They sent for reinforcements. Policemen, along with the SS and some regular army soldiers, came to the warehouse. After the incident at the house on Felberstrasse the night before they were taking no chances as they knew that these Jews also had rifles. They initially thought of gassing them out but the warehouse was too big. They decided to give the Jews a chance to surrender. If they didn't surrender, they would attack using an armored vehicle to minimize their own casualties. The distance between adjacent warehouses was fairly large and it afforded very little cover but they could have soldiers on the roofs of the adjacent warehouses and at each end of the side alley to set up a cross fire should the Jews try to escape through the side doors or windows of the warehouse. There were many vantage points where they could position themselves and have cover. They sent for a half-track truck that had a machine gun mounted on it that they could use to break down the front door. The street was not very well lit and it was a cloudy night. The clouds blocked the light from the moon at times so they brought some trucks with floodlights that they positioned around the warehouse. Once everyone was ready, the SS Captain in charge asked one of his men that spoke French to use the loud speaker to order them to surrender while simultaneously having the floodlights turned on and positioning the half-track at the end of the street ready to go and break down the door in case they refused. It was now about 1 AM.

The five escaped prisoners were startled by the voice on the loudspeaker and the sudden burst of light that came in through the windows from the floodlights. They were told to surrender and that they would not be harmed. They did not know how they were discovered but that no longer mattered. They talked it over and decided to fight since they believed that they would immediately be executed regardless of the promise made by the person speaking French. As soon as the flood lights were turned on, the Captain signaled for the half-track to approach the front door. Upon hearing the half-track approaching, which they thought was a tank; they quickly surmised that it would burst in from the front double door. The officer in charge decided to do this to let them know that they had brought in an armored vehicle so it would be useless to resist. They were given five minutes to surrender and come out with their hands raised without the rifles. They used the five minutes wisely. They rolled four of the full drums of lubricant up to the front double door, tipped them over and placed them about ten feet behind the door forming a semi-circle around the entrance. They pried off one of the drum covers and spilled all of the lubricant flooding the semi-circle right up to the door after stuffing some of the worker's clothes under the door to prevent the lubricant from leaking out the front door. This also formed a pool of lubricant around the door. They loosened the bung holes of the other three drums so the lubricant trickled out. After five minutes they yelled that they were surrendering and that they were coming out. This bought them an extra few precious minutes. They put another drum at the back door on its side, removed the bunghole cover and stuffed a lubricant-soaked rag in the bunghole to block it. They were now as ready as they could be under the circumstances and again yelled that they were coming out. Instead they took up positions around the warehouse and on the second floor balcony behind the boxes and anything else that they felt would give some protection from the expected fiery explosion and from where they could cover the front and back doors as well as the windows even though they felt that the high windows were the least likely entry points. Each of the men had a rifle. Two of them were very familiar with rifles so they were given the best vantage points. The woman was given the three grenades with the instructions to pull the pin out of one of them as soon as the tank started moving and throw it at the tank as soon as it crashed through the door. After waiting another two minutes the Captain knew that they were not going to surrender. Ten soldiers got into the back of the half-track. There were two soldiers in the cab with one driving and another one inside the machine gun turret. About ten soldiers lined up behind the half-track. They were going to closely follow the half-track into the warehouse, fan out and set up a crossfire with the half-track proceeding to the other end of the warehouse before letting the soldiers out. The half-track easily crashed through the wooden door with the machine gun going full blast and the soldiers running close behind. As soon as she heard the tank approach the door she pulled the pin and threw the grenade even before it crashed through the door. The drums exploded just as the vehicle smashed through the door. The fiery explosion totally engulfed the half-track as well as the ten soldiers running into the warehouse behind it. The explosion and fire incinerated all of the soldiers in the half-track. Some of the soldiers that were right behind the half-track were immediately killed and some were alive but on fire. Their painful screams were excruciatingly loud as some ran back into the street on fire while a few others ran further inside the warehouse. They were shot. Overall, eighteen soldiers were burnt alive or killed in the warehouse and three were on fire running in the street outside of the warehouse as other soldiers ran over to help them. Unfortunately, the opening random machine gun fire from the half-track killed one of the French men. The fire engulfed the front of the warehouse and made it impenetrable. The heat was unbearable so the French Jews moved further back into the warehouse. At this point there were not too many options. There was no access to the roof and as soon as they stuck their heads out of the side windows, they were fired upon. Still, they knew that they could not stay in the burning warehouse as the fire was quickly spreading and the smoke was quickly filling the warehouse. The only option was the back door. They opened the back door, which brought an immediate salvo of rifle fire. They lit the rag in the bung hole and rolled it out. When it came to rest on the other side of the alley, which was the back entrance of a hardware store facing the other side of the street, it blew up. The resultant explosion sent flames shooting up into the air and into the trees where three of the soldiers had taken their positions. They immediately caught fire and started screaming. The hardware store also caught fire. There were some soldiers on the roof that had to back away. In the back of the hardware store there was a storage room that had paint, turpentine and other items including nails. The fire quickly spread to this room. The resultant explosion knocked down the back wall and the fire quickly spread inside the rest of the store. The nails and other small items were propelled by the force of the explosion. While most of the nails were propelled within the store, some went through the side windows and some were blown out the back where the wall had collapsed as well as out the front door and windows creating a rain of shrapnel in the alley and the street in all directions. Quite a number of soldiers were wounded by the nails and other objects. Four additional soldiers were killed by this shrapnel. About ten soldiers were trapped on the roof of the store. They jumped to the ground to avoid the flames engulfing the store. Most of them suffered broken bones.

Three of the four remaining escapees, the men, ran from the back door of the warehouse and, as agreed, turned to the left throwing the two grenades ahead of them to clear the way. They decided that the woman should go into the work room and hide in the kiln chimney which she reluctantly did after giving them the grenades. The three escapees fired their rifles as they ran and managed to reach the end of the alley and run across the street. The Nazis did not know what hit them. They were in total disarray. More reinforcements as well as ambulances and the fire brigade were called by radio but it would take some time for them to arrive. Some of the soldiers pursued the escapees and managed to wound one of them before they disappeared into the row of warehouses on the next block. By now, the whole neighborhood was awakened by the gunfire, fire and explosions. They streamed out into the street to see what was happening. This made the pursuit of the three escapees even more difficult. The three men ran into the crowd and continued running until they reached a nearby park. They were noticed by many people since they were carrying rifles and helping their wounded companion. The people told the police who in turn surrounded the park with literally hundreds of soldiers. At dawn they moved in. The three remaining escapees managed to fire a few rounds before they were cut down in a hail of bullets. It took firefighters from four fire brigades in the city more than six hours to put out the fires, which had spread to five more stores adjacent to the hardware store.

In the morning light, the devastation that was caused was painfully obvious. There were 37 dead soldiers, the three French Jews killed in the park and the charred remains of the fourth French Jew that had been killed in the warehouse. Twenty four soldiers were burned to death. Two were shot, three were killed by the grenade thrown in the alley and eight were killed by the nails, three initially and five more later from their wounds. Twenty-two soldiers and policemen were injured. This was the first time that I had to list nails as the cause of death of anyone. The woman stayed in the incinerator chimney until the next night and quietly slipped out of the warehouse and the city. No one even knew that she had escaped.

We were hiding the thirty eight French Jews on the other side of the city. The timing could not have been worse. The fact they were French and didn't speak German complicated the issue. There was no way that we could prepare forged documents for them for train travel. There were thirty-eight people that we had to smuggle out of Vienna by the vans which, at eight persons per compartment, would require five trips. We had only two vans. We could not wait too long and keep them in hiding as the risk was too high. The Nazis were combing the city looking for the escaped Jews. Feeding thirty-eight people for any extended period of time would quickly exhaust our stored food supply and require purchasing a lot more food which was a prime give away to the Jew-hunters that someone was hiding Jews. Esther explained the situation to them. They were willing to do anything to avoid capture especially after I told them about what the Nazis did to the wounded prisoners at the station and what I learned about Auschwitz. One of them suggested that instead of eight per compartment they would be willing to travel less comfortably to maximize the number of people per van. After all, one of them said, they were packed into the box cars with absolutely no room to move so they would certainly be able to handle being somewhat uncomfortable in the van. We had not used the vans for this purpose for some time but we could easily reactivate them. The back door of one of the vans was opened and the one who suggested it got in. He looked at the compartment and concluded that they should be able to get thirteen or fourteen people into the compartment. This would allow some to sit while the rest stood up. They could take turns standing and sitting. The children would always sit. This was agreeable to all of them. This would only require three trips so we immediately decided to buy another van and fit it with the false wall. This was very easy. With the conversion of most factories to the production of war materials some large moving vans were readily available. These had mechanical problems and were too old to be used by the army. We were able to buy a van at a very good price the next day selecting one that was in the best mechanical condition. After having the engine and the drive train upgraded it was ready. All we really needed was for it to make the trip to Switzerland. We could leave it there of there was any issue on mechanical reliability. Our next discussion was what would be the best way to get them to Switzerland. We had always sent vans out one at a time but with the heightened security and the crackdown on black market smuggling the risk that at least one van would be discovered was too great. If one was caught the Nazis would go after the other two and possibly trace them back to us. We also had the old van that we purchased that could have a mechanical problem en route. We could not let the van travel alone. We decided to send the three out at the same time traveling together. Now all we needed was a reason for sending three moving vans to Switzerland.

We racked our brains and could not think of any cargo that would justify why three vans were traveling together. All of a sudden, Wilhelm had a brilliant idea. The Am Steinhoff hospital that had its patients euthanized in the T-4 program still had all of the beds and other supplies. He surmised that there may be other hospitals with the same surplus.

The allies had invaded France at Normandy on June 6, 1944 and were making substantial headway inflicting heavy casualties on the German army. The Allies dominated the air and were attacking trains in France. The rail lines in Germany were almost completely destroyed so transporting the wounded back to Germany was a problem. As a result the wounded were being treated in many field hospitals and small French cities near the French/German and French/ Swiss borders. These field hospitals and the hospitals at the small

French cities were not equipped to handle the number of wounded soldiers being brought to them. There were enough doctors and nurses since many doctors and nurses from France were pressed into service and there were some from Germany that volunteered to help but supplies were a problem. The allied bombings had devastated many industries and the remaining factories had been converted to produce war materials.

No one would miss the beds and supplies that were in these hospitals and in fact the administration would probably welcome the opportunity to get rid of most of the stuff. Wilhelm suggested "What if we suggested collecting these items and some additional necessities and arranging for a caravan of our vans to take them to France? Along the way we could make a quick detour to Switzerland to unload the French Jews before delivering the supplies." We thought that it was an excellent idea.

The next day Wilhelm called Am Steinhoff and some of the other hospitals in Vienna, particularly those that had former mental wards to see if they also had unused beds and supplies that could be used for the field hospitals. Without exception, they had surplus beds and linen and would be willing to donate them for such a worthy cause. Now to get the approvals.

Our first stop was to the office of Colonel Gaus. He saw us immediately. After the obligatory introductions and salutes, Wilhelm told him of our plan to collect all of the stored, unused beds and medical equipment and bring it to France to save the lives of German soldiers seriously wounded in France that might not make it back to Germany unless properly treated. Colonel Gaus thought that it was an excellent idea and commended us. He was clearly impressed by the way I managed the French Jewish train situation at the morgue. He asked about the route. I told him that we planned to head to Innsbruck and head southwest to enter France just north of the Swiss border. We were hoping that he would not suggest that we go instead to the Russian Front which was much closer but he didn't since there was still open rail service to bring the wounded to Germany. On the way out I asked about the French Jews. He said that they had accounted for all but 42 of them. At this point they had scoured the city and believed that they had either escaped out of the city or that the original headcount was wrong. They could not believe that so many would be able to hide in the city for so long not speaking German and as he aptly put it, "The Viennese hate Jews. They were glad when they were all deported. There is no way that they would help these French Jews," so they were leaning towards the miscount. I nodded agreement.

Wilhelm interjected changing the subject back to the medical equipment, "Given the humanitarian nature of the mission, perhaps the Swiss would let us go through Switzerland and enter France from Switzerland. The enemy would not likely be attacking in this area and we could let the Swiss authorities inspect the vans to show them that this was legitimate medical supplies. Perhaps they would even let us operate as part of the Red Cross."

We all agreed that this was a brilliant suggestion – for more reasons than Colonel Gaus imagined. However, the Swiss embassy refused to give permission for the vans to travel through Switzerland even though it was for humanitarian reasons. The embassy later confided in Wilhelm that they did not trust the Nazis at all and thought that the humanitarian cargo could be switched to a military cargo once in Switzerland.

Colonel Gaus prepared all of the paperwork: transit passes trough Austria, exit permits to leave Vienna with the medical supplies, a personal letter from him ordering full cooperation, etc. I thanked him. He thanked me. We saluted and left.

I decided that we should go through Innsbruck rather than around it since that route had the best highways and was the shortest route. Hans Kaupfner was now a General and one of the highest ranking SS officers in Austria. He was headquartered in Innsbruck. He was in charge of intelligence for the entire western part of Austria reporting directly to Kaltenbrunner. When he was promoted and appointed to his position I sent him a congratulatory letter along with some copies of the Vienna paper announcing his promotion and a bottle of very fine French champagne. He wrote back thanking me. I made it a point to have lunch or dinner with him a few times per year either on my way to or from France. Every Christmas we exchanged cards since I learned at dinner that he was religious – an anomaly for such a high-ranking Nazi. I called him and told him that we had just received approval from Col. Gaus to bring excess medical equipment to France that were being stored at various hospitals in Vienna. This would provide much-needed medical relief to wounded soldiers. He concurred that it was an absolutely excellent idea and fully supported it. I asked if he could send me a special travel pass for three vans full of medical supplies through his sector. He agreed without asking any further questions. He knew and trusted me. As soon as he hung up the phone he filled out the special travel pass and attached his personal card with a note on it thanking me for my support of the Third Reich. He dispatched a motorcycle with the travel pass to Vienna so it arrived the next day. Now I had the exit permit that would get us out of the city if we were stopped and two transit passes for travel throughout the country among other documents. Even though the pass issued by Col. Gaus was sufficient I also thought it best to call Col. Stryker to let him know what was going on. This way, should there be a problem where we could not reach col. Gaus, we could also call on him to resolve it. I also wanted him to know what I was doing as an additional service to the Fatherland. Wilhelm also called Col. Lange at the Gestapo headquarters for the same reason.

The next morning we sent two vans to Am Steinhoff due to large number of vacant beds there and the other to a few of the local hospitals where their surplus as much lower. Once they collected the beds and supplies they returned to the warehouse where we unloaded them, put in the false compartments with twelve people in one compartment and thirteen in the other two. The vans were reloaded with the medical supplies. It was decided that Wilhelm and I should go with the vans. While we did not expect any problems our contacts with the Gestapo and SS and our knowledge in dealing with the soldiers manning any roadblocks and checkpoints would be invaluable. We also decided to go during the day even though there would be more traffic thereby extending the time on the road since most of the smuggling took place at night. Due to the high alert we knew that every single car and truck could be stopped and potentially searched but we believed that we would likely not be searched given the purpose of the trip and our special permits.

As expected we were stopped at the first checkpoint just outside the city. This was normal but the fact that we had three vans and that the city was on high alert due to the escape raised a little more suspicion than normal. The guards looked at our papers and were just going to let us pass through when one of the guards suggested that they at least look through one of the vans. The guard proceeded to the third van, opened the back door and saw the medical supplies that were on the bills of lading. Still, three vans were suspicious and as they were debating what to do even though I also had the letters and permits. They decided to call the senior officer just to be safe. I mentioned that we were delivering much-needed medical supplies to France under special orders. I added that time was of the essence that every minute wasted could mean the difference between a soldier living or dying. I also showed him the documents from Colonel Gaus in Vienna and from General Kaupfner in Innsbruck. The officer admonished the guard and quickly sent us on our way.

Due to the escape there were now special patrols and additional checkpoints that could stop any vehicle to look for the escapees. The Nazis had developed an alternate possibility. Since three prisoners had held a family hostage there could be others that had guns and did the same thing. They could force their hostages to drive them out of the city and to Switzerland. Based on this supposition, which was much more plausible than a miscount, they intensified security. We were stopped five more times during the journey to the border. At each checkpoint I got bolder. At the second checkpoint we waited on the truck line for almost an hour but when we finally reached the checkpoint and showed the special passes, we were ushered through very quickly. At the third checkpoint I decided that we should not have to wait in line so we drove the lead van which was the one that I was riding in, out of line and up to the checkpoint. This was not too well-received by the guards on duty but when I told them our reason for traveling and showed them the passes and the letters they could not do enough to get us on our way. They sent a car to get the other two vans. We all passed through without further delay. At the next checkpoint we again pulled up ahead of all of the other vehicles waiting and showed the passes to the guards. The commanding officer at the checkpoint, Lieutenant Becker knew General Kaupfner as they had trained together. When he saw his note he mentioned this. I told him that Kaupfner and I were old friends. He asked about him. I updated the lieutenant who was most appreciative. I became even bolder. Noticing that there was a couple of motorcycles parked outside the checkpoint I asked the lieutenant if he could possibly spare one as an escort. He gave us two. I, of course, mentioned that I would be sure to tell General Kaupfner of his assistance. We hardly even stopped at the remaining checkpoints. One of the motorcycle drivers went on ahead and explained the situation and we passed through without even having to show any papers.

We arrived at the French border on the road to Strasbourg, which was about 100 km from Basel after about thirteen hours on the road. It was about 8 PM. We dismissed the motorcycle escort and they turned around and started back.

As soon as they left, we turned south and headed for the Swiss border. We crossed at night without much difficulty since we told them we had medical supplies that we were bringing to France via Switzerland for security purposes. As it was very late there was no one to call to get approval so the officer in charge decided to let us enter the country. They made a cursory inspection and let us through. We reached Basel in the morning. We proceeded to Dolf Fischer's place of business. He was prepared or us. He led us to a warehouse he owned where we were able to unload each van to free the occupants. We also removed the false compartment wall and the hinges. We reloaded the supplies. With the passengers gone each van was no longer full. We had decided in Vienna that it would not be in our best interest to send the vans to their destination with the false compartment in place as it could easily be discovered by the people unloading the vans. Since the bills of lading described each van as being full, we could not send them into France only partially full. Wilhelm had thought about this in advance and he had sent Rolf and Stefan ahead to buy additional supplies which they stored in Dolf's warehouse. They had bought enough to fully load each van. We filled the vans to capacity. The three false compartment walls and the hinges were left in the warehouse. At 7 AM the vans left Basel and crossed the border into France around 10 AM. We showed the papers and contents to the guards and they just let us through without examining anything. We drove to Strasbourg arriving at noon. We had called them from Basel and told them that one of the vans had a mechanical problem that would take at least six hours to repair which accounted for the time we spent going to and from Basel. As the vans pulled into the hospital area we were given a hero's welcome. All of the guards stood in parade formation and saluted as we drove by. The SS and Wehrmacht commanders of the city and the head doctor of the hospital were there to greet us. As we got out of the vans the band played the National Anthem. Everybody was singing with their arms raised. We were offered a very nice lunch which we accepted. There were a couple of speeches that basically had two themes. The first was that the Allied invasion was only a minor setback. They would be pushed back to the sea with casualties so high they would never consider coming back. The second was the great camaraderie that exists between German Germans and Austrian Germans. As one of the speakers said, "Again, the foresight and understanding of German values was evident when our Fuehrer reunited all of the German people of Europe!" The SS commander offered dinner and accommodations for the night since we had traveled non-stop from Vienna, which we also accepted. Wilhelm offered to help at the hospital even though he was quite tired. He worked for most of the night. At seven in the morning, we left Strasbourg and headed back to Vienna. The vans had been unloaded and much of the supplies were already on their way to other hospitals. We passed through the same checkpoints that we had passed through the day before. We were saluted at each checkpoint and given priority access. At the second checkpoint we were again provided with the two motorcycle escort which accelerated our return to Vienna. We arrived in Vienna close to 10 PM. I gave all of the travel documents and the card from General Kaupfner to our new forgery group so they could be duplicated and used again.

About two weeks after we smuggled the 38 Jews out of the country I had a surprise visit. At 2 PM on July 19 there was a knock at my office door. It was Colonel Gaus. He informed me that Gauleiter Baldur von Schirach was outside and wanted to see me. I stood up and saluted as he came in. He returned my salute. I asked him to sit down which he did. He again thanked me for my actions at the morgue regarding the "processing" of the French Jews and now for the humanitarian medical convoy. Gauleiter von Schirach informed me that he was going to recommend me for the Distinguished Civilian Service Medal for my work in supporting the Nazi cause in Austria. This was rarely awarded to someone born outside of Germany, which was the case since Austria was an independent country when I was born. The medal was for exemplary service on behalf of the Third Reich. Furthermore, he added that Col. Stryker and General Kaupfner had also written letters supporting the nomination. These, along with his letter, were sent to Berlin to the personal attention of Hitler.

I offered them some scotch which I kept in my office for occasions such as this which they gladly accepted. As we were drinking the scotch the subject of the deported Jews from France and the goings on at Auschwitz came up. He neither denied or confirmed that Auschwitz was a death camp. I poured him and Colonel Gaus another round of scotch. They got up, shook my hand, saluted and left my office.

In 1944 the general consensus among the more rational military and political people was that Germany was going to lose the war. The beachhead in France was firm and there many on the military high command that believed that the Allies could not be pushed back. Thousand of troops, tanks and supplies were pouring into Europe everyday. They were losing ground in Russia and Italy. Many believed that this was the direct fault of Hitler who was the Supreme Commander in Chief of the Armed Forces. Hitler believed that the attack on Normandy was a ruse. He believed that the real main attack would be at Calais, which shortest distance between France and England. Some say that he was acting on the advice of his astrologer. In any case, he held a number of Panzer tank and infantry divisions in reserve refusing to commit them to the defense of Normandy. The Allies were pinned to the beach for hours before finally breaking through the German lines. If the reserves were dispatched in time many of the generals believed that the invasion could have been stopped on the beach. Rommel, who had been transferred from Africa to supervise the defense of Normandy, was one of those that firmly believed this. Luckily for the Allies, he was not in Normandy when they attacked.

With most of the military targets in Germany either destroyed or moved underground, Austria was now a target for Allied air attacks. Key targets were the railroad lines, particularly the marshalling areas in major cities, oil refineries (there were six in and around Vienna) and all factories known or believed to be producing war materials. Given their air supremacy, there was no need for night bombings. The Allied air raids were very accurate. Collateral damage was minimal although in some cities where there were major German troop concentrations and communication centers that were located in populated areas, they were targeted and at these locations there was some collateral civilian damage. For now, Vienna was spared as were most city centers as there were enough military targets. But, no matter how you looked at it, the war had come to Austria. In Berlin there was an increasing realization among a growing group of high-ranking army officers that Germany could not continue along its current path. Something had to be done!

CHAPTER TWENTY FOUR

REVERSE OSMOSIS

"*Walküre (Valkyrie)!*"

> Colonel Count Klaus von Stauffenberg's code word that Hitler was assassinated and that his group could proceed to take over Germany

"Hitler is dead! Hitler is dead!"

These were the opening words from Mischa when he phoned me at the morgue. "We just received the news by telegram which was confirmed by phone from Berlin. Hitler has been assassinated in his headquarters, the Wolfsschanze (The Wolf's Lair) and a new provisional government was being set up by those that were loyal to Hitler and his ideals. They said it was an SS and Gestapo plot. We have just been ordered to arrest all senior SS and Gestapo officers with orders to shoot if they do not surrender peacefully so…..." Before he finished his next sentence he slammed the receiver down evidently as someone entered the office that he was using to call me. I immediately called Wilhelm and we both called the others in our group. We decided to risk getting together in case we had to make some important decisions regarding what course of action we needed to take depending upon who was taking over the government. We decided to meet at the morgue where I had our hidden radio. I was surprised to see nothing much out of the ordinary in the streets. While there were army trucks driving by there were no soldiers in the streets. People were obviously totally unaware of the situation and were strolling down streets oblivious to the turmoil unfolding around them. Some did notice the army trucks moving about but did not seem to pay too much attention to them. We arrived at the morgue around the same time. There was still nothing in the public domain.

Radios were still playing music and their usual programs. We just sat around and waited by the radio for the announcement.

Heading the Austrian operation for the conspirators was Captain Carl Szokoll who was an army district commander in charge of troop and supply movements. He was in charge of mobilizing the special Home Guard unit throughout Austria in case of an emergency. This was a special group of reserve troops in every major city in Germany and occupied countries that were to be mobilized if there was a civil emergency such an uprising of prisoners of war and impressed foreign workers. Not counting the Jews in concentration camps and ghettos, there were more than ten million forced laborers throughout Germany. The plan to use these Home Guard units was developed by none other than Col. Stauffenberg, the architect of the plot. The express purpose was to be able to suppress any civil disorder without having to call in the regular army or SS units from the field which would disrupt military operations. It would also take time for them to arrive in the troubled area. Hitler had enthusiastically approved the plan not realizing that it could be used against him. The plan was called Operation Valkyrie.

Captain Szokoll had a number of officers, mainly lower echelon who believed as he did about the need to kill Hitler to end the war. They infiltrated key areas in communications, logistics and security. Col. Stryker was to be in charge of the SS in Austria as soon as the current leaders were arrested. He was to replace Kaltenbrunner. When the word "Valkyrie" was received from von Stauffenberg by phone from the Wolfsschanze right before the phone lines were cut, the plotters were to activate the Home Guard in Berlin. Simultaneously, they were to send teletype messages followed by phone confirmation to all of the cities where they had co-conspirators that Hitler was assassinated by the SS in a plot to seize the government. Captain Szokoll was the epitome of efficiency. He mobilized the Home Guard to arrest Gauleiter von Schirach and his entire staff along with the hierarchy of the Gestapo at the Hotel Metropole and the SS at their headquarters. Within one hour, the Home Guard was mobilized and by the end of the second hour, they had control of all communications, the railroads, the highways, the arsenal and important buildings. Under Home Guard escort, all SS, Gestapo and

SD leaders were escorted to the old ministry building where Captain Szokoll was headquartered. Nazis were arresting Nazis. One of the most amazing aspects of Captain Szokoll's prowess was his ability to get his superiors to believe him and follow his orders. As far as they believed he was just reiterating the orders from the new government in Berlin.

In Vienna, the Home Guard was commanded by General Hans Gothenburg, a career army officer who had been wounded in the first few months of the war. He did not have full use of his left arm and walked with a limp from the wounds he sustained. He was well-liked and respected by his men and always followed orders without question. He was not part of the plot but when the order came from Berlin to Captain Szokoll who was in charge of mobilizing the Home Guard in an emergency such as this, that Hitler was dead he did not question the order – he obeyed. However, he did ask his adjutant to stay by the phone and radio to absolutely confirm the situation as he started to seize control of the communications and key buildings, which was the task assigned to him in such an emergency. By the time that his adjutant had called to tell him that Hitler was alive he had already completed his mission.

Captain Szokoll had a very good immediate superior officer, Colonel Heinrich Kodré, who was also not part of the plot but was great organizationally. When he was also told of the assassination by Szokoll and shown the telegram stating that Hitler had been killed by the SS he was asked to take charge of the arrests and bring the plotters to the old Ministry building. When the arrests were completed he entered the holding room and showed them the telegram that they received announcing that Hitler was dead at the hands of the SS who were plotting to take over the government. This was confirmed by phone. It was no secret that the hierarchy of the SS was openly critical of Hitler and the way that he was interfering with the war. Hitler had personally taken over military strategy and was making bad decisions, again which was rumored to be based on Astrology.

Col. Kodré was challenged by a number of those arrested but was impudent and hostile towards them. He despised the SS. They were arrogant, cruel and uncooperative. He believed that most of them were directly involved in the plot so he would await orders from the new government in Berlin before taking any action. Most of the prisoners just wanted additional confirmation. He refused the prisoners' every request. He wouldn't even allow anyone to go to the bathroom. Bad move!

Confirmation came about two hours later. Unfortunately, it was not the confirmation that the conspirators wanted to hear. Communications that had been disrupted by the conspirators had been restored. Hitler was alive. He had been wounded but not seriously. He got on the phone and personally spoke to the key people in command of the Home Guard to verify that he was still alive. The German High Command was now issuing orders that everyone connected to the plot was to be arrested. Hitler gave strict orders to arrest them and not to kill them. Hitler wanted a public trial. A few hours later, Hitler went on the radio and said that there was an attempt on his life but he was fine. He called on all loyal members of the National Socialist movement to act swiftly and decisively to arrest the traitors responsible for the reprehensible act.

The prisoners were released and Col. Kodré was immediately arrested. Surprisingly, Captain Szokoll was not arrested. He was of a subordinate rank to Col. Kodré and was believed to be just following Kodré's orders. Since the records seized by the Gestapo that were in the ministry building were compiled by him, his name was not on the list. This substantiated his loyalty and he was actually promoted. General Gothenburg was also exonerated. As soon as he had received the news from his adjutant he gave orders for the Home Guard to leave the buildings and release the men they had arrested.

Mischa was in the middle of all of this. His task was to arrest Eduard Frauenfeld, the chief of Propaganda for Austria reporting directly to Hitler with a small contingent of the Home Guard. Frauenfeld accompanied Mischa without any resistance since he did not know the reason why he was asked to accompany Mischa. Mischa, always the consummate politician, had not actually arrested Frauenfeld. He politely asked him to accompany him to the Ministry due to some critically important events that had just occurred. When asked what they were, Mischa feigned ignorance believing that it was not his responsibility to tell Frauenfeld that Hitler was dead. He just said that he was ordered to find him and bring him to the ministry. Good decision!

Upon hearing that Hitler was alive, Frauenfeld told the SS commander that Mischa was one of the good guys. As a detective and party member he was asked to assist in going through all of the files with the SS and Gestapo to help round up the conspirators in Vienna and in the other cities in Austria. Since he knew the city very well he could dispatch the arresting teams most efficiently. He did this with his typical enthusiasm and bravado – but not before calling us at the morgue to let us know what was happening. We were very disappointed in the news. We had all hoped that Hitler was indeed dead. We were just about to go on our respective ways back home when Hermann Schmidt had an idea. Since Mischa had access to the list of conspirators why couldn't we add some names to that list? We had compiled dossiers on many of the military personnel and civilians that were particularly anti-Semitic and had committed brutal acts against Jews. Why not include some of them in the plot? We stopped and turned around. "What a great idea!" Klaus loudly exclaimed. We returned to our places at the table and made a list of the worst among those that had done the most harm to Jews. Some were policemen that committed brutal acts others were those became new owners of Jewish businesses that they stole from the Jewish owners without any payment. Of these, we selected only those that had severely beaten the owners into submission or had arranged for them and their families to be sent to Dachau without even giving them a chance to emigrate. Others were party members that beat, robbed and sometimes killed Jews in the streets or in their homes. Finally, we added two government officials that had key roles in deporting Jews. There were eleven that made the list. We called Mischa and told him what we wanted to do. He not only thought that it was a great idea, he capitalized on it by having us add three more names to the list. They were three police officers that were directly responsible for the deaths of more than fifty Jews. They did not actually commit the acts, they ordered them. Since the Chief of Police was an identified conspirator, it was easy to include other police officers as supporting him.

Mischa came to the morgue at 2 AM with some of the files that he had secretly taken from the Ministry. He had to wait until everyone left the office. We worked until 6 AM and were able to duplicate the style of the lists and were even able to add most names to the existing lists in some blank spaces without too much of a difference in the typeset or handwriting since both were used to compile the lists. Only three names had to be added at the end of the lists (one to each page). Mischa returned to the Ministry at 6:30. There were already three Gestapo men in the office. They were rummaging through additional files. Mischa went to his desk and opened the center drawer. When he was sure his action would not be seen he put the list in the desk in it and went to get some coffee. Just as he was leaving the room one of the Gestapo men asked him about the list. Mischa told them it was in his desk drawer and asked if the Gestapo man wouldn't mind getting it as he really needed to go to the bathroom and get some coffee since he was there working until 2 AM. One of them asked if he had gotten any sleep. Mischa replied that he just went home to shower and eat and take care of a couple of personal things adding that the work he was doing was far too important to delay. Every minute delay gave more time for the traitors to escape. They nodded their agreement.

Fourteen men that had nothing to do with the plot were arrested, tortured and either executed or sent to prison for terms up to twenty years. It was extremely difficult to prove their innocence when the names on the list above them and below them admitted their guilt and gave details that only the plotters would know. When we had our next card game we reflected on the demise of these really horrible men. It was a cruel form of injustice but to us it was an injustice well-deserved.

The date will surely go down in history – July 20, 1944. We learned later that this was the most organized, elaborate and far-reaching plot to kill Hitler yet conceived. There had been many prior attempts but these were mostly by individuals or small groups and were not that well planned. This plot had hundreds of conspirators throughout Germany and the occupied countries with an entire provisional government set up to take full control of the government in Berlin. In Austria there were only a few key cities that needed to be taken over. Vienna was the most important city and had the most conspirators. We were very surprised to learn from Mischa that Col. Stryker was part of this group. He appeared to be fanatically loyal to Hitler as were all of the other SS officers that we ever met. Surprisingly, very few conspirators escaped or committed suicide. In a very unusual concession, Hitler agreed to let the families of the plotters live if they surrendered and stood trial. The trial was an enormous public spectacle. Their families were portrayed as innocent victims of their spouse's treason. Some even publicly denounced their husband or wife as a traitor and took the witness stand testifying against them, focusing on their "base moral character" and professing no knowledge of the plot. How much of this was voluntary and how much was coerced will never be known. To me, in retrospect, it was the only thing to do to save their lives and their children. While she did not testify, the wife and children of von Stauffenberg survived the war. He had already been shot before the trials began.

The day after the failed plot at about five o'clock I received a phone call at the morgue. It was Col. Stryker. He asked if I knew what was going on and that he had been involved in the plot to which I responded that I did. He was now being hunted. There was a pause but I did not say anything. He asked if there was any way that I could help hide him and his family perhaps at the morgue. He knew that he was asking a lot but felt that we had built a strong binding friendship over the years and he frankly admitted that he had no where else to go and no one else to whom to turn. He could pay well if I would hide them until the hunt for him shifted out of Vienna. Perhaps he could escape to Switzerland at that time. Unlike some of the other conspirators, he had set up an elaborate ruse in case the assassination failed that included a false escape route from Salzburg through Germany to Belgium where he had some old friends. With some good investigative work, the police and SS would uncover his mock escape plan that he hid in his home and would go off on a wild goose chase out of Vienna to Salzburg. But to make it work he and his family had to disappear now. When I asked him how he intended to escape to Switzerland he told me that he had some blank passports and official travel documents from which he could create new identities. He even had some Gestapo Seals and the requisite stamp. Gestapo Seals were very special stickers with glue on the back and the Gestapo insignia on the front with a warning that the box, crate, suitcase, etc. was not to be opened. These stickers, which were about five centimeters wide and twenty centimeters long, were applied to special shipments of secret or sensitive material. The purpose of the sticker was to indicate that the contents had already been inspected by the Gestapo and was not to be opened en route under penalty of being charged with treason. They were affixed across the box or suitcase in such a manner that it could not be opened without tearing it. A special large square stamp was applied to the edges using a rubber stamp and purple ink. Col. Stryker had all of this which meant that none of his luggage would be opened for inspection when he left Austria. He had thought of everything. We had been trying to get some of these seals ever since we learned of their existence. In his official capacity he had access to these items and had taken enough for his family and close friends that were conspirators but he decided not to risk capture by giving these items to other conspirators; hence, he had extras. He also had had extra blank passports that he would gladly give us in addition to money in case we ever wanted to leave Austria with real passports.

There was a moment of hesitation before he added that there was another reason that he called me. He mentioned the bottles of scotch and some other scarce items that I would often give to him which he knew had to be obtained on the black market. He thought that I could put him in touch with some smugglers and, for a price, they could smuggle him out of Austria and help him remain hidden in Switzerland for a few days until he was able to leave. He had a plan to leave from Switzerland to the United States as soon as possible but would not give us any details. We did not press the issue. He was sure that in this situation the SS and the Gestapo would violate Swiss neutrality and send death squads to hunt him down and execute him as soon as they were located. They would also execute his entire family.

As soon as he called and told me what he wanted I was already formulating the words for my negative response to his request. I was waiting for him to stop talking so I could decline but he just rambled on at times a bit incoherent and clearly in a panic. However, when he mentioned the extra passports, the travel documents and the

Gestapo Seals it changed the picture entirely. I asked him where he was. He replied that he was at a close friend's house just at the outer limit of the city in the ninth district but could not stay there for long as he believed that the SS or Gestapo would eventually search the houses of everyone he knew. I asked him about his family. He had two children, a boy of 17 and a girl of 15. I told him that I would help him and wrote down the phone number and address of where he was staying. I told him that it would take about one hour to make the necessary arrangements and get someone there to get them.

I called Rolf and Kurt and asked them to come to the morgue with one of the vans. When they arrived I told them what was happening. While neither of them had any love for Col. Stryker, they agreed that getting the passports, Gestapo seals and travel documents was worth the effort – and the risk. Kurt suggested that we just get the items and turn him over to the SS but I mentioned that he would surely tell the SS about the extra passports and documents that he gave to us and would certainly reveal my name. We clearly did not want to kill them so we decided to help them escape. I called Col. Stryker and told him that I would personally come to get him. However, Rolf mentioned that he was pulled over twice and had his van searched by the police on his way to the morgue. We couldn't risk using the van so we decided to take an ambulance.

Kurt, Rolf and I drove to the house where they staying with the red lights and sirens on. We turned them off about two blocks from the house and pulled the ambulance around the back of the house. I got out and went to the back door. They were already standing there. Col. Stryker and his family got into the ambulance. They had five large, heavy suitcases with them. I had his wife and daughter lie down on separate gurneys and inserted IVs in their arms. I wrapped some bloody bandages on their heads. I could see their revulsion at having the bloody bandages wrapped around their heads but they knew that it had to be done. Stryker and his son hid under the gurneys with sheets pulled over them extending to the floor. The suitcases were stowed in the area between the gurneys and the seats of the drivers and covered with sheets. They were really quite heavy. As soon as they were all in place we drove a few blocks from where they were being hidden and turned on the flashing lights and sirens as we sped to the hospital. We were flagged down by a police car and stopped. I jumped out of the ambulance when it stopped and demanded to know why we were stopped. I opened the back door as I told the officers of the horrible car accident and the two critically injured women that could die if not treated immediately. They looked inside the ambulance and apologized. They let us continue. However, we did not go to the morgue. Instead we turned off the lights and siren about one block from one of our safe houses and took them inside through the back alley telling him that this was only temporary. We liked the idea of hiding him in the morgue but wanted to wait until we felt it was safe. Since I worked closely with him my name would certainly be in his address book so it would be reasonable to expect a visit from the SS. He agreed and they settled in for the night with Rolf staying with them to make sure they did not do anything that would give them away such as looking out the window or turning on a light that could be visible to someone outside. This was supposed to be a vacant apartment.

The next morning two SS officers came to my office. I was with two co-workers when they barged in without knocking. "Are you Michael Baumann? One of them asked. I stood up and loudly said, "Yes, Heil Hitler!" almost hitting him in the face with my arm. He was startled for a second but had to respond, "Heil Hitler!" I asked what I could do for them.

"Do you know Col. Stryker?"

"Oh, yes. Very well. I have worked with him on a number of special projects. I first met him a few years ago when he came to my office and brought me this letter from the Fuehrer," I replied pointing to the letter. "I met him, you know. My father and I. Many years ago. I heard about the attempt on his life. I hope he is okay. There seems to be so much confusion."

"When did you last see Col. Stryker?" he asked.

"About two weeks ago. I went to his office. We have often worked together on the Jewish problem and other projects." I replied

"And you haven't seen him since?"

"No."

At this point about ten SS soldiers came to the office and stood outside the door. Without offering any explanation, they informed me that they were going to search the morgue. I knew from my experience that you never question anything that they do or ask.

"May I help? I know the morgue inside and out, every room and passageway including the ductwork and attic crawlspaces. I can get the master keys from the office that unlocks every door, window and storage area." I moved to the side a little so they could again see the letter from Hitler.

The two officers looked at each other and agreed so I went to the office with them, took the keys and asked if they wanted to start at the roof or the basement. We began a top-down search. I made it a point to have them look in every nook and cranny in the morgue. I opened every body-storage drawer and invited them to probe the bodies. I opened every cabinet large enough to hide a person. Every closet was inspected. We spent more than five hours searching the morgue. They clearly saw that I was most cooperative and extended myself well beyond their expectations. When we finished they thanked me and asked that I call the SS headquarters if Col. Stryker contacted me. I said that I would, still not asking anything. They were about to leave when one of the officers turned to me and told me that he was one of the conspirators in the plot to kill Hitler. I gasped and reeled back, "No way!" I exclaimed, "I would never have thought that of him. He seemed so loyal." I sat down, my face still contorted in disbelief as they left my office. That night using another ambulance we moved Col. Stryker and his family into the storeroom in the basement of the morgue that I often used when I stayed overnight. It had private access to a small toilet and washroom. I also brought some food to the room along with about a dozen blankets as there was only one cot in the room. Three of them would have to sleep on the floor. We told them that we would come as often as possible but during the day they had to be exceptionally quiet.

Early the next morning Kurt and I went to the storeroom with some food. We told them that as long as they were in this room they could not have any hot food or coffee. Hot food and coffee could be smelled by someone walking by the room which was supposed to be empty. In fact any food with a strong odor was forbidden. They understood.

We had already decided that the only people that would have direct contact with Col. Stryker and his family from our group would be Kurt, Rolf and me just in case he was caught and turned us in to the SS. We had a camera to take their pictures for the passports. We asked for all of the extra passports and travel documents as part of the payment. We had already told him that the operation to smuggle him and his family out of Austria using the smugglers that we knew would be very expensive. He did not seem to be concerned. We did not let him know that we were the smugglers.

The next day we told him that the price would be 50,000 Marks per person in advance. He opened his suitcase and showed us the gold, silver, jewelry and cash that was inside telling us to take what was needed. He picked up a bundle of cash and counted out 200,000 Marks. We were amazed. After an awkward silence of about a minute as we looked at each other and at the contents of the suitcase, Kurt asked him where he got so much wealth.

"From the stinking Jews, of course! It is amazing how much you can squeeze out of them. They would do anything to save their wretched lives. They would even sell their children to save themselves. They make so many babies that they would not miss one or two." He laughed.

We reeled back. When he saw our faces he said, "Don't worry, they are all dead. Well, at least I think they are. They have been sent to Auschwitz. Not many Jews get out of Auschwitz alive. So don't worry, no one will claim that any of this belongs to them."

Kurt had to restrain himself from lunging at him. I must admit that even though I knew him very well, especially after the T-4 program, I also had to restrain myself. We regained our composure and walked to the door without looking back. "We will be back later," I said. If he had a gun at the time there was no doubt in my mind that Kurt would have killed him.

By now the city was tightly sealed. Vehicles were stopped in the street, particularly trucks. The contents were thoroughly examined. Every vehicle leaving the city was searched from top to bottom, inside and out. Soldiers climbed up on all of the trucks to make sure that no one was lying on top. Outbound traffic almost came to a standstill. To speed traffic up, multiple inspection areas were set up at each road out of the city. Many roads were closed to outbound traffic in order to funnel the traffic through the checkpoints at a higher rate. Everyone in the city knew that they were searching for conspirators in the attempt on the Fuehrer's life. No one dared to complain if their house, business or vehicle was searched – no matter how long it took. A block-by-block search in selected areas was instituted by a combined force of police, army, SS and Gestapo personnel. His house was torn apart and they discovered his hidden escape plan. Salzburg was essentially shut down as literally a thousand police and soldiers descended on the city. The German-Belgium border was simultaneously sealed with micro-searches of every vehicle crossing the border. By now just about every known conspirator had been arrested or was dead.

We were amazed at this level of tight security until we found out that Col. Stryker was the only SS officer or soldier involved in the plot. Everyone else was from the army, police, government, civilians, etc. The SS were the most fanatical, die-hard supporters of Hitler and they were the first to be arrested when the coup started. To Hitler, he was the consummate traitor who had to be brought to trial and executed. He considered his participation in the plot as the ultimate act of treason and a personal affront to him. He was now the most wanted man in Germany.

I asked him why and how he got involved with the plot. He looked at me and nonchalantly explained, "Well, as you know, I had been a fanatic when it came to following Hitler's orders. I saw him as the savior of mankind be eliminating the Jews and restoring Germany to its rightful position in the world. Victory after victory reinforced my belief and my ardor. I truly believed that the Jews and the Communists were the cause of Germany's – and the world's, problems. My direct interaction with these Jews confirmed it. Look at all of the gold and silver and jewels that I was able to get from them after they claimed that they had nothing left. I was truly in favor of the T-4 program to eliminate those worthless, degenerate "subjects" as you called them, from society. I would have died for Hitler – at least I would have a year ago."

He paused and looked around at the four of us. He could see that we were extremely interested. "About a year ago, in August, I was called to Berlin to discuss the results of the T-4 program which had been officially stopped due to the public outcry. Hitler wanted to see about secretly reactivating the program. I was ecstatic. A chance to meet Hitler face-to-face! What an honor! There must have been twenty of us in the room waiting for him. All of a sudden he burst into the room ranting and raving about the war in Italy. How all of the Italians were degenerate and that they all should be killed. The Russian Front was next. How could any single German soldier surrender? They should all gladly fight to the death for him. They took an oath.. They were duty-bound. At the very least they should kill themselves rather than surrender. That was what the Japanese were doing. They didn't surrender. They died for their Emperor. The German soldiers have disgraced him. They have disgraced the Fatherland. He was thinking of arresting the families of these traitors as a lesson in case other soldiers believed that surrender was an option but Goering and Goebbels were against it. He went on and on for about thirty minutes. All of a sudden, he calmed down and started to talk about the T-4 Program as if nothing happened. He was attentive and cordial. We spent about one hour with each of us reviewing the situation in our respective cities. Globocnik was there and he just finished his report on Lublin. He had eliminated almost one million Jews and Poles. In addition, they shot every patient in institutions. There was no longer any need for a T-4 program in Poland. Hitler was very pleased. I was next but before I could give my report, an officer came into the room and handed Hitler a note. He was enraged. He stood up, banged on the table, started yelling at everyone and stormed out of the room. He never came back. About two hours passed before someone finally came back to the room and told us that Hitler was needed for some strategic input on the Russian Front. We reconvened the next day and found out that Kharkov had been recaptured by the Russians and thousands of German soldiers had surrendered. Again, they had failed him. They had surrendered. Hitler was not going to be available so we should all return to our respective cities." He stopped and bent his head staring down at the floor.

We could see how dejected Col. Stryker became at this point in his narrative. He paused and asked for some water. After drinking almost the whole glass he continued, "I was visibly upset. Everyone could see it. One of the Wehrmacht Generals turned to me and said, 'So, this is your first tirade?' At first I did not know what he meant and he could see that I didn't understand his question so he added. 'He does this all of the time. We never know what to expect!' With that he left the room. I stood there for a few minutes. By the time I left the room there were only two of us left. On the way out the other officer started to ask about my position and responsibility in Vienna. He could see the disappointment in my face. I was totally disillusioned. We talked a bit and he mentioned that I was not alone. He gave me kind of a weird look and abruptly ended the conversation at that point as he briskly walked out of the room. As I stood there alone I wondered what he was talking about. I returned to Vienna. I now realized that we would lose the war if his leadership continued. That's when I started to make plans to leave the country. I was planning to defect to the Allies but did not have a definite date set. About three months ago the officer that was alone in the room with me came to Vienna unannounced. He came to my office and started to ask questions about how I saw the war going, how I felt about the leadership, would I be willing to join a group interested in making some changes. I decided to answer each question truthfully but not to the point that was treasonous. I told him that I was very disappointed in everything but still hoped for victory. He invited me to dinner that night which I accepted. He came to my house at 8 PM with a car and driver and we went to the home of Captain Szokoll, the Chief of Police. I was surprised but did not say anything. There were about seven other men there. I did not know the others but soon found out that they were army and police officers. They explained that they were part of a group of hundreds of people that knew that Germany was going to lose the war under Hitler's leadership. They wanted to negotiate a peace before all of Germany was destroyed and all of its armies wiped out. Austria was already being bombed and it was only a matter of time before Vienna would meet the fate of Hamburg and other German cities. I listened and asked if I could think about it. They wanted an answer in three days letting me know the risk they were taking in talking to me. The next day I discussed this with my wife. She was not in favor of my participation. I was thinking of turning them down when I got word the next day that I was going to be investigated for stealing from Jews which was, in fact, stealing from the Third Reich. The source of the complaint was some Jews that I had promised to let go in turn for giving me what they had hidden but I deported them anyway. The authorities always received these complaints but as I had more than the usual amount they were going to make an inquiry. That day I joined the group."

He added, "My fear of discovery was unfounded. About three weeks later a Gestapo officer from Berlin came to my office. He told me that they had received complaints that I was extracting money from Jews and keeping it. He asked if this was true. I said no. He said okay and said that he would never take the word of a Jew over an SS officer and left. That was it! That was the extent of the inquiry but by now I was committed. My wife was still not in favor of my involvement but at that point we figured it could be a win-win situation. If the plot was successful I would be part of the government that successfully ended the war. If not, we already had an escape plan. Unfortunately, we were depending on some one in the Luftwaffe to fly us to Switzerland in a private plane that I had bought but he got frightened and reneged on his commitment once he learned that I was a conspirator. So, that is how we came to be here with you."

We were amazed at the story and re-iterated our commitment to help them escape to Switzerland. Under these extremely tight security conditions there was no way to get them out of the city – and even if we did we did not know what security measures were being taken within Vienna and throughout the country. The SS was operating with a vengeance never before seen in any of their operations. The fact that one of their own was involved was unthinkable and if they let him escape it would be an indelible black mark against them. All SS leaves were canceled throughout Austria and Germany. Every single vehicle was searched multiple times with the SS being the most thorough and the most ruthless. A residual effect was that anyone that happened to be smuggling goods into the country for the black market was discovered and arrested. Luckily, we did not have any vans out at this time.

We decided that we could not use a car or a van to get them out of Austria. The only viable way was the train, which was also heavily watched even though the SS believed that this was the least likely option for them. We suggested that they go in pairs – father/son, mother/daughter or some other such combination but they refused to be separated due to the uncertainty of not knowing what was happening to the other pair. They had considered this when they first fled but were willing to increase the risk in order to stay together, at least until they left Germany. With the authorities looking for a family of four with a teenage boy and girl, we felt that we had an impossible task before us. For now, at least, they were moderately safe in the basement of the morgue but there was always the danger of them being discovered even though no one usually went to that part of the basement and the morgue had already been thoroughly searched.

About a week passed with no let up in security. Hitler personally ordered that Col. Stryker be caught – or else! This was echoed by General Kaltenbrunner. The SS went to twelve-hour shifts for every officer and soldier as did the Gestapo. This made them even more surly than usual. Woe to anyone that complained about the security measures and very long lines at any checkpoint. They could be slapped, detained, arrested or maltreated in any number of ways at the slightest provocation. Even we were surprised by this level of brutality.

We were at our weekly card game. The entire evening was spent talking about various escape plans. One thing we knew for sure. We would need the services of Marie, our make up artist to disguise them. Still, a family of four matching the number and gender of the Col. Stryker family would be under closer scrutiny. We had no plan. Just before we were leaving, Carol just happened to remark, "Too bad he isn't Jewish. It would be much easier to get Jews out of the city and out of Austria than a Nazi Aryan."

We stopped dead in our tracks. What a brilliant idea! We could make them look Jewish plus we could make Col. Stryker and his son indelibly Jewish in the same manner that we were making Jewish men appear Gentile – with an extension – but with a penis that had been circumcised – a reversal of the process. We paused for a few seconds as we realized the risk. If they were caught and the extensions were discovered the authorities might realize that the process could work in reverse and they could start to examine suspected Jews more closely, especially those trying to leave the country. We, of course, would be arrested as we were sure that Stryker would identify us. We discussed the pros and cons some more and decided to do it. Unfortunately, there were no longer any Jews in Vienna that were typically murdered and brought to the morgue; they had all been deported so getting some circumcised penises would be a problem. We were sure that no one we knew would willingly give up their penis to help them escape. We had to resolve this.

The next day at the morgue while performing an autopsy I remembered that about 150 kilometers west of Vienna near Linz was Mauthausen, one of the first concentration camps set up by the Nazis. It was constructed in 1938 and had been expanded many times to include the nearby town of Gusen. There were granite quarries there which could be most economically mined using slave labor. Currently, there were about 50 sub-camps involved in mining and in war-related factories. While it was not a death camp like Auschwitz or Dachau, conditions there were deplorable and people were dying of disease, starvation and work-related injuries every day. I suggested that we try to get some dead Jewish males from there.

Wilhelm realized that the only way to get the bodies was for us to go to Mauthausen, select some dead Jewish bodies and bring them to Vienna. Access to the camps was highly restricted to only the SS. The key was to come up with a reason to have them release some bodies to take to Vienna.

In the Ministry of Information there was the Office of Ethnic Affairs. They were responsible for studying Jewish traits, customs and characteristics. Perhaps we could create some ruse there to get them to make the request. The Jewish issue had the personal priority of Himmler who headed the SS. No one refused an order from Himmler. So we decided that the request would come directly from Himmler. The only thing left was to make up a reason for the request. Then again, did we really have to? No one would question an order from Himmler, especially if it was stamped "top secret".

By now we had an excellently stocked forgery center. Due to our network, we were able to get actual forms, letterheads and stamps from various offices. All we needed was to make sure that we had the correct stamps and forms for top secret orders. We went to Col. Stryker and explained the plan. He recoiled with revulsion when he was told that he would have to "become Jewish" and at first refused but when he looked at his family sitting across the room he reluctantly agreed. We did not go into details about the extension but did say that he would have the genital appearance of a Jew. He immediately jumped up and said that there was no way that he would permit him or his son to be circumcised. We purposely delayed our response by moving back and conferring amongst ourselves to let him think about it before telling him that it was not necessary to go that far. He sat down relieved. In retrospect we wished we hadn't spoken that soon. We should have circumcised them as a condition of the escape but we also realized that they would be in too much pain to travel, that the wound and scar would look too fresh so it would have to be covered with an extension anyway. Moreover, it would be impossible to fit the extensions over their swollen penises to hide the new surgery – but the thought did cross our minds. We mentioned that we needed to prepare some top secret orders and he should let us know how they looked, what seals were used, etc. At that point Col. Stryker mentioned that he had some top secret files with him. He took them to give to the Allied forces in return for allowing him and his family to be taken out of Europe and perhaps even be given new identities in the United States, which is where he wanted to go to live. This was the first time he told us about this. He had been reluctant to let us in on his secret.

Top secret documents were placed inside a special envelope with special stamps and a wax seal at the back. He had some of those envelopes, the proper stationary and the metal stamp that was used to imprint the molten wax as it sealed the envelope. He refrained from revealing this initially as he did not want to tell us about the top secret documents that the was going to give to the Allies as their ticket to freedom. He had planned well for his escape. This was an unexpected additional benefit for our endeavor. We told him that we would need some of these items to facilitate their escape and that we would keep them as well as part of the price for his escape. He couldn't have cared less. He did not even ask why we wanted them. As far as he was concerned we could have just about everything they had in exchange for their escape. We took the letterhead paper and typed the following:

To:

Dr. Wilfred Schreiber

Office of Ethnic Affairs

Vienna

Upon receipt of this order, you are to arrange for the delivery of six recently deceased Jewish males from Mauthausen to the Vienna morgue. They should be between the ages of fifteen and fifty. You are personally to go to Mauthausen with the bearers of this order and take the bodies back to Vienna in one of your trucks. You will take the attached envelope addressed to the commandant of the camp which contains his direct orders. The bearers of this order will select the appropriate bodies which will be loaded onto the truck and brought to the central morgue. This is of high importance and priority. It is top secret. Under no circumstances are you to discuss this with anyone within or outside of your office. If anyone refuses to cooperate they will answer to me. Heil Hitler!

(signed) Heinrich Himmler

(stamped with the SS seal)

We prepared a similar order for the Commandant of the camp.

To:

Col. Franz Ziereis,

Commandant of Mauthausen

Upon receipt of this order you are to deliver six recently deceased Jewish males to the bearers of this order. They shall personally select the six males. This is to be done in strict secrecy. They shall not be observed during the selection process. Anything that they require should be placed at their disposal. This is of high importance and priority. It is top secret. Under no circumstances are you to discuss this with anyone within the camp. If anyone refuses to cooperate they will answer to me. Heil Hitler!

Signed (Heinrich Himmler)

(stamped with the SS Seal)

While this was being done we told Col. Stryker that having a circumcised penis was not enough to pass as being Jewish. He had to have a working knowledge of Judaism. We would have to teach him and his family the fundamentals since the guards often asked questions about the Jewish religion from the Jews that they were helping escape. We learned this from the father of a family that we helped escape. He was riding in the baggage car with his family when one of the guards, a very young man of 18 or 19 years old, came over and stared at him for a minute or two and told him that he came from a small town in Austria where there were no Jews, so this was the first time he was this close to a Jew. He started to ask him some questions about the religion and asked him to recite a prayer. He would repeat this on occasion when one of the Jews he was helping escape interested him.

And so began the crash course in Judaism. His wife and daughter were taught the Shabbat candle lighting prayer and ceremony. Col. Stryker and his son were taught the various prayers for blessing wine and bread and the candles on Chanukah and the four questions for Passover. For three days they spent nine to ten hours a day memorizing prayers, expressions and Jewish customs. We even gave them Hebrew names.

The day after we prepared the false documents we had Kurt and Johann dress up in SS uniforms. They proceeded to borrow two SS motorcycles that were parked in back of the SS headquarters. They just entered the building through the front door and walked to the back door. This was one of the security flaws I discovered from my many visits there. An SS soldier or officer could easily enter the building. The only time that they had to identify themselves was when they wanted access to the upper floors. So they walked through the building without any problem. Upon leaving through the back door they simply took two of the motorcycles parked there. Again, they were not challenged. After all, who in their right mind would impersonate an SS officer and steal an SS motorcycle? We rented a black Mercedes and put two Nazi flags on the front. Martin was the driver. One of our group members, Laurenz König, became a special agent from Berlin for a top secret program simply called J-14. Rolf accompanied him to drive the truck. With the documents that we had from Stryker and some of our own we were able to prepare the necessary credentials. They drove to the Ministry of Information. Laurenz entered the building, told the receptionist that he had a top-secret order for the head of the Ministry of Ethnic Affairs. Wilfred's secretary came down and escorted him to his office. Laurenz was shown into the office. After the obligatory Heil Hitlers he introduced himself. Without any conversation, Laurenz handed him the sealed order and waited while he read it. He read it and without a moment's hesitation he got on the phone and called the Commandant of Mauthausen telling him that he was personally coming there to get six bodies of recently deceased Jews stipulated in a special order from Himmler and that he would personally bring his order for his compliance with him. Here again, the Commandant had no reason to question the orders. If it were six live Jews perhaps he would have wanted confirmation but six dead Jews were of no concern. It was six less bodies that he had to burn and he just assumed that they were needed for some sort of medical experiments similar to the work that Dr. Mengele was doing in Auschwitz.

With Rolf driving the Office of Ethnic Affairs truck and Wilfred and Laurenz in the Mercedes, they left for Mauthausen with Kurt and Johann leading the way with the motorcycles. SS motorcycles escorting an official car were never stopped at any checkpoint which was why we set up the operation in this manner. Wilhelm had even given this operation a code name, "Operation Reverse Osmosis". Four hours later at 2 PM they reached Mauthausen.

When they arrived Wilfred and Laurenz were brought directly to the Commandant's office. He read the order and without a moment's hesitation personally brought Wilfred and Laurenz to a large open pit near one of the quarries. Rolf also went with them. "This is the Parachutist's Wall," he said smiling. "It is where we teach prisoners how to fly – but without a parachute!" The two of them stared down into the pit at the maze of contorted bodies. As they were standing there they heard a scream. Without warning the body of a man fell no more than ten meters from them. He was screaming as he fell. When he hit the ground they could hear just about every bone in his body break apart. He died instantly. Laurenz looked up and saw two guards peering over the edge laughing. They had obviously pushed the hapless man over the edge probably just because they were there. Laurenz was shocked beyond belief as the Commandant calmly said "See, there goes another flying piece of shit." The Commandant was smiling. Laurenz turned to Wilfred and saw that he was also smiling. Laurenz finally said, "I am sorry but we need the bodies in better physical condition."

"No problem," the Commandant said, "We have plenty of those too!" as he led them to another part of the camp near another smaller pit where the bodies of prisoners that were executed or died of malnutrition and other "natural causes" were located. The Commandant said that they were waiting to be burned but there was just too big a backlog so he welcomed the removal of the six bodies that we needed. There were about 100 bodies there. He apologized for the backlog saying that they were using all of the available prisoners in more important functions. He turned and left the three of them alone as the order requested. Laurenz asked Wilfred to wait a few meters away from the pit while he and Rolf went down the dirt incline to select the six males. This took much longer than expected. Most of the prisoners at Mauthausen were not Jewish. They were a mixture of political, criminal, and other undesirables, with a few Jews thrown in. Rolf waited at the edge while Laurenz entered the area where the bodies were piled up.

As he started the selection process he put on a surgical mask to stifle the smell of decaying bodies. He had to pull down the pants of each prisoner to inspect their genitals and pull them back up whether they were going to be selected or not. The smell was unbearable, even with the mask. He vomited at least three times but was able to select six Jewish males. He tied a red ribbon around their left leg. Once he had selected the six men he went to Rolf who helped him climb out of the pit. Wilfred could see that Laurenz was very upset. He was pale, coughing and not in the least bit talkative. Laurenz stayed by the pit and told Wilfred to go to the Commandant's office and request some help in taking the bodies out of the pit and to send the truck over to the pit. The commandant summoned a sergeant and told him to get some prisoners and follow Wilfred's orders. Ten minutes later the sergeant appeared with eight prisoners. The prisoners loaded the bodies into the truck and they left without even stopping by the Commandant's office to thank him.

The truck arrived at the morgue with the bodies at 11:40 PM. I helped them unload the bodies and put them on six tables in the autopsy room. As the Head of the Office of Ethnic Affairs was leaving he asked if I knew anything about this. I asked him to come closer and made him swear that he would not say anything to anyone about this, not even his family. He agreed. After swearing him to secrecy one more time, I told him that there was a secret project to re-animate dead men so they would be able to fight again and that they would not die again from bullets so that the only way to kill them again was to literally blow them up into many pieces. I added that it was decided to experiment with dead Jews first since they have small brains that are easily controlled. This would create an unstoppable army that would obey orders without question once their minds were programmed. This was one of the new secret weapons that the Fuehrer was talking about. I could see from his expression that he was absolutely amazed. He looked at the dead bodies, then at me and asked me if it was possible. "Nothing is impossible for our Fuehrer! How dare you question him! Heil Hitler!" I angrily said as I quickly ushered him out of the morgue.

I now turned my attention to the bodies. I was very upset once I viewed the bodies and had to sit down a few minutes before proceeding. Here were six men whose only crime was to be born Jewish. They had been worked to death. They weighed less than 50 kilos. Their bodies bore the scars of the whips of their oppressors.

I thought about the slaves in Egypt and wondered if even they had been so cruelly mistreated. I thought not. I did not even know who they were or where they came from. None of their family or friends would know for sure that they were dead. I recovered after a few minutes and quickly emasculated each of the men. With the help of Kurt and Rolf we put all six men into separate body bags and loaded them into one of the ambulances. Kurt and Rolf drove to the Jewish cemetery and buried them in a single grave. Some of our people had prepared this grave in advance. They waited for Kurt and Rolf to arrive, helped them with the bodies and covered them up. The last rabbi left in Vienna who was working for the Council of Elders was there to bury them. The rabbi was taking a great risk. If he was caught he would be immediately deported to Dachau since it was after curfew. The cemetery was not guarded or patrolled and most of the headstones had already been removed or defaced by the Nazis some time ago. The rabbi said the following prayer,

"Oh, Lord! Before you we stand; humbled in your presence. We have come to bury six men; to place them in your care for eternity. We do not know their names. We do not know where they were born. We do not know what they did in life. We do not know if they have wives or children. All we know is that they are Jews. And it is because of this that they have died. Oh, Lord, you delivered us from the oppression and slavery of Egypt. Could our suffering today be any less? We stand before you on the brink of extinction and beseech you to care for these six men as well as all of the others that have preceded them – and all those that will follow."

"Amen."

It was now time to convert the Stryker family to Jews. We called Marie and she came the next morning. We told her to make Col. Stryker and his family look Jewish. She laughed at the irony of it. This was the first time that she had this type of request. Everyone else wanted to look Gentile. She enlarged their noses and earlobes, darkened their eyebrows which made the enlarged nose appear even bigger. It took about three hours each to make the four of them "look Jewish". We took a photograph of each of them for their passports. When the passports arrived back at the morgue we showed them the extensions and gave him a crash course in the care and use of the extension such as how to urinate, the items he needed to carry such as the special pack of cigarettes containing the glue and the spare extension. We gave them the four extra spares due to the circumstances of their escape. They would have to pretend that they were Jewish probably until they reached the United States.

Carol sat with Stryker's wife and daughter while they were being schooled in Judaism. She really wanted to learn as much as possible about my religion.

As this was going on, we went to the south train station to see which guards were on duty. We knew a few of them that were willing to take a bribe to look the other way. At this point in time, with the war not going well, many of them were worried about their fate if Germany lost, which was a distinct possibility. Helping some rich Jews escape was very rewarding. They received a lot of money for it, much more than the reward for turning them in. In addition, if Germany did lose the war they could say that they helped Jews rather than kill them. To ensure the success of the operation, we would only give them half the money up front and rest when they were safe in Switzerland. As we had done this a few times before, the guards knew that we could be trusted to give them the balance of the money when the Jews crossed the border. Similarly, we knew that they could be trusted.

We quickly made the deal with Lothar and Fritz. Lothar was the young curious one so we knew that our efforts to "Jewdicate" the Stryker family would pay off. We set their departure for the next day.

That night, Wilhelm had another brainstorm and called me. "Since they are looking for a family of four with two teenage children, why not add another child to the family?" He already had someone in mind, Johann, the boy that switched the license plates on the SS trucks. I thought that it was an excellent idea. I called Johann's father who asked Johann if he would do this. He vehemently replied, "Absolutely!" In the morning he went to the forgery center and became their fifth child. When we told Stryker about it he was ecstatic at the idea commenting that "Aryan Ingenuity" always prevails.

At 3:45 we drove the family to the station to board the 4PM train to Zurich. Due to the tight security we had Bertrand Graber, who was still working at the station, arrange for them to secretly enter the railroad yard in a covered truck through the worker entrance and board the train from the side opposite the station. There was only one SS guard at the worker's entrance during the day so Wilhelm distracted him by asking him to look at something in the rail yard. We took this opportunity to smuggle the family into the station during the five minutes he was away from his post. When Lothar and Fritz saw the Strykers they were taken aback. He took out the photo that the SS had given them with the picture of the four fugitives. There was some resemblance but clearly these people looked Jewish and there were five of them. With his hand on the gun in his holster, he asked Col. Stryker and his two sons to step into the bathroom. Once there, he asked them to pull down their pants for the obvious reason. He clearly saw that they were circumcised. He was relieved and much more relaxed. As he was escorting them back to the passenger car, he told them of the manhunt for Col. Stryker but that he only had two children. During the trip Lothar, still a little suspicious made it a point to ask Col. Stryker and his family some questions about the Jewish religion which were all answered to his satisfaction. At the border, Lothar accompanied the Strykers through the German checkpoint. Here again the border guard also remarked about the coincidences of the facial features of these Jews with the Stryker family. Lothar told the border guard to go to the bathroom and "look at their dicks" which he did. Their passports were stamped and they were permitted to enter Switzerland.

About three weeks later, Hitler was informed that Col. Stryker had escaped and was believed to be in Switzerland but by the time he could send in a team of commandos led by Otto Skorzeny (who distinguished himself by rescuing Mussolini) the Strykers had left Switzerland without a trace. Col. Stryker had planned well recognizing that Hitler would relentlessly go after him and his family. He set up a number of false trails. There were quite a number of Jewish families in Switzerland that had illegally escaped from Austria that had no where else to go. Col. Stryker told us that he had arranged for three of these families that had two teenage children more or less matching the description of Stryker's family to get into Argentina, South Africa and Australia. He had planned very, very well for his escape.

Reluctantly, his wife agreed to split up since he felt that this was mandatory for his plan to succeed. They traveled separately out of Switzerland to further throw his pursuers off his trail plus there was much less risk of being caught going to Lisbon where they were reunited. They obtained political asylum in the United States Embassy arranged by the U. S. Consulate there due to the secret documents that he brought. Political asylum circumvented the quota limitation. If they had applied as refugee Jews they could have waited for months before being allowed to enter the United States. Johann, on the advice of his father, stayed in Switzerland until the war ended. Stryker gave him more than enough money to live very well for many years.

Hitler sent agents after each of the families of four that left Switzerland during that time period. Two months later he was told that they were not the right ones. The trail had gone cold. He decided to remove all traces of Col. Stryker as a conspirator. Since the SS was the most fanatic in their loyalty to the Fuehrer, there was no way that he wanted it to be known publicly that one amongst them was a traitor. Records were altered eliminating him as a conspirator. The official story was that he was not part of the plot but was a casualty of the plot. Col. Stryker was now listed as having been secretly killed by the conspirators the day of the assassination attempt as he had uncovered their plans and was trying to notify his superiors. His body was hidden by the conspirators but had been recently discovered. A sealed coffin was brought from Austria to Germany. Stryker was buried in his home city of Hannover with full military honors. His family was told that his wife was wounded in the attack on her husband and was in the hospital with the two children being cared for by a neighbor. This was done to cover her absence from the funeral. Because she was a material witness the hospital where she was recovering was classified so no one could be told where she was hospitalized. To this day, the participation of a high-ranking SS officer in the plot remains unknown.

CHAPTER TWENTY-FIVE
THE BATTLE FOR VIENNA

"Schirach looked at me and said, 'Skorzeny, my duty can be expressed in three words – victory or death.' What he wanted to say, Skorzeny noted sarcastically, was victory or flight. Five hours later the Reichsleiter left the city and sought protection with the retreating German Army."

> Otto Skorzeny commenting on Gauleiter von Schirach. Skorzeny, who had rescued Mussolini from partisans in July 1943, was now part of the Vienna defense force. Vienna surrendered seven days later.

I remember the morning when the Nazi troops marched triumphantly into Austria. The people of Vienna were exuberant.

I clearly remember Hitler's speech on March 15, 1938 when he promised the world to us. Vienna was a pearl and would be placed in its proper setting. The people of Vienna were exuberant.

I remember the Jews being removed from the economy and eventually from Vienna. The people of Vienna were exuberant.

I remember the dread of war turning to euphoria when Hitler attacked and defeated Poland in less than a month. Hitler's armies conquered city after city, country after country. When France surrendered we took to the streets in joyous celebration. Only the small island country of England remained in the west. The people of Vienna were exuberant.

When Hitler invaded Russia, we could not keep up with the victories as the army advanced to the gates of Moscow. The Communist threat would be eliminated forever. Even members of the clergy were in favor of this. All through the war, pictures of destroyed Russian cities permeated the newspapers and magazines. The people of Vienna were exuberant.

Even after the defeat at Stalingrad which was the first major defeat of the army in the war, the people believed in Hitler who promised a quick, decisive and victorious counter attack to stem the retreat of the German army. The people of Vienna were exuberant.

I do not remember exactly when they lost their exuberance but they clearly were no longer exuberant. Many families lost sons, husbands and fathers on the Russian Front. There were food, clothing and fuel shortages. Many Austrian cities had been bombed. Would Vienna be next? Defeat after defeat permeated the thoughts and conversations of the people. The barbaric Russians were advancing to the Hungarian border. Would Austria be next?

Vienna had been spared from Allied bombs for most of the war. While some other Austrian cities had been bombed in 1943, no bombs fell on Vienna. The other cities were selected based on their military value. All of the towns and cities that were production centers of war materials or transportation crossroads were bombed first. Civilian casualties in these attacks were limited to those living in the immediate target areas and a very few that were killed when a stray bomb missed its target. Innsbruck, which had very little war material production was not bombed until December 15, 1943.

By now, most of the above-ground factories and infrastructure in Germany and much of Austria had been totally destroyed. The factories just outside of Vienna and some of the factories within Vienna were now extremely important to the war effort. To protect the city, the Nazis built six tremendous concrete reinforced anti-aircraft towers. They had an advanced radar system that could direct the guns at planes that were as high as 6,000 meters which is where the high-altitude bombers flew.

On July 16, 1944, just four days before the ill-fated plot on Hitler, Vienna was bombed for the first time. The attack was centered on the railroads and stations, two oil refineries as well as some German gun emplacements and storage depots. This became the pattern for the first few months. The radar-directed anti-aircraft guns on the towers were quite accurate and shot down quite a number of fighters and bombers. Attempts to destroy the towers from the air proved futile. Aircraft losses over Vienna were the highest compared to almost all other Austrian cities combined.

On November 5 this changed. On that day about 500 planes bombed the entire city, which obviously included non-military targets. Almost every city block had houses damaged by bombs with many on fire. It was the first time that incendiary bombs had been used in Vienna. The results were devastating. Some fires had to be left to burn out as there was not enough fire fighting equipment to handle so many fires. Government and cultural buildings were given first priority by the firefighters so many residential homes and businesses were left to burn down to the ground. What made matters even worse was that the water supply in many neighborhoods was not working due to the bombs that either destroyed pumping stations or water pipes. Chaos reigned as people scrambled to salvage what few possessions they could safely get from a bombed-out or on-fire home or business as well as adjacent homes and businesses in case they caught fire from the unattended blazes. This proved prudent since many of the fires did spread to adjacent structures. The Allies decided that with Vienna being the center of Nazi activity in Austria that they wanted to break the morale of the people there and perhaps get them to revolt against the Nazis as had happened in a number of cities in Italy. This now entailed the open bombing of Vienna. Not one person in Vienna was exuberant. The war had come to them.

We decided that now more than ever that we maintain contact with each other after each air raid. While we were clearly concerned about each other's safety we also had to protect our own Jewish identities. If one of us were killed we had to at least try to retrieve the extensions. We could not risk discovery if one of us were injured and our genital subterfuge was discovered while in a hospital. That would surely lead to torture and death. We all agreed that this was mandatory. We also realized that this would become increasingly difficult as the bombings continued. Communications would likely be knocked out, public transportation was likely to be disrupted and we may have our own individual problems. Still, maintaining the integrity of our identities was much more important than personal concerns. We formed a chain by alphabetical order that included Mischa: Michael Baumann, Klaus Frühling, Mischa Kleinman, Wilhelm Roebling, Kurt Schultz, and Friedrich Steiermann. I would contact Klaus who would contact Mischa and so on. If anyone failed to be contacted by the person responsible it would cause the next person in the chain to find out why. We also set up a meeting point using specific streets that we would take between each contact link. If one did not hear from the other and physically went to find out why, they would be using the same streets and would likely run into to each other. We set the time as four hours after the bombing stopped.

With the Allied forces now fighting in Germany, a number of high-ranking SS officers in Austria were recalled to Germany. At this point we learned from some of them that old men and even children had been drafted into the army so they were needed to command these inexperienced draftees. They were not looking forward to their new assignments yet, to a man, they were still adamant in their support of Hitler with some even deluding themselves that a victory was still possible. As one of the SS officers told Wilhelm, "When they (the Allies) see how many additional armies we can raise, the cost in life will be so severe that they will have to retreat giving us time to rebuild the German army and air force with our new weapons that can send bombs to America. We will emerge victorious."

On January 17 tragedy struck. Kurt Schultz, the owner of the office supply stores, and his wife were killed in the Allied bombing. Tragedy struck again five days later when Friedrich Steiermann, the dentist, was killed. His wife, Magda, survived but was badly injured. She recovered but limped for the rest of her life. We were able to reach the bodies of Kurt and Friedrich before their ethnicity was discovered. I filled out the death certificates and they were buried in their family plots. With the numerous air raids there were just too many bodies to bring to the morgue. Special forms were created whereby the police would certify that the person had died from the air raid based on seeing the body and their papers. The family would bring the form into the office for a death certificate. If no one claimed the body it would be brought to the morgue where their papers would be used to try to contact the family. Due to the large number of deaths the bodies were stored in the basement until somebody showed up to claim the body. Due to health concerns we would dispose of all bodies within four days of arrival in the morgue. We took pictures of all of these unclaimed bodies, even if we still had them in the morgue since it was better for the families not to see so many unidentified dead bodies with horrible injuries, and wrote some information on the back of each photograph such as hair and eye color; birthmarks and scars; approximate age, weight and height; and any other characteristic that we felt would help in identifying the deceased. The pictures were posted in the lobby and hallways. At first we posted them randomly as we disposed of the body. Soon there were just too many and the random posting was too confusing so we segregated them by sex and approximate age. Soon, we ran out of space and had to expand the "walls of death" into other rooms of the morgue. We hired more people to control the crowds and set up stanchions to form aisles where people could walk in an orderly fashion to try to locate a missing family member or friend. It was a heart-rending situation. Whenever a loved one's picture was found the person or persons would cry and sometimes collapse on the spot. We had some of the people we hired standing by to assist the bereaved by gently taking them out of the line to one of the offices set up for this to complete the paperwork. In some cases the bodies were still at the morgue so the families at least had some closure in being able to bury their loved ones. For those that were identified after the four day residence limit, we had to tell them that the body was sent to the cemetery for burial in a common grave. Their misery intensified. Some rushed out of the morgue to the cemetery in the hope of recovering the body. I do not know how many, if any, were successful. I was glad that I was not at the cemetery as I envisaged people trying to get access to a mound of dead bodies and, if they gained access, trying to sort through them to identify a loved one.

On February 1, word reached us that Russian troops had liberated Auschwitz on January 26. The initial reports of conditions there defied our wildest thoughts of barbarism and human cruelty. We actually did not believe the initial reports thinking that the Russians were spreading false rumors to discredit the SS. They were taking many German prisoners but immediately executed known collaborators in the occupied countries without trial along with all SS soldiers and officers that surrendered. For the rest of February and through most of March, the Russian army was fighting in Hungary. They had to take Hungary before attacking Austria.

On March 20 the Russian army crossed the Austrian border across a wide front. They were still some fighting in Hungary but it was more to wipe out pockets of resistance. They decided to attack Austria across a wide front to prevent substantial reinforcements reaching Vienna which their intelligence reported was occurring from Italy and Germany. The Russian commander rightly suspected that Vienna would be the focal point of resistance. The Nazis were retreating but the retreat was orderly and the Russians paid dearly for each kilometer they advanced. The SS was in charge and the SS soldiers knew that capture meant instant execution. This was clearly in retribution for the atrocities committed by the SS on the Russian people. The SS were much more savage in their treatment of inferior Russians than the army. So the option was death in battle or death by execution. They chose death in battle. Greatly outnumbered they fought courageously. On March 29 Hungary surrendered. The Russians could now devote all of their efforts to taking Vienna.

Conditions in Vienna were rapidly deteriorating. Sanitary conditions were deplorable. Power and water were non-existent in most parts of the city. The bombings continued with less anti-aircraft fire. Fires burned uncontrollably throughout the city. Medical assistance for those hurt in the bombing was also almost non-existent due to the shortage of doctors and medicine. Many doctors had been sent to the Russian Front to treat wounded soldiers. Some hospitals had been badly damaged and were no longer open. The Germans were preparing to defend Vienna to the last man. According to Hitler, "Retreat (from Vienna) was not an option."

For the past two weeks Vienna was being reinforced. War-weary troops were streaming in from Hungary. Fresh troops were coming in from Germany. Retreating troops from Italy were sent to other cities such as Innsbruck. Overall, about ten different major military groups were defending Vienna. There were Panzer divisions, Waffen SS, Totenkopf SS, a full Panzer Grenadier regiment, a full Wehrmacht Army Group, and various remnants of the retreating soldiers from Hungary that were seconded to whichever military unit found them first. On April 1, the Russians were about 50 kilometers from Vienna. The next day, April 2 was an important day for Vienna.

On April 2, Waffen SS General Sepp Dietrich, Commander of the Waffen SS Sixth Panzer Army, was appointed as the "Defender of Vienna". The radio announced his appointment." Fortress Vienna" would be protected from the barbaric Russians. He gave his word.

On April 2, von Schirach urged all women and children to leave the city knowing that the ensuing battle would be extremely intense. The defenders were ordered to fight to the last man and von Schirach was determined to do this. Every hour that he held out was more time for the German army to regroup and counter attack. Unfortunately, there was no transportation available for any of the women and children to leave the city and they had no place to go. Only a few hundred managed to leave the city before it was surrounded by the Russian army.

On April 2, Wiener Neustadt and Sopron were taken. The Russians were less than 15 kilometers from the city center. Fighting was intense.

The Russians reached the suburbs of Vienna on April 4 but instead of attacking they proceeded to surround the city cutting off any possibility of retreat by the SS defending the city. This also allowed for a multi-pronged attack on the city rather than only attacking from the east. This was not expected by the Germans who soon realized that they were outflanked. The SS Totenkopf division defending the Vienna airport which was located outside of the city near Schewacht had to retreat into the city. Just before the Russians surrounded the city, the police loaded 109 Jews into a railcar and sent them to Theresienstadt. It was the last deportation of Jews and it occurred just three hours before the Russians took over that rail station. If it had been the SS, the Jews would have been executed not deported.

On April 6 the Russians attacked from six points. The main attack came from the north which, according to spies and resistance leaders was the least defended part of the city. For four days the defenders held out again making the Russians pay dearly for each city block that they captured. By April 10 most of the city was in Russian control. The Germans were now concentrated in Leopoldstadt, which was easier to defend since it was an island and most of the bridges had been destroyed or were very well protected. However, the entrenched Nazis were greatly outnumbered and were running short of supplies and ammunition. On April 13 Leopoldstadt fell and the Russians were in control.

There were two waves of Russians that descended on Vienna. The first wave was the army under General Fyodor Tolbukhin commanding the Third Ukrainian Front Army. By and large they were courteous and respectful of the people. The atrocities that the Nazis said would happen at the hands of the Russian Army proved totally false. There were a couple of incidents: some rapes, some looting and some vandalism but these incidents were the exception not the rule. The soldiers shared their food with the people, especially the children. A few spoke German which made it easier to comply with their orders. There were still a few pockets of resistance. Any captured SS soldier was shot and any SS officer was hanged in retribution for the killing and torture they inflicted on Russian civilians. Regular army officers and soldiers were taken prisoner and sent to a POW camp. Unfortunately, the Third Ukrainian Front army did not stay too long. The German army had regrouped about ten kilometers outside of the city. They had received some reinforcements so they decided to take a stand against the advancing Russians. The reinforcements, while large in number, were mainly young boys from 13 to 17 years old and old men that were bypassed for being too old to fight just a year earlier. This would be their first battle. Surprisingly, they stood their ground and fought very well. The Russian advance stopped – but not for long. The Third Ukrainian Army left Vienna and moved into battle as additional Russian troops entered the city. They were divided into two equal groups. One reinforced the troops that just left and the other half stayed in Vienna. These occupying Russians were horrendous. Rape was commonplace. Women, young and old, as well as teenagers and even some pre-teens were repeatedly raped. Homes, offices and stores were systematically looted. Civilians were shot for the slightest bit of resistance. Even protesting the rape of a child was often answered with a bullet. Food was taken leaving nothing for families.

Carol and I had left our hiding place in the morgue when we saw that the first contingent of Russian troops were not the vicious monsters that the Nazis portrayed them to be. We were totally surprised at the viciousness of the second group. About six of them came into the morgue. When I protested one of them hit me in the stomach with his rifle and another hit me in the back when I doubled over. As I fell to the floor a third soldier kicked me in the back. They left me alone on the floor, grabbed Carol and ripped off her clothes. She was totally naked. They knocked her to the floor and held her arms and legs apart. One of the soldiers opened his pants, pulled out his penis and proceeded to rape her. I staggered to my feet and pulled down my pants holding on to the wall to steady myself and pulled off the extension. "Jude! Jude!" I yelled over and over again. One of the soldiers holding her arm looked at me and immediately understood what I was trying to say and told the others that I was a Jew and not a Nazi. We were on the same side. He pulled the rapist off of her. They let her go and handed her torn clothes back to her. The one who pulled the rapist off spoke a little German. I told him that we were both Jews and had been hiding in the basement of the morgue for seven years with help from some co-workers. He told the others. They were genuinely apologetic. I must admit, I was surprised at the dramatic turn of events. That's when the soldier told me that they had been fighting the Germans in Poland and were among the first Russian soldiers to liberate Auschwitz. He told us about the death camp and the tens of thousands of Jews that had been killed there. There were so many that they could not even be cremated. The bodies were just piled up behind the crematorium or in large ditches that were not yet covered over with dirt. I stood there speechless. He added that this also contributed to the savage acts that they were committing in Vienna. Any people that could do this to other people did not deserve any mercy. Whether we felt that this was justified or not made no difference. Anarchy reigned.

Carol ran to the bathroom where there were showers and took a shower. The soldier had not climaxed inside of her but that did not matter. She was violated. The other soldiers left while the German-speaking soldier stayed with me for a few minutes more and warned us to go hide until order was restored. He cut off the patch from his uniform and gave it to me. The patch was a bear standing on its hind legs in a very menacing manner. This was the insignia of his regiment. He took out a small pad and wrote down the word friend in Russian in large letters and Jew in smaller letters under the word friend before signing it with name, rank and serial number and the name of his commanding officer. He told me to show this if any more Russian soldiers bothered us. As for the restoration of order, he thought that it would probably take one or two days more until some new commanders arrived and they started to set up a program to restore order. He grossly underestimated the restoration of order. It took more than two weeks for order to be restored and the regiment currently occupying Vienna to be moved to the front. The head of his regiment was a Colonel who hated the Nazis. He was also Ukrainian. His wife and two children and both their parents were killed by the SS. As far as he was concerned Vienna was as much a part of Germany as was Munich, Berlin or any major German city. The people overwhelmingly voted for Anschluss and fully supported Hitler before and during the war. This was retribution time and he let his troops know it. They could act with impunity – and they did. Until General Tolbukhin returned from the frontline he was in charge and he was going to make the most of it.

About 5,800 Jews still lived in Vienna when the city surrendered. This included the so-called "U-Boote" Jews (the German word for submarine, U-boat, was used to describe Jews that went underground into hiding with Gentiles or in caves in the mountains or in the city sewers), Mischlings who were part-Jewish (Geltungsjuden), members of the Council of Elders, and Jews married to an Aryan spouse. These people had not yet been deported due to the categories they belonged to but they lived in constant fear. The largest segment was Jews married to Gentiles. In 1943 the Jews in these categories numbered about 8,200 so quite a number had been killed or deported in spite of their non-deportable, protected classification.

The Russians swept across Eastern Europe wreaking havoc in their wake. They captured almost one million German soldiers and executed more than ten thousand SS soldiers. The Allies fought their way through France and through Germany meeting heavy resistance. City after city was besieged and captured. The Russian and the Allied troops met at the River Elbe on April 25, 1945 at Torgau in a highly emotional and well-photographed union of the two fighting forces.

Berlin surrendered to the Russians on May 2, 1945. Hitler had committed suicide in his underground bunker on April 30 after marrying his long time companion, Eva Braun. Dr. Joseph Goebbels committed suicide the next day with his entire family. The Russians did not release this information but there were rumors.

The war in Europe ended on May 8. There was now a mad dash by the Russians to take control of as many East European countries as possible. Germany, Berlin and Austria were partitioned between the four Allied forces: England, France, Russia and the United States. Almost one year later, on March 5, 1946, Winston Churchill made a speech at Westminster College in Fulton, Missouri where he first coined the term, "Iron Curtain" to describe the Russian control of Eastern Europe and the ideological differences between the East and the West.

The three remaining members of our card game (Wilhelm, Klaus, and I) met for the last time on June 18, 1945 in Wilhelm's house. Wilhelm's wife, daughter and son were there. I brought Carol. We invited all the remaining group members and Mischa. We were there for our last supper so to speak. We bowed our heads and had a minute of silent prayer to remember Kurt and Friedrich who had been killed in the bombing of Vienna. We prayed for the other members of our group that were killed in their mission to help others escape. We prayed for all of the people, Jews, Christians, Gypsies alike, who were mercilessly exterminated by the Nazis. We gave thanks for those that survived and for those that we were able to save. Overall, we estimated that we fitted about 110 Jewish men and boys with extensions that escaped in addition to supplying the males that stayed in Vienna. We also transported even more Jewish men to safety without the extensions. We were lucky, not one of the escaping people with the extensions was caught. There were a couple of close calls but to this day since everyone was sworn to secrecy, this episode in

Holocaust history remains an unknown, untold story – though there were some amongst us that wanted to go public with the story of our activities, which we now referred to as the "Extension of Life" for obvious reasons.

We discussed whether we should tell anyone else about our operation at our final dinner. There was much debate. On one hand some of the people wanted recognition for the life-saving work that they had done and to let Jewish people know that this could be used as a means to hide the fact that they were Jewish in times of peril. I was against letting anyone know about it but was not as persuasive as Mischa who simply said that the reason that we were so successful was that the Nazis never found out about it. If they knew that this type of ruse was being used, inspections of the pubic area would surely have been more intense and, as we all knew, if someone was really looking at the base of the penis for the extension, it would readily be discernable. Secrecy was the key to our success. Given the ongoing plight of Jews in the world, perhaps this should remain a closely held secret that we could pass on to our children and their children. Should the need arise perhaps it could be used again. It was Wilhelm who made the best argument.

"If we do not tell anyone then the process dies with us!" Wilhelm said. He had a point. So, at the end of the day we decided that the decision to disclose what we did would be at the discretion of the last one of us surviving. This could be done by the person directly or be a part of his Last Will and Testament. We all agreed that we would keep in touch with each other for as long as we lived. I prepared a written description of the process and the procedures used for the care and maintenance of the extension. This was given to a law firm in Switzerland along with a list of all of our names. Each of us prepared a will that included the notification of the Swiss law firm as well as the others on the list of their deaths. The last remaining member of the group would be able to get the envelope and decide what to do with it. If the last person did not ask for the envelope before he died it would be sent to his wife or eldest child and they could decide what to do with it.

We felt good, very good. Wilhelm proposed a toast, "To the people in our group that gave their lives to help others live. To the people in our group that were still alive that risked their lives and the lives of their families to help others live. To the people we helped; may they flourish. To all the Jews that died just because they were Jewish. To future generations; may they be never be subjected to such prejudice and cruelty."

We lifted our glasses and drank. The evening was great. We were all happy. We were exuberant.

CHAPTER TWENTY SIX

EMIGRATION

"We can never allow ourselves to forget what hate and the indifference of good men and women can do. We can never let the memory of the Holocaust fade away."

The Rocky Mountain Collegian on-line, March 5, 2008

Two dramatic events occurred in 1948. Israel became a country and I moved to the United States with Carol. She was pregnant with our first child – a son whom we named Robert. At first we were resolute in our decision to remain in Vienna to help returning Jews reclaim their assets but the number of Jews returning was very low. Most survivors did not want to return to Vienna so they immigrated to whatever country would take them. Of the few that did return, their claims were initially denied. The Austrian government was very reluctant to admit their role in the Jewish persecution. There were many hurdles. Restitution depended upon how their assets were taken from them. If they were confiscated by the Nazis in the official Aryanization process, very good records were kept. If they voluntarily brought their possessions such as gold, jewelry, furs and other items to the centers set up for these items, they were given the duplicate copies of the receipts. The originals were kept and were captured by the Allies when the city was liberated. Still, there was an issue of how much these items were now worth and where the money would come from. With property it was also difficult since the current owners would not give up the property without a fight. They had legally purchased the asset albeit at a fraction of the value but they said that what they paid was the market price at the time. The government finally set up a special office to handle the claims for restitution. For those that had their assets and properties taken in the period of the unauthorized, illegal wild Aryanization following

Anschluss there were no records so it was their word against the words of the current owners, many of whom were not the people that stole the items in the first place. They purchased or inherited the properties and said that they did not know that it was illegally taken from Jews.

It was a very frustrating two and a half years following the end of the war. Finally, with Carol becoming pregnant and Wilhelm's constant pleas, we decided to go to the United States. Wilhelm secured the necessary entry permits and facilitated the transition. We had some money saved and there was always a need for a mortician. I had a job interview arranged at the New York City morgue before I even arrived to the United States. On April 7, 1948 Carol and I arrived in New York City. Our first son, Robert, was born on June 8 – an auspicious beginning to our new life.

Wilhelm and I lived in New York. Once a year, we would invite the remaining members of our card group and their families to an annual reunion. Hermann and his wife made it a point to attend every reunion. Friedrich's wife, Magda, would occasionally attend. Twice Klaus came to the United States to join us. On the second visit he brought his new wife, Maria, with him. She was an Italian Jew who had survived the war in hiding in Venice. They had met at a United Nations conference on concentration camp refugees in Vienna. She had no family left alive and never returned to Venice after meeting Klaus. What little possessions she had were shipped to Vienna by the family that had hid her. They lived together for a few months and decided to get married. They had lost so much of their lives to the war that they did not want to waste a minute more. Klaus paid for the family that hid her to come to Vienna for the wedding and for an extended three week vacation which included traveling by train through Austria, Switzerland and France. Karl also offered them money but they would not accept it. The trip was enough. They had never traveled outside of Italy and really appreciated the opportunity. The man who had saved her life by hiding her at great risk to his own family walked her down the aisle as her father would have done had he survived.

In 1977 we finally had the opportunity to return to Vienna as I was attending a meeting in Paris which paid for my airfare. The only Nazi structures still standing were the six concrete anti-aircraft towers. They were so massive and well-built that conventional concrete cutting machines were not strong enough to penetrate the thick solid reinforced walls. Dynamiting them from the inside was much too dangerous due to the amount of explosives needed which would spread debris for a considerable distance. After many studies that showed the cost to chip the structure away manually would be very expensive, the decision was made to leave them in place. Rather than rebuild the notorious Metropole Hotel, the block was rebuilt with small commercial and residential buildings. The opera, churches and well-known public buildings were rebuilt and restored. The synagogue on Seitenstettengasse was restored. The morgue and hospital where I worked were no longer there. They were demolished with the land being used to expand the university. A much larger hospital was built at another location and the Central Morgue was not rebuilt. It was decided to set up a number of smaller morgues in different districts.

We stopped by the IKG office and asked about some of the people that we knew and were able to get information on some of them. Most had perished in Auschwitz. Those that survived emigrated. We had decided not to tell them that we were Jewish and survived the war in Vienna by using the extension. We just said that we were Gentiles that lived in Vienna during the war and were doing research for some friends. The IKG estimated that the Jewish population of Vienna was about three thousand but could not be sure. Of the 67,600 Jews deported from Vienna only about 2,100 returned. Not every Jew that returned to Vienna registered with the IKG or went to religious services. A special restitution service authorized by the government had finally been set up to compensate Jews that lost all of their assets to the Nazis. This took many years to accomplish. Due to the large number of claimants and the support that they had from various people and organizations, the compensation issue for undocumented theft was still being debated in Congress. We asked about the deportation records and were shown the house lists where

Jews that had been deported or had emigrated were crossed out. I asked for a copy of a page from one of these house lists.

We were amazed on how the city had changed. About 30 percent of the city was destroyed from the Allied bombings. New modern buildings were built in their place so it was not unusual to see a modern building alongside an old building built in the 1800s. There were also many more skyscrapers already built or under construction. Vienna was clearly modernizing. The bus and light rail system was restored and expanded. Mobility throughout the city was fantastic. We also went to Am Steinhof, the site of the T-4 euthanasia program for Vienna. There was a memorial plaque for the thousands of victims who were mainly children. The church there was not damaged in the war and was truly magnificent. The hospital was still operating.

We also learned that the town of my birth, Judendorf, had been completely destroyed by Allied bombs. The town was close to the Bruck train marshalling yard and had been used to store all of the spare parts for the trains. The resistance passed this information to the Allies and on November 23, 1944 the town was bombed by more than 175 planes. This did more to cripple Nazi train transport system than most of the forays against the rail system and stations. Tracks were easily repaired and the stations were no longer being used but spare parts were exceedingly hard to get with the destruction of most German factories where these parts were made. By that time the town was deserted. When the townspeople realized that it was the central depot for the spare parts they moved out. Because of this there was no one left to rebuild the town.

We spent four days in Vienna before leaving to visit other cities in Europe. The visit to Vienna was exhausting and highly emotional. Each night we would reflect on our experiences and on our losses of friends and family. We spent three weeks in Europe after the seminar in Paris visiting Belgium, Holland, Poland and Czechoslovakia. There was no way we could bring ourselves to go to Germany at this time. In Poland we visited Auschwitz which was located about one hour away from Krakow by car. It was one of the most solemn moments in my life. I cried as Carol comforted me.

We also visited Theresienstadt in Czechoslovakia. It actually looked quite pleasant. I closed my eyes and tried to envision it during the war with ten times more people living there than it was capable of supporting. It was difficult.

In 1988 we went to Israel for the first time to visit Esther, who lived in a small kibbutz outside of Tiberias near the Sea of Galilee and the Syrian border and Klaus, in Haifa.

We returned to New York where I continued to reminisce about Vienna but never again ventured out of the United States. We had three children, two boys and a girl. I would often tell them about the things that we did in Vienna – the people we saved, the Nazis we had to work with, the T-4 program, and many other things that characterized seven years of Nazi occupation.

When I knew that I was about to die, I spoke at length to my oldest son Robert and asked that he consider telling our story. I wanted to create a fitting epitaph for Karl, Mischa, Wilhelm and all of the others that risked their lives so that others could live. All I could think of was the Jewish Holocaust words, "Never Forget!"

"Never Forget!"

EPILOGUE

"Vienna was the only city in the history of the Holocaust where Jews actually looked to the Gestapo (and the SS) to protect them from the populace."*

Vienna and its Jews, George E. Berkley, Madison Books, 1988 (*author addition)

My mother died on January 18, 1988 of pneumonia. My father died on May 17, 1998. He simply died of old age. He was 91 years old. As I started to write his story, I decided to do some research on the various people that he worked for, with and against during his life in Vienna with the following results:

The Good Guys

Klaus Frühling stayed in Vienna for a few years. As a civil engineer there was plenty of work helping to rebuild the city from the ravages of war. In 1947 he married Maria. She was an Italian Jew in hiding in Venice. His last visit with the reunion group was in 1950. In 1951, they immigrated to Israel where he helped design and install irrigation systems for Kibbutzim. They had four children: three boys and one girl. He retired in 1986 and came to New York to visit Wilhelm and my father. In 1991 he passed away peacefully in his sleep. Wilhelm went to his funeral in Haifa where he lived with Maria and the one son that had not yet married. My father could not go due to a health problem.

Esther Kaufman immigrated to Israel where she became a nurse. Not content with that, at the age of 32 she went to medical school and became an obstetrician. She now felt that she had achieved her purpose in life – to help bring babies (life) into the world after being surrounded by death for so long. She married one of the professors at the medical school. They had one girl whom she named Carol.

Mischa Kleinman illegally immigrated to Palestine after the war ended and joined the Haganah, the Jewish armed resistance fighting the British to liberate Palestine and form an independent Jewish state (Israel). He was killed in the 1948 War of Independence against the Arabs. He had never married. He had named my father in his will as his sole heir. My father received a small package with some pictures, a medal he had been awarded in Israel, his Vienna detective badge, some personal papers, his wallet and a little money. I was with them when he received the package, opened it and looked down on this small legacy of a life devoted to saving others. He started to get depressed. We consoled him and my mother said that as small as his legacy was, he will be loved and remembered by all who knew him and all that he helped escape. Millions of other Jews did not even have this luxury. She was right. As my father put down the wallet a small piece of paper dropped out of one of the compartments. It was a toilet tissue that had been folded about six times. He remembered his demonstration to the other detectives in the precinct on how a Jew wipes his ass. He told the story to us as he unfolded the paper. We both laughed. Even in death Mischa remained the comic.

Dr. Isadore Nussbaum survived Auschwitz due to his medical training. He was forced to assist Dr. Mengele with his experiments which kept him, his wife and daughter alive. The day before Auschwitz was liberated he went into the supply room, took some poison from one of the cabinets and put it into the morning coffee of the ten remaining SS Death Head guards whose final orders were to kill as many Jews as possible before they retreated. He literally saved hundreds of lives at great risk to himself. He felt it was the least he could do as atonement for the things he had to do under Mengele. The three of them were granted a special entry permit sponsored by the Hadassah, a Jewish charity organization, to the United States when this became known. He arrived in the United States on May 14, 1946 but no longer practiced medicine. The things that he did at Auschwitz and the subsequent killing of the guards weighed heavy on his mind. He took his own life in 1947 after many bouts with depression.

Wilhelm Roebling and his family came to New York City in 1946. They met us at Ellis Island when we arrived. We stayed with them for a while until my father could afford an apartment in Brooklyn. Wilhelm resumed his medical practice after studying and applying for a license. He set up a unique office in lower Manhattan consisting of medical doctors, psychiatrists and psychologists specialized in treating survivors of the concentration camps and their families. This was extended to include former soldiers with war injuries and associated trauma. He established a world-renowned reputation in this area being one of the first in the profession to treat mental and physical disorders simultaneously. He died in 2002 at the age of 81. In spite of a number of requests to write a book about his experiences in the war he refused due to the pact that was made with the others not to talk about their actions as long as one other person in the network was alive. He kept that promise as my father was still alive.

Hermann Schmidt left Vienna for England in 1943 after Vienna had been emptied of Jews. He had to go back to law school since English law was very different from Austrian law. He passed the bar exam and set up his practice in Liverpool with his uncle who had sponsored him. One of his clients was a young man (confidential) who was suing his manager on some contract issues. Hermann won which allowed the man to join a singing group called the Beatles. Hermann moved to London a year later where he specialized in litigation in the entertainment industry. He was very successful. His daughter, who was eleven years old when he left for England, attended Oxford University and married an officer in the Royal Navy who was assigned to the Foreign Office. They lived in many different countries according to his assignment which she loved. They had three children, two boys and a girl. Hermann died in 1988 and on his deathbed said that his only regret was that he was unable to get more Jews out of harm's way before he left Vienna.

Magda Steiermann moved to the United States in 1946 to live with her son, Rudolf, who had gone to college there before the war. Rudolf fell in love with a Catholic girl whom he met in college and married her in 1945. At first Magda was angry due to the religious issue but she quickly relented after thinking about the plight of the Jews in Europe. Bringing up their children as Catholics would be much better than as Jews. She trusted no one any more. She saw what happened in Germany and Austria and while the United States was tolerant today who knew what the sentiment would be in twenty or thirty years from now? No, she rationalized being Catholic was much safer than being Jewish and even advised her son to destroy any records that indicated that he was Jewish just in case a Nazi-like regime was ever to gain control of the government.

The Bad Guys

Josef Bürckel the first Gauleiter of Austria, was either murdered or took his own life in September 1944. Rumors were rife that he was directly involved in the July attempt on Hitler's life and took his own life rather than face trial or was falsely implicated in the plot and took his life for the same reason. Some said he was murdered. The true facts may never be known. He was buried with full honors on October 4, 1944 with many high-ranking Nazis attending the funeral.

Adolf Eichmann fled Europe to South America. His identity was discovered by an Israeli intelligence unit while he was living in Argentina under the name Ricardo Klement. Interestingly, he was discovered because of his strong addiction to stamp collecting. His special areas of collecting interest were known by the teams of Israeli agents assigned to his capture. After many false leads they zeroed in on him at his house in Buenos Aires. He was kidnapped on May 11, 1960, taken to Israel where he was tried, convicted and executed for War Crimes.

Odilo Globocnik the first Gauleiter of Vienna was without a doubt the least known yet one of the most brutal of the mass murderers in the Nazi regime. He was personally responsible for the deaths of more than 1.5 million people, mainly Jews with a sizeable minority of Poles. After being dismissed as Gauleiter of Vienna he enlisted in the Waffen SS and distinguished himself with his bravery and leadership skills in the invasion of Poland. Himmler had always been a supporter of Odilo due to his unyielding loyalty and organizational skills. Based on his exemplary performance in the Waffen SS, Himmler convinced Hitler to appoint Odilo to be in charge of Lublin, Poland with the express charter of getting rid of all the Jews there and any other undesirables. He had found his milieu.

He excelled beyond the expectations of his superiors. He brought his mother there to stay with him and showed her his work. She was very proud of him. After all, it was she who had taught him his moral values which included a deep hatred for Jews. He committed suicide to avoid capture in May 1945.

Heinrich Himmler the leader of the SS and the man most responsible for the death of more than six million Jews and other people deemed undesirable was determined to survive. In April 1945 realizing that the war was lost, he deserted Hitler. He contacted the Swedish Red Cross offering to release Jewish survivors to them in return for amnesty. He also sent messages to the Allies requesting that he be the point man for surrender negotiations. They all refused. Hitler upon learning of his overtures to the Allies and the Swedish Red Cross was furious and ordered his arrest but Himmler had already fled. After these refusals, Himmler disguised himself as a common soldier and was making his way to Switzerland but was captured by the British. When he was recognized, he was told that he was going to be tried as a war criminal. He committed suicide using the poison capsule that he had hidden rather than stand trial and be convicted.

SS Brigadeführer Erich Naumann, commanding officer of Einsatzgruppen B, was arrested after the war ended, tried for Crimes Against Humanity and executed by hanging in 1951. At his trial he was asked if he felt that he did anything wrong. His response was that he, "considered the decree to be right because it (getting rid of the Jews) was part of our aim of the war and, therefore, it was necessary."

Ernst Kaltenbrunner, the head of the Austrian SS, was captured by a U.S. patrol on May 12, 1945. He was tried at Nuremberg for War Crimes, found guilty and executed on October 16, 1946. Even though he had personally interceded on my father's behalf a number of times I could not find any compassion for this cruel mass murderer. He was only repaying a personal debt; there was nothing redeeming about his actions serving the Third Reich.

Wilhelm Reisz, the head of the six-man Jewish Police Force (JURO) in Vienna was arrested, tried and convicted. He was sentenced to only five years imprisonment but he committed suicide in his cell shortly after the trial ended. When his family and former friends learned the details of his cooperation with the Nazis they sent word to him that as far as they were concerned he was dead and that upon his release he was not to contact any of them. Even his Gentile wife deserted him. Not one person attended his funeral.

Baldur von Schirach, the Gauleiter of Vienna, surrendered in 1945 and was tried for war crimes at Nuremberg. At the trial he was one of only two Nazis to denounce Hitler (the other was Albert Speer). He said that he did not know about the extermination camps. He also provided evidence that he had protested about the inhumane treatment of the Jews. His main defense was that the deportations had already started under Eichmann and his was a policy of non-interference so he was forced by his rank to continue what was already started. He was found guilty on October 1, 1946, of "crimes against humanity" for his deportation of 65,000 Viennese Jews to Dachau, Auschwitz and other ghettos, concentration and death camps. He was sentenced and served 20 years in Spandau Prison. On July 20, 1949 his wife Henriette divorced him. He was released on September 30, 1966, and retired quietly to southern Germany. He published his memoirs, Ich glaubte an Hitler (I believed in Hitler). He died on August 8, 1974 in Kröv.

Dr. Arthur Seyss-Inquart, the man chosen by Hitler to take control of Austria after Anschluss, took over the administration of Holland as Reichskommissar and Gauleiter after leaving Austria. He was a cruel and brutal administrator responsible for the deaths of thousands of Jews, Dutch prisoners and other undesirables. He was tried for War Crimes and executed on October 16, 1946.

Col. Orloff Stryker and his family were admitted into the United States under the political asylum system after he provided the top-secret information that he took with him. It was about the secret weapons the Nazis were developing. He made up a story about being a devout Catholic that worked in the Nazi headquarters in Berlin. With the Gestapo seals on their luggage none of their bags were inspected when they left Germany and with his status as a political refugee their bags were not inspected when he entered the United States on a military transport plane which landed at a military airfield. As such, he began his new life as a very rich man with the confiscated gold and jewelry from the Jews he sent to concentration camps. Once the U. S. authorities received the top-secret material they did not bother to do any additional background investigation. Obviously, there was no way he could be a Nazi even though there were some that questioned his ability to acquire such important information. Having lived in Berlin and Vienna they preferred a large city so they decided to live in New York City in a very fancy apartment overlooking Central Park, which turned out to be a grievous error. One afternoon about eight months after the war had ended he was walking down Fifth Avenue when one of the Jewish men that he had sent away to a concentration camp and survived recognized him. He yelled out his name at the top of his lungs, "Stryker! Stryker!" Stryker instinctively turned around and looked at him and immediately cowered and froze turning a grievous error into a fatal error. I do not know if Col. Stryker remembered the man or not but before he could say or do anything the man lunged at him calling him a Nazi murderer and strangled him with his bare hands as passersby just watched in horror. Only one man tried to pull him off of Stryker but the adrenalin rush gave him extra strength. He was not about to let go of Stryker's neck as it snapped under his pressure. The incident made the newspapers which was seen by Wilhelm who called me just in case I hadn't seen it. The man who killed Stryker, Sol Waxman, was tried and, was almost found guilty of killing the wrong man. Nazi records indicated that Col. Stryker was killed by the men that plotted to assassinate Hitler in 1944 and was buried in Hannover, Germany. However, when the picture of Col. Stryker was published more than thirty former concentration camp survivors recognized him and contacted the authorities. With so much corroborating testimony the Department of Justice asked the German government to exhume the body of Col. Stryker. When his coffin was opened it only contained rocks. Sol Waxman was subsequently exonerated. During the Waxman trial, Wilhelm wrote a letter to the newspapers, the police, the FBI and some Jewish organizations exposing the family as Nazis that came to the United States with assets stolen from Jews. They were deported back to Germany and their ill-gotten wealth was confiscated.

Caught in the middle

Cardinal Theodor Innitzer who initially welcomed Hitler grew increasingly disenchanted with the Nazis as they interfered with the church and persecuted the clergy. By the end of the war, he was openly antagonistic. He was directly responsible for saving about 150 Jews that had converted to Catholicism before Anschluss. The Nazis did not recognize religious conversion since they classified Jews as a race and not a religion. He continued to serve as the Archbishop of Vienna until his death in 1955.

Dr. Wilhelm Miklas resigned as President of Hungary after stalling as long as he could before agreeing to appoint Dr. Seyss-Inquart as chancellor to meet Hitler's demands. He was placed under house arrest and spent the war as a prisoner constantly worrying if he was going to be executed for his refusal to submit to the immediate demands of Hitler. He was released after the war by the Allies. He retired from public life and died in 1959.

Kurt von Schuschnigg was liberated in Italy by the Allies after having been a prisoner in Dachau and Sachsenhausen. He decided not to return to Austria. Instead, he accepted a position as a professor of political science at Saint Louis University where he taught until 1967. He quietly returned to Austria that year and died at Mutters, near Innsbruck, in 1977.

Franz von Papen Ambassador to Austria 1934-1938 was relieved on March 4, 1938 but continued to mediate with the von Schuschnigg government until Anschluss was completed. He was the Ambassador to Turkey until 1944. He returned to Germany and stayed out of government service. He was captured along with his son Franz Jr. near the end of the war at his home. He was tried at the Nuremberg. The court acquitted him, stating that he had, in the court's view, committed a number of "political immoralities," but that these actions were not punishable under the "conspiracy to commit crimes against peace" as charged. He was later sentenced to eight years in prison by a West German court for his participation in the Nazi government, but was released on appeal in 1949. He died in Oberasbach, West Germany, on May 2, 1969 at the age of 89.

AUTHOR'S PERSONAL COLLECTION

For more than 25 years, I have collected various Judaica items that included:

- Anti-Semitic paper money issued by cities, companies and stores including paper money that became worthless due to the rampant post-World War I inflation that were overprinted with anti-Semitic messages by the Nazis.

- Paper money and coins from concentration camps and ghettos.

- Paper money issued by Jewish cities and stores.

- Anti-Semitic postcards.

- Documents from concentration camps and ghettos such as ration cards, correspondence Anti-Semitic labels and stickers that were pasted on Jewish businesses, offices and homes including a label from a can of the poison gas canister, Zyklon B, used in the concentration camps.

- Yellow star armbands and stars that were removed from the uniforms in French and German.

- Anti-Semitic books, newspapers and flyers.

- A variety of other items such as a German passport with the "J" indicating that it was issued to a Jewish person, badges, forms, ID cards, etc.

The collection consisting of about 450 items was donated to the Houston Holocaust Museum in 2012.

ACKNOWLEDGEMENTS

<u>Vienna, Austria</u>

Holocaust Monument

Jewish Museum of the City of Vienna

Jewish Welcome Service, Vienna

Leonora Neuberger, superlative tour guide

Vienna Tours

IKG (Israelitischen Kultusgemeinde)

DÖW (Austrian Resistance Museum)

Sigmund Freud Museum

Other

Shanghai Jewish Museum, Shanghai, China

Jewish Tours of Shanghai, China

Zagreb Tours, Croatia

City Tours; Bratislava, Slovakia

Museum of Jewish Culture; Bratislava, Slovakia

City Tourist Authority; Ljubljana, Slovenia

BIBLIOGRAPHY BOOKS

1. Albrich, Thomas and Zweig, Ronald W. Editors. Escape Through Austria: Jewish Refugees and the Austrian Route to Palestine. London and Portland, OR. Frank Cass Publishers. 2002

2. Art, David. The Politics of the Nazi Past in Germany and Austria. New York. Cambridge Press. 2006

3. Beckermann, Ruth. Die Mazzesinsel (Matzoh Island). Vienna and Munich. Löcker Verlag. 1984 (in German)

4. Berkley, George C. Vienna and its Jews: The Tragedy of Success, 1880-1990s. Maryland. Abt Books and Madison Books. 1988

5. Browning, Christopher R. with Matthäus, Jürgen contributing. The Origins of the Final Solution: The Evolution of Nazi Jewish Policy, September 1939 – March 1942. Nebraska and Jerusalem. University of Nebraska Press and Yad Vashem. 2004

6. Brook-Shepherd, Gordon. The Anschluss. Philadelphia and New York. J. B. Lippincott Company. 1963

7. Bukey, Evan Burr. Hitler's Austria. North Carolina. University of North Carolina Press, 2000

8. Chamberlain, Houston Stewart. Translated by John Lees. Foundations of the Nineteenth Century (1899). London and New York. John Lane Company. 1911 edition

9. Cornwall, Claudia. Letter from Vienna: A Daughter Uncovers Her Family's Jewish Past. Toronto and Vancouver. Douglas & McIntyre. 1995

10. Edelheit, Abraham J. and Hershel. History of the Holocaust. San Francisco. Westview Press. 1994

11. Frankl, Adolf. Art Against Oblivion. Vienna. Art Forum. ND

12. Friedenrei, Harriet Poss. Jewish Politics in Vienna 1918-1938. Indiana. Indiana University Press. 1991

13. Feuerstein, Michaela and Milchram, Gerhard. Jewish Vienna. Vienna. Mandelbaum Verlag. 2004

14. Gilbert, Martin. Kristallnacht: Prelude to Destruction. Great Britain. HarperCollins Publishers. 2006

15. Grunwald, Max. Vienna (Jewish Community Series). Philadelphia. Jewish Press Publication Society. 1936

16. Herf, Jeffrey. The Jewish Enemy: Nazi Propaganda During World War II and the Holocaust. Cambridge and London. The Belknap Press of Harvard University Press. 2006

17. Hitler, Adolf. Translated by Konrad Heiden. Mein Kampf. Boston. Houghton Mifflin Company. 1971

18. Kurzweil, Edith. Nazi Laws and Jewish Lives: Letters from Vienna. New Brunswick (USA) and London. Transaction Publishers. 2004

19. Laqueur, Walter editor and Baumal, Judith Tydor, associate editor. The Holocaust Encyclopedia. Connecticut and London. Yale University Press. 2001

20. Maass, Walter B. Assassination in Vienna. New York. Charles Scribner's Sons. 1972

21. Maass, Walter B. Country Without a Name: Austria Under Nazi Rule 1938-1945. New York. Frederick Ungar Publishing Co. 1979

22. Meltzer, Milton. Never to Forget: The Jews of the Holocaust. USA. Harper Trophy. 1976

23. Parkinson, F. (Editor). Conquering the Past: Austrian Nazism Yesterday and Today, Detroit, Wayne State University Press. 1989

24. Pauley, Bruce F. Hitler and the Forgotten Nazis. North Carolina, The University of North Carolina Press. 1981

25. Perloff, Marjorie. The Vienna Paradox: A Memoir. New York. New Directions Books. 2003

26. Pick, Robert. The Last Days of Imperial Vienna. New York. The Dial Press. 1976

27. Poprzeczny, Joseph. Odilo Globocnik: Hitler's Man in the East. North Carolina and London. McFarland & Company. 2004

28. Reiffenstein, Bruno and Frey, Dagobert. Wien In Bildern. Vienna. Wien und Leipzig. 1928 (in German)

29. Rhodes, Richard. Masters of Death: The SS Einsatzgruppen and the Invention of the Holocaust. New York. Alfred A. Knopf. 2002

30. Rieger, Berndt. Creator of the Nazi Death camps: The Life of Odilo Globocnik. London. Vallentine Mitchell. 2007

31. Rigg, Bryan Mark. Lives of Hitler's Jewish Soldiers: Untold Tales of Men of Jewish Descent Who Fought for the Third Reich. Kansas. University Press of Kansas. 2009

32. Singer, Peter. Pushing Time Away: My Grandfather and the Tragedy of Jewish Vienna. New York. HarperCollins Publishers. 2003

33. Tent, James F. In the Shadow of the Holocaust: Nazi Persecution of Jewish-Christian-Germans. Kansas. University Press of Kansas. 2003

34. The Holocaust Chronicles. Publications International, Ltd. Louis Weber, CEO. Illinois. 2003

35. van Liempt, Ad. Hitler's Bounty Hunters: The Betrayal of the Jews. New York. Berg Publishing. 2005

36. von Papen, Franz. Memoirs. Translated by Brian Connell. New York. E. P. Dutton & Company, 1958

37. von Schuschnigg, Kurt. Austria Requiem (Left Book Club). London. Victor Gollancz. 1947

38. von Schuschnigg, Kurt. The Brutal Takeover: The Austrian ex-Chancellor's account of the Anschluss of Austria by Hitler. Translated by Richard Barry. New York. Atheneum. 1971

39. Wagner, Dieter and Tomkowitz, Gerhard. Anschluss: The week Hitler Seized Vienna. Translated by Geoffrey Strachan. New York. St. Martin's Press. 1968

40. West, Paul. The Dry Danube: A Hitler Forgery. New York. New Directions, 2000

41. Weyr, Thomas. The Setting of the Pearl: Vienna Under Hitler. New York. Oxford Press. 2005

Pamphlets

1. Bolshevism – Jewish Sub-humanity. (translated from Der Stürmer). USA. Third Reich Books. 2006

2. Catalog to the Permanent Exhibition. Documentation Center of Austrian Resistance (DOW). Vienna. Braintrust. 2006

3. Jewish Monuments in Bohemia and Moravia. Czech Tourist Agency. ND

4. Jewish Vienna – Heritage and Mission. Jewish Welcome Service, Vienna. ND

5. The Eternal Jew, volumes 1-4 (translated). USA. Third Reich Books. 2006

6. The Path of Remembrance through Leopoldstadt, Parts 1 and 2. Translated by Thomas Kellerberger. Vienna. 2008

7. The Roots of the Jewish Nation in Bohemia and Moravia. Ministry of Foreign Affairs of the Czech Republic, Department for Cultural Relations and Czechs Living Abroad. Prague. 1997

8. Streicher, Julius. The Jewish Question in the Classroom (translated from Der Stürmer). USA. Third Reich Books. 2006

9. Streicher, Julius. The Mongrel (translated from Der Stürmer). USA. Third Reich Books. 2006

10. Streicher, Julius. The Poisonous Mushroom (translated from Der Stürmer). USA. Third Reich Books. 2006

11. Streicher, Julius. Trust No Fox on Green Heath and No Jew on his Oath (translated from Der Stürmer). USA. Third Reich Books. 2006